Jenifer Kay Hood is one of the world's foremost authorities on Edna St. Vincent Millay. As a charter member of the Millay Society, Hood has had the opportunity to visit Steepletop, the poet's home in upstate New York, and has interviewed the poet's sister, Norma Millay Ellis, Millay's friends, biographers and other scholars. She wrote and performed *Fatal Interview*, a one-woman show about the poet which was featured on PBS, as well as *Bunny and Vincent*, a play about Millay's relationship with the critic, Edmund Wilson. She lives in Salem, Oregon.

For Deborah Wright and my sister, Willa, my own Norma.

Jenifer Kay Hood

YOUNG VINCENT

The Origins of a Poet

Austin Macauley Publishers
LONDON * CAMBRIDGE * NEW YORK * SHARJAH

Copyright © Jenifer Kay Hood 2025

All rights reserved. No part of this publication may be reproduced, distributed, or transmitted in any form or by any means, including photocopying, recording, or other electronic or mechanical methods, without the prior written permission of the publisher, except in the case of brief quotations embodied in critical reviews and certain other non-commercial uses permitted by copyright law. For permission requests, write to the publisher.

Any person who commits any unauthorized act in relation to this publication may be liable to criminal prosecution and civil claims for damages.

This is a work of biographical fiction. Names, characters, businesses, places, events, locales, and incidents are real but some incidents and events are the products of the author's imagination or told in a fictitious manner. The resemblance to actual persons, living or dead, or actual events should be researched and compared to accounts found in the end notes.

The literary estate of Edna St. Vincent Millay holds the copyright of all works by members of the Millay family quoted herein. Please contact the Millay Society (millay.org) for permission.

Ordering Information
Quantity sales: Special discounts are available on quantity purchases by corporations, associations, and others. For details, contact the publisher at the address below.

Publisher's Cataloging-in-Publication data
Hood, Jenifer Kay
Young Vincent

ISBN 9798895430712 (Paperback)
ISBN 9798895430729 (Hardback)
ISBN 9798895430743 (ePub e-book)
ISBN 9798895430736 (Audiobook)

Library of Congress Control Number: 2025900544

www.austinmacauley.com/us

First Published 2025
Austin Macauley Publishers LLC
40 Wall Street, 33rd Floor, Suite 3302
New York, NY 10005
USA

mail-usa@austinmacauley.com
+1 (646) 5125767

Acknowledgements

The poems and prose by Edna St. Vincent Millay are quoted courtesy of Holly Peppe, literary executor, and Frederick Courtright of the Millay Society (millay.org). Many thanks for all your help with the material. The cited works include the *Selected Letters of Edna St. Vincent Millay*, *Collected Poems*, *Distressing Dialogues*, and other works in the Millay canon, including excerpts from Millay's letters (published as *Letters of Edna St. Vincent Millay*, as edited by Allan Ross Macdougall, and *Into the World's Great Heart,* as edited by Timothy F. Jackson) and from Millay's journals published as *Rapture and Melancholy,* edited by Daniel Mark Epstein. Thank you also to Daniel Mark Epstein for permission to cite his biography of Millay, *What Lips My Lips Have Kissed*. I would like to acknowledge Dean Rogers of Vassar College's Special Collections and Archives Library for access to material from the college archives. Without his help I would not have first-hand knowledge or specifics of Vincent's grades, courseload, participation, how her various friends and instructors looked and so much more.

I could not have hung in there without the advice and guidance of my book consultant, Mary Bisbee-Beek. I would also like to express my gratitude to my friends—Lynn Millar, Debra Vassallo, Deborah Wright, Steven Mayfield, Pat Fuhrman and others for their assistance with the editing this work. In addition, I would like to thank all those long passed who shared their stories about Vincent with me, including the poet's sister, Norma Millay Ellis, her Vassar College romance Catherine Filene Shouse, Camden chums Corinne Sawyer and Martha Knight, biographers Nancy Milford and Joan Dash, and many others who shared memories in books and oral histories.

Lastly, I would like to thank my wife, Susan Taylor, whose many contributions in helping me complete the work are most humbly and gratefully appreciated.

Table of Contents

Foreword — 13

Part One — 17

   1. All I Could See — 21

   2. The Horizon, Thin And Fine — 27

   3. Look My Fill, into the Sky — 35

   4. Pressing of the Undefined — 39

   5. Immensity Made Manifold — 53

   6. The Creaking of the Tented Sky — 65

Part Two — 85

   Departure — 87

   7. The Ticking of Eternity — 88

   8. The How And Why of All Things — 101

   9. The Great Wound — 118

   10. Ah, Fearful Pawn — 121

   11. In Infinite Remorse of Soul — 138

   12. The Gall of All Regret — 146

   13. Every Brooded Wrong — 154

Part Three — 175

   The Penitent — 177

   14. Mine Every Greed, Mine Every Lust — 178

15. With Individual Desire	*185*
16. His Hunger as My Own	*205*
17. A Thousand Screams	*229*
18. An Answering Cry	*234*
19. The Compassion That Was I	*247*
20. Ah, Awful Weight	*255*
21. The Weight So Close About	*269*
22. Beneath the Weight	*272*
23. Quietly the Earth Beneath	*283*
24. The Crushing Weight	*290*
25. Full Six Feet Underground	*300*
26. My Tortured Soul	*315*
27. Deep in the Earth I Rested	*322*
28. Scarce the Friendly Voice Or Face	*333*
29. In My New Home	*340*
30. The Broad Face of the Sun	*353*
31. Close Sepulchred	*362*
32. Herald Wings Came Whispering	*366*
33. Startled Storm Clouds	*370*
34. One Black Wave	*374*
35. Happy Living Things	*379*
36. A Sense of Glad Awakening	*384*
37. The Rain's Cool Fingertips	*391*
38. Into My Face a Miracle	*394*
39. I Breathed My Soul Back into Me	*401*
40. Dark Disguise	*406*
41. I Know the Path	*413*

42. The World Stands Out on Either Side	*416*
Sonnet IX	*419*
End Notes	**420**

Foreword

Poets do not just appear. Their origin stories include circumstances, events, and, at times, a genetic attraction to the art.

Such was the case with the twentieth-century American poet, Edna St. Vincent Millay.

While composing this work of narrative nonfiction, I used not only the usual slew of biographies, but Millay's letters, journals and poems in an attempt to deliver the story of *Young Vincent* in the most authentic way possible, i.e., using her own voice. (It should be noted that the literary estate of Edna St. Vincent Millay holds the copyright of all works quoted herein.)

However, since Millay died two years before I was born, I do not have the benefit of having known her personally. I have met and interviewed many of her peers, friends and her middle sister, Norma Millay Ellis. I have attended conferences with experts, members of the Millay Society, and shared an evening with two of the poet's greatest fans, the actors Roscoe Lee Browne and Anthony Zerbe, discussing the poet's contribution to theater and the art of poetry. Consequently, I feel I have a pretty good handle on who she was.

Even so, there were instances when, for the sake of the narrative, I have had to extrapolate from available materials the circumstances of certain events, consolidate characters and develop situations based on what I know of college life, small-town gossip and sexuality. In doing so I hoped to generate as close an approximation of what her personality, childhood and youth were like as possible. In particular, since this is the story of the "Young Vincent", I have endeavored to think like an immature person.

Additionally, I have used the vernacular for the time to capture the period. For example, today we would say waiter for both male and female servers. In her day, the word for a female server was "waitress". Likewise, young women were referred to as "girls." Similarly, I have taken the liberty of composing some conversations based upon her journals and letters, interviews with principal characters, and from whole cloth given the scene being described. The endnotes are meant to be a guide for the reader to test my depiction. I trust that readers will do their own research to determine how accurate they think I am. You might want to consider the end notes a bibliography, although much of what I know comes from first-hand interviews and older biographies of Millay.

When checking my sources, please note that at times I will cite a section in an endnote that may refer to more than just that one sentence. I made this choice deliberately because otherwise I might be citing sentence after sentence and make it harder for the reader to just flow with the narrative.

Biographer and editor Daniel Epstein thought the character "Auntie Bine" was manufactured, just as the pubescent Vincent manufactured Mammy Hush-Chile. I disagree. Millay provides specific details about the home of her "Auntie Bine," which suggests she was a real person who took care of Vincent when she was a toddler. I believe this not only because of the details she provided in her journal entries, but also because Vincent and her sisters were often left with relatives. This was not at all uncommon at the time. For example, Alice Eastwood, the botanist who was Millay's contemporary, experienced just such an occurrence in her early life. Because I find Millay's recollections of her "Auntie Bine" credible, I also take Millay at her word when she describes a person or event unless I have reason to believe otherwise.

Even so, Vincent did tend to dramatize things. Although I do not have a degree in psychology, in my opinion Vincent's "rapture and melancholy" were early telltale signs of some pathology. Thus, I take certain journal entries with a grain of salt and try to use over fifty years of interviews and my common sense in developing what I imagine her character might have been.

Fortunately—and perhaps mistakenly—some of what follows is a combination of what her many biographers attest to as fact and what I suspect Millay experienced psychologically as a child. To start with, Millay's formative years were spent in unreliable circumstances. This makes for basic insecurity. If one is always the newcomer—or when the family is poorer than most of their neighbors—there is no basis for being sure-footed socially. Studies have shown that when the eldest child takes on the burdens of an adult too early, they tend to feel neglected. This void is filled by over-achieving in some areas and under-performing in others, as well as being controlling, manipulative, and resentful of younger siblings and peers. Older siblings tend to be preachy and teachy, assuming it is their role to be smarter than everyone else, whether they are or not. Eldest girls often try to play the role of mother when there is no adult around to fill that role. Older siblings develop a strong will and a streak of independence that is not always productive. If they have also been sexually abused as children, they tend to use sex as a coping mechanism as they get older. [1]

Much of this feels familiar to me, which is why I have gravitated toward the poet since I was a lass of sixteen. Like Millay, I spent my formative years in modest circumstances with parents who fought frequently. We moved at least six times by the time I was ten. Money was always tight. My parents divorced when I was ten. The neighbors viewed us as strange, too outspoken, a bad influence and thought we were overly dramatic. I also have two younger sisters who were born in a similar pecking order to Millay's sisters. After my parents' divorce, my mother would sometimes be gone long stretches, leaving me to care for them. Consequently, I imagine I have some inkling of the Millay family dynamics.

Finally, as a lesbian who dated men until I was 28, I believe I have a unique perspective among her biographers. For instance, my "gaydar" went off the moment I saw a picture of Elaine Ralli; when I met Catherine Filene Shouse, it was clear their sexual relationship had been primarily one of convenience, though they remained platonic friends after college. I also know how loneliness can be a cruel taskmaster, particularly when one is young and inadvertently insensitive to the feelings of others. You hurt people you wish you hadn't, and you sleep with people you know are not appropriate.

I think you will find that Vincent Millay learned many lessons in her youth that later served her in both positive and negative ways. She developed a keen appreciation of nature and the arts. Her highly developed observational skills became fodder for her poetry and came in handy when dealing with people. The poet knew how to be disciplined and precise when composing a work. This is thanks, in part, to the tutelage of her mother when she was a child. That is why I have recreated some of those lessons. Vincent felt things deeply and developed both compassion and discretion. On the other hand, the poet also learned how to manipulate people for her own ends. She put herself first, for better and worse. She made excuses, threw tantrums and was at times dishonest with herself and others.

As you read *Young Vincent,* I hope you'll take the time to enjoy the various Millay works I have quoted throughout the book, including *Renascence*, which is featured in the titles of each chapter, the poems that serve as preludes to each of the three parts of the book and as a coda, and to investigate the sources found in the endnotes to confirm the facts of her extraordinary life.

Biographers tend to go with what they understand or what makes sense to them. Consequently, there are places where I differ in my interpretation of Millay's life from others. Yet I value these published letters, poems, satires, reports and biographies because they give me a sense of how Millay was able to define herself depending on her audience. The works cited in the endnotes are the primary bases of my interpretation of Edna St. Vincent Millay's youth. When my interpretation differs, it reflects my deep dive into the history of the architectural, transit, social and cultural standards of the day and my own reading of who she was.

Part One

Intense and terrible, I think, must be the loneliness
Of infants—look at all
The Teddy-bears clasped in slumber in slatted cribs
Painted pale blue or pink.
And all the Easter Bunnies, dirty and disreputable, that deface
The white pillow and the sterile, immaculate, sunny, turning
        pleasantly in space,
Dainty abode of Baby—try to replace them
With new ones, come Easter again, fluffy and white, and with a
        different smell;
Release with gentle force from the horrified embrace,
That hugs until the stitches give and the stuffing shows,
His only link with a life of his own, the only thing he really
        knows...
Try to sneak it out of sight.
If you wish to hear anger yell glorious
From air-filled lungs through a throat unthrottled
By what the neighbors will say;
If you wish to witness a human countenance contorted
And convulsed and crumpled by helpless grief and despair,
Then stand beside the slatted crib and say There, there, and
        take the toy away.

Pink and pale blue look well
In a nursery. And for the most part Baby is really good:
He gurgles, he whimpers, he tries to get his toe in his mouth;
        he slobbers his food
Dreamily—cereals and vegetable juices—onto his bib:
He behaves as he should.

But do not for a moment believe he has forgotten Blackness;
>   nor the deep
Easy swell; nor his thwarted
Design to remain forever there;
Nor the crimson betrayal of his birth into a yellow glare.
The pictures painted on the inner eyelids of infants just before
>   they sleep,
Are not in pastel.

Edna St. Vincent Millay

1. All I Could See

1892

Henry Tolman Millay had tried to do right by his wife by renting the north side of a brand-new double house on Broadway Street in Rockland, Maine.[2] Outfitted with indoor plumbing and a spacious kitchen, the modest lathe-and-plaster home was more than they could afford yet he had managed to rent it in the dead of winter.

"Wait until you see it," Henry gushed as his wife waddled up the steps from the elm lined street. His smile was contagious.

"I'll believe it when I see it," Cora said, her feet swollen and her back aching.

"Oh, you'll see it alright, and you'll know I mean business when I say our baby will have the best of everything. You too if you'll let me. It's even got a lavatory." He laughed softly. "If you ask me, it's D.E."

Cora smiled and quietly shook her head. She knew that meant, "Damned Elegant."[3]

They had already been married for three years. Henry had won her hand with a combination of charm and good prospects. But that outlook had been squandered by drink and games of chance. Now they hung on, hoping that a child would shift the trajectory of their marriage in an age when divorce was something only the most common of folk did.

"I think we're past the threshold stage but close your eyes."

Cora laughed at the thought of Henry hoisting her and the unborn baby up and carrying them across the narrow threshold. She closed her eyes. The sound of the key unlocking the door was solid. Henry took her hand.

When they walked into the house, Cora could feel the warmth of the wood stove Henry had already stoked in preparation for surprising his very pregnant wife. The smell of the fire was comforting. As she stepped across the floorboards, she thought they might be oak, a major improvement over the pine boards they were used to. It was something about the sound, and Cora was always sensitive to the way things sounded.

"Now open your eyes, sweetheart! Welcome home!"

Cora looked up. An electric light bulb hung from the center of the room, its ornate shade the most generous thing the builder had supplied. She beamed. "Oh my, Henry. Can we afford this?"

"Like I said, our baby deserves the best and so do you. Besides, the landlord is a friend, and I got us a wonderful price."

Cora bit her lip. Henry's friends did not always fit that description. Sometimes they were more strangers than friends. Henry read her mind.

"He told me he was building the place last year and I said, when it's done, my wife and I would love to rent it from you if the price is right. When he gave me the price, I knew we could afford it."

It was already the end of January and Cora could feel the baby restlessly squirming inside her womb. She needed to sit down. She walked a few steps more and took advantage of a simple wooden chair that someone had left there.

"Are you not feeling well?" Henry asked, anxious to show her the rest of the bright yellow house.

"I'm fine. I just need a minute," Cora sighed. The crackle of the wood stove was comforting. The baby settled down. "Maybe he knows this is where he's going to live."

Henry's bright blue eyes sparkled. "That might be. We could call him Vincent, after the hospital that saved Charlie."

"Why not Charles?" Cora asked.

"There are dozens of boys named Charles, and I don't think we need a junior me, do we?" Henry teased. Cora laughed. "Besides, I think Vincent sounds more regal."

"Perhaps." Cora was non-committal. It was considered bad luck to name a baby before it was born. She ran her hands over her knees and legs. "Where's the kitchen?"

Henry sprung from the windowsill where he'd been temporarily perched. "Just through here. By the way, I have another present for you."

"Oh, Henry, another?"

"It's very practical," he replied as he gestured toward an upright piano just inside the dining room. "If you like I can move it into the parlor. You can give lessons and not have to leave the baby."[4]

Perhaps he really was taking responsibility for the family seriously. She opened the lid of the piano and poked middle C. "It will need tuning."

"No wonder, being in this cold house," her husband remarked. "The kitchen is just through here." There was a slight jog just to the left of the partially hidden staircase. She followed him into the modern room. "The stove is the latest model. Welly saw to that."

Wellington G. Singhi, the builder and occupant of the nearly identical south side of the modern Queen Anne duplex, had met Henry when the former tried to sell him insurance. The gregarious photographer turned real estate agent knew a sucker when he saw one. As soon as Henry mentioned his name Cora knew exactly who to thank for their apparent largesse. "Mr. Singhi, the Italian?" she asked, hoping against hope that she was wrong.

"The same," Henry replied.

Cora could picture Singhi, his thumbs plucking his broad suspenders, his scruffy goatee and unflattering forward comb-over.[5] She suspected he was from India, not Italy. Still the house was new and worth exploring. She rubbed her belly and then the smooth porcelain of the large cast iron sink. "What's next?"

"Are you up for taking the stairs?" Henry asked, gently slipping his arm around her waist.

"If you let me go first," Cora laughed. "That way if I fall, you'll be there to catch me."

Henry chuckled. "Good thing we had a hearty breakfast."

The couple made their way to the narrow and steep stairs that curved sharply from a door in the dining room. On the first landing Cora noticed some stained-glass panels in the small window that illuminated the stairs. It cast a rainbow of light across the steps as they climbed to the upper floor. After a short pause, she took a deep breath and pushed upward with her sturdy legs. Henry was close behind.

When they reached the top of the stairs, they both took a moment to catch their breath on the landing. "Left, or right?" Henry asked.

Cora replied without hesitation. "I want to see the lavatory."

Henry indicated a right turn. "It's just down the hall from the nursery."

Cora took the step up onto the second floor and then another two steps and looked to her right. The bathroom had a single porcelain sink, a claw-footed tub and a commode.

The pregnant woman stepped into the bathroom and shooed her husband out. An urgent need was one thing about having a baby's heel poking into one's bladder. She hiked up her skirt and sat down on the wooden seat. She smiled. This was a convenience. A roll of paper sat on the floor.

She finished her business and washed her hands in the basin. There was no towel. She resorted to using her skirt.

Henry pointed further down the hall. "The nursery is next door."

Cora walked the few steps to a small room at the back of the house. It was extremely chilly. "It's too cold for the baby," she stated flatly. It was the first sign of the disappointment Henry was hoping to avoid.

"Yes, but it's above the kitchen and there's a grate here and from the living room that will have the whole upstairs warm in no time." He stepped toward the hallway door and indicated the front of the house.

Cora marched past him. This was her first baby, and she wanted it to survive its first brutal Maine winter. She shook her head. An attentive Henry asked, "What?"

"I will never understand why they put a landing like that. If they made the stairs longer and little less steep one would end up in the hallway itself without having to step up depending on whether one is going toward the front of the house or the back." Cora stood looking at the landing and sighed. "We'll just have to be careful that we don't trip down those stairs."

Nevertheless, she did notice it was warmer toward the front of the house. She stepped into the bedroom at the center of the hall and found it more comfortable than the nursery.

Henry indicated the final upstairs room, "The lounge is already getting snug as a bug in a rug."

Cora quickly turned from the bedroom closet, walked into the hall and then turned left toward the large sitting area at the front of the house. It was the only room warm enough to give birth. "We'll put our bed in here until springtime," she announced.

There was little room for argument, but Henry tried anyway.

"There's no door. People will be able to see."

"That's irrelevant, Henry," Cora replied, as she stared through the grate to the warm parlor below. She noted that the grate on the ceiling of the first floor was much more ornate than the simple brass models on the floors of the second.

The room would be pleasant enough. "If you're squeamish you can wait in the bedroom or downstairs. I want our baby to be warm when he greets the world."

Henry could see there was no sense in trying to get her to change her mind, so he drew her attention to the windows. "The dormer window lets in a lot of light."

"The room looks a little out of balance with the small one beside it," Cora observed. "On the other hand, it keeps that corner well-lit and there's always that window at the opposite corner."

"I'll ask Welly if he'll give us a door to keep the heat in. Where do you want the bed?" Henry stepped toward his wife and slipped his arm around her waist.

"Over here, by the grate and this window. It should be nice and toasty here."

Shivering despite the passive grate, Cora hoped that the baby would live up to its name by rejuvenating their already failing marriage. She could see Henry had made an effort. The pine floors upstairs conducted the heat well enough, and the tiny room down the hall would provide a suitable nursery once the weather was warmer. Compared to the places the couple had already called home, 200 Broadway was indeed "D.E."

* * *

There was a fierce snowstorm the evening Cora went into labor. With her sister Clem at her side the restless mother heard her husband clatter down the stairs as he raced to bring the doctor.[6]

"Fool," she muttered. "His aunt is already on her way."

"You might need more than a midwife, Nell," Clem observed as she watched her sister pace the pine flooring. The Buzzell family nickname was always used when any of Cora's relatives were around.

Upstairs candles and kerosene sconces flickered creating a broken shadow on the wall.[7] All night long Clem kept a cool towel on her sister's head. The doctor arrived in a sleigh just before eight on the evening of February 21, 1892. A little more than ten more hours later the baby appeared.

"It has a caul!" Clem cried.

Cora became alarmed.

The doctor quickly wiped away the portion of the amnion that remained over the baby's head.

"Nothing to worry about, Mrs. Millay. She's just fine."

"Where was it?" the exhausted mother sighed.

"Over her head. Not to worry, little mother. There was a small hole over the top of her right ear." The doctor washed his hands in the basin Clem had brought for that purpose. He then gently wiped down the infant and wrapped her in a blanket Henry had warmed near the downstairs stove.

Cora had heard many stories from midwives about babies so blessed. The caul broken at the heel would be a dancer, at the toe one had to beware of broken legs. One broken at the back meant a heavy burden. Most relevant for a child born in the rocky seacoast town of Rockland, a birth veil meant the child would never drown. For Cora this meant her newborn would either be an actress or a singer. How could she know Vincent would be both?

When Henry entered the room moments later, he insisted the infant's caul meant his child would be brilliant and destined for a successful career. Spoken like a true gambler, Cora thought, betting upon something that couldn't be known. Nonetheless, she suspected he might be right given all the signs and wonders that presented themselves.

In the town square, bells began to ring wildly in celebration of George Washington's birthday. It seemed a propitious start for a child who would revolutionize American poetry. Yet in that moment all the Millays felt was relief that they had been blessed with a healthy baby girl.

They decided to name her Edna. Her middle name would be a tribute to the hospital in New York that had saved the life of Cora's brother. Together the name would be very grand, worthy of the caul she carried: Edna St. Vincent Millay.

2. The Horizon, Thin And Fine

1892-1895

The child was colicky, small and thin. As a sometime midwife and nurse, Cora was concerned and kept a close eye on her special baby. She wondered if at 28 she was too old to bear healthy children. Nonsense, she told herself, women had babies well into their thirties with no ill effect. Perhaps it was the caul. No, that was a good sign, an omen of good fortune. Cora comforted herself by peering into the child's eyes as they changed to gray green, with a head of thick red hair that shone bright as a newly minted penny in the sunlight. After a month there was no doubt: her newborn would survive.

During her recovery, Cora studied the baby's astrological coordinates. She noted that the child had been born during a waning crescent Sagittarius moon, under the sign of Pisces. The ephemeris showed the child's ascendant to be Taurus. She hoped the wailing infant was not the secretive stubborn child her astrology predicted.[8]

Within days, it was clear that Henry and the child had a special bond. He seemed to notice his daughter's needs before Cora did. It was as if she spoke to him from across whatever distance was between them. He would say, "Vincent needs changing," long before the infant squalled. At first this bothered Cora, but she'd seen fathers like this before and in time dismissed it as just another quirk of her handsome and bright husband. After all, why should she complain? Edna's birth seemed to generate a stronger sense of duty and fidelity in Henry.

* * *

Nevertheless, the baby's bed never left the upstairs parlor. When Vincent was only nine weeks old, Henry's parents suggested the family move inland to the small farming community of Union, Maine. That way, they explained,

Henry and Cora could afford their expenses by living closer to his family. The elder Millays offered the couple a spacious home within a stone's throw of the limited commercial district.[9]

Cora liked Henry's siblings well enough but found his father William as hard shelled as any Baptist that ever braved the water.[10] Consequently, she had concerns about the move beyond being far from her own family and living in a town so small the only doctor was several miles away. Disaster could strike in a place like that.

Regardless of her misgivings, that May Cora bundled Vincent up and with Clem's help took a buggy over mud rutted roads toward their new home, the third since her marriage to Henry and Vincent's second in three months. As they traversed inland, she took some comfort in the fresh spring meadows and flowering trees. The yellow forsythia danced in the mild wind as they passed, attracting the baby's attention.

"Be still," Clem said as she held the baby close to her bosom. Cora held the reins.

Suddenly, a train roared by. Startled from her somnambulant pace, the mare reared and took off at a gallop. The buggy rattled and jumped to and fro as Clem gripped Vincent tighter and her sister struggled with the reins. Both women immediately thought of their mother, who had died as a result of just such an event, as they endeavored to reassert control. "Whoa! Whoa!" Cora shouted, pulling the reins with all her strength. A quarter mile later, the horse finally settled down and both women looked to Vincent to see how she was taking the misadventure. The babe was sound asleep, a small smile at the corner of her mouth.

* * *

It soon grew obvious their infant daughter would have the best and worst of her parents' intellectual attributes. She would be smart but lazy, willing to take chances but quick to grow emotional, courageous when it was her idea and fearful when others pushed her along.

Both parents were delighted with the newborn's curiosity. The child seemed to notice everything around her even before she could walk. She would reach for the dangling strands of Cora's nightdress and inspect them as if they were something fascinating and not the drab woolen fasteners that did little to fend off the winter chill. Cora was happy to know her child had this trait because she knew Vincent would need it to address the hardships of the working poor.

Each parent noticed something different in their child. Her father noticed that Vincent had a tomboyish streak. This delighted Henry. It meant she might share his love of baseball and the outdoors. Better that, he thought, than being tied to the house in a faux version of domestic tranquility.

The infant soon began to experiment with sound revealing another aspect of Vincent's intelligence to Cora. She seemed to sing or at least have rhythm in her infantile mewling. Cora read poetry to encourage this trait, while Henry would sing the songs of his heritage in a tenor so sweet it always made the child smile, even when he was off-key.

* * *

Before long, Vincent was walking well enough to be left with her grandparents while Henry and Cora enjoyed a quiet time together on one of Union's many ponds. Henry loved to fish, and while Cora did not share this interest, she did enjoy cards. Sometimes she beat him at both. "Any crank on eugenics would say we were perfectly mated for the propagation of a family," Cora observed as he pulled a large trout from Cora's hook.[11]

"This is just beginner's luck."

"I'm hardly a beginner. I've fished with my brothers before."

Henry shrugged. He'd enjoyed many an outing with Bert and Charlie. "I suppose."

Despite proximity to Henry's family, the couple continued to struggle. Henry got a job teaching, which was nothing more momentous than him being one of the few men in town with a high school education. Cora found hair work and taught piano. Nevertheless, debts mounted.

* * *

It was a cheerless morning. Cora had finished the breakfast dishes and mopped the kitchen floor. Henry was already at work.

Baby Vincent rumbled through the house on both knees "helping" to dry the floor. Cora knew she had to finish a hair piece by the following day, but at that moment the harp-like weaving device seemed like an instrument of torture.

The laughter between them was broken. She was already pregnant with their second child. Would they ever get ahead? She scrimped on everything, yet they still rationed coal and wood as if they were the last thermos of water in an endless desert of want.

Vincent, ever sensitive to the household goings on, looked up from the floor. Cora investigated her steady gaze. What did a baby know of struggle? She realized that Vincent knew more than she could articulate. Bubbles of snot formed at her nose. Her wide green eyes fixed upon her mother. Time stopped between them. Cora began to wonder if the child's fingers, which were stuffed in her mouth, were clean enough to slobber over. The baby smiled. Tears rose in her mother's eyes.

Cora needed a break, so she retreated to her library and a favorite poet, John Greenleaf Whittier.[12] Even his name sounded like spring. As she left the kitchen and moved toward the parlor, she scooped up little Vincent and hoisted her onto her hip. The child's grubby fingers grasped Cora's threadbare dress as she leaned into her mother's soft breasts.

Cora sat down in the pretty rocker wealthy relatives had given as a wedding present four years before. Whittier was close at hand.

"This is the one," she said to Vincent. "I know you'll like this one."

Even though she knew her favorite poet had felt the influence of Emerson when he wrote, "Snowbound," she loved the rhythm of the poem. She began to read aloud, giving the words their meaning so the child would understand the mood if not the text.

> The sun that brief December day
> Rose cheerless over the hills of grey,
> And darkly circled gave at noon
> A sadder light than waning moon.

Vincent adjusted herself and sat up. The sound of the poetry being read was already a gift from her mother. Even if she didn't understand all the words, she knew how important that moment was.

> Slow tracing down the thickening sky
> Its mute and ominous prophecy.

Cora broke off. "Why do you suppose he did that?"

She investigated Vincent's face hoping for a reply. None came.

"Why would he rhyme sky with prophecy? I suppose we could just pronounce it prophe-sigh."

> A portent seeming less a threat,
> It sank from sight before it set.

Vincent leaned toward the book and stretched out her hand as if to turn the page. "Yes, I like that too," her mother said. "Sank from sight before it set. That's a lovely phrase, isn't it?"

Vincent smiled. Cora took that as agreement and continued to read the Victorian poem. Indeed, there were places where she had it completely by heart. The rhythmic sound of the recitation slowly eased the child's restless spirit. She took hold of the beads of her mother's necklace and pulled them toward her mouth. Cora didn't care. The enchantment of the vision painted by the poet had captured her. In her mind's ear she could hear the whinny of the horse "for his corn" and the cock's "querulous challenge."

By the time Cora reached "Peace in love's unselfishness" her heart had indeed stilled, and the child was deep in slumber.

The new baby kicked but neither occupant of the rocker stirred. Cora rushed toward the ending to the long poem; her voice having dropped to a husky whisper.[13]

> And while, with care, our mother laid
> The work aside, her steps she stayed
> One moment, seeking to express
> Her grateful sense of happiness
> For food and shelter, warmth and health,
> And love's contentment more than wealth.

Cora paused briefly at this stanza and looked down at her sleeping child. Vincent knew nothing of deprivation yet. "Love's contentment" was enough for her. Why, Cora thought, shouldn't I be similarly satisfied with my lot? There were others in town who had it worse, though not by much.

By the time she finished the poem's last stanza she felt better. She had journeyed with the poet's imagination from Malta to Memphremagog and now had a "grateful sense of sweetness near." The soft breath of her beautiful daughter gave her comfort like the poet's benediction. Cora was ready now to return to the necessary task of helping support their family.

She stood carefully so as not to wake the 18-month-old infant and made her way upstairs. Then she placed Vincent back in her crib. It was warmer there and the hair loom she laid out in the nursery beckoned. Throughout the day she labored, stopping only to feed and change Vincent.

The child sensed the urgency of her mother's task and the few pennies it would bring in. She busied herself with the small rag doll Cora had made, which included a bright copper wig fashioned from Vincent's own hair to add to the realism of the plaything.[14]

Just before three o'clock, Cora finished the task of weaving a realistic princess bang for a wealthy neighbor. It would bring in $1.25, enough for a ton of coal and a few items for the new baby should it be a boy. Otherwise, the child would wear hand-me-downs. The coal wouldn't last long, but it would be enough to give the newborn a fighting chance.

Laying in was a challenge because they needed the second income for just the three of them. Cora thought perhaps she could make a little extra cash by writing and selling her poetry, including a tribute to her firstborn, "My Comforter."[15]

> Sometimes, when the day is dreary
> Filled with dismal wind and rain,
> Sometimes when the frame is weary,
> Filled with nervous ache and pain;
> Then, across Earth's darkest shadows,
> Comes Life's dearest sweetest bliss
> As with sweet red lips uplifted,
> Baby whispers: "Onts a tiss."
>
> Sometimes when no sun is shining,
> And my head is bowed with grief

When it seems the sun's aligning
Never to bring me joyful relief
Someone comes on weak feet toddling,
Some gives my sleeve a tug,
And with eyes and arms uplifted,
Baby whispers: "Onts a hug!"

The fact was, at this point in her marriage Vincent was indeed Cora's only comfort. The child gave her life with Henry meaning. If it weren't for her first born, all she could see ahead was endless drudgery and constant moves.

* * *

Norma Lounnella Millay was a belated Christmas gift in 1893. Vincent was entering the terrible twos and became instantly fixated on her sister. Her new sister was very pretty and blonde and registered all sorts of sounds and smells her elder sister found fascinating. Of special interest was how her little sister was already singing.

Almost two years to the day after Cora's move to Union, the harried mother took her daughters to visit their Aunt Sue, Clem's twin, in Newburyport, Massachusetts. The long journey had made both children cranky, so she slipped them upstairs to put them down for a nap.

However, it wasn't long before she heard scampering feet.

"Are you in bed, darling?" Cora called up to Vincent.

"Yes, Mama."

The adults resumed their conversation. Just when they thought the children were fast asleep there was an enormous crash.

"We better go see what they're up to," Sue suggested as every adult in the room began the race upstairs. The geraniums that had graced the sill of a large bay window were gone except for a trail of dirt and petals emanating from the broken pot on the floor. Cora's eyes followed the trail and found Vincent but not Norma.

"Where's your sister!"

Vincent smiled and continued humming her own little song. The pillows meant to cradle their heads were beneath her and she straddled them like they were a pony. This "pony" was soon wobbling as the anxious adults scrambled around upstairs seeking the younger child. "Where is your sister!" Cora demanded again. The thrashing of the "pony" continued. "You rascal!"

Cora lifted two-year-old Vincent off her steed and threw the pillows aside. There was Norma. Geranium petals stained her lips and face. She spit them out and then took a huge breath and wailed so loudly every adult in the street knew exactly where she was.[16]

3. Look My Fill, into the Sky

1895

Cora trudged up the hill to the large white colonial.[17] She cursed the blackberry vines along the way as they snagged her dress and stockings. Vincent sat on her hip; her sleepy head buried in the folds of Cora's starched nursing uniform. Her friend Althea waited atop the hill, her arms akimbo at her sides.

"Is that the baby?" Althea called. The bundle she carried could just as easily have been laundry.

Cora waved. It would have to be enough of a reply.

Althea Norman had known Cora Buzzell since childhood. So long, in fact, that she was more like a cousin than a friend. Nonetheless, Cora was keenly aware of how people viewed the spinster at the top of the hill. There was gossip. Cora couldn't afford to be choosy. Someone had to care for the child while she and Henry figured out their next step and Althea had volunteered.

The house was well cared for except for the tall grass that Althea allowed to grow in favor of her privacy. It almost reached Cora's bosom. "Ahoy!" Cora called.

The toddler awoke and turned her head quickly this way and that to see what new adventure her mother offered.

"She's beautiful," Althea declared. "I see she got Hank's coloring."

Cora nodded and caught her breath as she gently put Vincent down beside a patch of wild columbine. "I hope this isn't too much of a favor to ask."

"Nonsense. You must need help, or you wouldn't ask. I'm happy to assist."

Cora turned her attention to the curious toddler who by now was chasing a cat through the tall grass. "Vincent!" she barked. The child froze in her steps and looked back. "Come over here and meet your Aunt Althea."

Vincent toddled back but again was distracted, this time by another patch of columbine. Althea knelt and greeted the child. "Do you like columbine?"

Vincent nodded. She liked this stranger.

"Shall we pick some for the table?"

"This is your Aunt Althea," Cora explained. "She'll be taking care of you while mama and papa find a new house."

Vincent's eyes widened. Had she heard and understood correctly? Her face began to screw up in fear. Althea handed her the flowers. "You'll be my own little girl for a time, Edna. We'll pick berries and make pies…" Althea noticed Vincent's fixation on the vibrant red variety as it contrasted with the bulk of its more pastel cousin. "There are many types of columbines, Vincent. Do you like to be called Vincent, not Edna?"

Vincent nodded and squeezed the bouquet tightly.

Her new guardian gently continued. "There are purple columbine and lavender columbine and even red orange, like this columbine."

"Bine!" Vincent grinned.

"Yes, dear," Althea smiled. "In fact, I'll be your Auntie Bine."

* * *

Althea understood the dynamics of Cora's relationship with Henry as a family member might. It might take a while, but it wouldn't be long before her friend returned for the child. In the meantime, "Auntie Bine" was determined to spoil the child just enough to ensure her devotion.

This started with recognizing that Althea might be a bit of a tongue twister for a toddler. Auntie Bine it would be. Vincent was given her own room for the first time, a small room just off the main bedroom that had been a nursery when Althea was a child. Next, she brought a small doll's house from the attic and purchased a couple of outfits that were big enough to grow into, not out of, as was the clothing Cora had brought along. Vincent seemed to thrive and for the most part was less of a bother than Althea thought she'd be. The endless questions, the frightened wailing, the bad dreams and skinned knees were just a part of any child's life. Few surprises meant an easier adjustment. Curious neighbors wondered aloud where she'd gotten the child, while others apprised them of a fired teacher and a hair weaver being too poor to afford to have a baby.

The broad, low house clung easily to the slope of the hill. It seemed to fit there, as if under the measured hammering of the years it had relaxed, unresistingly to become at last a part of the soil on which it stood. Its whiteness, surrounded by the wonderful green of the grass, was dazzling. Vincent had never seen grass so green. From her perch in the arms of an ancient elm tree the way the sunset looked in the windows of the house made it seem as if the old house had opened its eyes and blinked sleepily, and the big front door opened like a mouth as if to greet her. Auntie Bine was laying the snowy washing on the short green grass to dry. Perhaps that was why the grass was so green even in the peak of summer.[18]

Vincent watched as her mother descended the hill. Her loping gait already revealed impending birth, her third child in four years. Norma was staying with Clem. She would stay with this kind stranger. Auntie Bine's warm hand held hers with a gentle but firm grip lest Vincent dash toward her mother. But the child already knew it was better to be quiet, that mothers left, and fathers left, no matter how much you didn't want them to.

The furnishings in her temporary home were quietly elegant, at least two steps above the tenement the Millay family was moving from. Matching curtains draped the parlor, and the flower printed pink hurricane lamps burned softly when lit.

The room where Vincent slept was kept warm by the large stone fireplace that served to heat the whole house. Although spare, the former nursery was comfortable and quiet. Nonetheless, the whispered conversations of relatives and friends reached the child's ears.

"What? Another baby!"

"Why Henry can't feed his own wife let alone a passel of kids."

"Henry's alright. He's just hit a rough patch, that's all."

"I have to admit that Cora is not always the easiest person to live with."

"Don't you think the child is small for her age?"

"She's three. She seems fine to me."

It was not always easy to tell who said what, but little ears made big pictures, and the sense Vincent had was she was a scrawny burden to her troubled parents, and no one knew where she'd end up. It was the second chapter in a lifetime of insecurity. Oh, how she loved her mother, and oh, how she feared her.

At night sometimes her memory would conjure up her mother's soft voice singing quietly, reading verse or whistling as she sewed the smallest stitches or when she wove hair. Her father's presence was clearest when she heard her mother laugh. It was a laugh that sparkled, sending bits of bright light throughout the room. Those were the good times when her father had a job and brought in a steady income. These days that laughter had been less frequent, and when her mother told her she had to stay with her friend for a while there was no mirth, only strain.

When she woke up after that first day, Vincent was greeted by Auntie Bine in the kitchen of the old white house.

"Go outside and do your business and be sure to wash up before you come back," the kindly woman advised. The smell of bacon fat and fresh eggs was alluring, but the call of nature was stronger. The red head trained her hazel eyes on the adult. How could she explain her predicament? Auntie Bine had helped her the night before when it was dark, and the shrieking of the fox scared her. She needed help: the privy was too high to climb up on. She stared at the woman until she could take it no longer, ran out the door, squatted and let go.

Althea caught a glimpse of the frustrated Vincent. She shook her head. She'd have to build a shelf for the child. She didn't want to have to drop everything any time the girl had to go. Vincent went to the pump and managed to get a few drops of water from it to wash her hands. Her dusty feet would just have to remain dusty. She was glad to know the child took direction.

***

Her Auntie Bine provided a sense of stability in the chaos. Vincent would later remember the old white house set high upon a hill and the blackberries that provided even when her parents couldn't. But did she just create the patient caretaker to soothe herself? Vincent wasn't sure but she often recalled feeling treated as if she were Auntie Bine's own little girl. In her care, Vincent would be loved and welcomed, held and amused, treasured and coddled in ways her parents could not offer.

4. Pressing of the Undefined

1896-1900

Henry wasn't there when Kathleen Kalloch Millay was born but Mr. Gales soon was.[19]

Her father had been gone for a while. Such was the traveling salesman's life. Vincent never knew how long it would be before he appeared again flush with cash and full of promises. Each time her weary mother would take him back, happy to see the bills paid up and hear his bright laughter as he regaled her with stories of his travels. Given that his charm outweighed his ability to hold a steady job, its weight had worn a rut in her mother's heart that would soon break the wheel that carried her commitment to the marriage. Vincent heard stories about girls whose parents divorced. She already knew her mother would be viewed as the one who had failed.

Cora was not a steady church goer, but the opportunity to play the magnificent new pipe organ at the Congregationalist Church was too good to pass up. Everyone knew she played piano beautifully and so naturally she was the one to ask. Soon she was a regular and led the church choir. Naturally this brought her to the attention of the Reverend Mr. Gales.

The attraction was almost instantaneous. The lonely and disappointed Cora noted that his visit in the middle of dinner three days after Kathleen's birth was welcomed, and that he looked real cute in his bicycle cap. At this point Henry was no longer the fit man about town he'd been when she married him. Mr. Thomas Gales looked boyish and happy by comparison.[20]

Before long he was visiting daily. The pastor's concern for her family especially impressed Cora. He always asked after the girls and wondered how she and Henry were getting along. Cora was happy to help him in return. The reverend wanted to know what she thought of his sermons and suggested music to play to accompany them. He seemed like a wonderful friend to make and it lifted Cora's spirits as nothing had in a long while. He was so inspiring that she considered going back to school just so she could hold more in-depth discussions with him about logic. Even Henry liked the charismatic speaker. The lonely nurse found that her children and pets also found comfort in the well-dressed man.

* * *

Vincent was now five and Cora was teaching her to read by sharing poetry with her. It was a clever method, as poems rhymed, and sounds could be phonetically formed. The child practically gasped as she realized this connection. It made her a little sick, it was so exciting. This meant poetry was available to her, so that she could compose it and find new rhymes that others hadn't thought of yet. She became fixated on the word paramour. Cora explained the word was French. "What is French?"

"It is a language they speak in a land far away called France."

This was another revelation. It grew and grew in her mind until she became so giddy she would have fallen if she hadn't already been lying on the attic floor. An unearthly happiness opened suddenly outward like a door before her. *There are other languages?* She felt engulfed by a very tangible radiance as if she were standing in the path of the sun. This was a spiritual experience. She could scarcely imagine what was possible in the beautiful bottomless abyss of language, a place where every color of ecstasy moved like a cloud, drifting close, then away, and all there for her choosing. Overcome, she imagined a wind from depths unthinkable puffed out her pinafore from the tops of her black slippers.[21]

Given this response one can only imagine how she felt when Cora began to teach her how to read and play music. Another spiritual door opened wide, developing her ear for rhythm and balance, mood and dynamics.

The piano Henry had purchased had gone the way of most things from the double house in Rockland. Now Cora had a small organ they were purchasing from Cressey, Jones and Allen thanks to a deal Henry had arranged with the manager.[22] Together the gifted child and her mother played, some days for hours, with Cora working the pedals and Vincent plunking out the notes she could now read as well as she read words. One tune was a favorite hymn of Mr. Gales. Cora did not have the written music for it but knew the song by heart. She tried in vain to teach it to her daughter by ear.

One day, Vincent tried to master the hymn on her own while her mother was doing housework. After many failed attempts, her mother intervened. The poet watched as her mother's sudsy hands demonstrated the chords, the pink, yellow and pale green bubbles popping as her chapped fingers pushed down the keys.[23] As soon as Cora returned to the washing the child, aching with self-doubt, began to worry what would happen if her mother died? Who would teach her then? Certainly not her father, whose absences were becoming more frequent as the marriage disintegrated. Vincent checked to make sure her mother was out of ear shot, laid her head upon the cool keys and wept.

* * *

The oak swayed as it cradled young Vincent. The leaves shimmered in the morning light. It captured her throat. She let out a cry and tears began to flow as she gazed at the astonishing beauty. She couldn't move. She couldn't go back to that house and be a servant to the needs of everyone else.

It wasn't that the seven-year-old didn't love her mother and sisters. It was that she'd had a taste of being a child and she liked it. She liked being held and cared for. She liked the swaying tree. In its arms she could rest. In its arms the soothing whisper of Auntie Bine could still be heard. In its arms she was assured that all would be right, that all was not drudgery and obedience.

In the distance her mother called again. Cora's hardscrabble Yankee accent brayed above the whispers of the leaves. She couldn't escape it. She had to go home and face her responsibilities. All she really wanted to do was lay in the embrace of that tree and stare at the sky.

Vincent stretched her foot down to search for the familiar knot to ease herself down. Part of her hoped she'd miss it and tumble into the bearberry below. If she broke her leg or arm, she wouldn't have to do anything but lay abed all day. Her sisters would have to go to their Aunt Clara's, and she could stay home alone. Perhaps Mama would stay home and nurse her instead of sending her off to strangers.

But that wouldn't pay Mr. Wilson, the landlord, or Mr. Skinner, the grocer, or Mrs. Motta for the beautiful tulle Vincent wanted for her new dress. It was bad enough she'd have to sew it herself. She dislodged her sweater from a gall that poked from the back of the branch she clung to. With all the weeks her mother was gone, she thought, one would think their endless lack would be assuaged. Yet poverty remained like a free-loading relative.

Vincent looked at her half-frozen hands as they gripped the great elbow of the tree and lamented the chapped and blistered skin she saw there. One foot caught the palm of a lower limb, and then a knot caught the other. Her hands found the branches that made up the canopy as she moved downward, sinking into the depression that so often came with returning home. She did not fall or break a leg or arm. With her luck, she would have broken her writing hand anyway, so what was the use?

"I'm coming," she called, if for no other reason but to stop the embarrassment.

As she made her way along the frosty path, she could feel her mother's need.

"Where have you been all day?" Cora said as Vincent stepped through the door. She was careful to wipe her feet on the damp grass outside the door and again as she stepped on the rag inside.

"Out by Ethel's place," Vincent replied. That was, after all, the general direction she'd come from.

"I have a position in Rockport. I'll need you to make sure the girls are fed." Cora searched the ramshackle kitchen for an implement she knew she'd need. That and the herbs inside her bag would have her client right as rain in just a few days. She noticed Vincent's expression and smiled. "I'll only be gone a few days. Your father wrote to say he'd be home next week. He has a new position in Kingman."

Vincent frowned. Did that mean they would move again? Cora read her mind.

"Remember Ruth: 'Wither thou goest…' that's what you do when you're married."

"I don't think I'll get married," the girl replied, basking in the sensation of her mother's warm hand on her head. The comfort was short-lived. Norma came down the stairs in a rush of competing needs.

"Tell her it's mine," Norma cried.

"No!" three-year-old Kathleen protested. "I need it for my doll."

"You can have mine," Vincent offered. Kathleen, whom they all called Kay or Wump, clung to the small carving of a wooden dog their father had created for Norma's birthday the month before. Vincent's carving was older and looked more like a cat than a dog. Kathleen was not impressed with the offer.

"I don't want yours," she whimpered. "I want my own dog."

"Papa will make you one if you ask nicely," their mother replied as she pushed the last of her gear into a handmade bag.

The younger girls began to cry. They knew what the satchel meant. Mama would be gone, and no one knew when their papa would return. Vincent would be in charge, and she did not have the innate gravitas their mother possessed. All Vincent had was a way of tricking you into doing your chores and forcing you to go to bed. Neither of them had reached the age where chores of any kind, no matter what the enticement, held any reward.

Vincent stifled her tears. It had been a few years since Cora allowed her to cry just because someone had to make a living. She looked at her mother longingly. Why did she have to leave anyway? Her friends had mothers who stayed home and fathers who had jobs at sea or in the woolen mill. Some were even preachers or lawyers. It didn't seem right but every time she looked in the faces of shop owners, she knew it was necessary to lie.

"Now obey your sister," Cora said to the younger girls. "I'll only be gone a few days."

* * *

What Cora wouldn't say was she planned to send Henry away next time he came into town. That winter had been hard. His promises had been harder. Though a sharp dresser, Henry couldn't make a success in the haberdasher business. His gift of gab hadn't panned out in the insurance industry. His talent for teaching was squandered by a bad reputation. His drinking made him unreliable in every way a wife needs her husband to be. She was taking this job because it would give her enough money to rent a waterlogged house a friend from church offered.

Like her mother before her, Cora was engaged in an affair. So far as she was concerned, the scandal of divorce was worth the company of the Reverend Tom Gales—if he would have her. Rumors flowed like a Sunday hymn: thin, reedy and overly long. The simple-minded parishioners of the handsome brick First Congregational Church had too many questions. Why wasn't he married at 40? Why did he dress like an Englishman? Why was his vest cut to display his slender frame? How come the fabric of his frock coat was just the right shade to show off his limpid gray eyes? Chewing tobacco had been found in his shirt pocket. He was too friendly with the choir director, and she wasn't even a member of the church. Why did Cora spend so much time in the organ loft with him?

Nothing had happened, yet everything had happened. A brave and good man had appeared in Cora's dismal life who spoke with a voice that drew like-minded spirits to him. He matched her love of poetry and shared her love of music. He so inspired the 38-year-old mother of three that she began to imagine she could indeed move beyond her station. She could study. She could use logic to meet what he called "elective affinity."[24] He even shared drafts of his sermons with her, seeking her opinion in the manner of a man hungry for a strong, intelligent woman. He did little to allay wagging tongues.

The town's "little birds" spoke of how Cora wrote all his sermons. Ignoring Cora's own coloring, some claimed that dark-haired Kathleen was really Rev. Gales' child. Proximity meant nothing. The resonant closeness that hung in the air before, during and after choir practice was enough to start the rumor mill.

"Mrs. Millay, may I have a word?" the pastor asked with conventional stiffness. Glances amid the congregation did not disturb her husband, Henry. He let his wife's hand go and picked up Norma's soft pudgy fingers as they were freed from Cora's firm grip. Vincent sat on the opposite side, sensing something in the air but not knowing what.

When her mother stood next to the minister the reaction of the entire congregation explained what Vincent was only beginning to sense in her young body. There was something in the way her mother held her hips and swayed slightly as the reverend asked her a question. This was followed by a warm smile and a nod.

Henry saw nothing beyond his wife's normal charm. He understood why Cora liked the Reverend Mr. Gales. Henry was nearly as taken with the pastor as his wife was. When eyes fixed upon him as if to say, "Good God, man, why don't you do something?" Henry could see no reason to do anything. After all, Cora was his wife. These were his children. The reverend seemed far too fey to be a threat. In fact, when the church gossips became powerful enough to start a movement to oust the pastor, Cora wrote, and Henry circulated a petition to keep the man in the pulpit.[25]

Prayer and petitions did little to stop the controversy. Sick with worry that her only friend would soon be forced to leave Union, Cora could not keep her tongue, which only led to more rumors.

Things came to a head when a member of the choir gossiped that the Reverend Mr. Gales was not what he claimed to be. Terrified that she might lose the man she considered her affinitive mate, Cora railed against the tale tellers. It only made matters worse.

"If this church let's Mr. Gales go now, I will quit and never sing or play here again!"

The members of the choir looked at each other. Here was the confirmation they needed. "How's Henry?" one choir member asked with a cynical stare.

The passive-aggressive question set the exhausted woman off again.

"Mr. Gales is what makes this church a place of God! Do you recall that wonderful sermon about the threefold attitude of Christ? Toward his enemies, toward the hypocrites and toward those who believed in him. God bless him, I say! Can't you see the quality of elective affinity he brings to us?"

"Whatever he means by that," someone mumbled. Cora heard and continued digging a hole for her friend, not to mention herself.

By the time practice was over many who had been pro Mr. Gales had switched sides and Cora was so distraught she knelt before his pulpit for a final appeal to God. It was all for naught. Another vote was taken, and Mr. Gales was asked to leave Union forever.

The evening that he left town the Reverend Gales came to the Millay's home to express his thanks for their support. Hat in hand, he presented Cora with an inscribed copy of *The Poetical Works of James Russell Lowell.* This offering spoke volumes to the miserable Mrs. Henry Millay. Lowell shared her eldest's birthday, February 22. Mr. Gales knew she loved romantic poetry. He had placed a beautiful lace bookmark at the poem *She Came and Went*. It was all she needed to know.

* * *

Henry entered the back door of the house and lay down his fabric samples, wools and worsteds that men would order based on a sample suit in the window of Blackington's.

"Boo!" Norma cried as she jumped from behind the door.

The weary father leaned over to brush her head with his large hand. "Is your mother home yet?"

"Not yet, papa," Vincent replied.

"Is that my Kathleen I see hiding back there?"

The youngest giggled in response and jumped from her hiding place behind her elder sister.

Henry kissed Vincent's head and picked up Kathleen and began to sing to her, just as he'd done when Vincent was that age. A slight twinge of jealousy passed between them. The red head reached up for his hand as the family moved toward the parlor. The swirl of girls made Henry laugh. "Hey now, settle down."

"Are we going to have to move again?" Vincent asked bluntly.

Thanks to the inflation that followed the 1896 Panic, expenses were now so high that both Cora and Henry had to work. Yet it was clear to the seven-year-old that things were not going well.

Henry was startled. His eldest was beginning to have the same tone of perpetual disappointment her mother had. He searched her face for the origins of Cora's bitterness and was happy to see it had not yet infected her sweet innocence. "No. We get to stay right here in Union."

"Mama said you'd make me a dog," Kathleen cried into his leg. "I want two dogs."

"Then I want two dogs too," Norma stated.

"What happened to Rex?" Henry stared into his middle child's face.

"He's hiding," Norma replied. Ever since a confrontation between her parents a few days before, the blonde had hidden the carving behind a volume of Kipling in the Millay's small but well-appointed library of canonical essentials.

"Then I'll only have to make you one, won't I?"

Norma paused for a moment to consider the math. "Yes."

Kathleen looked at her sister from over Henry's shoulder and stuck out her tongue. "Papa, I want a big dog."

Vincent stepped in before her sisters could erupt into a sibling battle. "You've had a long day," she said dramatically. "You should sit down."

Henry smiled. "Has your Aunt Clem been by?"

The children's aunt was their emergency contact despite living miles away. Henry was actually asking if the girls had been alright.

"No," Vincent replied, watching as her father's tall frame slid into the worn Queen Anne chair. Cora's handmade red pillow eased the small of his back. "But Uncle Charlie came by with some eggs, butter and milk. Norma broke the eggs, so I made an om-eh-let." The word was the latest French word in her vocabulary, and she pronounced it carefully.

"Good thing Charlie's hen is quite a layer."

"Sure is, Papa."

"Is your mother out on a call? When do you expect her back?" Henry retrieved his pipe from inside his suit jacket. As he did a playing card fell to the ground. Norma picked it up.

"Here's your ace in the hole, Papa."

Although she didn't know what she had said, Henry wanted to be clear. "Only cheaters keep an ace in their pocket."

He tamped down the tobacco with his thumb and lit the pipe. Vincent loved the smell of it. "Where did you say your mother was?"

"Reverend Gales told her about a sick person in Rockport," a chastised Norma replied.

"He's a good man helping your mother like that," her father replied, drawing on the ancient Meerschaum with the head of a sailor.

"Perhaps he could find you a better job," his eldest suggested.

The observation stung. Even his daughter knew he was in trouble at his work.

"When can I have my dog?" Kathleen asked.

Henry turned his thoughts from his difficulty in keeping a job. "Go find me a piece of kindling from the pile, about this wide and this high and make sure it's plenty thick."

* * *

It was spring 1900. Vincent was eight, Norma not yet seven. Kathleen had just turned four. Cora's disappointment permeated the household like a skunk living in a crawlspace. After another losing night at cards, Henry found himself having to explain for the umpteenth time why he was late coming home.

Carl Thurston, the father of Vincent's classmate Grace, had beaten Henry for the last time at cards.

"You will leave now," Cora shouted flatly.

"Oh, darling, it's going to be…"

"It will never be better, Henry. Never. If you could be better, I would make a go of our marriage. But you won't. You never do. No matter how many promises you make. I have taken all I can. I want you to leave and never come back."[26]

Henry looked down at the suitcase his wife had packed in anticipation of this final contretemps.

Vincent looked at her father through the banisters. Norma was fooling with her doll's hair. Kathleen was down for a nap. It would be years until the poet saw him again. Meanwhile, all she knew was that her mother's mouth had the kind of grim determination that spelled finality.

Without a word Henry put on his hat and coat, picked up the suitcase, and walked out the door and past the bayberry, queen of the meadow and roses until he cut across the cranberry bog toward the train station.

Only Henry's brother Fred understood what motivated the expulsion. Clem and the rest of Cora's family thought she must have lost her mind. For Cora it was her last chance of happiness.

* * *

Vibrant fall leaves crowded the threshold as they stepped onto the porch of 78 Lime Street.[27] His black, high-topped shoes were splattered with the morning rain. The Reverend Thomas Gales was not carrying a Bible as he had when the leaves were green. He carried only his hat in one hand and Cora's callused fingers in the other. Vincent had just made a joke, and they all were laughing. Cora's chuckle was lighter and brighter than it had been in months.

"Who do you suppose that is with Nell," Clem asked the other relatives in the room. Everyone understood Cora's nickname.

"Vincent," Aunt Sue said matter-of-factly.

"No, the man's voice," Cora's sister clarified.

"Doesn't sound like Henry," their sister Georgia proclaimed as she started to stand to go to the door.

"Don't bother, dear. I'll get it."

She opened the door just as Cora's hand was reaching for the knob to let herself in. Vincent giggled as her mother tipped forward.[28]

Clem's face was stone.

Cora hesitated. This was not going as she'd hoped. She began an introduction but was interrupted.

"I know very well who you are," Clem snapped, directing her viperous gaze at the startled visitor. "You're the sanctimonious cheat who violated all the rules of decency."

Tom Gales dropped Cora's hand and croaked, "Perhaps we've come at a bad time."

This irked Clem even more. Using "we" as if they were husband and wife. "There is never a good time to take advantage of Cora's love of music and books, let alone depriving the children of their mother's time and attention and their father's love!"

The emphasis on "father" stung Cora. She searched for words as Vincent crept behind her skirts and watched silently. "Clem, dear, the Reverend Gales is in town visiting and…"

"Where is he staying?" her other sibling Sue demanded.

"Why, at the house, of course…"

This was the last word for members of the Buzzell clan. Vincent's cousin Ed, Uncles Charlie and Bert, Aunts Clem and Georgia, and her Great-Aunt Susan Todd all stood and went to the door. The hubbub scared the nine-year-old poet and silent tears began to stream down her face as her mother tried to explain.

"Look here, sir," Cora's cousin Ed said, taking Tom aside, while Clem, Bert and their Great-Aunt Susan Todd argued with Cora. "You best leave and go back to where's you came from. Eh yeh?"

Reverend Gales snorted at the colloquial version of *Okay*. "Then I shall go back to Cora's."

"And Henry's," Ed countered. Cora's soon-to-be ex-husband hadn't lived with the family for over a year and had never lived with her in their new rental in Newburyport.

Vincent's Great-Uncle Charles Randolph Todd appeared from another part of the house. Although elderly he was still a strong man.

"Let's go."

The two men began to lead the fallen pastor toward the train station.[29]

"I'll need my luggage," Tom Gales protested.

"What do you think, Uncle Charlie? Shall we take him by Cora's?"

"Best not give him any excuse to come back," he replied as they changed directions toward the nurse's modest rental.

It was clear to all that Cora had been a willing participant in Henry's cuckolding, yet they blamed Gales for taking advantage of her romantic disposition.

The trio were quite a spectacle marching through the small village. Everyone knew the Todds and by extension Clem and the younger Charlie. The man they were pushing toward the home of their new neighbor was a stranger and obviously an unwelcome one. The fact that Cora was still married made the man even more suspicious and Cora a target. The trail of gossip had already begun by the time they reached Bromfield Street.[30]

Meanwhile, Cora insisted on her innocence. The lie filled Vincent's ears with confusion. The man had already spent one night with them, and her mother seemed different somehow as the man led them in song and grace. She knew better than to be vocal in her fears. She watched as her mother and aunts railed at one another. Her Great-Aunt Susan eventually led Vincent away, placed her before a glass of milk and demanded she remain there. The removal to the kitchen was not far enough. The poet would have heard the family expressing their shame and disappointment in her mother from in any room in the house.

"I've lived in this town for years and in less than two months you already have tongues wagging," Clem scolded.

"He's just a friend."

"You think I don't know what was happening between your mother and my brother-in-law Gard?" Great-Aunt Susan's dredging of family shame from the distant past brought a high color to Cora's cheeks. To bring up her mother cheating on her father was a serious low blow. Besides, so far as the nurse was concerned, it was irrelevant. Thomas Gales was not Gard Todd, and she was not her mother.[31] She had suffered in silence for years during her marriage to Henry. She was only thirty-three after all. She deserved male companionship. Thoughts swirled through her head. "How can you be so blind to Henry's faults and Thomas' decency?"

Clem threw up her hands in disgust. "I'm not going to quote *Ladies Home Companion*, Cora, but I know that man is no good. He dumped his work on your shoulders and robbed your children of their father. You should have been devoting time to your children, not gallivanting all over Union with that man.

God knows Henry is not the most reliable bread winner, I'll give you that, but he's been as patient and decent as any man I know."

Cora choked back tears. Something in what was said triggered an old memory. Her mother had also been thirty-three when she left Eben Buzzell for Gard Todd. Was she repeating history? No. No! She had to believe the situation was different. She had a right to happiness, didn't she?

Newburyport, Massachusetts was a town of strong-willed women and Cora's relatives matched her blow for blow for every excuse she came up with. Henry gambled. Cora cheated. Henry couldn't keep a job. Cora was a nag. By the time they had worn themselves out with their neighbor enticing row, Great-Uncle Charles and Cousin Ed had put Tom Gales on a train never to return.

Watching her mother lose control of what had been a moment of joy carved a memory that birthed a plan in Vincent's mind. The truth was obvious. Cora's dependence on men and the wealthier members of her family made submission to them necessary. The Reverend Tom Gales relied on Cora more than he relied on God to get what he wanted, yet even that wasn't enough to give him power. Vincent knew that her parents argued about money. She knew both her father and Mr. Gales made Cora laugh. But neither man had the power of the Todds or Rickets. Her mother was dependent on them for one thing or another, most often money. It had always been like that. Vincent now understood an important fact: one had to have a lot of money to control her own life. One had to be canny, sometimes even cruel, to move people to one's will. It was a lesson that had been burrowing into her brain since her birth in that little duplex in Rockland. Poverty is what had made their seven moves in nine years necessary. The rich could move when and where they wanted. The poor had to move when and where their poverty carried them. Like flotsam on the sea, the Millay's had been tossed about all over Maine and Massachusetts on the whim of a force beyond their will.

Vincent looked at the expression on her mother's face. She knew what it meant. They would move again. When was anyone's guess, but soon. Then the nine-year-old realized something else. How would she ever make a friend if she never lived anywhere long enough to build sufficient trust for confidences?

Her mother fell into the davenport with a resigned thud as her aunts and uncles derided everything that she loved. By now Cora had pushed back the tears in favor of silent, stiff-lipped rage. Vincent wanted to come closer but childish logic told her that she was only a reminder of the disappointment her mother was failing at learning to live with.

5. Immensity Made Manifold

1901

Norma already looked ill, and Kathleen had diarrhea. Nine-year-old Vincent considered what to do. She was strictly forbidden from sending her mother bad news, but they all were sick. The sound of Norma's retching made her choice more difficult. She knew she was in charge, that she was responsible for making sure her siblings were safe and well. Her mother expected only good news.[32] It was part of her definition of being "a nice girl." That way when Cora came home all worn out, her children could help her get rested for the next assignment.

Vincent felt she had failed them all. Cora's letter had been curt and reminded her of her duty as the eldest. Yet Vincent had a headache, an upset stomach and, like her sisters, a high fever. She knew enough about her mother's work to know these were the very symptoms that kept their mother away from them. The poet's quandary lay in the fact they had no such luxury. They couldn't hire someone to risk her life for them. What about her aunts and uncles? Could they help? No. Her Great-Aunt Clara, Aunt Clem and Uncle Bert had their own health to consider.

Vincent knew she had to soft pedal in her reply:[33]

Dear Mother:

Thank you for your letter.

Vincent looked at the page. It seemed false. She pressed on.

The girls and I are not very well. I feel…

She scratched out "I feel" and replaced it with "Norma and Kathleen feel awful bad.[34]

I am getting along all right."

She knew that she had to tell more of the truth but make it sound light and childish, as if she had it under control.

"Norma and Kathleen have faces that are red as a June rose, I put cold rags on their heads with salt water and vinegar like you taught me. I think I should wear one two. We are almost sick.

Lots of love to you, your loving daughter Vincent"

By the time she finished the letter Vincent was starting to feel faint. The child reread the letter. It seemed soft enough but told the truth. They were all sick.

Vincent bundled the girls up and applied the compresses as she'd seen her mother do. The effort wore her out, but she remained dutiful, sitting in a chair as Kathleen cried and Norma whined.

Cora's reply came in the afternoon mail. She chastised Vincent for making her worry and insisted her eldest "write at once" to tell her things were well. "I am working awfully hard night and day and cannot stand it if I have to fret about you."[35]

The nine-year-old blanched. How could she say they were well when they all had nausea, diarrhea and extremely high fevers that wouldn't go away no matter what she did. Between dragging herself from one sibling to another, doing her best to nurse and calm them, Vincent herself was worn from working "night and day."

Vincent toyed with the idea of writing a letter to clarify but between her physical weakness and inability to comprehend her mother's reply she gave up in favor of sleep. Perhaps after a few hours' rest she would come up with some way to say how they were feeling without alarming her mother.

Cora fretted through the night. The following morning, she told her employer that she needed to go home to Rockport for at least twenty-four hours. Without a note from Vincent, the only way to clarify the situation was with her own eyes, ears and hands. She gave instructions to her employer's servant and walked the half mile to the ferry.

The trip from Vinylhaven to Rockland was wonderfully clear. Summer's last blush, she thought. In another few days her daughters would be in school, and she could return to work. The chug of the ferry's engine offset the lapping of the waves against the bow and created a rhythm that reminded Cora of how a heartbeat sounds in the chest of someone with pneumonia. She prayed for her children to have free lungs. It struck her that letters could only convey if a person was well enough to write. Cleary her eldest was either very sick or very lazy and might even be both. As the boat docked at the Rockland terminal that night,[36] Cora quickly raced to be the first to disembark. She had a two-and-a-half-hour walk ahead of her. The sooner she started, the better.

She was glad to catch a ride with an iceman as far as Camden. By now her head was filled with dread. She raced the rest of the way on foot. Would she arrive to find all three children dead? She pushed the thought out of her mind.

The children were asleep when Cora arrived. The house was cold, but her children were burning up. All three were deeply asleep. It was clear Vincent had tried to care for her sisters but had fallen so ill she hadn't even changed out of her fever-sweat-soaked day clothes before crawling into bed with Norma. Signs of vomit, diarrhea and caretaking were everywhere. A pile of wash rags, dirty nightclothes and half empty teacups littered the girls' bedside.

Cora quickly started the fire and began to make a blend of herbs for tea. Her experience told her the girls had typhoid. She placed all the soiled rags in a pot of boiling water and lye soap, then pulled a fresh rag and a bottle of alcohol from her medical bag.

She started with Kathleen who appeared to be the sickest of her children. Her sheets were soiled with urine and excrement. The nurse pushed her exhaustion aside and rolled Kathleen to one side while she tucked a fresh sheet on the opposite side of the bed. Next, she stripped the child's filthy nightclothes from her and washed down Kathleen's unresponsive body with soap and water, then alcohol, before rolling her onto the clean sheets and redressing her in one of Vincent's winter woolen night shifts. She then pulled the rest of the filthy sheets off the bed and pulled the fresh sheet over. The smell was putrid. She tossed the dirty sheets in with the rags.

Cora anxiously leaned in to listen to her youngest's chest. As she did a small clump of hair fell into her hand. Tears welled into her eyes.

"Kathleen!" she called.

Cora couldn't imagine losing any of her children, particularly Kathleen who looked the most like her. She listened again. The child's lungs were weak but showed no signs of pneumonia. The heartbeat was slow.

The nurse breathed a deep sigh of relief. She moved on to her other daughters and quickly determined she should start with Vincent.

At her mother's touch the poet opened her bloodshot eyes and croaked, "Mama?"

"Yes, sweetheart, it's me." Cora pulled Vincent's clothes off and began to wash her. "When did you go to bed?"

Vincent couldn't think. She had no idea what day it was. All she could dredge up from her aching body and fogged mind was concern for her younger siblings. "Normie? Wump?"

"They are fine. They are sleeping. I am here now." Cora drew a fresh night shirt over Vincent's head and shoulders. "Now you just rest."

"But I have to go to the privy." Vincent tried to stand but couldn't find the strength. Cora already had a bedpan ready to slip beneath her eldest. "You can go now. I'll take care of you."

Vincent was too tired to argue. She let the sickness gush and apologized for the mess.

"You're tired, Mama. You've been working night and day. I'm sorry. I'm sorry." She began to cry.

Cora cleaned her eldest daughter with the delicacy she would give a newborn, pulled the nightshirt the rest of the way down and tucked Vincent snugly under the covers.

"Now just sleep. Sleep as much as you want."

Her permission wasn't required for Vincent to fall deeply back into a fever dream.

Compresses of water, vinegar and salt water were applied to Vincent and Kathleen before Cora moved on to Norma. Like her sister she was glad to see her mother. She was ill too but had passed the most dangerous stage in the past forty-eight hours. Drifting back to restorative sleep, Norma looked up at Cora and smiled. "I'm glad it's you, Mother, and not Vincent."

* * *

Cora sat beside their beds day and night for weeks. There was no medicine or vaccine to help her battle the disease. Worse for Cora, there was no company but sick children that needed constant tending. Her bed was a chair beside them. The unrelenting overheating of their little bodies drained her. This went on from September through October.[37] The local doctor gave up, but their determined mother did not. She battled death like a champion. Nevertheless, Cora contacted Henry to inform him of the possibility he might never see his children again. After a short visit, the anxious father and mother argued for the umpteenth time about whose fault it was.

"Don't you see this wouldn't have happened if I had been there," he cried.

"You mean if you were working, and I had been able to stay home with the children."

"Please, Cora, take me back. I'm doing well in Kingman. I have a steady job and many friends. You've had to move, what, three times since we busted up? More? Our children deserve to know both their parents."

"If everything is so rosy in Kingman and your children are so important to you, why haven't you sent a cent of alimony?"

It went on this way for another hour before Henry kissed his girls and left, at last convinced their relationship was over.

Kathleen was hit the worse and the illness attacked her nervous system, resulting in uncontrolled twitching and even convulsions. The nurse would not allow the sickness to win. She rubbed her youngest day and night to banish the chorea from Kathleen's five-year-old body. The girls lost much of their hair. While they slept Cora washed and starched and ironed every stitch of clothes they had, every sheet and rag and towel were bathed in lye and alcohol.

When at last their fevers broke there was little time or energy for packing. It was nearly winter and another day in that drafty rental would have felt like tempting fate. They took only the essentials, clothing, the rocking chair, and Cora's treasured library. No one would take anything else for fear of the contagion.[38] The whole family returned to the area near Newburyport, where Cora's family offered to help. Their first stop was Ring's Island, a peninsula on the north side of the Merrimac River, to stay with her brother Charlie and his new bride Jennie.[39]

As the winter wore on, Cora and Clem consulted every book of herbs and remedies they could find, seeking to bring Kathleen and the rest of the girls back to full health. Norma seemed to respond the best. Yet she had always been the strongest child. The girls had lost half a year of school by the time they were well enough to attend Rings Island Elementary School.

Living with her brother began to wear thin by spring. On the day of the class photo the weary girls stood among the three rows of hardscrabble children looking worn but attentive to the photographer. Their hair was still short. Kathleen, in an odd military style coat with epaulets that overwhelmed her drawn face, stood in the middle row near Norma.

"Quit leaning on me," Henrietta Smithers complained.

"I'm tired," Vincent moaned.

"Well sleep somewhere else." The much taller and healthier girl pushed the poet left.

She tried to stand erect. Easily seven inches shorter, she could not battle her classmate even if she were healthy.

"Now stand completely still!" the photographer demanded. All the children endeavored to comply. Vincent leaned into her classmate again just as the shutter clicked. It was the only way she could stand without weaving.

Norma stood smiling in her best plaid dress, her dimples betraying a future flirtatious nature.

*　*　*

In 1902 finding a house to rent was difficult for anyone, let alone a divorced, unemployed mother of three, but somehow Cora managed to rent the Coffin House in Salisbury, two and half miles north of Clem and down the block from Charlie and his wife. Named for a person not an occupation, the Federal-style, two story home was already severely run down at a mere 67 years old, yet the home at 6 Second Street was the grandest they had ever lived in.[40]

Vincent found the home romantic, like something out of Charlotte Bronte. With nine shuttered windows facing the mouth of the Merrimac, the home spoke of a once prosperous family. She half expected Mr. Rochester to appear at any moment as she explored the home's infinite yard.[41] The call of the pheasant's eye narcissus enchanted her as they ran down toward the marshes where a plentiful harvest of clams could be had. Beyond that the harbor was choked with fishing boats and whaling ships.

Now settled, Cora found work in Newburyport. It seemed at last the family would get on their feet. The family moved in and cobbled together enough furniture from various relatives to be comfortable. This included moving Cora's enormous library into the attic where it was shared with neighborhood children.[42] Also shared was Vincent's new subscription to *Harper's Young People*.[43]

Yet the family continued to be confounded by prejudice and poor health. Some parents refused to allow their kids to play with the newcomers as they were the products of a broken home. Neighbors again gossiped about the consequences of Cora's marital status, and husbands were warned not to get too friendly. Despite being a hotbed of women's philanthropy, sympathy did not extend to women who might be a threat to the sanctity of marriage.

In an effort to ensure they could remain in the once upon a time mansion, the family took on a part time job packaging Seidlitz Powders for the local pharmacy. By now Cora was plagued with frequent headaches that seemed to grow in intensity the nearer she was to her menstrual cycle. In addition to bringing financial relief, the powders also served as a remedy for the miserable divorcée.

Despite the apparent stability of their situation, things were far from ideal. Money remained a constant concern. Cora was not officially divorced. Therefore, there was no means of demanding child support. While the laws still didn't recognize a father's responsibility for the welfare of his children, society did. Living apart from one's former spouse removed the benefit of this custom. Being divorced brought some sympathy.

Vincent was now ten. She took on more and more of the parenting responsibility. She had grown into an attractive child. Her mane of copper hair had grown back to her shoulders and was enhanced by hair pieces woven by her own mother. At school she was known for being unruly and frequently absent. Her mother's periodic absences had brought her into contact with the local baker, butcher, ice man, coal supplier and their landlord.

It was fall. Her mother was home for the first time in weeks. Vincent was still awake but pretending not to be. Her mother was calling from downstairs. She wondered if her mother had been drinking, which she did sometimes when the Seidlitz Powders weren't enough to cope with the migraines. The poet didn't like the way she sounded.

"Vincent! Are you awake?"

The girl lay quietly. Should she respond or stay still, willing the bed frame not to creak?

"I saw her light," a man said. His voice traveled up the stairs like a wraith.

"She falls asleep sometimes with it on."

"That's not very safe. Could cause a fire." Vincent identified the voice as that of their landlord. She cringed. Lately, she had noticed that whenever he was nearby his eyes were glued upon her. She pulled the covers closer around her body. The bed inevitably murmured.

"I better go check on her," the landlord said.

"I can go," Cora replied. She was not keen to have a man roaming around their residence for any number of reasons. "You can stay here and have another drink."

"No, I should go. It's my property and you're already late with the rent. I wouldn't want things to get any worse with the house catching fire."

Cora didn't know what to say. He did have the right as their landlord to inspect the rental, particularly as she was a divorcee. She again tried to discourage him but his raised voice with the same reasoning flustered her. The harried tenant finally gave her consent.

The excuse to creep up the stairs sounded ridiculous to Vincent. Nonetheless, she quickly blew out the lamp and pretended to be asleep. Maybe if he saw the light was out, he would know his precious rat trap was safe.

They had been living in the Coffin House for just over a year. Their landlord had seemed nice at first, but when he realized their father wasn't around his attitude had changed.

She heard him reach the top of the stairs and turn toward her room. Vincent held her breath. She prayed he wouldn't take the next step, that he would see her light wasn't on and return downstairs. Norma and Kathleen were spending the night with the Timmer sisters. There was no one else upstairs. Part of her wanted to climb out the window and shimmy down the drainpipe, but it was very cold, and any movement would draw attention. For a moment she heard nothing. Relief settled over her like an extra blanket. Then the door opened.

The lamp he held aloft sputtered slightly as he waved it to get a better view of the child. She could smell him before she felt his lumbering body take the liberty of sitting on her bed. Her eyes shot open.

"Hello, sweetheart," he said in a voice that reminded her of the doctor who had given her a smallpox vaccine. "I see you were awake."

She hated how his voice now had the tone of a father scolding his child. "Goodnight," she said and closed her eyes.

"Don't you want a kiss goodnight?" His hand pulled the covers from her shoulders.

"No, thank you," she said. His fingers now slid the nightgown off her shoulder. He leaned over and kissed her forehead. Her eyes opened wide.

"Goodnight," she said again.

"Ah, sweetheart." His voice had become husky. He brushed her hair from her cheek.

Why wouldn't he leave her alone?

"You have such lovely hair. I have always loved girls with red hair." She watched as he bent down and kissed her cheeks. The feel of his beard was scratchy, and he smelled of tobacco and brandy over the citrus wetness of Floris Special 127 cologne. It did little to mask the fact he hadn't bathed in over a week. His hands pressed down on her shoulders, and he kissed her mouth.

"Goodnight!" she shouted, hoping her mother would hear the desperation in her voice and come running.

The strength of his hands was too much for her, even when his right hand slid down her body. He took her left hand and placed it on his crotch. She ripped her hand from his distracted grip and tried to push him away. "No!"

The landlord ripped the shoulder of her nightdress and began to reach toward her private areas. She knew what this meant. "No. Stop!" Why wasn't her mother there? Why did she have to deal with this alone? Her father would have done something. She was sure of that. She freed her hand again as he adjusted himself to climb on top of her. With one mighty push she managed to put him enough off balance that she was able to free her right hand and slap him hard across the face, her nails grazing his cheek and knocking him partly off the bed.

"You little ratbag!" he sneered, rubbing his cheek as Cora's footsteps could be heard coming up the stairs. He jumped to his feet and pulled his coat down to hide his partially erect penis. "If you say anything I'll kick you all out."

Cora entered the room. She instantly knew what had happened but couldn't allow herself to believe it. "What's going on in here."

"Nothing," the landlord grumbled. He looked at Vincent. Her tiny hands were balled into fists. She had pulled the covers back up.

"Edna?" Cora said. The only time she used the poet's given name was when she was in trouble. What had she done?

The lie stuck in her throat. "Nothing, Mother."

"Good. Now say goodnight to Mr. Kinsale and go to sleep."

Her mother ignored the finality of Vincent's last, "Goodnight" and led the man from the room. The moment the adults left the room the girl jumped from the bed and shoved her dresser in front of the door.[44]

* * *

What happened after that Vincent didn't know, but when she woke up Cora had already left the house. The note she left on the front hall table said she would send money to the landlord from Searsport and that Vincent shouldn't worry. As a final note, Cora asked her eldest to work with her sisters to fill an order for 480 packages of Seidlitz Powders. She was then to take them to the pharmacist for payment and buy groceries. As Vincent absorbed her assignment, Norma and Kathleen breezed in.

"Have you had breakfast?" Vincent asked.

"And good morning to you, too," the girls chimed sarcastically. They began to giggle.

Their elder sister was in no mood for jokes at her expense. "Have you had breakfast?"

"Of course," Norma snapped, miffed at her sister's attitude.

"And not porridge," Kathleen beamed.

"Mama does the best she can!"

Concerned now, Norma approached. "Of course she does, Vince."

"That's right," Kathleen added.

"We need to package the powders. Mother left the papers and powder on the table. You two start. I'll be in after I make my breakfast."

"Yuck," seven-year-old Kathleen complained. "I hate the powders."

"Shush." Now it was Norma's turn to take care of Vincent.

The younger siblings marched into the front room and sat down before their task. Packaging the powders was a simple way to bring in much needed cash. Cora had laid out three half-teaspoons to measure each dosage. It was up to the girls to complete the monotonous task of scooping half a teaspoon into the precut papers, folding them up so the powder would not spill inside the box of twenty-four. Norma started in earnest, hoping to alleviate whatever it was that was making Vincent grumpy. Meanwhile, Kathleen began her usual technique of laying out six papers at a time because she was certain that made the day go by faster.

Vincent ate the heel of a loaf of bread, plying it with some of her mother's strawberry jam. The girls had picked the berries themselves from a wild patch they found in a clearing on a bluff overlooking town. There was a sweetness in that and for a moment the young poet forgot why she was feeling so blue. As she sipped her tea a ray of sun filled the icy kitchen. "Well, nothing we can do about it but pray," she muttered as she took her dishes to the sink. The girls would include the dishes in their housework later that afternoon before starting their homework.

The whole day was taken up with work. If it wasn't the Seidlitz Powders, it would be sewing and needlework to cover their corsets that otherwise would be miserable to wear. If it wasn't the dishes, it would be washing. If it wasn't schoolwork, it would be practicing piano, sports or Sunday School. Ten-year-old Vincent was already weary.

When she stepped into the front room the first words from her mouth were, "Wump, you're putting in too much. We'll never make 480 if we use that much."

Kathleen turned her nose up and snipped, "Who cares? I hate making powders anyway."

Norma stepped in before Vincent could explode. "People who take powders without enough medicine will care."

"Eh yeh, they won't be able to poop," Kathleen giggled. The powders were named after a small Bohemian village that had water with a purgative effect.[45] The three sisters began to laugh, with Vincent tossing six doses in one paper and proclaiming, "I'm saving this for Mr. Kinsale."

Kathleen followed suit. "This is for Mrs. Wilkerson." Riotous laughter ensued at the mention of the nosy neighbor. It became even louder when Norma's was designated for Tom Wells, the local bully. After they had laughed themselves silly it was decided that all packets except the few accurate ones Norma had made would have to be redone.

Vincent's role was always to make the drudgery of their household duties tolerable if not fun. She had to admit though, that she liked the game of "Corners" better than filling the packets. In that chore-easing amusement, each girl took a corner in the room and raced to the center of the room. Whoever got there last had to start the fourth corner and finish it with the help of the other two. Norma was glad that her elder sister seemed in a better mood. They sat at the table and had contests for speed, accuracy and overall symmetry of the packets. The local pharmacist, Mr. Clearwater, needed the extra hands. "Poor man," Cora had explained by way of enticement. "We just must help. Between his pharmacy and heart medicine business he's tearing his hair out. I told him we'd be glad to lighten his load." What she hadn't told her daughters was that she had begged for the work.

While Vincent was old enough to resent the assumption that they'd be willing to help one of the wealthiest men in town get wealthier, she had grown practical enough to know they had to bring in more cash. The task of generating twenty packages of twenty-four powders was broken up by a break for pea soup at noon.

"Why can't I have any bread? Norma asked."

"I'll make some later," Vincent replied.

"But why don't we have any now?" Kathleen asked, slurping the soup Vincent had warmed for them from a pot meant to last a week.

"Because we haven't any flour or any yeast."

"Can't we get some?" the blonde asked.

"Even if we got some—and we will get some just as soon as the powders are done—it would be hours before the dough rose and the bread was baked."

Norma knew very well how long it took to make bread. She just preferred going to the bakery. "I just think…"

"I'll get the flour and yeast when we bring these to Mr. Clearwater. In the meantime, eat your soup and shut up. And Wump, don't say "eh yeh." You sound like some ignorant townie. Say yes."

The younger girls were stunned. The switch from patient and kind elder sister to rage was startling. Norma understood this meant more was on Vincent's mind than the Seidlitz Powders and whether there was enough food in the house. They all followed their mother's admonition. "Tears can't put out a fire."

There was nothing anyone could do about their circumstances. It was best to just move forward and do all one could do to make good. Vincent planned to do just that.

As quickly as she had erupted, Vincent apologized. "I'm sorry, sweethearts. I'm just out of sorts today. Let's finish lunch and the powders so we can get outside and get some groceries."

"How many more have we got to do?" Kathleen asked.

Vincent surveyed the pile of folded powders. "It looks as if there are about 300 there. Let's package them up in their boxes so we know for sure. Shouldn't take us more than a couple more hours."

6. The Creaking of the Tented Sky

1904

It had been a bitterly cold winter. Some days it was so cold they had to pilfer the shingles from a dilapidated shack next door. The half ton of coal Clem had purchased for them just wasn't enough and Cora didn't think it proper to take the free coal the city offered to poor residents.[46] Instead she went into the neighbor's yard, threw the shingles over the fence, and waited for the girls to pick them up on their way home from school. They practically lived in the kitchen, as fuel was needed for both cooking and heating.

There were times when Cora wondered what would happen to her children should she die. It became a bit of an obsession that year.

"Now don't you worry, Nell," Charlie said. As usual he was using her family nickname. "I'm sure one of us could take one or two or all three in if it came to that."

This was not reassuring. Cora knew how much her children relied on one another. "I'd like the girls to stay together."

"Of course, you would, and that's the benefit of all of us living so close. They'd never have to be far from each other."

Cora smiled. God bless him, she thought. He really does want to make me feel better and he's only making me feel worse. She began to cough.

"Are you alright, sister?"

"Yes, it's just a tickle."

But it wasn't. Thanks to a poor diet and overwork, the nurse had a full-blown case of pneumonia. Within days the children were being cared for by relatives rather than being exposed. Discussions were had over which daughter would live with whom, just as Charlie had suggested, but by spring forty-year-old Cora had enough strength to care for a medical emergency involving her youngest. After the awful danger of chorea this was something far worse: polio. Cora blamed the humid climate. She became determined to move the ragtag clan back to Maine. Her first stop was Union to the home of a friend who owed her a favor. Next was the farm of Henry's brother Fred. The fresh supply of dairy products helped restore Cora's normal weight and the girls delighted in the farm animals and a beautiful pasture rife with blueberries.

But Kathleen was now experiencing severe nerve damage on her left side. It broke Cora's heart to watch her youngest try to keep up with Vincent and Norma as they scampered toward the fresh delights of wild berries. Cora gave her skullcap and vigorous rub downs with cocoa butter daily to try and restore the damaged nerve sheaths. It helped but the child still needed to brace her left arm between her legs to keep it from shaking while she ate the hearty meals from Fred Millay's table.[47]

* * *

Another Millay brother was next as the itinerant family kept moving toward a destination no one was certain of. Austin Millay was happy to have a woman around to cook while his wife was out of town on her own nursing assignment, but he was a mean drunk, so they moved on to friend and relative until they arrived at their Aunt Clara Millay's boardinghouse on Washington Street in Camden.

With Henry out of the picture, Vincent's Great-Aunt Clara Buzzell was often around, picking up the slack in the lackadaisical management of the household. Other relatives and friends of the family were also in the circle, but few had enough time to care for the lonely girl and her sisters. This meant that people expected Vincent to take on even more responsibility in caring for her younger sisters. Although her aunt played a pivotal role in the child's life, offering some quiet comfort off and on throughout her childhood, the eldest could only rely on herself.[48]

Kind, generous and fun, it was decided that Cora and Kathleen would stay with Clara as the brunette waif continued her recovery. The older girls would stay with their grandfather Buzzell in Searsmont, about two dozen miles north of Camden. This left Cora available to take a job nursing a famous piano and organ teacher, John Tufts. Every evening after leaving work Cora would return to Clara's and give Kathleen her rubdowns, her herbs, and her cod liver oil. This arrangement was confounded by the children's grandfather being unable to take the noise and racket of the two girls when blended with the noise of his own younger sons. It was plain the vagabond life would soon have to end.

* * *

Aunt Clara knew a man who owned a miserable hovel in Camden's Milltown neighborhood.[49] It was close enough that the girls could contact their aunt in an emergency and affordable. It had been unoccupied for quite a while and was considered abandoned by all but the landlord and the desperate Millay family.

To sweeten the deal the owner told Cora that she could have her first month's rent for free if they would do the cosmetic repairs that it desperately needed. The nurse jumped at the chance. There were clients galore in Camden and she was familiar with the neighboring towns.

With the girls temporarily housed with their aunt and grandfather, Cora spent the fall of 1903 making the home ready for occupation that winter. Located in a large field of tall grasses and adjacent to both the Megunticook river and lake, the shanty dwelling was situated near a path taken by the mill hands. Although it had no indoor toilet, there was running water in the kitchen of the L-shaped, four room cottage. The paper and paint supplied by the landlord were little more than a bandage on a gaping wound, yet Cora did her utmost to make it cozy enough to finally have a long-term home for her daughters.

* * *

The final divorce decree was received January 4, 1904. Now Cora would have legal recourse should Henry fail to do his duty and pay the $5 a week alimony. Between that and the life insurance she had purchased at Charlie's suggestion, the nurse finally felt like they were on the right track.

But for Vincent the past few years had been too much of an emotional strain. Bursts of rage competed with Cora's attempts to make their home a respite. Unable to cope with her lack of control, the poet spent hours hiking through the grasses and along the lake and river. Some days she'd run through the sleeping town[50] before dawn just to have some sense of being her own person. Conflicts with Cora became more commonplace as the poet entered her teens. There was something about the permanence of their drafty abode that gave the bewildered teen permission to vent long crushed feelings.[51] Banishment to the basement or her room was welcomed, though she spent hours sobbing uncontrollably. To steady their sister's wild moods, Norma and Kathleen would sneak her food and magazines, sing to her and tell her how very much they loved her.

Now that she was nearing thirteen, Vincent began to notice her feelings as never before. She tried to bury them with clubs and church attendance, but she was not made for the confines of Roberts Rules of Order. She had a sense that she was something more than these other girls who had lived their conventional lives in conventional ways. How could they know what she did? She interrupted. She argued. She made jokes. She sang impromptu songs of her own composing, with impossibly clever rhymes that half her friends could not understand.

* * *

In the rainy season the girls would strip and run outside in the tall grasses around the house before racing back where their mother waited with a terrycloth towel to rub down their bodies until they were as pink as scarlet bee balm.[52] These times of glee were offset by continued poverty. Despite the rent being cheap and a routine collection of wild fruits and vegetables, the feminine band of independent thinkers still could not make ends fully meet. The contradictions confused them all, but especially the poet who remained as often as not the primary caregiver.

She poured her confounded thoughts into a novel that spoke of a deep-seated sense of abandonment and loss. She wrote "Dear Incorrigibles" in a voice not unlike her mother's. The tale features Norma as fourteen-year-old Margaret, Kathleen as Helen, and herself as Katherine. The names spoke volumes about Vincent's emotional state. By giving herself a name similar to the real-life name of her youngest sister she expresses her own insecurity and need to be coddled despite assuring her mother that a "great big" girl is old enough to care for the younger children while the mother goes off to nurse a sick relative. It was a story all too real. It becomes even more so when the Vincent character tells her youngest sister a fairy tale about a motherless princess who lives in a palace where everything was made of gold and yet she remained unhappy. The attempted novel was never finished, though the poet would return to the theme of being a princess again and again for the rest of her life.

The home was far from a castle. In the winter its walls felt as if they were made of papier mâché. Yet the family had long since developed the ostrich defense posture. When things went wrong it was better to make a game of it than fret about it.

The gale force winds off the coast made cold colder. It didn't help that the house had been set in a gully, so part of the house was on land at the top of the slope and the kitchen and living room were at a very soggy ground level.[53] All sorts of perishables, even Vincent's yeast bread, had to be kept on the upper floor to avoid freezing.[54] The girls avoided going out to the privy and instead used basins. Even doing dishes was postponed, as the water ran icy cold, and it took far too much fuel to warm it for washing up. The inefficiency of the small woodstove on the sleeping floor necessitated employing the oldest method of staying warm: snuggling. One wintry morning, the clan was astonished to discover that despite leaving the faucet in the kitchen dripping, the pipes had burst, and the entire ground floor was covered with a sheet of ice. Matters were made even worse by the river runoff.

"Oh, dear!"

"What will we do? Mama won't be home until this afternoon."

"We have to clean."

"But how?"

Resourceful Vincent had a solution. "Go upstairs and get your skates."

At first Norma couldn't believe her ears. Yet she soon realized the inch thick sheet of ice provided the perfect skating rink. She and Kathleen ran upstairs.

"Get mine, too," Vincent demanded. She would tiptoe across the ice to the kitchen stove and start the fire.

The water in the sink was also frozen solid along with the dishes in the sink. It stung to break them free and unclog the drain but there was no other choice. She heard the girls coming down the stairs.

"I got yours," Norma called. "Hey, this is fun."

The *skritch* of steel blades on ice could be heard from the other room.

"Put your coat on and bring me mine along with the skates. I'll make us breakfast."

The youngest ambled down the stairs. Her gait had improved but was still uneven. She sat down at the bottom of the stairs and put her ice skates on. "What do you want me to do?"

"Start putting away Mama's books and bring me all the dishes out there."

Soon the girls were skating around the main room tidying and cleaning while the poet put the kitchen in order. Dishes were broken as they were pulled from the ice. Their breakfast of porridge was cold within moments of being served.

"By God, I've never seen it this cold," Norma remarked as she trembled with the frost.

Vincent worried Kathleen might get sick again. "Now you better stay warm, Wump. Maybe go upstairs and get a blanket."

Kathleen didn't need to be told twice. She got up and skated toward the staircase. She paused. "Do you think Mama would mind if I didn't take my skates off?"

"Just be careful you stay on the runner and tread carefully."

The sound of the wind whistling through the cracks in the siding reminded Vincent that they would have to dump the basins. When Kathleen came back Vincent had another contest for them. She pulled three matches from the box and broke the end of one. "Pick a match."

"What for?"

"Whoever gets the short match has to go out to the privy and dump the basins."

"Yuck! Can't you?"

"We all made the mess. Someone must be the one to clean it up. Besides, I've already made breakfast, and I have my hands full taking care of the kitchen."

The trio selected their matches. Ironically it fell to Vincent to do the deed. This only made Norma and Kathleen giggle.

There was something in that moment that enraged her. She threw her partially eaten porridge into the sink with a frigid splash. Norma and Kathleen stopped laughing and watched as Vincent used a knife to pry the frozen basins from the icy floor and marched outside toward the privy. Moments later she was thrusting the knife into a frozen tree. Again and again, she thrust it until she was exhausted with spent rage. She calmly returned to the house and began doing the dishes in water just warm enough for cleaning. Her siblings stared.

"Don't you have more cleaning to do?"

"Yes." They simultaneously replied and left the kitchen.

A stifled sob drifted toward them. "Do you think she's all right?"

"Vince is tough. She just needs a moment. It's hard on her."

"It's hard on all of us."

Norma shook her head. "It's hardest on her."

* * *

Spring 1905 came with beautiful colors from the dye works upriver. Pinks, reds, blues, greens and yellows flowed by the house in an endless cycle of rainbows. They belied Vincent's growing sense that there was no safety in that little house. It was true that Kathleen's gait had improved, Norma had begun to study singing, and Vincent had moved on from tales of thwarted princesses. But on Saturday nights, when a paycheck meant a drunken and quarrelsome parade past their house, a sense of danger was everywhere present.[55] Once it took all three children, flinging themselves against the front door, to close it, and bolt it, and just in time. After that, for what seemed like hours, there was stumbling about outside, and grumbled cursing. When everything was quiet again, the children lay awake for a long time, listening and not making a sound, and thinking sometimes of the inconspicuous little path at the back of the house which they could follow in the blackest of nights without making a sound, through the tall grass of the field to the banks of the river, and how there, if it should seem unsafe to cross the corduroy bridge a little further upstream, they could swim across as quickly as water-rats to the further banks, and hide themselves in less than a minute in any one of ten places where nobody on earth—not even with dogs and lanterns—and the itinerant mills hands never went about with dogs and lanterns—could possibly find them.

Vincent took pride in knowing the girls were able to put on a brave face when left alone. She never spoke to her friends about the men who wandered near their house or tell them her mother now slept in a hammock in the front room. As far as anyone knew Kathleen and Cora slept in one upstairs room and Norma and she slept in the other. They only saw the girl who could make anything fun, whose family was a kind of circus sideshow with always some unusual entertainment in the offing. Cora had managed to rent a piano and convince Mrs. French to give Vincent lessons. There was soon a telephone installed. Extra layers of newspaper and fabric scraps made the walls a little thicker and the front room less miserable in cool weather. Mineral wool[56] was wrapped around all the pipes. The ramshackle structure the Millay's called home began to take on the rough and ready personalities of its occupants.

Now that they enjoyed a tenuous stability, the girls started going to church regularly to build relationships in the community. This would benefit them in a few ways, including providing potential income sources, food sharing and tutors to help them catch up after years of haphazard school attendance.

It had been ages since they'd lived in the area and only a few of the surnames were familiar to Cora. One family, the Knights, had a daughter Ethel who was close to Vincent's age. They had met through the St. Nicholas League,[57] whose motto was, "Live to Learn and Learn to Live." It was an offshoot of a magazine Vincent subscribed to and would soon publish in. Designed for inquisitive minds and avid readers, the magazine published short pieces by Mark Twain, Louisa May Alcott and others, while also providing young writers with a chance at publication. Each month the League would sponsor a contest for the best essay, puzzle, drawing, photograph and poem. Winners won gold badges, second place silver, and those who won both got cash. It seemed tailor-made for Vincent. When she was fourteen, the poet had two poems accepted by the publication: *Forest Trees* and *Land of Romance*. The latter had won a gold badge.[58]

Having made a friend through the League was icing on the proverbial cake. Creating a club of their own was an even greater thrill. The Huckleberry Finners,[59] a group of girls dedicated to reading and sharing impressions of the work of Mark Twain, was soon a part of Vincent's abundant social life.

Both girls attended the First Congregational Church where Vincent would soon become fast friends with Abbie, the minister's daughter. At twenty-three she would be both mentor and foil to the budding iconoclast. For Abbie church was a place of fellowship and strict, seamless faith, which would sometimes put her at odds with both Ethel and Vincent. While the poet could be devil may care, and Ethel could make up mildly irreverent rhymes, Abbie's faith inspired her to create a girl's Bible study group which she called the Genethod. The odd name was based on Abbie's father's Welsh heritage, and it meant daughter, but Abbie decided it meant sisterhood.

Naturally Vincent was fascinated with the name, which sounded not at all how it was spelled. "Gah-neck-tahd…what a strange word[60]," she remarked.

Abbie puffed up like a fish. "It's not strange at all."

"I didn't mean anything by it."

"It's Welsh."

"That's what you said," Ethel said, hoping to calm Abbie down.

The tall, chestnut-haired Protestant shrugged.[61] She sidled toward the piano and began to bang out a hymn. Vincent and Ethel sang. After a hymn or two they discussed Bible chapters. Abbie was a natural leader and knew how to draw the members out and direct a conversation. Consequently, it was a tame group until it started to grow.

Vincent began to challenge the status quo, including Abbie's leadership. This created an odd dynamic. On the one hand Abbie's father was the pastor and thus it made sense in a small-town way that the older woman should lead the group. On the other hand, Vincent liked challenging notions of right and wrong, which made her attractive to her fellow teenagers.

Each Sunday, Vincent—and sometimes her family—would sit in the long wooden pews staring at the arch that read, "I Am the Resurrection. Christ is Risen."[62] To her right, Abbie would play the hymns her father had selected to go with the sermon. As they listened, Vincent's deep faith in the "God of Life" was stirred, but afterward the hypocrisy of those who preached tolerance disturbed her.

* * *

In 1907, Ethel convinced Vincent to keep a journal. By now she had already been in high school for a year, jumping ahead of classmates who found her confrontations with the school principal amusing.[63] She might have ended her education there if it hadn't been for Cora's determination that all her daughters would finish high school. It was hoped that the journal would keep Vincent's explosive temper under control and help her find her voice.

After a scandalous confrontation with her primary school principal over his annoying habit of calling her by any "V" name but Vincent, and Cora's subsequent brawl with the short-fused official in which he actually tried to throttle the nurse, Vincent sought to establish herself at Camden High School as the brainiest and most talented girl in class. This mask of self-assurance would bring her trouble before long. In the meantime, all it did was annoy people who knew what she really felt was overwhelming insecurity.

Her first journal, which she called Rosemary,[64] gave her an outlet that went well beyond recording the mere daily activities of a teenager. It spelled out her growing sense of being destined for something she couldn't define yet. In it she was able to voice her displeasure with Norma taking over her rocking chair and how it felt to be 16 and the oldest of three.[65]

The years had folded upon each other like an accordion, with the same airs and whines and whimsy day after day. But Vincent was growing in self-awareness and when she wasn't feeling like she was going to explode she was having impromptu outdoor parties with school chums.

* * *

The verdant grass around their home was tall enough to obscure which of the sisters or their friends was which. In a variation of "Hide and Seek," one of them would stand by the house with her eyes closed, count to ten, and then look for which playmate held what color silk ribbon aloft as the whole group ran willy-nilly through the field.

"Norma! You've got yellow!"

If the guess was correct the hand would drop, and the color would stop running. If it wasn't the mad dash would continue. It was the sort of game only the Millay sisters would think of.

Their parties were unlike any in town, because they had a type of spontaneity that was normally frowned upon. There was always something unique about them. Friends marveled at Cora's picnic fare of salmon and sardine sandwiches, various sweets and fruits, and Vincent's dramatic costumes. It was as if the Millays could bring sentimental novels like *Jane Cable* or *The House of a Thousand Candles*[66] to life. Over plates of warm fudge and through popular folk songs, Ethel and her sister Martha would linger long past their curfew just for a chance of a few more minutes in Vincent's magical presence.

Yet the poet did not feel confident that her secrets would remain safe with any of them. She knew she thought things that would be viewed as blasphemous if not outright criminal.

For one thing, she couldn't tell anyone about the men that lurked around the house. If she had it would be viewed as making trouble for the men that were helping keep the local economy going. For another, she was beginning to doubt the faith that brought her a circle of steady friends.

She started to hate Sundays. She was expected to make breakfast for Norma and Kathleen, then go to church and stay afterward to attend the Genethod meeting. But how could she when the church taught so many things that didn't make sense to her anymore. In truth, she was more pagan than Christian. God was everywhere. God was not one man who died in a country across the sea nearly two thousand years before. God was in the way the tide pools slurped and the wind blew through the trees. God was in her heart not a book. Doubt began to consume her. It wasn't that she didn't believe in a Supreme Being. It was how that being was defined by the people she loved. How could she talk to any of them about all that mystery when she was certain they wouldn't understand what she was feeling inside? It was as if her soul was too big for the rest of her.[67]

There were times when she wanted an excuse so much that she wished for the sky to just open up and rain cats, dogs, hammers, pitchforks, silver spoons, hayricks, paper covered novels, picture frames, rag carpets, toothpicks, skating rinks, Birds of Paradise, burdocks and French grammar texts![68]

In addition to these forbidden thoughts, her body was stirring with sexual desire she dared not speak of.

The lake was deep and cold, the sun all encompassing. The poet and her best friend were picnicking in the only shady spot they could find that hadn't already been overtaken by others seeking escape from the sticky air. Abbie looked at Vincent shyly. "Do you suppose we could swim in our drawers?"

Vincent wasn't sure. Abbie's shaky gait gave her pause. "Are you sure you can? The current's awfully strong sometimes."

The pastor's daughter tossed a stick into the inlet. They watched as it drifted down the lake toward the river. "It looks pretty slow to me."

"Perfect baptizing speed," Vincent giggled.

Abbie frowned. "How can you take our Lord so lightly?"

The poet remained quiet. She wondered how it would feel if she saw Abbie undressed. Had Abbie known love, the kind she imagined.

"So, shall we?"

Vincent knew she had to answer. She had swum in the buff with her sisters on many occasions, but this would be different. "Sure."

As Abbie pulled her skirt down Vincent found herself staring at the way her friend's corset met her hips. What she felt was forbidden. When the corset came off the poet fixated upon Abbie's shoulders and the curves below. She drew her inhale slowly. "Would you please loosen my corset? I think Norma knotted the lacing."

Abbie approached and gently began to undo the knot. As she did Vincent could feel her breath upon her neck. Abbie sensed what the younger girl was feeling and remained silent as she finished the task. Both trembled, but for different reasons: Abbie for sinful thoughts; Vincent with desire.

"There." Abbie loosened the corset, slipped away and walked into the water. Had she looked back she would have seen Vincent undress completely and her nubile body drift into the sun-dappled inlet. The lake partially cooled the feelings Vincent was hoping to forget.

"Race you to the island," the poet cried and took off toward a small island about two hundred feet from shore.

Abbie held back. Her limbs weren't strong enough. Instead, she took in the beauty of nature around her. It was a day that would soon appear in her own poetry.[69] For now it was enough to feel the cool stillness of the gentle eddy surrounding her.

Vincent looked across the water at her friend. They shared so much, yet there was no way to express what she felt.

* * *

When she filled her first journal Vincent was ready for a new confidante. "Rosemary" gave way to Mammy Hush-Chile, a black caregiver who, unlike her mother, would always be there to serve and comfort her. Camden was a town where abolitionists had once held sway, but that did not stop the teenager from imagining a "white-souled, black-faced cuddle-mammy." As a slave, Vincent's comforter had to stay with her.[70] Cora did not.

"Mammy Hush-Chile" was so nice and cuddly and story-telly when she was all full of troubles and worries and little vexations. It was a comfort to confide in her and let the cares roll off her mind. Having an epistolary confidante allowed Vincent to express all her anger and imagine Cora as a perfect mother.

Poetry was becoming another important way of expressing herself. The stories of her childhood made way for the first tentative verses. When her sisters left for school and she was alone Vincent would make two cups of tea in a little China blue teapot and imagine her mother sitting across from her, their faces illumined by the firelight of the crackling stove, while she recited the poems she had composed.[71]

Cora had given Vincent poetry, music and a love of literature. The budding poet would now dedicate a hand-stitched volume of poetry to her mother.

To My Mother,

Whose interest and understanding have been the life of many of these works and the inspiration for many more, I lovingly dedicate this little volume.

As she received the booklet, Cora felt a lump rise in her throat. "This is so beautiful, Vincent. How nicely you've printed out 'Land of Romance'."

"Thank you. I hope you like it," the small, delicate teenager said softly. She needed to hear the praise again.

"Oh, yes, of course. It's beautiful."

"There's an index."

Cora flipped to the back of the book. An alphabetical list of the sixty-one works rose from the page. "Oh, my! And you've even written down how old you were when you wrote them."[72]

Moments later, as she flipped through the volume, she found a poem she hadn't seen before. It brought tears to her eyes, for it was clear that Vincent felt it was her job to care for her as a husband might.

> Dearest, when you go away
> My heart will go, too,
> Will be with you all the day,
> All the nights with you.
> Where you are through lonely years,
> There my heart will be.
> I will guide you past your fears
> And bring you back to me.

Cora slouched and drew her hand to cover her face. Vincent mustn't see her cry. "Darling," she managed to mutter. "It's truly lovely."

* * *

The school paper had long called upon seniors to act as editor-in-chief. As a regular contributor to *The Megunticook*, Vincent knew she had a good chance of being named. As it was, even though she didn't attend lectures in the usual way, she was the only member of her graduating class to be published outside the high school paper.

By now she had won a silver badge from the St. Nicholas League for her poem, *Young Mother Hubbard*.[73] But that wasn't her only accomplishment. She was working on a new poem, a long poem that expressed some of her many frustrations with life in Camden and the sometimes-stifling atmosphere of her family home. She had a feeling about it. She sensed it would lead to being named class poet, a title she longed for with a passion born of hubris.

But poetry was not her only claim to fame. Her piano lessons with Leila French, practiced on a beat-up Mason and Hamlin organ,[74] were preparing her for her first recital. Her original compositions had even drawn the attention of her mother's former patient, Dr. John Tufts, a retired teacher from the New England Conservatory.[75] Although blind, the old man was startled with the young lady's inventiveness and variations on the compositions of Chopin and new works by Scriabin. When Vincent wasn't walking to the Cushing mansion to read to Dr. Tufts, she was playing for him and listening to him play in hopes of gaining some special trick that would assure admiration. Her activities even extended to playing a role in every play presented by the high school in 1909.

It was as if she were driven to prove something. She would show that she was as good as any of the girls in town, better even. Her artwork was admired, her poems won prizes, her music impressed a renowned expert, and she was a good enough actress to take any role offered to her. She would show them! She would be all the daughters of Zeus and Mnemosyne rolled into one.

That spring her family moved to a cute house at 40 Chestnut. In addition to having a wide front porch, the larger home was closer to town and had a bedroom for the girls that looked out onto the water. This was another demonstration of her excellence. Now her friends would be less hesitant to visit. She and her sisters would entertain friends in a style they aspired to even if they still weren't one hundred percent there yet.

The home became a favored retreat for the teenagers. For one thing, there were no parents around to scold them. For another, the parties, card games and impromptu meals conjured from seemingly nothing were enticingly unconventional.

Vincent's role as editor added pressure to her search for acceptance. She wanted *The Megunticook* to be the most wonderful school paper in the state. She would publish poems, write stories, edit the work of others and show all those boys who mocked her that she was as good as any of them. This would lead to the first of Vincent's many emotional breakdowns.

Football captains can sometimes be full of themselves. Add being handsome, the son of the local Baptist minister and class president and you have a nearly impossible combination. George Frohock was just such a fellow and Vincent's high school nemesis.[76]

Whenever the poet would try and speak George would lead a chorus of rowdy boys in shouts, catcalls, whistles and stomps until she stopped. It was George who encouraged their classmate Henry Hall to claim he couldn't finish a poem Vincent had asked him to submit to the paper. George knew, as did most students, that Vincent would simply finish it herself and put Henry's name on it as a favor she'd come to regret.

Everyone knew the red head was the best poet. The trouble was they also knew that she took great pride in that skill. As high school big shots will sometimes do, George and his cronies had to come up with a way of putting Vincent in what they viewed as her place. She was arrogant. She was opinionated. She made everyone else feel small, so it was her turn to feel that way. They knew they had to find a way to bring her down a peg without exposing themselves to punishment.

It began with a group decision to hold back on submissions to the school paper. This would force Vincent to ask someone for a piece. Everyone knew Henry had tried to impress the poet with his own verse and it seemed like chances were good she would ask him for a submission, particularly if others begged off. The plan was set in motion.

With only days before the paper was to go to press, Henry was instructed to call and announce that he hadn't finished the poem and that he wasn't sure he could.

"Oh, dear, Henry!" Vincent cried upon hearing the news.

"I'm sorry, Vincent, honest I am. I just have so much to do and…"

"I was hoping that with a little work and care you could produce some funny verses or something."

"Well, I started but then…"

Vincent was frustrated. There was already so much to do before press. It was her job to get it done. "Bring me what you have, and I'll finish it for you."

"Oh, gee, thanks, Vincent. I'll bring it right over."

The boys had managed to come up with something that they knew would appeal to the poet and have elements they'd heard many times in her work. Henry brought it by.

"Oh, this is better than…Um, I think I can get this ready for you. You don't mind if I fix the rhymes and meter, do you?"

"No. That would be wonderful."

After some quick goodbyes designed to prove how very busy Henry was, the schemer went to the corner and met up with George and the other plotters.

"Is she going to do it?"

"Yes, fell for it hook, line and sinker."

"Perfect. Now we've got to make sure everyone votes for it as class poem and names Hank class poet."

"What about the girls?" one of the boys asked.

"Don't worry about the girls. Most of them are just as sick of her highfalutin' ways as we are," George observed. As football captain he was almost universally admired.

Upon publication everyone rushed to Henry to congratulate him. Though the majority male class members were in on the ruse, others just thought that perhaps the short, dark-haired Henry had depths they'd never known. Vincent, in keeping with her sense of honor, never corrected that error. Instead, she remained confident that Henry's sudden rise to fame was too late to deny her place in the high school pantheon.

* * *

Norma came downstairs looking for a snack.

"Vincent?"

Her sister lay crumpled at the foot of the stairs, tears streaming down her face.

"What?"

"They've elected Henry Hall class poet."

Norma couldn't believe it. "Henry? That fat faced slug that played your father in the senior play?"

"The same."

"I...Are you sure?"

"I'm certain. The principal asked me to put it in next week's edition along with the valedictorian and everything else."

"What about..."

Before she could finish Vincent jumped in. "To think I put my arms around his neck and kissed him every night for weeks. Oh, I could strike my mouth! Ugh. I can feel the touch of him now. I laid my head on his knee and clasped his hand."[77]

"Who would vote for him?"

"Everybody. Even my friends. Corinne voted for me at least, but everyone else, they all voted for Henry, and I wrote the poem!"

"Wait? What?"

"You know how he was always writing me those rhymeless, meter-less things which I suppose he thought were poems?"

"Uh, huh...in juniors?" Norma knelt and took Vincent's hand.

"I've helped him take the only thing I cared about, and now...I despise him as I despise a snake." As much as the poet hoped to avoid tears her anger made that impossible. She felt like a volcano whose magma had reached bubbling point.

"But...I don't think I understand."

"Don't you see?" Vincent began to fume. She ripped her hand from her younger sister's and began to pace. "I needed something to fill a spot in the paper."

"Yes." Norma's voice was soft. She wished Vincent wouldn't take it so hard.

"So, I asked him to give me something. I figured I'd have to edit it, but..."

"I see. You made it good, put his name on it and..."

"Oh, he'll make a manly man someday, didn't have stiffening enough in his great big fat sluggish stolidity to get on his feet and tell them that the only poem he ever had printed in his life—*and the only poem he ever will have printed in his life*—had been half-written, wholly made over, and published *by me*!"[78]

Norma now realized the feeling behind the rage Vincent was trying not to direct at her. She had been the architect of her own downfall.

As if reading Norma's mind, the steaming redhead shook her fist. "Oh, it makes me white when I think that it was my own fault…and that I did for the paper. How can he sit there and smile at me with his round, red face! How can he speak to me with his great fat voice!"

"Maybe if you told Mama…" Norma began.

"Mama? I can't tell it all to Mama. Even if she knew everything that happened, she'd never know how it feels to *me*."

It wasn't long before the pent-up rage and its necessary venting made the poet sick.

Norma grew increasingly concerned as she watched Vincent become physically overwhelmed by the perfect complement to her sense of betrayal. She called their mother, who was in Rockport on a case. Annoyed at what seemed like an unnecessary intrusion, Cora prescribed oranges, sherry and milk.[79] Nothing worked to restore Vincent confidence. Norma called again, and this time Cora came running. She was surprised that her normally iron-willed eldest was so miserable. The strain stained the poet's face. Words that crowded behind her lips found other avenues of expressing themselves. The floor was littered with eggshells.

Over the next few weeks, Cora gave Vincent brisk rubdowns meant to push her mind into her body. The spring weather normally would have sent the poet outdoors, but she was far too caught up in the pain of her heart and mind to care about the piping plover seeking its mate.

Vincent retreated further as April became May, though she managed to attend the class group photo.[80] There, sandwiched between Corinne Sawyer and Stella Derry, the forlorn student sat looking and feeling alone and betrayed by the friends who just weeks before had stood smiling with her on the school's exterior staircase. Sensing her rage, no one touched her. Henry stood in the back row, raising his head to be seen over those of his classmates. George stood to her left, a smirk on his face and the toe of his right foot jauntily crossed across his left ankle. When it came time for the class's individual portraits, the poet refused to attend because she knew she'd be standing in line forced to make small talk with people she wanted to slap. Instead, she went to her family's old landlord, Wellington G. Singhi, to sit for a portrait that conveyed an innocence she did not possess.

*　*　*

Cora was furious with her daughter's friends. She called the few who had telephones installed in their homes to ask how they could have voted against her daughter. Some knew nothing about George and Henry's plan. They simply liked the poem. Others admitted their complicity but felt it wasn't their responsibility that Vincent took it so hard.

Of all the trials of the Millay clan Vincent considered the episode her first big disappointment.[81] When she entered the Camden Opera House for the graduation ceremonies on June 16, 1909, she avoided the gazes of her lesser peers.

"There she is."

"I never thought she'd be here."

"Wait until Henry reads the poem."

"I can hardly wait to see her face."

"Haha, serves her right, thinking she's so high and mighty."

"White trash."

"Is that her mother? I heard her father…"

Vincent forced the whispers from her ears. She concentrated on Martha Knight's lecture on Scottish folklore and Stella Derry's piano solo. She pointedly yawned when the boys spoke of the "Value of Higher Education" and "The Uses and Values of Electricity."

She could not, however, ignore Henry's recitation of the poem she'd improved enough to be intelligible. Every word that rhymed, every meter that beat with the clarity of a metronome, choked as it drifted from her ears to her heart. As the days had passed, she counted on Mammy Hush-Chile to serve up the bitter pill that had to be chewed until she felt better.[82] Now here she was, waiting her turn and her vengeance, as each of her classmates offered up what they hoped would win a ten-dollar prize.

She was the last speaker and the whole crowd held their breath, wondering what sort of composition Vincent would offer. Nearly every parent and teacher had heard of the prank played upon her.

The redhead lifted her head and walked toward the podium. She cleared her throat and used her magnificent voice to pound every doubter into submission. As she recited *La Joie de Vivre*, shame could be felt throughout the auditorium. She was bigger than any of them.

'Tis good to be alive on a day like this!
'Tis good to be alive! I will not miss
One joy from out of living: I will go
Through valleys low; where deep-set mountains throw
A shadow and shelter from the heat,
In cool retreat where shall no city street
Intrude its noise and scare the stillness sweet.

Deep draw I in my breath,
    Deep drink of water cold;
    There is no growing old,
There is no death.

The world and I are young!
    Never on lips of man,—
    Never since time began,
    Has gladder song been sung…

The recitation continued for another sixty-seven lines, stunning the audience and retrieving the power the boys thought they'd stolen.

Vincent, the true poet, won the $10 prize. The April prank had become a June triumph.

Part Two

Departure

It's little I care what path I take,
And where it leads it's little I care;
But out of this house, lest my heart break,
I must go, and off somewhere.

It's little I know what's in my heart,
What's in my mind it's little I know,
But there's that in me must up and start,
And it's little I care where my feet go.

I wish I could walk for a day and a night,
And find me at dawn in a desolate place
With never the rut of a road in sight,
Nor the roof of a house, nor the eyes of a face.

I wish I could walk till my blood should spout,
And drop me, never to stir again,
On a shore that is wide, for the tide is out,
And the weedy rocks are bare to the rain.

But dump or dock, where the path I take
Brings up, it's little enough I care;
And it's little I'd mind the fuss they'll make,
Huddled dead in a ditch somewhere.

"Is something the matter, dear," she said,
"That you sit at your work so silently?"
"No, mother, no, 'twas a knot in my thread.
There goes the kettle, I'll make the tea."

7. The Ticking of Eternity

1912

The telephone rattled against the wall as it struggled against the square of cotton fabric Vincent had installed between the bells.

The device had been ordered to help Cora spend more time at home, which turned out to be both a blessing and a curse. Clients could call for advice or, in an emergency, be assured Cora would be the first caregiver to arrive. The downside was its presence made silence unreliable. Vincent might be in the middle of composing a poem, bending under the terrible weight of the perfect word,[83] and suddenly the life-changing beast would spoil her process.

And it wasn't just Vincent. Cora might come home after an overnight shift and collapse with exhaustion and be interrupted by an overly anxious client worrying about a teething child. The telephone made Norma too popular and Kathleen too available. In short, the device was more trouble than it was worth.

Nonetheless, the incessant thud of the muffled bell made Vincent stand up from sewing her shortened corset and answer.

"Yes?" she said as she watched a titmouse flit through the tree outside their window.

"May I speak with Vincent Millay?"

"I am she." Vincent stepped as far as the receiver allowed to keep track of the bird's movement through the tree. The confused caller paused.

"Hello?" Vincent said. Disconnection was a frequent occurrence.

"Is your father Henry Millay?"

"Yes." The cheer-cheer of the chirping bird was far more interesting than the caller.

"This is the Kingman operator, Mr. Millay. Your father, is very ill and may not recover."[84]

The poet did not care if the operator did not understand she was a twenty-year-old woman. She was only stunned that the caller had told her that her father was perhaps dying. She remained silent, stunned by the news. It was hard to imagine his vivid blue eyes crowded with death.

Eventually the operator spoke. "Do you have any message for him?"

"I'll send a telegram," Vincent managed.

"Is that all?" the surprised operator asked.

"Yes." The tufts of the titmouse could just be seen in the crevice of the tree, but his "cheer-cheer" belied the mood in the room. "What is the address?"

The poet immediately called her mother and explained the situation. Cora told her where she could find the few dollars necessary to make it as far as Bangor. Meanwhile, she would call their family friends, the Duntons, about Vincent spending the night there. Cora's profession gave her an encyclopedic knowledge of the boat and train schedules. "You've already missed the noon boat to Bucksport, so you'll have to leave tomorrow morning. Be sure to bring that picture of you girls and the good one of me. Bring mourning clothes just in case, otherwise bring along your long underwear and an outfit or two. It's often colder up in Kingman this time of year."

It had been eleven years since she'd seen her father. In that time, he had moved almost as frequently as Cora and the girls had. Yet unlike Vincent he had remained in one town. The frequently unemployed, often ill, perpetually hard-up sad sack had never honored the court ordered child support of five dollars a week. If he had paid child support, they would not have had to move as often as they did. They wouldn't have to avoid the grocer, baker and butcher for fear of being quizzed about late bills. A dollar here or there was the best he could manage. Christmas promises became January regrets. Vincent lamented that she'd lived on sawdust long enough.[85] How could she and her sisters keep alive unless he sent something resembling dough every now and then? All of Henry's best laid plans came to naught as misfortune plagued him like a hornet at a picnic. Even his rental had burned down, taking all his possessions and hopes of success in the hotel fire. Now she was being summoned to Kingman, Maine as if they actually had a relationship. Perhaps he really did think about them a great deal even if he didn't manage to show it financially or even as a correspondent.

Cora told Vincent if he did die, she should find a way to see if he had any money tucked away despite his claims of poverty. "After all," the nurse remarked cynically, "you can't take it with you."

Her mother had been gone a long time. In summer 1910 she'd been away for over six weeks. In 1911 Cora spent more time with clients than at home with the girls. When the nurse was around, she demanded time alone to recuperate. Vincent was sick of being grown-up. She could feel the lines underneath her skin even if they didn't show. As it was her hands were stiff, rough, stained and chapped.[86] She loved beauty more than anything in the world and yet never had time to make herself so. So tired at night that she didn't even have the energy to brush her beautiful autumn-colored hair. She was tired of dresses that kicked around her feet, high-heeled shoes, hair pins, and conventions and proprieties. How she longed for the simple joys of the woods and fields near her Auntie Bine! She imagined tasting the sweetness of the rhubarb stalks as she peeled them to make ribbons to fashion a rhubarb leaf hat decorated with white clover and buttercups.[87] How she loved the old white house on a hill and the blackberries and clove that surrounded it! Her loneliness for her mother and childhood was so strong she wished for Auntie Bine to be her mother again.

Vincent was so busy seeking her mother's approval that she drew up a contract between herself and her sisters to keep the house in order during her mother's interminable absences. It assured her mother that she had convinced Hunk and Wump—Norma and Kathleen—to wake up every day at six and begin chores that were so perfectly synchronized that it was hard to imagine it was anything but a factory schedule. During a fifteen-minute period of morning ablutions, Kathleen would light the fire while Norma bathed, and Vincent filled and lit the lamps. Once Norma had completed her bath it would be Kathleen's turn while Norma made breakfast. Kathleen would then set the table while Norma finished making breakfast and Vincent took her own bath. Only then could the sisters sit down to a fifteen-minute breakfast and then dress, garden, make beds, do dishes and complete their "Corner" game of housekeeping. Kathleen would study while Vincent wrote, and Norma did wash. Even leisure was scheduled for a precise ninety-minute period from 3:30-5 p.m. A similarly tight schedule for the afternoon and evening included feeding the family cat, getting wood ready for breakfast preparation and the poet killing flies. Then they promised to go to bed at eight without fail.[88]

Now the question was, would the younger Millay sisters keep this schedule while she went to Kingman to see her father. Vincent worried that Kathleen would not study and drop out of high school. Norma, whose chief duties seemed to be cooking and keeping their clothing clean and mended, was boy crazy and very popular. Would she bother to hold up her end of their bargain? If Cora was gone who would be "mother"? Vincent needed to borrow a suitcase from her Aunt Rose.[89] Maybe she could ask her to check in on the girls now and then to make sure all was well.

After retrieving the suitcase, she threw some clothes, some poems, her journal and a volume by Robert Burns from her mother's library. She knew she'd need a distraction during her bedtime vigil, and she thought she remembered Cora telling her that her father liked Burns' work. She would read to him, just as she read to blind old Professor Tufts, her one-time piano teacher. Duty, duty, duty was everywhere.

When the girls got home later that afternoon, Vincent explained what was going on. Kathleen, who had very little recollection of the man they called Pa, only remembered the voice that sang them lullabies. Norma, stoic and detached, wondered if she might come along before realizing that being in Kingman would interfere with her role in planning a local fete. Their dinner, a humble plate of beans with remnants of ham hock, seemed tasteless as Vincent went over their amended routine while she was gone.

"But who will take care of us?" Kathleen asked, ever the baby of the family, even at fifteen.

"Oh, for heaven's sake, Kay," Norma chided. "We can take care of ourselves."

"Mother's case has pinkeye, so she won't be home for a while," Vincent cautioned. "You'll both have to do your part. There's some work at the grocer's and the Whitehall has posted something. Do what you can to help out Mother until I get back."

Normally, Vincent brought in the shortfall either by acting, selling poems, or playing the piano for the picture show. Now it would fall to her sisters to bring in the extra cash they needed. Norma nodded grimly. Kathleen remained oblivious.

After a fitful night's sleep, Vincent took the morning boat to Bucksport. The sixty-three-mile journey along the inland waterways of Penobscot Bay was scenic but brutally cold. Her eyes watered and sent an icy sting across her cheeks as the small transport boat made its way from Camden, to Lincolnville, Northport, Belfast and Searsport, then finally through the narrow passage of

Verona Island and into the Penobscot River, past Fort Knox and into the sleepy village of Bucksport.

The afternoon sun now hit the spires of the town's church which was set amid classic New England clapboard houses.[90] The Seminary Hill that rose behind the heart of the community reminded her of many of the towns her family had lived in through the years. Unlike many places where they had lived, Bucksport reflected the prosperity of its newer hydro-electric plant and the remnants of the town's logging and milling past.

After the boat landed, Vincent picked up her suitcase and walked the short distance to the simple, rectangular depot of the Bucksport Branch of the Maine Central Railroad. The next leg of her journey would be a trip to Bangor, a nineteen-and-a-half-mile trip. She telegraphed the Dunton's to tell them of her estimated arrival time and then stepped outside to wait for the train. Vincent hated the sulfur smell of the lumber mill as it collided with the sewage-tinged riverbank. It was all too much contrast with the beauty of the town. It smelled of death.

In short order the narrow-gauge spur line rumbled along toward Bangor and the sort of dreadful conversations one has in times like this. What would she say when people said, "I hope you get there in time"? It would be just too ridiculous to take the sentiment in the spirit intended. She hardly knew the man. The pun made her gently laugh. "Spirit intended," she muttered, hoping she'd remember to make a note of it for a story sometime. Other passengers noticed the sly smile of the girl with the mane of red hair.

Even at a distance, Bangor's Union Station[91] was the grandest depot she'd ever seen. Its tall clock tower stood like a steeple over the city. Its reflection in the murky waters where the Kenduskeag stream met the Penobscot River spoke of possibilities she had only dreamed of. The train paused as the drawbridge allowed a queue of lumber ships to pass to the waterfront for loading.

Now that she had arrived, the poet grew anxious. She'd only met the Duntons a couple of times and wasn't sure how much they knew about her. The city still bore the scars of a Great Fire the year before[92] and she wondered if her hosts had been impacted. If so, what should she say?

As the drawbridge came down Vincent recalled her mother's advice on how she should act during her overnight stay. For one, she knew it was expected to include the Duntons in everything she wanted to do. This would mean including Mrs. Dunton in her decision to bring flowers for her father's bedside. She already knew her hosts would feel obligated to give her the best available room in their home and to serve food they would not normally set for themselves. On the other hand, Mrs. Dunton would be unlikely to express regrets should she be unable to provide a private room due to the fire or say anything about whether Vincent's visit was an inconvenience. This meant the poet had to be especially sensitive to her host's signals and ask for very little. She would be expected to conform to household rules, which the poet already knew were unlikely to match the laissez-faire attitudes of her own family home.

She would have to reduce the urge to offer her opinion about things she heard, saw or consumed, particularly if she couldn't be complementary. In fact, this foray from the nest provided the poet with a greater challenge than any acting role, poem or employment she'd ever known. She would have to appear more disciplined and polished than she'd ever been.

The train pulled into the depot with a great burst of steam. Vincent stood and found her legs vibrating from the journey. Once on the platform she pulled her small, borrowed luggage from the row of various sizes and looked for the Duntons. They were nowhere to be seen so she worked her way through the palatial transit hub, marveling at its elegance.[93] The public facilities were far more opulent than any in Camden or Rockland. There was a smoker's lounge, a telegraph office, electric lights and radiant steam heat. Vendors offered coffee, tea, timetables, newspapers and snacks. Yet she still hadn't seen her hosts, so she decided to step onto Exchange Street and await their arrival. It didn't take long.

"Oh, my dear, I'm so sorry!" The Duntons had sent along their niece in the hope it would make the poet more comfortable. Mabel Dunton was three months older but seemed years younger. She hugged Vincent like a stranger acting familiar.

"Come along, child," Mr. Dunton said solemnly. "Mother has a nice supper waiting for you and your room's prepared."

"Yes, poor dear," Mabel repeated. "Come along."

Vincent allowed Mr. Dunton to take her bag as Mabel looped her arm in Vincent's, leading the way to their carriage. Two beautiful bays stood ready to carry them swiftly to their destination.

An automobile sputtered by. Then another. Although most vehicles were still horse-drawn, Vincent had never seen so many flivvers. It was the largest city she could recall seeing. Part of her was frightened; the other was thrilled.

Idle chatter was exchanged. The Duntons were full of stories of the Great Fire the year before and pointed out the empty spaces where various buildings had burned to the ground. Vincent was growing comfortable enough to allow herself to feel the exhaustion from thirty-six hours of little rest and too much emotion.

Within an hour they had arrived at the Dunton's comfortable home. Mrs. Dunton greeted her at the door and offered her a glass of sherry which Vincent eagerly accepted. They watched as Mr. Dunton walked up the stairs with her suitcase. "Your room is the first one on the right," Mrs. Dunton smiled. "We'll get you supper and then you can retire if you like. I would like to hear about your mother and sisters, though."

Vincent nodded. "Thank you. It will be so nice to have a bit of rest before seeing Pa."

"It's been a while, hasn't it?"

"Yes." The poet wasn't sure what she should respond to. "Mother is fine."

"Is she still doing hair pieces?"

"Sometimes," Vincent replied and accepted another glass of the golden liquor. "Mostly she works as a nurse."

Mrs. Dunton knew what that meant. "She must often be gone. How are the girls?"

Vincent felt her legs go wobbly. "Do you mind if I sit?"

"No. Of course not, dear. Whatever was I thinking? You must be all in." Her hostess indicated a chair and sat down in another facing her. "So, the girls?"

Vincent settled down and took another sip. She wanted a refill but dared not ask. "Norma is about to graduate from high school and Kathleen is starting her junior year next fall."

"Will you be going to college?"

Vincent frowned. It was the thing she wanted most in the world, to further her education enough to escape the tiny tourist town she called home. Mrs. Dunton pressed on.

"Mabel is starting at Wellesley next fall, that is, unless she marries her beau."

This last bit of gossip set Vincent's teeth on edge. Why were the two things mutually exclusive? She censored herself and remained silent, grateful for the excuse of travel-fueled exhaustion. The conversation was interrupted by the arrival of Gladys Niles. Vincent was instantly taken with the new arrival.

"Good evening, child," Mrs. Dunton said cheerfully. "This is Cora Millay's eldest, Edna. Edna, I'd like to introduce you to our granddaughter, Gladys Miles."

"How do you do?" the poet extended her hand. "Most people call me Vincent."

"Then I shall too!" Gladys replied with a broad smile.

"We're very proud of her," Mrs. Dunton added. "She is studying law at the University of Maine."

"Are you?" A female lawyer wasn't unheard of. There was one who practiced in Rockland in an office not far from where Vincent was born. Yet to see someone her own age engaged in the pursuit of a law degree was surprising.

"Yes. It just fascinates me. My folks tell me I am facing an uphill climb, and of course I am, but if we are ever to get the vote or some sort of improvement in the lives of girls and women there must be a few sacrificial lambs." Gladys and Vincent laughed.

"Are you going to college?" Mrs. Dunton asked again.

"Perhaps," was all the poet could say.

Gladys suspected a story behind the stoic reply. "What's stopping you? You're not still in high school, are you?"

Mrs. Dunton frowned at Gladys' directness. "There's no excuse for prying."

The law student was chastised. Vincent came to her rescue. "It's not offensive. To me, that is. I graduated but my family's finances don't really allow for college. I hope to publish some poetry and earn my way through."

Mrs. Dunton frowned slightly, a movement the ever-observant Vincent caught.

"Of course, this may not be entirely practical. I may have to use my skills as a typist or work as a teacher."

Her host's frown rose to a veiled smile. "That's very wise."

"What sort of poetry do you write?" Gladys asked.

"Oh, any kind, I suppose," She took the last sip of her sherry. "I love poetry in three different ways. For one, intellectually it is a real challenge."

"How so?" Gladys asked.

"Just consider the skillful rhymes of Robert Browning or, for that matter, the clever satires of Alexander Pope."

"You said three ways. What are the other two?" Mabel broke in.

"I believe there's a spiritual element in poetry. For example, the thirty-third Psalm: 'Praise the Lord with the lyre, make a melody to him with a harp of ten strings, sing to him a new song, play skillfully on the strings with loud shouts'."

Mrs. Dunton was now fascinated with their young guest. "And the third?"

Vincent hesitated for a moment. It would be her hostess who asked about the most controversial reason for loving poetry. When she could pause no longer, the poet replied. "Listen to Shakespeare. 'Shall I compare thee to a summer's day, thou art more lovely and temperate…'."

Her enraptured host listened as she recited the Bard's great sonnet. Vincent finished, paused and added, "There's a sensuous quality in some poems that truly moves me. This last thing about verse, the rhythm and the color and music of poetry strikes me as the most intense. All three elements reflect life itself, don't they? After all, I am one part brain, one part soul and three parts flesh and blood. That is the way with a great many people who wouldn't admit it even to themselves."[94]

"Oh, my!" Mabel blushed.

"That is fascinating. You make a wonderful argument for poetry and your defense of your attachment to it," Gladys observed.

The conversation was interrupted by the sound of a bell. "That must be dinner," Mrs. Dunton said.

Her husband appeared from the staircase as if on cue and walked with them into the dining room. A heavy-set Irish maid was serving the food. Vincent realized she might soon be in such a position and sighed.

"Yes, I understand," Mabel noted in response. "You must have so much on your mind with your father and all. Father, do you suppose it would be all right for Edna to have another glass of sherry?"

The exhausted guest inwardly thanked her otherwise dull but well-meaning peer.

"Of course. Bridget, please pour for us all," Mr. Dunton replied.

Vincent ate as if she hadn't had a meal in weeks, a fact not lost upon the Duntons.

"Your family must have tough times of it with just one income."

"We all work," Vincent said in a tone she knew her mother would disapprove of. "I type, and..." Vincent hesitated. It was probably not a good idea to let it slip that she spent time on the road with a traveling acting troop the fall after graduation. "Norma waits table at the Whitehall Inn, and Kathleen takes whatever work she can get."

"Of course, dear," Mrs. Dunton said gently, with a sharp glance at her husband, niece and granddaughter.

The simple meal of mutton, potatoes and field greens combined with the sherry brought on a sudden need for sleep. "I'm sorry if I sound ungrateful. I'm just tired, I guess. I only wanted to say we all chip in and get by."

"I've never known anyone to work harder than your mother," Mr. Dunton assured her. "If she passed her work ethic on to her girls you're likely doing very well."

Mabel noticed Vincent's eyes squinting against the urge to sleep. "You best get some rest before you fall into your plate."

Vincent chuckled. "And what sort of guest would I be if I did that?"

"A welcome one," Mrs. Dunton replied with a reassuring smile.

It was soon settled that Vincent would take the early train for the ninety-minute journey to Kingman. Bridget was assigned to alarm clock duty at three a.m. so Vincent would have time to dress and eat before Mr. Dunton would drive her to the 4:30 train.

The poet awoke without prompting and dressed immediately. She would not walk through the house in her night dress in the wee hours at home. She threw her sleepwear back into her suitcase and carried the bag downstairs, meeting the sleepy Bridget on the landing.

"Goo' mornin', Miss," the indentured Irish servant said. "I trust ye had a goo' night's rest."

Vincent was taken with her accent and smiled. "Yes, thank you, Bridget. Is anyone else awake yet?"

"I heard Master Dunton stirrin' a bit ago. He's always up with the lark, so don' be worryin' ye puttin' him ta-enny trouble."

"That's good to know," the poet replied. Bridget took her suitcase the rest of the way down the stairs before placing it by the front door. The house guest went toward the dining room.

Mr. Dunton was already seated and eating his breakfast. A morning paper lay on the table before him.

"Oh, bless my soul! I didn't think you'd be up and dressed already," he remarked after a warm, "Good Morning."

"Yes, I slept so deeply that I was wide awake at 2:30. I can see why my mother considers you such great friends."

"Our pleasure, Edna. Or do you prefer Vincent? Cora always uses that."

"Our family and most of my friends call me Vincent which is why I feel you must as well."

"Thank you for such an honor." Mr. Dunton buttered his toast. "Please sit down. I'm sure Bridget will be in with your breakfast in no time."

Moments later Bridget appeared with a rasher of bacon, poached eggs and bread. "Ye'll be wantin' a goo' breakfast to make it through yer day, Miss."

"Bless you, Bridget," the poet said, lifting a piece of bacon to her mouth. Mr. Dunton frowned slightly and realized she was Cora's own child. After all, the bacon was crisp and dry. Why not use her fingers? Vincent was oblivious and ate another piece before slicing the perfectly poached eggs and sopping up the yolk with still warm bread.

Mr. Dunton watched the ravenous youth. It was clear she rarely ate as well as they did. "I understand you write poetry."

"Yes. I'm working on something now. I call it my "down underground" poem.[95] Because it's about...," she hesitated a moment. How much could she tell him? "Renewal."

"Oh, an ode to spring?" he asked.

"Not exactly." How could she explain to this simple man what her new poem was about when she hadn't even finished it? She decided to deflect. "I recently had something published. Would you like to hear it?"

"Yes, I would," Gladys appeared at the entry to the dining room and sat down next to her grandfather. "Good morning, sir."

Vincent paused and waited for her to get settled. She liked her new friend. Having Gladys there made her feel more empowered. "It won a prize. I used it to buy a copy of Browning in the sweetest brown leather binding."

"Where was it published?" Gladys asked.

"St. Nicholas Magazine. I know that's for baby stuff, so this is the last thing I can publish with them."

"Let's hear it," Mr. Dunton smiled.

"It's called 'Friends'." She cleared her throat and stood up. Gladys, Mr. Dunton and even Bridget watched as a veil came over her like a person possessed of some mystical power. "The things I loved I may go to see. I may lie in them no more. But I stand at the door of the used-to-be, and dream my childhood o'er. I sit at my window alone. I hear each voice and I know that I miss through them all the sound of my own as it rang in the long-ago."[96]

The girl with so much promise seemed adrift. Too old for a publisher of children's verse, too unknown to find an adult publisher, too poor to self-publish. It seemed all doors were shut to her. "You mentioned you were working on something," Mr. Dunton almost whispered. "May we hear some of it?"

The poet began with what fragments she had. What she offered was unpolished and seemingly simplistic, yet there was something in the power of the imagery that confirmed what the poet expressed as the three elements of poetry. "That was beautiful," Gladys sighed. "Of course, I can see where you haven't fully finished it, but if this is a sample of your work, then I believe your success is assured."

"Agreed," Mr. Dunton said, wiping a determined tear from his cheek. The girl's voice had so moved him an involuntary drop had escaped his eyelid.

Gladys looked at Vincent and realized she'd made a lifelong friend. It was something she hadn't quite expected. The pair exchanged appreciative smiles.

"We best be off," Mr. Dunton declared. He stood and went to pull Vincent's chair back for her. She rose and looked around the room. Her eyes scanned every corner, committing it to her photographic memory. She had felt welcomed. While the Duntons were friends with Cora, they had judged her by her own merits and that felt good.

All her childhood she had been Cora and Henry's daughter. Before her parents' divorce, she had been judged by her father's gambling debts. Afterward she was measured by her mother's decision to cling to a man she loved and as the wild eldest child of an errant parent. This was the first time she felt measured as herself.

In a few hours she would be standing by her father's bedside trying to figure out how she fit into her parents' lives. It had been so long since she had seen him, she scarcely understood anything but what other people had said about him, and thus, about her.

8. The How And Why of All Things

1912

When she arrived in Kingman's tiny train station, she was surprised to find a territory a fraction of the size of Camden. Yet somehow the village of 708 souls had a large high school atop a hill above the Mattawamkeag River that bordered the sleepy community.[97]

Standing on the platform was the handsome daughter of her father's physician. The stranger's approach was confident because by then the few souls who got off the train at Kingman had already been claimed.

"You must be Vincent Millay," she said, sticking out her large hand in greeting. "I'm Ella Somerville. My father is your father's doctor."

"How do you do?" Vincent replied, immediately fascinated by the woman. She noticed there were paint stains on her fingers. "Do you paint?"

Ella looked at her hands and laughed. "Yes. I guess I should have done a better job at cleaning up."

"Oh, no need to worry about that. I've always said that if it came to a choice between living in a neat room and giving up poetry, I'd live in a mess."

Ella laughed. She liked Henry's daughter. "How about we go home to our messy house? My father can fill you in on Henry's condition."

The pair climbed aboard the doctor's buggy and took the short drive out Kingman Road to his residence where Vincent was encouraged to consume a cup of coffee. She would need some before going to the robin's egg blue home of Yannis Boyd where her father was boarding.[98]

Despite Ella's keen repartee, she spoke to Vincent in a manner that felt strange given she hardly knew her father. That trite phrase "Brace up" seemed to be on everyone's sympathetic lips.[99]

The speech she had practiced on the train kept running through her mind as she climbed the stairs to the room where a virtual stranger was coughing deeply. A man who looked just like Andrew Carnegie greeted her at the top of the stairs.

"Good morning. Before you go in, please understand it is best to keep your father quiet. He is very ill."

"Are you Dr. Somerville?"

"Gracious! Where are my manners? Yes, child. I am Beverly Somerville. Your father calls you Vincent, is that right?"

"I suppose," the poet replied. It occurred to her that she wasn't completely sure *what* he called her outside of the family. "Last time I saw him I was nine so, actually, I'm not certain."

"There, there," the kindly white-haired man said, taking her hand in his. "It's good then that you're able to see him now. But, please, for his sake, only stay a few minutes. He must rest."

Vincent suspected that everyone from Ella, the Boyds, the nurse and doctor expected her to faint dead away. Instead, she realized she wasn't nervous at all. In fact, what everyone else viewed as admirable calm was in fact numbness.

The sound of her father's catarrh led her to his room on the left. "Hello, Papa dear," she said just as she'd rehearsed except her voice was actually reedy.[100]

Henry's eyes opened slightly. She caught her breath. He had eyes the color of the spring sky. She watched as if frozen as he struggled to sit up. "Vincent! My little girl…"[101]

"Oh, I wish my eyes were as blue as yours so they might match my hat." Vincent marveled at her self-absorption in light of the occasion.

Her father, exhausted by the effort of sitting up, replied with the humor that so often won over Cora. "You can't very well change your eyes, but you could change to a green hat."

Vincent laughed. Though he smiled his eyes had already closed. She sat down in a bedside chair and took his hand. His eyelids fluttered like the wings of an injured bird. She grew concerned. Her father drifted back to sleep as if the small effort of acknowledging his daughter was too much for him.

Dr. Somerville came beside the bed and took Henry's other hand. He frowned. The pulse was very uneven. "I'm glad you're here. He may have only a few more days."

* * *

That evening, Vincent wrote a small postcard to her family saying she had found her "Papa very low."[102] The picture showed the town's cross streets, Main and Marginal, a depiction that belied the tiny community's small but active downtown.[103] A few words about Somerville's broad forehead and white beard explained her notion of why she thought he was the "spittin' image" of Carnegie, but otherwise the note said little.

Vincent's mind was elsewhere. There was something about the doctor's daughter that she found particularly compelling. Across the room, Ella played piano under a painting she had completed. It seemed as if they were kindred spirits. A peaceful Chopin nocturne followed and sent the poet's head drifting toward the attraction she couldn't help but feel.

Ella caught the aura from the corner where Vincent sat at a small writing desk. Her playing slowed and she turned to look. Vincent was indeed lovely, and Ella wondered if her own curiosity would be reciprocated. As she hit that last E flat major chord of Opus 9, the painter knew she would ask Vincent to share a bed that night. Where it would go from there was anyone's guess.

Vincent addressed the postcard and looked at Ella. It didn't matter if she was a woman, or older, or even that she was the daughter of Henry's doctor. Ella had stirred something in her that she had previously reserved for her imaginary beloved. Watching Ella rise from the piano bench and come toward her sent a shiver up her spine, but that was nothing compared to the sensation when Ella said quietly, "Shall I sleep with you tonight?"

The poet's eyes shot into her lap and then back to Ella's face. She felt as if a dark secret had been revealed to this total stranger. Ella's lips were inviting, but her father was expected at any minute. The poet felt her body tremble and grow faint. Yet her desire was stronger than her weakness. Ella awaited her reply.

The sensation of rising from the chair had a dreamlike quality. She could not feel her feet touching the floor and still she moved toward the artist in a misty fog. Ella took her hand.

"Let's go upstairs," she said gently, her breath coming in shallow gulps. As their hands met, Vincent's feet landed on the ground. Was she really doing this? Was she going to actually have her first sexual encounter with a girl? She reminded herself that it wasn't Ella's womanhood that attracted her. It was that Ella had aroused her inexperienced libido.

They made their way to the attic guest room. Each creak of the stairs sent a chill down their spines. Would they be found out? Their bodies moved in synch, as if part of a choreographed ballet of love. Their fingers intertwined and their lips met as they stepped into the small dark room.

As items fell off their trembling bodies, Vincent found herself forgetting entirely how others might feel about the Sapphic moment. She helped Ella take down her hair and allowed her friend to return the favor. They climbed into bed, anxious and awestruck by their attraction. Fingers explored, mouths tasted and in short order both women had achieved climax. All night they balanced between the dream of love and the call to sleep. By morning, Vincent realized her emotional life would never be quite the same.

* * *

The following morning the two were still talking about this and that, especially their dreams and goals. Ella confessed that she imagined herself married with children by now, but if it didn't happen, she might become a world-renowned painter. Vincent told her the latter suited her better, and cited Ella's large copy of Edwin Landseer's *Newfoundland Dog*.[104] "That is truly fine, Ella darling," she cooed as she visualized the huge black and white canine in a setting of green fields and blue water. She stopped her effusive praise to kiss Ella's bare shoulder. The older woman stroked Vincent's hair.

"I can hardly wait to read your finished 'down underground' poem. What I've heard so far is marvelous." They snuggled closer against the wintry chill.

"I smell coffee," Vincent muttered. "Does that mean we have to get up?"

"I'm afraid so, sweetness." Ella sat up and reached for her corset. "I'll have to sneak down to my room first though."

"Do you think anyone heard us?" Vincent grew concerned. She might be sent home before her father died, which would necessitate another trip to Kingman by someone else, and who would take them after what she'd done? Panic began to overtake her as Ella silently dressed. "Your mother, oh my! What would she say? What would your father say? I'd never see my father again."

Ella turned to look at the younger woman. She was so much more naïve than the sophistication she claimed. "My dear, my parents are on a different floor on the other side of the house. It's quite unlikely they would have heard us, let alone imagine what we were up to. Now, get dressed and come down in about fifteen minutes. That will give me time to dress in something new and be at the table before you arrive."

Vincent reached for Ella's hand and kissed it, her fearful tears mixed with the moisture of her lips. "Bless you."

The artist leaned over and kissed the poet. "See you in a little bit."

The door closed before Vincent could respond. Ella's matter-of-fact demeanor was reassuring. She put on the simple green dress she brought for daytime, then brushed her waist length copper hair until it gleamed. The process took longer than the fifteen minutes Ella had suggested. Her pen delayed her departure an additional five minutes as she began a guilt-laden apology to her imaginary "beloved" for cheating on him, which morphed into a paean to Ella's naked beauty.

As she descended the stairs, Vincent could hear Ella's bright laughter responding to something her father had said. The sound made the poet's flesh dance.

"Good morning," she said with a smile as she entered the dining room. Ella sat beside her mother near the end of the table. Beverly Somerville sat opposite finishing a soft-boiled egg and toast with marmalade jam.

"Ella tells me you are to stay a while," Dr. Somerville said cheerfully. "That's wonderful news."

"How's Father?" she said too quickly, then added, "Yes, if that's alright."

"I believe you're a tonic, Vincent.[105] I may call you Vincent, mightn't I?" The doctor put down his toast and looked at his wife. "Mother, is it alright that Miss Millay stays with us a few more days?"

"Why of course it is," the short, stout immigrant replied in an accent so thick the poet could only make out the meaning by the smile on Mrs. Somerville's face. "She's certainly worked magic on our Ella."

Her daughter smiled. "Indeed, she has."

Vincent went to the sideboard and selected a breakfast roll, some cheese and a ruddy cheeked apple before drawing a cup of coffee from a copper urn. The brew was already tepid.

She sat down next to Ella, who rewarded her with an affectionate pat with her lap hand. Dr. Somerville noticed his guest's blush and misinterpreted its cause. "Did you sleep well, Vincent, or were you up all night sick with worry?"

Ella stifled the desire to giggle. Vincent blushed deeper. "I slept…fitfully."

"It's no wonder, Beverly," Maud Somerville chided her husband. "Poor child. Her father at death's door and that unfamiliar bed."

"I'm certain, Mother, that Miss Millay is just fine in that old bed."

Vincent laughed nervously. "I think you're right, Mrs. Somerville. It's not a terrible bed. I've slept in much worse."

The poet's disquiet made her sweat. This was made worse when Ella explained the guest mattress had once been her own. All she could think to say was, "I'm the eldest. Poor Norma and Kathleen always get my hand-me-downs. When I was younger, I even wore my mother's old clothes."

"You poor dear," Ella said sincerely. "I'll see to it that you get something new while you're here. Something just for you."

Vincent didn't argue. While she was able to make a new dress for herself now and then, it would be quite another thing to purchase something that was actually fashionable.

Before long it was time for Dr. Somerville to begin his rounds, starting with a visit to Henry Millay.[106] Vincent tagged along, taking along a book by Robert Louis Stevenson she'd found in the Somerville's library and the volume of Robert Burns she'd brought from home to amuse herself.

On the second day of her visit Henry did little but sleep, awakening only long enough to say, "My baby," before drifting back to sleep. Still, Vincent kept vigil. The interruption for dinner at noon lasted only as long as it took her to consume it. Her father slept despite the ministrations of Saoirse; a tall, strong looking girl brought in from Bangor.[107]

By the fourth day of her visit, it was clear that Henry wouldn't die, and Ella was smitten. In celebration the young women went shopping, bought fine new dresses and then went dancing at the local Odd Fellows Hall. The local swains immediately noticed the attractive stranger. Not only was she a tantalizing blank page, but she was also a better dancer than any girl in town.

Ella could not allow jealousy to interfere with Vincent's enjoyment of her freedom. They both became enchanted with the violinist for the Kickapoo-Laguna Traveling Vaudeville Medicine Show,[108] but it was Vincent who was hoping to illustrate distance. She loved Ella, but now that she had tasted it, she loved freedom more. The attentions of the dark-eyed fiddle player and the various beaux of the Kingman community were enticing to the theoretically virginal newcomer. What would sex with a boy be like now that she had violated her pledge to her imaginary "beloved" with a woman? A torrent of sexual yearning had been unleashed and every fantasy from heads in laps to orgasm had been fulfilled. Now she wanted more and there was no one in Kingman to tell tales back in Camden.

The stronger her father became the more she went out. Dances, theater performances, motion pictures, hikes, day trips to Bangor for shopping and amusements were on a daily menu arranged by Ella for the enjoyment of her lover. The painter loved to see the look on Vincent's face when she announced their daily calendar. It was a way to further the attraction as much as it was a way to get out of the house and away from her parents' supervision. While the first and last events of the day were allotted for visiting Henry, Vincent found that sitting at his bedside lost its urgency when compared to the pleasures of being beyond the reach of her mother and sisters.

Meanwhile, Cora was getting frustrated. Although Norma was eighteen and close to graduation, her nature was not consistently dutiful. Vincent could be relied upon to lead the girls in their chores. Norma and Kathleen battled constantly. Her eldest kept her informed about what was going on. With Norma, Cora was always the last to know. There were things to be done that weren't being done. Cora wanted Vincent home.

Norma was likewise unhappy with Vincent's lack of correspondence. Her senior year was being stymied. Not only was Vincent not there to help with her French finals but she wasn't available to carry the load while she enjoyed the frivolities of her senior year.[109] In addition to not writing with news of their father, there was a very real fear that her elder sister may have decided to disappear entirely. In midnight conversations Vincent had intimated as much. Norma knew she was looking at foregoing the usual senior parties in favor of making sure household operations met Cora's exacting standards. Her anger at being abandoned by the poet, someone she admired above all others, was building with each day.

In fact, no one in the household was satisfied with Vincent's short messages. They seemed designed to be more dutiful than reassuring. Although she wrote on March 4 that Henry was expected to get well, there was no mention of when she would get home. It seemed to them that her purpose for being in Kingman had passed and her duty was now to return. Why should Cora care if Henry was popular.[110] She knew how charming her ex-husband could be and how easily people were taken in by him. Had her daughter been taken in too?

Vincent felt she was telling them what was most important. She didn't dare be honest about why her visit had lingered so long. Dr. Somerville was now taking her driving every day, sometimes with Ella but mostly just the two of them. He enjoyed the twenty-year-old's conversation and ability to recite poetry and plays from memory. On one drive they saw a dead deer hanging from a tree and the good doctor told her that it had likely been killed by a bobcat.[111] She had never seen anything like it. Her mission of mercy was now daily escapades through the rivers, lakes, hills and valleys of her father's adopted hometown. The heady combination of male attention and sexual attraction made Vincent loathe returning anywhere with institutional familial memory.

The local Methodist church welcomed Dr. Somerville's guest with open arms and readily accepted Ella's suggestion that Vincent sing Schumann's "Ave Maria" for them. Henry, sitting at the window of his room across the street, heard his daughter's rich contralto voice and shed tears of joy. Every success was his and no one in town was aware of any failure in his daughter's character. Even Vincent felt as if she fit in better in Kingman than she ever had in Camden.

The inquisitive eyes of local boys and the Medicine Show violinist further tantalized the poet. She began to lose her grip on appropriate manners and slipped into the old habits of being too sharp and opinionated. In a town of 700, her flamboyant disregard of social mores was soon viewed as the product of a broken home. Given the community's love for Henry, there was only one person blamed for Vincent's transgressions…for now.

Every night Ella would sneak from her room to Vincent's for nocturnal play. She loved how the poet rolled her Rs when reciting Robert Burns. Each tongue doing a cunning dance, the serpentine dance, the butterfly dance, drew Ella closer.[112] They were experimenting with techniques that would have made them blush only a few days before. Ella would read from her personal copies of the *Rubaiyat of Omar Khayyam* and Honoré Balzac. The volumes' mildly salacious content spurred on their attraction. Vincent began to call Ella "Grapefruit," a reference to her pink, round breasts. Vincent became "Little Plum." While they danced waltzes and Schottisches with the boys in town, flirted shamelessly with the itinerant fiddle player, and celebrated the novelty of Vincent's visit, their nights belonged solely and secretly to them.

Norma was the only person Vincent confided in, suggesting that the romance was there without going into detail. The middle sister, always a confidante, read the news with a mixture of relief and envy. She knew how stultifying life in Camden was for the poet. She understood why Vincent would linger. Yet the longer the poet was away, the more Cora leaned on Norma to pick up the slack at home. Testy letters were met with more tales of conquest and fun in Kingman. The poet had been gone close to three weeks, two weeks beyond her brief note saying how well Henry was doing. What did Kingman, a town a quarter the size of Camden, have that was more fun and interesting than home? Sure, the blonde understood that the familiarity of Camden could breed contempt, and yes, finding a new friend was enormously attractive given how many bridges had been singed in the whole class poet debacle, but didn't her own family mean anything to her? It was a mystery Norma simply couldn't fathom.

As for Cora, she considered a different approach. She wrote saying how pleased she was that Vincent had new friends and asked if she had shared the photograph of herself in her stiffly starched uniform with Henry. She suspected making nice with Henry would be enticing to Vincent, who had grown to love her father deeply. Yet the poet's fifteen-page reply did little to reassure her mother that she would be home anytime soon.

Homelife in Camden continued to devolve. Fights between Norma and Kathleen seemed to go nowhere. The small sums Vincent had brought in to help with accounts had taken a pinch out of their already skimpy budget. Cora tried to take in more work, but she was slowing down. Her chronic headaches grew worse. Complaints by the grocer, butcher and landlord became unavoidable. Things were coming to a head and not just in Camden.

Vincent's celebration of her freedom was starting to wear thin at the Somerville home. Maud had started noticing her daughter's mooning gaze at the poet. She became uneasy. What hold did the charming poet have over her? One morning she got her answer.[113]

The young women came down the stairs laughing. They often did. Only this time there was another layer to the hilarity. In the past, they spoke to each other in fake Scottish brogues, each testing the other for how intelligible they could make the accent and still be understood. Other times they would humorously argue over the point of sheets, with the poet taking the position that satin sheets were miserably uncomfortable—though she'd never slept on them. But this morning they were discussing the clock in Vincent's room.

As they giggled it became clear that Vincent spent a good deal of time in front of the mirror. "If you didn't spend so much time staring at yourself you would have remembered the clock," Ella laughed.

"But you *do* like the way I look," Vincent countered. The cheek of this irked Mrs. Somerville, but it was what Ella said next that made her concerned.

"Of course, sweetheart, but if you wound the clock yourself my ankle wouldn't be all swollen and bruised."

It was now clear they had been sleeping together and judging by Ella's admiring glances it had been going on for some time. Mrs. Somerville understood that Vincent was likely used to sharing a bed. Sisters often do. In fact, she had herself back in Newfoundland where she'd met her husband. But they were prosperous now. There was no need. She hesitated as the guest and her daughter continued their story, which her husband was finding amusing.

Perhaps Ella slept with Vincent to make her feel at home. If that was the reason it would be perfectly gracious. After all, Ella was also the poet's host. Besides, Ella had many suitors, and Vincent had drawn more men to the house seeking a wife. Yet something with the story remained disquieting.

"You know, Father, how cold the nights have been" Ella began. "I'll take all the covers I can get but Vincent doesn't like anything over her body."

Beverly Somerville laughed, his beard crinkling in alignment with his cheeks, "Go on."

"You know how the clock is up there in the guest room. If it isn't wound nightly, it just stops working entirely and you must take it to Mr. Connor for repair."

"I've paid that bill often enough."

"I asked Vince if she'd wound the clock, and she said she hadn't and she wasn't going to."

"Oh, my," Mrs. Somerville said for more than one reason.

"So, I told the little minx that the clock had to be wound, and she best get to it."

The younger woman began to laugh uproariously. "I told her she was right. The clock must be wound."

Dr. Somerville enjoyed the story. Nothing about it seemed odd. Vincent continued.

"There was a *lo-o-ong* silence. It was almost like you could hear the clock slowing down. I knew Ella was thinking she hated to get up and I was glad I didn't need to."

There was something in Vincent's phrasing that told Mrs. Somerville the poet was aware of the spell she'd cast on Ella, and it troubled her. Still, she tried to smile, and the young women continued their story.

"Stubborn mule! Then I got up and started toward the bureau, only it was pitch black."

"And she didn't want to strike a match because the shades were up, and she didn't want to put them down because—"

"I'd only have to put them up again," Ella interrupted.

"Well, if you weren't so lazy this story would be completely unnecessary," Vincent laughed.

"Why did you worry about the shades being up?" Mrs. Somerville asked, suspecting she knew the answer.

Ella and Vincent paused, cast a quick glance at one another and continued as if the question hadn't been asked. "I was just scratching and pawing around, trying to find the clock, which was ticking away, echoing around the room like it was the Swiss Alps instead of the attic."

Dr. Somerville began to howl as he imagined the scene, adding a "tick-tick-tick" embellishment.

Vincent continued the tale. "She asked where the stand was about the tenth time that she stubbed her toe."

"And you took no pity on poor Ella?" Mrs. Somerville asked with a forced smile.

"Not one bit," Ella laughed. "I just kept saying, 'where's the stand, where's the stand'?"

"So, I said, 'where's the wall'?"

The doctor, his daughter and houseguest were now practically falling out of their chairs as Vincent performed the scene with dramatic effect. "You'll need to find the wall first, Ella! You must be drunk!"

By now, Mrs. Somerville was fit to burst. Why did Vincent think Ella was drunk? What sort of influence was this cheeky devil. Manners told her to hold her tongue.

"And you know how normally the clock is on that pretty little stand between the wood stove and the bureau?"

"Yes," her father sputtered through his laughter.

"Well, of course, Vincent had to move it!"

"Now, Ella, you know I planned on writing a letter to my family. I had to wheel the stand over to my side of the bed."

"But I had forgotten all about it, so I am fumbling and crashing when Vincent could have just reached over and wound the clock without moving an inch!"

"So why didn't you wind it?" Mrs. Somerville asked.

"Because I was sick of winding it and it was Ella's turn."

Ella stood up and began illustrating fumbling in the dark even as the sun streamed through the dining room window. "I can't find the wall. I can't find the stand!"

"Well, finding the wood stove will be easy. You can start there," the redhead giggled.

Ella turned back toward her parents to finish the story. Everyone's meal had gone cold, but no one cared. "But then, for some reason I realized the clock was ticking away somewhere near the bed. I managed to get to the stove, lit a match and sure enough the clock was sitting right there on the stand next to the bed, and Vincent started to laugh, and when I got over how I'd been torched we both were laughing fit to die because the little minx knew where the clock was all along!"[114]

"I didn't actually," the poet countered. "I only realized it about a minute before you did, but it serves you right."

"I knew it!" Ella replied and gave Vincent a wink before sitting back down.

Mrs. Somerville visibly winced. There was an intimacy that went beyond friendship, of that much she was certain. "What were you doing in there anyway?"

"Keeping me warm," Vincent announced, oblivious to the fact that Dr. Somerville was now taking notice of the pair.

"What do you get out of it, Ella?" the kindly doctor asked. He was still behind his wife in awareness, but he had noticed something was troubling her.

"She reads me Robert Burns." Ella was beginning to sense her parents' concern.

"Ella likes the way I troll my Rs." The poet hoped someone would find that amusing. No one laughed.

"By the way, Miss Millay," Dr. Somerville said with a formal tone that let Ella know he was now unhappy with their house guest. "Your father is out of danger."

Seconds ticked by before he added, "Thanks to you."

"So perhaps now would be a good time to return home. I'm sure your mother and sisters are missing you," Mrs. Somerville added with a look toward her husband.

Ella could feel tears welling up in her eyes as Vincent replied in more subdued tones, "Yes, of course. I'll make the arrangements right away."

Her eyes fell to the gentle start of an early spring snowfall. Part of her wished it would become a brutal storm, another realized she was growing weary of Ella's romantic needs. As far as her feelings for her family, she knew she was having much more fun enjoying her father's company than she ever would by returning to the drudgery of life in Camden.

* * *

After Dr. Somerville left on his rounds and Mrs. Somerville left for a meeting of the local chapter of the Ladies' Health Protective Association, Ella and Vincent sat glumly in the parlor mulling over the latter's departure.

As fate would have it, a letter from Cora came in the morning mail. It spoke of a contest with a $500 prize. "Perhaps you should finish your down underground poem and submit it," her mother had written. Now she could think of leaving the Somerville's as her own idea.

"Well, I suppose it makes sense," the poet noted. "I can't get anything done here."

Ella wasn't sure if her lover was teasing or in earnest. "What if I come with you?"

"Silly grapefruit! You're the reason I can't get anything done." Vincent's face screwed up in a smile that was only vaguely reminiscent of humor.

"Stay then. I promise I'll leave you alone to write. We could find a place of our own."

"And how do you propose we support ourselves?" the poet asked, all too aware of how relationships die for lack of income.

"I could…" Ella began.

"So could I, but the truth is, in a town this small it wouldn't be long before your parents' suspicions would be on the lips of half the town, and we'd never find work. And before you mention it, I've moved enough in my life to start moving from place to place as an adult."

Vincent studied Ella's face. She realized there was one more gambit to nip in the bud. "Don't even think of my father supporting us. You know as well as I how lost a cause that is."

They discussed the timing of Vincent's departure for Bangor and decided to tie it in with a performance of a traveling theatrical troupe. Although she didn't say it, the poet knew this would give her two days to mend fences and make plans. Now that she had been made aware of her effect on women, she wondered if Gladys Niles would be available for such sport. She thought better of it. The Duntons were too close to home. A night in Bangor with Ella, then a night at the Dunton's home with Gladys. It was too much. She knew she was wicked and part of her relished the thought. Still her mind went back to Cora's letter and the plaintive one from Norma that accompanied it.[115] She needed help with her French, or she wouldn't graduate. Norma couldn't handle Kathleen. Their mother demanded too much. They needed Vincent's help. Vincent was being selfish staying away so long. The finger of blame for the family's woes came down hard upon her heart. They were moving yet again. Creditors gave them dirty looks. It was all her fault. Vincent sighed deeply as she laid down the indictment.

"What's wrong?" Ella placed her warm hand on the poet's shoulder.

"Nothing. It's just better that I get home. We'll stay at the Dunton's for a night and then you must return to Kingman, and I must go back to Camden. It's the only way, sweetheart."

Vincent's endearment was sincere. Indeed, Ella did have a sweet heart. It would not be too long before one of her many beaux would ask for her hand. Whatever they had together would be over and be only a memory shared in shy glances across the room. Meanwhile, Vincent promised a night of mutual pleasure before her departure. It would have to suffice.

She found the clothes she bought stretched the limits of the suitcase, so many of the hand-me-downs she'd arrived with were left behind. So were many other things. She had shed the last of her notions about family loyalty. Now that she had met Henry, she realized that she was not responsible for her mother and sisters. She loved them. She cared for them. She would do almost anything to make them happy, but her own happiness also mattered, too.

That night Mrs. Somerville insisted that Ella check in with her before retiring and as a result Vincent slept alone for the first time since her arrival. It felt right though she missed the physical warmth.[116]

* * *

The next day she crossed the street to the big blue house where Henry was a lodger. "Good morning, Papa," she said brightly.

"How are you, daughter?" Henry's face had regained its color, and he was freshly shaven.

Though she hardly knew him, there was a void in her life he seemed to fill. "You've probably heard I'm headed home later. I'm going to miss you, Papa."

"Of course, you are, and I will miss you. There will be no one to serenade me on Sundays."

"The church has a lovely choir. You could leave your windows open." Vincent longed for a compliment and received one.

"I suppose. But no one can sing like my Vincent. Why, everyone who visits me has a story about you. It seems you made quite an impression this past month."

"It's not quite a month yet," Vincent muttered and began to cry.

Henry understood. It couldn't be easy for such a spirited lass to be stuck in Camden looking after her younger siblings and at Cora's beck and call. "I could write your mother and ask if you could stay longer."

"No. I must get home. Norma's about to graduate and…" Her voice trailed off. She couldn't tell him the real reason for her departure. Besides, all Mrs. Somerville had was suspicions and she had been a guest for a good deal of time. Henry anticipated her thoughts.

"Well, like old Ben Franklin said, 'fish and visitors smell in three days'."

"And it's been over three weeks." Vincent forced a smile. Henry chuckled and held out his arms for a hug. His grown daughter was so tiny and bird-like she felt like a small child. She whimpered into his chest. "I just hate to leave you, Papa. And Ella."

Henry was already aware of the gossip but chose to ignore it. His neighbors often responded to outsiders with unfounded tales. He also understood how it felt to be lonely even when surrounded by one's family. Vincent's tears broke his heart.

"Now that I'm fit again, I can host you myself."

The poet's heart briefly leaped. Henry sensed her excitement, but not the resignation that followed. "When I get my own place, I'll send for you."

While he meant it to be hopeful, Vincent had been on the receiving end of his promises too many times to have faith in them. It was just another of his dreams.

"Of course. In the meantime, we can write more often."

"Yes. Yes, I'd like that. And send me your poems. I like what I have heard so far, and you can send me clippings and news of all the gossip in Knox County."

Their conversation waned like the moon from bright and clear to dark and almost invisible. Vincent walked back to the Somerville's home where Ella waited to go with her to Bangor.

* * *

The rails squealed as they wended their way toward the city. Vincent and Ella sat across from each other as if in preparation for their inevitable parting. Ella tried to keep their patter cheerful but neither woman relished the trip. For the painter, the three and a half weeks had been a revelation. Vincent had inspired some daring brush strokes and a move toward an impasto technique. The poet had discovered the next movement of her work in progress.

Although she hadn't shared many of her additions with Ella, Vincent's poem of suicidal angst had become one of liberation. She wondered if she would have felt the same had her father died. Probably not. Their renewed kinship and the fresh conversations with the Duntons, Gladys Niles and Somervilles had shown her there was indeed life beyond the coastal hamlet she called home. In Bangor she was treated with gentle consideration. In Kingman she had become something of a celebrity. Everyone wanted to hear her sing, read her poetry, dance with her and get her thoughts on the news of the world. Her schoolgirl French was almost exotic to the modest folk of the tiny community she was leaving behind. She'd been pampered as a child of a dying man and eventually spoiled as a miracle worker. Her mother's controlling demands, and the endless needs of her sisters were just a few of the picks and spades that had almost buried her creative spirit. Poverty, misunderstanding, and lack of education also contributed. Now it seemed like her mother was saying, "Come home, come home, and finish that poem so maybe we can use the $500 to get us out of debt." She wondered if her mother was also submitting poems in the vague hope that some largesse would give them a cushion for once. Where the railcars had sung, "Hello, Papa." on her way to Kingman, they now screamed, "Leave me alone. Leave me alone."

    The couple spent the night in Bangor, checking into a hotel across from the Playhouse before heading to the theater. Nothing about the play was amusing. Ella's tears annoyed the poet. The next day she called the Duntons and said she'd arrived on the afternoon train. This subterfuge was designed to give her a break from the needy voices that surrounded her the past few days. After walking Ella to the station, Vincent wandered the streets half hoping she'd run into Gladys, Mabel or another of the Dunton clan. The rest of her wished to disappear in the city's crowded streets. She window shopped past Woolworth's, the Bijou Theater and the charred remains of the grand library that had been destroyed in the fire. Everywhere the sound of hammers and saws belied her sense of desolation.[117] She had a light lunch at a small café on the ground floor of the Bangor House Hotel. Despite the flavor of the food, there was still some hint of smoke in the meal. From there she made her way to the train station where she worked on her poem before meeting the Duntons.

    Her second stay with the Dunton family was confusing. After picking her up and celebrating her father's recovery, it seemed as though they couldn't wait for her to leave. Gladys confided that Cora had sent her grandparents a letter when the poet had failed to write for a week. No longer viewed as the dutiful daughter off to visit her father before he departed for the Pearly Gates, Vincent was now seen as an ungrateful child who must be put up as a favor to her mother. Although her kinship with Gladys was on par with her previous visit, she found the Dunton's perfunctory attention to her travel needs disquieting. It was as if she were already facing down the disapproving glares of Camden's conventional citizens.

9. The Great Wound

1912

Boarding the train felt like letting go of a daydream. The ride to Bucksport and the ferry to Camden were dismal, punctuated by a pallid gray light. This was not a rain sent by God to wash the dirt from her longed-for grave. This was a featureless and uninspiring drizzle that only served to remind her that once home the reasons for longing to be down underground would again be plain.

Norma met her at the ferry dock. "I was starting to think you'd forgotten all about Mother and us kids."[118]

Vincent feigned a smile and a moment later realized she'd actually missed her middle sister. "Oh, Hunk!" Tears began to fall from her eyes.

The blonde was concerned. "Did Papa die after all?"

"No, no, Papa is fine. In fact, Dr. Somerville says it was a miracle. He said I must be an angel of mercy."

"The way I hear it your halo is a little askew."

"You don't know the half of it," the poet winked, recovering. "I'll tell you on the walk home."

By the time they arrived home, Norma had heard most of what Vincent would say about Ella. She hardly knew what to think, since included in the story were tales of men both women had danced and flirted with throughout the time her elder sister was in Kingman. Besides, Norma knew first-hand about all the beaux who had tried to reach a similar level of intimacy with Vincent right there in Camden. Ella seemed to be a bit of an opportunist, Norma warned, to which the poet replied that if Ella was, so was she, for she had welcomed the painter's advances.

In fact, the whole adventure had helped her understand that her sexual desire was more based on a strange chemical reaction than societal norms. This fascinating perspective was interrupted by the return of Kathleen.

"It's about time!" The young brunette laughed before sweeping Vincent into her arms for an extended hug.

"When is Mumbles expected?" Vincent asked. The house was filled with boxes for their move to 82 Washington Street. The poet hated the idea of having to move across town and closer to the high school.[119] Their tenement was drafty and damp, but they had lived in it longer than they had lived anywhere.

"Mother has a client over that way and said we should meet her at the new house. I think it's her way of getting us to haul boxes full of books," Kathleen shrugged. "Let's take the lightest ones and leave the rest to the new landlord."

"The new landlord is moving *us* in? He must be desperate." Vincent observed cynically.

"No, the house is lovely. He's a friend of Uncle Fred. He's the mill foreman."

"It smells over by the mill," Norma complained.

"It's not so bad. It just smells of soggy sheep," Vincent laughed.

"Baaaaa," Kathleen brayed as she started checking boxes in search of the lightest. Ever since her serious bout with typhoid she avoided anything that might cause a strain. The tallest of the three sisters found her desired boxes and urged her sisters to find their own. "I'll take the small one and my suitcase," the poet quickly announced. This left Norna with the heaviest of the lighter boxes. Yet, if the truth were told, Vincent's burden was the heaviest of all, as her suitcase had gained a few pounds in her absence.

They walked past the village green on their way toward Washington Street. The last of the snow was melting in the damp grass. As they neared the corner of Spring, Cora saw them coming and rushed to greet her eldest daughter.

"There you are!"

"Hello, Mother," Vincent exclaimed, embracing her tightly. "I missed you all so very much."

"You sure couldn't tell it from your letters," the elder woman said, still miffed by Vincent's absence. "I'm glad the prospect of submitting your poem to *The Lyric Year* was enticing enough. I couldn't think of anything else you might find worthy."

Vincent closed her eyes to contain herself. Her mother's passive-aggressive attempt at humor made it clear she would pay a price for her neglect. She loved Cora. Cora loved her. In fact, there was plenty of love to go around.

What was missing was honesty. Each member of the household held secrets from the others, including how she really felt about their relationships. Kathleen's jealousy banged against Vincent's abundant ego. Norma's vanity pushed against her elder sister's talent. All the girls butted up against their feelings about being left alone so often. Vincent's taste of freedom remained in her mouth like a faded penny candy. She continued to suck the juice of it despite her mother's abrading.

That night she discovered she would finally have her own room under the oblique embrace of the third-floor roofline, she would situate herself in front of a window and work on the poem that would eventually be her ticket to freedom.

At that small desk things seemed possible again. Her life was at last aligning with the path she'd long imagined. In that quiet corner she could imagine herself in Ella's embrace, switch that for Gladys, and then for the imaginary, endlessly dutiful, patient and kind beloved she'd been trying to conjure for two years. Alone with her thoughts the down underground poem unfolded like crocuses from the cold, damp earth of spring.

The change in direction manifested itself in another telling way. The loopy right facing schoolgirl script of the past month was shifting to a tightly wound leftward facing scrawl of barely legible text. She wasn't sure what had caused the change in her handwriting, but she suspected it was being untethered from the moorings of convention. The journey to Kingman and back had loosened something inside her and try as she might she could not put herself at anchor again. For better or worse, Vincent Millay had experienced freedom, and it had liberated her.

* * *

She did the minimum required to keep her family satisfied until something came along that would free her from Camden forever. She tutored Norma and Kathleen. She kept the house clean enough to keep her mother almost satisfied. She ran errands and performed odd jobs to keep extra money flowing in, but from now on at least some of what she earned would be used to buy sweet little things for herself. In time, she would be able to buy her mother and sisters whatever they wished, but now was her time, and she would take advantage of it.

10. Ah, Fearful Pawn

1912

The patter of rain on the garret's tin roof cheered her. Letters from Ella and Gladys, needy and chatty respectively, inspired her. The gloom of winter that once made her consider suicide had become a rainbow over Penobscot Bay. No matter how hard the rain fell, Vincent knew she'd never have to hear it without sensing the warmth of the sun elsewhere. She had experienced the sensual power she had over strangers and knew she could use her seductive wit, voice and body to get what she wanted in life. Her midnight assignations with her imaginary beloved faded in favor of the real memories of the force she wielded over people. She would not be alone. She would be loved for herself, not the relationship she had with another.

The down underground poem continued taking shape all through April and May of 1912 until she was satisfied enough with it to walk to the Camden High School office for typing. Her alma mater was pleased to host the star student under its mansard roof. Many knew she was destined for something greater than the sleepy confines of their town. As she worked and reworked the long poem she now called "Renaissance," doting teachers and old adversaries wondered why it had to be typed at all. Vincent knew better. What little she shared during its conception and germination was received with astonishment. But it had evolved far past what anyone but Vincent knew. It would be her passage.

Her "ticket" was mailed on the last Monday in May to the contest her mother was also keen on winning. Vincent had little doubt "Renaissance" would receive a prize, but just in case she mailed her other submissions under different covers, but always under the name E. Vincent Millay.

Watching the smoke billow from the twin chimneys of the high school felt like her dreams going up as May became June and June, July. Had she been tripped up by hubris yet again?

Naturally there were things to celebrate during the wait for the reply. Norma's graduation offered pride and satisfaction. The sisters had been practicing a duet of Vincent's own humoresque to sing during commencement activities at the town opera house. Norma took the soprano, and Vincent sang the alto part. Their role in commencement did much to allay Vincent's remaining feelings about Henry Hall stealing her poem. Besides, unlike the other household necessities, singing with her sister was an enormous pleasure and a way to help Norma overcome her own disappointment at not being cast in the senior class play, an operetta called *The Elopement of Ellen*.[120]

Nevertheless, as the days ticked by the poet grew increasingly anxious about her submission. Had it been received? Did it get lost in the mail? Vincent wrote to ask if the poem had been received and was assured that it had but was still given no clue as to its reception. She tried to busy herself with new work. She made gifts for the weddings of friends, including her dearest pal, Ethel Knight.[121] She socialized, went to dances, took part in weddings and baby showers, anything to keep her mind off the fate of her poems. She wrote letters to her father and answered Ella's letters until she couldn't.

The endless needs of her family and friendships were enough to discourage her from any other entanglements no matter how pleasant the memories of Kingman were. There were suitors, of course, but they were the foolish boys of her hometown, not the exotic and much older men that had fascinated her there. The memory of the Violin Man fiddled with her heartstrings, yet she was savvy enough to know he lacked the stability and financial ease she imagined her beloved would have.

The poet had mixed feelings about all the marriages that June. She knew that Ethel loved Lerois Hodge, but she didn't know why. To her Lerois was a dullard without wit or sex appeal. On the one hand, these had been her friends, girls and boys who were classmates and sometimes rivals. Marriage for a woman meant an end of normal socializing. So why would Ethel or anyone else settle for someone like Lerois? Husbands ruled the roost, Vincent knew that. On the other hand, marriage was said to provide stability. Marriages that failed were usually viewed as the woman's fault. Too much pride, too much vanity, too much of a prude…Too much of a nag, too slovenly to keep a man who simultaneously might be abusive, controlling or lazy, but had to be viewed as worthy of a wife's loyalty.

Vincent was keenly aware of how her mother had been branded and that made a strike against her for being her mother's daughter. Her hand-to-mouth upbringing was another. If "boys would be boys," why couldn't "girls be girls"? Kingman and Bangor had revealed a life outside of perceptions. As a stranger she was defined on her own terms, and this pleased her. She could control what a future husband might think of her, or even if she wanted one. Who knows, she laughed quietly as she remembered her secret, she might even settle for a wife. A wife would be expected to do housework, while Vincent would write.

* * *

On Monday, July 17, 1912, Vincent returned home from gathering blueberries to find her mother waiting at the door with an open envelope.[122]

"Read it! Read it!" Cora exclaimed.

"It's for me?"

"Yes. Read it."

The letter was already damp from her mother's sudsy hands. "You read it already?"

Vincent set the basket of summer supplies on the table near the door. She bit her tongue and pulled the moist letter from inside the envelope. Her eyes dashed across the page until she read the words, "Cordially Yours, The Editor."

"Girls! Girls!" she cried. She dared not address Cora directly in that moment for fear her tongue might betray her unhappiness with Cora's presumptuousness. A tumble of feet flew from upstairs.

"What?" Norma breathlessly asked.

"Your sister's—"

"Let me tell them," Vincent interrupted.

"Of course. I apologize."

"What is it? It's not Father, is it?"

"No, no. It's good news. *Renaissance* has been accepted by *The Lyric Year*."

"That contest?" Norma asked.

"Yes."

"How much did we win?"

Vincent ignored her sister's wording. "They haven't decided yet. They want some biographical data."

"I hope I'll hear soon," Cora remarked, confirming Vincent's suspicion that her mother had also submitted some work. Her mother was a good poet, and there was no shame in submitting just in case, but somehow it didn't feel right. Vincent pushed the feeling back and kept reading. Wouldn't it be galling if her mother got top prize and she did not? The thought reappeared. She'd be happy. That's what she'd be. She'd be happy. It felt like a mantra. What her mother would do with the money and what she would do were two distinctly different things, though she didn't wish to articulate it.

"You will," the poet observed and reread the letter.

"Do you think one of us will win the prize?" There was an odd insecurity in her mother's tone that made her sound more like a peer for a moment.

"I don't know. He said he liked 'Renaissance' tremendously." Vincent hoped her mother would share her joy in being published in a book and not just a magazine.

There remained a reservation in Cora's reply. "Yes, dear, that's wonderful. It really is. I'm proud of you but we really need the rent money, and I was hoping…"

Before she could finish the sentence Norma jumped in. As usual she was more sensitive to her sister's feelings. "It's just marvelous, Vince! Imagine, your poem has been selected from thousands of submissions by Messrs. Wheel and Braithwaite and whoever this is." She shook the letter for emphasis. Then in a nod to her mother she offered, "And you too, Mumbles, money would be nice of course, but the important thing is you've been selected for publication."

Cora smiled and touched Norma's arm. Always the peacemaker, her beautiful middle child. "Yes, that's right, for Vincent, that is. I haven't gotten word yet."

"They'd be fools not to include your poem. Think of it, mother and daughter in the same volume. I can't wait to tell Kenneth."

Despite her attempt at conviviality, Cora's disappointment flooded the room like a bolt of lightning. One moment she'd be swollen with pride, the next a cloud would darken her mood. Vincent had long since become sensitive to when the flash would occur. At any moment Cora would need to lie down with a headache.

The poet began to mentally spend the prize money. She'd give some to her mother and sisters, and she'd take the rest just for herself. Even if she only won the second or third prize of $250, she would feel as rich as Croesus. She might even be able to go to college, a dream soon dashed by quick calculations.

"Wait until Kathleen gets home," Norma said as she took Vincent's hands and began to quick waltz through the parlor. "She'll be green with envy."

"Or red with rage," the poet giggled.

"Now girls," Cora chided, shifting to a more appropriate response to her daughter's good fortune. "Wump may yet hear about her submission, and we all know she'll be pleased to bask in your success. Congratulations, darling! Let's all hope for the best and be content with whatever the outcome is."

Norma was rereading the letter when she began to giggle. "He thinks you're a man."

"I'll disabuse him of that notion soon enough," Vincent replied with a wink.

"Vincent!" Cora cried with only a trace of actual disapproval. As a nurse and midwife, she knew how often hormones outweighed common sense. Nonetheless she liked the idea that her daughter might wait a while before marrying.

"He's probably some sweaty old man like Mr. Singhi," Norma laughed.

"Ugh!" Vincent and Cora said simultaneously. To Vincent anyone who adored poetry as much as she did would have to be smart and dashing. She theorized the editor might also be the publisher, Mitchell Kennerley. The slight amount she had found in the local library only revealed that he was British born publisher of Oscar Wilde and Walt Whitman, all things that assured her they would be simpatico should they ever meet. She decided to write the man who called himself "The Editor" in hopes that a possible relationship with an attractive girl from Camden might improve her chances for a prize.

* * *

"Dear Editor," she wrote in the privacy of her garret, her tongue firmly planted in her cheek. "It may astonish you to learn that I am no Esquire at all, nor even a plain 'Mister'. In fact, I am just an aspiring 'Miss' of twenty."[123] As she relayed the details of her birth and background, she admitted her reason for submitting the poem in her gender deceptive manner. "It was in the hope that you, too, would think me a man, that I signed my name as I did, with its feminine Edna just initialed."

While she didn't explain specifically why she preferred the legerdemain, the reasoning would have been obvious to anyone who knew her, The Millay girls were well-aware than women were undervalued at best and frequently overlooked. By entering her work as a potential man, she felt she had a better chance of being taken seriously.

The poet further admitted that one of the reasons she submitted to The Lyric Year was the presence of Edward J. Wheeler on the judging panel. He was an "old friend" who once placed her in the money when she submitted to *St. Nicholas Magazine.* Vincent's cheeky confidence assumed the other two judges, William Stanley Braithwaite and Mitchell Kennerley himself, would be swayed by Wheeler's affection for the child poet.

Her reply to the questionnaire then took a more directly flirtatious turn. "If I were a noted author," she wrote, "you would perhaps be interested to know that I have red hair, am five foot, four inches in height, and weigh just under one hundred pounds; that I can climb fences in snowshoes, am a good walker, and make excellent rarebit."

The comely redhead paused and debated correcting the lie about her height. The truth was, she was only five-foot, one inch tall—on a good day. She decided it wouldn't matter as she would be wearing heels when they met, which she was certain would happen sooner or later.

She finished her list of attributes as might be expected, given that she had little idea what the editor was looking for when he asked for her characteristics.

"And, if I were a noted author, I should not hesitate to tell you that I play piano; Grieg with more expression than is aesthetic, Bach with more enjoyment than is consistent, and ragtime with more frequency than is desired."[124]

In short, she described herself as a very modern woman, impudent, sensual and well-read. The Editor soon understood E. Vincent Millay knew the Rubaiyat by heart, could quote Ibsen with ease, and in a pinch could be handy on a boat. Finally, she admitted she was not a noted author and would quit lest she bore him.

* * *

Vincent waited with anticipation, certain that her new friendship would lead to grander things. She was also terrified it would not. The time away had spoiled her for anything less than success. Two weeks went by. She began to wonder if she'd dreamed it all, or, worse yet, perhaps she had seemed so cocksure of herself that she had been disqualified. The unsatisfactory activities of eldest daughter and partial bread winner compounded the wait. How could she get lost in her knitting when something so enormous had been teased before her?

The waning moon of August 6 brought a reply at long last. Only by the time she received it the new moon blues had set in. She tore open the envelope so quickly that she ripped open a corner of the letter. "Dear and True Poetess" it began. Vincent was over the moon. She raced to her room to enjoy the missive in privacy of the very garret where she had completed her selected entry.

The Editor explained that others in the review panel had found her long poem worthy but were confused when her other entries did not appear as strong as *Renaissance*. Was someone playing a trick on them? Was she truly the author of the magnificent 214-line lyric poem? The other poems had struck him as likely produced by a 20-year-old girl. Then he found another short poem he liked by someone with the same last name. Could the long and shorter pieces be by the same person and Vincent the poet of only "La Joie de Vivre" and "The Suicide"?

The fact that the short poem he liked was Cora's solicited no correction by Vincent. The Editor told her it was not strong enough to be among the hundred selected for the volume, but it did explain the dual-faced nature of the quality of the submissions. He found "Renaissance" both very finished and very crude.[125]

As she read the letter, she knew which parts were which. Her time in Kingman was very productive. Between the socializing and sexual play there were hours of time when solitude allowed her the quiet to think of her poem critically. Parts she wrote at home before the trip were fraught with the depression that made her wish to be "down underground." Parts written during her trip showed it had given her the will to live again. Those additional verses explained her view that her world was indeed, "no wider than the heart is wide."[126] Polishing done at home, changes of tense, word choice and corrections to the meter were flawed by constant interruptions and demands on her time.

The flirtation continued. So much so that the poet became certain that she was in the money as far as the publication went. Whether she received the grand $500 First Prize or second or third's $250 didn't matter. That money would give her enough to help her family and escape the suffocating sameness of her small town. Meanwhile, she had to be sure to keep the editor on the line. If that required shameless flirtation, so be it. If it required directly suggesting he might take her virginity, so be it. She would do what it took to survive.

Keeping peace at home was another matter. Her mother had received none of the attention of the mysterious editor. While this gave Cora pause, she was wise enough to know Vincent had more talent for poetry. What mattered to her was making sure her daughter didn't blow her chances with letters so frank they might appear unladylike. She was also concerned about making ends meet in the larger rental. Now that Vincent had a room of her own it seemed only logical that she would carry at least a third of the expenses.

The poet did not share this assessment, although she was willing to help. Consequently, when Norma asked her to help out at a party, she accepted the invitation.

The Whitehall Inn was one of the few decent hotels in Camden. Once owned by a sea captain, the resort had spacious, well-appointed rooms, a wraparound porch overlooking the harbor, and one of the better restaurants in the area. Norma worked there as a server, maid and amuser of guests.[127] With her thrilling soprano voice and a spirit ready for play, the middle Millay sister was a favorite with guests. They admired her hands and the way she spoke. This inevitably led them to ask if there were any more sisters like her at home.

Norma was happy to oblige. She spoke adoringly of her mother and sisters, skipped over her father and bragged that her elder sister was about to be published in *The Lyric Year*.

Curious but oblivious guests wondered if her sister would be attending the staff party. For some reason they assumed she worked a different shift. Norma told them no, that Vincent was shy and besides, she didn't work at the hotel. Undeterred, they told the gregarious blonde she ought to invite Vincent to the masquerade ball.

"Why not?" Norma asked the poet when she returned from her shift.

"A better question is why?"

"It would be a lark," the blonde replied as she brushed Vincent's long copper hair. "We dance so well together, and everybody is dying to meet you."

"Oh, Normie, you know how much I hate going out. Maybe Kathleen could go with you, or maybe Mumbles."

The blonde knew that Vincent always managed to pull herself out of her isolation if a friend were having a shower, which many of their friends were that year. Ethel's engagement and her sister Marion's wedding shower had brought the poet out of her garret twice in June. Not only that, but her elder sister was also hosting a tin shower that Tuesday and attending a linen shower at Alice Wadsworth's on Wednesday. Why was she hesitant to attend a ball, especially when she had always been keen on dress up events?

Nonetheless, Norma had noticed that Vincent was increasingly prone to locking herself away from others. She had first noticed it before she visited their father. Now it seemed even worse. All she seemed interested in was writing her editor and corresponding with the women she'd enjoyed relationships with during her journey that spring. What socializing she did was limited to things she felt she couldn't get out of and still consider people friends. "Come on, Vince. It will be fun, I promise you can leave anytime you like, but at least be my date."

The poet looked at Norma's pleading face and realized that her sister was not about to give up. Something inside her said it would probably be worth it. Oh, alright. "Let's see some of these tony people who come for the summers."

* * *

Although the poet had some misgivings, her younger sister set about creating a Pierrette costume out of yards of white cheese cloth with black pom poms down the front.[128] The sleeveless bodice was low-cut, and the skirt fitted snugly at her waist. When combined with a black velvet mask with a rosette of red crepe, the redhead looked younger than her twenty years. Vincent was delighted with the look of the commedia dell'arte character. It suited her mood: sad, lonely and desperate for some relief from the poverty that kept her chained to a life of limitations, but willing to accept the hand of someone she did not love. It also gave her the excuse for being quiet, since the traditional Pierrette role is performed in mime.

The day of the party arrived. It didn't take long for Vincent to get into the spirit of things. To the delight of guests, she proved herself a worthy Pierrette, miming her surprise and enthusiasm for winning best costume and dancing the Turkey Trot, Bunny Hop and Camel Walk between one step spins across the floor with her younger sister. As the August 29 event wound down it became clear much more would be expected from the local celebrity.

The guests had retired to the music room for ice cream and cake. Although billed as a party for the staff, the truth was the staff was expected to entertain the inn's guests. Norma, of course, knew this and told a guest, "Ask Vincent to sing some songs. Ask for the *Circus Rag*. You'll see! Nobody is better than my sister."

Vincent gave her sister a look like she'd been telling tales she ought to have kept to herself.[129] The poet was keenly aware of what it would mean if she refused. Norma would pay a price with the management. Her energy was flagging but despite her pique, the encouragement from guests proved enticing. She began to play and sing her own rag, with Norma helping with the "Step right up" choruses.

> You must have heard that circus rag,
> Years ago when you were a kid.
> Now the same old wag gets the same old gag
> Off just as he always did.
>
> Right this way, ladies and gents!
> Just a quarter of a dollar, only twenty-five cents!
> Step right up! Tickets here!
> We make it just a quarter to a pretty girl, dear.

Some of the guests got up and began to dance. One gentleman took Norma in his arms in hopes that the event's Best Dancer would improve his Grizzley Bear stomp. Laughter rippled through the room and soon others joined in the chorus as the poet and composer replayed the song a second time.

Her next selection was an even bigger hit with the crowd. Mr. and Mrs. Blanchard started a chorus of "encore" when she finished her original song, "Sun's Comin' Out." Like the one before it, the song was repeated over and over, followed by others, with requests from the inn's more than thirty guests for even more. Cheers and applause rang out, filling the poet's head with pride. At last, she thought, people are seeing me for what I am. It was as if she'd been transported back to Bangor and Kingman. Her head spun, trying to recover more tunes to ply the influential crowd.

She finally settled on another original, "Who Will Go A'Maying?" The guests were mesmerized by the performer's magnificent contralto despite the tune's derivative melody. "I will, I will," cried Mrs. Geier. "We all will!" The room nearly glowed with energy as the guests, finally exhausted from dancing and raucous sing-a-longs, began to sit down to finish their desserts.

"Ask her to recite *Renaissance*. It's going to be in *The Lyric Year*." Norma cried almost too loudly. Yet the guests seemed to welcome a recitation. While most guests had no idea what that meant, by now they were convinced they were in the presence of genius and one guest, Mr. Walter Geier, requested the recitation.

The poet, still in her Pierrette costume, turned around on the piano bench to face the guests. She knew the long poem by heart, and as her voice spread through the room there seemed to come a universal but silent request for quiet. Even the staff paused. Norma found herself more entranced than she had ever been. "All I could see from where I stood…" she began. As if by some signal every guest's head turned to take in their own views. With each stanza the enchantment grew deeper. No one moved. Breathing became quiet.

In the crowd that night sat a wealthy middle-aged matron named Caroline Dow. As she listened to the girl whom she had thought frivolous moments before, she realized the young woman was something beyond a sleepy tourist town. The cadence, the deceptive simplicity of the verse, revealed a child who must do more than change the sheets at a bed and breakfast. As Vincent's voice reverberated with the final stanzas, Miss Dow felt a tear sneak from her eyelid.

The power of the completed work, performed in public for the first time, caught the room unawares. The applause rattled the dishes. Vincent thanked everyone and eagerly accepted the praise being heaped upon her. Few could adequately put into words what the performance had meant to them. Norma, beaming with pride, considered their response as proof that the Millay girls were indeed different than all the Ediths and Mabels of Penobscot Bay. They were a special breed, created by the stern hand of an unconventional mother.

After the girls cleared the tables and the guests retired to their rooms the hum inside the Millay sisters made it clear to both of them that something extraordinary had happened that night. While Vincent remained relatively quiet and self-effacing, Norma was effusive.

"Did you see how Miss Dow looked at you?"

"Who is that?"

"The one in the dark blue dress with the white lace bodice, somewhat tall?"

The poet thought for a moment. "Oh, that woman about Mother's age. Who is she?"

"I think she's the head of the YWCA," the blonde replied with a grin that spoke volumes. As usual she exaggerated the importance of the visitor. It was true that Dow was affiliated with the women's association, but only as the head of the New York Chapter.

"Is she married?" Vincent asked out of the blue.

"I don't know." Norma pulled a thread from her sweater, balled it up in her fingers and tossed it aside. "She came alone, but she seems to know most of the ladies here."

Vincent wasn't sure if that meant she knew the women of Camden or the guests at the hotel, but it didn't matter. As she had done the summer before with the theater company, Vincent had made a conquest in the room. It amused her to know she had that effect on people.

The sisters walked in silence for a long while. Eventually Norma could contain herself no longer.

"Do you suppose she's rich. I mean very rich?"

"I suppose, but I don't think she's a Rockefeller."

"We should ask Mother. She's nursing Mrs. Dow's friend, Mr. Chesborough."

Vincent thought for a moment. If Miss Dow was rich, she couldn't afford to make any mistakes. What if she called? What if she wanted to see her? Was Norma, right? "What makes you think she's taken an interest in me."

"The way she cried at the end of 'Renaissance'. I just know she was deeply moved. Maybe you could be her companion. Rich ladies often have companions to fetch them things and keep them company. Maybe she'd take you to Europe."

"Ugh," the poet replied. "I don't want to keep some lonely old lady company."

"It's better than waiting table or packing up powders for the pharmacist," Norma correctly observed.

"I suppose. If she took me to New York, I could get a different kind of work or find a publisher or…" A great thought occurred to her, a dream she had been squelching for two years since graduation. "Maybe she could send me to college."

"I don't think companions are allowed to do that. I mean, companions need to be close at hand," the blonde replied, missing her sister's point entirely.

"Oh, hang being Miss Dow's companion," Vincent snapped. She hated how Norma would throw a damper on a wonderful fantasy by adhering to the reality of their class.

By the time they reached home the conversation had shifted to the party itself. Each woman held her prize ribbon loosely, cherishing the recognition from Norma's employers, their peers and the guests of the Whitehall Inn. The triumph of Vincent's performance was set aside for gossip about Ethel's upcoming wedding and Kathleen's final year of high school.

* * *

The next morning Vincent was aroused by the sound of feet climbing the stairs. The steps were brisk and light. She pushed a pillow over her head and prayed whoever it was would leave her alone. "Vince! You've got a phone call," Kathleen's voice had somehow gotten a light Irish lilt.

"Tell them I'll call back," Vincent mumbled.

"Norma says you're going to want to speak to her."

Vincent sat up. "Who?"

"Miss Dow."

Suddenly awake, the poet scrambled to put on her slippers and robe before dashing downstairs. By the time she got there Norma was telling Kathleen all about the previous night's performance. "I bet she wants Vince to be her companion."

"Why didn't she ask last night?" the younger sister asked as she ate a slice of bread lathered with the last of the butter.

"I don't know, but…"

"Hush!" Vincent said as she reached for the receiver. Her two siblings crowded near her to hear their sister's call.

"Good morning."

"Oh, yes, good morning, dear. I hope the call didn't wake you."

"Not at all," Vincent lied. "I've been up for hours."

Norma and Kathleen made faces at each other that almost made Vincent laugh.

"That's good to hear. I am a great believer in Poor Richard's adage, 'early to bed, early to rise, make a man healthy, wealthy and wise'."

"Of course," the poet replied. She waited for Miss Dow's response.

"Oh, my, where are my manners? This is Caroline Dow. I'm a guest at the Whitehall Inn. I heard you recite last night. I simply can't get you off my mind."

"You're too kind."

"Or your poem!"

Caroline Dow, daughter of an American elite, knew people and in Vincent she saw the daughter she would never have. "I'd like to speak with your mother privately. When might she be available?"

The redhead was temporarily confused by the request. "Did I do something to offend you?"

"Of course not! I've spoken with friends and we're going to send you to Vassar."

Vincent nearly dropped the phone. College? Some women she had never met would pay for her college. The poet could hardly believe her ears. "You'd pay for college. At Vassar?"

"That's what I want to speak with your mother about. We'll have to determine what would be needed."

Vincent resisted the urge to say, "Everything." Instead, she took a deep breath and replied. "Mother is out. She may even be there now."

"At this hotel?" Miss Dow asked. Now it was her turn to be confused. Was her mother a member of the staff, an owner or a guest?

"Yes, she's been asked to care for Mr. Chesborough," Vincent explained. "She's a nurse." The poet figured this sounded more professional than she would do almost anything for money. Wig maker, nurse, journalist, herbalist, pharmacy assistant...her mother had done it all with varying degrees of success. "Nurse" sounded more professional.

"Oh, yes, he's been poorly," Miss Dow replied. "The hotel manager said he would call someone in. How coincidental that it is your mother."

Vincent thought it was more kismet than coincidence. "Is there anything else I can do for you?"

"Yes. I'd like you to come to the inn again this evening for dinner and recite your poem to some friends of mine who may want to help you get to Vassar."

"Honest?" Vincent exclaimed. "I'll be there. What time?"

"Seven-thirty. That will give them time to get to meet you and settle in. You may bring your charming sister and mother if you like."

Vincent wanted this moment of triumph for herself. As much as she loved Norma, she knew her sister's enthusiasm might be off putting. Her mother would know better. Besides, Norma could be her stand-in at Alice's party. "My mother and I will be there."

"Please bring any other music or poetry you have composed."

"I will." The poet's head swam. She should finish "Who Will Go A'Maying?" No doubt she would have to spend the day preparing her best clothes, music and poems for that night's opportunity.

The matron and her protégé signed off the telephone.

"College!" Norma cried.

"Not just college, Vassar!"

"I wonder if she'd help me go too," Kathleen said. She would graduate the following year and, like her elder sister, had designs well beyond the confines of Camden.

Norma had never liked school. She had visions of an operatic career or perhaps she'd be a famous actress like Madame Bernhardt.

Still, Miss Dow's interest in the family proved they were special and above the yokels.[130]

"Let's get you out of high school first," the poet replied. It was a role she had taken so often it was second nature. As surrogate mother to her younger siblings it was her job to inject discipline into the dreams of Kathleen and Norma. Cora was usually too exhausted or ill to offer more than a pained smile at the whims of her children.

Vincent quickly consumed breakfast and went to her room. There was so much to do in preparation for that evening's command performance.

* * *

When Vincent and Cora arrived at the Whitehall Inn that evening, they were met by fourteen expectant faces. The group included men and women who represented the aspiring upper classes. The Geiers of shipping and milling fame vied with the Esselborns for a seat near the guests of honor. Georgiana Skilling Bangs, a member of the Daughters of the American Revolution, thought she was better suited to be a judge of the Millays' character than recent immigrants like the Esselborns. The fifty-two-year-old reporter and author Day Allen Willey thought certainly he should sit close enough to hear every word of every poem in order to judge the quality of Vincent's verse. Although he had made his considerable reputation as a writer of scientific papers and was in the midst of planning a trip to explore the Rockies, he made sure everyone knew his connection to the *Baltimore World* newspaper.[131] It seemed as if everyone at the table had something to offer the starry-eyed poet, yet both Millays were cynical enough to cast a wary eye at their would-be benefactors.

As dinner commenced, Cora asked as many questions as were asked of her daughter. If Frederick Geier spoke of taking poems back to Cincinnati, she was quick to politely ask what he would do with them. Mr. Willey explained he could assure publication, but Vincent's mother recognized a rogue's face when she saw one. Cora nudged her daughter. It was a signal that had long meant, "Be still."

Watching their interactions, Miss Dow observed not only Cora's protectiveness, but also her wit. This was no simple country nurse. Here was a woman who had instilled a love of learning and art in her daughter. It was clear she'd made sacrifices in her quest to raise three children alone.

Most guests assumed the staid, forty-nine-year-old nurse was a widow making ends meet. No one, not even Caroline Dow, knew she was a divorcee. As Vincent spoke of the books and music she loved, every ear was attuned to the way she used language. While her voice was pleasing it was replete with colloquialisms that just wouldn't do at Vassar.

"Perhaps she could go to Smith first," Mrs. Blanchard whispered to Pauline Esselborn at the far end of the table.

"That might help, and I'm certain my husband could do something about that drab homespun," she replied. Her daughter had caught the eye of the most eligible bachelor in the room, Frederick August Geier.[132] Mrs. Esselborn discreetly turned to Juliet and asked if she might have some clothes that would fit the poet. Her daughter, aware that the handsome and kind-face mustachioed man had more interest in her than the poet, agreed.

For her part, Vincent couldn't believe how wonderfully kind and charming they all were toward her.[133] It was probably the grandest thing that had ever happened to anybody, she thought. At least she knew it was the most reinforcing thing that had ever happened to any dream she'd ever had.

The response to the dessert performance was even more enthusiastic. Cora reveled in seeing her daughter transfix the audience of well-to-do patrons. It meant there was hope for Norma and Kathleen. Perhaps they might also want to publish her own poetry.

Neither woman could fathom Vincent's good fortune. Every time the poet thought of it, she could practically swoon. It even seemed as if she might have at last conjured her beloved in the form of The Editor of *The Lyric Year*. Things were coming together at last.

11. In Infinite Remorse of Soul

1912

As summer turned to fall excitement turned to annoyance. The wait was interminable. Aside from invitations to visit and a promise by Mr. Willey to take her work to a literary agent, Vincent remained stuck in Camden. Miss Dow assured her that she was gathering the necessary funds for admission to Vassar for the following year, but there was still no word of certainty.

Meanwhile, her editor at *The Lyric Year* had finally sent his picture in response to her flirtatious pressing for details regarding the publication.[134] He assured her in mid-September that it was his opinion that "Renaissance" would win the competition, particularly if she made some changes to the poem, including changing the spelling of the title to the American spelling "Renascence," dropping the use of "suddenly" and allowing some of the poem's events to happen quietly. The poet realized immediately that he was right and figured that if these corrections improved her chances, she would be a fool not to take the suggestions. She also reworked seven other lines she had noted. By the time the proof pages of her poem were sent on September 21, she was delighted to have such a helpful editor because it was clear he had her interests at heart.

Was he her "beloved"? Was he the one she'd been conjuring for years with monthly incantations? She didn't even know his name yet, but she did know he was tall and thin, with straight black hair, dark eyes and a sly grin, not to mention a wife and baby.[135] It wouldn't be the first time she'd captured the heart of an older man. Even Walter Geier had given her *The Instructive Game of Poets*, a deck of 52 cards in thirteen groups of four poems per rhymer. It had struck her as odd that a man fourteen years her senior would treat her like a child, especially since it proved how little he knew her. Although her editor was her senior by the same number, she quickly knew that he did understand her. When he revealed his name in a letter a few days later she understood why.

Her editor was Ferdinand Earle. The poet and painter was just the sort of man she imagined her beloved to be.

"Several have prophesized that you have the best chance for first prize," he teased. What did that mean? The decision has not been made yet. Who were these "several people"? She was well-aware that men often made promises they couldn't keep so she warned him that if she were disappointed it would be a terrible blow. Her skepticism notwithstanding, Earle invited her to join his family at Vinderholm, the estate his father had built on the site once occupied by George Washington during the American Revolution.

His enthusiasm for her visit was not shared by his wife, however. Being wife number two, she knew exactly how likely it was that someone might be wife number three.

The exchange of letters grew increasingly familiar. "If I could believe that I have encouraged and helped you with my big, clumsy venture I would be most gratified. When your name is pronounced only with whispers of awe, it will be my secret prize to believe I had the privilege of discovering your worth before anyone else."[136]

Vincent thought the flowery modesty was false and wondered why it would occur to her he was really referring to her virginity. Nevertheless, she thought his venture was far from "clumsy." To her it was "big" and "splendid."[137] She gave him credit for making her year "miraculous."

Her reply gave him pause. He realized that he might be leading her down the proverbial garden path. In truth, it was Edward J. Wheeler that held her future in his hands as far as the prize went. Earle needed to find a way to keep her engaged without admitting he'd overstepped his bounds in far too many ways.

"I realize you are a woman, and not the mere elfchild I let myself imagine," he began. "I am half very sorry and half very glad."

What did that mean? Was he saying he liked thinking of her as a child? Perhaps even preferred thinking of her that way? Her mind raced back to her old landlord, the man whose hands had fondled things they shouldn't have before Cora's timely interruption. Vincent pushed the thought from her mind and continued reading. In two more weeks, he would know the chosen winners and couldn't tell her. "What you read between the lines, I should not be responsible for, should I?"

This incensed the poet. He'd all but told her she was in the top three. Why did he seem so coy? She kept reading and learned that her editor's wife had begun reading her letters and that while he was "glowing with wild, uncontrollable delights" his wife was not. Therefore, he confessed, he was not sure how the poet would be welcomed in their house.

The writing on the wall would have been plain to Cora, but Vincent's immaturity was unable to take in his meaning. Instead, she replied to his question about how she came to write *"Renascence"* at such a young age.

"If it will make you happier to know just what your friendship has meant to me, then please understand this; the sky had to cave in on me, of course, before I could write 'Renascence'." She went on to explain that she'd "dug up" the narrator of the poem, but not herself. "It was you who, in your enthusiastic 'discovering,' accidently exhumed me."[138]

Vincent realized she sounded too broken to remain atop his display of treasure and added, "Now we won't talk about *that* anymore."

* * *

Earle soon realized that he was indeed dealing with a young woman he had led to believe was in the running for a reward. He had to let her know that while he was attracted to her, liked her, was her friend and editor, he must protect her from flights of fancy that might soon result in singed wings. "You must promise me, dear, dear Tom Boy, never, never to write to a strange man as you have written me."[139]

The poet read the pages of his letter oblivious of the disappointment lurking there. "Dear, dear…never, never," sounded more like the pleading of Pauline fending off the advances of Simon Legree. She wondered if they could talk about the weather and return to a less confusing correspondence, yet she pushed further toward him, made certain by her naivete that he was indeed her "beloved." That he was twice married didn't matter. That he wrote mediocre sonnets, painted passable art and played an expensive Cremona violin seemed irrelevant. She had enough love and talent for them both. The desire that her brief romance with Ella had awakened now stormed inside her. Hers was a love that needed to be broken like a wild horse before she'd take the bit.

"If you could know how almost annihilatingly I want to hear you play that violin! Or how I would come straight back home again and be turned for the rest of my life, if not for one evening I might listen to Wagner music with a man who *knew* how I love it! Savage passion! There could be no savage passion in you that would not find itself again in me! I am not big enough to love things the way I do!"

The poet looked at what she'd written in reply to his letter, which had tried to temper their epistolary affair with reality. She decided she needed to add something to assure him she'd understood his letter, lest they get caught up in the Sturm und Drang of Wagner's Träume violin concerto. Rather than rewrite the letter, which she would have had she known how far she'd gone overboard, she awoke from her dream and played at being chastened.[140] "I had not meant to say so much. It is shockingly bad form to be so unreserved. Dear me! What will you do with me now, Mr. Ferdinand Earle? Scold me, shake me, or pat me on the head?"

Vincent laughed at the idea of the man under her spell would ever pat her head as if she were a child told to run along and play elsewhere. "Don't dare!" she added. "O, I *have* to giggle."

The question was, how would she test his mettle if she had to pretend innocence? By openly flirting she was not only measuring her power over others, but she was also examining how much fortitude he had in the face of temptation.

* * *

Cora read Earle's letters with a mix of maternal pride, envy and fear. Here was another man with a roving eye and a taste for younger women. On the other hand, their financial situation made the prize he seemed to promise worth the risk. After all, he was in New York, married and admitted to sharing Vincent's letters with his wife. Edward Wheeler had once judged Vincent worthy of a $10 prize for her submission to *St. Nicholas Magazine.* Perhaps between Wheeler and Earle there would be $500 to go toward the family coffers.

As weeks continued to go by the excitement of August turned into the skepticism of October. Was Earle just stringing her daughter along as a method of seduction? Was Miss Dow less well-connected than she seemed? Were *The Lyric Year* and Vassar just two more Sisyphean peaks that would never be reached? Her daughters, all three of them, but most especially Vincent, were caught up in the hope both mountains promised. What would happen to them if it was all an illusion?

Finally, after a dozen more promising letters, Earle regretted he had to leave "a trail of fire across Vincent's dreams."[141]

The poet read the letter of October 14 in stunned silence. It was two weeks before the scheduled announcement of the winners, yet it was plain that her editor knew something that flew in the face of months of assurances. "Would you hate me if they snubbed you?"

What did that mean? She knew but did not want to believe it. He had been telling her for months she'd win a prize. If not first prize, second or third. He was the one funding the prize money. Why would he say that if he didn't mean it? What a weakling! What a scoundrel! She considered all her shameless flirting, the growing trust that was now shattered. She wanted to smash his Amati violin. She wanted to tell him he was old and ugly. She pushed her pillow into her mouth and screamed. How dare he?

Eventually, she realized that he also had the power to remove her poem from the volume entirely. This would affect Miss Dow's efforts to send her to Vassar. She had to push down the rage that was now making her fingers tremble. Wiping back her tears, she wrote back to him back October 15.

"I shall not hate you. But I shall cry all night long the night I got that letter, and I hope all night long you will lie awake and know that I am crying. I wished once to make you glad in return for the gladness you had given me, and now, by the same token, I would make you wretched. I desire that you cannot sleep that night for thinking of my wretchedness."

A tear puddled on the page. He obviously had no idea what that money would mean to her let alone her family. As a man who had never had to worry about money every single day, Earle couldn't know what the $500 would mean to her. "You had not thought of that," she scolded. "I would choose not to think of it myself if I had any choice."

By now the weak, lonely, latchkey child was in full-throated rage. Here was the man who had invited her to New York when he knew his wife and son were away. The man who had suggested he might sneak into Camden to meet her.[142] She admitted her flirtation was chiefly done due to being twenty and Earle being the only man friend on whose shoulder she could cry. The confusion trampled her mind like hobnail boots. On the other hand, she needed him because men responded to tears better than her mother or sisters. On the other, she hated how much of a fool she'd been and blamed him for it. The same suicidal thoughts that had given birth to "Renascence" now reemerged stronger than ever.

"I haven't in all the world one friend who is stronger than I," she wrote. The butt of her palm was stained with ink. She didn't care. "I need someone to make me do things, and to keep me doing things, and keep me from doing things."

This was no idle threat. Her life seemed to spin without meaning. Loads of praise and promises but scant else. She found herself lapsing into almost Dickensian baby talk, the last refuge of the deeply disappointed.[143] "I feel so small and shrunked up. I am honest 'fraid you have to use a big 'nifying glass! Please, sir, I am sorry for my badness, and will you write me a letter to cry on?"

How could she know what was in his head? Would she realize how terrifying her letter would be? He could see the headlines, "Lyric Year Poet Kills Self: Family Blames Editor." This was not the sort of letter he needed even as he waffled in his choices for the top prizes. On October 15, 1912,[144] Earle wrote to the publisher, Mitchell Kennerley, that he thought she should get second place if not first despite the voting of the other judges. He wrote Vincent saying the poems were "almost judged" that same afternoon. The irresolute editor wrote Kennerley again on October 25, perhaps after reading Vincent's plaintive letter, and championed the poem for first prize.

* * *

Fall fell deep and long. The poet remained in her room. When Earle wrote again telling her that most "friendships, relations and acquaintanceships were as bloodless, frigid and stark, with no becoming drapery in the form of mystery and romantic atmosphere, with no bared elbows and throats,"[145] she sobbed, not only for the loss of a means to escape Camden, but also Earle's apparent desire to push her away entirely. If his communication was meant to soothe with phrases lamenting that he had no news for her, that the question of who won was "still an open one (shut at the outside ends)," the majority of his cut and pasted letter gave her the impression that he shared her assessment with the world. People only pretended to care. They flattered and flirted, promised and promoted, but in the end, it was all about what was in it for them. In her bitterness and resentment Vincent was just another girl he might entice with kind words and effusive praise. It was easy to see why she thought so when one considers how quickly the bounty of summer turned to the barren limbs of fall. The famous autumnal colors of New England meant little to her. They too seemed like a lie. All glitter and glamour hiding the icy depths.

* * *

For his part, Ferdinand Earle, Jr. was chafing under the scolding of his wife. In a moment of Freudian slippage, the libidinous editor had left a letter from Vincent where anyone could see it. It was a letter he had asked for, one that was frank and revealing. It made no bones about her desire for sex and even her willingness to sleep with him so she would get a prize.[146] The stunning revelation was the last straw for his wife. Their marriage began to crumble, and although he would write to discourage Vincent's affection, the damage was done.

Now he had to deal with the vengeance of another scorned conquest. When Vincent replied to his "patch work letter" on November 15, she did so with barely veiled rage befitting one of the Furies.

"Let me congratulate on your impersonation of a genuine man. How can I be expected to understand a person who got his education in France, his business methods in Siberia, his behavior in vaudeville and his brains in a raffle?"

Like a wounded animal, Vincent struck out with claws in a vain attempt to avoid pain. She asked for the letters she'd written to a friend because they had landed somehow in the hands of a complete stranger. "I am wild, if you like, but I stayed in my burrow for a long, long time—nibbling your straws and snapping your fingers, but always just a little bit out of reach. Until at last, I got to trust you so much that one day I ventured out for a minute—and you threw rocks at me. And I will never come out again."[147]

The poet's understandable pique elicited a thoroughly unsympathetic response. Vincent exploded with a kind of strained emotional ague. She admitted no tears, only referred to the "strange and terrible sound" of her mother weeping, an echo that she would never forget.[148] Several replies were attempted but the redhead could find no words because she felt as though she didn't even know the man who was sending the curious letters that threatened exclusion from the publication.

Instead, she realized with bitter delight that Earle's hand had been forced when a third party, Jessie Rittenhouse, received an advance copy of the book and proclaimed "Renascence" the "best thing" in *The Lyric Year*. As she was a founding member of the Poetry Society of America, Earle couldn't afford to snub Millay's entry, which Rittenhouse[149] called, "one of the freshest and most original things in modern poetry."[150] To further confound Earle's tit-for-tat revenge fantasies, the wealthy Chicago poet and critic pitied the judges if Vincent's work didn't get first prize. Like any man who finds his planned retaliation thwarted by forces greater than his own, Earle sent along Rittenhouse's assessment with a poorly disguised wish that Vincent never write another poem. "What more could you hope for? You might as well retire and rest on your laurels the rest of your life."

As if a twenty-year-old could retire. He was well-aware of her ambition. She had revealed far more secrets than she should have. As usual she had mistaken male friendliness for actual respect. It wasn't the first time, nor would it be the last. She would never forget Earle's manipulation of her self-confessed naivete.

12. The Gall of All Regret

1912

While Cora wept, Vincent became ever more determined. She wrote Caroline Dow to confirm she would not lose her other summer "prize."

Indeed, Miss Dow admitted she could see why Vincent might think she had been forgotten. Still, the matron assured the poet she was working toward finding funding to send Vincent to Vassar. Meanwhile, the matron needed to know what she had studied at Camden High School and where she stood in the class rankings. The patrons of so lofty an enterprise wanted to know their money would be well spent. Who were her favorite authors? What were her extracurricular activities? Was she physically fit and from a suitable family? Miss Dow knew better than to tell anyone that Vincent's parents had divorced, or that Vincent had been so disruptive in high school that she had been barred from attending classes and had to study at home.[151] Instead, she emphasized the poet's multiple gifts and Cora's enviable library. "Oh, of course, and she's had piano lessons, attends church regularly, even taught Sunday School..." the respectable and respected president of the New York YWCA would explain. Consequently, Vincent had to be careful to avoid impropriety, including being too theosophical or esoteric. The wealthy could tolerate a girl from an unconventional background, but not a heathen who eschewed many traditional Christian precepts.

This odd conflict between the temptations of Earle and the admonitions of Dow struck Vincent as amusing. She would wear whatever mask that would achieve her goal, while at the same time remain true and committed to those closest to her. In other words, though one might criticize her cynicism, one couldn't fault her loyalty or honor. It was a dichotomy that would cause consternation in everyone who knew her.

But Miss Dow wasn't the only one searching for a way to educate the erratic Miss Millay. Another guest from that night at the Whitehall Inn wanted

Vincent's feather in her cap. Mrs. Esselborn sent a copy of "Renascence" to her Smith-educated friend Charlotte Bannon who in turn passed it along to the new head of the Smith College English Department, Ada Comstock.

Miss Comstock was as much a rebel as Vincent, but she knew Smith couldn't be too lax in whom it sponsored for admission, so she asked as many questions as the Vassar dean. Her queries also included why a woman of non-traditional college age wanted to further her education. Vincent knew enough about college to know that Vassar had more prestige and, more importantly, it was much further away than Smith's Northampton, Massachusetts campus. Yet the poet didn't want to blow her chances of a college education and was willing to by admitted to either campus. True to her nature, she told Miss Dow about Smith's firm offer to support her throughout her years there so long as Vincent passed the entrance exams.

Caroline Dow was conflicted. She knew her protégé would benefit regardless but felt strongly that the country college of Vassar would be less distracting than the proximity to the distractions of home. However, so far, she had only raised enough for the poet's first year in Poughkeepsie.[152]

The collegial tug-of-war delighted Vincent. Though it seemed to be taking forever to resolve one way or another, the battle between the rival women's colleges and the sponsors who sought her entry gave the poor girl from a broken family a confidence that allayed the disappointment of losing *The Lyric Year* money.

* * *

Cora had noticed the change in her daughter with a mixture of pride and worry. Who would tutor Kathleen in her senior year of high school? Who would act as a chaperone to the girls who had blossomed into independent and desirable young women? Who would bring in extra cash, since Vincent seemed to be the only one willing to take the bit when things were tough.

"When is Miss Dow coming for another visit?" Cora asked one November evening over dinner.

Vincent looked at her mother quizzically. "How should I know? I suppose she's in New York."

Cora decided to try again. "Is she still arranging for Vassar?"

"Of course, Mother. In fact, she's already raised $600."

"That's not enough," Norma declared. She actually had no idea how much it cost, but she knew college was more than $100 per year or Cora would have found a way to make it happen, just as she'd found ways to get them piano lessons.

"And Miss Comstock at Smith says if I pass the entrance exam, I might be able to go there," Vincent replied, ignoring her sister's remark.

"Who is Miss Comstock. Have I met Miss Comstock?" Cora asked.

Kathleen looked at her sisters, then at her mother. Although close in age she had felt distant since their bout with typhoid years before. Norma caught her gaze and stuck her tongue out at her before winking. As younger siblings their role was to attract attention away from the conflict plagued the household. Yet neither Cora nor Vincent had noticed the exchange.

"No, Vincent replied as she reached for the basket of freshly baked bread."

"Is she related to the Comstock mine?" Norma asked.

"If she is, I bet she is very rich." Kathleen added, waving a hand to indicate she would like bread as well.

Vincent became annoyed. It was hard enough to cope with months of ambiguity let alone deal with her family's clueless speculation. "I don't think so. She wouldn't need a job if she was."

Cora was still not satisfied. "Who is she then? Miss Comstock, I mean. What does she do?"

The poet sighed and explained it all. Her mother remembered Pauline Esselborn as a strait-laced, chatty, nouveau riche daughter of an immigrant.

"Maybe she could give you some new clothes," Kathleen suggested. As the tallest of the girls, she often had trouble with hand-me-downs. She hoped the wealthy woman would give her an outfit that fit for a change.

"Miss Comstock or Mrs. Esselborn?" Norma teased. "You'd be pretty loud clanging around in silver."

Vincent laughed at the image. "You know very well who. Miss Comstock is more interested in my brains than how I dress."

"But of course, when you meet her, you'll dress appropriately," Cora fretted.

Her eldest daughter felt like she would scream. Were they being deliberately obtuse? "Of course, Mumbles."

"What if you applied to both colleges, just in case." Cora's smile reflected the pride she had that two schools were vying for her daughter.

Exasperated, Vincent replied. "That's what Miss Dow suggested I do." The butter that had melted on her slice of bread was on the verge of being rancid. The ice from Lake Chickawaukie had melted almost two days before and there was no money for more. She ignored the soapy sour taste and took another bite of bread. The evening's fare was a pot of beans. The family ate that sort of meal as often as Vincent's sensitive stomach allowed.

"How long until you'll know?" Cora prodded again.

"As long as it takes," the poet replied barely masking her frustration with the topic at hand. She took a breath and hoped to soothe her mother. "Don't worry. It isn't like *The Lyric Year* with some man playing me for a naïve fool. This is a sure thing. These women mean business."

"I hope so, dear." Cora returned to her legumes with more hunger than desire.

* * *

They were still scrounging for Thanksgiving dinner when her copy of *The Lyric Year* arrived. Somehow it was a disappointment. She decided the red leather binding with the gold leaf lyre reflected the man who promised the moon but delivered a rock. Nonetheless, Cora gushed with excitement. "Look! Isn't it wonderful? Come here, girls. Come see what your sister did."

Kathleen stepped forward and carefully took the volume from her mother's hands. She thumbed the uncut pages. "Where is it?"

"Here," Vincent poked a spot just past the center of the book. "Page 180."

The young brunette flipped to the page just as Norma entered. "It came?"

"It came."

The women passed the book around three times. Vincent thought the placement was odd.

"It's not at the beginning." It's not at the end. It's not even in the middle. She forced a bitter chuckle. "It's right where people stop paying attention to the book."

"That's just silly, Edna," Cora said firmly.

The poet knew what using her given name meant. She was not conforming to her mother's dictate. "Yes, ma'am."

Norma proudly touched the page. "Just think of it. A book. A real, leather-bound book. Not just a magazine or the newspaper, but a book."

"Too bad Mr. Wheeler didn't put you in the money." Kathleen observed.

"Yes, and have you read that stupid one about the *Centenary of Robert Browning* that got second place? Norma had pronounced 'centenary' with an extended 'Cen-ten-ARee,' mimicking the accent of Miss Dow as she began to read George Sterling's prize-winning entry. As unto lighter strains a boy might turn from where great altars burn, and Music's grave archangels tread the night, So I, in seasons past..."[153]

"Couldn't stand its bloody sight." Vincent improvised sarcastically. The women began to giggle, making fun of the unfortunate Mr. Sterling. While all of them were familiar with Browning, even loved his work, they thought the $250 prize winner was a slice of hammy iambic pentameter.

Vincent gasped. "The ceaseless trumpets of the war on Good." She thrust her hands for dramatic effect into the air. "Ah, thou, ah, thou...Perhaps I misunderstood?"

They howled with laughter until the humor became fury.

"How could they give second place to that?" Kathleen wondered.

"Perhaps you did something to Mr. Earle to discourage him," Cora suggested, looking closely at her eldest daughter.

Norma, the only one besides Vincent to know to what extent she had encouraged him, scoffed, tipping the book toward her mother's gaze. "I doubt that. It says right here he thought she should get first prize."

"That's right, Mother," Kathleen added. "After all, Mr. Wheeler and Mr. Braithwaite didn't choose her at all. Majority wins."

"Sadly," Norma finished in case their mother and sister misinterpreted Kathleen's logical explanation.

* * *

It wasn't long before a train of apologies and opinions flooded into the Millay household from people similarly flummoxed by Vincent's loss. The following day, in addition to an unexpected letter from her father, the poet heard from fellow contributors Arthur Davison Ficke and Witter Bynner who expressed their belief she should have won all the prizes. Orrick Johns, the actual first place winner,[154] sent an encouraging note calling his achievement "an unmerited award,"[155] as did the other second place winner, Thomas Augustus Daly. His poem *To a Thrush* reflected the mid-Victorian sensibilities of the older judges. Louis Untermeyer, the preeminent poetry anthologist and critic, felt that her poem had "a direct and often dramatic power."[156] Even the publisher Mitchell Kennerley expressed his misgiving about the judges' selections. Then, in the November 30 holiday issue of the *New York Times*,[157] Jessie Rittenhouse singled out "Renascence" in a review of *The Lyric Year* that made it clear that while Earle and Kennerley were to be commended for such a project, their idea of which poems were worthy of cash prizes left a lot to be desired. Sure, she admitted, there were flaws in Vincent's poem, but they reflected her youth. "That a poet so young should have so personal a vision of humanity, nature and God, such a sense of spiritual elation, of mystical rebirth, and present it to us with the freshness of first view—is certainly worthy of recognition." Then, in what most young poets would have considered the piece de resistance, she received a letter from the Poetry Society of America on December 12 asking if she had any unpublished work they could share with the club's members, followed by a notice on December 17 that she had been voted into their membership.[158]

* * *

Although the attractive young redhead had the poetic world at her feet, she felt letdown. In addition to an ongoing correspondence with Ficke and Bynner, who had initially thought she was "a brawny male of forty," the publication of Earle's compilation reminded her patrons and the folks at Vassar of her application to the college. It was determined that she did not qualify based on her high school grades and activities, but if she could pass a year at Barnard she would be accepted to the much more prestigious college. Miss Dow hadn't counted on this setback but was so determined to place the poet that she accepted the challenge. As the president of the YWCA, Miss Dow was confident housing would not be an issue. The organization had just expanded into a massive residence, meeting space and training center at 610 Lexington Avenue at 52nd Street, New York.[159]

On December 18, 1912, Vincent's opinion of the women vying to help her was born out when Marion LeRoy Burton, the president of Smith, dangled a full scholarship starting in fall 1913.[160] Not to be outdone and still convinced the poet would be better served by Vassar, Miss Dow dashed off a note trying to be impartial but clearly indicating her choice. She had gathered enough money for a full year and had the beginnings of a second at the esteemed college in Poughkeepsie.

"Mother, wait until you hear this!" Vincent wrote to her mother who was working on a case in Rockland. "My head is a howling wilderness. On the one hand, she puts in her little words about the country life at Vassar, the next she's leaving the decision entirely to me. Every once and a while I have to shriek with laughter over the dead funny of it."[161] It was odd. She was the master of her destiny for the first time in her life, yet still at the mercy of well-connected upper-crusters.[162]

* * *

1912 came to a close with a flurry of congratulations, reviews and even a request for her autograph from a Chicago fan. Arthur Davison Ficke was so smitten that he sent her books by Vachel Lindsay and himself. Christmas had an air of success around it, with a stunningly large haul of volumes, including another book by Ficke, *Breaking the Bonds*, and William Blake, who, surprisingly she'd never heard of, and a fountain pen, paper knife, and three boxes of Crane's Linen Lawn handkerchiefs.[163]

While basking in all the abundance, Vincent planned Norma's birthday party for Sunday, December 29 (although her actual birthday was the day before). Like many holiday babies, Norma often felt unseen on her birthday and her precious sister wanted to make sure this wasn't the case in this year when so many of her own dreams were manifesting. She spent the day cooking, invited Kenneth, Marion and the rest of Norma's friends, and dressed in an elegant yellow chiffon. She read aloud a letter with birthday greetings from her father, sang a special birthday song, passed along Cora's gifts and greetings and did all she could to acknowledge the ways in which Norma, more than anyone in her family, had been supporting her throughout the interminable waiting for word on college and publication.

"Vince," Norma whispered as her sister passed around a tray of homemade canapes.

"What?"

"Your dress."

Vincent looked down and realized that somehow the chiffon was being shredded and leaving behind a trail of small slices of fabric.

"Goodness!" She set the tray down and raced into the kitchen. Norma followed.

"Why did you go in here. You need to change," Norma said. Another slip of the chiffon fell to the floor.

"What is causing this?"

Norma looked at the material. "Don't ask me. What did you wash it with last time?"

Vincent thought back. Although she did the washing, it was really Norma who was better at anything related to fabric. "Cold water, soap."

"Did you twist it? Wring it, rub it on the wash board?"

"I didn't use the washboard."

"But did you wring it?"

"It had a stain so I…"

"Say no more. Go upstairs and change. I'll keep things going down here."

Vincent slipped through the crowd toward the staircase. Every time she bumped into someone another feather of fabric dropped. Norma followed to distract in case anyone else should notice. "Now I know what Cinderella must have felt like when the clock struck twelve,"[164] Vincent whispered before dashing up the stairs.

* * *

The last day of 1912, a year that had been filled with extremes of all types, was a lovely day.[165] It began with a clipping from Louis Untermeyer of a review he'd published in the *Chicago Evening Post* on December 27. She decided his remarks were the loveliest to date about her infamously snubbed poem. What an honor it was and so very much needed at that moment. She had bought a new journal for recording just such events in the coming year.

13. Every Brooded Wrong

1913

On January 6, 1913, Vincent received two important letters and a few that simply annoyed her. Ella was still hoping to see her. Gladys wondered why she didn't choose another college entirely. Mitchell Kennerley, still benefiting from the reaction to *The Lyric Year*, sent Vincent a copy of the January issue of *The Forum* in which someone named Charles Vale reviewed *The Lyric Year* and singled out "Renascence" as the volume's most important work.[166] Finally, Charlotte Bannon advised Vincent to take the bird in the hand, a full ride from Smith over the maybe of Vassar.

Of course, Bannon understood that the poet needed to be diplomatic and express her gratitude and appreciation to Miss Dow and all the rest who had been so kind, but what President Burton offered was a definite certainty. Bannon closed her letter with a line that was the surest form of flattery to someone like Vincent. "I want to be your great friend and I will be, if you let me."

Like Miss Dow, Mrs. Esselborn, Mr. and Mrs. Geier and the rest, Charlotte Bannon felt hemmed in by what society required. Helping Vincent gave them all an opportunity to vicariously experience Lord Byron-like freedom to live as they chose.

To hedge her bets, Vincent began to fill out the Smith application, but it didn't take her long to realize she'd have to make an appointment with the newly hired principal of Camden High. Although Smith College was, in the final analysis, her second choice, Miss Dow had only raised $800 so far and she thought a bird in the hand was better than nothing, even if she did worry about being seen as a jenny-come-lately by her Camden High classmates who were already juniors at Smith.

Vincent knew him only as Kathleen's principal but sensed that if anyone would be sympathetic to her desire for an education it would be Principal Dwinal.

She made an appointment to see him after church on January 12, 1913.

* * *

Vincent knew it was time to break up with her imaginary "beloved." After all, she was nearly twenty-one-years-old.

At this point she had not actually met any man who came close to her ideal. Her correspondence with Earle had whet her appetite for the real thing far more than the fiddle player in Kingman. Now the probing, patronizing letters of Arthur Davison Ficke stirred her imagination. She was beginning to see that her "beloved" had only served as a goal and would never be a fact she could conjure. The men who now presented themselves to her seemed much more likely to fulfill her fantasies.

Consequently, on the night of January 10, 1913, she had a last ceremony to honor the "beloved" she had so desired.[167] In the dim light of her garret she stripped and pulled her ceremonial ring and journal from their hiding place. The chill brought her nipples tight and her flesh alive. She began to write in the journal she called "Sweet and Twenty," and speak in a whisper as she wrote her final message to the imaginary source of true love.

"Some people think I'm going to be a great poet and I am going to be sent to college so I may have a chance to be great—but I don't know—I'm afraid—afraid I am too-too little I guess to be very much," she confessed to the only person she was actually real with, a male version of herself.[168]

Kneeling before the candle in the dark, the redhead revealed her darkest fear. She would end up like her father: all potential and no real success. Losing *The Lyric Year* prize had acquainted her with how fickle dreams could be. So had many other events in her life, such as Henry Hall stealing the title of class poet and not being asked to continue with the theatrical troupe she'd joined after high school. Being virtually booted from the Somervilles and the Duntons. She wasn't good enough for Vassar. She would have to excel at Barnard to prove to all those people that she was worthy of their investment.

"After all," she continued, her breath rising before her in the chilly room, "I don't want to disappoint people, and perhaps tomorrow I won't feel like this, but it seems to me that all I am really good for is to love you—and that doesn't do any good."

The poet paused and reached for the quilt that covered her bed and draped it over her naked form. In a few days she would meet real men, and important people of both genders. Real people expected things her imaginary lover never would. That's why she was so good at loving him. He never questioned why she acted in certain ways, her moods or her omissions.

Soon she would have to impress the provost of Barnard, Harriet Munroe, members of the Poetry Society and even Miss Dow. Who else would be there she didn't know, but she knew what she faced in New York was a day of increasingly challenging tests that she wasn't sure she was up for.

The candle sputtered from the breeze of the quilt and when it settled, she continued, her voice growing more plaintive. She had been strong for so long. She had helped her mother support the household for over ten years already. She had gone to school, buttressed her friends and helped raise her siblings. She desperately wanted someone to lean on, someone to take all the burdens away—or at least shoulder the hardest one of all, finding inspiration, time and will to work hard.

"Perhaps I could be a great poet or nearer to it if I had you, and if you wanted me to. Dear, I think once I saw you I could write and write and write! If I could just hear your voice over the phone wire—and know it was you—I could work and work and write and write!"[169]

Vincent pulled the quilt closer around her petite frame. Like most women of her time, she had been trained to believe that a man would rescue her from the life of a virtual scullery maid. Yet, at the same time, she resented this mythology. It was her work that had liberated her and women who had championed her. She reached under her bed and found a white triangular box.

This final conjuring had to be the most sacred yet. She prepared for the completion of the ceremony by pricking her finger with a hat pin she'd found in the white hat box, then let the blood drip on the pages of her journal so the blood might sanctify her efforts. The poet closed her eyes and said a soft "amen" before placing the journal in the hat box. She then kissed the ring, took it off and dropped it gently beside the journal.[170] It rattled to stillness.

The candle was nearly spent. Satisfied with her ritual, Vincent put the lid on the box, kissed it and then dropped candle wax to seal its contents. Now that she was leaving, she knew Norma would claim her room. Thus, sealing the box served two purposes: keeping the sanctity of her imagined romance as near virginal as she was, and providing potential evidence should her sister's prying eyes ever open it.

Her heart elevated by the liturgy, Vincent blew out the nubby candle, slipped on her nightgown and threw back the covers of her bed. The quilt was pulled up from the floor with her free hand. All was quiet. The last embers of the stove in the front room had already begun to cool and were no longer sending their warmth upward to the sleeping quarters.

"Heavenly Father," she prayed. "Please help me make a good impression with the college people. Please help me to find the right words not to be a disappointment."

She paused. Did she even believe in that kind of God anymore? Nevertheless, she continued, thinking it good manners if nothing else to bless Miss Dow and Miss Bannon and everyone else who had been of assistance in manifesting her dream of college. She then blessed her mother and sisters before finally turning again to her imaginary beloved. "Darling, darling, darling, thank you. I would kiss you now, now and now. Give me strength. I am so little. Give me strength."[171]

Icy clouds parted and moonlight streamed into the room as if answering her plea.

* * *

She was planning to attend a performance of the play, "Freckles," when a letter from Miss Dow was set before her.

"Looks like you've got another letter from your Aunt Cah-line," Kathleen remarked as she went toward the stove and tossed in a chunk of coal.

Vincent looked at the letter. What would be the excuse now? She set down the tea she was drinking to help her stop coughing and used her new letter knife to open the thick missive. She began to read.

"What's she saying now?" Kathleen was becoming more engaged in the ongoing mystery of whether or not her elder sister would go to college. She felt surely if Miss Dow could find money for Vincent, she could find some for her.

"She says I must make up my mind. Apparently, she has enough money raised for me to start at Barnard in the fall."

"Don't you have an appointment with Principal Dwinal tomorrow about getting your Smith application in order?"

"Yes, but she's really adamant about making up my mind. I prefer Vassar but…"

"She still hasn't raised enough money."

"Right."

"What do you plan to do?" Kathleen sat down beside her sister and looked into her eyes. Although they often fought, it was less like cats and dogs and more like rough housing kittens. She loved Vincent and knew her well enough to know that it took her a long time to make decisions, but once she made one, she was committed.

"Let's see what happens with Mr. Dwinal tomorrow," the poet said. She set down her crocheting and sighed. "Whatever happens, I guess I'm going to college. God willing."

* * *

Little had changed in the two and a half years since the poet had graduated in 1910. Because it was a Sunday, the halls and grounds of Camden High School were empty. Her steps echoed in the hallway as she made her way to the principal's office—a path she was well-acquainted with for reasons good and bad.

"Miss Millay?" Principal Dwinal called out as he heard her approach.

"Yes," Vincent replied, stepping into the immaculate office.

"I would know you anywhere," he said with a smile.

"Yes, Kathleen is my…"

"Of course, Kathleen, but because the whole town knows you—or so it seems—I understand you'd like to go to Smith College. A fine school."

His voice trailed off. Zelma Merwyn Dwinal was only eight years older than she was.[172] His square jaw and steely stare belied a just and thoughtful heart. The Camden school board had hired him after he spent five years as a principal in the Richard and Livermore Fall School District, but the appointment was delayed by another honor. In 1910, Maine's Senator Frye called on Dwinal to serve as a police officer for the United States Senate. While the post was not to his liking, Dwinal took the opportunity to study law at

Georgetown University before returning to Maine to serve as the principal of Camden High School in fall semester, 1912.

The poet studied his handsome face. Was *he* her beloved? There was a sternness behind the friendly turn of his mouth. His nose was short for his face but thin and aquiline. She knew he was married with children. She decided his high cheekbones and steely gaze were a bit intimidating, while his mouth spoke of an honest man who would likely be a wonderful kisser.

Vincent's reverie was interrupted by a question. "What do you need from me?"

"I'll need all my records. That is, I need a letter from you detailing that I graduated, the clubs I belonged to, my grades…that sort of thing."

"Well, let's start with the extracurricular activities, shall we? Then we'll get to your grades." Dwinal pulled a note pad and pencil from the top drawer of his desk.

"You want me to tell you?" the poet asked.

"That would be easier."

"But what if I lied?"

Her insouciance amused him. "I'll know," he winked. "Besides, Mrs. Henderson already pulled your file for me."

Vincent laughed nervously. Dwinal joined in, but only from a place of confidence.

She rattled off her memberships, her activities, and her interests as he took notes. She started to tell him her grades when he held up his hand. "I've got those. I just wanted to see what sort of girl you are. Now I shall write the cover letter. Meanwhile, why don't you start filling out the rest of the application? If you're not sure what to write, just ask. I know the ropes with Smith, what they want to hear. I already know they'd be lucky to have you."

Vincent breathed a sigh of relief. The application felt daunting. She was afraid of being tripped up. By the time she left the office she was more confident that one way or another she'd go to college.[173]

* * *

Two days later she decided to bake instead of doing laundry as prescribed by her self-designed schedule. The smell of bread, rolls and cake filled the house as she wrote to Miss Dow and Miss Bannon telling them both what they wanted to hear. She laughed and thought of the *Rubaiyat of Omar Khayyam*. All she needed now was a jug of wine, but there was no thou to lie beside her in the wilderness. Barring that, so long as she had the house to herself, she decided she would work on an idea for a poem.

Her mother's brief return home the previous day had reminded her of all the reasons she preferred Vassar. Cora's motherly love was both missed and suffocating. She asked a million questions about Mr. Dwinal, including a severe warning about the importance of a chaperone when visiting older men. Vincent knew she hated the notion of having a third wheel around as much as Norma did when her boyfriend Kenneth came to call. Of course, Cora was right. The town was full of people who might judge her and thereby jeopardize her scholarships. But she also knew how awkward it felt to watch Kenneth try to take Norma's hand while she was present. The limitations of her world were many, made even sharper when Cora came home with orders and demands. It almost felt as if Cora had brought the blizzard that appeared after Vincent returned from visiting with Mr. Dwinal. The urge to rebel against her mother's order precipitated the baking spree despite the pile of laundry.

Nonetheless, she loved her mother. Cora was a touchstone. Vincent and her sisters were both pleased and stifled when the family matriarch suggested it was probably a good idea that she come home every Sunday now that she had a regular position at a hospital in Rockland. Their carefree days were rapidly coming to a close. Cora's long absences made their waning freedom feel broader. In her imagination, the poet could tell herself that Norma and Kathleen were roommates, not sisters. If their mother were around, they would remain children expected to obey every societal convention.

Sitting there in the quiet house with only the sounds and smells of baking to keep her company, Vincent was relieved that Norma had decided to go to Rockland with Kenneth and their mother, and that Kathleen was out with her friend Hope. The rhythmic clomping of the moist dough on the kitchen table and the tactile nature of its texture had reminded her of the sounds and feel of the snowy path through the woods on her way home from Principal Dwinal's office. The wintry path reminded her of the depression that came with *The Lyric Year* verdict. She was glad she was alone with no one to tell her it was wrong to be sad.

* * *

The following morning, Vincent awoke to the sound of sleet hitting her window. There was a certain quiet in the air. She knew she was alone in the house.

As she descended the stairs the fading smell of coffee hovered in the air. Crumbs blanketed the kitchen table. Half a loaf of the bread she baked the day before was gone, as was most of the butter. She frowned. The pie safe had not been raided.

There was still some coffee in the pot. The poet pulled a cup and saucer from the cabinet and poured the lukewarm brew. The first biscuit from the pie safe already tasted stale.

The familiar pull of despair dropped over her. *The Lyric Year* was out. Many were already calling "Renascence" the best thing in the book. She had read their copy from cover to cover and still didn't understand why she had lost in every way but publication. Added to that was how up in the air college remained. Despite the eloquence of Principal Dwinal's letter of recommendation, Vincent was not sure she could pass Smith's entrance exams. She already knew she hadn't passed Vassar's and would have to take remedial courses elsewhere. But what if she failed those courses too? Disciplining herself to study for the Smith exams was proving harder and harder as the futility of the enterprise grew more likely. Even if she did pass, Miss Dow still didn't have enough money raised to get much past her first year of school.

She sipped the tepid brew and chewed the biscuit. Too much soda, she thought. Her consideration of the meal matched her mood. The poet was about to let herself cry when she heard Norma and Kenneth enter the still house. They whispered among themselves. Soft giggling could be heard from the foyer as they hung up their coats and hats before taking off their galoshes. It reminded her of her mother and Mr. Gales. "Vincent?"

"In the kitchen."

Norma and her boyfriend walked in the door and saw the poet sitting glumly at the table.

The blonde knew by the look in her elder sister's eyes that Vincent had descended into a familiar dark place. "What's wrong?"

"Oh, nothing,' the poet replied. She knew Norma would not believe her."

"Yes, something," the blonde countered. "Right, Kenneth."

"Right." The handsome suitor had no idea what he'd just assented to.

"I was just wondering if Miss Dow was ever going to find enough money to send me to Vassar."

"Didn't Miss Bannon say you have a full scholarship to Smith? You sent your application, didn't you? I saw you catch the postman just as Mumbles and I were leaving."

"You don't miss a thing." Vincent smile was sardonic.

"So, what is wrong?"

"What if I don't pass. What if I fail their entrance exam, just as I failed Vassar's?"

"Now, now, sister. Get ahold of yourself. Miss Dow wrote to tell you that didn't matter, that you could make it up. Besides, Principal Dwinal could help you."

"Yes, but..." the poet protested.

"No 'buts,' Vince. No buts. You're going to be fine. You're different. We're different.[174] Different people get noticed," Norma replied sternly. It struck Vincent how much she sounded like their mother at that moment.

"Especially if they are different in a good way," Kenneth added. This struck them all as hysterical.

"That's better," Norma said, taking Vincent's hands in hers. "Now get dressed. They are showing a new picture at the Comique that we'd like to see."

"Oh, don't forget these," Kenneth said, holding up a small package.

"Mother found us these sweet slippers," Norma explained gleefully.[175]

Vincent inspected the straw slippers her mother had sent. "Oh, they are so darling! Of course, I can't wear them outside, but you must thank my mother when you see her, Kenneth."

"I will, gladly."

Vincent noted his willingness and wondered why it was that Norma had found such a nice boy, and she had not. Then she realized she had rejected many a Kenneth as too dull or ignorant to sustain her interest.

"Just let me get dressed." The poet stood up and took the last sip of her coffee. She was glad her sister had appeared when she did. She dashed upstairs with slippers in hand. "I'll try these on right now!"

"Your sister sure is moody," Kenneth said just as Vincent was out of earshot.

"I think it comes with being a genius," Norma brushed a tangle of hair from his forehead. "We were all sure she would be in college by now."

"I remember," he noted. He sat down and pulled the blonde onto his lap. They kissed but no more. Moments later Vincent appeared.

"Uh-uh-uh!" she winked with a wag of her finger. "I'm supposed to be your chaperone."

"Some chaperone you'd make," Norma laughed. The sisters knew that she was referring to Vincent's affair with Ella. Kenneth just smiled, tapped Norma's shoulder and they both stood up.

"Shall we?"

The sisters and their escort exited the house and turned left toward the center of town and the brand-new Comique Theatre. They strolled three abreast with Kenneth in the middle. Residents and business owners stared. Vincent and Norma ignored the whispers in favor of discussing Robert Louis Stevenson and the film adaptation they were about to enjoy.

"I've always thought the name Dr. Jekyll sounds more evil than Mr. Hyde," Norma remarked.

"Maybe he is," Vincent countered. "After all, he's the one who invented the serum."

"What does the serum do?" Kenneth asked, hoping to contribute something to the discussion.

"It makes Dr. Jekyll's real personality come through," Vincent replied.

"Sounds like liquor."

"Maybe that's what Stevenson meant," Norma observed. "I hadn't thought of it like that."

"I think we all have good and bad sides," her elder sister observed.

"That's true."

"Don't tell me more or you'll spoil the flicker for me," Kenneth pouted.

The girls looked at each other and smiled. "We've read the book." They walked a few steps more when Kenneth got a strange look on his face.

"Say, I'm a little short."

"I'll say," Vincent giggled.

"Ken's not short. He's taller than me. That's all that counts," Norma countered with a laugh. "I think he's perfect."

Kenneth shook his head and offered a good-natured grin. "In any case, um, I was hoping…"

The girls stared at him. He fingered the dollar in his pocket. If he paid admission for all of them and purchased popcorn he'd have to walk back to

Rockland in the cold. He muttered, "Never mind," as they approached the theater.

Vincent took pity on him. "Here's a quarter. That should cover my share."

"Gee, thanks," the relieved beau replied.

They left the theater an hour later discussing the merits of the moving picture, but Vincent's mind was only partially engaged. She was beginning to see there was a Good Vincent and a Bad Vincent. Even as they spoke of the performances in the film, she realized how flawed her own performance was.

"Why would they change the pompous aristocrat into a pious preacher?" Norma asked.

"Huh, what aristocrat?"

"In the book, the man Mr. Hyde kills an obnoxious rich man," Vincent explained. The cobblestones of the street they crossed were smooth but uneven. Norma nearly tripped. Kenneth caught her.

"Whoa! That was close," Norma said. "Thank you, sweetheart."

"Of course."

Kenneth's chivalry irked Vincent for some reason. Her mind kept wandering despite their proximity to one another.

"Vince?"

The poet heard her sister's voice as if in a dream. She looked over at the couple. "Did you say something?"

"Yes. We were wondering what you made of the sets and make-up."

"You've done professional acting before, after all," Kenneth noted. "You would be better than Florence La Badie was, that's for sure."[176]

Vincent blushed. She agreed the leading lady was aptly named. "I'm pleased you think so."

"What did you make of him?" her sister asked, speaking of the man who had played the dual role of Jekyll and Hyde.

"He wasn't bad. I really believed in his transformation into Hyde. The make-up was awfully amateurish, though. Yet his body did seem to get smaller."

"Do you think it was two actors? He seemed so much shorter than Hyde."

"The program said James Cruze played both," Norma countered.

Vincent could feel herself being pulled away as the couple argued the merits of the film. Good Vincent was the one who baked bread and tolerated ignorance. Good Vincent kept house and turned over nearly every dime she earned to her mother. She had done so for nearly thirteen years. Good Vincent hosted when she didn't want to, walked her sisters to school, helped them with their homework, lied to the landlord, smiled at the hypocritical preacher and the parishioners at the First Congregational Church, and made and repaired her own clothes. She was maniacally good. Responsible, disciplined and polite to the point of distraction. Good Vincent didn't cry even when she was miserable because her mother was too tired to hear it and her sisters too dependent on her good humor to comprehend it.

Bad Vincent hated her family. Hated Camden and its nosy, judgmental, small, and hateful minds. Bad Vincent wanted to cause a scene and smash things until they were splattered with debris and tears. She hated the endless waiting game of how long it took Miss Dow to raise enough cash to send her to Vassar. She hated taking exams she'd never pass. How long must she smile and be understanding? How many times must she recite "Renascence" like a trained monkey to convince people she was worthy? How wide did her smile have to be? How demure did she have to pretend to be when all she wanted to do was scream? "Arghh," a muffled growl spilled from her lips.

Norma and Kenneth laughed. "That's perfect," the blonde giggled. "That's exactly how Hyde would sound."

She made herself laugh with them. Somehow her outburst had coincided with a conversation about how different sound motion pictures would be.

"I read that some of those actors have very thick accents, like Polish or something," Kenneth offered. "Maybe they already know how to have sound and don't want to risk it."

"Maybe. But with all the actors in the world and people who want to be famous."

"Like you," Norma interjected.

The poet smiled a genuine smile. In that moment Good Vincent really loved her sister. "I don't know if I want to be famous so much as heard and seen outside this crummy town."

"Camden's all right," Kenneth shrugged.

Having let Bad Vincent temporarily escape, the poet reverted to her more conventional self. "Oh, it's pretty and all, and there are all sorts of nice folks and things to do. I guess I just have wanderlust. I want to meet more poets and writers and musicians…"

"You will, believe me," the blonde smiled. "Why, you get letters from people like that already. It won't be long before they start appearing at our front door and you will want them to go away."

"I'd prefer appearing at theirs."

"Like whom?"

"Of course, I'd like to meet Mr. Ficke and Mr. Bynner, or even Mr. Donnor who wrote me such a nice letter." Vincent stopped to adjust her skirt before they stepped into a soggy bit of slush at the curb.

"And that Mr. Earle," Norma baited.

"Just so I could spit in his eye," Vincent snapped.

"But someone not in your book. Who do you want to include that's not in your book?" Kenneth asked as he lifted Norma across the most egregious puddle of the winter of 1913.

"Sara Teasdale. She's in the book, but that's who I'd like to meet."

* * *

The slippers were so cute and comfortable she couldn't bring herself to take them off. The events of earlier that January 15 afternoon hung over her thoughts as she puttered through the house, doing the long-postponed laundry, sewing and cleaning.

While Norma hung the laundry in exchange for borrowing Vincent's nicest frock, the poet lingered over her tasks in the hope it would make that night's meeting of the Huckleberry Finners come sooner.

She needed to see old friends. It seemed like years since she'd seen Abbie Evans, Ethel Knight, Stella Derry, Corrine Sawyer and the rest of the gang. In summers they'd swim, sail and hike, explore the woods and climb Mount Battie. Al fresco lunches and wild fruits and flowers had once filled every free hour. Now it seemed like all she did was wait.[177]

There was a warmth in seeing them all again. Although some members had married, enough of the old clique attended the meeting to remind the poet that she was indeed loved and had made an impression on the lives of her fellow classmates.

"Why, without you I never would have passed Latin," Eleanor Gould gushed. "That sentence construction business was murder."

"Oh, it's not so hard," the poet beamed. "It's just a matter of—"

"Never mind that," Stella interrupted. "Let's talk about the fun things we did."

As the afternoon progressed, the free spirited, trustworthy confidante soaked up the camaraderie so much that she almost forgot the rehearsal of *A Pair of Burglars* that she was required to attend.

The play by Byron P. Glenn was a farce perfectly suited to Vincent's sense of humor. She could see herself in the role of Vera, a debutante who repeatedly refuses her sweetheart's marriage proposal because he dislikes her father's sugar bowl. Yet as the first born the bowl's heirloom status seems rightfully hers and not her sister May's. Although less than twenty minutes in length, the setting and rhythm of the one-act satire amused her and helped her forget she had to make up her mind about college.

* * *

Each day passed with another distraction. On January 16, she went to the pictures again, only this time with Martha Knight, Kathleen, Norma and Kenneth.[178] The following day, Kenneth and the poet's sometime beau Harold bought a load of groceries, and the foursome made several delicious dishes for supper including steak and onions. She caught a cold, admired Norma's new outfit and hat, played poker, practiced piano, attended play rehearsals and corresponded with her growing list of poetic admirers.

By now that list included Louis Untermeyer, who sent her a copy of his book, *First Love*. How she wished she could attend the Poetry Society meeting in New York. Her mother kept telling her to be patient, that her time would come, and Good Vincent just nodded and smiled while Bad Vincent fumed. "Doesn't Mother understand what I am going through?" she thought as she breathed through the anxiety that expanded with each passing day. The crumbs being dropped by Miss Dow, Mr. Ficke, Mr. Donner, Miss Monroe and Mr. Untermeyer just seemed like a tease that no amount of steak and onions would assuage.

Nevertheless, there were mornings that engrossed her, such as January 24, 1913, a frigid Friday poker night organized and designed by Norma and Kenneth as a means of lifting her from the muck her life now seemed mired in. The pair put up decorations and signs in the family's library that read, "The Poker Joint." Norma got an old advertisement for Velvet Tobacco and hung it along with photos of boxers to give the room a sporty flair. To further set the mood, Kenneth came attired in a green visor and garters on his sleeves.

As the trio sat around the table they kept adding to the tableau. Norma put on her honey of a hat,[179] a brown beauty that gave her the air of a gun moll, while Vincent competed by smoking a little Fatima cigar and wearing several strands of beads. To further her character study, the poet began to try out different accents that she'd heard when listening to town visitors and the itinerant mill workers. Her current favorite was a slow Southern twang.

"Ah do wish Ah-d hear-ah from Aunt Cah-o-line," she drawled as she lay down a pair of fours.

"Who?" Norma asked, folding.

"She probably means Caroline Dow," Kenneth said, adjusting his visor. "I'm afraid you lost this hand, Miss Millay." He set down two pairs, jacks and aces.

"Ah doo dee-clarah, you rye-t! Suppose Ah could dee-all, suh?"

"Why certainly, Miss Edna," Kenneth's attempt at a drawl was not as accurate, but it made everyone smile.

Vincent took the cards and expertly shuffled. They were playing a game of five-card draw. Norma picked up each card as it was placed before her, giving away her hand with every expression a card wielded. Kenneth, a far better player, kept his hand faced down until he was sure he could control his reactions. Vincent did the same.

"I'll take two cards," Norma said, setting down the cards in the middle of her hand.

Kenneth studied his hand before asking for a single card.

Vincent dealt herself three and threw three buttons into the pot.

"I'll see your buttons and raise you two," Norma giggled.

"I'm in," Kenneth set down five buttons. Vincent tossed in two. There were now fifteen buttons on the table. Playing for cash was out of the question.

Vincent's hand was the best of the evening so far. She had three nines and a pair of fives. Things were going her way for once. "Ah'll raise you five buttons."

Norma laid down her hand and reached for a cigar. "I'm out."

Kenneth studied Vincent's face. Was she bluffing? It was hard to tell with the acting and all. He decided to call her bluff despite the fact he had almost nothing but the beginnings of a straight. He threw down five buttons.

"Read 'em and weep, suh!" Vincent cried.

"Hang it!" Kenneth sighed and laid down his lowly hand.

Vincent joyously pulled the twenty-five buttons toward her and laughed. "Good, suh, Ah think you all been licked!"

"Kenneth conceded and suggested they head to the kitchen for refreshments. Norma took his hand." "Don't worry sweetheart, you'll get her back after a break."

"I doubt it."

"Don't be such a sore loser," the poet and card shark chided in her usual voice. "Your luck will change. Mine did. Maybe I should always play using a Southern accent."

Kenneth smiled. "You girls are a pip! Are there any of those cookies left?"

"There are plenty of cookies, but only one Vincent," the blonde replied.

* * *

The following Tuesday, January 28, 1913, Vincent received a letter from Miss Dow in the morning mail. It told her in no uncertain terms that she must be prepared to come to New York and spend the spring semester at Barnard in preparation for a Vassar education in the fall. Suddenly the whole idea of college was very real. She could delay her decision no longer.

Vincent mulled over her largesse. On the one hand she had a prestigious college practically begging her to attend there at no cost. On the other, while Miss Dow had only raised about half the money she would need, Vassar offered her an opportunity to mix with girls of an entirely different ilk.[180] The young woman who had memorized the *Rubaiyat of Omar Khayyam* would be able to meet girls from Persia and Syria. The pianist who adored Bach and Wagner could meet someone from Berlin. The dreamer who had played for a performance of the Mikado could actually meet a real Japanese girl at Vassar. She didn't want to be like so many others from Camden High School, attending the closest women's college. She wanted to travel far from home, literally and figuratively.

There was so much to do before she could leave. First, she had to honor her commitment to perform her role in *A Pair of Burglars* on January 31.

Next, she would have to pack. After spending the night at her Uncle Bert and Aunt Rose's in north Camden, she had to go to Rockland on February 1 to pick up a tailor-made suit, a new hat, new rubbers and a brown leather travel bag.[181] She was certain the travel case she had purchased earlier and the hand bag she had bought would be plenty to hold everything she needed, but that afternoon, when she got home from her shopping spree, she discovered she would have to add the contents of an emergency package from Miss Dow to her luggage. It contained a new coat, gloves, train tickets and a schedule, spending money and a letter telling her what to bring and who to look for when she arrived in New York.

Perhaps her most demanding pre-departure chore was writing several difficult letters. To begin with, she had to write to Ella and let her know it was over. The painter had continued to beg Vincent to come back to live with her in Kingman. While Ella had tried to be subtle, to not seem too desperate, to be supportive of the poet's collegial dreams but she was far from successful. Vincent's attitude had now changed. She loved Ella, but her horizons had broadened. Men found her attractive, captivating and embraced her ambition. These weren't boys: limpid eyed, overly eager, obvious. These men were sophisticated and older. If she had been wiser to the ways of the world, she would have known some of these prospects found her youth as alluring as her poetic skill. Most were eighteen years or more older than she was. Miss Dow tried to caution her, but being a spinster, the YWCA president was not taken seriously by the hormone fueled lass. Although Ella shared her enthusiasm for the sport of man chasing, her heart had already been captured by Vincent. The poet knew she would have to be at least somewhat unkind to distract the painter from her dreams of domesticity. It was the one loose end that simply *had* to be tied before she could leave Maine.

There was also the issue of Mr. Kennerley, who now was pestering her for a full volume of poetry. What if she were exposed as a talented amateur with only one good poem in her? Vincent had doubts about her ability to create full volumes since she was a child. Maybe the only reason she had won the St. Nicholas prizes is because she *was* a child. After all, the one adult poem she had submitted had not won anything but an Honorable Mention. Her post-adolescent voice was still being formed. Was she mature enough to be taken seriously? She had to find a way to keep him engaged but beg off for at least a while longer.

Finally, she had to write to Miss Bannon to tell her of her decision. It would be the hardest letter of all.

* * *

Miss Bannon was disappointed.

The poet had chosen someone and somewhere else. She couldn't be bitter about it. Miss Bannon knew Vincent's future lay with freedom. Trying to tame her was like dancing with bees.

Vincent's letter telling of her decision had arrived in the morning post. Bannon's desire to lift the poet from down underground was evident in her afternoon reply.

"I do not want them to conventionalize your spirit. One can learn anywhere—but I want you to learn to think and dream for yourself. Do not think everything that is told you is necessarily true—because what you want is freedom to think and freedom to range among dreams."[182]

Bannon had seen it all before. How many friends did she have who had wed and bred? More than she could count. The sensitive ones broke under the yoke of societal demands. The strong ones had miserable marriages devoid of warmth and filled with resented children. The few who had found the courage to divorce limped through life under the stigma of perceived failings. She knew almost instinctively how fragile Vincent was despite her bravado. In Vincent's eyes Bannon saw a deep inner loneliness that comes from trying to be yourself in a world that expects more than your soul can give. The pressure on an attractive and accomplished girl to marry had cut short so many women. One needed the right sort of guiding hand. She was certain Professor Conrad of Smith was just the sort of person to help Vincent navigate the system. After all, Charlotte Bannon feared Miss Dow was the sort who was likely to keep Vincent on a short leash. Of course, she had no proof of this. It was only her own experience nudging her toward caution. Just in case, Bannon wanted Vincent to know she had a lifeline if she wanted one. "I shall always be interested in you—if anything happens that you cannot go to Vassar, write me at once and I shall be your friend again—and again."[183]

* * *

Despite all her prayers for deliverance, Vincent was having trouble letting go. She had tea with her friend Martha on February 2, 1913, and wrote letters and spent hours typing. It was as if she was dragging her feet, despite Miss Dow's generous offer. Like many young women the phenomenon we know as "impostor syndrome" was at play. What if she failed? What if she couldn't make friends? What if all the people who were so nice in their letters were actually ogres? Subconsciously, the poet had serious doubts about college which she masked with activities and chores meant to delay her required departure. Even her January 31 journal entry said, "*If* I go to New York next week."

On February 3, 1913, Vincent got an anxious telegram from Miss Dow telling her she *must* arrive by the following day. Even then the poet procrastinated. She packed and repacked, never sure of what dress or personal items would be best to bring along despite Miss Dow's list of necessary items. The poet did more typing, baked bread, wrote more letters, sewed some old clothes and packed her new travel case for the third time before going to a party at Corinne Sawyer's house that evening.

Consequently, it wasn't until the morning of February 4 that she boarded the northbound Maine Central train, thanks—as much as anything else—to Cora's frantic push in response to Miss Dow's telegram.

The train leaving Rockland was an hour and a half late.[184] Fortunately, the short journey on "The Pine Tree Route" to Portland did not conflict with the schedule of the Boston and Maine Railroad's new "State of Maine Express" line between Portland and New York City's newly opened Grand Central Terminal.[185]

Her more worldly cousin George met her at the Portland Depot and transferred her travel case from the narrow-gauge local to the larger train's luggage car before helping the poet get situated in Pullman Sleeper Car A, Berth 10 Lower. They then walked through the train to the club car and sat for a moment before the express left the station.

"So, you're going to college," he offered by way of small talk.

"That's right."

"Why New York?"

Vincent looked at him. He wasn't as dull as he looked. They rarely saw each other and when they did, they had little to say. Still, it was handy having a man to make sure her case was moved from the local to the express train. "Because if I pass my classes there, I can go to Vassar, and what girl wouldn't want to go to Vassar?"

It was almost as if she were daring him to come up with a name.

"Well, good luck, Vince. Make us proud."

"Don't I already?" she laughed. George joined her.

"You certainly have."

Outside a porter called, "Board! All Aboard!"

"I guess that's my cue," George smiled, shook her gloved hand and moved toward the exit. "Don't take any wooden nickels."

"I won't. Give my love to your folks."

The great train rumbled and then began to slowly exit the station. George waved until she couldn't see him anymore. This would be her grandest adventure yet.

As Vincent wandered through the moving train, she noticed for the first time how much larger it was than the cars she was used to. The luxurious Pullman cars had all the latest comforts, including Cumberland Club Cars for lounging, plush reclining seats,[186] and dining cars for lunch, supper and breakfast the following morning. The baroque interiors hinted at a luxury Vincent had only seen in the largest theater in Bangor, and even then, it was a step up. She imagined the train must look like a miniaturized version of the Cobb Mansion back home in Camden. "Just think," she thought, "I'll travel Pullman all the way."

After a delectable dinner the poet decided to retire to her berth to read herself to sleep. The bed was lovely and comfortable, and she drifted into an easy slumber. Sometime in the night the train stopped for no apparent reason. "I wonder where we are and why we're not moving," she mumbled. Vincent knew that Boston had no north/south rail connection so her train would bypass it.[187] Consequently, it was likely they were somewhere between Lowell, Massachusetts and their destination. She reached out and drew up the shade ever so slightly to get a look. In the dark was a large factory blanketed by a brightly lit sign reading, "Brockton Die Company." That explained where they were, but not why weren't they moving. After some time, they began moving again, and she drifted off into a much deeper sleep.

Five hours later, the poet and soon-to-be college student woke to the porter calling, "New York! New York, ladies and gentlemen. Grand Central Terminal, ten minutes!"[188]

Part Three

The Penitent

I had a little Sorrow,
    Born of a little Sin,
I found a room all damp with gloom
    And shut us all within;
And, "Little Sorrow, weep," said I,
"And, Little Sin, pray God to die,
And I upon the floor will lie
    And think how bad I've been!"

Alas for pious planning—
    It mattered not a whit!
As far as gloom went in that room,
    The lamp might have been lit!
My little Sorrow would not weep,
My little Sin would go to sleep—
To save my soul I could not keep
    My graceless mind on it!

So I got up in anger,
    And took a book I had,
And put a ribbon on my hair
    To please a passing lad,
And, "One thing there's no getting by—
I've been a wicked girl," said I;
"But if I can't be sorry, why,
    I might as well be glad!"

14. Mine Every Greed, Mine Every Lust

1913

Grand Central Station was the largest structure she'd ever seen. It dwarfed the depot in Bangor. As she stepped from the train carrying her scrawny overnight bag, she tipped the porter ten cents. It felt generous to the naïve girl from small-town Maine. Her eyes struggled to take everything in. The Beaux-Arts style structure was brand-new, having opened only three days before her arrival on February 5, 1913. She guessed it was just after seven a.m.

Echoes bounced from the 125-foot ceilings festooned with 2,500 electric lights depicting the stars one would see in a Mediterranean view of the zodiac.[189] The enormous windows at the south end of the terminal made her blink her eyes in wonder. People were moving to and fro across the 35,000-square-foot, granite and marble concourse at a pace she'd never seen people move. Miss Dow had said someone would pick her up at the station, and that she should just wait until Mary Alice Finney identified herself. She stood and watched, searching for a friendly face. Would Miss Finney know who she was? The faces she saw reflected a multitude of nations. Surely with a name like Finney she would be Irish. The poet didn't dare attempt a journey to the ladies' lounge. She searched for a clock. Grand Central's Information Booth was graced with a shiny four-sided brass clock. It read 7:23. Someone would be there soon. She inhaled slowly and tried not to look as terrified as she was.

In the rush to get her aboard the Maine Central train to Portland the previous day, her mother had neglected any sort of checklist that would have helped her avoid embarrassment and Vincent was too flummoxed by the summons to be much use in the packing department. She had no brush. Her long red locks were a mess. All she had to tidy up before exiting the Pullman car was a borrowed comb. Accordingly, the best hairstyle she could manage was pigtails.

"Miss Millay?"

A voice behind her roused the poet from her tremulous reverie. Vincent spun around. "Yes?"

"Hallo, I'm Mary Alice Finney. Miss Dow sent me. Is that all you have?" She pointed to Vincent's petite canvas bag.

"No. I have a case too."

Mary Alice sized up the situation. The poet looked like a lost child.[190] "We'll go to Baggage and then out for an ice cream soda. Would you like that?"

Vincent smiled and followed Miss Dow's efficient assistant as she briskly marched toward Baggage Claim. Mary Alice told the porter there where the case should be delivered, took Vincent's bag from her and made her way through the crowds to the Commodore Passage, looking back on occasion to make sure her charge was still with her.

The scene outside was even more overwhelming for nearly twenty-one-year-old Vincent Millay. Mary Alice hailed a cab and helped Vincent inside. "Huyler's!" Mary Alice demanded.

"Oh, my!" she exclaimed as the cab pulled away from the terminal. "What's going to go there?"

Mary Alice followed her gaze. "A giant clock and some Roman deity; Mercury, I think, flanked by Hercules and Minerva."

Vincent didn't want to ask too many questions because she didn't want to be thought of as some hick. Nonetheless, her many internal queries were partially solved when her guide explained the history of the new landmark.

"Who designed the clock atop the information booth? It's simply spectacular."

"That was done by someone named Bedford, I think." Mary Alice's business-like but friendly demeanor explained what she knew about the terminus they had just left and where they were going. "You're lucky. Miss Dow's made sure you have a nice room on the eighth floor of the National Training School building. Now this is Lexington, and our building is at 52nd and Lexington. Huyler's is on Broadway, on the other side of Central Park near Columbus Circle."

Vincent tried to take it all in. Names and places came fast and furious. She studied every landmark and thanked God she had a photographic memory for places. It had come in handy every time she had moved as a child, and this was the biggest move yet. Mary Alice explained that they would register her for college after the freshman took a nap and had lunch, but first they were having a little treat to pick her up. It was funny, but it wasn't until then that she started to feel tired. Yet adrenaline recharged her with every new piece of information that was fed to her.

After sweets at Huyler's, Mary Alice gave her a short primer on the subway system while they walked just over a mile to Vincent's newest residence. "Do you like to walk?"

"I walk almost everywhere at home," the poet replied.

"Good, because walking is a great way to get to know the city. It's four miles to Barnard from the Y, but you could take the subway or a bus. Taxis are too expensive. Just remember, the numbers get higher the closer you are to Barnard, so if they get lower, turn around and head northwest. Got it?"

Vincent nodded.

"And don't let anybody you don't know help you."

The poet giggled. "I don't know you."

Mary Alice laughed. "That's good, right. Yeah, any stranger you aren't expecting to pick you up in a strange city." They both began to laugh. "Here we are."

Before her was a modern eleven story brick structure. Vincent caught her breath.

"Impressive, isn't it?" Mary Alice observed. "We couldn't have done it without Miss Dow. She's the whole thing here. Let's get you situated and in a couple hours I'll take you to lunch and then some appointments Miss Dow has arranged."

It occurred to the poet that Miss Dow was a serial arranger. She had arranged the dinner at the Whitehall Inn with potential donors, arranged a workaround after she failed the Vassar exam by a convincing the director of Columbia University's Journalism School to find a way for the poet to audit classes at Barnard, and, as of her arrival in New York, had somehow raised $1200 toward her Vassar expenses. It seemed like something out of a modern-day fairy tale.[191]

The unmarried YWCA administrator was committed to the virtues of thrift and industry. Despite her love of the arts, Miss Dow did not love the profligacy and sloth of many artists. To her mind they required education and disappointment to tamp down their natural tendencies. She did not want her "little protégé"[192] to be spoiled by too much praise. The *Lyric Year* results had humbled the poet, but she still displayed some of the brashness of a gifted and undisciplined soul. The patron had managed Vincent's entry to college, but she wanted to be certain Vincent got no special treatment when it came to her classes and thus had arranged for her to be interviewed before she was enrolled.

Mary Alice led Vincent to her room on the eighth floor. Though Room 840 was small, it was just right for a young woman awestruck by the sheer scope of the city.[193] From her window she could see everything—just buildings everywhere, seven, eight stories to ones that seemed a million to a billion tall. She found herself staring at the washing drying on top of and between buildings and heard them flap and flap so that it seemed like applause. Children playing tag on roller-skates on the sidewalks below, smokestacks and smokestacks, windows and windows and signs high atop factories and cars and taxicabs in a plethora of colors and designs that were simply astounding. She couldn't believe all the noise but embraced it like the hum of a modernist symphony, a cacophony that for some reason she found restful.

Her travel case had already been delivered, and Vincent put things away rather than sleep. How could she sleep while so much was going on? She laid down and stared at everything, taking it all in to be sure she could recall everything about it. It wasn't a dream. She was really here, in New York and in a few minutes, someone named Mary Alice would take her to Columbia to meet with the journalism professor and then Barnard to register for the classes she had to take in order to start at Vassar in the fall.

Before she knew it there was a knock on the door. A woman's voice called out her full name. She realized she'd drifted off and jumped out of bed and raced to the door. Mary Alice raised an eyebrow. "Good afternoon. Did you get any sleep?"

"A little I guess."

Mary Alice noticed that the poet was still in her traveling outfit, including a hat. Both were hopelessly out of fashion.

"We'll go to lunch and then to Dr. Williams's office for the entrance interview. If all goes well, we'll register you at Barnard this afternoon," she said in her chirpy way. "Are you ready?"

"As I'll ever be, I guess."

After a quick lunch in the dining room, they exited onto Lexington Avenue and made their way toward a subway station.

"Is that really Park Avenue? The real Park Avenue?" Vincent cried, much to the bemusement of Mary Alice. "Oh, look! It's Central Park."

"I know," her companion nodded drolly.

"That's the Church of St. John the Divine. Do you know that was started the year I was born?" the poet asked.

Mary Alice looked at Vincent. Although young herself she was taken aback by the poet's naivete and enthusiasm for things she took for granted. "Yes, that's right. You're not Catholic, are you?"

"No. I'm not sure I'm anything other than Christian. I left the Methodist church a few years ago, and the Congregationalist church before that." When the poet noticed her guide's expression change to concern, she added, "I pray every day."

Mary Alice breathed a sigh of relief. It wasn't long before they approached Milbank Hall, a red brick building with limestone columns and terra cotta details that further dazzled the poet. "They haven't finished Pulitzer Hall over at Columbia,[194] so you'll be meeting Dr. Williams here."

Vincent barely registered what she had said. "I must remember to thank Miss Dow," she whispered to herself as her eyes scanned the impressive edifice. She followed her guide up the stairs and into a crowded, book-lined office on the third floor. Mary Alice knocked and, upon hearing a single word, swung open the door.

"Dr. Williams, this is Edna St. Vincent Millay. Miss Dow sent her. Miss Millay, this is Dr. Talcott Williams."

"Pleased to meet you," the redhead began, extending her hand in greeting.

Believing and acting are two different things. Vincent could act like a successful genius, humble but gracious, simple yet challenging, but she did not believe she was those things. Standing there in front of the sixty-three-year-old journalism professor, she hardly thought herself worthy of his friendly but inquisitive gaze.

"Miss Dow's told me many wonderful things about you. Tell me, why do you want to go to Barnard?"

Vincent felt her mind go blank for a moment. Dr. Williams had a long face, a bushy mustache and thinning hair, yet his eyes were compelling, as if capable of seeing past all artifice. They were a journalist's eyes, watchful for signs of obfuscation and subterfuge.[195]

"I want to do better on the Vassar exams and Barnard is a wonderful school and…" If she had stopped there Williams might have denied her entry, but as she ran on, he could see how truly sincere she was in her quest for knowledge.

After a few more questions and blessedly briefer answers, Dr. Williams wrote a note to Dean Virginia Gildersleeve at Barnard seconding Miss Dow's recommendation. Vincent accepted the note and thanked the professor, who in turn reminded her that whatever writing she did she must always remember to interpret society fairly but directly.

As they walked down the stairs and across campus to the offices of Dr. Gildersleeve, Mary Alice suggested trying to be briefer in her answers. "Dean Williams likes long answers. Dean Gildersleeve does not. On the other hand, I think you'll like her. She's very kind and sensitive."

Although Virginia Gildersleeve didn't require Dr. Williams' second of Vincent's application, after meeting the poet she was certain that, given her background, it might be necessary to "treat her gently."[196] The poet was allowed to register for two English courses, a French class and one in Latin. Vincent's one-time occupation as a typist filled the registrar's final question. The poet stood at attention, realizing this meant she would fulfill her work requirement by typing—a conformity she was hoping to avoid. Gildersleeve recalled Miss Dow's caution, "Success is not always the best tonic for young artists."

Another note and another trek to the registrar's office. She was already feeling the crush of convention and she hadn't even started her classes. She noticed how people looked at her and she blushed when realizing how even the smartest clothes in Rockland were nothing compared to the styles in New York. Standing there in her pigtails, having been forced to remove her hat out of respect for her betters, with a dress that screamed rural America, Vincent grew more self-conscious by the minute. Yet after the seemingly endless paperwork Mary Alice had a surprise for her. On the way home they would be stopping at Lord & Taylor for a new wardrobe.

The poet was astounded by the largesse and grateful that Miss Dow would arrange for her to fit in. She chose pumps with what she called "eleven-inch heels," boots, gloves, a handbag, handkerchiefs, silver cuff links, a parasol, shirt waists (including two with high Robespierre-style collars), and—to the poet's unabashed delight—a dark-gray chinchilla coat with a rolling collar.[197]

If Miss Dow was hoping Vincent would not be spoiled this was not the best start!

Happily, there was an ulterior motive in making sure the poet was presentable to high society. Those who met her were more likely to forgive her rough edges if she dressed well. Like Shaw's Henry Higgins, Miss Dow, working in concert with Mrs. Esselborn, made sure her charge appeared worthy of their investment. Vincent's personal selection of a white silk scarf with tiny yellow roses spoke of her modest roots as did her Maine accent which she tried to mask by imitating the Mid-Atlantic tones of the great actresses of the day and the elocution of her Barnard classmates.

Vincent desperately wanted to fit in, to live up to everyone's expectations, but she also chaffed at the reins Miss Dow held. After returning to her room and placing her New York fashions on top of her old clothes, she slipped downstairs and outside to explore the city on her own. She noted bus lines, locked in where the subway could be caught, roamed Columbus Circle and Central Park and—being careful to keep track of every penny as Miss Dow requested—purchased some hand lotion to start the process of moving from "scullery maid" to fashionable freshman.

15. With Individual Desire

1913

Classes were murder, but Vincent persevered. Despite the rigors of her four classes and her work as a typist, the poet filled her days with amusements of all types, and often alone, a fact not lost on Miss Dow. While the accomplished administrator knew her protégé was capable, she knew New York City was not Camden, Maine. New theaters, new attractions, stunning new skyscrapers dotted the horizon everywhere one looked. What sort of people would Vincent meet if she went to the International Exhibition of Modern Art at the Armory? Miss Dow had heard things about Augustus John and Toulouse Lautrec that would curl one's hair. As far as Miss Dow was concerned, venturing south of 42nd Street was risky business. God forbid a girl like Vincent should go to 25th and Lexington Avenue and spend twenty-five cents to view that strange new art that looked like paintings a child might do.[198] What ideas might fill her head? Vincent needed discipline and exposure to the right kind of culture.

As for the poet, she had already visited the new but unoccupied Woolworth Building. At fifty-five stories tall, it was more than fifty stories taller than any building in Camden. Its thirty-four elevators would take her up or down by express or floor by floor. Vincent had never seen anything like it, and it frightened her a bit, despite the fact she was awed by its magnificent lobby. It reminded her, inside and out, of pictures she'd seen of Westminster Abbey in London.

New York was indeed the center of the artistic universe. It was filled with theaters, concert halls, galleries, museums and movie houses. The carnival nature of the city most enjoyed by the poet was the top deck of the double-decker buses. There she could sit in the open air and absorb the city at her leisure. When not exploring the city by bus or subway, Vincent would venture out to the various islands of Hudson's Bay. It did not escape her notice that she was again viewing a world made up of large and small islands set in a bay, yet the expanse of her world was widening.

*   *   *

On Saturday, February 8, 1913, her status as the muse of Maine offered a delight she had dreamed of. The long-admired Sara Teasdale wanted her to come to tea.[199]

Vincent wrote her family breathless letters about this and other privileges she was enjoying thanks to the pull she had courtesy of being Caroline Dow's pet project. She had received "very irregular special consideration"[200] in her placement and was able to attend all sorts of concerts and events she never would have been able to experience in her hometown. It seemed as if she had forgotten entirely who held the strings, academically and economically. Although the poet was in for a rude awakening, for now she did as she pleased, including visiting people Miss Dow would not have found suitable companions.

Vincent stood before the Martha Washington Hotel and considered what she would say when she met her idol. Maybe she should ask Sara about her experience publishing with Putnam, since they were already asking about publishing Vincent's first volume. Was that too personal?

The Martha Washington Hotel was a twelve-story residential hotel for women only smack dab in the heart of midtown at 29 E. 29th Street, just one block east of Fifth Avenue. It was close to all modes of transportation, had 150 well-appointed rooms or 500 apartments to choose from, a milliner, a dress shop, a shoeshine parlor, and two restaurants, one private, another public. As Vincent stepped into its vaulted lobby she marveled at the elegance of its coffered ceilings, marble floors and oriental carpets. She knew that reputable hotels usually discriminated against single women, so she was not at all surprised to see the only clientele were the fair sex. By now she was getting used to the size and scope of New York, yet it surprised her that anyone would build a large hotel with women alone in mind. In fact, she found it tremendously amusing that the only position deemed worthy of a male employee was that of bell boy! Even the elevator operators were women. It thrilled her to discover another place where the only patrons and most employees were women. Between her residence at the YWCA and the restaurant of the Martha Washington Hotel she never had to see a man's face unless she chose to, which was a kind of freedom in itself.

As she approached the front desk to ask for directions to the Tea Room, Vincent immediately recognized her luncheon companion.

"Good afternoon." Sara Teasdale smiled.

Vincent had seen photos of the older poet before, but she was surprised to find her less ethereal than she expected.

"Good afternoon, Miss Teasdale. I'm…"

"Yes, of course, Edna Vincent Millay." Sara took her arm and began to lead her toward the Tea Room.

"St. Vincent." The redhead corrected before realizing her rudeness. She blushed.

"Naturally, the rhythm is better," Sara chuckled. Vincent was relieved. Sometimes, the things she said were taken the wrong way. She smiled back.

"Do you have a middle name?"

"Trevor, and they spelled my name with an 'h'…S-A-R-A-H."

"Why did you change it?"

"Numerology," Sara quipped.

Vincent studied her face. Her mouth had a thin upper lip; her cheekbones were high; her nose was long; and her eyebrows were heavy. She wasn't pretty in a conventional sense, but Vincent found her compelling.

"I understand you're from St. Louis," Vincent offered by way of small talk. "Have you ever met Samuel Clemens?"

At that, Sara laughed so loudly that heads turned. "I'm afraid he runs in a different crowd these days."

Vincent began to giggle. Of course! How could she have been so stupid? Clemens had been dead for three years and Sara's success hadn't come until 1907. She was relieved that Sara would take it so well and not tease her rudely.

They entered the Tea Room and were guided to their table by a beefy woman with short hair and an artificially feminine manner. Vincent couldn't help but stare. It was the first time she'd ever seen a woman like that. Sara was non-plussed.

Vincent hated it that she gushed to the point of idiocy. This happened now and then, despite her attempts to be smart and sophisticated. It seemed strange that she would be the hayseed and Sara the sophisticate. They talked about poetry.

The young poet was glad Sara did not ask her to recite "Renascence." She discovered that not only did Sara Teasdale know her poem well, but she could tell how much time had elapsed between the sections and which ones Vincent had reworked in the hope of masking those lapses. This encouraged her enough that she shared the beginnings of *Journey*, a poem that would take Vincent another seven years to finish. Her new friend loved the imagery and remarked how anyone, anywhere, could appreciate how it felt to look back at loneliness and sigh even as one felt compelled to move forward.[201]

Sara, by contrast, was flattered that the smart and frank young woman before her had memorized huge bits of her poem, *Helen of Troy*, from Teasdale's recently published volume.

"I just loved the lines, 'Yet life is more than death,[202] How could I learn the sound of the singing winds, the strong sweet scent that breathes from off the sea, or shut my eyes to Spring?'" Vincent exclaimed as she passed Sara the cream container.

"I can see why, given 'Renascence' and that new poem you're working on." Sara's fingers lightly touched Vincent's as she took the porcelain vessel from her hand.

The two women stared at each other. "How would you like to stay for dinner?"

"That would be wonderful," Vincent replied without hesitation. There was a paper she had to write for Dr. Carpenter, but that could wait until morning. Sara Teasdale wanted her to stay longer.

They discussed more than poetry while they waited for dinner. It felt like they were truly more friends than poetic rivals or even pupil and mentor. The older woman's delight in Vincent was clear. Sara's sense of isolation in New York disappeared. Yes, there were men avidly courting her, but here was a woman friend, just eight years her junior, who spoke her language and saw the world in a similar manner. It eased her and suddenly made the city come alive in a way it hadn't before.

"What shall we do in the meantime?" Vincent asked.

"Have you ever ridden the Fifth Avenue bus?"

It seemed like an odd proposal, but the younger woman was game, so they left the hotel and walked the block to the M7 stop. As the vehicle drew near, Vincent stifled a laugh. It was almost like a carnival ride in its splendor, much fancier than the other buses she'd ridden since arriving in New York. It had flowers and ribbons galore decorating the vehicle. They stepped up the creaky stairs as the barely horseless carriage idled at the curb before sitting on the simple wooden bench seats.

"We'll sit on the driver's side until 42nd Street and then switch benches on the way back," the transit veteran explained. "The scenery is just wonderful from up here."

The women held on as the bus lurched forward.

"There's a suffragist group who rents space in my hotel that uses this line to spread the word about votes for women," Sara noted as they rumbled along the thinly paved thoroughfare.

"Oh, which one?"

"I think they are called the Interurban Women's Suffrage Council. You are for suffrage, I take it?"

"Votes for women? Of course!"

"What are you doing Monday evening?"

"Having dinner at the Untermeyers with Miss Dow. Why?"

"Too bad. Jane Addams is speaking at a suffrage rally at Carnegie Hall. I thought we could go together." Sara smiled.

Vincent was silent for a moment. She'd been putting off the Untermeyers for too long, and she wasn't sure how Miss Dow felt about the vote. On the other hand, Sara was asking her if she'd like to hear Jane Addams in person. No one like the suffrage leader had ever spoken anywhere in Maine, so far as she knew. Addams's summer house in Bar Harbor was not spoken of and therefore didn't seem to count.

Sara sensed her position. "Some Council members were on this very bus last week," she began. "They had a banner that said, 'Votes for Women' right up here where we're sitting." She patted the front panel of the upper deck.

"I would have loved to have seen that." Vincent lamented. "If it wasn't for the engagement with the Untermeyers—"

"Never mind. There will be other opportunities," Sara interrupted. "It's important to cultivate people like Louis and his wife. They know everybody you should know."

Vincent nodded. "Still, I wish I could go with you. My mother admires Miss Addams so much and would be so happy to know I saw her in person. When I think of my mother and all she's had to go through while still not being able to vote, it just makes my blood boil."

"Tell me more about her." The bus screeched to a halt at 42nd Street, and the new friends switched sides of the bus and continued their chat. The younger woman spoke of her mother lovingly and spoke of how the whole family had lived under the shadow of divorce. Sara listened silently, aware for the first time of the extent of Millay's deprivations as she stood looking at those "three long mountains and a wood."[203] It made her sad as she thought of the girls living in an icy shack in Mill Town, alone and without comfort. It was far from her own upbringing, which was one of the reasons she admired the work of Jane Addams and Hull House. Somehow, despite all that, this girl beside her had written an extraordinary work of depth and complexity well beyond her years—or, she thought, perhaps because of it.

* * *

The jealousy and confusion were palpable. Arthur Ficke was married. Ferdinand Earle was married—barely. Vincent sat in the emotional wings, awaiting her entrance into the New York literary society. She hated everyone.[204]

Earle was about to embark for Europe. He told her it was an attempt at a second honeymoon, but she knew it was his desire to escape from her.

She was anxious. Before her were commitments she wasn't sure she wanted to fulfill. She decided to ditch classes.

Sitting in the café at Barnard, she did her best to exude 'don't touch me' vibrations. Norma had written, scolding her for not doing more for the family. Didn't her sister know how expensive New York was? How having to meet people and dress well were budget items as surely as food and rent? Another review from Louis Untermeyer created the capstone of her mood. Must "Renascence" always be thrown in her face like an unwanted child?

Of course, Vincent had overdone it. She had attended nearly every speech, dinner, concert, play, and meeting she was asked to, and she naturally fell ill because of the strain. Ever since the typhoid bout in 1901, she had to be careful about how hard she pushed her body. Yet she pressed on. Sometimes she couldn't tell the difference between being in class and being in bed. She'd feel her eyes drooping and her breath fluttering as she struggled to take in the day's commitments. The poet carried the curse of her breed. She could sense the anticipation of others, which gave her nervous spells, faintness, and unrelenting exhaustion. Poets, she told herself, must do this. This is how we're made.

On February 19, 1913, she walked up Riverside Drive for the first time. She noticed the outfits of the dressage riders, looking for all the world like characters in a Henry James or Edith Wharton novel. She continued up the path, her eyes ablaze with the enormity of New York. In that moment she wondered if Wharton's character, Undine Spragg, was related to Sara Teasdale.[205] Here was the place, the very exact Riverside Drive, where the heroines of so many books she had read went riding.

Her family wanted more than she could give. Her patron wanted more than she could give. Barnard and all the wonderful girls and teachers there wanted more than she could give. Where was the space for her?

The day progressed. Vincent attended a sublime piano recital at Aeolian Hall. Then returned to the Y for a reading of a novel in a Canadian dialect, all while somewhere in the building a girl in a pale blue satin dress trimmed in vivid red chiffon played violin in the recesses of the estrogen wonderland that was the YWCA.

* * *

It was meant to be an early birthday gift. Miss Dow and Mrs. Trowbridge, a matron of about fifty who found Vincent "delicious," announced she would join them for a performance of *Madame Butterfly* by Giacomo Puccini on February 20.

From the moment she stepped into the ornate opera house, she knew she would love Grand Opera.[206] Sitting between women whose approval she needed, the poet dared not be effusive. Yet she couldn't be oblivious to the lyric soprano's voice. Just ten years older—almost to the day—Geraldine Farrar was a revelation. There were other girls at the Y who envied her. They called themselves Gerry-Flappers.[207] The woman before her was not like the often obese and elderly traveling performers she'd seen in Camden's small opera house. Farrar was young, beautiful, and had an intimacy in her voice that made Vincent feel like she alone was hearing the secrets of Madame Butterfly. "Oh, how I wish I could hear it again tonight, and tomorrow, and every day thereafter." Vincent was crying as they broke for intermission.

"You're enjoying it then?' Mrs. Trowbridge asked, her chin jutting forward like a peacock.

"Truly," the poet began, wishing she could contain her excitement. "I really ought to hear it three times right off. It's the only way I'll really understand it."[208]

"I told you it would make you weep," said Miss Dow. She gently took Vincent's purse and removed the white silk handkerchief with the yellow roses.

"I never cry at the theater. I guess I just feel things too deeply—too deep, I suppose even for my own heart. Yet I am weeping like a fool at the opera." She dabbed her nose almost imperceptibly, just as she'd seen other Barnard girls do—the girls without patrons, the girls with parents who could live at the opera should they care to.

"That's all right, dear," said Mrs. Trowbridge. "This is your first time, after all, and it is such a beautiful opera."

"Mr. Puccini is a wonderful composer," Miss Dow added.

Vincent swallowed hard to push back the feelings that were about to overwhelm her. She'd learned long ago that people didn't like displays of emotion.

"What do you think of Miss Farrar?" Mrs. Trowbridge asked.

Vincent struggled to explain her response to the soprano. "She's simply marvelous! Now I can see why the girls were so jealous when I told them where we were going."

Miss Dow frowned. "We must be careful not to appear as if we're playing favorites," she observed, speaking of herself in the plural.

Vincent instantly realized the gaffe. She often had to hide the generosity of her relatives from her sisters, though Kathleen was a favorite of her Uncle Charlie. She focused on her siblings before replying. "Oh, yes. I see. I apologize."

"No need for an apology, my dear," Miss Dow smiled. "Let's just remember that gossip is not our friend."

*　*　*

Vincent soon discovered the benefits of secrecy. Her twenty-first birthday was awash with cards, gifts, and even a surprise costume party. How the girls managed to disguise the reason for dressing up like Martha Washington was still a mystery to her, but when she arrived at Saturday dinner and discovered a tall classmate in a stunning George Washington costume, the jig was up. A huge birthday party was delivered with hoots and hollers, followed by an appropriate minuet with her costumed "husband."[209]

There were so many greetings that she was further surprised when several packages arrived the following Monday. She wrote Cora a letter of thanks for the pretty satin slippers with rhinestone buckles she had sent, along with a collection of hair combs to make up for the one the poet had forgotten to bring. Yet even as Vincent wrote it, she felt a bit like an impostor. Here she was in New York, being waited on and feted while her mother and sisters were still struggling in Camden.

The city had a fascination for the poet. She was already an old hand at elbowing her way to a seat on the subway and grabbing the streetcar as it rumbled past. From her window, she could see everything and nothing. Buildings—just buildings, seven or eight stories to heights so high she lost count of the floors. She imagined she could see the noise, which was as ubiquitous as the soot.

She realized the city had changed her somehow. In two days', she would attend her first meeting of the Poetry Society.[210] There, she would be expected to be both dynamic and composed. She hated having to smile and be charming. Life in New York was its own kind of dichotomy, different from the one that she struggled against at home. The letters from her family expected her to be the same person she'd been in Camden, but how could she be? New York had stolen her heart as surely as the Reverend Gales had taken her mother's. Maybe New York was a better fit for her temperament. Regardless, her education was in more than French and Latin. She was being schooled in the ways of society.

The Poetry Society provided one of her first lessons. Although a relatively nascent organization, the enthusiasm of its members and founders was contagious. Each member paid a dollar to join.[211] Many of its members had read and admired "Renascence," including several who were convinced she'd been robbed of *The Lyric Year* prize. In addition to Society founders Jessie Rittenhouse, Edwin Markham, and Anna Branch, Vincent was able to commune with Edward Wheeler, her stalwart supporter for seven years, ever since he bestowed the St. Nicholas Gold Medal Prize for *The Land of Romance* in 1906.

When Mrs. Trowbridge introduced them, Wheeler was a bit taken aback. The young redhead looked as if she were still a child, except for her steady, intense gaze.

"How do you do?" Vincent took his hand with a light curtsy.

"Such a pleasure," he smiled.

"Do you remember me?" She knew full well he did.

"Yes, your 'Land of Romance' was quite wonderful."

Vincent nodded as if to agree with him. Mrs. Trowbridge looked down at her feet. The poet felt her heart jump. "Uh, thank you."

"And 'Renascence' was a fine follow-up to your juvenilia," he added, having successfully thrust through the young poet's pride to reveal the vulnerable core of the artist. His smile broadened the deeper she blushed.

"Yes. Thanks," she sputtered.

"'Renascence' was quite marvelous, I think," Mrs. Trowbridge remarked.

"Of course," Wheeler replied. "That's why it is in *The Lyric Year*."

Mercifully, they were being approached by Jessie Rittenhouse and Ferdinand Earle.

"Sophia, is this our young genius?" Jessie asked.

Earle instantly recognized Vincent and managed to veer off to speak with another member while still being within earshot. Vincent had not noticed him.

"Why, yes!" Mrs. Trowbridge exclaimed. Vincent noticed how the heavy-set woman's pert nose and double chin seemed to quiver with delight at making the introduction. She had never known her chaperone's first name. So far as she was concerned, she was Mrs. Samuel Breck Trowbridge.

"Is Caroline with you?"

"No. She's on vacation, if you can believe it," the architect's wealthy wife replied. "Miss Millay, may I introduce you to Miss Rittenhouse?"

Vincent's smile broadened. "Pleased to meet you. How do you do?"

"Delighted. I'm so happy you could make it. Have you brought anything new to share with us tonight?"

The young poet's cheeks grew warmer. She had nothing finished. She begged off, saying she felt the Society was too distinguished for someone like her.

"Nonsense," Jessie replied. "It isn't meant to be a formal group at all. We like to think of it as a salon, a place where poets can gather to read and discuss their work."

Vincent felt like she'd just landed in paradise. Miss Rittenhouse was so welcoming and unaffected that she felt instant relief. The redhead had tied the word "Society" to so many of the stuffy organizations her pristine chaperone and absent benefactors belonged to that she hadn't realized this was a place where she'd really fit in. "Oh, bless you. That sounds lovely."

"How about this? We shall have a little gathering in your honor. Does March 9 work for you? It's a Sunday, I think. Would that give you enough time to prepare?"

"Why, yes!" Vincent quickly replied, while simultaneously wondering when she would find time to create anything worthy of reading before the membership of the nation's premier poetry group. She quietly thanked God that "Renascence" was so long.

"May I meet this ravishing creature?" A tall, handsome man with a white beard appeared beside Jessie. Vincent noticed how immaculate his beard was, his broad, high forehead, and intense gaze. A westerner, he had all the brash openness of the frontier. Although sixty-one-years old, Edwin Markham's vibrance captured the younger woman's imagination. She had read *The Man with the Hat* and been impressed with its economy.

"Edna, this is Charles, er, Edwin Markham," Jessie said. "Edwin, this is Miss Millay."

"The girl who wrote 'Renascence'?" he nearly shouted. "I can hardly believe it. Is that true?" He gave the young poet a lascivious wink.

"I'm afraid it is."

The color that rose to her cheeks emphasized her gray-green eyes and sent out a kind of clarion call to the many poets present. Who was this attractive young lady? Those Mrs. Trowbridge didn't know, Jesse did. Introductions to Amy Lowell, Anna Branch, Ezra Pound, and William Butler Yeats were made. Vincent's head swam as her head filled with poems by each one.

"How are you finding New York?" Markham asked.

"It's so inspiring. Inexpressibly so. I heard all sorts of stories about it, and so many are right while others are so wrong."

"For instance?" Miss Lowell asked. She could barely stand and leaned heavily on her cane for support.

"Well, I'd been told the public library was magnificent."

"Which it is." Miss Branch observed.

"And the subway was awful, which it isn't," the young redhead continued.

"Beauty is in the eye of the beholder," a scruffy but fascinating Ezra Pound muttered under his breath.

"Not to mention the view from my room—"

"She's staying at the Y. I'm hoping to convince her to move to my Three Arts House in spring," interrupted Mrs. Trowbridge.

"All these buildings, St. Patrick's Cathedral, the St. Regis Hotel…"[212]

"Breck Trowbridge designed that, you know," Jessie noted.

"Oh, my! Really? It's just charming, charming…So many roofs and things, you know, warships and chimneys and brewery signs…so inspiring."

"Indeed, particularly the latter," Markham teased, and they all laughed.

"And Madison Avenue Presbyterian! Oh, it's just tremendous!"

"You do get around, don't you?" Anna Branch laughed. Mrs. Trowbridge frowned. How could she not know about these forays so far afield?

"You mustn't let yourself become too bohemian, child," she chided.

Sensing a captivated audience, the young poet rattled on, even as the group made their way to their seats. "I am not so bohemian by half as I was when I arrived."

"What do you mean?" Jessie asked. "I thought you came from some little Yankee village in Maine."

"Oh, I do. But, you see, here in New York one must be one or the other, whereas at home one could be a little bit of both." Vincent noticed the look on Sophia Trowbridge's face and realized she was probably saying too much. "Where shall we sit?"

Mrs. Trowbridge forced a smile. Her perfectly tailored suit and pleasant face returned like a scarf dropped from her lap. "I think I'll go freshen up. Sit wherever you like, but please save me a seat."

"We shall." Jessie smiled, gently positioning herself as a replacement chaperone. She realized even more than the poet that Vincent had said too much. "Come along, Vincent. That is what you call yourself, isn't it?"

"Yes, my family has always called me that; and now so do my friends." The poet's smile spoke of the grateful relief she felt for the anthologist's intervention. At that moment, she caught sight of Ferdinand Earle as people were taking their seats.

"Then that is what we shall call you. Charlie Markham now calls himself Edwin. We're all used to it by now." Her laugh was playful, not wicked.

"Perhaps I should sit with Mr. Earle," Vincent suggested. "I was hoping to spend more time with him in person."

"Speaking of avoiding trouble," Jessie replied. "Ferdinand is a lovely man, but he has a terrible roving eye."

"The Untermeyers warned me." Her erstwhile editor smiled at her from across the room.

"Then they probably also warned you about the importance of propriety, even in a city like New York, especially when one is reliant upon the good will of benefactors like Mrs. Trowbridge."

The young redhead looked at Jessie, her eyes scanning the elder poet's face for trust. It was clear the older woman had her interests at heart. "I might have said too much."

Jessie nodded silently.

"I must confess that I have sometimes amused myself at idle moments by the diffusing of indiscreet letters to Mr. Earle when I would now give half my kingdom to recall, but at present I am prudent to the point of Jane Austen."[213]

Jessie roared at the analogy.

Vincent was delighted by her laughter. "I left all my bad habits at home—bridge pad, cigarette case, and cocktail shaker."

Now others were laughing. The charming girl continued, with each new item on her list eliciting another burst of good humor. "I brought all my good habits—diary, rubbers, and darning cotton."

"What's so funny?" Mrs. Trowbridge asked as she re-entered the circle.

"Vincent was listing all her good habits," Jessie replied.

Mrs. Trowbridge looked confused, but seeing smiles all around, she assumed it was perfectly harmless fun.

The group sat down and quieted as William Butler Yeats began reading his work. He had barely noticed the redhead—almost as if she were as common as the lasses in his native Ireland. Instead, he communed with Ezra Pound, who had taken a seat within reach of the revered master.

As the meeting broke up, Ferdinand Earle finally approached his epistolary romantic interest.

"Vincent? Ferdinand Earle."

"I am very glad to meet you, Mr. Earle,"[214] she stated simply. She actually wanted to say, *oh, we know one another!*

"I just wanted to say congratulations on making such a big splash tonight. I understand you're at Barnard. That's marvelous. Might I have your address?"

"I think it is better if you kept writing to me at the Camden address. I never know where my career will take me. You understand?" She smiled so broadly that he almost believed her.

"Perhaps we could go out..." he began.

"I'm afraid I can't. Mrs. Trowbridge is taking me home from here. Perhaps another time."

"I'm sailing for Europe tomorrow. Perhaps I could send you a postcard."

"Please do."

"Do what?" Jesse asked as she approached along with Mrs. Trowbridge.

"Send a postcard." Earle frowned. These women were clearly acting as chaperones. He wanted to see Vincent alone. He hated how they'd left things after the publication of *The Lyric Year* and his "jigsaw puzzle" letter. "Well, nice to have met you in person, Miss Millay. Au revoir!"

"Au revoir." Vincent watched as Earle slinked away.

"What did he want?" Mrs. Trowbridge and Jesse said almost in unison.

"Oh, you know. Thank God, I have more sense than I did a year ago. Last year, I would have called him like some desperately lonely child, but that is not how I'm running things now." Vincent picked up her wrap and looped her arm with Mrs. Trowbridge's.

"Wise girl!" Jessie smiled. "I'll call you about doing a reading next month."

* * *

The routine at Barnard was a challenge. Her insatiable curiosity about the literary and musical world of New York battled with classes and the commitments meant to foster further investment in her education and career. She loved all the attention she received, especially when overwork landed her in a sick bed. Back home, she had to work through illness to fulfill her duties as the eldest. Here she was fussed over and pampered almost as much as when she visited her papa three years before.

She often overslept, a fact that had necessitated currying the favor of Y's prized cook, Nancy. The tawny domestic was an odd confidante for the poet, despite how she called her original diary Mammy Hush-Chile. Vincent would come in late begging for a biscuit or fruit—just something to tide her over until lunch—and spend time discussing her English composition class or the difficulty she was having translating two and a half pages of Horace from Latin. Nancy would smile indulgently and knead her dough or decorate a cake for the seemingly endless birthday parties.

Much to Dean Gildersleeve's dismay, Vincent would cut classes altogether, choosing instead to work on the poetry she had promised Miss Rittenhouse. Other days, she would revel in translating French as she watched her clothes dry atop the roof, the sun gleaming through the fabric as it danced in the wind. Barnard was giving her a form of independence she had never experienced, and she wasn't exactly sure what to do with it. Relationships blossomed, and opinions were exchanged. Good Vincent was aware of the need to do well and put in enough work for Monsieur Muller and Miss Goodale to pass her French and Classics lessons, while Bad Vincent conspired with her neighbor to meet curfew and men, particularly the former.

Miss Dow returned on March 2, anxious to know how her protégé was doing. Inquiries were made, and while Vincent was not viewed as saintly, she had been performing well enough in her classes to forgive the occasional foray into the more bohemian corners of the city. The Untermeyers were viewed as suitable mentors despite their Jewish faith. The Mitchell Kennerleys less so. Nonetheless, Dean Williams had mostly good things to say about Vincent's deportment, and Mrs. Trowbridge's main complaint was the poet's tendency to blurt out truths that were better left unsaid.

Two days later, Vincent cut classes to attend a Poetry Society luncheon honoring the English poet, Alfred Noyes. The way she viewed it, such an event was its own kind of education. Most of the usual faces were there, but a new face was particularly welcome. She studied it and liked what she saw. It was a man she'd been corresponding with for over a year, ever since her fellow *Lyric Year* contributor had written to exclaim that she couldn't possibly be female.

Now standing before her was Witter Bynner, the best friend of her "spiritual advisor," Arthur Davison Ficke. Bynner's prematurely balding head, kissable lips, and intense gaze were just the sort of features she imagined her "beloved" would have. His eyes bore into her, and the questions he was asking seemed to indicate he still had doubts she could be the author of "Renascence."

"Do you mind if I smoke?" he asked.[215]

"Not in the least." Vincent watched his elegant fingers pluck a cigarette from a silver case, which he then offered to her. She glanced toward Miss Dow and declined. He expressed surprise, his long eyelashes blinking over sensitive eyes. "You don't smoke?"

"Not here, certainly." Vincent nodded toward the contingent of patrons she was still cultivating.

"Then you have no prejudice against it?"

"None whatever." Vincent watched as he rolled the cigarette across his lips to moisten it before he perched it between his lips on his right, close enough that she might smoke it with him. He smiled.

"I'm glad of that.[216] My sister used to think it was dreadful, and now she smokes more than I do."

Vincent laughed. "It's hard to imagine you with a sister."

"It happens."

The friendship continued to bloom. When they met again on March 9, 1913, the day Jesse Rittenhouse had set aside for a party in Vincent's honor, they spoke for a long while, brushing off the approaches of those outside their echo. Vincent was intrigued by the immaculately dressed man with the lovely, sonorous voice. Consequently, she was especially thrilled when he asked if he could recite "Renascence" as a tribute to her. "That would be lovely."[217]

When Bynner stood to toast Vincent, the young redhead noticed how people stopped speaking. Normally, there would be a period of shushing before a speaker's voice was heard. On this occasion it was as if no one wanted to miss a word of what he said.

Her lips anticipated every verse, and yet she found that hearing her poem recited by someone else was a revelation. There were ways in which he emphasized certain passages that helped her understand why he would think her a "burly man of forty-five."[218] She waited for the applause to die down before telling him how much she enjoyed his reading. "That was beautiful, Mr. Bynner."

"Thank you. I'd like it if you called me Hal. I take it I'll hear you read at the next meeting of the Society."

"Miss Rittenhouse wants me to, but I honestly don't know if I'll have anything ready."

"I'm sure you must have something," he winked.

"Just some things that were published in St. Nicholas."

"Aren't you a little old for that publication?"

"Well, I'm not over forty, Hal," she teased.

He laughed. "That was Ficke, not me. I thought you would be closer to 30."

Their laughter turned heads. "Have you seen the International Exhibition?" he asked out of the blue.

"Yes. I must admit the Cubist work is not to my taste. I couldn't make hide nor hair of Duchamp's *Nude Descending the Stairs*."[219]

"I could see it, but I didn't understand it," Hal remarked. "What did you make of the Impressionists?"

Vincent considered what she would say. "Some of it I liked very much. Mr. Matisse's work was interesting, but it hardly seemed like the female form."

Hal laughed. "I would have said the same thing. In fact, one could say it was very like a cross between Michelangelo's women and the work of a Fauvist."

"Like Messieurs Braque and Derain?"

Hal nodded.

"I rather like Dr. Derain's work," she continued. "It captures mood so well. I suppose I like more realistic work. Do I sound terribly conventional?"

Now Hal laughed. "Not at all. Modern art takes some getting used to."

"Like jazz."

"Correct."

Topics rose and fell between them like petals in spring. They discovered they both enjoyed ragtime in moderate doses. Hal spoke of his love for Asian arts and photography. Vincent told him how happy she was that the man Anna Branch had invited for her amusement had favored another of the fourteen attendees. Yet Hal did not respond as she hoped he might to that revelation. It was obvious he was not interested, even though she would have provided the perfect cover for his natural proclivities.

Sara Teasdale had wandered over in the midst of this exchange and was bemused by Vincent's flirtation. "I think I'm more likely to fall in love with Miss Millay than Mr. Bynner is," she whispered to Jessie Rittenhouse, who was seated to her right.

The host replied with her own confession. "I suppose all of us will sooner or later. One can't help but find her fascinating."

* * *

Indeed, a few days later, Jessie Rittenhouse informed her that Hal had said some nice things about her.[220] Neither woman was sure what that meant, as Jessie was well-aware of Hal's sexuality and Vincent was still questioning why he never seemed interested in kissing her.

Once again, Vincent found herself wondering why every man she was interested in was either married or would not reciprocate. She thought perhaps it was because they were all literary types until she discovered the handsome pitcher for the New York Giants, Christy Mathewson, was also unavailable. Men were more interesting if they were older, but those who were older were usually married. Boys her age usually wrote bad poetry in the hope of winning her. Little they said surprised her. The girls at the Y were fun, but the proximity to Miss Dow discouraged her from pursuing anyone but Sara Teasdale, whose interest didn't seem stable. The older poet was still mooning for the vagabond poet Vachel Lindsay, and the other man Teasdale was dating, Ernest Filsinger was, in Vincent's estimation, a dull fop. She could not understand what a woman like Sara would see in the author of books about commercial business in Latin America.[221]

One thing that the young poet knew about Sara was how much she longed for financial stability. Perhaps this was the reason Sara even bothered with Filsinger. Whenever they met for tea, Vincent could tell which of the two men had Sara's ear at that moment. Sara was always more cheerful when she'd been in the company of Vachel, but she was more generous when she'd been around Filsinger. When in Vincent's company, she seemed playful. Vincent wondered if it would be possible to establish a relationship to satisfy the sexual urges she was repressing. She wasn't sure. Meanwhile, as Sara's friend, she was always there to hear the emotionally fragile and reserved older woman's ongoing confusion.

"You know Vachel, and I think you met Ernst at the last Society meeting," Sara began.

"Yes." Vincent took a moment to sip her tea.

"What did you think?"

Vincent wanted to be polite, but Sara was a friend, not a stranger who required delicacy. "I'm sure he is a fine provider, but he is rather dull."

Sara didn't need to be told which of her suitors her fellow poet meant. "And what of Vachel?"

Vincent did not hesitate. Lindsay was clearly the better choice if Sara sought a man who was sympathetic to her poetic drive. "It's clear he adores you. Besides, I think he understands you."

"You mean he understands my poetry?" Sara replied, reaching for a madeleine from the selection offered by the Tea Room.

"I mean your poetry and who you are as a person—or should I say how *I* see you?"

Sara sighed. "It always comes down to; should I marry a genius who writes marvelous poetry, or a fine, handsome rich fellow who enjoys *my* poetry?"

"And offers more stability."

"Yet, like a candle you light at noon, I just don't feel a need for him."

"On the other hand," Vincent countered. "When would you find time to write if all you had time for was cooking and cleaning for a poor man?"

Sara frowned. "Yes, I'm afraid Vachel would consider me an appendage designed for wifely duties. Ernest is well off enough that I'd have help."

The pair were quiet for a moment. Vincent considered her own options. A boy in Texas had sent a crazy mash note; some guy named Munroe was as much of a kid as she knew he'd be, and another man suggested that if she allowed him to deflower her, she would never be satisfied with another man, to which she replied, "What makes you think I'm a virgin?"[222] She wondered if Sara was. Finally, Vincent broke the silence.

"No matter who you choose, it should be someone kind, someone who knows how lovely you are."

Sara smiled shyly and blushed. It was as close as any woman had ever come to flattering her in that way. "You're too kind."

"Not really," Vincent laughed. They both knew there was a perceptible hint of truth in that statement. "If anything, I'm lucky."

Sara felt more comfortable changing the subject, so she asked if her young friend heard much from her old friends in Maine.

"I got a letter last week from my old pastor."

"In Camden?"

"Yes. Reverend Evans is my friend Abbie's father. I've told you about Abbie, haven't I?"

"I believe so." They paused as Sara refilled their teacups.

"He reminded me that the chance of a lifetime has come my way—like it did with Abbie—to attend college and that I must make use of that gift from God."

"How sweet," Sara said, plunking a lump of sugar in Vincent's tea and another in her own.

"Of course, he feels I should be the finest woman in my power because the only immortal poets were men." She began to laugh, with Sara quickly joining in.

"I'm so glad you're mortal." Sara giggled.

"So am I. It's so much more fun."

"Men can be so…"

"Yes, can't they? He needn't worry. I am quite settled down. I run in my rut now like a well-directed wheel. Sometimes, it is true, I feel I am exceeding the speed limit. But I seldom skid, and when I do, there's very little splash."[223]

It didn't matter that she had guessed Sara's adjective for what men can be. What mattered was that they both knew their futures did not require the presence of a man. The women laughed softly, sharing their mutual feeling as only close friends can do. Men were half the equation of humankind, but not the whole of it.

The young redhead looked up at a large wall clock that hung over the service area. "Oh, my gosh! I must go. I must prepare for my Classics' exam."

"We should have a walk next time," Sara suggested.

"I'd like that. Right now, I must be a good girl and bury my head in Horace for a few hours before dinner."

"Oh, that is a challenge. He is terrific, though, isn't he?"

"The other night, I got so engrossed that I missed dinner. Reverend Evans may go on about virtue being its own reward, but it's darned unsatisfying when you're hungry."[224]

"You can come here for dinner anytime. Even if the kitchen is closed, I always have a little something in my room."

"Oh, Sara, could I?" The young poet grinned.

"Certainly, otherwise you'll be a little too mortal." The friends laughed and embraced.

"I wish I didn't have to go, but I'm afraid if I don't, I'll never make it to Vassar."

16. His Hunger as My Own

1913

Mamaroneck, a sleepy seventeenth-century settlement on the coast of New York's Westchester County, was just the sort of place for an up-and-coming publisher like Mitchell Kennerley.[225] In addition to *The Lyric Year*, Kennerley's small, independent press balanced the scandalous work of English modernist writers like Christopher Morley, D. H. Lawrence, H.G. Wells, and Oscar Wilde, as well as the so-called obscene poet Walt Whitman, with romance novels and spiritualist tomes by Elsa Barker to make ends meet. His gift of gab was his tool for convincing the naïve Vincent to publish her first book of poetry.[226]

However, before he could do that, he had to be sure she had the right combination of high-brow poetry and sex to generate sufficient interest to pay back his investment.

The Lyric Year was already a sure-fire success. At least three hundred copies had been sold between the poets, their families, and friends, and more than two hundred more had been sold purely by virtue of the reviews of the publication and the scandal of Vincent losing the top prize. All this put money in his pocket.

Mitchell Kennerley already knew that E. Vincent Millay was an attractive, flirtatious twenty-one-year-old. This and her talent made her a potential gold mine. Now all he had to do was cultivate a friendship. Based on what he knew about her childhood, this meant he had to bring her to his home in Mamaroneck. But how? He was married, and his wife was already on alert. Perhaps his cousin, Arthur Hooley, who had reviewed *The Lyric Year* under the pen name Charles Vale, in *The Forum*, could cultivate a relationship. After all, he had said "Renascence" was the best poem in the volume. How could she resist a man who had written, "There have been some suspicions that the soul of America was becoming flat, but the sky will not cave in while there are such poets to uphold it." Arthur was single and literate, even if he was shy and had a speech impediment.[227]

He arranged for Vincent to visit his office after spring break. It would provide the perfect cover for an invitation to his bayside home. Meanwhile, he had to make sure Arthur was on board.

* * *

March 1913 droned on, with classes becoming progressively more challenging, and her hunger for physical companionship growing.

At Easter, she went to three different churches: Catholic ("dreadfully oppressive"), Madison Square Presbyterian led by the inestimable Reverend Doctor Charles Parkhurst,[228] and an evening service at Calvary Chapel, where Vincent was certain she heard angels singing with the choir during a performance of the Hallelujah chorus.[229]

After a generous dose of religion on Sunday, she joined Mrs. Trowbridge on Monday, March 24, for a day of shopping. Although she knew she should feel grateful, she couldn't help being disappointed by the dresses she could afford. In one of life's great ironies, the wealthy women helping Vincent through school did not think her worthy of truly beautiful things. The poet couldn't bear anything that looked or felt cheap. Yet being forced by her circumstances to wear items that didn't meet her standards, she hated how she looked. She wanted at least one graceful dress.[230]

There it was before her. It was sweetest thing she'd ever laid eyes on. She looked positively languorous in it. Though the price tag mocked her.

"Well," Mrs. Trowbridge began, negotiating for a smaller tab, "if you could limit yourself to that one dress and a couple of accessories, I suppose you may have it."

"May I? Oh, Mrs. Trowbridge, you'll never know how much this means to me. The dress makes me think of summer and iced tea on the lawn, with a breeze once and a while just to remind myself to breathe."[231]

Mrs. Trowbridge laughed and signaled to the clerk that Vincent could have the dress.

Yet on the following Wednesday, Fate found a way to pay her back for her good fortune when she was charged a seventy-cent late fee for a book of Milton she'd taken from the library and never looked at. Which was offset again by the good fortune of being able to move around the corner into a larger unit at the Y: Room 863. She loved it. Besides more windows and a view of downtown, the room had a quirk that made her feel as if it were made for her. The lines to the hot and cold water had been switched, so the cold came out hot and the hot came out cold. It made her feel at home somehow, perhaps because of the crazy shacks and tenements of her youth, which had little or no hot water on demand. [232]

As April got into full swing, the poet's good fortune continued. Kennerley, following his plan and his taste for poetry, gave Vincent a check for $25 for two poems that he published in his magazine, *The Forum*. Both *God's World* and *Journey* were poems she had shared with Sara previously, and the imagery harkened back to "Renascence," a fact not lost on the publisher. The pinkish-lavender check was the first one she'd ever received that wasn't some kind of prize. It felt like magic to open the envelope and read Mr. Kennerley's letter inviting her to his office on April 18. It seemed as if she'd broken her hoodoo of "all praise and no profit."[233] Now she was on her way. She could feel it. Her friends Sara Teasdale and Louis Untermeyer had been crazy about the poems, but that alone was of no use. It was cash she needed. Her family was poor, and sending along the income was a small way to make up for all the bragging she'd been doing in her letters home.

The following day, Vincent put the check in an envelope with two letters. The one to Cora begged her, "Please do something to make everything easier for yourself. Shoes, dear—or have your glasses fixed if they are not just right. I'd like it so much if each of you would get some tiny little thing that she could always keep."[234] As she watched the check fall from the envelope and drift to the floor, the nurse thought it providential that it should land in the glow of the noonday sun through a broken window.

Norma and Kathleen were dismayed at the changes in Vincent's tone. Cora was not. The nurse knew her daughter was the sort of person who would be discreet in everything but pride. Sooner or later, she reasoned, Vincent would get her just desserts, and while she wondered how this would affect her eldest, she was certain Vincent would find a way to rise above it. As for her younger children, there was the inevitable sibling rivalry that comes with tales of shopping trips and grand opera. As for Cora, she couldn't be bothered with replying. While she was happy that Vincent was finding publishers for her work, she had more immediate concerns. Work was drying up and without the income her eldest contributed to the expenses, life on Washington Street was anything but certain.

The nurse tried to concentrate on the positive, just as Reverend Gales had taught her. Vincent was making her mark. She had been paid $25 for just two poems. At this rate, Vincent would be able to support the whole family within months. Cora told herself she needed to remember that and that her eldest was receiving a free college education. Perhaps Miss Dow could be convinced to send Kathleen as well, or help Norma open a milliner's shop. If Vincent were a success, Norma would be too. Cora was sure of it. In addition to being a designer of marvelous hats, her middle child had the best singing voice and was a wonderful actress. Vincent could write plays and songs for her. Vincent would get her degree, return to Camden, and, like Emily Dickenson, live quietly in the family home writing verse. Cora knew this was fantasy, but somehow thinking this way comforted her.

The response from Norma was tepid and downright cool from Kathleen. Saying "she could keep" was so much less personal than "You will keep." Kathleen was direct. She pointed out her elder sister's habit of relating shopping trips, fashion shows, concerts and plays. "How do you think it feels to us, when Mother hasn't had a new pair of glasses in years, and Hunk and I are still wearing your hand-me-downs, to learn about your shopping sprees?"

* * *

In the week before her trip to Kennerley's downtown office, Vincent applied herself to her classwork. She caught up on reading, traded *Songs of Sappho* for *Alice in Wonderland* at the Columbia library, wrote overdue papers, translated the wrong odes of Horace, cleaned her brown silk waistband with a toothbrush just as her classmates had advised, and managed to fall in love with an auburn-haired Yalie three years her senior that she met at a party. The only problem with the latter accomplishment was she was too likely to spoil him when she was the one who hoped to be spoiled. She so wished she was a nice girl![235]

Her conversations with Monsieur Miller were bringing French to her lips in a manner approaching a first language. Everyone she knew in the city had at least passing fluency. Hers was getting so proficient that she was anxious to expand to German. Sadly, that would have to wait until her Latin translations met the exacting standards of Miss Goodale.

Her obsession with sex continued. Ever since her brief affair with Ella, she hadn't been able to quell her desire. Her Yale man was smart, funny, music loving and darned sweet, but she knew it was unlikely she'd ever see him again. Nonetheless, Mrs. Trowbridge knew exactly what she was thinking and made a point of discussing him with her. It made for a miserable day. Once again, she was being asked to rein in her keenest desires and most ardent wants. It had been that way all her life. The praise and punishment for her natural gifts never seemed to stop.

Despite the warnings of her chaperone, Vincent went through with the long-planned meeting with Kennerley. He struck the naïve schoolgirl as trustworthy and attractive. All she could see was his pipe, and all she could hear was his British accent, which he emphasized for effect when exclaiming how much he hoped that she would publish with him. The poet, still unsure if she had enough material for a full volume, demurred. She was also aware of how such a move would be interpreted by Miss Dow and her other patrons, who hoped she would go to press under the Harper Brothers or Houghton-Mifflin banner.

The prospect of playing at the same level as Sara, Hal, Harriet Munroe, and the Untermeyers was daunting. When she received Mr. Ficke's book, *Twelve Japanese Painters,* the week before her meeting with Kennerley, she could not put it down. It made her feel drunk.[236] His descriptions were staggering. Would she ever be able to describe anything as beautifully as he did? The pheasant's "snow-clogged feet," the crane in the sunset, the "wild geese that rush across the moon." She felt his Earth-Passion[237] matched her own. Yet she still wasn't sure she could sustain her rapture long enough to produce a volume, even a slim one.

"My dear girl," Mitchell Kennerley said in his most tantalizing voice, "you needn't worry about your work not measuring up. You made *The Lyric Year,* and perhaps this year you'll be among the cash winners."[238]

"There's to be another *Lyric Year*?" she cried. This would be a chance to save her family in a way that she could scarcely imagine.

"Of course. The first issue made such a splash, thanks in part to your wonderful poem, that people are just clamoring for another volume."

"Did I miss a year? I don't recall one from last year."

Kennerley realized he might be overstepping his ploy, so he doubled back. "No, no. You see, because of the whole controversy about the selection of the winners, and Mr. Earle's unavailability during his second honeymoon, we had to postpone the second volume. But everyday someone calls and wants a new issue, so we are planning to make the announcement as soon as Mr. Earle is back from France."

Vincent was so taken with the elegantly dressed older man that she completely ignored the timing issue with Earle's travels. Instead, she exclaimed that she would submit *Journey*.

"I'm sorry. The new volume will be for new work only. I've already published and paid you for your wonderful poem, so you'll just have to produce something just as wonderful as 'Renascence'."

"But..."

"As I said, you needn't worry about your work when you have an editor like my cousin. He'll be sure to steer you precisely where you need to go." The tall man lit his pipe and leaned back in his chair, gauging her response.

Vincent inferred the editor she was talking about was Charles Vale, not Ferdinand Earle, whom she was not at all anxious to work with again. "I'd like to meet Mr. Vale before I commit."

"That's fine, fine! Mrs. Kennerley and I would love to have you out to our place in Mamaroneck." His voice began to pick up speed as he sensed his opportunity. "My cousin lives there too. We could have a small gathering so you could get a good look at someone who *truly* appreciates your work. How does May 18 sound to you? The weather will be lovely, and your friend Mr. Bynner will be there to tell you about his experience publishing his *Tiger* play with us."

* * *

In the month between the meeting with Kennerley and the trip to his home in Mamaroneck, the poet found herself working as a typist, a job she loathed, for one of the school's administrators. It was not only boring; it wore her out. That, added to classwork, washing, and shopping, not to mention the endless socializing, made that spring's fever higher. When her Aunt Clem sent her the star-shaped, white arbutus, Vincent became dreadfully homesick.

Enveloped in the fragrance of the blossoms, the poet remembered family outings in the Maine woods.[239] The cement and steel of Manhattan blocked her. She needed greenery. She needed to hear birds—not the choked chirps of English sparrows from the crevice and shelf under her window,[240] but the glorious, full-throated joy of country birds. She needed to see the unblocked wind. She needed to smell the salt spray and the thick, fishy smells of seaweed and lobster traps.

After two more hours of typing for Miss Adams, the miserable redhead decided to do some shopping. Between the small amount she earned from the secretarial task and Miss Dow's allowance, she had just enough to send a used opera cloak to Norma.[241] She could see her sister twirling around in the coat, her hands stuck deep inside the pockets as she spun. It made her smile, but she was so lost in her longing that she temporarily got tangled by the river-bound streets.[242]

The closest she got to greenery was the Polo Grounds, where she watched the Giants beat the Phillies 7-0. She missed her Red Sox and swore if they ever played against the New York team she'd drop the Giants. The man who took her to the ballpark was surprised by how much she knew of the game, viewing it as a plus since most girls he dated were bored to tears with the sport. But Vincent loved it. She cursed the umpire's bad eyes when a Giant struck out and praised his calls when a player was proclaimed safe. Yet a day spent in the stands was no match for the feeling of grass between one's toes.

A homesick loneliness overtook her ability to concentrate. If she couldn't even finish a poem, how could they expect her to make it through four years of college? Doubt began to fuel her insecurity. What if she was only a flash in the pan? What if people were right when they said *The Lyric Year* judges were right to choose more experienced poets? Her mind was eased when Jessie told her *The Forum* that featured her two poems was about to be published.

"You were what?" Jessie pulled at her beads nervously.

"I was worried I might have to return the $25."

"Oh, my dear, don't be silly. That's the last thing that would happen."

Vincent blushed and changed the subject. "Do you ever have trouble finding the right words?"

Jesse paused. The young genius was feeling doubtful. She knew how that felt. She knew she would need to be honest but reassuring. "Yes, sometimes. I just try to let go of the search. Do something else. Take a walk outside. It will pass."

But it didn't. Vincent walked up Riverside Drive, stared through the fences at Gramercy Park, and strolled down the quiet lanes of Central Park, where gardens still flourished and yet creativity eluded her. Small scraps of verse dribbled from her pen. She needed more than the sight of trees and flowers. She needed the sounds and smells to be unobstructed by the rush of the city.

Someone at the Y recommended that she try to assuage her desires with a trip to Staten Island, including a visit to the Goddess of Liberty on the way over. This made matters even worse. Now she knew there was beauty somewhere near her everyday reach. She, who loved beauty more than anything in the world,[243] would go back to her comfortable but closed-off room. She couldn't wait for the trip to Mamaroneck.

* * *

The brick house was a monument to Gilded Age wealth. Mitchell Kennerley was not home when she arrived, but the servant who greeted them seemed to have a script memorized.

"Miss Millay, Mr. Bynner, Mr. Kennerley is delighted you are here. He has been delayed, but Mrs. Kennerley and Mr. Vale are expected momentarily." The servant took the young poet's suitcase with the new E.S.V.M. monogram and led them to a large and comfortable library. She then nodded toward a chair and withdrew as silently as a cat.

The poets looked around the room in a kind of dance, crossing back and forth and meeting in the middle before crossing to the opposite corner. The selection of volumes rivaled that of the Camden Library. Even her mother, who had one of the largest private libraries in Knox County, would have been put to shame. Vincent perused the titles, noting that the short wall consisted of books Kennerley himself had published. There was an odd assortment of romance novels by Kenneth Brown, Edith Wharton, and Rex Beach and spiritualist books by Elsa Barker, Upton Sinclair, and Lord Dunsany, as well as a section of American poets, including multiple copies of *The Lyric Year*. Their pages were uncut. What intrigued her most were the volumes by English authors and Americans considered too racy for public consumption, including Walt Whitman, Thomas Hardy, and D. H. Lawrence. She was about to delve into *Sons and Lovers* when a tardy bell rang in her head. "Mr. Vale?" Wasn't he the man who had written such a rave review of "Renascence"? She couldn't remember if Kennerley had mentioned it. As if on cue, Hal said, "It should be fun for you to meet Charles Vale. He's a big fan, you know."

"I wondered about that just now."

"I suppose I must have read your mind. I wonder if there are any books here on that topic," he laughed, gesturing toward the volumes on mysticism.

Vincent smiled back. By now, she knew Hal was fascinated by Eastern religions, particularly the work of Lao Tsu. "This is quite a library."

"You haven't seen the music room."

"He must be very rich." Vincent's curiosity was piqued. Now she must see the music room. She guessed there would be a grand piano, a harp, and perhaps even a pipe organ. Her mind briefly wandered to her blind teacher, Professor Tufts. He had been dead for five years.

Hal considered what to reply. He settled on "He married well" before pulling a volume halfway out of the bookcase and shoving it back in.

"Do you think it is important to do that?" she asked. Vincent had a terrific crush on the bow-lipped man. She could offer nothing but love.

"To do what?" he asked. He had settled into a chair with a volume by Goethe.

"Marry well."

Hal thought for a moment. "If by well you mean marrying someone wealthy, I think that depends on what your own needs are. Yet as far as I'm concerned, I think one needs to be happy, to follow the dictates of one's heart."

"So, you think people should marry for love," she stated, now having abandoned Lawrence's book in favor of tracing the lines of a sculpture by Rodin.

"Well, let me put it this way," the ever-inscrutable Hal began. "Love should be enough, but often it isn't. But if it is, one should embrace it."

Vincent didn't know what to make of his answer but thought it must be wise. She could see why Hal and Arthur Ficke were such great friends. Both spoke in a way that made her feel as if she were in the presence of some mystic. She was about to ask him to expand on his idea when they heard voices in the next room.

"Oh, that will be Helen and Charlie Vale," Hal said, bidding Vincent to join him in walking toward the sound.

"You're here!" Helen Kennerley almost shouted as she met them in the doorway of her husband's study. A tall, lean man with sallow cheeks and deep-set eyes followed Helen like an attendant butler in a mystery novel. "Miss Millay, may I introduce you to our cousin Arthur?"

The older, quiet man cleared his throat.

"Uh, sorry, Charles Vale. Charles Vale, Edna St. Vincent Millay. Vincent Millay, this is Charles Vale." Helen hoped the multiple introductions would make Arthur Hooley's pseudonym stick.

Vincent had noticed the shift in names. Surely a cousin would know a name. She decided to let it go in favor of thanking Mr. Vale for *The Forum* review.

"You're entirely welcome," Vale replied. "It was a remarkable piece of work for one so young."

"How kind." She nodded smartly and did a small curtsey, imagining that's what an English person might do to an older person who looked like a miserly lord in a George Eliot novel. "Do you know Mr. Bynner?"

"Certainly," Vale looked toward the handsome though balding author of exceptional haiku and terribly controversial short plays. "Hal."

Bynner nodded. If there was more than a passing friendship, it escaped notice.

Vincent let her eyes drift between the two men. So far, Hal had been friendly but apparently disinterested in her charms. Mr. Vale, however, was staring at her with a curious expression. Perhaps he was her beloved.

An automobile pulled up, and a man with an extensive collection of photographic equipment got out. He entered with a clatter.

Helen seemed bemused by the photographer's entrance. "And this is Arnold Genthe. Mr. Genthe, Miss Millay, Mr. Bynner and Mr. Vale."

The forty-four-year-old German immigrant gave each member of the party a courtly bow. Vincent was immediately taken with him. His chiseled features reminded her of pictures she'd seen of Jack London. There was a good reason for the comparison. The author had sat for Genthe many times.

"Mr. Genthe is also staying with us for a few days," Helen explained.

"I've seen your marvelous photographs of San Francisco after the earthquake," Hal remarked. He noted the handsome photographer's high forehead and piercing gaze.

"Thank you. I have admired your striking *Tiger*." Genthe's Prussian accent gave the statement a kind of mystery.

Vincent reflexively giggled. Something about the accent and the combination of striking with *"Tiger"* struck her as funny. "It is just such a vivid image," she smiled.

Genthe smiled, and Helen laughed. "Why yes, sometimes English makes it difficult to express myself."

"Oh, but the play is striking, so your description is apt. I think your English is very good." Vincent reached for Hal's arm. He looked at her fondly, then turned his attention toward Genthe. The poet and translator already knew the photographer's work. Now he hoped to know the man. With Vincent on his arm, his interest could not be confused with flirtation.

"What brings you to the Kennerley's?"

"I'm here to take a portrait of Helen and the children."

"We've been meaning to have Mr. Genthe here for a while," Helen offered.

"How long will you be here?"

"I'll set up this afternoon and use the morning light for the shoot. It's ideal through that window." The photographer nodded toward a large picture window.

As Genthe brought his equipment toward the study, Helen made sure her other guests were well primed for the evening's socializing.

Hal silently nodded toward Vincent, who caught his signal and released his arm. The handsome poet and playwright followed Helen to the liquor cabinet.

The air of the country estate began to filter through Vincent's lungs. She felt herself relaxing. From every window there was greenery—the sort of view she hadn't seen in months. In the distance, the sparkle of the harbor gleamed against the hulls of sailing boats. She inhaled deeply. The salt air blended with the smell of freshly mown grass to incite an intoxicating blend of memories. She half expected to see Cora and the girls come around the corner. Yet, when they didn't, she was surprised to discover that her homesickness didn't so much reflect her relationship with them as the environment of coastal Maine.

Mr. Vale noticed her gaze. "It's a lovely view."

"It makes me think of home."

"Those 'three long mountains and a wood'?"

She laughed, resigned to forever being linked to her breakthrough poem. "Yes, though I was actually thinking of the view from Dr. Tuft's, my piano teacher's home."

"You studied with John Tufts?"

"Yes, briefly, a couple of months. Before that, I was taught by my mother, and then by Mrs. French, a local woman Dr. Tufts recommended."

"Mitchell has a beautiful Bösendorfer in the music room. If you play as well as you write poetry, I'm sure you'd be welcome to give us a performance."

Vincent knew that many of the best pianists insisted on that brand. Yet her ear was attuned to something else: Vale's slight speech impediment. It was a combination of a lisp and a stutter over the letters "p" and "f." His deliberate pronunciation of Bösendorfer was the giveaway. Again, her fear of being found out overrode the Englishman's flattery. "I'm grateful you think I'm capable of playing such a fine instrument."

She looked down at her hands, absently spreading them as if she were reaching for an octave with her fingers. Vale noticed.

"You have such lovely hands, Edna. Well-suited for the keyboard."

"The only keyboard I seem to be thumping these days is the typewriter," she laughed self-consciously.

"Working toward a book for Mitchell, I hope." Vincent noticed his crooked and missing teeth when he smiled.

"No. I'm afraid I pay for my expenses by doing work for Miss Adams at Barnard, where I go to college," she replied. "Nine hours this week in addition to my schoolwork."

Mr. Vale noticed how the young woman appeared disturbed by the necessity of work. He decided to put a positive spin on her apparent distress. "At least your finger muscles will retain their strength."

They both laughed. "Shall we take a walk around the grounds before dinner?"

"Oh, yes, please!" Vincent cried.

After taking leave of their hostess and the other guests, the pair exited the large brick home and strolled down the hill toward Pelham Bay. Their walk would be brief but monumental, because during their brief stroll Vincent had already fallen a little in love with the gentleman, despite the fact he was old enough to be her father.

They had spoken of all sorts of things in the twenty-four minutes they had been gone. How James Fenimore Cooper had written *The Last of the Mohicans* while a resident of Mamaroneck, how politicians and Episcopal bishops had called it home, how the Japanese magnolias were about to bloom, and how the journey to New York by train was quick and productive as it gave one a chance to read the newspaper or edit copy, as Vale had for *The Lyric Year* two years before, ahead of one's arrival in the city. They seemed to have no end to the things they could discuss. By the time they returned, Mitchell Kennerley had arrived to greet them.

"I'm so glad you two are becoming friends," he cried as he watched them saunter up the drive.

"Why is that?" Vincent asked.

"Because...um, Charles will be your editor when I publish your first volume."

"Will he? How wonderful!"

Helen arrived at the door and called them in. The appearance of two young boys, Morley, aged eleven, and Mitchell, Junior, aged seven, delighted the poet, who was again transported to her childhood along the Yankee shore. Each child hugged their father briefly, stared wide-eyed at the young redhead, and sneered at Hal and Charles. As they walked toward the dining room, Kennerley made his affection for his cousin clear to the poet. "You're lucky. Few men have the sympathetic insight and taste to discern what is truly abiding and distinguished in literature. To have such a man at your side will be an undoubted gift, Vincent. You must listen to his advice. He is truly a genius."[244]

"Having spent some time with him I do indeed consider myself blessed," she nodded quietly. She watched as Charles pulled the chair for Helen and helped settle the children. While not ready for children herself, Vincent was delighted to see a man of such elegant manners and carriage interacting within the circle of bohemian intelligentsia.

After a meal complemented by stimulating conversation on topics ranging from gardening to politics, the group retired to the music room where, despite her protestations, Vincent played piano for the group, delighting them with Liszt and her ragtime originals. Then all but Helen and the children recited poetry to one another. Once Morley and Junior were tucked in, fine brandy and cigarettes fueled more discussion until they went their separate ways, finding their guest rooms amid whispered thank-yous and wishes for pleasant dreams.

* * *

But Vincent could not sleep. Now she had two men who fit the bill of "beloved," perhaps even a third in Mitchell Kennerley himself, though she didn't like the idea of breaking up a home as hers had been. She and Norma had been about the same age as Morley and Junior when their mother fell for Reverend Gales. She imagined her father would be especially unhappy if she followed her mother's example. What she didn't know yet was how much Kennerley and her father had in common. As far as she was concerned, while both men possessed the gifts of gab, salesmanship and a gambler's spirit, the publisher was the consummate professional, elegant, urbane, and successful. The poet didn't know how a trail of debts followed Kennerley, just as doggedly as it did her father. To her, the only difference was that Cora was not an heiress whose wealth made experimentation and failure possible.

As her mind toyed with all the potential romantic outcomes, it also scanned other options in her life. There was Barnard and all the classwork she was avoiding by being at the Kennerley's for the weekend. There was Vassar, still an unknown Elysian field. There were the many women she found attractive but avoided lest Miss Dow cut her off. There was poetry and music and theater and family and all the rest of the things she emotionally stumbled through.

Only nature seemed constant. In that she and Arthur Ficke agreed. Nature was the only thing that did not disappoint, because even in death, Nature became beautiful. Her soul traced the thousands of memories that gave her poetry, from her mother reading to her as a child to the way the trees bent to the wind from Penobscot Bay. Poetry, in fact, all art, originated from nature. Her sexual desire came from nature. She could feel her menstrual cycle coming on and the accompanying rush of hormones that urged her to touch herself, as if answering some ancient aboriginal call. She took a deep breath, capturing a column of sea air that had made it through a crack in the windowpane of her room. She thought of Charles Vale, then Hal, then Arthur Ficke—whom she still hadn't met. She thought of Gayle, Ella and Sara. A mélange of possible lovers made her skin flush with excitement. She brought her left hand to her mouth, shaping the thumb and index finger as if they were lips, still deciding who she would be kissing. Her other hand lazily fondled her pubic area until her arousal was satisfied.

She eventually relaxed and slept, awakening only when the boys burst into her room to ask if she knew where their mother was. It all felt so familiar. She half expected to find Norma and Kathleen at the bottom of the stairs.

"Bonjour," Hal said as he passed her on the landing. His hair was still damp from a shower, and the scent of Burma Shave and Penhaligon's English Fern aftershave trailed after him. The fresh blend of soap and warm, woodsy spice lingered long after he ducked back into his room. "Bonjour," she returned as his door clicked shut and she entered the Kennerley's well-appointed bathroom, where moments before Hal had been singing.

She imagined what he'd look like under his robe and found herself again obsessing over which of her many male choices would be the first to have her.

She moved through her morning ablutions automatically, throwing in some singing herself, returned to her room, dressed and began her descent downstairs. Hal was speaking with Mitchell and Helen. Charles had returned to the city by the early morning train. Arnold Genthe was somewhere on the grounds.

Breakfast was a boisterous affair as the children exchanged double-dog dares and adults discussed the day's activities. Helen chided her children about the necessity of remaining fresh in their personally selected outfits. "Mr. Genthe is taking our pictures after breakfast." She took Morley's hand and pulled him toward her, adjusting his tie and collar before smoothing his unruly dark hair. Satisfied, she drew Junior to her side and asked, "Are you sure you want to wear that peasant blouse for the photograph?"

"Yes. I think I look beautiful," the boy replied.

"Beautiful?" Hal laughed. "Don't you mean handsome?"

"Do you think I look handsome?" Junior asked, tugging at his short pants.

"Why, yes, I do," Hal cried.

"I do, too," Vincent laughed. "I think you look like a character out of Dostoevsky."

"Dos-ef-ski? Who's that?" Morley asked.

"A Russian writer," Helen explained.

"Does Pa publish him?"

"I'm afraid not," the boys' mother answered.

"I'm a Russian," Junior announced.

"By way of Ohio," Mitchell laughed wryly, staring at his seven-year-old namesake with a bemused grin.

Helen smiled. "Never mind your father. Finish your breakfast and wash up. Mr. Genthe has asked us to join him in the study at 10:30, and we mustn't be late."

The children wolfed down what remained of their meal and raced after each other up the stairs.

"Ah, peace and quiet," Hal said. "I don't know how you do it, Helen. They are quite a handful."

Their hostess ran her fingers around her Florentine neckline and primped her dark curly hair, which was worn up with a small fringe of bangs. "Oh, we have help. The nursemaid allows them to dress themselves. Of course, she makes suggestions. I suspect she was the one who convinced Morley to wear a suit. But Junior has his own mind when it comes to things."

"Like his father," Hal noted.

"Naturally," Mitchell laughed. "Helen, darling, will you need me in the pictures?"

"I don't think so," she smiled indulgently.

"Good. I was hoping to get a ride in before lunch."

Vincent remained keenly observant of the whole tableau. She had never been close to a family with such contradictions. Helen's impeccable upper-class manners and Mitchell's acquired elegance were as if reality and theater had been blended. She watched as Helen's dark eyes watched Mitchell finish the folded newspaper on the table to his left.

"Did you sleep well, Vincent?"

The redhead felt jolted from her reverie. "Excuse me?"

"Did you sleep well?" Helen asked again.

"Oh, wonderfully. I heard a titmouse this morning as I was dressing. In the city, all you hear are English sparrows and finches, and of course the pigeons and doves."

"So, you're a bird lover," Helen asked.

"My sisters and I used to compete over who could identify the most number of birds."

"My guess is you were probably the winner," Hal observed.

"Actually, when my mother participated, she got the better of us all. My sister Hunk—I mean, Norma—was very good. We were pretty evenly matched for our ages. In fact, Kathleen beats me often now that she's older. Of course, we're on the honor system."

"You trusted each other?" Mitchell asked.

"Yes, of course. Why, there's no one I trust as much as Norma." Vincent finished her breakfast and asked to be excused.

"Of course, dear. Here you are your own master."

With family and schoolwork top of mind, Helen's words could not have been more welcome. Vincent retrieved textbooks from her room and went to the coastal boardwalk. There, she found a bench and attempted to study French. Although her teacher liked her sense of humor, that didn't help when conjugating verbs. She would pass, she thought, with little effort, but somehow the ease with which she tackled the language in high school eluded her amid the myriad accents of New York. She closed her eyes and thought of home.

The moment her lesson began to take shape in her mind, she thought of having seen Sarah Bernhardt in *Camille* the week before. "Ah, elle était mérreilleuse!" The play was the most wonderful thing she'd ever seen, heard, or even imagined, particularly the last act.[245] Her patrons could not have known how much of a fan she was or how she'd clipped pictures of the "Divine Sarah" from magazines and posted them about her room as a child. A wave of gratefulness came over her. She just had to do well. If for no other reason than that her patrons were the very people who allowed her to realize her dream of seeing the French actress in person.

She resolved to spend more time speaking French. This would help considerably if she were ever to come to full facility with the language. She wished she could do the same with Latin, but short of finding a kindly priest to converse with, most of her Latin work was strictly bound to the classroom.

The clock along the boardwalk told her it was time to return to the Kennerley's. Helen was going to drive her to the station for the late-morning train. As she walked back, she savored every moment. She felt at home in ways that home did not. She made a note of that for a future poem and almost skipped back.

* * *

The flying horses of Coney Island whirled around to the sound of the automated calliope. The girls on her floor had decided it was too fine a day to be stuck on campus and dragged her away for a day at the beach the moment she returned to the YWCA.

The foray into the Kennerley's world marked a new phase in her life. Now she felt as though no matter what happened with college, she could somehow find her way in the world. There were people who found her interesting, attractive, and fun, even without a degree. On the other hand, the largesse of her patrons gave her far more than Mr. Brewster, Professor Trent, or the rest of her collegiate instructors. It gave her opportunities like seeing Bernhardt in *Camille*, hearing Yeats read his own work with his marvelous Irish brogue and discussing poetry with Sara Teasdale. Vincent became determined to knuckle down and make herself worthy of their faith in her.

The day at the Brooklyn shore had been the perfect bookend to the yachts and dogwood blossoms of Mamaroneck. Now she had to prepare for her final exams as the last vestiges of her Fievel Flying steed circled her mind.[246] There were English, Latin, and French tests ahead, as well as hours of practice conversations with classmates and her YWCA Training School friends. She knew she would have to achieve the highest marks if she were to enter Vassar in the fall. She had already filled out the paperwork required to get credit for her classes, so she felt there was no slowing down. She couldn't make excuses. The voices of her mother, Miss Dow, and Miss Bannon echoed in her head: "Knuckle down!"

* * *

Yet all her pledges were forgotten after a rather curious adventure in Central Park.

Vincent was going to meet her friend Alene Stern for a splendid meal at an uptown restaurant. As the poet made her way from the Y, she entered Central Park. Normally, she avoided walks in areas where she might be kidnapped or approached by strange men, but her longing for greenery gave way to her usual common sense.

She had left her umbrella behind, assuming the gray clouds sufficiently wrung out from an afternoon downpour. The park had the usual scents of spring, and the young redhead was so inspired by the beauty she ignored the first warning drops of a late spring monsoon. Instead, she forged ahead, losing her way altogether as she admired the azaleas, violets, and peonies, not to mention the cherry and crabapple blossoms that blanketed the green grass with pink petals. It seemed like a dream world, and by the time she realized she was lost, she was soaked to the skin.[247] The poet's long hair, so carefully arranged atop her head, began to frizz and loosen. The tree where she sheltered to get her bearings dropped flowers and twigs into her head, further adding to her disheveled appearance. Her new calfskin boots began to squeeze her feet as the material shrank. There was no one else in sight. It was only when she made it to the Columbus monument that she realized she was too far south for her rendezvous at 106 W. 73rd.

Having corrected herself, she traipsed across the sheep meadow to Eighth Avenue and then Columbus before heading north, arriving at the below-ground café gloriously saturated. She hoped she wouldn't run into Mrs. Trowbridge, who lived just three blocks away.

Alene rushed toward the poet. "Goodness! What happened to you?"

"I got lost. No umbrella," Vincent laughed through chattering teeth. She shook the twigs, petals and rain from her hair, much to the dismay of the maître d'.

"Would mademoiselle like a towel?"

"Oui!" she replied, ever anxious to practice her French. Alene went to the coat check and asked if they had any items left behind. The laughing clerk handed her an enormous man's overcoat. It would have to do. Between the towels, the coat, and the mirrored wall of the foyer, Vincent was hardly presentable, but Alene's ranking with the owner made dismissing the couple out of the question.

As usual, they gossiped, doing their best to ignore the stares of other patrons. Vincent decided to explain the reason for her distraction. She could not get Charles Vale out of her mind.[248]

"He looks, I imagine, much like Uriah Heep or Fagin," she explained to her dog-loving friend. Alene had graduated from Barnard before the poet's arrival and was thus viewed as a suitable companion by Miss Dow.

"Do you mean he's Jewish?" Alene asked, polishing off the amuse bouche at the Café Anglais.

"Oh, no, at least I don't think so," the poet replied. "He's just so English-looking."

"What do you mean?" The waiter refilled Alene's teacup and removed the service in preparation for the next course.

"He has…Now this won't sound right…You'll think him odd."

"Go on."

"He has a rather thin face, with deep-set eyes, a long nose, and a kind of pointy chin."

Alene tried to mask her confusion. Here was a lovely, attractive young girl discussing a man over eighteen years her senior, and he did indeed sound like one might imagine a Dickensian villain.

Vincent read her friend's face. "And he has big ears and eyebrows that come across his forehead." Suddenly, Vincent began to laugh. Relieved, Alene joined in.

The poet continued. "Yes, he sounds awful, I suppose, but he's just so fascinating."

"Sounds like an undertaker," Alene giggled. "I suppose he wears tweed and one of those silly, hopelessly out-of-fashion ties."

"Yes, but he's just so…"

"I know, fascinating. Honestly, Vince, I cannot understand what you see in him when there are so many younger, attractive, and wealthy boys at Columbia."

"That's just it, Alene. They are boys. When Charles speaks of poetry it is as if he had a poet's soul, like he knows my every sorrow and regret."

"If you don't watch yourself, you'll have something else to regret," Alene offered in a tone of caution.

"I know," Vincent said, not wishing to admit how much she wished his long, thin fingers would push the damp, stray hair from her forehead as she'd seen him do with his own course, dark locks.

They finished their meal with a change of topic and a bottle of wine that went straight to the poet's head. By the time they parted, it was very late.

* * *

Vincent was not the only one thinking of her seemingly realized beloved. After her French exam, a call came through from Helen Kennerley inviting her to spend the weekend in Mamaroneck. There was a dance at their country club, and Charles didn't want to be the third wheel.

When the poet agreed to go, she knew she was breaking her word to Miss Dow. She was obliged to have dinner with her patron and Mrs. Trowbridge. Yet she would lie a hopeless lie because it was sure to be found out. She claimed the soaking of the previous night had given her a cold and conspired with a neighbor to block all calls and visitors. Her word of honor was already becoming threadbare, and yet she persisted in her pursuit of the unmarried cousin of her host.

It turned out that Charles was a marvelous dancer. His pace matched her own. As their palms met, she felt a shiver that told her she would break another promise she had made.

By the third turn around the floor, she knew that her instincts were right. Not only had Charles revealed his real name, but he had suggested they go for a quiet walk.

"It's likely to rain," she said.

"True," the sad-faced man replied as he lifted her off the floor and swung her around.

"You could come by my room," she countered as they dipped.

Vincent caught her breath. What was she thinking? She knew what that meant. She was expecting her menstrual cycle and was worried about what would happen until she realized that, as a theoretical virgin, she would bleed anyway. They continued to dance, turning, swirling, and dipping to the Grizzley Bear. The poet's love of dance, coupled with Arthur Hooley's (aka Charles Vale's) desire to embrace in the only socially acceptable way he knew. Before the quartet returned to the Kennerley's estate, Vincent and Arthur had made plans for when their tryst would occur.

Arthur left her room shortly before one a.m. Her head swam. It had been nothing like she thought it would be. She lay there wishing he had stayed and thanking God he had not. No matter how hard Vincent tried, sleep eluded her. By now, her menstrual cycle had begun in earnest and the mess made her consider taking a long, hot bath. The trouble was she'd have to go down the hall, past the Kennerley's and Arthur's rooms to get there, and the risk of waking the occupants of either room was too great. She threw the covers back and shrugged. The bathing pitcher was her only option. She would make her apologies to the staff if she had to. Meanwhile, a quick sponge bath and the homemade menstrual pads she packed would have to do.

The hours ticked by, and upon hearing the cock's crow, she realized that if she didn't get to sleep, she'd have to think about the ramifications of her intemperance.[249]

Over the course of the next few days, Vincent was amazed by how little she cared about the loss of her virginity or even that she had broken the promises she had made to Miss Dow. Bad Vincent reigned supreme.

The end of the term had come, and she needed to pack for home. She had mixed feelings. "He" was in New York. Her family was in Maine. While the homesickness had somewhat abated thanks to her visits to Mamaroneck, her heart longed to see her mother and have a nice, long confessional with Norma. Seeing Kathleen all grown up and ready to graduate would also be fun.

Yet Helen Kennerley called like a siren from her suburban retreat. Her insistence rattled Vincent. She felt like a fool. There were excuses like hearing Helen's friend sing, having dinner with the Drakes, or viewing Beatrice Howe's exquisite pastel drawings, but Vincent knew Helen's real motive was getting her lifelong bachelor cousin married.

Sitting across the table from the man she now knew as Arthur confounded the poet. She watched as Miss Howe's upturned nose twitched as she dismissed the pollen count, but what really concerned the poet was how Beatrice addressed "him."

"Mr. Vale, you look like a man who suffers with allergies," the artist suggested. "How do you cope?"

"I don't."

"Don't what, Mr. Vale?"

"I don't suffer from allergies."

"He does look like someone with allergies," Vincent teased. "Doesn't he, Helen?"

Helen hardly had time to reply when the Drakes chimed in to agree. "My brother has terrible hay fever, and his eyes have dark circles just like yours."

"So does my sister," Vincent lied. She could see she was getting a rise out of her lover.

"Perhaps we should take Ar…Charles at his word," Helen said.

"What do you think, Mitchell?" the poet asked her would-be publisher.

He laughed. "I suppose if he did have allergies, he'd know it."

"I didn't know until Dr. Kellogg told me that is why I have frequent headaches," Miss Howe replied.

Vincent was enjoying every minute of the exchange. "How fortunate you must be to have been in his care. I've heard the Battle Creek Sanatorium is simply marvelous for what ails you."[250]

"Oh, yes," Miss Howe offered, hoping to be delicate. "You must undergo a strict cleansing regimen, eat a vegetarian diet, and submit to all sorts of treatments, but you do feel ever so much better afterward."

"What sort of treatments?" Bad Vincent asked, hoping to extract a confession of multiple enemas.

"She doesn't have to tell us that," Arthur said sternly.

"Why, *Charles*?" the poet asked, emphasizing Arthur's alias for effect. She was rewarded with an icy stare.

"Perhaps Mrs. Thorp could heal us with another song," Helen suggested.

"Oh, I don't mind telling. It's really rather interesting. There's hydrotherapy, of course, strictly cold water though," Miss Howe began.

"I've heard they have electrotherapy," Vincent smiled. "That sounds like it would be painful."

"No, not really. I mean, it is at first, but after a while it just feels like static electricity," the artist explained. What followed was a discussion of everything that happened at "the San" except the daily enemas Miss Howe had undergone.

Finally, Mrs. Thorp herself got up, went to the piano, and began to play and sing "Die Fledermaus" as the most effective means of avoiding Vincent's continued goading of both "Charles Vale" and Beatrice Howe.

As the group broke up an hour later, the still-fuming Arthur insisted Vincent "take the night air for her health." By now, the poet had been so taken by Mrs. Thorp's rendition of "The Laughing Song" aria that she'd almost forgotten her playful attempt to yank Arthur's chain.

The night air was unseasonably warm and filled with the scent of new growth. Arthur took her far enough from the house that a heated debate would not be heard and then growled, "Why did you do that?"

Vincent looked up at the barely visible, waning crescent moon. It was as obtuse as her reply. "What?"

"Humiliate me," he said flatly. His nasal voice sounded even more like a whine than usual.

"I don't know what you mean," she said, and bent down to remove a fallen branch from the path.

"Of course, you do, you silly child," Arthur began. "That whole business about my health when you know very well how healthy I am."

"Because you sometimes have enough energy for sex?" Vincent bristled. "That's no accomplishment. A dying salmon will spawn."

Arthur's mouth stiffened. He waited to control himself before saying, "You're being damned nasty, Edna."

"Am I?"

"You know you are. The difficulty is I don't know why." He moved away from her. She did not miss the warmth of his body.

"And I don't know why you insist on using a pseudonym. Is there some skeleton in your closet I should know about?"

"I have my reasons."

"But surely your own cousin shouldn't be forced to be a party to such tomfoolery."

"She understands," he replied. The dull gray of the night's reflections made his face even duller.

"Well, I don't. In fact, I think you should be open with me about why. After all, we're together. Aren't we?" Vincent's long fingers rested on her hips.

"I suggest that has been a massive mistake," Arthur replied.

Vincent stared at him. Whatever thoughts she had of Arthur being her "beloved" were already melting. "Fine. I think you're right. If you can't be honest with me, what's the point?"

"None whatsoever," he replied and began to walk away. Though he hoped she'd follow and apologize, she had no such desire. She took the opposite path, back to the Kennerley's.

17. A Thousand Screams

1913

Yet, three weeks later, they made up. Vincent was actively enticing Arthur with a black swim suit that made her glad her hair was red.[251] He was complimenting her immaculate diction and the way she'd learned to project her voice. Over the few months at Barnard, she had also cultivated a fashionable Mid-Atlantic accent that reminded him of the upper-class girls he'd known in England. More outings and stolen kisses in the woods extended the length of their brief romance.

Vincent's forays between New York and Mamaroneck began to swing toward longer stays in the country. She somehow kept missing Miss Dow, who apparently was beside herself with worry and disappointment. The poet did manage to find a way to visit the dean of Columbia's journalism school, Dr. Williams, and his friend Katherine Hubbard, who advised Vincent to heed her father Elbert Hubbard's warning concerning one's reputation. "Many a man—or woman's—reputation would not know his—or her—character if they met on the street. To avoid criticism, do nothing, say nothing and be nothing."[252]

"If I were you," Dr. Williams agreed, "I'd leave a message for Miss Dow asking her to call you when you're in town. I know how hard it is for young people to remember that we worry about them, but a quick call would help her feel her trust isn't misplaced."

Vincent nodded but neither admonition could keep her from seeing the patriarchal Englishman. Sexual desire overcame her usual sense of self-preservation. She realized what a chance she was taking. but couldn't bring herself to care. That is, until Miss Dow finally reached her at the Kennerley's home.

"Hello, I've been meaning to…"

"My dear, please do not try to charm me when I know perfectly well what's going on down in that den of iniquity!" Miss Dow snapped.

"I'm perfectly chaperoned," Vincent countered. She could hear her mother's warning voice. Cora had told her eldest how important it was to maintain a blameless existence so long as she relied on Miss Dow's patronage.

"Ha! Do you call staying at the home of a known adulterer, a man with friends of such dubious character that they must resort to false names, a man who owes money to nearly everyone in New York, suitable?"

The poet was taken aback. Miss Dow had never spoken so harshly to her. She also did not know the true state of Mitchell Kennerley's apparent wealth. "I believe his wife's family...," she began.

"Nonsense, dear girl! Sheer poppycock. She was cut off without a penny when she married that rogue."[253] Miss Dow had clearly done some digging and what was exhumed smelled rotten.

"I...I didn't know," Vincent said softly. She looked around the expansive house and suddenly noticed the threadbare furniture.

"And that man who calls himself Charles Vale, that editor? Do you know his true name is Arthur Hooley?"

Vincent could feel sweat beginning to drip down her sides. Vassar was at risk. She had to be careful. "Yes, he told me."

"And you think such a man is suitable?" Miss Dow's voice cracked. "After all I've done, we've done, for you. How could you be so ungrateful?" She began to cry but continued railing. "Do you think people will invest in a girl of questionable morals? Do you think one poem makes you above common decency?"

Chastised, Vincent replied, "No."

"And what of me? Do you know what people are saying about me?"

"No, I don't, Miss Dow. I am so very sorry." For the first time in weeks, Good Vincent poked her head out from behind her Bad twin.

"They are saying I am an old fool. That I've been taken in by an ungrateful wretch from a broken family. It would be quite a different thing if your attendance and grades illustrated a commitment to making good, but you could hardly call them stellar." Miss Dow took a deep breath, exhaling slowly before finishing the dressing down. "I expect you to be back in New York promptly, so we can discuss your future in person."

"Yes, Miss Dow. I will," she said. The poet felt rotten about making her generous benefactor cry, but her contrite feelings did not extend to whoever had spilled the beans about her activities in Mamaroneck.

Miss Dow added one more admonition. "I expect you in my office at four o'clock Wednesday afternoon, and when I say Wednesday, I mean *this* Wednesday, June 4th!"

"Yes, yes, I understand. Uh, huh. Goodbye." Vincent returned the handset to the receiver.

"Damn 'em!" she almost shouted now that Miss Dow was fully twenty-one miles away.

"What?" Helen asked. She could see Vincent's flushed face and sensed the call did not go well.

"I wish they'd keep their mouths shut."[254] Vincent slumped into a chair. She placed her head in her hands, dismayed. Arthur entered the room.

"What's wrong, child?" he asked. "Tell me."

"Miss Dow heard some new cussedness about me and is heartbroken," Vincent cried. The conflict between embarrassment and anger was evident in every word.

"Will she cut your funding?" Mitchell asked, having been drawn from his study by the poet's cursing.

"I don't know. I hope not," Vincent stood up and began to pace. "I feel awful about it, of course, but I'm also very angry. Who would have told her?"

Arthur slipped his arm around her shoulder. He began to wonder as well. He'd said something to Ferdinand Earle in confidence. Was he the source? Miss Rittenhouse had seen them laughing together at a Poetry Society meeting. Maybe she figured out what was going on. Would Helen or Mitchell have said anything? Hal Bynner had been there the evening they met.

Vincent was making the same catalog with the addition of Alene Stern, her neighbor and others in her circle at school. Suddenly, she found herself angry at Arthur. She shrugged his arm off her shoulder and renewed her pacing. "Herbert Kaufman. It would be just like a newspaper man to broadcast my private affairs."

"I'm sure he would be careful," Helen soothed. "I've known him for years. He's very discreet unless there's a story to be had."

"I don't think you're helping, sweetheart," Mitchell advised. "Seriously, Vincent, don't worry. I'm sure Miss Dow will be alright once she reads the new poems you've been working on. She'll see how good the country air has been for you. I'm sure of it."

The poet stepped away toward the stairs. "I'm afraid I've lost my appetite. I'm going to my room."

Arthur started to follow. A quick look by Helen suggested it was better to leave the young redhead alone.

The following morning, Vincent woke up to find her hair damp with tears. Her face was white and her throat sore.[255] How could she have been so stupid? She prided herself on adamantine silence,[256] but, somehow, she'd confided in the wrong person. She felt as if she were dying. So did Arthur. Their misery hovered over breakfast like a hornet at a picnic. Mitchell tried to lighten her mood by announcing that someone had found her signet ring in the sand after she'd asked him to hold onto it and he'd dropped it. His story only reminded her of how much Miss Dow distrusted him.

Arthur suggested a walk in the woods. She agreed. Whatever spy had revealed the affair would be unlikely to be lurking in the woods. They broke from the established path. Their hands trembled for different reasons.

"I feel awful," he said.

"Me, too." The poet caught sight of a towhee in the branches overhead. A squirrel skittered down a nearby branch and startled them both.

Arthur pulled her toward him. The effort felt half-hearted. It mirrored her feelings. Nevertheless, the editor didn't want his paramour to lose her opportunity thanks to him. "What are we going to do?"

He knew how the world worked. People who have little are always beholden to the kindness of those who had much. Someone once told him he was a reflection of his cast—and not a good one. Although related to Helen Morley Kennerley, his branch of the family tree had born inferior fruit.

"I don't know," the poet replied, reflexively kissing him. She leaned into his chest hoping to hide her growing indifference to his presence. At this point, the relationship reflected proximity more than passion. He had not satisfied her once in the three times they had engaged in sex, and, frankly, the act was already becoming routine. Courtship had its benefits, but consummation had its limits, especially with a man unaccustomed to women throwing themselves at him. Too often she found herself thinking of the pleasures in Ella's arms. How they laughed and played together. Arthur was brilliant and fulfilled her need for a mature male in her life, but he was unimaginative in bed and quick to climax. Lately she would masturbate after he fell asleep just to finish what he'd started.

The couple remained so silent a doe tiptoed by with two newly born fawns. The poet and editor watched as the deer disappeared into the woods. Finally, Vincent spoke.

"I think we'll have to break things off, at least for now."

"I suppose that's the only solution," he replied. Part of him was relieved, part of him regretted denying his cousin the hope he might have found a woman he could commune with. He kissed Vincent passionately as if putting an exclamation point on their decision. She responded accordingly but was able to ignore any feelings of arousal. She decided it was better to remember him with lust than disappointment.

18. An Answering Cry

1913

The time had come to leave Barnard and make her way home. The journey would be circuitous.

Vincent's first stop would be her Uncle Charlie's in Bristol, Connecticut. Her mother's brother welcomed her with open if wary arms. Word of the poet's indiscretion had made its way through the family grapevine.

The local boys could sense the presence of a willing partner, and she had her pick. There was Torchy, a little redheaded Jew with beautiful brown eyes and an instant feeling of fellowship with her.[257] There was her on-again, off-again Yale suitor Henry. A boy named Jimmy brought her roses and invited her to Lake Compounce amusement park. Now that she'd had the forbidden fruit, she was keen to sample another variety. Even her Aunt Jennie's dreadfully dull Rebecca Club social was made tolerable by the presence of numerous boys.

Of them all, Henry seemed the likeliest candidate despite the fact he was engaged to a girl in Minnesota. This did not stop him from inviting Vincent to stay with him at his home near the lake. She had to admit her acceptance of the invitation was a little unconventional, even for her.[258] Remarkably, the couple avoided a liaison despite four hours of canoeing along some of the Lake's more private sloughs. Vincent kept him talking about his bride to be.

When she returned to her uncle's home on Monday there was a letter waiting for her.

"Looks like it's from that Miss Dow," Vincent's Uncle Charlie observed. "Do you suppose she knows about you gallivanting all over Lake Compounce with that boy?"

"Not unless you told her," the poet snapped. "Besides, nothing happened. He is a nice boy, and I was a nice girl. He's engaged, after all. We're just friends."[259]

"Is that what you call it," her Aunt Jennie mumbled.

"Nice girls don't spend the weekend without a chaperone," Charlie Buzzell retorted.

"Honestly! Don't you trust me at all?" Vincent cried. She opened the letter and quickly read it, half expecting her uncle to be right. Miss Dow asked her to return to New York immediately. Her heart sank. What new piece of gossip had reached her ears? Did her patron know about her flirtation with Mitchell Kennerley as well? "I must go back to New York for a day or two. Would you please drive me to the station?"

"She's going to drop you. Just you wait," Aunt Jennie sniffed.

Vincent bit her tongue and handed her aunt the note. "I'll go put a few things together."

"Better hurry," her uncle noted. "The train leaves in an hour."

* * *

Ironically, when she arrived in New York she was greeted by Miss Dow's ever faithful assistant, Mary Alice. The poet had seen little of the Irish immigrant since the day she helped her enroll in Barnard months before. Mary Alice informed the poet that Miss Dow was unavailable until Wednesday because there had been a death in her family. Vincent had to laugh. She had been scrupulously obedient and came immediately, and yet because Miss Dow had failed to make arrangements for a place to stay in the city, Vincent would have to spend Monday and Tuesday in Mamaroneck.

The reason for the delay gave Vincent pause. It reminded her of how fragile life is and in turn made her think of her own little band of women back in Camden. "Hunk" and "Wump," her sisters Norma and Kathleen respectively, were her best friends in many ways and their mother, while stern and Victorian, seemed to accept her boy chasing with equanimity.

After two days with only Helen Kennerley for company, Vincent returned to the city feeling chaste and respectable. She took a bus to the Y from Grand Central Station and took the elevator up to the ninth floor.

"Oh, Aunt Caroline!" she cried upon seeing the grief-stricken Miss Dow. "Was she very close to you? You poor, dear thing."

Miss Dow's black satin dress shimmered in the light of the tearoom. She reached out her hands to take Vincent's outstretched hands. Both women wore gloves, so the sensation was especially warm.

"Dear child! You *are* a dear, dear child!" the older woman said, tears welling in her eyes. "Edina was an old friend from my own days in school, almost a sister. It was just so sudden."

Now Vincent understood why Mary Alice had said it was a family member. "You must be heartbroken," Vincent observed sincerely. She had a few friends at Barnard and the thought that any should die made her eyes respond well in empathy.

The pair were seated at a table by the window that overlooked the busy Manhattan streets. As they sat down, Vincent calculated whether it seemed she would be sent home without ever seeing Vassar. That was not her sense of things. There was another reason why Miss Dow had to see her. She was flooded with shame. She realized she had wronged Miss Dow in several important ways and was glad for the opportunity to make up for her lapses in decorum.

They ordered lunch and avoided the true purpose of their meeting until the food arrived. Small talk would do until they could discuss matters without interruptions. Miss Dow's friend had been a year older and helped the executive find her footing in college. Vincent asked questions about what was happening with the Poetry Society, Mrs. Trowbridge, Miss Gildersleeve and Dr. Williams. Neither mentioned where Vincent had lain her head the night before.

When the soup arrived, Vincent took the opportunity to start their next conversation with an apology.

"Before you read me the riot act, which I deserve, may I just say how sorry I am for causing you so much pain."

Miss Dow studied Vincent's face. She had become aware of the poet's ability to manipulate things to her advantage. She determined that the apology was sincere and chose to speak frankly but gently.

"You know, Edna, that I was a girl once," Miss Dow began. "Of course, that is just the sort of thing a person says when they are about to scold you."

They both laughed.

"This event, Edina's death, reminded me of how green I was when I first came to Bryn Mawr," she continued.

Vincent nodded.

"The fact is, I know how easy it is to get one's head turned. It's something I feared might happen and why I was disappointed when you were unable to go directly to Vassar."

"Yes, that may have made things smoother," Vincent agreed.

"But since that was impossible, I hoped being closer to me would give you the structure a girl such as yourself might need."

"But New York got in the way," Vincent smiled.

Miss Dow agreed. "Yes, New York did."

The matron paused.

"You see, there is so much you have yet to learn about the ways of the world, what people will say if given the slightest chance."

The poet nodded solemnly as their club sandwiches arrived.

"When those who can help you hear rumors, they naturally come to me, just as people in Camden report to your mother."

Vincent didn't want to tell her patron there was just as much gossip about her mother and sisters as there was about her. In fact, she was surprised Miss Dow hadn't heard it—unless she had and was discreet enough not to mention it. "Of course."

"So, the truth is, if I'm going to remain your advocate I must be assured, we must be assured, that there will be no more episodes like the one with Mr. …um…Vale."

For a moment Vincent was confused, then she realized Miss Dow's effort to be delicate. "I understand."

"Your grades, frankly, were not as strong as we would have hoped," the matron continued.

"Again, I truly apologize," the poet replied. She had gotten decent grades but had to admit they could have been better.

Miss Dow smiled but continued. "I suspect that it is partly my fault, taking you here and there when you should have been studying."

"Oh, but I learned so much," Vincent cried. "I had never dreamed I would see Sarah Bernhardt or had tea with Miss Teasdale, who is such a dear."

"You know how much I enjoy the Poetry Society meetings but not everyone is a suitable companion for an impressionable girl such as yourself."

"Yes, Miss Dow," the poet contritely replied.

They paused and ate their meal. Vincent looked at the shadows that crisscrossed through the room as the afternoon sun filtered through the windows. They looked like crucifixes of light. When they finished, Miss Dow continued, only now with a more upbeat tone. "You should know I have now managed to raise $1600 toward your first year at Vassar."

Vincent's heart leaped, but she wondered how much more could have been raised had she not been the subject of gossip.

Miss Dow anticipated her query. "Now I could have raised far more had you not spoiled your reputation."

"But…" Vincent protested.

"Please don't offer excuses, Edna. Excuses are the children of sloth."

"Yes, Miss Dow."

"I have assured your patrons that you are just a small-town girl overwhelmed by the bright lights and sinful ways of the big city."

"I'm so grateful for your support." Vincent hated the trite condescension but had to admit her patron was at least partially correct. The city had overwhelmed all her best laid plans to be a diligent scholar.

"You are welcome, Vincent dear," Miss Dow continued. "I have assured everybody that once at Vassar you will put your head down and study."

Vincent smiled. Now that Miss Dow was using "Vincent" instead of "Edna" she knew the harshest words had left her patron's lips.

"Now I know you're older than most freshman and most of the girls you'll meet at Vassar will come from much more sheltered families and communities," the matron added as she poured them both a second cup of tea.

"True," Vincent nodded. "Even the girls at Barnard have different backgrounds than mine." The poet then told a long story about a classmate, Ida Rolf, who was studying chemistry. Her example didn't impress Miss Dow, who was well-acquainted with that member of both the Y and Phi Beta Kappa.

"I am aware of Miss Rolf," Miss Dow chided. "She has some unconventional ideas of her own."

Vincent shrugged.

"In any case, if you do well this first year at Vassar there are people who will expand their generosity and others who will step forward with enough funds to hopefully allow you to be a part of the graduating class of 1917."

Something in those words stirred gratitude in Vincent's soul. She was reassured. She would graduate.[260] She hadn't lost her opportunity. Everything was going to be alright. A new round of pledges left her lips.

"I am so glad to hear this, child," Miss Dow smiled. "I'll make the arrangements for your tuition to be paid and send along a check for incidentals."

"Bless you, Aunt Caroline, bless you!"

"But be warned," Miss Dow cautioned. "If there is further foolishness, we may find ourselves up against it, and I am afraid you'll bear the brunt of that misfortune."

* * *

The following day Vincent was back at her Uncle Charlie's. All her pledges to Miss Dow somehow didn't hold sway in the presence of her aunt and uncle, who were appalled that she'd accept a box of chocolates from a boy who was engaged. Her friend Henry and the other Bristol boys were just too much for her mother's brother. "Perhaps you ought to be moving on to your Aunt Clem's," her Aunt Jennie recommended when she returned from a sing-along by the lake.

"I'll write," the vivacious young flirt replied.

"We already have. She's expecting you on the morning train," her uncle replied.

The poet blanched. What had she done that was so God awful? She had planned to spend a month with the uncle she was almost named for, but after three weeks she'd been called to New York for three nights. Now, just one day after her return, her aunt and uncle wanted her to leave again. It reminded her of all the times she'd been shunted around from relative to relative, then dropped at a friend's house, even a kindly friend like her dear Auntie Bine, as a child. She choked back tears. She didn't want to give either of them the satisfaction of knowing she was hurt. She should have just gone directly home.

The following morning, she took the four-hour train ride to Boston.[261] She amazed herself by making it across Boston, a town notorious for confounding travelers, to the ferry terminal all by herself. That afternoon the alluring ingenue was enjoying her Aunt Clem's much more relaxed company in Newburyport.

* * *

The poet would never forget the sight of the carefully drying herbs that lined the crown molding of Clem's fragrant kitchen. Pennyroyal for insect repellant. Tansy for killing lice. Chamomile for a restful sleep. Yarrow for an upset stomach. Boneset for a fever. Ointments and oils of all sorts lined the pantry.[262] Clem's herbal pharmacy ranged from facts to folklore, with many of her decoctions being more effective for their placebo effect than reality. This didn't matter to Vincent. All she knew was her Aunt Clem's remedies smelled like home and in that she found peace.

It had been several years since they'd spent time together. She'd only been a girl then. Now she was a young woman. Her aunt's amusement at Vincent's celebrity did not come into play when expressing her opinion of the unchaperoned poet's frequent forays in Clem's automobile. After a daylong loop from Newburyport to Gloucester to Beverly Farms and back, Vincent got an earful.[263]

"Who do you suppose is paying for the upkeep of the Magic Carpet?" Clem asked, referring to her car.

"I filled the tank," the poet protested.

"Yes, you did, and I thank you for that, but there's much more to it than just gasoline."

"I'm sorry." Vincent wasn't.

"Gallivanting around all over town…a hundred miles! Land's sake! Why you better not end up like Nell."

It took the redhead a moment to remember that the whole Buzzell clan called her mother Nell, not Cora. "Oh, I'll never end up like Mother."

"You best not." Clem was making beans and gestured with the ladle, sprinkling bean juice over the stove and her apron. Vincent tried not to giggle as the bean juice flew in every direction. "Your mother had a fine man in your father.[264] She just threw away a lifetime royalty of happiness, she did. And for what? When I think of what it has cost you girls it just makes my blood boil."

Clem stopped and studied Vincent. She realized her niece was not fully listening to the familiar lament. She took a deep breath and decided to try another tact. "Now I know you got that lovely poem published, and people are making a big fuss, but youth is wasted on the young. You must plan things out. Take them seriously. When you go to Vassar, you'd best put your head down and get to work. You don't want to end up like your mother raising three children on your own, even if you do manage to find a kind fellow like Henry."

"Is there anything I can do to help you with dinner?" Vincent asked, desperate for a change of subject.

Clem sighed. "No, dear, just set the table." As an afterthought she added, "By the way, your mother sent a letter. It's on the mantel."

* * *

The nudge from Cora was irresistible. It reminded Vincent of all the reasons she loved her mother. The letter reflected the tireless, disciplined and endlessly supportive parent that Cora displayed when they were ill or in trouble with convention. The poet prepared to leave for Camden immediately after supper.

The journey was long and exhausting. Each station became more familiar and yet it wasn't long before she wondered who she would find in her hometown. Thanks to Norma's steady paycheck from the telephone exchange and renewed child support from her father, the family was, for once, relatively stable. This allowed Cora to dedicate more time to her eldest and assured Vincent did the necessary preparations for life at Vassar. Cora was ready to be soothing because she was not struggling as much.

Vincent arrived in Camden the following day and walked to the family's rental home. As she walked the familiar streets, friendly and not so friendly faces greeted her. It seemed as if she knew everyone. Her clothes now reflected New York fashion, and as she moved through the town gazes of envy and appreciation greeted her along with the usual whispered gossip. By now, everyone in town knew she had gone to Barnard and raised a stir in New York. Some had heard rumors of an extramarital affair with Mitchell Kennerley—or some other older man no one knew but of whom they felt perfectly comfortable discussing without benefit of fact.

When she arrived at the Washington Street house her mother and Kathleen were waiting by the door, because word of her arrival had already reached them through the town network of gossip.

"Vince!" Kathleen cried, running to her and taking the overloaded suitcase from her hand before dropping it on the ground.

"Wump!" The poet threw her arms around her youngest sister and the two began to dance around.

Cora stepped into their circle with tears in her eyes. She kissed Vincent's cheeks repeatedly. "Why didn't you say you were coming on the morning train?"

"I wanted to surprise you," Vincent smiled, her own eyes moist with tears. "But it looks like it wasn't much of a surprise."

The phone inside the house was ringing. Kathleen dashed to answer it.

"Is she there yet?" Norma asked from the telephone company's switchboard.

"She just got here."

"Connecting you now," Norma said loudly, a sure sign her supervisor was hovering nearby.

Kathleen rushed back outside. "That was Hunk."

"Was?" Vincent asked.

"She had to hang up…"

"Mr. Wyant is very strict," Cora finished.

Vincent remembered Mr. Wyant from when he ran the hardware store in town. He was always certain someone was stealing from him and shadowed every customer that came in. Before long the local boys discovered that if they sent one of their numbers in to lead Wyant to the back of the store, anything at the front was fair game. She laughed at the memory. "When does Norma get home."

"About 5:30 usually," Kathleen replied.

"How is your aunt?" Cora asked.

"Fine. A little angry that I took the Magic Carpet out for a spin."

Cora was about to chastise her eldest when a neighbor appeared.

"So, what happened? Did you flunk out of Barnard?"

Cora bit her lip. She hated the gossip. Vincent hated it more.

"No. I did not. In fact, I got As and am going to Vassar in the fall."

"That's not what I heard," the stiffly starched biddy replied.

Cora stepped in. "Well, I don't know who you are talking with, because my Edna is going to Vassar. It is all arranged."

"Is it?" The neighbor sniffed jealously and turned on her heel.

"Oh, how I love Camden," Vincent said sarcastically.

"Never mind her, Vincent. Her daughter has to spend another year at high school being tutored by Principal Dwinal."

Kathleen hoisted Vincent's suitcase and performed a remarkably apt impression of the neighbor as she marched into the house. Cora and the poet began to laugh. "Let's go inside. The mice are better company."

After working hours most of Vincent's long-time friends and nearby relatives came over to see the college girl. Corinne Sawyer and Martha Knight marveled at Vincent's chic wardrobe. Norma and Kathleen modeled what they could fit into while the poet received her stream of visitors. Already the redhead was feeling a tickle in her throat, but this did not stop her from continuing to socialize. "Everybody gets a cold when they first get home," Corinne reminded her.

"Because one gets allergic to sourpuss neighbors," Kenneth joked.

"That must be it," Norma seconded her long-time beau. "Old Mrs. Coons has cooties!"

* * *

The poet's friends were not the only ones to notice Vincent's wardrobe. Cora had observed the outfits with a mixture of delight and fear. Her daughter was already carrying herself like she was above the local folks, and as a mother of three girls she was keenly aware of the underlying jealous tension in their impromptu fashion show. Such emotion could result in bitterness from all sides, particularly if Vincent didn't do well in school. She had to find a way to keep her eldest's feet on the ground.

Vincent had two months to prepare for life at Vassar. Cora knew this meant her daughter would have to spend the summer doing more than relaxing. She would have to keep up with her language studies, math, and write enough poetry to earn the extra cash the family needed. While some thought writing a poem was simply a matter of inspiration, Cora knew better. It required enough discipline to get past the ego and strip away all but the essentials. Vincent could be disciplined, but she was so brilliant that Cora worried she would become reliant on her ability to outshine most of her peers. At Vassar she would find girls just as brilliant, from well-to-do families with the means for private tutors. In Camden, Vincent was a star. In college, she'd be just another clever girl. Cora knew her daughter was capable of so much more. It was her job to make sure Vincent remained rigorously disciplined in her studies for the Vassar exams and the college itself.

By Wednesday June 25, 1913, whatever physical reserves the poet had were gone. She lay basking in the ministrations of her mother, younger sisters and the unrequited adoration of Martha Knight. Good thing, too. By afternoon, Cora had been called away to Rockland by Dr. Roland Nasgatt, the town's forty-year-old physician, leaving the poet to resist the urge to play with old friends. Vincent failed miserably in this discipline. Despite a relentless cough, she continued to accept visitors and invitations, including one from Norma to attend the community's Thursday Night Dance.[265]

In 1913, the tango was all the rage. Depending on who one spoke with, the dance was either an incredibly delicious bit of fun or a pathway straight to hell. Vincent, of course, loved it and all the other disreputable dances like the Turkey Trot and the Slit Skirt. All required the couple to press against each other and move erotically in sync across the dance floor with cheek, chest and hips seductively close. Unlike many New England towns, the tango had not yet been banned in Camden. Nonetheless, there were breathless whispers and aghast faces as the beautiful, blonde Norma clutched the fresh-faced redhead as they moved across the floor. The nature of the tantalizing tango steps was made even more scandalous by the unseasonably warm weather. It was a miracle Norma did not catch Vincent's cold. Eventually they sat down with Kenneth, who did not know the steps and chatted amiably despite Vincent's miserable cough. It was as if the whole town was being exposed to what a mere nine months in New York would do to a girl. Local parents took note.

After a while, a town boy dared ask the poet to join him on the dance floor. She had watched the set up among his friends from the corner of her eye. Hushed whispers, stares, pointing fingers and finally the selection of Avery Singleton to be the victim. Since everyone knew Kenneth was dating Norma, the obvious choice for their experiment was Vincent, who sat waiting like a spider for her prey.

The lanky lad two years her junior approached. "Miss Millay, my name is Avery Singleton. May I please have the next dance?"

"Avery, you know I'm with Kenneth," Norma teased.

Flummoxed the dark-haired scion of the woolen mill foreman flushed bright pink. "I mean Miss Edna."

"Of course, you did," Vincent said. "You must not tease the *boy*, Norma." The emphasis was not missed as she stood up. Her hair was at the level of his shirt buttons. "My, you're tall."

"Yes, miss," Avery smiled and took her hand. They approached the center of the dance floor closer to Avery's friends. Although the music being played was not a tango, Avery attempted to thrust his knee between Vincent's legs after a quick nod from his pals. Vincent was having none of it.

"Mr. Singleton, this is *not* a tango," she cried in feigned horror.

Avery blushed even brighter, loosening his grip and stepping back. The pair performed a perfectly passable Turkey Trot. By now, Vincent was smiling as it was unlikely a boy from Camden would know the latest dances, let alone be able to dance as well as her sister. Avery's friends were beginning to whoop with delight when suddenly his father stormed toward the boy. "We'll have none of that!" he cried, just as his son and the poet were putting their backsides out and dipping.

"But Father!"

"No buts, son. I'll not have you making fools of us by dancing with that Millay girl."

Vincent shook her head then smiled wickedly at the man. "Are you cutting in?"

"Certainly not!" the red-faced foreman bellowed as he led his son from the floor.

Watching it all were Norma and Kenneth, who were laughing themselves sore at the sight. Kenneth jumped to his feet and stepped through the dancers to join Vincent who was dancing a solo after the loss of her partner. While not as skilled as Avery, he was willing and fun, not to mention he saved the poet from humiliation. As the music stopped a few seconds later, Vincent coughed and suggested they all head home. Norma agreed and the trio left to the bemused stares of their peers.

* * *

Lying in bed that night, Vincent couldn't help but let her mind wander to the reaction of Mr. Singleton. It wasn't that she minded so much. Some so-called proper folks had avoided her family her whole life. Sure, they all had friends. They made it through high school, attended church and shopped in the same stores. But they had always been viewed as odd. It struck the poet that the people of New York wouldn't care much that her parents were divorced. They would just think it was something to do with her being an artist. Creative types were tolerated in New York. Mostly, anyway. She had run-ins with Miss Dow and school provosts, but people in New York didn't stare and point as if she had a wart on the end of her nose.

She blew her nose and laughed. *I think I must be allergic to Camden.* There was no one to contest this theory. Vincent realized that the things that were charming about Camden were just as delightful in Mamaroneck without all the askance looks. The only thing missing in the latter seaside town was her sisters. They had so much fun at the dance despite the whispered gossip and Mr. Singleton's outburst. Kenneth was fun, too, for a local boy. Norma's beau was going to bring a basket of delights the following morning so the three of them could sit out the storm and nurse Vincent's cold, so she'd be well enough for the Sunday School picnic on Saturday, June 28.

She didn't want to miss seeing Abbie, Ethel and the rest of the old crowd. Maybe they could convince her that Camden was truly home.[266]

But, of course, this is home, Vincent sniffed. *Mumbles is here, Hunkus is here. Even Wumptywoons. My sisters and my mother are my home, I think.* She pulled the covers up under her chin. It was so confusing. When she was in New York she wanted her Mama. When she was home, she wanted New York and all the people who really understood poetry and language and the theater. Cora was more sophisticated than most of their neighbors, but she hadn't traveled. Theirs was the best library in town, but it paled beside the New York Public Library. She thought of her tiny mother's warm embrace and how they all giggled at certain adventures she recounted. It was thrilling to share all her exploits with them, and yet she resented having to explain so much. The same was true when she told stories to her dearest Camden friends. If she was going to be a success, she had to be around people who knew more than she did, not less.

The clock struck two. She closed her eyes against the three-quarter moonlight. Tomorrow was approaching like a comet.

19. The Compassion That Was I

1913

July arrived and Vincent celebrated her independence with a trip to Lake Megunticook. After a month of being the third wheel beside Norma and Kenneth, the poet at last had Fritz Boehler as an escort.[267]

As the foursome paddled atop the still water, she found herself wishing Fritz could dance as well as he rowed. The attentions of the Cornell University student was tainted by jealousy. If Kenneth talked about some trout he caught, Fritz's catch had to be bigger. If Norma liked a motion picture, he had to like it more. Yet Vincent didn't care enough to forego his courtship. It gave her a much better excuse to avoid studying for Vassar's rigorous entrance exams.

The poet's ambivalence concerned her mother much more than it did her. If she failed again, there was little chance Miss Dow would risk her reputation further. Was Vincent serious about school? Cora wondered. Her daughter did seem to be enjoying the process, but only in the abstract. Didn't she realize how it would change her life? Didn't she see how she was spoiling Kathleen's chances of also being championed? Cora didn't worry about Norma. Her middle child would make do. The blonde was as determined as she was gregarious. But Vincent—with her wavering discipline and touchy moods—made it difficult for Cora to know how to express her concerns when she returned from Rockland the following day.

It had been Kathleen who brought Vincent's scholastic neglect to Cora's attention. Being caught between the children was something the nurse dreaded. Yet she knew her youngest had a point. The ripple effect on the family would be a tsunami. Kathleen spoke of nightly parties, male visitors, a messy house and Norma's influence. There were card games, afternoon picnics, alcohol and running each other ragged. "I want to be a good sport, Mama. Honest, I do. But Vincent's just selfish."

Cora looked at her youngest. Kathleen had nearly died of typhoid when they were children. She still walked with a limp. She was dark and had the look of someone concerned that each breath would be her last. "I'm sure Vincent is just blowing off steam after all her hard work in New York. She'll settle down."

Both knew this was just an excuse.

"But..."

"Hush now, baby," Cora said, taking her hand. "You sister will do what's right. She loves you and Norma so much. She's always put you first when I'm gone. Maybe she just thinks she neglected Norma and you and wants to make up for lost time."

"That's just it. She never has time for me. She's always off with Norma and Kenneth and Fritz Boehler."

Cora blanched at the mention of the Boehler boy. He was not the sort of man Cora wanted for Vincent. "Tell you what," the nurse replied, "Mrs. Norton is on the mend. Perhaps I can ask Dr. Gordon if it's all right for me to take a few days off."

Kathleen smiled. She had gotten her way. "Please don't tell her I said anything."

"Of course not. You did right by bringing this to my attention."

* * *

"Hunk! Wake up!"

"What?"

"Mumbles is coming home."

"Oh dear." The pretty blonde turned over in bed. Kenneth's jacket was draped over a chair. Vincent silently wondered if he had spent the night. Norma stretched and turned over in bed. "Vince?"

"Yes?"

"When will she get here?"

"She called this morning. She said she'd be here in time for supper."

"Oh, my!" Norma stretched and turned back over. She glanced at Kenneth's jacket. She caught her elder sister's knowing smirk.

"He went home at four."

"I didn't say a thing."

"You didn't have to," Norma yawned. "He must have been freezing."

"Warmed by thoughts of love," her elder sister teased.

Norma ignored her and stepped out of bed before heading to the lavatory. Vincent dashed downstairs. "I'll start the coffee," she called as her bare feet flew down the steps. She knew she'd have to clean from garret to cellar before her mother made it home.[268] With Kathleen gone for the night she knew it would be a major task for just the two of them, especially since Norma was prone to dawdling.

Kenneth called and volunteered to mow the overgrown lawn while the sisters cleaned the house. The flurry of activity must have startled the neighbors. The poet imagined them laughing. They hadn't washed dishes or swept the floor in days.[269] The skittering cockroaches and lazy gnats would have to be discouraged from appearing too numerous. The canned goods in the cellar would have to be organized to put the older jars in front. Carpets draped over the clothesline were beaten until they practically gleamed. Norma cleaned the bathroom in exchange for avoiding the mess in the kitchen. By the time three p.m. came around, there was still more to be done, but Vincent knew she'd have to start the beans that had been soaking for two days and prepare dough for soda bread. As Kenneth kneaded and Norma picked rejects from the soaking legumes, Vincent raced upstairs and quickly bathed. Everything had to look like their mother had left it.

In the brief moment she allowed herself to relax in the tub, the poet realized how much she missed her hardworking mother—and that she would never be that sort of woman. When it came to housekeeping, she would rather live in a mess than miss a dance or an inspiration. After a quick scrub, she dressed and dashed downstairs just as Norma was lifting the tureen onto the stove. The bread lay where Kenneth had left it and was rising in the pan.

"Go on, clean up. I'll finish the beans," Vincent said, brushing a damp strand of copper red hair from her cheek.

"Have you cleaned your room?" Norma asked as she started up the stairs.

"Yes. I did that first thing. You better clean yours…and give Kenneth his jacket."

"I'm not doing Kathleen's side," Norma stated flatly.

"Your side is a bigger mess," her elder sister noted. "It's spilled over to Kathleen's side."

"Oh, all right," Norma huffed and began her ascent.

Vincent dropped onions and selected spices into the beans, she realized she'd have to set the stage very carefully for her mother's arrival. She plotted the setting she would create to appear more disciplined than she was. The smell of the beans as they simmered spread throughout the house. Soon it would be time to put the bread into the oven. Perhaps she could lay out her test exams or some books to illustrate a commitment to preparing for Vassar. What about hanging some fresh cut herbs or putting some on the counter near the ubiquitous pot of beans? As the poet prepared the plebian meal, she imagined Cora's homecoming. Perhaps some cut flowers from Cora's cherished garden could be placed on the table. Kenneth was looking for something to do. Her mother's arrival would be like so many others through the years, starting with a joyful and heartfelt reunion and ending with a lecture about doing more and doing better. Upstairs, Norma's voice could be heard singing, its dulcet tones filtering through the grate above the stove. Vincent smiled. Hunk had a lovely voice, the best of them all. It would be another piece of the staging should their mother arrive at that moment.

An hour later, the bread was in the oven, the beans on their way to being done and a bouquet of summer flowers was propped inside her mother's favorite vase on the dining room table. The middle and eldest children were busy darning and studying respectively when Cora and Kathleen arrived home hungry and disheveled from a day of travel.

"Mother!" Vincent cried, standing up and pointedly setting *Principles of Economics* aside.

"Mama! Kay!" Norma said, gleefully setting aside her dreary task.

Mother and daughters embraced.

"Something smells wonderful," Cora said, pretending the familiar scents were some gourmet meal. "I'm famished."

"Me, too," Kathleen said as she helped her mother remove her coat.

"Have you girls eaten yet?" the nurse asked.

"We were waiting for you," Vincent smiled. "That way we could all have supper together."

The feelings were more than sincere in that moment. Every time Vincent saw her mother something like relief caught in the poet's throat. The threat of death or abandonment had been a constant since childhood. Seeing Cora's prematurely aged face above her wilted uniform filled the poet with grateful admiration.

Cora started for the kitchen. "No, Mama, you're tired. You just sit at the table. It's already set. You too, Kathleen. Hunk and I will serve you."

Over dinner the conversation sparkled with gossip and laughter. Cora told of her client's illness, secure at the discretion of her daughters, while Norma spoke of almost nothing but Kenneth. Vincent explained that Fritz was in town for the summer holiday but would be heading west for Cornell the following month. Of course, she still referred to him as "Mr. Boehler" when speaking to her mother as the poet was keenly aware of how anything more familiar would be interpreted. Kathleen showed off a new outfit she had purchased in Rockland and recited a poem she was working on. The meal was as tasty as poverty allowed.

When they finished, Cora joined her daughters in cleaning up before they settled in the parlor to pursue whatever amused them. The ticking clock marked the time. An hour, then two, passed with nothing more than idle chatter. At eleven p.m., Cora announced they should retire.

Vincent shrugged. She was already twenty-one, Norma nearly twenty, and Kathleen, the baby of the family, had just turned eighteen. To be told when they would go to bed seemed a little much after months of dictating her own schedule, yet they all obeyed like automatons. Watching Norma and Kathleen leave to go upstairs, Vincent noticed her mother seemed to linger as if willing her eldest child to lag behind. *Here it comes*, Vincent thought. *I'm to be admonished for some infraction or another.* Still hoping to avoid the customary rebuke, the poet put a foot on the first step of the staircase.

"Vincent?"

"Yes, Mother."

"I'd like a moment alone before we go upstairs."

Vincent lifted her foot from the first step and set it back down on the main floor. She returned to her seat and sat down; her body resigned to what would come next.

Cora took Norma's chair, which was closer to the poet. From where she sat, she saw Vincent's evening study was no more than a volume of Edith Wharton's latest, *The Custom of the Country*. It struck the nurse as an appropriate volume given the message she hoped to deliver to her sullen eldest daughter.

"How have you been since I've been gone?" Cora asked by way of introduction.

"As you'll recall I had a dreadful cold last week..." Vincent clasped her hands in front of herself to reduce the urge to scream.

"But you're better now?" Cora absently reached for the knitting she'd been occupied with.

"Yes, just a little tired," the poet hinted.

"What I have to say shouldn't take but a minute." Cora set the knitting down again and reached for Vincent's hand.

"Yes, Mother." The source of the poet's exhaustion was clear.

"People in Camden talk."

"People talk everywhere," Vincent blurted.

Cora frowned. There was a new independence in her daughter that made their talks increasingly problematic. "Yes, they do. But what concerns me is what I hear from our own neighbors."

"Oh, Mama, our neighbors are just a bunch of busybodies with nothing better to do. Why do you let them worry you so?"

"Perhaps because I know what might happen should Miss Dow hear of your escapades all over the county with Fritz Boehler, a boy who is engaged, or dancing the tango with your sister and Mr. Singleton's son."

"It's just harmless fun," Vincent sighed.

"Perhaps, but what about that Englishman you wrote us about. The one who writes you all those letters. Are you going to marry that Englishman?"

"No. It's all off and it's all over."[270] The thought of having to explain Arthur Hooley to her mother was beyond her temper at that moment.

"And what of your examinations? You've hardly cracked a textbook since I left," her mother continued.

"Yes, I have," the poet replied.

"A novel, Vincent. A novel. Not a serious book. You may have *Principles of Economics* beside you, but I would imagine you've barely opened it since you returned home. There's more French, Latin, History and whatever else you've neglected. What will happen if you fail this time?"

"Miss Bannon says I can come to Smith anytime I like."

"You'll need to pass the Smith examination as well..." Cora countered.

"No. Miss Bannon says I have a full scholarship waiting anytime I want to use it." While true in theory, the poet's hubris troubled her mother.

"And what of Vassar? What about Miss Dow? Do you realize what that would mean to a woman who has fought for you and been so kind and..." Cora began to cry, weakened by exhaustion from a long day rehearsing this conversation in her mind.

"Miss Dow will understand."

"And will Miss Bannon promise Kathleen a scholarship?"

Vincent felt like a butterfly who had recently escaped her cocoon only to be pinned for a collector's shadow box.

Cora seized the moment.

"I understand, child, really, I do. I was young once too. Yet you have a duty to others, if not yourself."

"Yes, Mama," Vincent could feel her own tears welling up as Cora's dried.

"Study. Give Kathleen some pointers. You need to spend more time with her, so she'll be ready when her time comes."

It suddenly dawned on Vincent who the "neighbor" was. Her younger sister's frequent visits to Rockland were now explained. The poet bit her tongue. Now was not the time to get into a fight with her mother. "Yes, Mama."

"Of course, enjoy your time off. Vassar will be exceedingly hard at first, so you'll need to be rested enough to discipline yourself to the task at hand," Cora continued, temporarily repositioning the pins that held her daughter down. "Yet you must study. You must be prepared. You can't count on 'Renascence' to do it all for you."

Vincent felt her throat constrict as tears began to fall past her eyelids. She wanted to shriek, to yowl like a tethered beast. She had published half a dozen poems since *The Lyric Year*. She called Sara Teasdale, Jessie Rittenhouse, Witter Bynner and Arthur Davison Ficke friends. She was close to publishers, playwrights and world-class musicians. Who was her mother? Just a country bumpkin with a little talent, and dreams that she used to pin down her children as if they were specimens she could glory in. She dared not say any of this. She hated herself for even thinking those thoughts. Cora had sacrificed so much; she'd gone without so they could have piano lessons and a library that was the envy of even the richest and most educated people in Camden. There was no room for her anger at that moment. All she could do was cry. Cora took her expression as a cue to embrace what she thought was a penitent child. Cora had no idea what her daughter's actual feelings were, and, truth be told, neither did Vincent. All the poet could feel as she accepted her mother's warm embrace was how much she had missed her. As emotions caromed through the spectrum of rage and love, she began to see that hers were not the feelings of a twenty-one-year-old. They were the heartsick yearning of a small child asked to provide more than she knew how to give, a nine-year-old girl seeing her mother for the first time in weeks. Her sobs were filled with loneliness and the frustration of abandonment.

20. Ah, Awful Weight

1913

By the following week, guilt and duty were again her masters. After a letter from Vassar Dean Ella McCaleb, Vincent had buckled down to all the tiresome little duties she'd been putting off for ages. She wrote reassuring letters to Miss Dow, studied for her exams, and worked on some poems in hopes of earning the rent her mother needed.[271] Meanwhile, other family demands resulted in Kathleen becoming a fifth wheel in her adventures with Fritz, Norma and Kenneth. Her little sister went almost everywhere they went, including picnics, canoeing, motion pictures and stealing cherries from a neighbor's tree.

From almost the moment her mother left on a new assignment, Vincent began to explore disobedience—only now with an eye for Kathleen's penchant for tattling. Yes, she studied her geography, American history and Latin, but she couldn't let a summer of fun go entirely by.

Childhood meant long winters and brief summers. Weather was a constant, for it dictated everything. Summer meant gathering berries and fruits for canning and devouring. Spring meant flowers and rain. Autumn's colors were legendary. Winter was for bitter cold and skating on the face of nearby ponds and lakes. As Vincent matured, she began to consider just how her life had been directed by the mandatory activities of the seasons. That summer of 1913 was no different. Only this year carried an awareness of the briefness of her time for enjoyment and the limits the weight of duty placed upon her.

The poet also noticed how much she was counting on Vassar for escape before the full weight of winter's demands were upon her. Poems came to her frequently now, and while some would take months and even years to complete, she knew she would not have any other profession. Acting was fun, but there were elements of it that reminded her of the requirements of her family. While she and Norma would write and perform witty scenes for their friends, that was the limit of their collaboration. Music was a pleasure almost akin to sex but required being someone else's voice. With poetry, she could indulge her need for solitude and quiet. Poetry carried both the pleasure of creation and spiritual satisfaction. True passion came with entering that place where words tumbled out, where a turn of phrase was ferreted from the senses, where sunlight and rain had a dozen meanings.

The peculiar pattern of the local weather brought rain in the midst of a sunny day. Outdoor pleasures were often thwarted by sudden downpours, but the poet had learned to take them in stride. Fritz, Henry, and other suitors competed with old friends like Hazel and Martha for the opportunity to lay in a hammock giggling until the moon was high.[272] Soon she would be saddled with compulsory study and rules that were positively mid-Victorian. Summers were made for fun regardless of humid drizzles and stiff sails in Penobscot Bay.

Her relationship with Fritz Boehler was inconsistent in nature. That is, it was neither here nor there. He loved to sail but could not dance.[273] He wanted her but was honor bound. Looking into his gray eyes aboard *The Comfort* bound for Great Spruce Head Island, she realized that he, like the twenty-nine others in their party, was haunted by the specter of conformity.[274]

This awareness evinced itself in her changing relationship with Norma. Her sister was evidence of what would happen should Vincent not pass her entrance exams. Norma was working at the Whitehall Inn again, the very place that had brought the poet to the attention of Miss Dow and, by extension, Vassar. If she didn't study, they both would end up accepting meager tips from wealthy tourists.

Conformity had never been Vincent's strong suit. In fact, she took pride in being thought special. On the other hand, assent was the only way she could escape the rigid confines of her hometown. Consequently, when Norma brought her a letter from Vassar while studying, the poet couldn't help but feel gaslit.

"Damn!" the poet shouted just as Norma exited the room. Vincent threw the geometry book she had borrowed from Fritz across the room. It smacked against the mantle and dislodged a small porcelain dog which fell with a crash even the neighbors could hear. "Damn!" she cried again and began to cry.

From the other room, Norma debated whether to go to help her elder sister. The letter obviously contained bad news, but what? She knew nothing about geometry. She considered herself lucky to understand what little math she managed in high school. Vincent's tears made the decision for her. She poked her head through the kitchen door.

Vincent looked up. "Read this!" She thrust the crumpled letter at her sister. "Am I reading this right?"

Before Norma could even reach for the paper, Vincent screamed, "I'll never go to college."

"What happened, darling?" Norma asked. Her awareness of Vincent's struggle with conformity combined with the knowledge of how much the whole family was counting on Vincent to transform their fortunes. She took the paper from the poet's hands and read. Norma couldn't believe her eyes. "What? Does this mean the whole time at Barnard was pointless?"

"That's *exactly* what it means."

"But that isn't fair. You passed your courses and..."

"That doesn't matter," Vincent sniffed. "As a 'non-matriculating student,' whatever that means, all that work is moot. Vassar won't even accept the credits. I must do a complete exam. It's like starting from square one."

"Now, now, I'm sure Miss Dow can fix it," the blonde cooed.

"That's just it. She can't. According to this Barnard was supposed to prepare me for certain parts of the Vassar exam, not substitute for them."

Norma knew what this meant. She wondered if the Whitehall Inn would give Vincent a job. Their mother would be miserable. Kathleen would be furious.

"In fact, Dean McCaleb even says the entrance examination will present a larger problem than usual.[275] I'll have to master a third language, work up my Latin prose, study ancient history and do more math. And what's strange is she says I might be able to get by with American history and Latin."

"Wait a minute, American history instead of ancient history?" Norma's mind raced. It made sense that Latin would be a third language: English, French and Latin. But history? They had both had done well enough in high school to pass both world and American history. The blonde couldn't help with anything at a college level. Yet she couldn't imagine her brilliant sister failing at anything.

"And listen to this, I simply don't believe it." Vincent began to sob.

"What?"

"In my last letter to Dean McCaleb I sort of, you know, begged off, hoping she'd let me in on the basis of my grades at Barnard. I told her I was distressed by everything in the sample examination, and, instead of having at least some pity for my situation, she says..." She waved her hand toward Norma who returned the letter. Vincent's hands shook as she scanned the letter for the right place. Her chin trembled. "She says, 'If you are really so desperate and ill-prepared as your letter suggests, then perhaps you have no right to try for Vassar this year.'"[276]

The poet took a deep breath before continuing. "'...the disappointment of those who are interested in you would be nothing compared with the possibility of your attempting too much. No one wishes you endanger either your health or your best development, but this is only a college,'" Vincent let out a wail. "*Only* a college!"

"But doesn't it say something like everybody has to play by the same rules?"

Vincent folded her arms down on the desk and began to shake with fury. Finally, she lifted her head up and glared at her sister.

"Vassar isn't just a college to me. It's my only ticket out of here."

Norma was taken aback. She thought her sister liked Camden and all the fun they'd been having. Why the summer had been filled with adventures, and Vincent certainly had her share of beaux. "Camden's alright."

Vincent realized she'd said too much. The look on Norma's face broke her heart. "Of course, it is, Hunk. I got you and Mumbles and Wumps and all the rest of the gang. I'm just frustrated. That's all."

The poet stood up and the sisters raced into each other's arms. Both were crying now. The idea of separation hit Norma hard, but she knew it was necessary if they were ever to rise out of consistent poverty.

Norma hoped to brighten the gloom that had settled over them "Didn't she close the letter by saying she'd be willing to help? Write her back and ask for help. Do whatever you have to. Tell her you'll do whatever it takes. I'll help in any way I can, Vince. I promise."

"Thanks, Hunk, and I'm sorry for being such a baby." The poet's apology was sincere in intent if not in fact. She didn't think she was acting like a baby at all, but as the eldest Vincent knew it was her job to be the "boy" and complain as little as her sensitivities allowed.

Norma went to a shelf and found a book. "Here's a copy of *Common Sense*," she explained. "Even I understand it. And I think Mama as a copy of the Constitution and Benjamin Franklin's autobiography."

"Bless you," the poet cried, taking Thomas Paine's skinny volume in her hands. Now her tears reflected the love she felt for her sister. "Dear Hunk!"

* * *

The summer of 1913 continued with the partially chastised poet doing more study and less dancing. The lifeline Dean Ella McCaleb had offered proved invaluable. It allowed Vincent to use her wit and wiles to capture the professor's sympathy. Soon letters greeting her as "dear child" arrived with subtle hints of topics and areas the poet should concentrate on.[277]

As for Fritz, Kenneth, Norma and the rest of Vincent's gang, all made sure she didn't study too much. There was swimming, motion pictures at the Comique Theatre, and poker games that lasted well into the night. Curious friends who had heard tales of her fabulous new wardrobe stopped in.[278]

August reminded Fritz he had to go back to college. He knew by now that Vincent was not willing to take to the saddle of married life. At times when he looked at her, she almost seemed small enough to be a child. Yet whether reciting verse or learning to swim the crawl, Vincent was what she had always been. The mystery of her remained intact. Like most boys he found the fun-loving Millay girls a nice change from the staid society types that populated Camden in the summer. He was smitten with the redhead from the wrong side of the tracks.

He would always remember that August, especially one night when she summoned him to her bedside.

It was as if she were playing Camille. Her garret was festooned with Chinese lanterns and candles. Her red kimono matched her red blanket. Her red hair was down, flowing over her shoulders like a princess in a fairytale. He couldn't take his eyes off her.

"Oh, Fritz," she coughed, then extended her hand dramatically.

"How are you feeling, Vincent?" he asked, taking the chair from the desk and placing it beside her bed. He liked her in red. The fading light blended all the colors until the room seemed ablaze with unrequited desire.

"I suspect too much play, and not enough work has made Vince a very sick boy," she teased.

Fritz laughed. He settled his gaze on her bare neck. "You should cover your neck and chest."

"I thought you'd like to see them." Vincent drank the tepid tea Norma had brought up before his arrival.

Fritz grew uncomfortable. She was so forward. He wasn't sure how to respond. His father had warned him about gold diggers and cautioned against succumbing to his youthful urges. "Well, of course, you do have a most wonderful throat."

"Which will someday be strangled,"[279] she interjected with a grin.

He laughed again. His gray suit matched his eyes perfectly. Vincent wished he would take it off and keep her warm in bed. They stared at each other for a long time.

"How are your studies going?" he asked, deflecting her flirtation.

"I'm working on algebra now. I hate it, but I hate geometry more."[280]

He smiled. "I really like geometry."

"Good God, why?"

"You can use it for all sorts of things," he explained, using his hands to delineate an example. "For instance, if you want to determine the distance between here…and here," he tapped his toe and looked down, "to here…and then to there," he nodded toward the desk.

"Why not just get up and use a ruler?" the poet challenged in jest.

"You know what I mean."

"Of course," she giggled.

He realized it was hopeless. He wasn't there for a lesson. He had to change the subject. "How's Latin coming?"

"I'm getting some help from Professor Haight," she replied. "Dean McCaleb has been referring people to me. I'm getting all sorts of help in preparing for the exams."[281]

"That's nice of her. What else do you have to master?" Fritz adjusted himself in the chair.

"American history… But if I can't vote, what do I care about American history?[282] Besides all I know about the history of this country is one verse of 'The Star-Spangled Banner'." She draped her hand over her throat and pretended to sing.

Fritz laughed. Vincent eyed him seductively. He knew he would have to leave by the expression on her face. "Really, Vince, you should rest instead of yakking with me. You'll never get over that cold if you don't."

"I've been resting all day." Her eyes danced. "Kiss me."

The lad was shocked. It wasn't as though they had never kissed. They had done that and a lot more. But here in her bedroom, festooned with candles and draped in Chinese red silk? He could scarcely believe his ears. "I'd catch your cold."

The look she gave him left her next remark moot. "I can't think of a nicer way to share it."

Fritz did not want to be caught in such a position. "I must get home. Dad needs me to help him with the automobile early tomorrow."

"Have it your way," she pouted. She hoped her quick acquiescence would entice him to stay a while longer.

If he had waivered, the sound of Kathleen's feet on the stairs would have settled the matter.

"You need more tea, Vince?" she called through the closed door.

The poet put her index finger to her lips. "No, dear. I'm going to bed."

"Alright. Goodnight," Kathleen called.

The couple waited for her steps to recede.

"I better go."

"I suppose so."

"Tomorrow?"

"No. I have to study, besides…my cold."

Fritz stood up and moved the chair back to the desk. "Goodnight."

"May flights of angels guide thee to thy rest," Vincent giggled as she listened to her suitor's retreat.

* * *

Vincent did indeed stay in bed studying. She had to admit she felt lousy. There was no means of avoiding the drudgery of math, so she simply went with it, occasionally stopping to ask the birds for their opinions.

It was a lazy summer day. The sun streamed through the window and across her bed making dappled shadows courtesy of the large elm outside. With their mother gone, her sisters took the opportunity to go swimming. The poet didn't mind. It gave her the chance to formulate answers, and sleep in peace and comfort.

As the day stretched on, the poet switched to reading *Common Sense* in hopes some American history would sink in. Dean McCaleb had continued to send suggestions of what to study—most of which she found incredibly dull. At least Paine's book was a scant forty-seven pages long. She found his arguments for an egalitarian government compelling, particularly in light of her suffragist sensibilities. She wondered if noting that in an answer essay would be well-accepted. Given Vassar's status as a women's college she thought it should be. It read like a sermon. She liked that Paine thought an honest man was worth more than the "crowned ruffians."[283] It was like all those people who thought themselves better than her mother, when at least Cora was an honest, hardworking woman.

An incongruous thought dashed through her mind. She did not love Fritz Boehler. Yes, he was attractive. He was as smart as the local boys. But he was not sophisticated. He was so busy blending in with the ordinary mores of rural Maine that he had no foresight beyond the tip of his nose.

She read on, hoping some of Paine's polemics would sink in. Her eyelids began to droop and before she knew it, she was waking up to the sound of Norma racing up the stairs. By now the shadows had lengthened. She calculated it might be around three o'clock.

"Hi!" her middle sister stepped into the room without knocking. The room was stuffy. "You need some fresh air." Without asking, Norma opened the window and let in a gentle breeze. "That's better."

"Thanks," Vincent croaked. Her eyes blinked against the remaining light. Her mouth felt pasty. She took a deep breath through it and reached for a soiled handkerchief. "What time is it?"

"About three-twenty. How long have you been asleep?"

"I don't know." The poet yawned. "I suppose a couple of hours."

"Best thing for you," Norma replied in a tone that Vincent recognized as their mother's.

"Is there anything to eat?"

"There are some greens, bread and a bit of cheese left."

"Too bad there's no wine," Vincent quipped, returning to her cherished *Rubaiyat of Omar Khayyam*.

"Want me to get you some?"

"I suppose I ought to come down and make supper anyway," Vincent replied, slipping on the same red kimono from the night before. "Would you start some tea for us? I'll be down in a minute."

There was something of duty in her voice, a responsibility to be the primary household manager in Cora's absence. It also gave her an excuse to quit studying. The dinner she prepared was a simple stew made using the cheapest of salted meats and a few vegetables from their garden and some plantain for the benefit of Vincent's deep, raspy cough. It was one of the many herbal remedies the poet had committed to memory under her mother's tutelage.

* * *

The following day, Norma and Kenneth appeared with a handsome young man named Joseph Neil.[284] While the poet immediately took a liking to Joe, she was almost upset that her sister would interrupt her studies with such a tantalizing prospect. "Men are such a bother," she whispered to her sister as Norma's beau and Joe left the room. "It's got to stop."

"I thought it would perk you up," Norma teased.

"Well, yes, Mr. Neil is simply delicious, but I can't get distracted. I've got to get better, and I may as well study so long as I'm sick."

"Suit yourself."

The sisters parted, but not before the seed Norma had planted took root. Why should she limit herself to Fritz? Vincent resolved to take her erstwhile suitor aside at the next opportunity.

It wasn't long before Joe Neil was her escort to parties and picnics. The poet lamented that Fritz was so dreadfully cut up about it. She didn't enjoy hurting people.[285] The look on Fritz's face when she told him he couldn't come up anymore stuck with her like a penny nail in the sole of a boot. Still, Joe was willing while Fritz was not. He could dance and he had a sense of fun. The only problem was Norma took her advice by breaking up with Kenneth for the umpteenth time.

Vincent wasn't used to sharing men with her sisters. They had their suitors. She had hers. Now the poet had to study, Norma was available, and Joe liked them both. Most of the sibling rivalry was met with humor. Other parts were met with a passive-aggressive form of double dating. When she wasn't studying, she'd invite Fritz to join them and mercilessly flirt with them both. Her friend Hazel could hardly believe she had the gall, but Vincent only shrugged and said, "Yes, I did." The scandal sent tongues wagging as far away as Searsport and Rockland, where their mother got wind of the menage. More scolding followed, assuaged somewhat by how much studying the poet was finally doing. Once again, Kathleen was called upon to act as a spy. This worked to turn Joe's head more toward Norma.

On the warm, dim evening of August 21, Vincent, Fritz, Norma, Joe and Kathleen paddled across Sherman's Cove to the rocky shores of Sherman's Point.[286] The location was at the end of a long spit that created the southeastern edge of a crescent-shaped cove. The trees caressed the water and, although the moon was waning, there was still plenty of light to enjoy their lengthening shadows in the water near Northeast Point. Scarcely populated, the spot was a perfect location for a late al fresco supper. The boys built the fire while the girls made coffee and set Joe's lobster traps. Their wee boat had enough provisions for quite a feast. Aside from the coffee, the group brought fresh greens, potatoes and corn which they cooked in the husk amid the coals. The fishing poles were shared, and it didn't take long to know what they would have as their first course.

"You got him!" Norma cried as Fritz scrambled over the rocks to play his catch. Once in a more stable location, he easily hauled in a large flounder.

"I've got potatoes ready for the coals," Kathleen added. It reminded her of all those years they struggled as children. She had to admit: the scavenging and stealing were still at play even now when they had all had jobs. Vincent felt it too, only she was too caught up in watching Fritz land the fish. Joe kept one eye on his traps, another on the girls who danced around the fire like a coven. With the potatoes and corn cooking in the glowing embers, it was likely the meal would be eaten in stages. *No matter*, Joe thought. The narrow, rocky strip of land had long been a spot where lovers would snuggle by the fire and smooch. Joe looked at Kathleen, who was poking the coals, repositioning the vegetables. Why did they all have to be so darned attractive?

"Oh, my!" Vincent called out as Fritz proudly held the flounder aloft. "Well need more than that."

Norma took the fish from his hands as he removed the hook. "This is plenty."

"We might have lobster in a minute," Joe called.

"I don't suppose anyone remembered butter," Kathleen giggled.

"No, but there's salt and pepper in my bag."

The hours passed with stories and discreet "walks" along the shore, though proximity kept things from going too far. They sang, recited poetry and shared dreams. Vincent was struck by how beautiful Kathleen's recent poems were and told her so.

"You're not the only poet in the family," she replied with a good-natured grin.

"I suppose you both inherited that talent," Fritz said thoughtfully. "After all, your mother writes poetry, too."

"Does your father?" Joe broached delicately. He'd heard many stories about the Millay girls and wasn't sure it was appropriate to bring up their patronage.

"He sings," Vincent said proudly. "He has the most beautiful voice and a wonderful sense of humor."

"I'd like to meet him one day," Fritz replied, taking Vincent's hand and kissing it.

"That's unlikely," Norma said. Her tone was perhaps a little too blunt.

The group grew quiet. The waves were breaking hard against the rocks, causing the fire to sputter. Joe asked, "What time do you suppose it is?"

Vincent looked up at the stars she knew so well. "About eleven, I think."

"That wind is getting nasty," Fritz observed. "We better head back."

The group gathered blankets, gear, empty lobster traps and piled into the boat. Fritz and Vincent began to row but were faced with a sudden squall.[287] They couldn't get the boat around enough to catch the wind. They all became concerned.

"Let me row," Joe urged Vincent.

"No. The current is too strong, and we mustn't rock the boat. Stay there."

Kathleen, who was near her sister, offered to scoot over and help with the rowing.

"We'll just go round in circles. We best let the tide carry us into that small cove, tie her up and walk home," Fritz suggested, knowing it was easier to steer the boat than row against the tide.

All agreed, though they were facing a three-mile walk through rough terrain. Vincent and Fritz pulled with all their might toward the cove. As they got to shore, rain began to pelt them. Joe jumped out and helped get the boat high enough on dry land so that they could safely tie her up. The storm was rapidly passing, but the water continued to be too rough for rowing. Each member of their party grabbed something from the boat. Norma carried the picnic basket, Joe his lobster traps, Kathleen the blankets, Vincent fishing rods and kitchen utensils, and Fritz oars. Thus burdened, they began their trek back to town through fields and thickets, their clothes soaked with rain, mud and sand.

Over an hour later, they arrived at the city limits. "We must look a sight," Kathleen noted, as an older couple stared through their window at the rag tag group of friends.

"I wouldn't be surprised if they called the police," Joe remarked.

"We better keep our voices down. It's awfully late." Vincent adjusted her load.

The poet's supposition was confirmed when they passed the Comique Theatre. It was already 12:30. "Mama is going to be livid," Norma said.

"Your mother? How about mine?" Fritz laughed. He knew as well as the others that boys lived by different rules.

Trudging toward the Millay home, Joe couldn't help but realize that the girls would be chastised, but not severely punished. His sister had come home once a mere fifteen minutes past her curfew and wasn't allowed out of the house for the rest of the summer. He watched as the girls cooperated to develop their story. His admiration grew, and yet part of him was repelled by their laisses faire attitude toward lying.

By the time they reached Washington Street all were exhausted. Cora sat on the porch with her arms folded tightly over her bosom.

"Kathleen! What happened?"

"We got caught in…"

"Did I ask you?" Cora glared at Vincent.

"No, Mama," the poet hung her head. Suddenly she felt four years old.

"We went to Sherman's Point," Kathleen began.

"That place?" Cora looked at the boys. "You may leave now."

Fritz and Joe almost ran away.

Kathleen continued; their excuse forgotten under her mother's icy glare. "We had a picnic but by the time we headed home a squall…"

"Vincent, how long have you lived by the shore?"

"My whole life, Mother."

"So how is it that you didn't notice the weather changing?"

Vincent hardly knew how to answer. "It…"

"It came on suddenly," Norma interjected. Before their mother could reply, the middle Millay sister finished her thought. "Honestly, Mother, you should have seen Vincent row. She was rowing so hard."

Now Cora's anger turned toward the boys. "And why weren't the boys rowing?"

"Fritz was," Kathleen chimed in. "Fritz did and Joe would have except he had cut his hand on the rocks."

"I about lost my mind," Cora stormed. "I didn't know where you were. It was getting later and later. I know what happens to girls who…"

Her hesitation spilled out in the looks she gave her eldest daughter.

"We've been good, Mama," Norma said.

"They have. I chaperoned. The boys were perfect gentlemen," Kathleen offered.

"Maybe not perfect," Vincent added wryly. The look on her mother's face told her it was not the time for levity.

"We'll discuss this tomorrow, young lady," Cora glared. "Now you all get to bed."

* * *

The blow up lingered over the house for days. Oddly, Vincent was grateful. It gave her space to study without interruptions. Aside from the necessary retrieval of the rowboat, the poet managed to stick to the necessary tasks and then some.

Given the bohemian atmosphere of the house, the usual sounds of Norma and Kathleen arguing were complemented by the intermittent burbling of her friend Ellen's infant daughter. The poet's friend had sought refuge from her abusive husband and found a willing babysitter in Vincent, who was amazed by how much she loved little Gwendolyn.[288]

"Did you see that?" she laughed.

The baby was howling, and Cora's annoyance had turned to concern. "No. Has she been fed? Changed?"

"Of course," Vincent replied, feeling her own sense of annoyance. She'd been caring for infants since she was six. "Wee thing saw her fist and managed to hit herself in the eye with it."

She began to laugh even harder. Cora was not amused. "That's not funny."

"Not the poking herself in the eye part, but the way she looked at me as if I had done it."

"I still don't understand what you find entertaining in the poor child hurting herself."

Vincent bit her lip. How could she explain? What was funny was how startled the baby looked, like a vaudeville comedian. She knew her mother wouldn't understand no matter how she explained it, not in the mood she was in.

The weather had turned from glorious summer to an unseasonably chilly early fall. Vincent huddled in her new green and orange sweater.[289] If it weren't for the baby she would escape to her garret, but for now the best she could do was keep quiet and wait for her mother to leave for an assignment. The ticking clock reminded her of too many deadlines. Feed the baby, change the baby, help with dinner, reply to letters, clean her room, study for the Vassar examinations, there never seemed to be a moment she could truly call her own. It was all too much, particularly when Fritz, Joe and Norma were calling like sirens from the cliffs above the harbor. There was no time for play or poetry. The weather gave her a good excuse for staying in, but it didn't stop the passage of time.

21. The Weight So Close About

1913

The exam was much harder than she anticipated. Her memory, usually a reliable ally, seemed to escape Vincent the moment she stepped into the room. The stern blue eyes of C. Mildred Thompson glared as she began the history portion of her test by noting that she was "prepared in American history at my home in Camden, Maine in the hammock, on the roof and behind the stove."[290] Her insouciance did not charm the disciplined professor.

Professor Thompson wasn't the only one concerned. Miss Dow had heard from Dean McCaleb that Vincent might prove a problem to her patrons. The poet's haphazard study habits were not likely to be tolerated by Vassar, which in turn might not only risk her funding, but embarrass the generous and kind matron. While Ella McCaleb found Vincent an interesting and promising young woman, she wasn't sure how well she'd do after the first year.[291]

The poet joined her classmates in the post exam ritual of meeting Dean McCaleb for the verdict on their results. As the line grew shorter, Vincent's anxiety surged through her body. Already a couple of prospective classmates had been gently let down. The look on their faces filled the poet with dread. Would she join them in a tearful exit? Finally, she stood before the woman she'd only known through correspondence. The dean looked at her pet project for a moment and smiled. "Well, my dear, what did you do?"[292]

"I did my darnedest," Vincent replied solemnly.

"I suppose you did. However, you did not pass your examinations."

The poet gasped. Tears began to well in her eyes. What would Miss Dow say? Worse, what would her mother say? She knew it would mean a stream of "I-told-you-so's." She numbly took the examination papers from the educator's hand.

Dean McCaleb knew she had managed to terrify the woman before her, perhaps enough to elicit some discipline moving forward. She waited until the flush of Vincent's face turned to a look of determination before concluding. "Nonetheless, I've decided we'll take a chance on you."

The poet's heart leaped. She was in! She would go to Vassar. The pride she felt made her feel slightly faint. "I don't know how I ever repay you. Oh, Lord, bless you!"

"You'll have your work cut out for you though," McCaleb warned. "College is not a stroll. It is a hike, and a steep one at that."

Vincent knew exactly what she meant. How many times had she taken the easier path up Megunticook? The climb up the mountain was stony and in places steep.[293] She considered the times she woke up at half past four, wondering what wonders she'd find along the way. Running through the sleeping town she'd arrive at the base of the landmark, all too often taking the less challenging trail. Yet she realized in that moment that whenever she had taken the less traveled path, the sights, sounds and smells were far more rewarding when she reached the summit in time to watch the sun come up over Penobscot Bay. Dean McCaleb had said just the right thing.

"You're a darling," the poet cried, hugging the startled academic. "Thank you!"

***

When the poet arrived at Mrs. McGlynn's boarding house for young ladies she was greeted by Agnes Rogers, her sophomore guide. The pair instantly hit it off, in part because Agnes was already familiar with "Renascence". "You will be pounced upon by *The Miscellany* people," the mousy brunette remarked. "Just in case you don't already know, *The Miscellany* is the college magazine."

Flattered, the poet thanked her for the welcome note she had sent even before Vincent was accepted.

"Oh, we send them to all the freshmen. It's a way of figuring out what sort of girl each one is."[294]

Agnes studied the young woman with the brilliant red hair. She wasn't fashionably pretty, but there was a luminous quality to her, as if she were lit from behind. Agnes wasn't alone in seeing this aura around the poet. Other tenants approached them, hoping for an introduction to Vassar's latest celebrity.

Among the admirers was her roommate, Olive Burke.[295] Although several years younger than Vincent—as were all the freshman that year—Olive had the sort of English mannerisms that made the poet self-conscious. As one of only two McGlynn girls with a New England accent, Vincent worked hard to maintain the Mid-Atlantic accent she had mastered at Barnard so she could mask her rise from poverty.[296] The instinct for self-preservation blended with her desperate need for acceptance among her wealthier classmates. She wanted to fit in as she never would in Camden, because at Vassar she could make up her own story. Talent and ambition would have to be enough. The poet resolved to use her exceptional powers of observation to discern who was truly important.

"Who's that?" she asked as she watched a professor march by the group.

"Her?" Agnes asked. Vincent nodded. "That's Professor Jenney. She teaches German."

Vincent quickly excused herself and ran after the respected instructor.

"I just wanted to say something," the poet began when she had caught up.

Bemused, Professor Jenney took the measure of the younger woman. "Yes?"

"I am going to love German."[297]

"Will you be in my class?"

"Yes," the poet replied, grinning.

"And you're a freshman?" the professor asked, answering her own question.

Vincent studied the professor's expression. "I know my work has not been very good yet, but it is going to be. By Christmas I shall be the best in the class."[298]

"You must be the poet everyone is talking about."

"I suppose I am."

The professor noticed a small element of doubt behind the hubris in Vincent's reply.

"Then I am certain we'll meet again. Right now, I must be off."

The poet watched the preoccupied linguist as she strode onward.

Agnes and Olive raced toward her. "What did you say to her?" they asked almost in unison.

"I told her I was going to love German."

Agnes was perplexed. "But you're not taking German yet, are you?"

"Not yet, but I may as well make an impression now."

22. Beneath the Weight

1913

Her room at the head of the stairs was not unlike the one she once shared with Norma. Olive had already taken the bed nearest the window and the desk. The poet would have to cope with the noise from the stairwell. Vincent placed her suitcase atop the bed and began unpacking. The small dresser could barely hold what she'd brought.

"Oh, my!" Olive smiled. "You have so many clothes."

"Miss Dow has some friends who make sure I am well-dressed. I guess they don't want me to look like a country bumpkin."

"Well, they have succeeded."

"Do you have any room in your armoire?"

"A little. Maybe Mrs. McGlynn has something in the basement. They tell me that girls sometimes leave things, and the stuff goes right downstairs," the seventeen-year-old explained. "My, that's a lovely dress."

Vincent held up a gold brocade evening gown. A simple tiered net collar, cuffs and hem provided a delicate balance, while the three-tiered drapery at the rear was accented with sewn in ribbons.[299] "I was thinking I would wear it tonight at dinner."

"Of course, you'll want to change from your traveling clothes, but nobody here wears anything that beautiful. Something simple but more formal will be fine," Olive remarked. She ran her hand over the fabric of Vincent's dress. "What else did you bring?"

An impromptu fashion show began. Soon other girls were offering their opinions and admiring the poet's wardrobe as they passed in and out of Olive and Vincent's open room. In time, Vincent decided upon a modest blue wool crepe frock embroidered with small yellow columbine flowers.

"I'll hold a spot for you at the table," Olive said brightly. "Come on, girls, we have to let Vincent dress."

Soon the thunder of stairs shook the whole wing as a dozen women descended to the dining room.

Just as the poet was slipping the selection over her head, she heard a masculine giggle and looked down to see the feet of a woman named Margaret, who called herself Jack, standing in the doorway.[300] Vincent blushed when she realized Jack was looking at her with unabashed lust.

"You horrid thing!" Vincent cried in mock horror. "I shall close my door at once."

"No, you don't. I'm coming in." Jack oozed the confidence of an upper classman.

"You can't!" Vincent almost screamed. She wasn't sure how she felt about a woman being so brazen. She reached for the hook to close up the back of her dress. "It's not proper."

Jack just smiled.

"All right then, come on in and see if I'm all hooked up."

Jack entered the room and closed the door. She walked in and set her hands on the back of Vincent's shoulders. "We're going to be friends."

"Are we?" Vincent glanced backward and smiled.

"Yes," Jack replied. She kissed the nape of the poet's long neck before finishing the last hook.

Vincent felt a shiver run down her spine. She soon learned Jack was a sophomore and studying biology. Jack watched the hair on the back of the poet's neck dance at her fingertips. "Yes, we'll be friends." She took Vincent's hand. "Come on. We don't want to be late for supper."

***

The flirtation with Jack was short-lived, but Vincent thought herself lucky to be little. Tall girls usually played the role of boys. She had to be a girl.[301]

Between the whirlwind of social engagements and getting used to the discipline of college life, the poet found herself quickly overwhelmed. Within days of her arrival, she was joining others in planning a feast for the following Friday, September 26, 1913. It was her first foray into campus politics, and she took to it like a hummingbird to a lily. Most of the women at McGlynn's were Kathleen's age. Accordingly, the group decided their "big sister" would be proctor for the wing. This responsibility was something Vincent should have declined, but she found herself unable to say no. As usual, the poet dove in headfirst and damn the consequences. She wanted to be both secure and popular, a delicate balance in a room full of comparatively spoiled younger women. Her tendency was always to keep an eye out for the next move, as if she were playing chess. How much territory could she take, how much could she lose and still win? It required enormous energy to be calm in the face of risk.

One evening, Olive tipped over her ink bottle all over everything. Vincent had to quickly stop her history homework—assigned by the dreaded C. Mildred Thompson—and comfort the poor kid.[302]

"It's ruined," the seventeen-year-old cried, looking at both her dress and the braided oval rug between her bed and the desk.

Vincent threw her towel over the rug and quickly flipped the rug over. "See? It's hardly bled through."

"I want my mother," Olive wailed. Tears blended with the stains on her sleeve.

"There now. We'll ask Catherine if Filene's sells them," Vincent attempted to soothe, hoping she was saying and doing the right thing.[303]

Olive looked at herself in the mirror she frequently primped in front of and realized there was a streak of ink under her nose. She cried deeper tears. "I look like a man."

"Now, now…No, you don't," the poet replied. "Take your dress off and put on my dressing gown."

"It won't fit."

She helped Olive change, and then used cold cream over her roommate's inky mustache. The poet had to admit the dress was a lost cause. The girl continued to drown the silence with her sobs. Vincent suggested she go to the bathroom down the hall and take a quick bath. The cold cream jar was added to the bundle the older freshman offered. Meanwhile, Vincent blotted what she could from the rug, desk, chair and floor and replaced some of the ink in Olive's bottle from her own supply.

Satisfied with the efforts, the poet prayed Olive would return without more cries for her mother and father. She already found Olive's homesickness trying, whether it was actively or passively expressed.

"What's going on?"

Vincent looked up to see Catherine Filene.[304]

"Speak of the devil," she muttered.

"What's that?" Catherine asked.

"Oh, I had just been thinking of you. Olive upset her ink bottle and ruined her dress and rug, so I was wondering…"

"We might have something in our Automatic Bargain Basement that Olive can afford," the tall, high-cheek-boned debutante remarked.

Vincent was struck by how she would make a wonderful boy for the Halloween Dance. The poetic side of her noticed how Catherine held herself like a young prince who is such a snob that even a girl like Olive was considered bargain basement material.

The Filene's Department Store chain had a flagship store in the heart of Boston. Its new beaux arts style store had been completed the year before, although Vincent was already well acquainted with the brand. The company's scroll-like logo had a character similar to the striking granddaughter of its founder.[305]

Though Vincent hardly knew her, one could not miss the commanding presence of Catherine Filene. With a name almost as melodious as Edna St. Vincent Millay, Catherine's father also had a similarly memorable name, Abraham Lincoln Filene. The sophomore had a Boston Brahmin accent and an imperious way that intrigued the poet.

Catherine remained in the door as Vincent finished the cleanup. Occasionally they eyed each other.

"Are you coming to the dinner Friday?" Vincent asked. Catherine was not part of the planning committee.

"I might," the proud girl stated. She waited for Vincent's response. None came. It frustrated her.

Olive could be heard coming down the hall. Vincent's dressing gown was damp and had its pockets stuffed with tissues. "Oh, hi Catherine. Did Vincent tell you what happened? I just ruined my dress."

Catherine nodded and offered to call her uncle and arrange to have some samples sent up.

"No, thank you. I've called Mother and she's bringing me some things from home. Meanwhile, I'll just borrow something from Vincent."

The poet's head swung around. She'd offered her dressing gown, not her wardrobe. The casualness of Olive's assumption reminded her of just how young her peers were. Still, she didn't want to raise ill feeling.

"Yes, my blue serge is not unlike the tea gown you lost. Shall I get it out?"

"Can she see what else you have? The serge is so middle class," Catherine asked, smiling broadly.

Again, the poet reserved her reaction to the class-conscious woman's remark. She was still uneasy about using the Mid-Atlantic tones she affected.

"Certainly." Vincent opened the armoire nearest her bed.

The Bostonian poked her head inside and turned to Vincent with an appreciative smile. "You have exceptional taste."

"You're too kind."

Their exchange of glances communicated volumes that Olive had never read.

"Well, I suppose I should be off," Catherine said. "I've got Sandison in the morning."

"You're taking Latin?" the poet asked.

"Yes, ugh. My second year of it."

"We should study together sometime," the freshman redhead suggested. At least they had that much in common.

"I'd like that," Catherine replied, although all Vincent could see at that point was her back.

The celebrity student stepped back into the room to find Olive had put on a nightgown.

"Any luck?" Vincent nodded toward her closed armoire.

"None, thanks," Olive sighed. "I'll just wait for Mother to send some things. She'll know just what I need. My mother always does. Papa is very rich, you see, and our clothes must always be from the finest…" She hesitated, realizing she was being rude. "Thank you, Edna, I mean Vincent. It was awfully nice of you to clean up after me."

"Nothing at all, Olive dear," the poet replied as she returned to her history textbook.

*　*　*

Olive didn't need fresh clothes after all. The following day she was called up and sent home. Although she wouldn't discuss it, there was a rumor she was more social than scholastic, and her grades and attendance made it impossible for her to remain inside the college's esteemed halls.

Vincent was delighted. At nearly twenty-two, she had wanted a lonesome room in the first place.[306] Besides, she couldn't abide the younger girl's constant laments about the joys of home. The poet wasn't sure if that was because she sometimes missed her own family or if it was the annoyance of Olive's soggy tales of how wonderful her folks were. Regardless, she was glad to have the room to herself, particularly now that she had connected with Catherine.

Fewer interruptions did not mean she was any less confused or overwhelmed. Six classes a day, chapel, homework and rules, rules, rules soon had her head spinning so much that she was never sure if she was supposed to be speaking German or French. Algebra and geometry continued to confound her. The joy she felt in her English classes was constantly challenged by the pink and gray college she was starting to hate.[307]

Adding to the strain of the social requirements of the Friday Spread was the early appearance of her menstrual cycle. No longer on her sisters' monthly schedule she had switched to that of the twenty girls at McGlynn's. It surprised her. She had spent her last drop of energy on making the dinner event unique, so in some ways things were no different than at home. There were rules, there was judgment, there were limits, demands, duties and requirements to perform even the simplest of tasks.

The girls who resided at McGlynn's were from at least upper-middle-class families. Vincent knew she would never measure up unless she continued to get support from Miss Dow and the others who measured her by her talent. Her mother and father certainly would never be able to endow a new building or wing, so it was up to her to press on.

When overwhelmed, the poet would skip classes she was doing well in and attend those she was not. History was one of those classes she knew she had to attend no matter what. Miss Thompson made it seem as if history was always in the wings about to enter on ponderous tiptoe at the cue proceed.[308] The past had plagued the poet all her life.

Nevertheless, Vincent knew she would match her self-imposed deadline of being the best in her German class by Christmas, and thanks to her mother reading her *Morte d'Arthur* as a child, her sophomore level class in Old English was coming along well despite challenges with conjugating verbs. While Malory's prose telling of the King Arthur legend was in Middle English, she quickly discovered her capacity for languages was geometric. The space between those versions of English told her how she could get from Malory's English to where Professor Fiske wanted her to be in Old English. Perhaps learning to transition from Middle to Old English would help her to master mathematical geometry. It helped that her old friend "Jack" had demonstrated how math applied to other things she was interested in. Astronomy, music, and languages all involved measurement and distance. Geometry was just a question of learning how to calculate the shape of things. If she could master the milieu of campus life, surely, she could find the key to passing her math requirement.

Cheerful letters from Norma and visits from Miss Dow helped, as did the occasional note from Sara Teasdale, Mitchell Kennerley, Hal Bynner and her old beau Arthur Hooley. They reminded her there was a place for her in the future and helped her calculate how to get there. Nevertheless, she could only admit to the strain she was feeling in letters home. In fact, her family's compassionate ears were about the only thing she truly missed. They understood her. They knew about her tendency to push herself too far. She could complain to Norma and know it would go no further. She would send Kathleen geometry tests and be thanked. Even carefully couched letters to Cora provided relief, as they reminded her of why she was going through all this in the first place.

Norma's notes overflowed with gossip from home, including her ongoing on-again, off-again relationship with Kenneth. Vincent quickly wrote back telling her sister to dump Kenneth immediately and find someone who would consistently make her happy. It was advice Vincent was deliberately avoiding taking herself. She had realized that one of the advantages to a women's college was she could have her pick of the ten girls who played boys whenever there was a dance.

The Halloween Dance at McGlynn's featured chocolate cigar smoking women in men's suits and well-dressed young ladies waiting to fill their dance cards. Vincent's initially included one dance with Catherine Filene, who asked for another.

Between numbers, the poet struck up a conversation with Agnes, who had come by to chaperone the all-female dance.

"Where did you learn to dance like that," Agnes smiled.

"That's nothing," Vincent crowed. "You should see my sister Norma and me doing the tango."

"You tango!" The alarm apparent in Agnes' voice almost made Vincent laugh out loud.

"Yes, and the Figure-Eight, the Open Boston, and..."

"Oh, my—" Agnes interrupted.

They watched as a particularly boyish classmate dipped her partner as part of the Heavenly Rest steps. Both were impressed.

Agnes remembered something. "I heard that you wanted nothing to do with Catherine, yet you've danced with her this evening."

Vincent smiled wickedly. "She'd give a lot, I think, to have me chase her around. I don't go near her."[309]

"You seemed awfully close to me," Agnes winked.

"You're right, of course, but I am not about to let her boss me around."

"That's smart." Agnes started to tap her feet to "Midnight Choo-choo Leaves for Alabam'." Vincent resisted the urge to pull her onto the dance floor.

Catherine appeared beside them with a glass of punch for Vincent. "Our dance is coming up. Drink up!"

The poet just smiled. She took the glass, examined it and then slowly drank it as their second dance number played. Catherine didn't know what to make of her friend. She imagined Vincent would be delighted to have someone to offset her poetic flights of fancy with a firm hand. Vincent just did whatever she wanted, but in the most pleasant manner imaginable. It was confounding because Catherine could neither dominate nor chastise her. It made for an irresistible balancing act that Vincent delighted in.

When the next song started it was Catherine following Vincent to the floor. They danced a brisk Turkey Trot which by then was already going out of style. Next came a ballad and Catherine begged for the opportunity to take the poet into her arms during "Till the Sands of the Desert Grow Cold."[310]

"We missed a dance," Catherine began. "Let's make up for it."

Vincent smiled coyly, gazing up at the boyishly dressed sophomore. "Wasn't that our second?"

"Well, yes, it was, but...but...I'd love to dance a third."

The poet just smiled.

"Please?"

"I suppose," Vincent said and allowed herself to be drawn into Catherine's arms. With her hair parted on the side and tied tightly atop her head, the would-be swain was deliciously close to the forbidden fruit the poet was "learning" about in hygiene class. Catherine held her tight.

"What shall I call you, *boy*?" Vincent demanded.

Catherine was taken aback. She looked down at the impish grin of her five-foot, one-inch dance partner.[311] She then understood.

"How about Fil, like Phillip, but spelled like my last name."

The poet smiled and buried her face in her partner's shoulder. "Hold me close, Fil," she whispered.[312]

"Fil" could feel herself blush. She obeyed. Eventually, she screwed up the courage to ask permission to take the next step after a Halloween Dance.

"May I haunt your room tonight?" she cracked.

"Only if you bring me some spirits," Vincent giggled.

Agnes, who had been watching from across the room, realized the futility of her job as chaperone. Desire was rampant in the room full of young women. They virtually swam in hormones. She identified at least three couples who would sleep together that night. There was little she could do about it short of warning them to be discreet. Sex among the girls was an open secret at Vassar. Few would cling to lesbian life after graduation. Many would deny any such liaisons had taken place. Somehow, Agnes knew Vincent was neither virginal nor fully heterosexual. Catherine would soon marry while Vincent would float from lover to lover as stable as a soap bubble.

* * *

The term went on. Vincent made her room reflect her own taste, which others found remarkably cute when it was clean, which wasn't very often. She continued to push through geometry, history and German, but took great delight in being one of two freshmen allowed to take Mademoiselle Conrow's sophomore French class. Nevertheless, she only started going to chapel when she overheard the French instructor say that while Vincent was a brilliant student, she might not last the year because she was so often late, cut classes and refused the most rudimentary of disciplines, such as chapel and hygiene class. The redhead realized she had nowhere else to go.[313] That meant if she had to endure chapel she would. If she had to take hygiene more seriously, she would. It was a necessary evil to adhere to college rules. Consequently, she occasionally cleaned her room and remained discreet in case Miss Dow should appear with her allowance and a new dress or two.

Settling in was aided by the attentions of her female suitors. In addition to scandalizing the campus by walking hand in hand with her "Fil", the poet was now actively and successfully seducing her downstairs neighbor Katherine Tilt. Bad Vincent reveled in playing them off one another.

One night Vincent was sitting in her room listening to someone play Dvorak on the piano downstairs. Outside her door the steps of fellow students could be heard going up and down, and in and out of each other's rooms. She stood up in her blanket bathrobe and wandered down the hall with an armload of books. She ran into Fil.

"Oh-ho! where are you going?"[314]

"Where do you suppose?" Vincent began to descend the stairs.

Fil hardly knew what to say in reply, but she began to stew. An hour later, she marched down to Katherine Tilt's room and burst in. "Oh, I beg your pardon. Perhaps I interrupt. You two *turtledoves*!" the galoot growled in her insolent way.

Katherine became flushed with embarrassment, but Bad Vincent pretended she could have cared less. She was happy that Katherine was now aware of her relationship with handsome, great big child.[315] She faced Fil and said, "You may leave now."

Fil looked at the poet as if struck. Discretion meant she could not make a scene. She slipped upstairs and awaited her next summons to Vincent's bed. Katherine, on the other hand, was now jealous and thus easier to seduce. Vincent thought it had all worked beautifully.

Yet the truth was Vincent liked them both. Fil was a strong and committed lover, generous and satisfying, though not terribly bright. She had the sweetest, most charming smile when she wanted to be decent for a while.[316] On the other hand, Katherine was beautiful, elegant and cultured, with a brilliant mind and a shy manner that was endearing. While Fil tried to dominate, it was the poet who held the cards. When Vincent returned to her room later that night, she lingered on the landing weighing the place between the brute and the beauty, between passion and chastity. It was a dilemma that matched her generation as it transitioned from Victorian to Edwardian. McGlynn's was still, and the few who chose to sleep together had already made their choices of where to sleep. Standing there in the quiet, Vincent realized she had three choices. She could return to her own room alone, lay in Fil's arms smelling the pungent brandy of her skin, or enjoy the anxious depth of her platonic connection with Katherine. "Ah, well," she sighed, "Katherine will get nervouser before it's all over. And it will be good for her."[317]

The next day, Vincent went downtown with Katherine, who acted as if she were thoroughly resistant to the poet's attentions. It bothered Vincent enough that when they returned to McGlynn's she immediately went to Fil's room to report her annoyance. The boyish paramour consoled the redhead beautifully.

23. Quietly the Earth Beneath

1913

Seated at her desk, Katherine looked every inch a Seven Sisters scholar. Her hair was in braids bundled at her crown, and she embraced a book like a lover. "I'm glad you're here."

"Are you?"

The arc of light from the oil lamp she preferred cut across Katherine's shoulders revealing the steel of her spine. Vincent loved how her posture gave Katherine the air of Guinevere. The poet slipped off her blouse and placed her breasts against Katherine's shoulders. "Don't," the beautiful woman croaked.

"Why?" Vincent asked like a two-year-old.

"You know," Katherine replied. "It's…a…a…sin."

The poet pulled away, only to kiss the nape of Katherine's neck. The kiss was accepted. Vincent ran her hands across her shoulders, sending chills up and down her body. "Vincent."

The strange mixture of misgivings and anticipation surged through the poet. She paused. For once, Katherine did not. Instead, she guided Vincent's hand to her breasts.

"Are you ready?" the poet asked, again leaning her breasts into Katherine's body as the latter rose from the chair. She turned and looked down at Vincent. Although taller, it wasn't by much. "May I kiss you?"

Katherine nodded and allowed the poet's mouth to meet hers. Until now the closest they had gotten to sex was holding hands and snuggling overnight. This was something else entirely. She found herself responding to the more experienced woman. After removing Katherine's dress, Vincent's hands quickly moved to her corset. "You don't need to wear this." The corset fell to the floor like cherry blossoms.

"What's next?" Katherine asked, taking in the echo of falling garments.

"You'll see," the poet replied, taking in her prize. Katherine was lovely, shapely, and soft. Katherine closed her eyes as if that might make what she was feeling less potent. Vincent undressed and pressed her body against Katherine's. They kissed again, this time deeper. The poet could smell her partner's arousal and slipped her hand between the beauty's legs. Katherine shuddered at her touch. Hesitancy rocked her momentarily before the couple embraced atop Katherine's swan's down coverlet.

* * *

As dawn dipped its pink bud over the horizon, Vincent awakened and remembered why she was there. Outside the world had been quietly inoculated with snow. In two weeks, she would be in New York for the Christmas break. Her publisher had sent up a secretary to see if she was working on the promised volume. He had also sent another thing she wanted: news of Arthur Hooley. While she connected with women, that didn't mean she wasn't anxious to have a male lover.

But, she wondered, how was sex with Arthur so different from what she enjoyed with women? Primarily, he was a sometimes-true version of what hands approximated. Women like Katherine had similar traits of literary genius but shared his ambivalence about physical pleasure. Her sandy voice, a sound not unlike the tide that comes in at dawn, spoke of someday, when all the poet cared about was now.

This was a different now than that of her childhood, when the immediacy of need, danger, debt and silence were the endless call of her family's now. The now of physical pleasure filled a deep inner void, a longing for connection, a desire to be held and comforted, to come first above all else.

The poet took a deep breath and brought herself back to the moment. The trees whispered. The flutter of pigeons rushing for a winter source of food met her ears. In the far distance the jingle of sleigh bells spoke of the season. She took another breath and exhaled with a sigh.

She looked at the curve of Katherine's wrist. Vincent was the inside spoon. They had finished with the beauty wrapping herself around the poet like a cup of water in a desert of need. But the poet wanted to get up. Her hair was still damp with Katherine's tears. She realized that Fil would have been more able to satisfy her physically, but Katherine filled an emotional need. Torn and confused, Vincent debated wresting herself from Katherine's arms or resting in them. The latter seemed right at that moment.

* * *

Letters have a funny way of finding the wrong eyes. Miss Dow was concerned. She had heard rumors. Nothing specific, of course. Just a suggestion that perhaps Vincent had missed too many classes because she was visiting Catherine Filene.

"Oh, Miss Filene? I hardly know her."

"I understand she lives on one floor above you." The furrows of Miss Dow's middle-aged forehead were taking on a life of their own.

"Oh, her. We know each other in passing, but just to and from the bath."

"One needs to be careful, Edna, er, Vincent." Miss Dow looked at a point behind Vincent's shoulders, afraid of what she'd see if she looked directly into her eyes.

Teacups faintly rattled. They finally looked at each other. Vincent knew that every road she took Miss Dow may have also taken. Did she understand the seductive nature of nubile girls blending or the sweet warmth between their legs, the deep pleasure filled sighs that accompanied orgasm?

But Miss Dow had remained *Miss* Dow, while Vincent had become mistress to whomever she chose.

"Truly, Miss Dow, surely you understand how Miss Filene and I might like to spend time together. School is so demanding."

"Are you improving in geometry?"

Vincent inwardly smiled. Her maneuver had been successful. "Well, enough," she said, taking a moment to be truthful. "I do struggle with it at times."

"That's what school is for, dear. It helps us past the struggle, so things become natural for us."

The poet looked into Miss Dow's gray bovine eyes. She really was a dear. They sipped tea, savoring the moment like a brandy caramel.

As Vincent lifted her teacup to her lips, she smelled Katherine on her fingers. Each time she sipped there was Katherine. Sometimes she compared how Fil and Katherine smelled. Each touched something different in her. Was it possible to love two people at the same time? Her mind wandered away from the staid confines of midday tea. She wanted to see one of her lovers. Would this lunch never end?

As if one cue, the waitress came and presented the bill.

"Will there be anything else?"

Vincent and Miss Dow looked at each other, silently agreeing, two peas at either end of the pod.

"That will be all," Miss Dow said, taking the check from the waitress's outstretched hand.

Vincent recognized the waitress as a "boy" she had danced with. She had been grand at tango, leaping and jumping, but lacking in imagination. She lowered her eyes. She needn't have bothered. The prospect had been too drunk to remember her.

In the quiet between paying the bill and exiting the student run lunchroom, Vincent saw Fil walk by. Torn, she fidgeted. Fil had seen her but dared not respond. After all, it was a women's college, not Sodom and Gomorrah. Warmth permeated the space between them. *Surely Miss Dow will notice.* But no. Chastity has its own form of deafness.

She inhaled her lover's scent as she passed. Her eyes filled with tears she dared not shed. She thanked God it was cold, and she could blame it on the sting of freezing weather. Out of the blue, she could see Cora in her mind's eye. It was a very old memory.

"I'm leaving. You take care of the girls."
"But…"
"No buts, Vincent. None. You will do your duty."

The poet silently choked back the feeling as she relived the twelve-year-old moment. *"Yes, Mama."*

Her memory slipped forward a few years. Which one would come next? There was a figure in the distance. Was it Papa or Mama? The poet realized it didn't actually matter. Her duty always seemed to take precedence over her own ambitions. Vincent returned to the present. Her patron's capacious waistline made a path for the slender freshman.

As the last of Fil's sweetness drifted away, Vincent found herself lifting the smell of Katherine Tilt to her nose. "How lovely," she whispered to herself before speaking aloud to her patron. "I better go study for my history final tomorrow."

Miss Dow peered into the poet's face. "Yes, you must and do look harder at geometry. You did so well in the entrance examinations, I would have hoped for more by now."

Vincent didn't dare disabuse her of that mistaken impression. "Yes, ma'am. I guess we just have started some problems I can't get my head around."

Her patron looked down at the pixie of a girl. "I know you mean to do well. A lot of people are counting on you."

Vincent sucked in guilt. She no longer cared for her own sake. She would complete Vassar because, like so much else in her life, it was a means to an end, a duty she must fulfill because she had to, not because she wanted to.

"It was lovely to see you," Vincent embraced her patron.

Miss Dow opened her walrus leather clutch and pulled out a check. "Your allowance."

"Oh, my gosh, Miss Dow! I forgot all about it."

The older woman studied Vincent's face. She had learned to look more deeply when dealing with the poet. "Not entirely."

Vincent sheepishly grinned. "Well, yes, not entirely."

"Be careful, dear. Little pictures have big ears."

The poet was taken aback. "Why, Miss Dow?"

"Good afternoon, child."

Vincent watched as the dour woman who had made her situation possible walked down the colonnade. She again marveled at how her life had changed. Less than two years before she had been considering spending her life with Ella, working odd jobs, scrubbing, scouring and lamenting that her life was at a dead end. Now she was standing on the campus of Vassar, lauded by successful poets, and pursued by men and women. Her eyes scanned the view around her as she marveled at her good fortune.

She considered her promise to study and began to walk toward McGlynn's. When she got there, Miss Dow's warning rattled in her brain. She stopped at the landing. Where would she go? Only the memory of Fil's scent lingered, but Bad Vincent climbed the stairs.

"Come in," Fil's voice traveled from a familiar corner of the room.

Vincent turned the doorknob and entered. Fil was lying on the bed in an inviting position. Her feet were on the floor and her knees bent over the edge, her head propped up with pillows and resting on one arm. In her other hand was a textbook. Vincent knelt beside the bed and ran her hands inside Fil's thighs. "Sorry I didn't greet you out by the colonnade."

"I get it. That was Miss Dow, wasn't it?"

"Yes," Vincent's hands slipped inside the undergarment and gently brushed Fil's pubic hair. "I've missed you."

In an instant Vincent went from atop to beneath the taller woman. The poet submitted to her desire. Fil was swell looking and swell feeling.[318]

* * *

The final dance of the year challenged Vincent's role as proctor. Late night preparations and dance lessons rumbled through her wing.

The back and forth between Fil and Katherine confounded everyone but Vincent. She knew exactly what she was doing. It wasn't that her affection oscillated. It was her desire. She and Fil would host an invitation-only tea one night, and the next Katherine would be in her room asking if she could unhook her dress. With all the preparations for the last dance of the year, few people noticed the carom as the poet bounced from room to room, glancing off lovers and friends with equal randomness.

This unpredictably had a side benefit for the cautious poet. It kept crushes at bay. Not only those directed at her, but, more importantly, those she felt. Getting too close would hobble her. More than anything the poet longed to control her own destiny, and love had a habit of checking her independence. Besides, she wasn't one hundred percent sure love could be trusted. Her experiences with that emotion told her that love was fickle and an unreliable measure of community.

Vincent had a favorite dress that season.[319] It was tan and had a short train. She wore it—and not much of anything else—because it drew attention while keeping people from approaching her from behind. It also assured that residents of McGlynn's would notice her when they entered the room. If she chose to dance with someone other than Fil, she would make a show of lifting the train, which fluttered like tail feathers, making Fil jealous. It wasn't that she meant to be cruel. She just knew how things would change, because so much had changed so often in her own life. A new year would soon be upon them, and with new year came semester examinations[320] followed by new classes and other new things.

24. The Crushing Weight

1913

Cora waited anxiously. Vincent was due home for Christmas break. Apparently, her publisher had told the poet she needed to spend some time in New York before going home. The nurse knew this was a lie. Her daughter was seeing that man. Vincent didn't know how much she knew. But news travels, particularly when money is tight and there are friends who might know when Vincent might be sending money home.

It was true. Mitchell Kennerley had sent an invitation to the overworked poet, ostensibly to begin preparing her first volume. Yet it was plain it would not be an all-business meeting. This was the "not true" part that Cora sussed out from slips of Norma's tongue, and curious notes from Miss Dow.

The Kennerley's home was a home with children, and as such it reflected every holiday whimsy. A tree, garlands, packages, sweets and company—lots of indulging company. Vincent arrived to learn that "Uncle" Hal and Cousin Arthur were to join them. The poet was thrilled by the opportunity to employ her seduction technique on men after having so much luck with Fil and Katherine. Hal with his Cupid's Bow lips would be there for her to flirt with while she was also having liaisons at Arthur Hooley's cottage not far from Mitchell and Helen's estate.

Her stay in the New York coastal village was perfectly logical on the face of it. Mitchell was going to publish her first book, that much had been agreed upon. It was also true that challenges with the construction of the New York Central line made going by way of the New York, Westchester and Boston Railway a necessity.[321] That she would choose to visit the Kennerleys during the holidays was what gave Cora pause.

As for Vincent, she didn't want to miss the opportunity to see the man she had decided she was actually in love with, though they had never consummated their attraction: Hal Bynner.[322]

She arrived first. Helen Kennerley had set her up in a room at their house just in case funders from New York visited. Otherwise, most of her things were sent to Hooley's cabin.

Yet until Arthur arrived, Vincent looked for Hal at the new train depot at Mamaroneck Avenue and Harrison. Straining to see her fellow poet, the smitten redhead leaned on her tiptoes against the car door. Mitchell sat silently behind the chauffeur with a bemused expression. She was so young. Helen would never be so obvious.

It wasn't long before the object of Vincent's affection appeared carrying a simple leather bag. She could barely contain herself as she watched him scan the roadway for Mitchell's automobile. "Hal!"

The handsome bachelor turned his head this way and that, seeking the owner of the voice. Vincent's distinctive alto was somewhere in the crowds. He had not been told she was joining in the Christmas merriment.

The dreamy-eyed traveler finally caught sight of a tiny hand waving at him from across the street. He raced down the steps of the Italianate station to the waiting vehicle.

The couple lunged at each other. He couldn't believe his eyes. Vincent's low-cut dress revealed soft, fulsome breasts. "Sorry about my décolleté," she said with a wink.

"It's fine," Hal replied, blushing bright pink. It was confusing to feel attracted to a woman. He had never shown interest before, yet he couldn't take his eyes off her body.[323]

Vincent concentrated on his eyes. Hal's long eyelashes kept blinking as he stared at her, and she was convinced it was the proximity of her naked breasts that enticed him. She had wanted his attention for a year and now she had it.

They discussed her poetry on the ride to the Kennerley's with Mitchell directing their discreet chauffeur through the construction zone. After a friendly greeting, Mitchell internally wondered how the dynamics would change when Arthur arrived on Monday, December 15.

It didn't take long to find out. Once the older man was added to the mix the pace of conversation quickened with the center of attention being the comely redhead. All three men vied for her attention as they sensed something was different about her. It may have been her engagement with the Vassar scene, or her ability to seem ambivalent while also enticing.

Only the poet knew exactly what it was. She had fine-tuned the art of playing with people. She was charming, circumspect, quick to laugh, easy to flirt with and had become remarkably urbane in the last few months since they'd seen her. Even her voice, which was already a standout feature, had a more pronounced upper-class quality.

Hal was fascinated.

"My, Vassar seems to agree with you, Vincent."

"I admit. It's growing on me," she laughed.

"Not growing too much, I hope," Arthur noted. "I really can't stand these nouveau riche phonies."

The poet frowned. "You don't know the girls. They are really quite lovely once one gives them a chance."

She had said chance as if it were spelled with a "w"—"chawnce."

Hal laughed. "Yes, that's it. You've mastered it."

"What?"

"The whole Back Bay dialect. It's rather marvelous, I think."

"I probably have picked it up from my friend Catherine Filene," Vincent explained.

"Is she related to the department store people?" Helen asked as she wrestled a cigarette butt from her son's mouth.

"Yes. Her father is Lincoln Filene."

"What a splendid man he is," Helen replied. "I've never heard of any employer who treats his employees as well."

Mitchell nodded. "We don't do much business with them personally, of course, since they don't have a local store, but we sell some books through them. Helen shopped all day when we went to Boston to sign the agreement."

"The dress I wore yesterday was from that trip," Helen noted.

Vincent looked at Hal and Arthur and realized they were growing bored with all the talk of women's fashion. "How about some poker?"

The men assented; Helen begged off. "I'm afraid card playing is bad for the health...of my wallet," she giggled. "It's time the boys went to bed anyway."

The host and guests moved to the library where a card table was ready for action.

The men were soon disabused of their notion that Vincent would be an easy mark. The game was played for matches in place of dimes. Each player pledged to make good in actual cash once the game was over. While Hal was hopeless when it came to a poker face, Vincent's face remained pleasantly immobile no matter how good her hand was. By the time their play ended, she had won all but two hands and had won enough to cover her losses and then some.

"I think I'll go to Filene's on my way home," she grinned as she slipped $23 dollars into her purse. She walked to the bar cart and poured herself a glass of sherry.

Hal laughed. "And you'll spend it all."

"Most likely, but I'll also buy presents for Mama and the girls."

Arthur frowned. He didn't have any money left for presents, having squandered the last of his earnings on poker, horses and a small gift for Vincent. He hoped Helen would help him make rent. "I'm going to bed."

Vincent smiled at him from over Hal's shoulder, but the older man only shook his head, "Goodnight," she called after him.

"Sleep well, old man," Hal said.

"Yes, goodnight," Mitchell said, carefully avoiding the use of a name for his nom de plumed relative. "I think I'll find my wife." He rose up from the hard Windsor chair with a stretch. "Goodnight, Vincent, Hal…"

Hal stood as the two older men left the room. Vincent nodded toward them as they exited before leaning seductively into Hal's back. She wrapped her arms around his middle and squeezed before reaching up to place her tiny palms flat against his chest.

The handsome poet and translator found himself aroused despite Vincent's gender. He put his hands over hers. "You know, I used to shop at Filene's when I went to Harvard."[324]

"Um-hmm," she kissed his mid-back. It was a poor substitute for his neck.

Hal turned and faced her. Looking down, he smiled softly. "I'm afraid I may be the Witter of your discontent."

Vincent laughed at the pun. "Perhaps, but do I care?"

"You might," he smiled again and leaned down to kiss her.

When their lips met a strange recognition was ignited. She realized he had not kissed many women. He saw that she had. They stared at each other for a long while. "Shall we go upstairs?" he suggested.

"I think so," she replied. They turned out the lights and quietly made their way to his room.

Their lovemaking reflected both his inexperience and her willingness to please. By the time it was over, neither felt satisfied.

Vincent soon realized the love she felt for Hal was different, more of a meeting of minds than a matching of souls. As they lay beside each other he asked if she had poems he could read.

"No," she admitted. "Mitchell is after me, but a poem cannot be forced. You know that. When it comes it comes. Besides, with schoolwork and all, how would I ever find time to put together anything good enough?"

"To think that everything you do is so good. I wish you'd write something ordinary."

"No, you don't," she replied. It was true.

"Still, I'd love to hear you recite some of your new things."

Vincent paused. Nothing new was ready. He'd read "God's World" already. Finally, she selected something short that she thought he might like. "So long as we were discussing Filene's," she laughed and sat up, "I've been working on this one. I don't think it's quite finished. It's called 'Sorrow'."[325]

Sorrow like a ceaseless rain
Beats upon my heart.
People twist and scream in pain—
Dawn will find them still again;
This has neither wax nor wane,
Neither stop nor start.

People dress and go to town:
I sit in my chair.
All my thoughts are slow and brown:
Standing up or sitting down
Little matters, or what gown
Or what shoes I wear.

The echo of the words on Hal's heart hurt. He was quiet as he let his mind absorb the poem. At last, he spoke.

"There is the 'brawny forty-year-old male' again." He winked at her, knowing she'd taken offense when he and Arthur Ficke refused to believe she had written "Renascence" three years before.

She smiled and asked what he thought of "slow and brown."

"I like it. I suppose you mean like dung?"

Vincent began to howl with laughter, so much so that she had to push her face into a pillow. Hal followed suit until they had wound down to quiet titters. Despite their attempts, Hal thought he heard someone stirring in the next room.

"I had better go back to my room," Vincent said.

"I suppose so," Hal replied, rolling over and propping himself on his elbow. He watched as Vincent wordlessly dressed. His fingers drummed his temples as she lifted her bloomers over her hips and then drew her chemise over her head. Her evening dress required his help. He rose without being asked and went to her.

"Don't change it," he said softly as he buttoned the back of the dress. He kissed her back with each button. It excited her, but not enough to reverse course.

"Change what?"

"Slow and brown. It works, and, besides, it will be our private joke."

Vincent turned and kissed his cheeks. "Agreed."

* * *

Two days later, on December 17, Vincent and Arthur were playing honeymooners in his modest Mamaroneck cabin.

Hal had gone home the day before. The poet wondered if her pursuit had chased him away. Yet Helen spoke of Hal getting a call late in the day from Arthur Davison Ficke saying he was in New York and wanted to see him about some writing project they were starting. She wasn't sure who to believe, but more importantly she wished there was a way to go to New York herself so she could meet Ficke, her other Arthur. The long-time pen pals had revealed so much of themselves in letters she felt as if she was missing out. Yet the comely redhead knew it was even more important that she took advantage of her time with Arthur Hooley before going home and facing whatever demands would come from her family.

After driving Hal to the station, the Kennerleys drove Vincent to Arthur's modest country abode. The couple had decided that whatever was going on it was none of their business. Arthur was already ensconced in his tiny home in preparation for her arrival. Vincent had made it clear that she loved both men.

What could the Kennerleys say to either of them that wouldn't come off as condescending or illiberal?

She was greeted by an inviting fire in the capacious hearth.[326]

"Brr," Vincent cried as she entered the modest dwelling. She stamped the snow off her feet and removed a beautiful blue cape she'd received from someone who had purchased it in London.[327]

"My, what a lovely dress," Arthur exclaimed. His English accent intrigued her, and she privately considered how she might incorporate it into her growing linguistic repertoire. In keeping with the season, she was wearing a long, green dress accented with violets.

"Thank you," she smiled. Her eyes traveled around the room. She wanted to remember everything.

"Dear me! Where are my manners?" Arthur got up from his Windsor chair and cleared a spot on the divan. "Please sit down."

Vincent knew the piece of furniture served a dual purpose. It was both a bed and a couch for visitors who happened to come into the fifteen by eighteen-foot room. Accordingly, it was near the fireplace in the corner of the room. Arthur's wingback chair sat opposite the divan, only facing the fire. An upholstered rocking chair was next to a small table and chair that served as a desk. Beside the undersized cookstove was a narrow table with only one simple rail back chair. It had a cabinet above it for dishes, utensils and basic food stuff. For the two of them to dine together, Arthur would have to pilfer the desk chair. An armoire that sat against the wall near the rocker finished the room. Nothing matched. There were only two windows, and the door opened to the center of the room. The privy and well pump were outside. Though smaller, it reminded her of some of the places she'd lived in as a child.

Vincent sat down. Arthur noticed her shoes. "Those are almost like princess slippers."

The poet smiled. "Have you ever seen a princess's slippers?"

"If I were in London I might."

They both knew this was unlikely. Nevertheless, Vincent laughed. "I believe you might,[328] and you'd ride in her carriage over hills and heaths in a suit of armor like Don Quixote."

"No, child. I would much rather ride like Sir Galahad in search of the Holy Grail."

He leaned over and kissed her before sitting down. It was a chaste kiss, carrying none of the expected passion. "I have a present for you."

Vincent couldn't help but be stunned by this. She wondered if she had anything she could offer in return. He placed a tantalizing box in her hand. It was not as small as a ring, and perhaps too large even for a bracelet. Inside was a small volume of the *Iliad* in Latin, nicely bound in English leather, measuring only four by six inches. Her eyes filled with tears.

"It's alright?" he asked. His saturnine face reminded her of a Dicken's character, but she still didn't know which. "I recall you read Descartes' *Second Meditation* in Latin just for the intellectual adventure of it."[329]

"It's exquisite, Arthur," she patted a spot beside her.

"Not just now," he smiled.

"You do know I adore you," Vincent replied. She thumbed through the volume by Homer.

"Oh, child, child, let's not talk of love."

The poet quickly understood they were repeating a scene they had started at the Kennerley's the year before. She rose and walked toward him. "Then perhaps we should make love."

He allowed her to sit upon his lap and kiss him, but felt the light was too bright for anything more. She leaned into his ear and whispered, "If I were a fairy I would take you back to England, to the Derby races."

Arthur laughed. "You rather look like a fairy, Edna, with your tiny body, jade eyes and copper hair. I shouldn't wonder if you might spread your wings and take me wherever children go."

"I wish you'd stop seeing me as a child. I'm a woman, or have you forgotten?" She lifted his hand and placed it upon her left breast.

He withdrew his hand and placed it chastely upon her hip. "In you there are so many possibilities. I would be loath to leave you with any memory that you might ever wish to obliterate."[330]

"How could I forget a room like this?" she asked. "It's as if I've stepped into some long forgot, enchanted, strange, sweet garden of a thousand years ago."[331]

"Like a fairy story."

"No. This seems very real, like I've been here before, which of course I have if only briefly last year."

"So much has changed," he said sadly. "It seems like Vassar has changed you."

"Why I'm just as I have always been," the poet replied. She looked around the room and noticed the dust that had settled upon the hearth beside his pipe stand and brandy bottle. It stirred a memory. "Remember the day when you picked the first sweet pea and brought it into the Kennerley's library to show me? The whole room smelled of their garden yet for some reason all I wanted to look at was your eyes, your beautiful eyes."[332] She kissed his eyelids and then his mouth.

"Yes, Edna. I do remember," he replied, coolly accepting the kisses. "I brushed the flower against your innocent, girlish lips to try and get you to focus on it." He ran his finger across her mouth.

Vincent wanted him but she knew the moment had passed. She damned the limits he placed on their contact. "Only you didn't kiss me. You kissed my hair instead."

He nodded solemnly and searched her face for the child he loved.

"That first sweet pea! I wonder where it is?[333] It seems to me I laid it down someplace, or perhaps I pressed it into a book or in one of your letters. How I would love to go back to that sweet summer afternoon with you."

"Yet here we are in winter."

As if on cue, a log broke in the fireplace and rumbled down to the hearth. Sparks flew and in a moment Vincent and Arthur were standing, he bending to the errant embers and the poet wishing they could kindle something more between them.

Arthur's confusing signals continued throughout their two days together at the cottage. He would say something romantic, like suggesting she shouldn't sit in the rocking chair they had moved by the fire because he might always want her there, or read poetry he had composed in her honor.[334] The rest of the time, she thought he was just a big old bear swinging at her in his decadence, such as the time when he saturated his handkerchief with her cologne and said, "One can get by without women, if he has perfume…and vermouth."[335]

In response she would read him Swinburne's "Triumph of Time," emphasizing the lines, "Had you loved me once, as you have not loved, Had the choice been with us that has not been."[336]

The beginnings of the illness that would kill him were hovering over him like the last glimmer of light upon a hill after the sun has set.[337] She could sense it even if she could not see it. By the time the week was over, she knew the final embers of their love were fading on the hearth.

25. Full Six Feet Underground

1913

The local electric trains to Camden were not running due to a power outage. Nonetheless, Norma and Kathleen were there to greet her with a friend who owned a sweet little four-seater for the drive home. The girls were excited to see their sister so they could see the latest fashions, and, of course, because she seemed to be transforming before their eyes.

Vincent had spent every nickel of her poker winnings and part of her December allowance on a trip to Filene's in Boston during a layover on her way home. She wanted to make an impression by looking more like a wealthy tourist than a townie home for Christmas. Besides, Norma had said there was a Knights of Pythias Dance the following Wednesday, on Christmas Eve, and she wanted to look her best.[338]

On the way home after her misadventure in Mamaroneck she imagined how she might pin her skirt on the green curtain of the lower bunk of the sleeper car with a man's coat on the upper berth as a kind of signal. It made her laugh how much this would shock people. [339]

A stop in Portland to visit Aunt Sue did little to prepare her for the brittle face of her mother when she arrived.

"So, you've arrived," Cora said.

Vincent kissed her. "It's so wonderful to be home."

"If it's so wonderful, why did you have to spend five days with those people?"

The poet ignored the remark. Her "Aunt Calline" must have advised her mother of what type of people frequented the Kennerley's home. She still wondered who Miss Dow's spy was. A maid, a neighbor, perhaps even Helen?

Cora watched as her eldest entered the house. She had to admit Vincent was looking fine. The poet walked with a level of confidence she'd never seen before and it both thrilled and disquieted her. Her Vincent looked and sounded like a college girl. That alone was an accomplishment Cora could lay claim to. After all, it was she who had prepared Vincent for that possibility. Yet Cora suspected this might also change their dynamic.

As the girls ripped through the latest fashions in the poet's suitcase, including some items that reflected the rising hemlines of the coming year, the nurse wondered about what awaited them in the sealed gift boxes. She did not want to look above her station…or below it.

The whole town knew that neither Vincent nor Norma were virgins. While they put on a good front, boys will talk. Kenneth had become possessive. Fritz had turned his attention elsewhere.

Cora had her own chaste romance with the husband of one of her patients. The wife wasn't expected to live, but it would require a move to Rockport and Kathleen still had a semester in school. How she managed to keep the flirtation buried from prying eyes God only knew. Even her daughters did not suspect.

That night over dinner they discussed school, including the poet's first term, Kathleen's pending high school graduation and her hopes of following Vincent to Vassar.

"I wish we had more time together," Kathleen innocently began.

"Next spring you should come directly home so we can enjoy the nicer weather together," Norma added.

Cora's face turned iron, a look the girls were all too familiar with. Somehow someone had said something or done something that displeased their mother. They waited for the eruption while passing the potatoes.

It finally came just as Vincent handed the bowl to her mother.

"If she can be dragged away from those people!" Cora snarled.

"The Kennerleys?" the poet said quietly. She hoped the calmness of her tone would keep her mother from continuing.

"You know who I mean!"

Kathleen got up from the table ostensibly to refill their pitcher of water.

"Mama, you don't know them. They are very respectable people."

"Miss Dow doesn't think so, and I respect the opinion of a Christian woman like her than a man who sells pornography!" Cora's visage had a quality that once had turned her children to stone.

Vincent understood her mother's reference. Kennerley had recently been arrested for selling a novel considered salacious. "Mother, Mr. Goodman's book, *Hagar Revelly*, is far from obscene. We've been accused of worse."

"That's exactly what I mean," Cora stormed. "A book about two sisters in New York and what poverty leads them too…It's just disgusting."

"It's practically the story of our lives," Vincent replied. "Not all of it, naturally, dear. We've never been prostitutes. It's only what might happen if not for your strength."

Norma smiled. Her sister was getting better at using flattery to dispel their mother's eruptions.

Kathleen came back to the table and refilled everyone's glasses.

Cora was momentarily silent, but it wasn't the praise of her eldest child that cooled her tongue. It was the realization that no matter what she said or did the world was changing and with it her daughters.

"All my business is here," Cora said in a non-sequitur that drove each child to look at one another in confused astonishment.

Vincent managed to put the remark together. "No one is saying we're moving to New York, Mumbles. My friends are my friends because they understand me."

Now it was Cora's turn to look confused. "And we don't?"

Norma decided it was time to take a stab at clarification. "I think what Vince is saying is Mr. Kennerley published the revelry book because he understands people like us and believes the world should too."

The poet smiled. Norma was close but the truth was more complex than that reason alone. Kennerley understood her need for freedom—a fact she dared not mention to her family. "Of course, you understand me. In fact, when I tell my friends at college about my family, they can scarcely believe it. No one is as close with their family as I am."

Again, the subtext had to remain unsaid. It was true that Vincent bragged about her family to friends, and that some were envious of the closeness they shared. Yet few knew the extent to which Vincent hid her true feelings, not just for her family but her friends as well.

Cora stared at her children. The lull in conversation lapsed into another topic. Sure, Vincent would love to attend the Knights of Pythias Dance. There were sure to be at least some boys who could dance the latest steps. Besides, Norma and Kathleen might meet boys who met some measure of their mother's Victorian sensibilities. Cora wasn't aware of her eldest's calculations. She only knew there was no point in trying to take them all on.

Kathleen was getting that funny twist in her face and Cora knew this would soon result in a scene of one kind or another. It was a mixture of both fear and pique that she had first seen on her youngest's face when they all had typhoid as children. Kathleen had been the sickest of them all and there had been moments when Henry and Cora were certain they would lose her. Her little face would wrinkle in a way not unlike a child about to pass an enormous bowel movement, a mixture of surprise and discomfort that would either result in a flood of tears or odd nervous laughter. Kathleen had not been fully normal since. Cora worried where the temperamental veneer would lead as her youngest grew older. Would she be able to stand the rigors of college, or would she be better off taking a non-demanding job here in Camden where she could be close to the ministrations of her mother?

* * *

When the phone rang the following morning, Cora had already left for work. Norma and Kathleen had slept in and only Vincent was up to take the call.

"Hello."

There was a brief pause before she heard her Uncle Bert's voice. "Why, Vincent, you're home."

"Uncle Bert!" the poet cried. Here was a chance for a break from Cora's relentless judgement. "It would be great to see you. Are you coming down?"

"No," her kindly uncle laughed. Whether he was aware of her intent was anyone's guess. "In fact, we were calling to see if you had made it home, but I see you have."

"How is Aunt Clara?"

"She's fine. She was thinking you might stop in on your way home or when you're headed back to Pough-keep-sigh."

Vincent ignored his pronunciation of the college town. "I'm so sorry I didn't stop in," she said. This was sincere. She loved her mother's brother. "I had thought of stopping but I already stopped overnight at Aunt Sue's and figured I best get home."

"Yep," her uncle laughed. "Your mother called saying you were late getting there. I don't know why she worries so much. You've always been a sensible girl."

"Bless you," Vincent smiled. She wondered if inviting herself up would be too presumptuous.

"When did you get home?"

"Saturday afternoon. It took forever what with the bridge down in Wiscasset," she explained.[340]

"I heard about that. Awful nuisance," her uncle said cheerfully. "Perhaps you'd like to come up after Christmas on your way back to college."

This was her opportunity. "Actually, Uncle Bert, if it's all the same to you, perhaps I could come over tonight."

"That would be swell! Your Aunt Rose will be delighted. When should we expect you?"

"I'm free today. I'll just throw a few things together and come for a night or two. There's a dance on Wednesday I promised the girls I'd attend, but otherwise I'd love a nice long visit."

They finished the call just as Kathleen lumbered down the stairs.

"Who was that?" she asked with a yawn.

"Uncle Bert. They just invited me to spend a couple of nights with them, and before you say anything, I'll be back for the Wednesday dance."

"I wasn't going to say anything," Kathleen protested.

"Good," the poet replied. She lifted the darning she had started the night before from the end table and began to sit down.

"I just wondered what Mother would think," Kathleen looked out the window. "Has the mail arrived yet?"

"Not that I know of," Vincent replied. "Don't you worry. She'll be fine with me visiting Uncle Bert."

"You know how she was last night," the brunette said in almost a whisper.

"Yes, I do, but she was just worried about me, and she doesn't know Mr. Kennerley. If she did, I know she would find him charming."

"I think that's what she's afraid of." Norma's laughter could be heard coming down the stairs.

Vincent joined in. "She'd probably be suspicious of Prince Charming."

Kathleen began to laugh. "I suspect she thinks every man is a Lord Byron."

"Yet unable to write poetry that's worth a damn." Vincent giggled as she laid down her darning and walked toward the kitchen to make a pot of tea.

The sisters exploded in laughter and for a moment Vincent reconsidered her desire to escape to her uncle's house. The moment didn't last long. On the kitchen table was a note from their mother with a list of chores none of them wanted to do.

"Tell you what," Vincent said as she returned with the news. "I'll finish my darning and iron, if you two bake the bread and beat the carpet." Cora hadn't listed house cleaning so that needed task wasn't mentioned. As an afterthought, the poet only added, "…and one of us should shovel the walk."

Norma frowned. She was still mooning for Kenneth, and he planned on coming over. Maybe he could clear the path to the door.

Their tasks assigned, Vincent quickly packed an overnight bag with only the most necessary items before finishing her darning and speeding through the ironing. Norma and Kathleen flipped a coin for which of the other onerous tasks they would complete.

The long walk to her aunt and uncle's home reminded the poet of what she loved best about Penobscot Bay, despite the miserable weather. The blue sky peeking through the gray mist, the brutal whirl of the wind pushing birds back, the dark mottled silver green of the spruce trees along the way reminded her of all the Christmases she had enjoyed with her family before her exposure to the very different world that was New York.

She realized that while she loved her family, the Pandora's Box of the outside world held too many treasures for her to remain satisfied with their merry band alone. Even the sight of her aunt and uncle standing on the porch felt constricting considering what she now knew. Still, it felt good to have a short respite from the suffocating love of her primary family. She knew them too well, loved them too much. The Latin proverb was true, "quod nimia familiaritas pasid contemptum." Familiarity did indeed breed contempt.

"Edna!"

She heard the call but ignored it. No one but strangers called her that anymore.

"Edna!"

The call was more insistent and closer as she turned to look at the voice.

"Your head is certainly in the clouds," her Aunt Rose said as their eyes met.

Vincent laughed. "Oh, sorry, I guess I didn't know you meant me."

The poet quickly studied her aunt's face. Rose did not have the careworn look of her mother. Vincent was overcome with shame: how could she cause her mother so much grief?

"You look just as always," the young redhead cried, embracing her uncle and his wife.

"And you're prettier than ever," Uncle Bert observed. "You're really growing up."

"Growing up, Bert? Why, Edna's already 21 and in college. I'd say she's been grown up a while." Rose paused as she realized why her niece had not responded. "Oh, my, you prefer Vincent, don't you?"

The poet grinned. "Of course, with family and close friends."

"No wonder she didn't respond when you called." They all laughed as they stepped inside the comfortable home. Uncle Bert took her bag and Aunt Rose looped her arm.

Their home felt familiar and yet different. After a brief chat they helped her settle into their small guest room. Vincent concluded she loved these relatives deeply, perhaps because she felt so loved.[341] *"It is the same as I feel when I'm far from my family. Maybe distance is what I need to see it."*

Rose soon called her down for dinner. Vincent had already changed into dinner dress before she realized that it was unlikely her aunt and uncle would make a similar adjustment. Knowing it was rude to hold up the meal by redressing, she descended the stairs.

"Wow!" Uncle Bert blurted. She looked stunning in her new dress from Filene's.

"You didn't have to dress for dinner, dear," Aunt Rose said with a warm smile. "We're family."

"I'm sorry. I guess I'm just in the habit now. It's required at McGlynn's."

"Oh, my!"

"Well, all I can say is it's a cracking good-looking dress," her Uncle Bert added. "They'll be jealous back at Vassar."

There was a reverence in the way he said the name of the school. What a wonder it all was. One of their own going to college. It felt like something out of one of Cora's fantasies.

Over dinner, Vincent told her aunt and uncle all about her life at Vassar, leaving out parts that might find their way back to her mother. They laughed and expressed the approval she needed. The chicken dinner was as good as anything she'd had at McGlynn's, and the conversation warm and comforting.

* * *

By the time she went to bed, Vincent had only one question: "I wonder why people love me so."[342] As she sat looking at the icy night sky, the smells of dinner had quelled to a tasty memory and the sounds of her relatives reduced to a distant snore.

The poet pondered her relationships. Fil, Katherine, Arthur, Hal, Fritz—and those she admitted to no one—danced through her heart like a carousel. Each person had their own qualities and her desire for each was so different her head spun with possibilities.

Fritz had given up on her although he flashed moon eyes when he wasn't glaring. Katherine's embrace was tempered by fear of scandal. Fil was possessive, demanding and willing to try nearly anything. Arthur was not really interested in sex, although she had managed once or twice to consummate their poetic symmetry. Her relationship with Hal was a lot like her bond with Katherine, more spiritual than physical—but for different reasons. He could appreciate beauty, even get aroused by a woman who wasn't looking for marriage, but his eyes only settled on men. By now Vincent knew Hal was more in love with his married friend Arthur Davison Ficke than he would ever be with her. The poet's "Spiritual Advisor"[343] was less interested in Hal than he was in any woman he could get his hands on. In fact, as Vincent would later find out, Hal's dear friend and her epistolary confidante was more like her in temperament than anyone currently in her circle of romantic interests.

But there were also her familiar connections to consider. Her father was ill again after more than two years of robust health. She hardly knew him. Her memories were fonder than their quantity deserved. At fifty, he was a man who had been sick rarely but when he was it was severely. His health, she surmised, was not unlike his employment history. Although she didn't know it yet, this period of illness would be short, and her father's death wouldn't come for almost twenty years. Ella had written with the news of his illness hoping she could entice the now much more experienced poet back to Kingman, but by now Vincent viewed her first lover as no more than a pen pal.

The steady ticking of the banjo wall clock began to invade her mind as it wandered, blocking her thoughts as she tried to imagine what life might be like in England with Arthur Hooley. She saw herself in a little town on a hill. From that high crest[344] she imagined the world that had given birth to the much older man. It was a world of Victorian manners and sensibilities, of starched collars and murderous corsets. *No wonder,* she thought, *he cannot bring himself to abandon those mores. How could he be such a modern thinker when he is such a prude?* She could never go back to the old-style corsets and endless hours of sewing fancy corset covers to shield her from whalebone stays. Times were changing. Even in her short life she'd seen enough to know the days of group corset circles were over. Yes, women were still bound up in clothing designed to keep their walk to a mincing gait—even if hemlines were rising, shoulders dropping and waistlines loosening to allow at least some freedom of movement. All those things—sex, Arthur, history, style, social politics—swirled in her head until at last she fell into the arms of Morpheus, the most satisfying lover to date.

* * *

Tolerance was almost in view at the Knights of Pythias Dance. The Knights, dressed in their fraternal regalia, were kind, benevolent and even generous, but there were limits to their tolerance.[345] Camden's subordinate lodge had forty-three members, most of whom were middle-aged men of prominence. The few "Pages" who remained eligible bachelors immediately spotted the three Millay girls. Brunette Kathleen, blonde Norma and redhead Vincent made quite an impression, though some wondered about the differences in coloring. The rumors had drifted through the town like the smell of distant smoke. There were all sorts of accountings for their lineage. Nonetheless, this didn't deter the young Romeos who asked them to dance.

All the sisters were excellent dancers, particularly Norma, who made it her business to learn all the newest steps and then teach her sisters. Vincent now knew a few even Norma hadn't heard of. Few men knew a third of what the sisters knew. Still, as the three comely girls swirled around the dance floor, heads turned. Vincent made sure they all had dresses of the latest fashion and Norma had created small corsages to match each dress.

It didn't take long for a recently promoted Esquire to approach the poet as she waited for a chance on the floor. He had fashioned a baldric from an old saddle cinch strap, embossing "F * C * B" for the Knight's motto, "Friendship, Charity, Benevolence" across it and the figure of Samson straining against the pillars at the top of the scabbard so it appeared the Biblical strongman was pushing the guard of his sword apart.

"May I please have this dance?" the tall, pleasant-faced man of twenty-three asked.

Vincent looked him over. She liked the homemade gear that dressed up the rather ordinary sword. "I'd love to."

George Henry was a good dancer and matched her steps well, even though he knew only a few of the more modern moves. They enjoyed a passable Grizzley Bear before breaking into a Turkey Trot.

As they moved across the floor, Vincent learned that George had come from modest means, but a recent inheritance gave him some options, one of which was joining the Knights of Pythias and opening his own saddle shop.

"That explains your sash."

"Baldric," George corrected. "It's called a baldric." He seemed to stand a little taller as he said the word.

"I take it you ride?"

"Of course. A horse has a soul. Not like these new-fangled flivvers."

Vincent smiled through her disappointment. The only thing she liked more than the latest fashion was a sporty new automobile.

"Do you like to ride?" George asked hopefully.

"Yes." It was as close to honesty as she could muster.

The six-piece orchestra brought the rag "Waiting for the Robert E. Lee" to a close and the drummer did a roll and cymbal splash to signal an announcement. The voice of the Grand Knight of the Lodge boomed.

"Ladies and fellow Knights! There will be a drawing for a turkey at the end of the next tune. Knights are now passing out tickets. Good luck!"

At that moment, a man of about sixty handed Vincent and George slips of paper with numbers on them. The poet glanced around to make sure Norma and Kathleen got one as well. Having three chances improved their odds considerably. Her siblings nodded in reply from across the room. The band began, "When Irish Eyes are Smiling." Vincent considered it a good omen.

The waltz was George's best step and Vincent used the opportunity to gently suggest she would not be available for dates because she was going to college in New York. Neither mentioned writing letters. As the singer warbled "sure they'll steal your heart away," every couple on the floor slowed and looked down at their numbers.

With another cymbal crash at the end of the song, the Grand Knight announced, "Sixty-three! Who has number sixty-three?"

The poet's eyes grew brighter. The family had been wondering what they would have for Christmas dinner. Before the drawing, it looked like they would be limited to beans and greens in pork fat.

"Sixty-three!" the man called again.

"That's me, that's me!" Vincent cried. Her sisters raced to her side. The Grand Knight approached to check the slip of paper. George beamed almost as much as his dance partner.

"Sir, I am honored," he said, bowing to the older man. It was part of the dictates of the order.

"Esquire, you have indeed brought charity to this fair lady." The Grand Knight drew his extremely ornate sword and tapped the bowed shoulders of George.

Vincent looked bemused as the sword was pushed back into its scabbard. George had nothing to do with winning the turkey. Why would he get the credit?

"Oh, Vince, it's so exciting!" Kathleen cried. A turkey would be meals for a week, and a wanted change from their usual gastronomical monotony.

"Oh, what fun to bring it home to Mother," Vincent exclaimed.[346]

"Do we have sweet potatoes?" Norma asked.

As the girls discussed side dishes, George basked in reflected glory. "I'm so happy for you and your family."

"You're so kind," Vincent replied.

When the music started up again, the poet found she couldn't muster enough interest when balanced against the prospect of seeing her mother's face brighten. Her sisters shared her doldrums, leading them to huddle in a corner away from their dance partners as soon as the music stopped.

"There's a dance in Rockland tomorrow," the blonde offered. "We could go there after Christmas dinner."

"My boy is a terrible dancer," the youngest Millay moaned. "My feet are killing me."

"Then let's go!" Vincent directed. "I'll go up and get the bird. You go outside and wait for me."

Moments later, the poet emerged with an eighteen-pound turkey in a large burlap sack. She hadn't counted on it dripping and she found she had to hold it away from her body to avoid spoiling her new dress,

"It's almost as big as you are," Norma laughed.

"Good golly! How are we supposed to get it home without ruining our clothes?"

"I'll wrap it in my old coat," Kathleen offered.

"And walk home in the snow without one?"

"It's stopped snowing and it's not too far."

"It's three-quarters of a mile!" Norma cried.

"It's worth it," Kathleen replied, her mouth getting that stubborn look it sometimes got when she felt ganged up on by her sisters.

Vincent looked at her younger sibling. She knew a solution had to be found as it was already thirty-degrees and getting colder.[347] "How about this? Let's all wear our coats inside out and take turns carrying the bird. That way if there's any mess it will be where people can't see it."

Norma and Kathleen nodded. They set the turkey on the ground, quickly switched over their coats, and started their trudge toward home. Vincent took the first turn.

When they arrived, Cora was wearing a knit cap over her head for warmth and had just added the last of their coal to the fire in anticipation of their arrival. It was plain she had done without heat in the girl's absence. Her business was going through another dry spell, and she was behind on the rent.

"What have you got there?" the nurse asked.

"Wouldn't you like to know," Norma teased.

"Close your eyes and stick out your hands," Vincent demanded sweetly. "Be ready for something heavy."

As Cora complied, Kathleen could contain herself no longer. "Can you believe it? Vincent won us a turkey!"

"What?" their esteemed "Mumbles" replied as she accepted the bird. She looked down and began to cry. "How…how?" she blubbered.

"The Knights had a drawing at the dance."

"How much did it cost?" The concern etched on Cora's face overcame the joy she felt.

"Nothing. It was just a drawing," Kathleen explained. "Vincent had number sixty-three, I had number forty-seven, and what did you have, Normie?"

"Twenty-eight; and as luck would have it, Vince won."

"The odds of one of us winning were pretty good," Vincent interjected.

"So, see, it's all perfectly fine," Kathleen soothed.

Cora was torn between delight and fretting. The prospect of a turkey for Christmas dinner won out. There was something wonderfully Dickensian about it, with Kathleen as Tiny Tim, her body and mind still bearing the scars of childhood illness, Norma as Bob Cratchit's eldest daughter Martha, and Vincent as…Cora hesitated. Who was Vincent? Scrooge's nephew? The Ghost of Christmas Present? Perhaps she belonged in another Dicken's story. Was her eldest Steerforth, a charming rogue with loyalty and concern for only herself? No. Her talented, smart and fortunate daughter lovingly offered enough food for more than a week. Cora realized she could preserve the bone broth. She could mix it with barley and have it as a casserole and a soup. She began to cry harder as she took in what a difference this sudden good fortune made for them.

"Merry Christmas, Mama." Vincent began to cry herself.

By now the turkey was too heavy for any of them. They teamed to carry it into the kitchen and put it in the ice box until morning.

"How long do you think it will take to cook?"

"About six hours. I'll have to put it in brine first thing, then in the oven by ten or so." Her eyes scanned the collection of herbs that hung around the kitchen window. She began to pull a select few down. "We'll need butter."

"I'll get it tomorrow," Norma suggested.

"The stores will be closed," her elder sister corrected.

"My friend Paul has a cow," Kathleen said. "Maybe we could get some cream and churn it ourselves."

The idea of freshly churned butter took Cora back to her childhood when a lovely cow devoted her entire life to the Buzzell family. "That sounds just right. Call him first thing."

"He doesn't have a phone. I'll walk over in the morning." Kathleen yawned and leaned into the door frame. "I think all the excitement has caught up with me."

"Me, too," Norma blinked.

The contagion of yawns drew Cora to conclude they should all go to bed.

* * *

As she stared at the ceiling of her bedroom, the poet once again embraced the love she felt for her family. How they struggled! Tomorrow, the girls would benefit from Vincent's poker winnings and the pure chance of drawing the turkey, but otherwise each month was a game of roulette. Cora's client base for wigs and hair pieces grew smaller every year thanks to changes in fashion, and her age made it tougher to get nursing jobs. There was also the cost of making sure the family remained educated and connected to the world of their peers. Cora had long sacrificed items for herself to provide books, music lessons and other middle-class incidentals they could ill afford. It was a way to assure her daughters married well—or at least could support themselves. A tear escaped the corner of Vincent's eye as she realized how intolerant she was being. Of course, her mother would be gruff. Anything the poet did would reflect on the desirability of her sisters. Her face flushed with guilt. The rush of emotion exhausted her. Soon a deep and restless slumber let her ignore the icy room.

* * *

Christmas began with nut meats and a single orange each. Eggs were being saved for a less bountiful day. The women spent the day cooking and cleaning in preparation for their planned Christmas feast.

The meal was as delicious as it was plentiful. In addition to the turkey, the family enjoyed beans, greens in pork fat, boiled potatoes and a mincemeat pie.

When it came time for the gift exchange, Vincent surprised her sisters with pretty, embroidered serviettes and her mother with a hat that was more in fashion than the ancient nurse's cap she usually wore. Yet the previous night's resolutions to be more patient with Cora fell away when her mother's response to her gift was a lecture on economics. If she hadn't already planned on going to the dance in Rockland with Norma and Kenneth, Cora's less than gracious response sealed her determination to get out of the house.

The poet was able to show off her tan gown with the train, which never failed to elicit attention, while Norma had the opportunity to dazzle Kenneth in the soft, lemon-yellow gown Vincent had purchased for her. The attention drawn to the elder Millay girls made many of the attendees wonder how the pair happened upon such fashion when many knew their rent was already over a month late.

The rumors didn't stop. They brewed in a wicked snowstorm the following night. A few of the old crowd came to the Millay home for a little party, but otherwise the most moving moment of the holiday was a gift from Fritz, a book they had discussed; George Bernard Shaw's *Pygmalion*.

"Good old Fritz," she remarked as she unwrapped the brown paper and twine.[348] "He didn't forget." She remembered the boy who had briefly caught her fancy before and during that wicked excursion to Sherman's Point the previous summer.

Yet Fritz's kindness wasn't reason enough to stay in Camden for the rest of the Christmas break. Her mother, sisters and even Fritz felt like anchors, not wings. She longed to be away, safely tucked away in New York with her books and admirers. A short visit with her Aunt Sue in Portland only emphasized the reasons she felt she had to escape. She wanted to be back at Vassar. That was home now. Next year she would live on campus as a sophomore. Housing would be quite different than at McGlynn's. Less private in some ways, more so in others. She could hardly wait to see where she would be assigned.

On December 28, 1913, she boarded the train back to New York. In the berth above hers a young man was quietly breathing. She wondered what he looked like and tried to imagine some onboard beloved. Soon she was matching his breathing to her own. She drifted to sleep, her finger stuck in the pages of Shaw's tale of a girl changed by circumstance, created in the image and likeness of a man who thought himself capable of modeling the ideal woman. She awoke with a scream that matched the shuddering screech of the brakes as the train rumbled over the switchbacks carved out of the Appalachian Range.

26. My Tortured Soul

1913-1914

Arthur was there to meet her at the station. She had been waiting for twenty minutes already. She tracked him down.

"Good afternoon," he said in that odd formal way of his.

"Darling!" she cried, swinging her arms toward him like an actress in an Edison movie.

Arthur looked down on her. His eyes were gray as clouds.

"Have you got us a taxi?"

"Yes, yes," she panted. All efforts of appearing indifferent were failing. She had to have him before she went back to that pink and gray college.[349] She took his bag for a moment and then handed it to a porter. "Number 32," she blurted.

The porter understood. At the curb, a virtual zeppelin was parked with its driver alongside it. "Missy wants ya to wait. She'll be here directly," the porter explained in his fading dialect.

Vincent liked to think New York made everyone smarter, even the Negro. Her thinly veiled bigotry was tempered by a marginal awareness of how servitude felt.

Arthur and Vincent meandered a bit on the way to the cab. "I've really missed you," the poet said, staring into eyes captivated by nothing but his own doubt and pain.

Should he tell her he was dying? He knew it even more closely than the doctors. His eyes had the look of a cat's eye marble.

He reached for her and pulled her close. His lips brushed against her cheek. Arthur was forty but looked sixty. Vincent was not quite twenty-two. Was that Einstein fellow right about time? She studied Arthur's face as one might a map. Where was he going?

Where were *they* going?

She thought she heard him say, "Sweetheart," as he squeezed her hand.

"I love you, too."

"Let's talk when we're at my place," he emphasized.

Vincent dropped her eyes. She was always too forward. Everyone had warned her. She needed to appear indifferent. She wasn't, of course. In fact, she cared dreadfully what people thought. It was just that love always seemed to get tangled into sex.

They rode toward Arthur's New York apartment in near silence. Other than the bland ruminations of how well they had slept the night before and how bitterly cold it was, their conversation gave no hint of their friendship.

Desire was a demanding mistress. If it wasn't Hal, it would be Arthur. If it wasn't Arthur, it would be Katherine. If not Katherine, Fil. And if not Fil, some obliging benefactor or professor. Vincent knew how to be discreet. In fact, it was her one saving grace. She just wondered how she managed to attract and be compelled toward such disparate people.

Some months before, as she and Arthur lay chastely beside each other, Vincent had whispered, "How do you define love?" He didn't answer. The question had apparently been for herself.

Love, in that youthful moment, was, in truth, the quiet breath of satisfaction her partners made when they reached orgasm. Emerging from the dark domains of discipline, the girls let go perhaps too easily. Vincent had yet to feel that particular glow, but she knew how to share it with others. Why wouldn't Arthur take her again as he had one drunken night against a tree in the park near the Kennerley estate. It had been the most exciting tryst of their year-long affair.

She watched as the sun set against the skyline. But what if love was something beyond what she presently knew? A perpetual student, the poet knew her perspective had changed dramatically since "Renascence." Now her life was one narrow island and its far-flung suburbs.

The cab reached Arthur's apartment building. They split the fare, and each carried their own luggage.

"Entréz s'il vous plait!" he smiled.

The miniscule residence was much like his cabin near the Kennerleys. His ever-present pipe stands. A rather large and dark armoire with some kind of family crest. A barely made bed. A desk with piles and piles of papers. A floor to ceiling bookcase overflowing with essential knowledge. Other than indoor plumbing and a slightly larger kitchen, Arthur seemed to prefer places where there was only room for himself.

They ordered in from a neighborhood Italian place halfway up the block. As they dined, they exchanged ideas. She knelt before Arthur and rested her head upon his knee, while he stroked her hair. It was just as she had imagined it would be with her beloved. This, the poet sighed, was love.

The tension between them grew. By ten o'clock, she had to ask.

"Dearest?"

"Yes, my love," he replied in a tone that may as well have been "my aunt." He raised her chin toward him.

"Don't you…um…want me?"

The poet knew she had to push back any emotion that escaped her trembling chin.

Arthur knew he had to tell her. "I'm sick."

"Sick?"

"I might be dying."

Vincent took this in. Death was no stranger to her. But nobody that mattered had ever died before. Distant relatives, of course, had died, whom she had never seen or saw for an hour, and couldn't really be said to have lived at all.[350] But Arthur?

"Of course," she muttered.

"What's that?"

"I was just noticing that I've known you were ill for some time."

Arthur was struck by this. She didn't seem to notice much of anything he felt. "You noticed?"

Vincent nodded. It wasn't a premonition. It was the result of noticing his frailty and attributing it to why they no longer had sex.

"Oh, darling, how can I be so cruel?" he said in a manner more grand than necessary. The poet looked at him askance and he said it again, only this time in a softer tone. He added, "You do not deserve cruelty."

"I'm glad *you* think so." She forced a laugh hoping to sound flippant.

He reached for her hand and turned her palm upward and kissed it, then cradling her head in his hands. This allowed a corralled tear to jump its fence.

The poet had to go back to Vassar in two days. Should she stay with a dying man? What about her mother, Kathleen, Miss Dow, Miss Haight, and all the rest of them? For that matter, what about Mitchell Kennerley, their mutual friend and the one who brought them together?[351]

"What's wrong?" she asked.

"Cancer or something, I'm not sure."

Vincent had once delivered medicines and changes of clothes to her mother when she was tending a man with late-stage cancer. She shuddered at the thought and did not want any more details. The memory of the man in her mother's care was horrid. His emaciated, unshaven face and yellow-gray pallor had given her bad dreams for weeks. She pushed the memory aside and imagined Arthur's naked body beside her own. They had only been together that way a few times. She needed to feel him inside her again. It would not happen that day or night.

* * *

The following morning, they got up and sat in their nightdresses drinking tea. Barely a word passed between them. The First World War loomed in the world outside their bubble. There was a film at the Bijou based on Conan Doyle's "*Study in Scarlet*," and Mary Pickford was still "America's Sweetheart" in *Cinderella* at the Odeon. Yet they both knew they couldn't sit still long enough to enjoy anything. A sense of desperation crept over Vincent, and she didn't know why. Was Arthur serious when he said he was going home to Newcastle-Under-Lyme?[352] The silence between them pressed down upon her heart. She had to speak.

"Arthur, do you know who said, 'I sometimes think that all great passion is like a kiss in mid-battle—a difficult peace between oil and water, between candles and dark night'? Do you not think it is very beautiful?—'a *difficult peace*'!"[353]

"Yeats, I think," he replied before returning to the newspaper.

Vincent leaned back and wished for a more detailed reply. She gave up and went back to her new book.

"Don't do that." The sharp voice startled her. She looked up, still not sure who had spoken.

"Did you say something?"

"Yes. I said, don't do that, that thing with your knee. It makes your hands look ugly."[354] Arthur pointed toward her raised left knee and the entwined fingers that held it close to her chest. She loved his hands, and the fact he was pointing at her hands and calling them ugly made her sad. Why was he so cruel? She dropped her knee and put her hands primly in her lap. "You old bear."

The Englishman said nothing. He put down the paper and retrieved a volume that was never far from his bedside. *Ivanhoe* was required reading where he came from, and he remained intrigued by its immortal page after page conceived in a mortal mind.[355]

"Read to me," she asked after a time. She watched as his long fingers turned the page. "Please?"

The editor looked up and studied her. She looked so sweet and boyish sitting there. If it wasn't for the sweep of long copper hair draped over her shoulders, he might be able to imagine her one. His tone softened. "If you like."

Vincent leaned against the bed, closed her eyes and listened as his perfect diction practically sang the words of Sir Walter Scott. "For he that does good, having the unlimited power to do evil, deserves praise not only for the good which he performs, but the evil which he forebears."[356]

"Would that I was Rebecca tending to your wounds," the young redhead sighed and reached up for his free hand.

Arthur smiled but did not reply. He pulled his hand gently away from hers and turned the page. He decided that it was as good a stopping point as any in the novel. He set the book down and stood up. "Shall we get dressed and go for a walk?"

It was more of a command than a suggestion. It was also a diversion. Outside her moon calf eyes could not plead so desperately. He knew what she wanted. He didn't know how to make it clear to her. When they first met her innocence and tomboyish attitude was almost stirring. He knew some people knew things about his taste that he didn't want Vincent to know. Harriet Munroe was heard to call him one of Vincent's pet pansies, but he wasn't like Hal Bynner. The fact that Hal had shown any interest in Vincent was quite amusing given what everyone knew about the handsome translator. Perhaps the almost masculine quality of her desire was what had attracted him in the first place. The difference was that Hal liked men close to his own age. Arthur liked them very young. Vincent was now too mature to arouse his fantasy of pubescent romance. While still comparatively a child, particularly when it came to her obsession with him, Vincent had ceased being obedient and now danced to her own drummer.

As for the poet, she didn't understand any of it. In all the hours they had spent together he'd been most ardent upon their first meeting, when the virginal flush of her cheeks still lingered. She had no competition, at least as far as his cousin Helen Kennerley knew. Was Vincent too stupid to understand his brilliance or too brilliant to be the child he seemed to desire? Vincent did not let herself imagine he was like the landlord who plagued her whenever her mother was out of town so many years before. He was, he had to be, her beloved. He was exactly as she had imagined him. He read aloud to her as she knelt at his feet. He allowed her to kiss his hand and never demanded sex in the anxious, greedy way some boys and men had. Theirs was a romantic love, imbued with a kind of sacred purity. Nonetheless, the poet's sexual awakening had thrown the doors of chastity off their hinges. She wanted sex. She needed sex. It helped her feel seen and connected. It gave her control. To be the most tremendous lover was her goal. The *Rubaiyat*, Plato's *Symposium*, the *Aeneid*, the *Song of Solomon*, the poetry of Homer and Sappho were her inspiration. While some of the girls at Vassar were thinking of other girls, others were thinking of men, but not men like her beloved editor.[357] How could Arthur be the manifested creature of her incantations and *not* desire physical intimacy? Was something wrong with the spell she had cast?

They walked to the corner of Lexington and 41st before the smells of a bakery drew them in. It was the sort of excursion that usually sidetracked the unspoken conversation about sex. Today, the diversion was only partially successful. After the sweet delights of the newly opened McMurphy's, they discussed how it compared to Veniero's or Ferrara's in Little Italy or Glaser's in Yorkville. When Arthur said Ferrara's was better overall, all Vincent could think to ask was, "Then why didn't we go *there* for breakfast?"

Arthur sighed. "Child, you mustn't get in a tizzy over something as ordinary as a bakery."

The poet bit her tongue at the word "child," but persisted. "I'm not. It's a simple question. Why not go to the best place? Why did you choose McMurphy's?"

"Because it's new," he replied with a snap. "I like things that are new."

"Is that why we never make love anymore?" Vincent pouted. "Because I'm 'not new'? And, by the way, I am not a child in love with you to be patted and sent away or to be scolded and shaken."[358]

The older man looked down at the "child" beside him. "Let's go back to my apartment."

Once within the confines of his apartment, a lengthy and explosive scene followed, carrying well into the afternoon. Finally, as the tension mounted, he began to yell at her, "You wicked boy!" culminating in grabbing her and violently throwing her over his knee. Vincent was taken aback. She struggled against his anger fueled strength. Why was he calling her boy? He began spanking her, hard. "Is this what you want, you wicked boy? Is it?" he screamed.[359]

All Vincent could do was cry. There was nothing more to say. He'd injured more than her pride. The fire was out by which Arthur stood and said aloud those lovely verses while his voice shook. The fire was out by which she read to him the "Triumph of Time." The fire was out which burned that first night in his little house, when he had said, "I guess it's fun living alone, sometimes." He didn't really love her then, if he ever did. Arthur only loved the tireless and vivacious girl who looked seventeen. No one had ever guessed her secret, eating sorrow.[360] While Arthur retreated to the solitary comfort of his books, Vincent packed and left for the Y. She could not, would not, look back at his flushed and tormented face. Something had been broken in Vincent's sense of idealized love on December 30 amid the screaming and violation. It would remain a date wedged in her memory as surely as the moment she knew Ferdinand Earle had only been playing her for his own designs. She often wondered if Arthur thought the nearly nineteen-year age difference between them gave him the right to consider her a child to be spanked and scolded. She thought not. Her relationships had already proven to her that she was wise beyond her years. Her naïveté was such that she even imagined she would never be fooled again. What she didn't realize was her self-defined maturity was the product of pride, the kind that comes before a fall.

27. Deep in the Earth I Rested

1914

The weekend at the Y was an exercise in self-restraint. Miss Dow and other benefactors were gently but firmly insisting she use her time studying to ensure she'd make it through another year. She was beginning to hate the YWCA almost as much as she hated Vassar. A visit with Sara Teasdale somehow interfered with a visit from another Arthur, her spiritual advisor, Arthur Davison Ficke, Hal's great friend.[361] It was probably just as well. The imposition of rules and social demands made any fulfillment of their three-year flirtation impossible. Besides, Vincent felt like a kid in a candy store on the way to the dentist.

When at last she returned to Vassar on January 5, 1914, Vincent realized that she didn't hate it as much as she imagined. The poet was greeted by her classmates with excitement and requests for participation in more things than she could possibly do. Besides taking the role of Princess Daisy of Pretentia[362] in the fall production for the sophomore party, Vincent had learned there was a contest sponsored by the college's magazine, *The Miscellany*. Prizes for the best poem, story, essay and play were being offered along with $15 in each category.[363] Immediately she knew she would submit her story "Barbara-on-the-Beach," but what else?

There was a piece she'd been working on that she was certain would make a bigger hit in a college full of women than anywhere else in the world.[364] It might even do a lot for her in making her professors more forgiving of her frequent absences from class. "Oh, well, she must be writing a poem," she imagined them saying when it came time for scholarships for the following year.

The composition was *Interim*, a two-hundred-line elegy from the point of view of a man who has lost his wife. It had been years in the making. In fact, she had started it before she began "Renascence". The influences of her youth were fraught with meaning for the 19-year-old who had composed with work, particularly Milton's *Lycidas* and Shelley's *Adonais*.[365] These classic pastoral elegies, like nearly all her work, relied on natural images to make her point. The thinking was that everyone has watched a flower fade, or a butterfly flicker the last wave of its wings. Submitting this poem while she was lurching into another period of wondering about God and Death made sense.

It seemed appropriate that the young woman who had written about being a man buried "six feet underground"[366] in "Renascence" would cast herself as the man's dead wife in *Interim*. The book, table and room portrayed in the poem were, in fact, Vincent's own bedroom in Camden. The 8 ½-by-6 ½-inch brown bound book held all the grief of that little girl who had been left in the doorway of Auntie Bine's farmhouse.[367] What faith she had expressed in her brave hand was matched by her doubt that she would ever escape the deprivations of her family life.

She'd written the poem around the same time she wrote an essay on faith. She had concluded that things were real only as one believed them to be, just as surely as one's universe is bound by the circumstances of one's life.[368] In 1911, the year she wrote both the poem and the essay, the radius of Vincent's world was indeed, "no wider than the heart is wide."[369] The notion of being in college was as foreign as the concept that she was the queen of France. Now, three years later, not only was she in college, but she would soon play the role of the Queen Marie of France!

Interim had also come to mind because it seemed to reflect her relationships with Arthur and Katherine. The loss of her effeminate male lover sparred with the deeply held religious beliefs of her female one. She longed for the prior summer with Arthur at the Kennerley's estate. They had been so wholly one it was hard to imagine they would ever be apart. Yet they were, and whether she'd ever see him again seemed a question best placed before God. As for Katherine, they had originally come together like the wings of a bird, rising and lowering with faith that somehow that alone would keep them from plunging to earth. It was faith that kept their love aloft, not truth. The poet knew there was only so much truth one could tell. People had to take things based on love or faith.

While Vincent knew *Interim* was not her best work, she understood that it had enough merit to be considered. Still, she needed her mother's approval before submitting it, relying, as she so often did, on the woman who had introduced her to poetry in the first place. Cora approved of the plan and suggested she submit works in all categories. The notion that her daughter might be able to send home as much as $60 eased the nurse's troubled mind. How much could she confess to her daughter? Cora could only imply. It was a conversational habit born of want that her daughters also employed. With Cora's stamp of approval, the poem was added to *The Miscellany* submissions by E. Vincent Millay.

In the meantime, the redhead settled back into academic life. Moonlit walks with friends became impromptu fetes on the bleachers as the girls sang, played mandolin, told jokes and performed scenes from the plays they were studying. Tutoring sessions with friends evolved into philosophical discussions.[370] Flirtations blossomed, including when, ten days after the semester began, she saw Katherine Tilt on January 17, 1914, and they came together with a crash.[371] By the time they picked up the pieces, resolving both their sexual desire and their frustration with one another, things were quite wonderful.

The poet thought it was funny how her attitude toward Vassar was changing. She laughed at herself for now considering its esteemed halls as "my college." She laid claim as if she owned the place, which, in a sense, she did.

* * *

The poet was now viewed as integral to campus life. Fellow students sought her out for her opinions on all sorts of things, including if she thought they were missing something by skipping chapel. Although she couldn't say exactly what, she had to admit they most likely did. "We've gotten so sort of skeptic and scoffy here that if anybody has a real thought, she's ashamed of it and keeps it to herself."[372]

"I wouldn't say we're ashamed. At least I wouldn't say that about Kim. She's a regular missionary," the poet's classmate Dorothea observed.

"True, but maybe we're missing out on what's best in each other by mocking another girl's opinion. Do you know what I mean?"

Her friends pondered for a moment. Finally, Harriet spoke up. "Maybe we should get together and read the Bible or something instead of chapel. It will practically be the same and…"

"That way we won't lose the loveliness of the Bible," Dorothea noted.

"And Kim can't call us heathens anymore," Vincent laughed. Her friends joined in.

"Harriet's got the biggest room. Maybe we could meet over there. That is, if that's okay with you, Harry." Bee asked, a little sheepish at her assumption.

"Sure," the statuesque brunette nodded. "Does ten o'clock tonight work for everyone?"

The group nodded. Vincent realized she didn't have a Bible but said nothing. She'd have to borrow one from her mother.[373]

* * *

Miss Dow—now affectionately deemed "Aunt Calline"—supplemented the poet's meager allowance with gently used hand-me-downs. Some were hopelessly out of fashion, while others were too big and needed to be taken in. One item, however, suited her in ways she found hard to express.

"Oh, Aunt Calline! It's sweller than any dress I have ever seen.[374] It's simply regal in every scrap of material. Unquestionably this season's style." Vincent pressed the satin afternoon dress to her body.

"I'm so glad you like it, dear," the portly benefactor replied.

The poet swirled around, watching as the very soft panniers at the side of the dress swung ever so slightly from where they ended in a row of buttons. The dress was the French style in length, and it clung to her body showing off her figure. "What do you suppose they call this shade," Vincent asked as she pet the delicate fabric. "It's sort of a violet-gray, isn't it? Or is that just the light in this room?"

"I'd call it mauve, even though that's usually more violet than red. In any event, it looks lovely on you. It complements your eyes quite magnificently."

Vincent dug inside her armoire and pulled out a metallic, gray-colored shoe to see how it would go with the dress. Satisfied, she slipped on the other and stood in front of the mirror. "I love it!" She adjusted the long sleeves with their purple plushy velvet bands. "With my hair at one end and these shoes at the other it's rather nice."

"Will you need some extra funds for the Wanamaker's event?" Miss Dow asked. Her charge's excitement had become contagious. McGlynn's had announced it was hosting the department store's spring fashion show, and the older woman knew how important it was for Vincent to look well among her peers.

"That would be so wonderful, Aunt Calline. I cannot thank you enough."

"Just be certain that you study hard for your examinations," her patron warned. "Exams are right around the corner, and we don't want people saying all their money was good for was making sure you were well-dressed."

Miss Dow's attempt at humor fell flat. *Does she have any idea how very hard I'm working?* The poet forced a smile. "They won't. I can assure you of that," Vincent replied, thinking of the mostly ill-fitting and out-of-fashion clothes she'd just been presented with. While she appreciated the gesture and offer of cash for the fashion show, reminding her that she only deserved them if she was good irked the poet.

"Well, I best be off," the kind and generous patron said as she stood up from Vincent's desk chair. "Here's $20. That should be enough for everything you need. Now remember, one should only replace items as required, not because they are out of fashion."[375]

Again, Vincent drew her lips upward in artificial agreement. If she had her way, she would never be out of fashion. "Yes, Aunt Calline."

* * *

The poet had passed her first semester examinations with a "B" average, much better than anticipated. Vincent was certain she would flunk history and geometry, and barely manage German,[376] but somehow was happily surprised to discover she'd gotten "A"s in both French and German, a "B" in Old English, and managed "C"s in the fields she hated most. Fortunately, her participation in a variety of clubs, committees and plays made up for her less than stellar performance. "After all," she joked with Katherine, "One can't be expected to be a genius in everything."

"Tell that to my parents, will you?"

"Certainly," Vincent laughed and switched papers with her friend. It was a habit now for them to share work in progress to have fresh eyes on old problems.

"You missed an apostrophe here," Vincent leaned over to show her on-again, off-again lover and always friend. "Otherwise, this page looks fine."

"Thanks," Katherine handed Vincent the page she had corrected for her and pointed midway down the page. "I added a comma here. I think that's right."

The poet looked at the page. She silently read the sentence and then used her pen to mark over the penciled correction.

Her second semester at the college had begun six weeks before on February 2. She hoped she'd do better in algebra and trigonometry than she did in geometry. The poet had no such qualms about continuing with English, German, and French. Now she was working on a paper for her Chaucer class with Professor Fiske. She was feeling confident, having read *The Canterbury Tales* as a child.

"Will you still be moving to North Hall next fall?" Katherine asked.

"I'm not sure anymore."

"It's where all the doings are."

"So I've heard."

"Good grief, Vincent, if you really want to get ahead you have to know the right people."

"True. The trouble is my budget," she confided. "I wanted to. But it costs more, and Miss Dow is having a hard enough time of it."

"Oh, you'll be fine." Katherine looked at the penciled corrections Vincent had made on her homework. She shrugged and filled them in with pen.

"I hope so. Now what I really want is for the college to stop the annoying process of subjecting us to prolonged execution each semester."

"You mean exams."

"Yes. I don't understand why a monthly written wouldn't suffice."

"I think it's because they like to torture us, like a cat batting around a mouse before biting its head off."

"You sound like Dr. Salmon."

"Maybe the new president will change the policy."

"Good old Dr. Taylor. He'd just love to go off to a pasture someplace," Vincent giggled as she visualized the retiring president of Vassar.

"I hope whoever he is lets us have more speakers like Inez Milholland. Her lecture last month was thrilling."

"Wasn't it? I have a feeling that someday I'll know her, or maybe that gorgeous husband of hers."

"I think it's marvelous that he lets Miss Milholland keep her name.[377] I wonder if Dr. Salmon will ever get married?"

Vincent rolled her eyes. Katherine could be so clueless at times. "I don't think she's the type." Vincent set her pen down and stared out the window. "She's right, you know, about education.[378] Latin is more than Latin. Eliz…Miss Haight has proved that much to me. I came here to learn, not to simply be taught. History is just dust if it isn't made relevant to the present and future."

Katherine pressed her blotter over the page and started to speak but abandoned talk in favor of noticing how beautiful Vincent looked in the evening twilight.

"What are your plans for summer?" she eventually asked.

"I think I'll spend it in New York."

"You're not going home?"

"I don't know. I miss Mother and my sisters, but I wonder if it wouldn't be wiser to cultivate my connections in New York, particularly if I'm moving on campus in the fall."

"Maybe a little of both?" Katherine said, trying to imagine how her own parents would react if she decided not to come home.

"Maybe."

* * *

To test her theory, Vincent decided she would rather spend her spring break with the Kennerleys than her own family. As soon as school let out at 11:20, March 27, 1914, she caught the first train, one that would only go as far as Mamaroneck.

During her visit, Arnold Genthe would photograph her in a tan linen spring dress she purchased after seeing it among the Wanamaker's offerings. The tailored dress somehow mirrored the shape of the Japanese magnolia blossoms at Kennerley's estate. Its white muslin collar emphasized her shoulders, so they appeared broader than they were. The waist, in turn, seemed smaller, like the blooms that spread up and outward from the leafless branches.

Standing there in her friend's garden, she looked precisely as one would imagine a poet might. A little lost, her mouth set in a determined version of a Mona Lisa smile, and her fingers twining around the branches as if they were a lyre, the now twenty-two-year-old betrayed little of the disappointment she felt in the absence of Arthur Hooley.

To Mitchell Kennerley it looked like the cover of a book.

"Honestly, Vince, one must strike while the iron is hot. People are already forgetting 'Renascence'."

"Obviously you haven't," the poet countered.

"Well, of course, I haven't. It's my job to cultivate the work of people I admire. Those pieces you recited at the Poetry Society last week tell me you probably have plenty of work for a slim volume."

Vincent balked. "I'm just not sure they are ready. Sometimes it takes me years to finish something. I want to make sure each line is perfect. I can't do that if I'm being rushed. Besides, editors are always changing things. How do I know you'll respect the way I've laid out my work on the page? Harriet Monroe often ignores my line breaks, and I've known her longer than I've known you and she claims to honor people's work no matter what theory it is written under."[379]

Mitchell leaned back and pulled his pipe from the inside pocket of his suit jacket. He didn't want to scare her off. Someone was going to snatch her up. He wanted it to be him.

"I promise you: if I so much as misprint a comma I will reprint the entire run at my own expense."

The poet looked at him and said nothing. In the days that followed, the publisher made several more attempts at selling her on the idea of signing with him, even enlisting the help of his wife and their other house guest, the photographer Genthe. Yet Vincent demurred. Now was the moment to think about Vassar and Miss Dow's pledge to try and get enough funding for Kathleen to join her at college. She couldn't afford to distress her benefactor by signing with the publisher of what Miss Dow considered pornography.

This determination was born from Cora's most recent letter. Her mother had lamented that if things didn't turn around soon, she would be on her knees crawling around after Miss Dow so Kathleen could go to school.[380] It was a rare admission of how bad things were at home. While Norma's letters obliquely hinted, Vincent's situation made it easy to ignore those suggestions. But her mother's admission opened her eyes. While she loved her family more when they were at a distance, she didn't want to disappoint her mother or alienate Miss Dow. If helping her family meant cultivating the friendship with

Miss Dow, toying with Kennerley, or submitting some of her best work to *The Miscellany* for a mere $15 prize, so be it.

Nonetheless, there was another, more important, reason for putting off Kennerley. Although publication would have provided larger checks, the poet's dedication to her art was even greater than to her family. She had already discovered the importance of cultivating her poetic crop before harvesting. Nothing could convince her to publish a book before she was ready. Between school and extracurricular activities, finding time to perfect a poem was in short supply.

When she returned to school on April 7, she was so overwhelmed with study that she hardly had time to spend putting together a volume, let alone mooning over romance. Her friendship with her Classics professor, Elizabeth Hazelton Haight, was blossoming and consumed many hours. Middle English with Christobel Fiske filled her heart with tales of knights of old and often resulted in tears of Arthurian regret. Extracurricular drama classes with Gertrude Buck, who had started Vassar's Theater program, were a joyful distraction as they allowed the poet to get lost in the adoration of fellow students.

The truth was, Vincent needed a means of emotional escape. Besides a drug-infused bout with a toothache that put her out of commission for two days[381] and bemoaning the loss of Arthur, her family's letters were filled with need. Consequently, when *Interim* won *The Miscellany* prize on May 21, 1914, she immediately sent the money home to her mother with apologies for not sending more. "Please, please don't feel bad that I've let it go for so little. I shall do more, much better, or it won't matter. And it will do a great deal for me here, both with the faculty and the girls. Please don't mind, dear."[382]

While the money was sent to Cora, a second letter to Norma conveyed the sense of loss she suffered after the break-up with Arthur. "Everyone lies when they tell you time will heal all wounds. More likely all heels wound time. I miss him everywhere. There are a hundred places where I fear to go because they remind me of him in some way or another, and even when I find some place with no association with him, I find myself remembering him because he never was there."[383]

* * *

She had also decided to move to North Hall. It was a part of her plan to fertilize her career by having the strongest connections possible. As luck would have it, she drew a lovely corner room with windows on two sides and room for everything.[384] "Fil" and "Harry" would be just down the stairs from her and the other members of their prayer group, Margaret and Kim, one more floor below that. Her excitement about living on campus in her own single, top floor room overlapped with a final meeting with her history professor, C. Mildred Thompson. The instructor was furious. She wondered why, given how poorly Vincent did in her entrance exam on the topic, she couldn't be bothered to attend her pre-examination meeting with the teacher who felt she wasn't worthy of Vassar in the first place.[385]

Vincent looked at the stern task master. For some reason Dr. Thompson was not succumbing to her charm. "I didn't think it would matter."

"Why didn't you think, you naughty little thing?" Dr. Thompson glared.

Vincent shrugged. "Because I got a C."

A slight smile crept over the corner of Dr. Thompson's mouth. She took a deep breath. This student was incorrigible. The poet managed to be clever enough to carry her fifteen hours of classwork a week plus mountains of extracurricular activity. Genius? Perhaps. Maddening? Certainly.

"You'll need to do better than that with Lucy Maynard Salmon's class on how history informs literature. Your answers will have to be less lengthy and more precise. And they should bear at least some resemblance to the questions asked."

"Duly noted. The good news is 'Periodic Literature: It's Use as Historical Material' has at least something to do with my major." The poet's smile was just short of a smirk. Dr. Thompson was her "sworn enemy."[386] The correction of Thompson's notion of what the fall class would be about was typical of the passive-aggressive way in which Vincent confronted those who did not like her.

Dr. Thompson nodded and walked away without a single word.

* * *

Summer 1914 arrived, and Vincent was still ambivalent about how she'd spend it. Sara Teasdale had invited her to spend some time with her in New York. Similar entreaties were made by the Untermeyers, the Kennerleys and

Mrs. Trowbridge, her patron and frequent New York chaperone. The choice about the latter invitation was easy. No. She would not be joining her former jailer for the summer. However, the others were harder to say no to. The freedom she would enjoy in their company was more than enticing. On the other hand, she missed the familiarity of her kinfolk. She didn't have to be "on" for them. She could be as silly as she wanted to be. They wouldn't require her to recite "Renascence" for the hundredth time. They wouldn't care if the hem of her skirt was perfectly sewn. She could confide in Norma, spar with Kathleen, and would be pampered by her mother if she got sick after overdoing it. Given all the demands of college life, she decided Katherine's suggestion came the closest to what she really wanted to do. With the rigors of exams fresh in her mind, she knew her first stop would be Camden.

28. Scarce the Friendly Voice Or Face

1914

On the train home, the steady ka-chunk of the wheels as they rattled over the track found its way into a dream.

In it, a conductor called out the names of people and not towns, and when she asked him when they would arrive in Rockland he answered, "When we get there, Miss." It troubled her as she gazed out the window to rolling hills of people's faces. Forests became limbs and steam rising off lakes became people's breath. She awoke with a start to the whine of the train entering a tunnel.

The next morning, she still couldn't get the dream from her mind. Elizabeth Haight was a town she could see. Fil was a mass of vines that at one point held the train back. Katherine got off the train in her own town. Arthur was a station without any signs of life.

When she actually saw Norma at the Rockland station, the poet asked her sister what she thought the dream meant.

"Seems simple enough," she laughed. "People are just way stations in your life."

"That's mean."

"I'm sorry, darling, I didn't mean anything by it. You asked; I answered." The blonde studied Vincent's face. Every time she saw her now, she looked different. "Mumbles and Kathleen are meeting us at Dillon's for breakfast. We should get going."

The poet was quiet. Meeting the remainder of their merry band at the small café felt odd. She wanted to go home. Why were they going out for a meal? Weren't they hard-up? Norma anticipated her question.

"Kathleen's got a job there now. I guess she wanted to see you before you get so inundated with all your Camden friends that you don't have time for us."

Vincent ignored the swipe. "Are any still around?"

"Of course! Ethel Knight had a kid, and Mary Pendleton is planning her wedding. You *did* get an invitation?"

Vincent realized she hadn't opened the letter yet, figuring it was just some gossip from home. Some gossip? This was news! "Yes. Have you met him?"

"Harold? Naturally. They've been going steady for years, haven't they?"

It was true, yet hearing the words made Vincent feel like an old maid. They approached the café and Kathleen, who had been clearing a table, caught sight of them and dashed outside. The girls embraced in the middle of the street before heading toward a booth, where Cora sat in wait.

"Did you sleep on the train, dear? You look a little tired."

Vincent removed her hat. "Hello, Mother."

Cora stood up and embraced her weary daughter. Why had that been the first thing she said? She resolved to be friendlier. Perhaps remarks like that were why the college sophomore didn't write more often.

"It's so wonderful to see you, dearest," she offered with a genuine smile. "I'm just concerned about you. Never mind what I said. We have you home for the whole summer. Let's enjoy it."

The poet breathed a sigh of relief. "Oh, Mother, I have so much to tell you. What a wonderful summer we'll have despite me having to bone up on my Latin prose."

"Oh?" Cora bit her lip. "You did pass Latin, right?"

"I haven't taken it yet, at least not at Vassar," Vincent explained, wishing she didn't have to. Hadn't her mother understood when she explained this at Christmas break? "I've been studying with Dr. Haight, in preparation for my fall class."

"The Latin you took at Barnard didn't count?" Kathleen asked.

Vincent shook her head. It still irked her that nothing she did at Barnard had counted. "No. I thought I'd already told you, Wump. That's why you should study like the devil. The classes I took at Barnard were meant to prepare me for Vassar, not as a substitute, though I still don't see why. In any event, I'm still behind the other girls, which is why Dr. Haight has taken me under her wing. I'll have to spend most of my time studying like I did last summer."[387]

"We were all looking forward to spending time with you," Kathleen began before catching the look on her manager's face. "I better go."

"Of course, boating, hiking, picking berries and all the rest," Vincent assured her as Kathleen turned to leave. "We better pretend to order tea or something."

The group laughed and Kathleen scribbled on her pad. "Yes, ma'am, right away!" The sound of the giggling women attracted the attention of the locals, but no one particularly cared.

* * *

The summer of 1914 was much like the prior year, except that Vincent had come to love Vassar and found it worth the trouble of preparing for her sophomore courses. The popularity she enjoyed in a place without memories was intoxicating. She couldn't wait to go back. She made plans for her new on-campus room and all the ways she would make it come alive with flowers, magazines and newspapers.[388] She plotted how to get a second cot and desk from seniors who had graduated. She would bring her personal tea set from home and then buy a small alcohol teakettle to warm water. Hers would be the cutest room, a place where people gathered and socialized. There would be impromptu poetry readings and study groups would relish her hospitality.

Meanwhile, life in Camden provided fun as well as wearing times that summer. Kathleen could be both amusing and a pill. Cora would be warm and loving one minute and harsh and judgmental the next. Norma was a pal, but at times the poet wished she could just be left alone to study. Boys were less an issue than they had been, though older men continued to look upon her with fascination.

The twenty-two-year-old's beautiful copper mane framed her long throat. Her mysterious mouth had lips that were a natural cranberry red and the envy of every woman who needed lipstick to enhance her own.[389] She considered her forehead extraordinary despite the multitude of freckles that resided there and across her impudent, aggressive and critical nose. Yet male assumptions about her were a bother.

* * *

There was one event that differed from the previous summer, and that was a short visit with her father.

Henry was still living in Kingman and, for the first time in his life, almost thriving. He had sent his eldest daughter a gift for her birthday and had yet to hear a word of thanks. He thought her ungrateful. The only way to convince him that she had indeed received it and sent a note of thanks was to take a short break from the Camden side of the family. This time she would bring Norma along as a foil for Ella Somerville's attention. Norma would sleep with her in a daybed at her father's, and the pair would giggle through the night just as they had as children. Daughters and father would share the dance floor.

Nevertheless, it quickly became obvious that Ella's intoxication with the poet remained. The moment she heard that Henry had a visitor from Camden, the artist practically flew across the street to the rooming house where the school principal held court with his beautiful daughters.

While Vincent and Ella had continued their correspondence, the poet quietly made her newfound confidence clear to the painter. Ella's was not the only heart she could wrangle. In the two intervening years, the poet had slept with two men and four women. Her sexuality had grown from a fascination to near pathology. As far as Ella knew, Vincent was still the nubile virgin who needed to be embraced to feel attractive. Now it was clear there was something different in Vincent's flirting, a willingness to experiment with anyone who caught her eye. While the poet had toyed with the Violin Man in 1912, back then she would not have acted on that flirtation. However, Ella was certain the poet would do so without shame in 1914.

Henry looked at his daughters when they first arrived with a mixture of pride and curiosity. It was obvious they were no longer girls bound by the conventions of their hometown—or Kingman, for that matter.

Vincent had stopped calling him "Papa," and started calling him "Dad," reflecting the customs of her wealthier classmates.

Norma just stared as if determining which of her parents she most favored.

Henry realized that his middle daughter had not seen him since 1900, when she was nearly six. Now almost twenty-one, she looked at him with curiosity, not love. His handsome features and quick wit impressed her, yet even years later this brief visit would be more about the Somervilles and Kingman than it was about her father. Kingman was new territory and had new men to conquer, just as it had been for her sister in 1912.

The short visit provided Norma with a longed-for escape from what she called "Camdenburg."[390] Instead of being stuck at home while Vincent was off shopping, going to concerts and dances, and getting buckets of admiration, the blonde would get her opportunity to be the belle of the ball.

The blonde's envy reflected her frustration with being Cora's newly preferred house manager. Norma didn't care about going to college. That was not an aspiration she shared with her sisters. She did care about the hand-me-downs, literal and figurative. Her insecurities had few outlets. She was considered the most conventionally pretty, but she did not consider her gifts the equal of her sisters'. Having an opportunity to be in a new place with fresh eyes viewing her helped her see what Vincent had tried to explain after that first visit to Kingman. The liberation from town gossip, the fresh start, and being able to bask in the reflected light of her much-loved father brought a sense of relief she would carry long after they returned home.

It was the last time either of them saw their father alive.

* * *

As summer vacation drifted toward fall 1914 semester, Vincent knew she would make good on her decision to enjoy both the comfort of family and her connections in New York.

By now the train trip to the city had become familiar. She arrived at Grand Central at 7:20 a.m. on September 8, 1914, handed her luggage to the ubiquitous Red Cap, then rushed to Miss Dow's apartment for a quick visit before racing to the Plaza to meet Mitchell Kennerley for a nine o'clock breakfast.[391]

"Good morning," the elegant editor said as he extended his hand.

"Good morning!" Vincent was struck for the umpteenth time by how appealing he was.

"Have you ever eaten here before?"

"No. It is rather splendid, isn't it?"

The maître d' pulled out her chair and waited until she was comfortable before leaving. A menu lay before her. Reading it, she tried not to gasp at the Palm Room prices.

Seeing her response, Mitchell smiled with a gentle laugh. "Order what you like."

The poet realized she was rather hungry and ordered a full breakfast from the French language menu. "Why not just write it in English?"

He laughed heartily. "You got the French menu?"

"Yes. Didn't you?"

He shook his head. "Good thing your French has improved. Would you care for a cigarette?"

"No. I'm afraid someone might be here that knows I do not smoke," she replied with a wink.[392]

Mitchell began to laugh so long and hard that Vincent wondered if he was making fun of her. Of course, she smoked. She'd been smoking regularly for over a year now. She did all sorts of things Miss Dow and the other New York patrons disapproved of. The Plaza was just the sort of place someone like Mrs. Trowbridge would frequent.

They discussed Vincent's coming year at Vassar and what she was writing. She spoke of *The Miscellany* prize, and lamented the time it took to polish anything for submission. She pointedly wished she had an editor she trusted. Aware of her tactics, Mitchell carefully avoided the topic of Arthur Hooley and changed the subject every time she brought up the need for an editor. Vincent took the hint. Still the meal was relaxed enough for the poet to accept Mitchell's invitation to continue their discussion at his new Lexington Avenue office.

When they got there, he almost immediately offered her a jar of Page and Shaw orange candies as a means of sweetening talk of publication. Again, she waylaid his offer with excuses.

"But why? Jessie tells me the stuff you read the last time you were in town was wonderful. You've published at least eight pieces already and read four new ones by Jessie's account. That's practically a book right there."

"Honestly, Mitchell, I just don't have time. There's school and all the extra things I'm doing to get on the good side of the faculty and Miss Dow. I barely have time to start a poem much less finish one. Please be patient."

"But think of the money you could bring in…" he began.

She cut him off. "It would not be enough to finish school—and Miss Dow and others have been perfectly clear about how they feel concerning any involvement with you. I want to finish at my college."

Mitchell dropped his head into his lap, took a deep breath and faced her. "By God what have they got against me? Never mind. I know. It is the D.H. Lawrence business, isn't it?"

Vincent nodded. "Yes, that and the Goodman book." She noticed Arnold Genthe's portrait of her among the magnolia blossoms on his wall. "That's really rather lovely."

The lanky publisher filled and lit his pipe, then stood up and walked toward the print. "I think I'll use it as the frontispiece when you do sign with me."

By now, Vincent had become absorbed in Genthe's composition. It appealed to her vanity and yet she didn't feel worthy. Genthe was the chosen photographer of celebrities like the actress Billie Burke. "How could a man like that find me of interest?"

"You're beautiful. That's why," Mitchell pronounced. "There's no use being modest. We know each other well enough for the truth. You're vain and rightfully so."

The poet wasn't sure how to take his remark. "Yes, but there are…Let's face it, I've only made one small splash in an ocean of talent."

"But what a splash! Do you realize if you were to live in New York you would never lack for work?" Hyperbole aside, the publisher believed strongly that she would never be forgotten if "Renascence" were the only thing she ever published. It was his whole motivation for wanting her to sign with him. Sure, she had said she would work under his imprint, but she had yet to sign. His future would be secure so long as she published with him.

"That's foolish," she replied, now accepting the cigarette he offered from a walnut and silver case on his capacious desk.[393] "I would have to do far more than that to make a dent in a place like New York—though I must admit I'm trying."

The pair laughed. Vincent inhaled deeply. She was happy he found her beautiful. Nonetheless, their mutual attraction went no further than also giving her a box of chocolates and a lengthy novel to read.[394] Both had their loyalties to consider. Besides, Vincent was canny enough to know when flattery had ulterior motives. "Renascence" was a wonderful poem, to be sure, but at this point it felt like an illegitimate child. People kept throwing it in her face. She was destined for more, she knew that, but she wasn't sure what. Would poetry earn her a living? Acting? Composing? Or would she end up teaching somewhere, hoping to find someone else with potential she could guide toward its realization? She simply would not let herself believe in that fate. She would be a poet. One who was recited, admired and memorized by lovers long after she was gone.[395]

29. In My New Home

1914-1915

The reemergence of Bad Vincent started with the move to North Hall and her proximity to some awfully nice juniors.[396]

Here among the older girls Vincent felt more alive. Gender roles were even more confusing. Now age contributed to which partner would play what. Some girls did without sex altogether. Others made do with what was available. Then there were girls like Elaine Ralli.

Born of a wealthy Greek immigrant family, Elaine was Vincent's opposite in almost every way. Though three years younger, Elaine was already a year ahead of her at college. Loud, aggressive, demanding and rich, Elaine spoke Continental French so fluently that even Vincent's Canadian professor Mademoiselle Conrow had trouble keeping up. While the poet had been a poor latchkey child, Elaine was raised by French governesses and traveled frequently to Europe as a child. Her family's wealth gave the biology major an ease around finances that Vincent would never have—even years later when wealth and fame brought her millions. Elaine's intense eyes and sureness of bearing reflected never having to worry about being supported. She would not have to buckle under like Vincent because she was not a charity case dependent on patrons. Elaine played field hockey, rode horses and excelled in all the classes Vincent struggled with. Yet the attraction to the loud, olive-skinned junior was immediate. Soon Fil was forgotten. Katherine played second fiddle. Another conquest, Isobel Simpson, was deployed as a weapon to provide jealousy. It made people uncomfortable to have the poet and her mannish companion strolling arm in arm around campus. Bad Vincent didn't care. Elaine was all muscle.[397]

Elaine's tendency to dominate the indomitable poet extended itself in ways that previously would never have been tolerated. If Vincent was talking with a group of friends, Elaine would drag her off mid-sentence to show her something she found interesting, or to satisfy a sudden sexual urge. While Vincent had a virtual train of girls following her, Elaine was the first "boy" that insisted the poet follow *her*.

"Come with me!"

"But we were discussing…"

"Hang it, Edna, I want you to come with me. You've got to see this."

"What?"

"Never mind what. I want it to be a surprise."

The pair climbed the stairs of North Hall and passed the room Elaine shared with Virginia Kirkus.

"Where are we going?"

"You'll see."

A huge bouquet of French pink roses blended with pussy willows [398] sat in a Tiffany vase atop the small table in North Hall 903.

"How did you get in my room?"

"I asked the Residence Clerk to let me in," Elaine grinned. "I was just going to leave them here, but I decided I couldn't wait to see your face."

"They're beautiful." The poet scooped a group of blossoms into her palm and inhaled their fragrance. They must have cost a fortune in fall. "What kind are they?"

"Rosa Meinostair." Seeing the poet's puzzled expression, Elaine added, "Sweet Mademoiselle."

Vincent smiled. She had to admit the huge bouquet had a certain artistic flair. "That's very sweet, darling."

Elaine shut the door with one hand and pulled the sophomore closer with the other. They began to kiss. Vincent loved the feel of the peach fuzz on Elaine's face. Now she was glad Elaine had interrupted the chat she was having about her upcoming role as Marie de France in the *Pageant of Athena*. Succumbing to the urgency of Elaine's desire, they fell onto Vincent's undersized bed.

Elaine reached beneath Vincent's dress and pulled her tango knickers down. The stronger girl lifted the poet's legs over her shoulders and pulled her pelvis toward her. Excited, Vincent reached up for her lover, but Elaine gently pushed her hands down. "My turn," the Greek commanded. Elaine rolled the poet's skirt up and stroked the inside of her legs until her labia shone with moisture. Elaine's presence was so masculine that Vincent half expected her to enter her as a man might. A dildo had not yet been purchased.[399] The medical student probed the area with her thumb before pausing to look at the poet's face.

"You should undress." Elaine stood up and watched as the obedient poet began to undress. Vincent could hardly contain herself. She wanted to kiss Elaine's breasts. The Greek said "No," then began to stroke each revealed bit of flesh.

"Please," Vincent begged as she finished undressing. Elaine nodded.

Naked, tingling, the poet unbuttoned Elaine's blouse and unhooked the front of her Ovida brassiere. Vincent threw her mouth against Elaine's right breast before she could protest. The poet reveled the beauty of those curves. Her lover's areola reminded her of a wild carrot, with its crimson central eye, and her breasts were as round as an onion blossom.[400] Elaine allowed the pleasure of Vincent's lips for only a moment. It was too feminine a posture. Again, she gently pushed Vincent back into the bed, only this time she slipped her fingers inside her lover. It wasn't long before a wave of roiling pleasure dispersed over Vincent's naked form.

Sated, Vincent pulled Elaine down on top of her and kissed her eyes, ears, neck and mouth. "Please finish undressing. I want to see your body."

As her lover acquiesced, the poet noted Elaine's supple back, her strong brown arms, the curve of her mouth, and her sunburned curls as she hastily and abstractedly flung down to the floor, having raked them, arm after arm, over her head, her white silk blouse and brassiere, and how, before their silken susurration had subsided, they were as close together as it is possible for two people to be.[401] The poet traced Elaine's muscular limbs with her fingertips and cooed, "I love your body."

They started again, only this time Vincent took the lead by reaching down and fondling Elaine until she moaned a deep growl of satisfaction.

"I've heard the French kiss there," Vincent pointed.

Elaine blushed. "Have you done that before?"

"I haven't done that with any girl."

"Do you want me to?"

"Yes."

"Maybe later."

Vincent pouted. Elaine yawned. "Let's cuddle for a while first." This led to more sex but not what Vincent was after. Eventually the pair drifted into a shallow sleep.

* * *

It hadn't been the first time. In fact, it wasn't even the second or third time. Yet the woman sleeping beside her had struck a chord Vincent wasn't sure she wanted to hear.

Elaine wasn't pretty. She wore her hair in a shorter bob than most of the girls who excelled at sports. Yet she had a smile that lit up the room and a laugh that drew you in whether or not you got the joke.

Miss Dow would certainly not understand the attraction. At times she wondered herself. But lying there in her narrow bed Elaine looked sweet beside her. The poet used her free arm to brush a tousled lock from Elaine's forehead.

Elaine stirred at Vincent's touch. "You're insatiable," she said sleepily and turned to face the smaller, fairer woman beside her. Despite their age difference, the poet looked younger and far more delicate. The couple took a moment to stare into each other's eyes before they kissed.

Elaine glanced at the clock and frowned. "We better get up. I've got chemistry and you can't afford to be late to physics again."

"I'll say you've got chemistry," Vincent laughed. The two girls made the bed per dormitory regulations and made a mad dash for the communal sinks and toilets. There was no time for a bath.

Their main hall dormmates knew what made them so late.[402] Vincent had had a platoon of lovers since entering college and rumor had it there were even more in her past, including men. Nevertheless, a whispered, "What does she see in her?" struck Vincent's ear like a tuning fork and she made a very deliberate flirtation with both Fil and Katherine to demonstrate her freedom to everyone in the communal space. As she was speaking with Fil, Katherine joined in. Both had been supplanted in the poet's affections by the most masculine of all, Elaine.

"How are you doing in physics this time around?"

"Oh, about the same, but I'll fail if I don't study more."

"You'll be fine," Fil said, speaking from experience. "You'll just have to turn on the charm. It always works."

"But even Vince has her standards. Dr. Saunders isn't exactly her cup of tea," Katherine observed.

"Never stopped her before," an eavesdropping senior remarked as she passed.

The remark stung Good Vincent. Was that how people viewed her? Bad Vincent spit out the toothpaste, ran her tongue over her teeth, rinsed and then smiled into the mirror. "I guess that will have to do."

"It will do, sweetheart. Boys aren't looking at your teeth," another classmate observed.

"Neither are girls," Fil offered with a wink.

"If they did, they'd notice you," Vincent flirted just as Elaine returned from the commode.

"Vince, it's time to go." The swarthy biology major took the poet by the hand and pulled her away.

"But…" Vincent protested, though part of her loved Elaine's take-charge attitude.

"You've got to get to class. I'll take you."

Their schoolmates stared in shock at the way Vincent was allowing herself to be manhandled by the possessive athlete. No one messed with Elaine.

When they were outside, Vincent confronted her. "I do wish you wouldn't do that when I'm speaking with my friends."

"Sorry, darling," Elaine said, her voice plaintive. "I just don't want you to get into trouble."

It was always that way. Elaine would do something to annoy Vincent, and the poet would exact an apology doomed to be forgotten within hours.

* * *

Vincent lay in Elaine's arms at dawn on a fine day in March 1915. The Eastern bluebirds and Magnolia Warbler called outside as the sun sent its dappled radiance across Vincent's messy room.

"What are we going to do about summer?" Elaine's attempt at casual conversation held a deeper meaning.

"My plan is to go home to Camden. Miss Dow's allowance only applies to the school year now."

The poet lazily fondled her lover's thick fingers. The dishes from the previous night were alive with ants arriving after winter's hibernation. Across the room Elaine's blue serge day dress was casually draped over a chair. Her under garments were on the footstool. Vincent had left her clothing on the floor.

"Mine doesn't," Elaine remarked.

"What doesn't?"

"My allowance. I can go anywhere I like." In the nine months they had been together the biology major had finally learned that Vincent did not enjoy assumptions.

The poet paused the gentle stroking that had kept them both awake after a night of lovemaking. She had told Norma all about Elaine, and even mentioned her to Cora and Kathleen, but she wasn't sure how her friend would be viewed if seen in the flesh. Her eyes fell to the curves of Elaine's breasts, with their large, dark russet aureole and tightly pinched nipples. They were surprisingly smaller than they appeared when she was dressed but still larger than her own. The contrast between her white-pink, freckled skin and Elaine's Mediterranean hue stirred her imagination. "You're like a pirate."

"Huh?"

"Your skin. It's like a pirate's."

"Have you met any pirates?" Elaine laughed. The warm, deep chuckle entranced the poet.

"No, but they say pirates used Penobscot Bay as a hiding place."

"Wouldn't that make you a pirate? After all, you stole my heart," Elaine turned to kiss Vincent. The warmth of the sun excited the exhausted couple.

Vincent couldn't resist a yawn mid-kiss. "Sorry, sweetheart."

Elaine stretched out her arms, which caused Vincent to cling to her to keep from rolling off the narrow bed. They both yawned this time. "We've got to get some sleep."

The couple adjusted themselves into a comfortable position and closed their eyes. "When we were little, my sisters, both of them, used to sleep with me on a bed this size."

"I know you were little then, but how could all three of you fit?" Elaine asked, brushing Vincent's left shoulder with her right hand.

"We slept like sardines in a can."

Elaine's laugh rang out. "I envy you. You sound so close. I wish I had sisters."

"I'd love you to meet my dear family. Knowing them would tell you so much about me."

"If they are anything like you, I know I'll love them just as I do you."

"Oh, Panda," Vincent teased, using her pet name for the athletic upperclassman. With a middle name like Pandia she couldn't resist. "Maybe you should come visit us this summer. Then you'd have three sisters."

"Could I?" She pulled the poet closer.

"Certainly." Vincent snuggled into Elaine's shoulder and before they knew it both women were drifting toward Sunday slumber.

The sugar lump on the table nearby was black with ants now. The sounds outside the door grew as students returned from chapel. The wind through the nearby elms whistled quietly. Before long Elaine was deep in dreamland, snoring lightly as she descended into worlds only she could know. However, Vincent only managed to sleep a few moments before she realized her family could not afford a house guest.

* * *

Despite her best efforts, Vincent's grades in her sophomore year were only slightly better than the year before. Top marks in Latinate languages and English clashed with middling ones in other courses, even the ones she enjoyed. Nonetheless, Miss Dow continued to find funding, thanks in part to Vincent's performances in various school productions, and providing French lyrics to "Claire de Lune" for the farewell party for her professor, Georgiana Conrow, who pronounced the lyrics "C'est exquis!"[403] These contributions to campus life made the donors less apprehensive about funding the student with the laissez-faire attitude toward attendance and classwork. Yet the donations had grown smaller and mostly went toward her tuition and housing.

The $20 a month she received as spending money seemed to evaporate. Most of Vincent's clothes were the same old blend of shabby rejects that were either out of fashion or far too large. Some she even passed along to a clothing drive for war refugees. As hems went up in 1915, Vincent used some of her allowance on thread to raise the hemlines of older outfits or otherwise append them to suit the fashion of the day. The occasional extra cash her blessed Miss

Dow could manage usually went for something brand-new—and if it wasn't enough to cover the cost of the outfit, the poet's skill at poker quickly made up the difference.

There were now only eight weeks before the campus emptied for summer. Vincent realized she would have to tell Elaine about the financial restraints of her family. Cora had written expressing dismay at such an invitation with the forewarning that if Elaine were going to spend the summer with them, she would have to pay for room and board, no matter how close a friend she was.

On April 12, 1915, as they were leaving the one required class they had together, Vincent suggested walking toward the riding stables together.

The couple held hands. Many women did in those days. No one would bat an eye if it wasn't so plainly obvious what was going on between them. As they turned the corner past the Main Building, Vincent finally spoke.

"Darling, I'm afraid I have some bad news."

Elaine stopped short and dropped the poet's hand. "What?"

The athletic biology major was always on the lookout for rejection by her far more popular lover. She heard the whispers about Vincent's various liaisons, but the poet's discretion made it easy to deny the rumors. Elaine was sure this was the beginning of a Dear Jane moment and braced herself. Her heart fluttered like a captured bird's.

"Well, we may be able to get around it," Vincent began, gently taking Elaine's hand and bringing it to her cheek. There was no one around to see them. Most girls were studying for finals or preparing for their graduation ceremonies.

"What!"

"It's not us," the redhead soothed. "It's my mother. My family, actually."

"What? What did you tell them?"

The poet had seen the look in Elaine's eyes before; jealousy, frustration, suspicion had clouded over her face. "Nothing. I mean, I told them you were my friend and…"

"You didn't tell them about us, did you?"

Vincent knew she needed to be more direct. Attempting to soften the blow wasn't going to work.

"We can't afford for you to stay with us this summer."

"You don't want me there." Elaine knew that many of her past lovers felt insecure about having her around their families. She thought Vincent's family would be different. Her usual confidence melted away when it came to her looks.

"No, no! I do! It's just that, well…" she hated to admit it, "my family can't afford another mouth to feed."

Elaine paused. She knew Vincent's family was of modest means, but she was thinking like Isobel's family was middle class. Not poor. Not very poor. What could she say? How selfish she had been. "Oh."

Vincent looked at her friend and began to cry. The admittance broke down what remained of the illusion that she belonged at the expensive women's college. The difference between her and others academically was marginal, but the difference economically was cavernous. Her second-hand dresses, restrictive allowance and the fact that without the generosity of others she never would have gone anywhere near college. Her involvement in campus activities was her currency. She could look like one of those bored rich girls trying to justify their existence by being a whale in a lake. The poet sat down on the grass near the paddock.

The wealthy girl sat down beside her. "It's not a problem."

But Vincent still hadn't said the part she was most ashamed of. She decided it was time. "If you want to come after all, um, maybe you could…uh…pay room and…My mother is…"

"Of course!"

The poet stopped, looked at Elaine in grateful hope and decided to go with what seemed like a satisfactory price. "Could you give us $5 a week?"[404]

As spoiled as she was, Elaine was not entirely sure if that amount would be too much. "I'll ask my mother."

"What about food?"

"I can live on grape nuts and salad."[405]

That Elaine didn't know how precious a salad was in the Millay household gave Vincent pause.

"What sort of things do you like to do?"

"Riding."

"Of course."

"And sailing, I have a little boat of my own or I could rent one."

Vincent began to calculate costs and figured they had best leave the details to her mother. "We'll work out the details, but I'd love to have you there."

As the days of cramming and exams continued, the poet was in a near constant state of exhaustion. Things got worse when she heard from Norma. Their mother was very sick and the whole family was three months behind in their rent.[406] Cora hadn't worked in months and had forbidden Kathleen from working until she took her Vassar entrance exams. Vincent had received the Coe Fellowship, but would only receive it if the family managed to cover the rest of her costs.[407] The money Vincent had promised after her poems "The Shroud" and "Sorrow" appeared in *The Forum* was spent and, as it turned out, that rogue Kennerley never did pay her![408] She began to toy with posing for art classes.[409] Her blonde middle sister, Vincent's most reliable confidante, was even considering a move to Boston where she could work in a milliner's shop and make enough to support the family…maybe. It weighed upon the poet like a Sisyphean rock.

Norma managed to make the weight even heavier when she told her how their mother longed to hear from her.

Vincent had to admit she hadn't written often because she had little to say to her mother. If she complained, she was chastised. If she told her what her grades were, Cora wanted to know why they weren't better. If she mentioned a play she was in, Cora wondered if she wasn't wearing herself out at the cost of better grades and scholarships.

To top things off, it seemed the family Vincent hoped to show off to Elaine was far from presentable.

While Vincent was grateful for all her mother had done for her, she was in no position to help unless she got a large scholarship she had applied for. Otherwise, all she had was her monthly allowance and whatever she could make from poetry submissions. Those funds were usually sent directly to the family, but such checks were few and far between. She already knew that if she didn't come up with the money for the prior semester's bill, she might have to forfeit her room.[410] Vincent lamented that it took so long to write a poem worthy of submission yet knew how important it was to only submit her best work. She had written to Norma to explain. "Darling, I understand how much the family needs cash, but I have to be careful lest I become that annoying amateur whose poems are tossed in the trash before they are even read."

Norma appreciated her sister's dilemma but didn't understand why she couldn't get a loan for what the family needed. After all, she had borrowed from their mother. Not only had Vincent never paid it back but she had never even mentioned it in all the time she'd been away at college.[411]

Tensions were high in all directions and sleep was in short supply. Vincent knew she must write both Norma and her mother immediately, and not some perfunctory note. What she wrote needed to be reassuring, tender, kind and filled with expressions of remorse. She started with the words, "I love you."

"If I don't get the scholarship I very likely won't come back here so I'll get a good job and help out at home. One reason I've been doing so many plays and things here is so the college will want to keep me."

"Elaine is going to ask her mother if she can come to Camden in the summer and board with me. She knows all about us. Her people don't, but she does."

* * *

But her lover really didn't, not fully, not yet. Elaine was so coddled she had no clue what actual poverty looked like. It came down to Elaine's mother to bring some sense to the girls' plans. It was Daisy Ralli who wrote Cora with a sensitive and generous offer.

"The two of them seem to have made all the arrangements without consulting their mothers and I am wondering whether it will be convenient to you to keep Elaine for the length of time she wants to stay," the much wiser woman of the world wrote her counterpart in Camden.[412] She had registered Vincent's second-hand clothes and knew her manners were likewise. "I feel that it would be an imposition on you unless you allow me to pay her way. I know that she is a spoiled child and an extravagant one, in the bargain, and every additional member of a household adds to the expense. So please let me know how much I ought to contribute."

The relief Cora felt was palpable. Elaine had already started helping Vincent to send home extra cash. This letter eased the pressure entirely. Cora quickly calculated the amount she would need to get the landlord off her back and keep the family whole through the summer, including their house guest. She weighed this against seeming greedy. With a sizable but credible amount determined, she wrote Daisy Ralli a note of thanks.

The nurse was now 52 but looked many years older. The weight of being a single mother landed on Cora's face like a threshing machine, pruning what remained of her youth until the wisdom gained would land upon her tongue for use in the survival letter.

Dear Mrs. Ralli:

My sincere thanks for your concerns regarding Elaine's stay with us this summer. It is true that Edna often gets ahead of herself before checking in with me.

Because we are saving for tuition for both Edna and her sister, Kathleen, your offer is most welcome. I have enclosed an accounting that I believe will cover all the necessary expenses.

I sincerely hope to meet you and your husband one day soon. Please know I will do everything in my power to treat Elaine as if she were my own daughter.

Sincerely,

Mrs. Cora Millay

The invoice, cleverly disguised as an estimate, called for $120. After all, a week at the Whitehall was $15 plus meals. If Elaine was going to be there all summer, it would easily cost far more at the hotel, and that didn't even include the various entertainments Vincent was hinting at.

Mrs. Ralli had said Elaine was spoiled. She'd want something nicer than baked beans for dinner. In fact, she had already told Vincent she was fine with grape nuts and salad. Cora looked again at the calculations. She wished she could pad it more. If their situation continued as it was, the requested amount would account for half their annual income that year, yet all it would do is cover some of the back rent and the grocery tab. God alone knew what it would take to get them through the winter. Weariness squeezed her until she was all but wrung out. When added to the trials of the change of life Cora felt like she would explode.

Kathleen and Norma wondered why their mother insisted on playing the martyr. Hers was a force that carried everyone along with her, whether they wanted to go along or not.[413] Watching their mother agonize when Kathleen could easily take a job and study in her off hours frustrated her youngest. Norma agreed. Cora was being ridiculous and the blonde resented being the sole bread winner. Cora took any position she could but offers were getting fewer and farther between now that she looked as sickly as her patients. Of course, there was love and appreciation for her sacrifices, but her stubborn insistence that they'd somehow manage did nothing but put everyone on edge.

Vincent knew how it felt to be caught up in that whirlpool of misery. She hated it. Nevertheless, she felt she owed her family, especially given the enormous benefit she was receiving thanks to their involuntary limitations. The love/hate balance that flooded her with guilt was at times overwhelming. If Elaine had simply taken the disappointment in stride the machinations between their families would have been unnecessary. Now, in addition to begging them to spend money they didn't have to make Elaine comfortable, Vincent had to find a way to tell them how to behave and how to fix up the house so they could avoid feeling shame.

30. The Broad Face of the Sun

1915

Having successfully crammed enough to almost earn a "B" average, Vincent wrote to her sisters from the model comfort of the Ralli's New York penthouse. The letter read like she was bringing home a fiancé.[414] It cautioned them against being "too gorgeous" and recommended a "simple shirtwaist and skirt." The daughter of a wigmaker pointedly noted that "no one *ever* hears of false hair" at college.

She then became specific: "Don't be too powdery." By this she meant that her sisters, especially Norma, wore too much make-up. Kathleen was supposed to play powder and curlers cop, and Norma was assigned to make sure Kathleen wasn't "too in earnest about anything."

But her strongest advice for first impressions was directed at her mother. Norma was to make sure that Cora's hair was "lovely" and to have everything she wore be "just as dainty as possible." Given that Cora was an elfin woman, the idea of being "dainty" meant not too overbearing.

Vincent's stage management also included a request that things be "homey." By now the poet's impression of an ideal setting for familial bliss had been shaped by the apartments of her wealthy friends, patrons and classmates, particularly the Rallis, whose sprawling Upper West Side apartment included the "homey" smells of expensive tobacco, fine wine and discreet cleaning products.[415]

After a weekend at the Ralli's, Vincent was anxious to have Elaine love her family as she did. Ironically, this did not mean as they usually were, but as she wished them. The qualities in her sisters and mother that she loved the most were at odds with the first impression they'd make.

The poet and her lover boarded a train, shared a sleeping berth, and made their way to Rockland, where Elaine hired a car to drive them to Camden. This extravagance was only the first hint of how the coming months would be spent.

When they pulled up to the modest Cape Cod-style two-story shingled residence, Elaine almost allowed herself to wonder if this wasn't an abandoned summer cottage. Vincent had warned her that her family home was modest and far from luxurious, but she was not prepared for its condition. To add to her disquiet, the moment they walked in the door Elaine was almost overcome by the odor of Djer-Kiss, a lemon and honeysuckle scented bath powder the seemed to have been used in every room of the house.[416] Vincent's mouth twisted into a tight smile as if she were holding back a scream. After brief introductions, Elaine watched as the poet invited her sisters to join her in making tea.

"What did I tell you?" Vincent snapped through gritted teeth.

Norma looked askance. Kathleen wasn't as thrown.

"We cleaned! Why, you could lick the floor. And see? Norma doesn't have a stitch of make-up on except a little lipstick and rouge."

"I'm not talking about that. You look fine. It's the smell of that damned Djer-Kiss. It makes me sick to vomiting."

"We had to bathe, didn't we, in order to meet your *exacting standards*," Norma mocked.

"But did you have to use the bathwater everywhere?"

"All we used was Bon-Ami. That's French enough for you, isn't it?" Kathleen growled.

Vincent realized their voices were raising and the tea not being made. She calculated that if she started the process her sisters would follow suit and things might settle down. She was wrong.

As Norma got the special occasion tray from the shelf over the ice box, she grumbled about how Vincent never seemed to be satisfied with what they did. "You're up there getting things paid for and you expect us to fix up the house as if the Queen of Sheba were about to arrive."

"And she's no Queen of Sheba…More like the king," Kathleen observed.

"Hush, she'll hear you!" The poet put the kettle on to boil and stoked the embers of the breakfast fire. She then began to search for the family's fancy China. "Where did the good set go?"

"Mother sold it to buy groceries."

Vincent couldn't believe her ears. It was the one truly nice thing Cora had gotten out of her marriage to Henry. "Mumbles let her wedding dishes go?"

* * *

Cora looked across the modest living room at Vincent's dark-skinned, muscular and mannish friend. She hardly knew what to say. It was almost as though Elaine was a prospective husband. Why she even wrote letters for Vincent sometimes and had purchased gifts for the whole family.[417] Cora was glad her daughter's paramour was rich, but there were family jewels missing from the occasion.

Elaine noted the threadbare furniture and worn carpets. The family's attempts at cleaning only made the home's shortcomings more obvious, not less. She had adjusted to the smell of heavy perfume, but now she had to find a way to see past the extent of Vincent's poverty.

All the small talk in the world couldn't overcome the misgivings of the two women. Both were relieved when the Millay sisters emerged from the kitchen with a weak pot of tea and mismatched dishes.

As they went over the activities the Millays had planned for their guest, Elaine looked at each of the women in turn hoping to discover an ally. At that moment she could find none.

Cora's hair, which was pulled away from her careworn face in a White Carnation style, seemed out of place in the shabby room. Kathleen and Norma had styled each other's hair in a style called Reverie. There were no hair pieces. Their clothing, some of which Elaine recognized as Vincent's rejects, was clean and pressed. Yet there was something sad about their appearance that forced their guest to keep returning to the most mundane of subjects lest she embarrass the family with questions about travels abroad or other things that were normal topics in her usual circle. As their discussion continued, Vincent hit upon something they all could agree on.

"You should hear Norma sing."

"I'd love to."

"Come on, Hunk," Kathleen urged, her face finally relaxing into a genuine smile. "Vince can play piano for you."

"I'll turn the pages," Cora volunteered.

The family's beat-up Weber was opened and, much to everyone's pleasure, it was still in tune. After a whispered consultation, the poet and her sister performed "Ave Maria," followed by a solo performance by Vincent of "Claire de Lune," which gave way to a series of rags she had composed. With the rags came dancing and with dancing came a breakthrough with Kathleen, who accepted Elaine's request to join her in "tripping the light fantastic."

Before long Cora, Norma and Kathleen went into the kitchen to make dinner. In keeping with Vincent's pleas for a good first impression, dinner was squirrel stew passed off as Lapin Chasseur lest Elaine's finer sensibilities be aroused.

"They eat rabbit in France all the time," Kathleen hissed sweetly as she and Vincent served the meals. Cora's homemade huckleberry wine would have to do as a libation. By the time the evening was over most of the tension had been relieved. Whatever concerns Vincent felt were replaced with worries about whether her family could keep up the façade of genteel poverty.

* * *

Over the course of the next few weeks, the Millays slowly let down their guard and returned to their normal manner of approaching the world. Cora became less "dainty," Kathleen more sullen, Norma more outspoken and Vincent more bossy. The neighbors became inquisitive about the stranger who seemed thoroughly infatuated with the town's famous poet. Friends who knew Vincent in high school made polite inquiries. Some wondered if Elaine was evidence of what happened to educated girls. "They downright lose their femininity," one man noted as the girls passed his shop. "Girls are best when they don't know too much," his friend agreed.

Elaine likewise allowed herself the privilege of not giving a hang what anyone thought. As the young women wandered the poet's favorite trails, Elaine permitted herself the occasional smuggled embrace behind blackberry brambles and under water where they swam naked. Although spoiled, the biology major had never experienced such freedom. She grinned with pride as she flexed her muscles for the sisters, demonstrating a talent for making her breasts and biceps dance to a song Vincent made up on the spot. Waves of hilarity rang through the woods as the Millays' favorite swimming hole became a nudist colony. It was only when they heard the voices of a rowdy group of boys that they quickly dressed in their bathing attire. When the boys arrived, they were so disquieted by the stranger's physical presence that they retreated into the safety of town gossip.[418]

On the way home, the sisters watched as Elaine lifted Vincent over her shoulder and traversed a narrow creek while the poet giggled with absolute delight at the astounded faces of her siblings. By the time they reached the house, the quartet were muddy and damp, the precise opposite of everything the college influenced Vincent had warned against. The couple dashed up the stairs to change for dinner. Norma and Kathleen made their way to the kitchen where Cora was making dinner.

"Do you need help, Mama?" Norma asked.

"No. The beans are nearly done, and I found some greens to make a salad for Elaine."

"That Elaine is the strongest girl I ever saw," Kathleen remarked. "She picked Vincent up and carried her halfway down from Hosmer's Pond."

"Oh, my!"

"And she can make her muscles jiggle."

"Really?"

"Yes, Mama. She really is a dear."

"Very sporty," Norma added, hoping that sounded diplomatic enough.

"That's for certain," Cora mumbled under her breath before dribbling some oil and apple vinegar over the wild greens she had gathered that afternoon. "You girls set the table, then go up and get dressed."

Norma nipped at the salad as she exited the kitchen while Kathleen hung back. "Are you alright, Mama?"

Cora sighed. She had hoped she would be poker faced. "Oh, Mr. Dickey came by this afternoon. He wants the rest of what he's owed."

"Didn't Elaine's mother send enough?"

"Well, yes, I suppose, but I didn't count on the vultures descending. As soon as I gave Mr. Dickey two months back rent and brought the grocer up to date, Mrs. Murchison wanted the money for the dry goods account."

"Oh, Mama! Please let me go to work."

"No. You must study. You must do far better than Vincent did with her entrance exams. Miss Dow tells me your sister did not even get a full "B" average this term, and that's after she's gotten used to school, has a private room and whatever other excuse she's using."

"Which is more than likely Elaine."

"Precisely. Consequently, it's getting harder for her, Miss Dow, I mean, to find patrons for your sister's education. If she wasn't in all those plays and things, she would probably have been kicked out long ago. I don't want you spoiling your chances like she seems so determined to do."

"But Mama…"

"No. That's final." The nurse was suddenly overcome with a hot flash. "Goodness!"

"What is it?" Kathleen noticed the color of her mother's face was bright pink.

"Nothing. Look, your sister did such a nice job with my hair the other day that I might be able to go out and find work if she did it again. It made me look quite elegant; I think."

"It certainly did," her youngest replied. It was true that the tightly drawn coiffure had made the difference in her affect.

"Now go upstairs and get dressed. Dinner will be ready in about ten minutes."

* * *

The summer continued to test Cora's skill at stretching what was left of Elaine's room and board money. Squirrels, fat back, oysters, clams, stolen fruit and fish heads were manipulated into whatever fancy sounding dish she could conjure.

"We're having bouillabaisse again?" Vincent would cry, knowing that in fact there was very little fish in it that hadn't been someone's bait hours before. Wild anise, which grew in abundance near their home, masked the fishy smell while canned tomatoes, and fresh garlic and wild onions helped with the flavor.

Elaine remained keen to try anything Vincent would eat. She did not complain but offered to buy a chicken which became two meals thanks to her host's culinary ingenuity. The hikes and picnics the women went on became extemporaneous foraging expeditions, demonstrating a frequent resource of the Millay clan.

It was on one of those walks with Norma that the blonde heard someone say something about a "Boston Marriage."[419] She knew what that meant, and it was embarrassing. Her elder sister and Elaine were being called Lesbians. The word caught in Norma's throat. So long as Vincent's philandering was based in an all-girl college, she could ignore the gossip, but now it seemed like the whole town knew Vincent was a Sapphist.

While she personally didn't care, Norma knew it was already hard enough to keep her head up in the close-minded town without having the added burden of that label. Elaine was sweet and obviously adored Vincent, but she was as close to an obvious butch as Camden had ever seen. It troubled Norma that her elder sister would return to college and not have to cope with the rumors when she would have to bear the burden of yet another undesirable label.

So it was that one day when the four of them were launching Elaine's cute little sloop, the *Watch Your Step*, that Vincent was confronted by a townie.

"Never knew you was an invert." [420] His voice rattled off his nasal cavity as he stared at Elaine. The small vessel had been delivered by servants after she had written to her parents asking if they could send it along.

Vincent looked at the man. He had been a classmate in grammar school and not beyond that. She likewise decided it was best to ignore the remark, if only out of courtesy to Elaine.

Kathleen did not. "Shut up, Al!"

Vincent and Norma turned away. Elaine, busy with finalizing the details of their route, hadn't heard a thing. Al raised his voice so the stranger could hear. "So now yer goin' out with a bull dagger."

A flush rushed up Elaine's body. Never a great beauty, she did not think she was that obvious. She felt embarrassment and rage at the same time. No one had ever openly called her that. She bit her tongue for Vincent's sake.

"Better her, than you, you uneducated lout," Kathleen countered. Vincent wished she would just shut up.

Another man decided to voice what so many others in town were thinking. "Eh yea, if dat's what's happens when youse go to college I'd rather me sister stay home and be a natural girl."

Elaine dropped the map into her boat and helped Vincent, Norma and Kathleen into the knockabout. The young brunette was about to respond when she felt her elder sister's iron grip silencing her. Within seconds the quartet were putting around the harbor, hoping to get as far from the dullards as possible.

The single-masted pleasure craft had gaff-rigged fore and aft sails which Elaine maneuvered expertly and silently as they left the dock. With the help of the Millay sisters, who were competent sea women themselves, it wasn't long before the main sail was fluttering in the bay wind and the jib properly set at close reach.

Vincent, who was unsure how much knowledge Elaine had concerning sailing in unfamiliar waters, now relaxed and cuddled against the vessel's

"Captain." Once the wind was at precisely ninety-degrees to the sails, the premed student also relaxed.

Though they had arrived at beam reach upon the water of Penobscot Bay, Elaine remained troubled. Vincent had warned her about the people of Camden, but she didn't think people would be so blatant. She looked at Kathleen, who sat on the port side ready to manage the jib. Vincent's younger sister had only made the confrontation with the townies worse. She should have ignored the taunts. Elaine then looked over at Norma, who sat to her left as far to the edge of the craft as she dared. The blonde was looking away from them all, staring at the horizon, silent and obviously ill at ease. Why did a perfectly lovely day have to be infected with this poison?

Elaine wrapped her right arm over Vincent's shoulders and tacked gently, avoiding any extremes. The fingers of her right hand felt the poet's right nipple respond to her touch. Suddenly it was clear. She was not naïve. She knew people like her were considered freaks. What was really bothering them was not that she was a lesbian. It was that Vincent had been drawn to her, the stranger in their midst, and not some local boy.

She heard a click and saw Kathleen pull the camera down. The photo had captured the whole awkward moment.

* * *

At the end of August, Elaine packed her bags and retreated to her family's summer house in Bellport, Long Island. Located in Suffolk County, the community had much in common with both Camden and Mamaroneck, only it was far more welcoming. Just across the water from Fire Island, Bellport was the home of many artists, writers and craftspeople who served the tourist trade and wealthy New Yorkers who owned summer residences there.

There is a certain civility in a small town where neighbors rely on neighbors for everything from a cup of sugar to shoveling snow. Camden had reached the congested point where residents didn't always feel a need to be civil. Bellport, with only 400 year-round residents, did not. The Rallis had chosen a place where their daughter would feel welcomed while also having the sort of amenities rich New Yorkers desired. It was a community of suffragists, women athletes, and white wicker chairs. As sailboats glided over the Great South Bay, ferries carried visitors to Fire Island, a place where people like Elaine would hardly be noticed.

Elaine and Vincent had agreed the poet would join her in Bellport in a few days.

Yet the poet knew this was unlikely. Although she had told Elaine not to be frightened about being apart, there was a part of her that had been stung by the incident at Camden Harbor. Everyone in town was now talking about it, and while she could go home to Vassar, her sisters and mother had to live there. Norma's reaction alone had dampened her ardor like a summer squall.

She had lost her sense of balance in the relationship.[421] Elaine could not be discreet, at least not as discreet as polite society required. While Katherine and Fil were able to put on a good show, Elaine could not—even when she tried. Vincent liked being inscrutable. She knew she would have to let go before the relationship with Elaine defined her. While people might whisper about her dating an older man, it was not unheard of. Arthur Hooley was socially acceptable; Elaine would never be. She adored Elaine's lovemaking. In fact, she enjoyed sleeping with women, which is why she embraced any person she found desirable. But there was an obvious difference between what could pass as a schoolgirl crush and a lesbian relationship.

31. Close Sepulchred

1915

The fall term began. Vincent moved to a smaller room in North Hall, which the school's new president, Henry Noble MacCracken, had renamed Jewett Hall after the first man to hold that position. By choice she signed up for English, German and Spanish. By necessity she enrolled in philosophy, history and economics. It was a heavy load, six courses, but MacCracken had made it clear that she needed to buckle down if she wanted to graduate with her class.

To counter the misery of coursework, the poet remained active in French club, drama club, choir, and her private prayer group. She entered every poetry and stipend contest in hopes of raising cash, and although she didn't get the scholarship she hoped for, she was able to publish in the Vassar *Miscellany* and occasionally was paid for work published in *The Forum* and *Poetry Magazine*. Kennerley was still pestering her for her promised volume and Miss Dow was still concerned with her purity.

By now, all who knew her knew Vincent was in love with love. She cherished it for the poetry fuel it was. Nevertheless, Miss Dow felt it necessary to have a long chat with the poet when they met for their monthly luncheon.

This time the matron had brought several suitable dresses and a smaller than usual check. Vincent was worried. How should she interpret this? It wasn't long before Miss Dow got to the meat of the matter.

"Now of course you are the mistress of your own production,[422] and, as always, I do not wish to make unreasonable demands, but that poem, 'The Suicide' was just obscene."

"Obscene?" Vincent replied as she rummaged through the hand-me-downs. For once most of them would need no alteration.

"I may not be a literary woman, but I must say there are some ways in which I can help you to navigate friendly avenues."

"Uh-huh," the poet grunted and held up a pink chiffon gown with the tiniest stain. She was certain she could embroider something to mask it.

"I believe, perhaps, that you are unaware of dangers, both physical and temperamental, of absorbing the attentions of individuals who are a hindrance in spite of the pleasant things they bring."[423]

"So, you'd like me to do what?" The annoyance of yet another hurdle was clearer than Vincent wanted it to be. She softened her tone. "These dresses are beautiful, Aunt Calline, honest they are. Believe me, dear, I plan on applying myself this year. I'm already involved in the college's fiftieth anniversary celebration. I'm to play Marie of France. The poet, you know."

"That's fine, child. Wonderful news. It is also important to me that in the next year or two you guide yourself and what you publish carefully. More of my friends have seen you now, and if their influence—and funding—is to be had you must tread in the right direction."

Vincent smiled as she put away a powder blue suit that still had the cardboard shapers in it. "Yes, I understand, Aunt Calline. The grapevine among the rich is very short."

Miss Dow smiled. She loved the image and felt comforted by it. "Precisely. Because of your gifts, Vincent, life will present some complicated problems for you."[424]

The matron hesitated before continuing. She was no stranger to the goings-on in women-only institutions. There were rumors and she knew what they would mean. "Your friend, Elaine Ralli."

"Yes?"

She realized the best way to get Vincent to do anything was to seem neutral. "Is she the one whose parents are in trade?"

Vincent set aside something that hadn't been in fashion since she was in grammar school. "Yes."

"She's very athletic." Miss Dow hoped the expression would feel bland enough to seem merely observational.

"She rides dressage."

"Isn't that interesting."

"And plays hockey."

"Ice or field?"

"Field, I think." Vincent was so consumed in the latest batch of clothes she wasn't paying attention to the subtext of Miss Dow's questions. Now she caught on just as Miss Dow had hoped.

"She may not be the kind our friends would like."

The two women looked at each other. An understanding had been reached.

"Honestly," Miss Dow continued. "I do believe you have both courage and strength, and yet I see such pitfalls. You have an idealism which means ennobling the lives of others. I don't want you to be the sort of poet who thinks freedom means license, or who thinks you can touch pitch without being spoiled. The world needs your words because they brighten, strengthen and, I think, illuminate the path to life's great fundamentals."

Miss Dow noticed that Vincent had again drifted toward imagining herself in the blue dress. The poet nodded and merely said, "You're a dear."

The matron watched her protégé for a moment. Had she misunderstood Vincent's apparent comprehension of the issue at hand? She would have to be more direct. The poet's benefactor raised her voice ever so slightly, just enough to signal she wanted to be heard. "I know this sounds like a sermon to you, dear, but it is not so intended. My concerns merely mean love and my great interest in your many gifts."[425]

Vincent lifted her eyes. Shame overcame her. Her eyes filled with tears. She realized for the umpteenth time how much she appreciated her "Aunt Calline," yet this time it felt as if it had registered somewhere different within her. Without Miss Dow's assistance she would not be in her third year at Vassar, nor would she be dressed in finery—even if it was second-hand. She thought back to the way her clothes looked in Camden. While she had always endeavored to dress well, budgets would have prohibited expensive materials, much less items from Filene's or Wanamaker's. Now she wore clothes she had only seen in magazines. More importantly, her mother and sisters had also benefited from that long-ago chance of fate at the Whitehall Inn. Engulfed by regret, she spoke softly. "You are such a dear. What did I ever do to deserve such kindness?"

"You wrote a very lovely poem, and I hope to see many more in that vein."

The poet already knew Miss Dow wasn't fond of "The Suicide." What would she think of "Indifference"? Most likely she'd hate it. Nevertheless, Miss Dow's message had made it plain she would have to get serious about spending less time with Elaine.

As the poet walked Miss Dow across campus, she looked at the many faces who had already fallen away from her life. The reason was clear. When one is tangled in a web of possessive love, no matter how delicious or desirable, one cannot reach out, nor does anyone feel safe reaching in.

* * *

Later that Thursday afternoon, as Vincent was walking toward the anniversary pageant rehearsal, she ran into a friend from first year German, Frances Garver.

"Come on back and get some fudge. I've made some in the candy kitchen[426] and I'm giving it to people I love."[427]

While Vincent realized Fran "loved" as many people as she did, she also knew that Fran was just the sort of person Miss Dow would approve of. As an Oregonian, Fran's family was far enough away that it was unlikely they would get wind of any liaison. Because one of Fran's eyebrows was slightly higher than the other, she always had a sort of quizzical look about her oval face. Her best feature was her beautiful blue eyes, which held you tightly in their gaze, as if reading your soul.

"Oh, do you love me?" the poet flirted.

"Yes, I always have," Fran smiled.

Although Vincent already had plans to spend Friday through Saturday at a lakeside resort in Mohonk with Elaine, the poet decided then and there to spend Saturday night with Fran.

32. Herald Wings Came Whispering

1915

She had been called "Princess" ever since her portrayal of Daisy of Pretentia the prior year at the Sophomore Party.[428] Now she would be called Marie of France after her standout performance in the "Pageant of Athena" staged on October 11, 1915.

Looking tall and regal in her white satin gown with a train so long and wide it took two girls to carry it, Vincent had the carriage of a queen and the loyalty of fifty subjects, some carrying cushions, others rugs, while one employed a parasol to protect her from the sun while still another fanned her highness lest she become overheated.[429] With her beautiful red hair down, she looked like a drawing by Maxwell Parrish.

Faculty, board, students and family members swarmed around her after the performance. "That was wonderful!"

"I completely believed you were the queen of France."

"What year are you in?"

"Are you the girl who wrote 'Renascence'?"

Vincent lapped it all up, though she was no longer the same girl who wrote her most famous work. Elaine, standing nearby, basked in reflected glory. Vincent was polite but showed no outward affection. All those years of playing poker were paying off. Few suspected she was anything but a virginal twenty-two-year-old actress.

Professor Elizabeth Haight approached. Her kiss enraged Elaine, but the Greek knew better than to make a fuss in the moment. Vincent did not like scenes unless she made them.

"Oh, Vincent, you were simply marvelous," the Latin professor cried, lightly kissing her again on the mouth. As they embraced Miss Haight whispered, "Te amo."

"Pretiosus es mihi," the poet whispered back.

It was a good thing Elaine wasn't within earshot.

Miss Dow finally made her way to the adored poet. "Oh, child, that was fine, fine!"

"Aunt Calline!"

"We should have little trouble funding your senior year now."

"Thank you. You've been so good to me. Will Kathleen be here too?"

Her patron smiled. It was so like Vincent to always infer a little more was in order. "We're close on that. See over there? The gentleman in the dark tweed overcoat with the black tie? That's Henry MacCracken. He's taken over as president of the college. Have you met him yet?"

Vincent nodded and peered toward the young academic. He was handsome enough. Not a fuddy duddy like President Taylor. At thirty-four, MacCracken was ideally suited to lead the women's college. A strong advocate of suffrage and a liberal politically, there was another advantage for Vincent: his specialty was English Literature. "Oh, yes, I had the pleasure just after he arrived. I guess he wanted to meet all the girls. Who is that woman standing next to him? The one in pink?"

"That's his wife. A lovely woman who is as smart as she is beautiful. Go talk about Shakespeare with him," Miss Dow hinted. "He'll like that."

Vincent obediently wandered in the direction of the new president. She was determined to win over the academic.

"Good afternoon, sir. My patron, Miss Caroline Dow, suggested I ask you about your Shakespeare class next fall. I don't know if you remember me. I'm Vincent Millay."

"Don't you mean Marie of France?" he smiled.

"Perhaps I am at the moment."

Marjorie Dodd MacCracken sized up the brash junior and determined she was no threat. "Yes, but what will you be in a few hours?"

"Just a lowly student," Vincent feigned humility with just the right touch of humor.

All laughed. Additional admirers circled the poet in her new location. Between their congratulations and praise the poet spoke with the president about Shakespeare.

"Have you appeared in any of his plays?"

"No, but I know it knocked the wind clear out of me when I opened my mother's gargantuan copy of Shakespeare and read the passage from *Romeo and Juliet* about the 'dateless bargain' and death keeping Juliet as beautiful as she was in life."[430]

"Yes, that is a remarkable passage. Have you read *Midsummer*? I imagine you would make a tremendous Puck."

"Do you think so? In Drama Club we've been considering whether to stage *A Midsummer Night's Dream*."

MacCracken nodded his approval.

"Is your mother a teacher?" Mrs. MacCracken asked.

"No. My father was, and principal and superintendent too," she replied as she signed a program for a gushing admirer. "My mother is a nurse…and a wigmaker." She looked down at her shoes. She wished she hadn't added the latter profession. Her embarrassment at her humble origins had overcome her pride in her mother's great skill.

"Honest work," MacCracken declared, easing her discomfort.

She was immediately taken by his delicacy. "Bless you. Yes."

Confident that Vincent had made enough of an impression on her own, Miss Dow approached with Mrs. Trowbridge at her side.

"I see you've become acquainted with our protégé," Mrs. Trowbridge smiled. She nodded toward MacCracken's wife. "Marge."

"Nice to see you, Sofia. How's your genius husband?"

"Likewise. He's fine."

There was a moment's pause while Vincent extricated herself from the embrace of a freshman. An amused MacCracken looked on and then turned to the poet's patrons.

"Seems as though Miss Millay has a knack for making friends."

The group laughed nervously. "When do you take the reins, Henry?" Mrs. Trowbridge asked.

"I already have."

"He's been busy as the devil the past week," Marjorie MacCracken noted.

"I thought attending today's anniversary event would help me to get acquainted with the families, and the college's various celebrities," he nodded toward Vincent with a wink.

As the group nodded in agreement, a figure stepped between Vincent and the newly hired executive. "Dr. MacCracken, so pleased to meet you. I'm Elaine Ralli, a senior, class of 1916."

"A pleasure. You were unable to make our appointment, as I recall. I hope you're feeling better."

Vincent's head turned toward Miss Dow, hoping the action would reassure her patron that Elaine's appearance was just a coincidence.

"You're a biology major, right? Top of your class?"

"Yes, sir." Elaine ignored the steel-edged glare of her former lover. "I'm pre-med. Biology and physics."

"You're aiming to become a physician. That's marvelous. We need more female doctors. Don't you agree, Miss Millay?"

"Um, yes," she smiled through her frown. Elaine knew the look in her eyes. It was a performative smile the poet had perfected for just such occasions.

"I take it you two know each other," Mrs. MacCracken said, reaching for her husband's arm in a subconscious gesture that showed she knew exactly how well.

"Yes."

Miss Dow took Vincent by the arm. She realized the predicament the poet was in thanks to Elaine's appearance. "Well, I'm sure there are many students and parents who would like to have some of your time. Come along, Vincent, I'd like you to meet some of my other friends."

When they were out of earshot and while Elaine and Mrs. Trowbridge were still conversing with the MacCrackens, Miss Dow offered her thoughts on Vincent's most recent performance. "You handled that well. It looks like you've made another ally."

"Which one?" The poet arched an eyebrow in a comical manner.

"Dr. MacCracken."

"Yes, I think we'll get along very well." The freshmen who had held Vincent's train were long gone and the weight of the costume was beginning to tire the poet. "I best go inside and dress for dinner."

"Yes, shall I save you a seat?"

"Please." Vincent gathered the train in a bundle and started toward the residence she still called North Hall.

"Perhaps your charming friend Miss Tilt could join us." Miss Dow called.

"I'll ask her."

33. Startled Storm Clouds

1915

It wasn't long before word spread on campus that Vincent was again playing the field. It seemed as if everyone fell in love with her. Nevertheless, the new and old "friends" she made were more carefully selected for their seeming heterosexuality and well-placed parents. Miss Dow signaled her approval with a modest raise in her allowance.

What none of her prospects and patrons could fathom was that Vincent's only real love was her poetry—though Elaine soon felt this with a cyclonic certainty.

The redheaded junior had stopped sharing her poetry with Elaine. When the Greek asked why, Vincent only shrugged. The truth was she was now sharing it with Fran Garver, who was soon as enchanted as her predecessor.

One night in late October 1915, as she lay in bed reveling in her luck at having captured the attention of Vassar's own Marie of France, Fran noticed how exhausted the poet looked.

"You know something, sweetheart?"

"Hmmm, what?"

"Never mind. It's morbid."

Vincent was now curious. She rose from where she rested on Fran's chest. "What is?"

The sweet-faced soul only patted the poet's tousled hair. "Relax…rest…"

Vincent let her head back down and kissed Fran's nipple before turning her head back. "What's morbid."

"You look so tired."

"That's not news," Vincent laughed.

"When I looked at you, I felt something I hadn't felt since my mother died."[431]

The poet sat up. She had worn herself ragged between coursework, rehearsals and performances, not to mention juggling four women.[432] How she wished to just lay down in the long grass and close her eyes. She sighed in spite of herself. The poet could listen to the catbird calls all afternoon.[433] "How do you mean?"

"I was holding her hand, like I'm holding yours now."

Fran became choked up remembering the half-hour she spent comforting her mother just before she died. She explained that her mother smiled at her happily, closed her eyes and died. "Vincent, dear, you had the same beautiful expression in your eyes a moment ago. You seemed so peaceful."

The poet agreed it had been a morbid thought but smiled. "I feel peaceful because you're such a dear. You give me a place to rest. I have so much I need to do, yet I come here, and you just let me relax. I can't tell you how valuable that is to me right now."

Fran kissed Vincent's eyes shut and eased her down upon her breast. This was not foreplay. It was concern. Her fingers gently stroked the poet's head until she fell asleep.

It wasn't long before their naked bodies were entwined in slumber. However, they only slept for a scant hour before the poet awoke, looked at the clock and tried to get out of bed without waking the "child" she loved enough to supplant Elaine. *"That's ironic,"* she whispered to herself as she dressed. *"When Arthur calls me 'child' I hate it, yet I call Fran that."*

Just as she finished the thought, Fran awoke. "Where are you going?"

"I promised Professor Washburn I'd come in and discuss attending her psychology course next term," she paused and rolled her eyes. "What we must do to get our degrees."

Both women laughed but for different reasons. Fran because she knew what Margaret Floy Washburn had to endure to be the first woman in the United States to get a doctorate in psychology; Vincent because she imagined what Dr. Washburn would say about the whole "child" thing.

The poet finished dressing and began to slip on her shoes. "I can't imagine why they require that course."

"Maybe they are hoping it will help you deal with your profession or your children," Fran laughed again.

"The only children I have are my poems and *they* are the only thing keeping me sane in this place."

"You know, if you don't marry when we're out of here, I shall earn a million and you shall write and we'll divide the money, and when it pleases you, you'll visit me and do exactly as you wish."[434]

Fran stood up and kissed the poet tenderly. "If you don't leave right now, I shall make love to you."

"Is that a promise?" Vincent giggled as she turned and dashed out the door.

* * *

The truth was another lover awaited after Dr. Washburn. In light of the poet's reputation for cutting classes, all the psychology professor wanted to discuss was her attendance requirements.

As the semester continued, Vincent made good on her promise to Miss Dow. Her grades improved as her Elaine distractions diminished. The advantage of her other paramours was they were as afraid of social conventions as the poet's patron was.

While still aglow from her performance as Marie of France, Vincent took the role of the male poet Marchbanks in George Bernard Shaw's *Candide*. It was another critical success. Classmates marveled at how well she played a man.[435] The college awoke with her contributions. Her name was everywhere. More poems were published in the Vassar *Miscellany*. More students followed her for hints about coursework. And, of course, clothes were now exchanged as freely as ideas.

Meanwhile, Elaine sank into a deep depression. Vincent's visits to her room were fewer and their assignations further apart. They had spent the last few months passing each other with hostile whispers, while knowing the passion that sat between them was like an inevitable train wreck, one that hovered in the future like bad memories from one's childhood. Yet it wasn't long before the biology major realized she had been dumped in favor of girls who met criterion she would never reach. Elaine wanted more of her time and begged, "Please say yes," in a plaintive tone that further discouraged attachment. The Greek's love for Vincent slowly began to consume her right mind. She wrote of her longing, noting, "Have you heard the rain? It is cold tonight and I'm too restless for rain—only for the touch of you—will I ever not want that?"[436]

As for the poet, Vincent found fodder in her words, making notes for future lamentations about the loss of her seductive power. "The rain is full of ghosts tonight that tap and sigh upon my glass and listen for reply…"[437]

The humiliation of simply being a conductor of rhyme began to eat at Elaine. "You have not spoken to me for so long about your poems and I dare not ask—will you not say something—surely some day you will find time to say something to me."

The future doctor tried to remain light when dealing with the poet, but the desperation of her love soon overwhelmed Elaine and she experienced a mental and emotional breakdown that overcame the strength and power that had so attracted the poet. What started as a visit to the infirmary became an extended holiday convalescence at home. Daisy Ralli fed, bathed, and dressed her daughter, and would sit on the porch and take long walks with Elaine in the bright winter solstice sun. By the time Elaine returned to school in January 1916 to finish her pre-med degree, Vincent had moved on completely.

34. One Black Wave

1915-1916

Christmas 1915 with her family was a bleak affair. Without the extra few dollars Elaine had been giving her every month, their situation had gotten even worse than the previous summer. Cora had managed to find part time work at the local pharmacy, while Norma's waitress salary was combined with income from the hats she designed.

Needing just a few more dollars to avoid being late with the rent, Cora finally relented and allowed Kathleen to work part time at the Comique cinema. Between the three of them and whatever Vincent could pinch off from her $25 a month allowance and poetry sales, the Millays remained only one month behind in the rent Mr. Dickey demanded, $37 behind with the grocer and, thanks to Cora's job at the pharmacy, their debt on toiletries and other sundries was diminishing.

Nevertheless, the rumors about the family had reached the point where every vendor's patience was at a loss. If they could just hang on for another two years Vincent would have her degree and be able to come home and get a job that offered enough income to support them all. Then anything Cora and Norma earned would serve to pay off the old debt and help Kathleen with her expenses at college.

Since the October 1915 break-up with Elaine, the poet had taken up a renewed correspondence with Arthur Hooley. His replies held the same ambiguity they always had. It was maddening. He would suggest that men and women couldn't understand each other, and that only a man could understand his lack of interest and depression.[438] Nothing she said could convince him to renew the former state of their relationship. To make him jealous she told him of her various conquests at Vassar. He remained unmoved. "Edna, even if you had cared for a girl, and even if you had given yourself (so far as you could) I do not think I should care, greatly. No, I should not."[439]

Although she still hoped to see him, she soon realized it was hopeless. It had been nearly two years since they'd seen each other. Whether she desired Arthur as a man or confidante, it was plain he had no interest in the woman who was no longer his "child." She tried to take it philosophically. Who was he that she should be kept awake as many nights are there are days weeping for his sake? There were other men, braver men, kinder men, even men who were adorably stupid. Why was he the one man on her mind?[440]

Arthur may have been the only man the poet thought of, and she might have even regretted anything she'd ever said to him, nonetheless, she had withheld parts of herself. There were many things she had not let him see.[441] There were the moods only her family knew. Now and then, when she was particularly low, the ministrations of a classmate came as a response to a mood or thought. But Arthur had not seen them because they reflected the internal debate between Good Vincent and Bad Vincent, and not the cute, amusing way she discussed her feelings in her letters.

These times of deep fear and insecurity were masked with true bravado concerning faithfulness (which she found stupid) and were complemented with false statements that nothing had ever hurt her. Many things had hurt her; not winning first prize for "Renascence" for one, Ferdinand Earle's manipulation of the naïve nineteen-year-old for another. Yet those pains had callused over like a yogi's feet after years of walking on hot coals. She pushed any thought of the pain away until it bubbled over to the surface, delivering a mood she would hide from Arthur and other outside intimates. It would create a poison inside her that would eventually require more and more substances and sex to allay.

It was this self-absorption that generated a snare for unwary lovers who thought they could be the sole exception to Vincent's otherwise single-minded allegiance to herself. Nevertheless, as much as she eschewed intimacy, she was terrified of being alone. This gave women like Fran and the poet's latest conquest, Isobel Simpson, a route into her heart that became a trap. Once closed, they would be used until she was done with them, not because she wanted to hurt them, but because she could not help herself. Sooner or later, they would want to hold onto her in the same way her family did. Such closeness was untenable. The few who managed to break down her defenses usually did so with humor and acceptance, not great dramatic scenes and slavish devotion. The people who most interested Vincent were the people who kept their distance. They were safer.

Starting with being left with her Auntie Bine as a toddler, the family's frequent moves, her parents' separation and divorce, and her mother's frequent absences, the poet had learned to distrust proximity. This was proven when Ferdinand Earle used his power as an editor to manipulate her into trusting that her family would soon be free of financial care. Even Miss Dow, kind, generous and steadfast as she was, had not been able to deliver all she had promised. It had reached a point where every relationship was a test. How much can I abuse you before you give up? Can I really trust you? Am I worthy of the attention I am getting? Will you abandon me too? Do I deserve love?

People who were secure enough to act as if they cared less were partially able to earn her trust. In her fashion she remained true to all of them, but those who managed to keep their distance were the most attractive of all—and if her mother disapproved of them, all the better.[442]

Consequently, her longing for Arthur was a product of his lack of availability. As far as she was concerned, it wasn't necessary to be a man to understand what the word "girl" meant to Arthur.[443] What did he think the word "man" meant to her? Had she known how greatly one girl's beauty and presence—sometimes even her absence—could disturb another girl's peace of mind, she might not miss Arthur at all. After all, she was glad there was an Anactoria for any Sappho at Vassar. Such relationships had taught her there was no reason to say harsh and foolish things about an ancient Greek philosopher or modern English poet, people who the world often condemned and punished.

Vincent just wanted the editor to touch her again, to look at her and bring her back into herself.[444] Yet she was glad when he confessed that he was miserable when he thought of her at night. By her logic, that torturous dynamic must be a form of love, the push-pull of lovers, the useless battle between the Montagues and the Capulets, a fight so old no one could remember why the feud began in the first place. She recalled spending the night before the fire in his little Mamaroneck house while the rain dripped across the eaves. He hadn't loved her then, when she most loved him, but now that the fire was out for her, it was sparking in him.[445] The agony of the on-again, off-again romance added dimension to a beautiful but otherwise frustrating game of so-called love.

* * *

Although she endeavored to devote herself to study, it was incredibly frustrating to learn that her grades in the fall 1915 term had slipped. She told herself that her average grades in economics and history were because she hated those subjects, but how did that account for her "C" grade in German? The "B" she got in philosophy reflected her fascination with Plato and Epictetus, and her "A" in Spanish probably had something to do with her tutor, the Nicaraguan poet Salomón de la Selva. She knew she had to do better if she wanted to graduate. Yet Bad Vincent was always able to drag her away from study. Whether it was a new sexual partner, or a smoke in the campus cemetery, she could not be disciplined by anything but poetry.

When the second semester began on January 31, 1916, Vincent took secondary classes in philosophy, English, Spanish, French and added first-year courses in psychology with Dr. Washburn and in "The Opera" to fulfill her music requirement. The heavy load was not the least of her worries. She was still obsessing about Arthur and her family's increasingly desperate letters concerning finances.

* * *

The truth was, although she was mature in some ways, the poet still didn't know how to control her tendency to overdramatize nearly every event and relationship in her life. This became abundantly clear in when she was selected to play the lead in John Millington Synge's *Dierdre of the Sorrows*. It felt so real to her.[446] So real, in fact, that she became caught up in the suicide scene and actually stabbed herself through the leather jacket of her costume. Although it was barely a flesh wound, it illustrated how deeply she had stepped into the tragic character who kills herself over her lover's grave. As a result of her growing reputation as an actress, reporters from the Poughkeepsie *Eagle*, the *Enterprise* and the *New York Tribune* were sent to review her performance, with the latter describing her performance as growing in "intensity, building toward a successful crisis."[447]

Yet the poet didn't trust this kind of praise. She wanted it from the man who mostly ignored her, a distant, emotionally unavailable father figure who she believed was capable of speaking to her as an equal. Her immersion in the role of Dierdre had helped her realize it would not be absurd if he loved her, but how absurd it would be if she loved him. "People fall in love with me, and annoy me, and distress me and flatter me and excite me—and all that sort of thing. But no one speaks to me. I sometimes think no one can. Can you?"[448]

35. Happy Living Things

1916

The urgency around money was growing all consuming. On March 13, she heard from her family that they would be kicked out of their home at 82 Washington Street. She couldn't bear thinking of the fence of morning glories next to their home that greeted her every morning as she went off to Camden High, Hosmer's Pond or up Megunticook. But it couldn't be helped, so why think of it?[449]

The poet continued submitting works in the hope of publication in *Poetry Magazine, The Forum* and the group of literary magazines that were cropping up all over New York. In February, she had taken the time to write an essay for the Helen Kate Furness Prize, thinking her expertise in Shakespeare might tip the scales of success in her favor. She had even begun to seriously entertain putting together a book for Mitchell Kennerley.

Yet she was beginning to see that when it came to preparing a manuscript for publication, time was not her friend. It was always more demanding than she could possibly deliver. Classes, rehearsals, relationships and the requirements of being a protégé took hours she wished to apply toward her only real love, her poetry.[450] Somehow, she would have to make time if she wanted to be taken seriously after graduating the following year.

* * *

That spring was rainy but unseasonably warm in Poughkeepsie. Buds appeared in the pine boughs earlier than usual. The fragrance of blossoms made it difficult to stay indoors studying. Yet, if she wanted to graduate with her class, she would have to force herself to ignore the season's siren call.

Fortunately, her new roommate's reserved nature left space for quiet. It was part of what made her so desirable. Isobel Simpson rarely interrupted

Vincent while she was composing, rehearsing or studying. On top of that, the Classics major had a great sense of humor. Consequently, she provided welcome relief from the demanding distractions of Vincent's junior year.

The poet was now twenty-four. Isobel was only twenty. In addition to a fondness for Greek and Latin poetry, the couple adored Kipling's *The Jungle Book*,[451] which they frequently read to each other. To further break the monotony of study, they left silly letters addressed to "Best Beloved" in odd places in their shared dorm room. Isobel's sense of fun was a blessing after the break-up with Elaine. She soon became Vincent's "Little Sphinx," so-called because of her inscrutable silences; while Vincent was given the moniker "Slimy Serpent."

Vincent was trying to make sense of Dr. Riley's remarks about her most recent philosophy paper. He had accused her of being a fraud whose thinking was "sloppy." His sarcasm ate at her confidence. Normally she liked his approach and how he put the various theories together, but he had not been pleased with her work and had asked her to write a paper on the "intellectual duality" of the American Idealist Jonathan Edwards. He suggested she read chapter three of his book, *American Philosophies: The Early Schools*.[452]

Isobel lay on her back next to Vincent. Her left foot was anchored in her right thigh. She shook the March 7 issue of the *Poughkeepsie Eagle* like a butterfly to flip the page.

"Say, did you hear about C. B. Reardon?"[453]

"No," Vincent replied, half to her professor and half to her "friend."

"He bought himself a new Studebaker hearse."

"I bet no one wants to ride in it," Vincent dead panned.

They both roared with laughter. Little nibbles met lips. Finally, Isobel asked, "Are you going to the organ recital tomorrow?"

"What time?"

"Why?"

"Will we be out of bed by then?"

"Probably. It's 4:15 in the afternoon."

"Wonderful!"

Isobel's nibble became a gentle bite.

"I've got to get through this text," Vincent lamented.

"How would a philosopher describe us about now?"

The poet thought for a moment. Was Isobel giving her a hint or just something to think about? A few seconds passed. "A philosopher would say our loyalties were divided."

Isobel knew this was the correct answer academically, but was it the right one among friends? "And what, pray tell, my little slimy snake, are your loyalties?"

Vincent looked into her partner's eyes and decided it was better at that moment to view Isobel as a roommate.

"My loyalties, my very little Sphinx, are to Vassar College, my family, my friends, and you—in no particular order." Vincent winked. "Thank God theology is not in the mix, or I'd be as conflicted as this Edwards fellow was."

Isobel wasn't sure of the meaning but realized a contest was useless. Vincent was who she was. Praying to be visible in a room of mirrors while chasing a goddess was an exercise in futility. She switched legs. After a decent interval she turned the page of the newspaper and asked, "Are you going to attend the vocational conference?"

"I thought I might go to the one on jobs in publishing houses."

"I take it you're thinking of living in New York."

"Eventually, later maybe."

Vincent returned to study, but Isobel was puzzled by the idea of Vincent living in the huge city. The poet had once told her how much she loved the woods, and adored greenery. How many hours would she have to spend walking in Central Park and anywhere else a tree would grow to fulfill that need? Isobel's furrowed silence slowly pried words from the poet's lips. "Why are you worried?"

"I just can't see you living there, that's all. You already told me how suffocating Barnard was."

The poet remained quiet and then leaped from the bed and raced to the typewriter they shared, "Spirit of the Trees, which is the undying Spirit of Love, enters the Hearts of the People. The nations unite and go out together singing."

It was the missing link in what would become the convocation poem in 1917. Isobel sat there stunned. She had often seen this poetic birth and it was precisely why she loved Vincent so much. The magical brilliance of her process. Had Homer been like this? Aristophanes? The classic essence of

Vincent's prose fueled her mind with utopian dreams. "Do you actually believe that is possible?"

"Maybe. That is, people would have to change a lot, I suppose but..." Vincent shuffled through some papers. "I started something. It's not finished yet, but..."

"I'd love to hear it."

"It's rough."

"That's alright."

Vincent stood up, turned her chair around and leaned forward, a cardboard bound notebook in her hand. "Out of night and alarm, out of darkness and dread, out of old hate, grudge and distrust, sin and remorse, passion and blindness, shall come dawn and the birds..."[454] the poet paused and set down her workbook. "That's as far as I've gotten."

Isobel let a quiet drop of dream juice escape her eyes. "That's tremendous! Are you going to submit it to *The Miscellany*?"

"Maybe. It depends on how long it takes to finish." Vincent picked up the book and erased a word. "Actually, I was kind of thinking I'd submit it for the convocation next year."

"You mean when you graduate?"

"Yes."

"But what about the war?"

"Dr. Salmon knows what I mean..."

"You read this to her?" Isobel did her utmost to remain detached.

"In a manner of speaking."

"What did she think of...of..."

"I call it 'Song of the Nations'."

"What did Dr. Salmon think?"

"I didn't read it to her."

"Oh." They sat across from each other, the intellectual sparring exciting them both. Finally, Isobel leaned toward the poet. "Then how do you know that she knows what you mean?"

"Because she writes about balance. Balance will only come when women share power."

"Isn't it the other way around? I mean equal power is only possible when there's balance, that is, balance between the sexes."

Vincent looked at Isobel quizzically for a moment before replying. The twenty-year-old watched as the junior calculated the poem's meter.

"There are different types of power," Vincent finally began. "Men have political power and intend to control our social power politically. Balance is contingent on men and women sharing both political and social power. Or, at least, allowing women to have sole possession of social power long enough that women can educate themselves and their children to respect women and men equally."

"Have you run any of this by Dr. Riley?"

"No. He won't like it."

"Then why are you poking the bear?"

"Because the bear, as you call him, and rightly so, is one of those instructors who is better at telling you what someone else said than coming up with anything original. That's why, if I ran it by anyone, I would run it by Dr. Salmon. She would know what I meant."

They both laughed before Isobel got serious. "You really ought to just give him what he wants and save that suffragist stuff for Washburn or Salmon. Just say something like Edwards explored the 'inner and outer life to develop a sense of wholeness between the secular and the divine.'[455] At least I think that's what he said."

Vincent laughed. "I'll think about it."

36. A Sense of Glad Awakening

1916

Vincent's forays into New York continued to hold a deep fascination. She found the tremendous heights of the buildings scary, like they were giant castles of the king in her beloved *Morte d' Arthur*. The buses, automobiles, and carriages that choked the streets clattered so in the concrete canyons that at times she wasn't sure where the sounds were coming from.

At the same time, being able to read her work before audiences and connect with other poets, dramatists, actors and musicians made her feel as if she'd been dropped into Renaissance Florence. Her friends Mitchell Kennerley, Harriet Monroe, Sara Teasdale and Hal Bynner were included in this delicious urban soup. It bubbled with imagination, even if it didn't always smell as wonderful as it tasted.

By now, Vincent could read and write in seven languages, although one of them was only spoken in Catholic churches, and her Greek was barely passable. She could test her growing language skills with the variety of dreamers who came to the city in search for the "pots of gold" they'd heard of back home in Italy, Spain, Germany and France.

Vincent loved learning. Isobel's knowledge of the Classics helped her with Greek and Latin, just as Elaine's competency in chemistry and physics was applied to her unappreciated theories about psychology. She absorbed it all, feeling her mind and heart expand well beyond the borders of Camden and even New York.

More poems were published in *The Miscellany*, and more plays were being produced. She was becoming a woman under the watchful eyes of Miss Dow, Dr. MacCracken and all her favorite teachers and friends. Meanwhile, her letters home became fewer and fewer. What could she say? She was tucked away in a dorm room, secure of her place in the world—at least for now. She was busy with a dozen things that served as a perfect excuse for avoiding the pressure from home.

The leavening agent at Vassar College was the school's uniform.[456] It was especially welcome during Vincent's junior year when her family was virtually homeless. The silver gray and pink outfit was reminiscent of a naval midshipmen's garment. Of course, some "middies" were purchased at Filene's or Wanamaker's, while others were hand sewn. Nevertheless, uniforms served to equalize the girls during classes. The only time their costumes were competitive was in the evenings and at special events, like the annual Junior Prom, which in 1916 was held coincidentally on Washington's Birthday.

"They're having a birthday party just for me," Vincent giggled.

"Who will you take?" Fran asked.

"I'm taking my cousin Chester," Isobel offered.

The poet looked at the two women who would not be her date. Arthur would raise too many questions. He was too old. Hal? Maybe, but she doubted it. Who else did she know? The face of Elaine's older brother came to mind.[457] Sure, Victor was dark-skinned and diminutive, but she knew he'd be available.

"I think I'll ask Elaine's brother."

Fran and Isobel looked at each other and then at the poet.

"Are you serious?" they asked almost in unison. The idea was less than tasteful. They both knew how Elaine continued to moon over Vincent. Why would she even consider Victor Ralli? It was just cruel.

"You're thinking of Elaine, aren't you?"

"Well, we know how she…," Isobel hesitated. The romances between women were rarely spoken of in detail when they reached the fully Sapphic.

"I think that's all in the past. In fact, we ran into each other a few days ago and had a lovely chat. We're friends now, and I know Victor is a terrific dancer."

Doubt continued to muddy the air, but the topic was dropped in favor of what they'd wear. Miss Dow had recently brought an oversized but beautiful yellow chiffon gown with golden butterflies on the shoulder and fur trim along the hem. With Isobel's help it could be fitted. Vincent herself would do the altering.

Victor Ralli was floored by the invitation. He had no idea what the true nature of his sister's relationship with Vincent was. All he knew was that he found the five-foot-one-inch redhead sexy and fun ever since they met after his performance in the Vassar Alumnae Play in the previous fall.[458] He immediately said yes. Elaine stayed home.

Heads turned as the pair walked into the ballroom. Victor, his head held high and beaming with delight, held Vincent's elbow as they made their way through the crowd.

Tongues did more than wag. A few seniors who were familiar with their romance wondered if Vincent had the courage to come with Elaine dressed as a man. Others expressed surprise at her escort. He didn't look like her type at all. Although normally men were forbidden as if they were apples,[459] Vincent seemed the sort of girl who would attract a more erudite, polished looking date. Victor was a man of workman-like temperament. As far as he was concerned, if Vincent would accept him as a suitor he would bunk with the janitor.[460]

What appeared to be cruel to most of the attendees was actually thoughtless. Unless she was angry, Vincent was not the sort of person to be deliberately savage. She just didn't think her social experiment would impact the participants. There were times when she was manipulative, and even consciously so, but that was usually when there was a means to an end. She had no interest in Victor except as a date who could perform the latest dance steps. Consequently, she hadn't understood the shocked looks on Fran and Isobel's faces. After all, she was always careful to be discreet. She watched what she said when interacting with rivals. Yet here she was at a dance with a discarded lover's brother.

As juniors and their dates marched into the hall, President MacCracken and his wife led the way. After brief remarks, he sought the poet and her date out.

"You look fine this evening, Miss. Millay."

"So do you," she replied. The hem of her gown was a shocking eight inches from the floor.[461] Even with heels on this allowed more than half her calves to show. Vincent turned her attention to "Prexy" MacCracken's wife Marjorie with a sincere complement. "I just love that frock."

"Thank you, Vincent." Marjorie's smile indicated her pleasure in the compliment and amusement at Vincent's second-hand gown. She recognized it as one she'd seen a friend wear the prior year at an event in New York City. Vincent had missed the lapsed stitches of the butterfly embroidered at the shoulder. It was the very reason her friend had donated it to the YWCA.

"I don't believe I've had the pleasure," Dean MacCracken nodded toward Victor.

"Oh, Lord, where on earth are my manners?" the poet replied. "This is Victor Ralli. His sister is my friend Elaine that you met after the 'Pageant of Athena.' She's graduating in June."

MacCracken smiled. He knew the rumors but found himself pleased that she had brought such a stalwart lad to the dance. He hoped it would bode well for Vincent's senior year.

Fran and her date Howard, a law student senior from Yale, approached. There was something about Howard that reminded Vincent of Hal Bynner. He blinked his large brown eyes vacantly like a man lost in a sea of women.

"Hello, Fran!"

"Vince!" Frances Garver raced across the room and took the poet's hand. "This is Howard. Uh, Howard, over here."

The tall, immaculately dressed man wandered toward them from where he'd been waylaid by a pal from his fraternity. "Hello."

"This is Edna Millay. The girl I mentioned."

"Hello."

"Howard is a wonderful dancer. Is this Victor?" Vincent's date stepped forward and took Fran's hand.

"I'm sorry. Yes, this is Victor Ralli. This is Fran Garver."

Victor recognized the name his sister had mentioned to their mother over the Christmas holiday. He couldn't remember the context, only that Elaine didn't seem happy.

"Good evening," he said with a slight bow that further impressed MacCracken.

The orchestra started in with "Pretty Baby" and Vincent grabbed Victor's hand. "Oh, I love this song. Let's dance."

The couple and many others made their way to the dance floor for the first dance of the evening. Victor had a steady beat as the couple completed a difficult Turkey Trot maneuver. "I hope they play a tango," he confided as they swung around amid the other couples.

"You tango?"

"Yes. I *love* it!"

The poet's estimation of Victor grew. Maybe the dance would be a lot of fun. Neither of them knew the college board had strictly forbidden the tango.

During a sappy version of "The Light of My Hometown," Vincent observed, "My sisters and I sing better harmony than the so-called Peerless Quartet."

"I imagine you do," Victor smiled.

Vincent added a fifth harmony as they circled the dance floor before they ran into Isobel and her cousin Chester Arthur Simpson.

"Hello!" the poet called. "Geez, you look swell, Isobel." It didn't miss Chester's gaze that Isobel's roommate was more than that ranking implied.

"Vincent, come meet my cousin."

Victor Ralli skillfully guided his date closer to her friend.

"How do you do?" the redhead smiled.

"Edna St. Vincent Millay, this I my cousin, Chester Arthur Simpson. Chet, this is Edna St. Vincent Millay. I call her Vincent."

"Were you named for the president?" Vincent asked.

"I was. Are you a history major?"

Vincent laughed. She'd come dangerously close to failing her entrance exam thanks to her limited knowledge of history. "Oh, my, no."

"No. She's a poet, a playwright, and actress and a composer."

"My major is English."

"I'm in insurance."

"My father used to sell insurance."

"Oh? Who is he with?"

"Can't say," Vincent replied as the orchestra brought up the pace with a rendition of Walt Jeffries' "Everybody's Crazy on the Foxtrot."

Vincent and Victor maneuvered away. He was truly an excellent dancer. "How do you know her?"

"Isobel? She is my roommate."

"I didn't know you had a roommate. Elaine said you had a private room."

"I did, but that was just the luck of the draw. It changes every year. Besides, I can't afford a single room anymore."

"That's too bad. Oh, oh, I like this one," the poet and her date perked up at the strains of "Sunshine Dad."

Victor had mastered several slide and glide turns created by Vernon and Irene Castle. "I hope they play *The Alabama Slide*," he said as they turned past Chester, Isobel and the MacCrackens. Fran's date was sitting by himself and drinking punch. Where Fran had gone remained a mystery for the rest of the evening.

As the night drew to a close, Vincent noticed Victor's hands were getting more familiar. The attraction simply wasn't there no matter how well he danced. If anything, she thought of Elaine. The difference between the siblings was as plain as their genders. As masculine as Elaine was, Victor was not feminine enough. Vincent loved the dichotomy between the sexes and most enjoyed a delicate balance between the two. Victor would never rest on that fulcrum.

Until she came to Vassar, she had not realized it was possible for others to feel this way. Writers like Plato and Oscar Wilde were victims of a narrow-minded world.[462] So far as she was concerned sin was a manufactured construct designed to keep people hamstrung by judgment. She wondered it might have been better if Jesus had said, "Let him among you who has sinned all sins, cast the first stone."[463] It wasn't that she didn't believe some things caused pain. That was obvious. Yet minus judgement how would the pain be defined? To her the Golden Rule was a sufficient boundary. She endeavored to be true to that limitation, to only do to others what she herself would tolerate. *Perhaps,* she mused, *a poet does not need to sin at all, except in the heart, in order to know that it is no question of stone-throwing at all. It often happens that I am very, very sorry for everybody.* She remained surprised when people's thresholds were lower than hers.

* * *

Kennerley wrote that May telling the poet he was publishing three of her works in the last issue of *The Forum*.[464] "The Suicide", "Witch-Wife" (which may as well have been called "Which Wife?") and a sonnet called "Bluebeard". The latter retold the tale of a murderous husband with a twist. In her version, Bluebeard was simply disappointed that his wife had disobeyed his command not to enter a room in his castle. He leaves her with the keys and departs. He had kept the room to himself "lest any know me quite."[465] The hidden secret of the room is the part of himself he wishes to reserve as his own. It is clearly Vincent saying, *Leave me to myself. No one can own me. I have my secrets. I am holding in reserve a part of myself you can never know.*

And you did profane me when you crept
Unto the threshold of this room tonight
That I must never more behold your face.
This now is yours. I seek another place.

37. The Rain's Cool Fingertips

1916

Cora sat on the ferry for hours. She had to earn some money. She had heard that women in the most remote islands and towns of New England still wore hair weaves. When she couldn't find work as a wigmaker, she washed or dressed hair.[466] The family was again relegated to sharing space with relatives. It seemed the harder she hustled the farther behind she got.

The nurse lamented allowing Kathleen to work part time, blaming that on her youngest daughter's failure on the Vassar entrance examination. Kathleen would just have to spend another year in serious study. Cora was not giving up. Kathleen would join her sister at Vassar. Vincent would make nice with a hair washing client who was also attending the college. Her daughters would climb socially through the good graces of the wealthy.

Yet Cora's plans were not at all appreciated by her eldest daughter. While Vincent was disappointed with the result of Kathleen's exam, she had zero interest in meeting her mother's client.

By now, Vincent had established herself on her own terms, and her mother's meddling in the hope of reflected glory seemed gauche to Vassar's leading lady. If Cora was hoping to hear from Vincent, it was a desire she'd soon regret.

"It doesn't make any difference whether you wash their heads or their floors, they have nothing on us, unless we give it to them," she wrote furiously. "As long as we consider ourselves their superior and they can't get the idea out of their heads, they have nothing on us, and can't get anything, you see? The girl you want me to approach is a non-entity at Vassar. I am not."[467]

"You haven't gotten me into a mess, dear. But you must *never* again invite anybody to see me unless I have said it is somebody I want to see. People can say anything they like about me and my family conditions, but they cannot visit me unless *I* want them."

Vincent had learned one of the most difficult lessons of life. Shame feeds upon itself. If she allowed shame to enter her mindset it would consume her. Cora's interference and the conditions by which the poet had somehow managed three years of college could not become garments she wore for all to see. If she allowed her mother's well-intentioned intrusion into her social life, she would soon have no social life. She would be the daughter of a woman who washed girls' hair. Although Vincent loved her family, she was not going to allow her past to determine her future. Her identity, carefully and truthfully crafted, was a small-town girl of modest means who had made good through her wit and talent. No one needed to know anything else.

* * *

That summer, the poet traveled from place to place, cultivating relationships on her own terms. She spent time at the YWCA and Miss Dow's apartment while further exploring the magical city that had been her playground only three years before. Mamaroneck became a second hometown. The Poetry Society welcomed her readings. Stages in Greenwich Village were interested in her as both an actress and a playwright. Everywhere she went, even when she briefly went home to Camden, she wore the mantel of Vassar College detachment.

Norma was still her closest confidante. She completely understood her sister's letter to their mother. "It would be like bringing a friend home and all she sees is your parents fighting. Of course, it was embarrassing!"

"More than that," Vincent replied. "It was downright confounding. How would such a girl be able to accept me as an equal if Mother's hands had been scrubbing dandruff from her scalp?"

Norma laughed at the image. Like Vincent she was mortified that Kathleen had not passed her exams—even with Vincent's help, copies of prior tests and almost one-hundred-percent free time to study while Norma held three jobs to help the family stay afloat. Her pride in her elder sister was enormous. Vincent had mostly "A" and "B" grades. Her "C" grades in psychology, economics and history were the only things barring her from a higher-grade-point average.

"What are you going to study next year?" the blonde asked as she braided Vincent's long hair.

"I'm taking a class in Shakespeare with Dean MacCracken."

"That should help."

"And Techniques in Drama…"

"That should be fun."

"Victorian Poetry…"

"Of course."

"Italian, Spanish and Art."

"Another language?" Norma cried. "Why?"

"It's the only one I haven't taken," Vincent laughed.

"How many is that?"

"Six, plus English, I think."

"And you're fluent in all of them?"

"Well, not all. I'm comfortable now in French, German and Latin. I have a way to go if I'm to say I speak Greek. They have different letters, so it's harder. My Spanish is improving but sometimes I mix it up with French or Latin. I figure Italian should be a breeze since it's halfway between Spanish and Latin—either that or it will just mix me up more," Vincent laughed. It was an odd concept, a kind of linguistic goulash.

Norma chuckled as she tied the end of her elder sister's braid. "There."

"Thanks, Hunk," Vincent said, eyeing herself in the mirror her middle sister held.

"It's nothing."

The two sisters looked at each other. There was an unspoken understanding between them. Norma knew Vincent would not be spending the summer tutoring Kathleen the way Cora wanted her to.

38. Into My Face a Miracle

1916-1917

Vincent entered her final year at Vassar in Fall 1916. The class with MacCracken would try both their patience. She excelled in Gertrude Buck's inaugural drama class. A second psychology class with Dr. Washburn proved that required courses do not share universal fascination.

Before long she was president of the Spanish Club and rehearsing the lead role in a new play by John Masefield, *The Locked Chest*. There could be no doubt she was "somebody" at Vassar.

The character of Vigdis opens the play by singing cheerfully about the man she loves. The audience was not only struck by her lovely singing voice but also by her comic timing. As possible ghosts, bribery, betrayal and murders abound it's all a "fair fight."[468] Eventually it's clear that Vigdis, the long-suffering wife of the querulous Thord, is more of a man than any of the men in the cast. Vincent relished the part.

The role of Vigdis would be a triumph and spread her fame even further than "Renascence" had. As luck would have it, friends of the playwright attended the play's December 9 debut. Not long afterward, Vincent received a fan letter from Masefield himself.[469] The Englishman invited her to send him samples of her poems. It seemed only the beginning of an incredible final year.

Thanks to the machinations of Vassar Dean Ella McCaleb, Kathleen had managed to secure a year at the Hartridge School in New Jersey to prepare for Vassar. It was a stab at following in Vincent's rather enormous footprint, and it seemed to be going well. Her sister's equivalent to Miss Dow, McCaleb had arranged for Kathleen's enrollment and Miss Hartridge herself was delighted with the recommendation. She found the young brunette a dear; disciplined, polite and studious.

Based on her own experience, Vincent suspected that Kathleen's improved disposition had more to do with being away from home than a sudden change in personality. Kathleen was normally very serious and often petulant. She hoped Kathleen would not make the same mistakes she had.[470] Their rivalry was the result of having an elder sister who ordered her about for years as a surrogate mother whenever Cora was out of town. Though Vincent had tried to make the most of their poverty, she also had too much on her shoulders as a child to be capable of motherly wisdom and compassion. Resentments had grown through the years, with Norma the usual go-between.

While the blonde loved both her sisters, she usually adored Vincent. She was old enough when their parents divorced to understand the position Vincent had been put in. Her chief complaint, which she avoided expressing, was how often Vincent would crow about attending the theater, enjoying a fine meal, and dressing in clothes so far beyond the Millay's budget as to be another world entirely. Her discomfort with Elaine was not mentioned. Her annoyance with the poet's superior attitude was mostly internalized. As far as she was concerned, Vincent was the family's best hope of escaping the deprivations of poverty. If she got mad at all it was when Vincent criticized the family. Meanwhile, she would be encouraging, supportive and a sounding board for all of Vincent's notions.

* * *

Winter 1916 had dug in its roots. Vincent, pleased with her final year's progress, was happily preparing to join her adoring friend and fellow poet Salomon de la Selva at the home of Professor Richard Austin Rice over the December 1 weekend. Vassar's head warden, a Miss Palmer, had explained how that date would fall after students were supposed to return from Thanksgiving holiday. Vincent didn't care. With Thursday classes being shifted to Friday, and Fridays to Saturday, the opportunity for a romantic getaway seemed a wonderful way to break the monotony of classes. They would be ostensibly chaperoned by Professor Rice and his wife, Salomon's great friends and fellow members of the Williams College faculty.[471]

The weekend in the Berkshires was idyllic. She loved the blue hills of the area. In addition to a piano concert of music by Chopin, Bach and Schumann by Mrs. Taylor, the wife of the head of Romance Languages, there were hikes and shared poetry. Yet Salomon was far more entranced than she was. He offered expensive perfumes and incredibly slavish love letters in exchange for very little. But he was simply not her type. Too young, too round, too boyish and worst of all, too available.[472]

* * *

With Christmas looming, the poet was delighted when Harriet Monroe published "Kin to Sorrow", "Afternoon on a Hill", and "Tavern on a Hill" in *Poetry Magazine*. This brought in a much needed $16, almost all of which went to pay back rent. With the new year would come tuition and more expenses; she would have to write many more poems before she was caught up. Meanwhile, there was a small amount brought in by posing for the art classes.[473] The poet thought it ironic that she was posing nude, when her mother had been scandalized by Kennerley publishing *Hagar Revelly*. Regardless, she would have to be very sparing, or she would find herself in arrears.[474]

* * *

President MacCracken felt he could best serve his students by not only leading the college, but by participating as an educator. He knew full well that Vincent was a problem student. After all, he had discovered that she had been barred from in person attendance in high school because she was viewed as too disruptive in class. Accordingly, Vincent's assignment in his English Drama course was to write plays.[475]

When she did come to class, which wasn't often, she sat dreamy-eyed and wrote, or she'd stand in class and start reciting Shakespeare out of the blue. His observations about the Bard of Avon were seeping gently into her subconscious. The first play she produced for Dean MacCracken was *The Princess Marries the Page*. Her reflection on the prized fairy tales of her childhood included plagiarizing her own childhood story, "Dear Incorrigibles."[476] The Princess is sitting in a tower reading when she hears the merry sound of the Page's silver pipe. She finds it annoying and asks him to stop. After all, she's the princess, isn't she? But he refuses, so naturally she becomes intrigued. This leads to the discovery that he is a spy seeking a way to ruin her father, the King.

The couple discover their feelings are mutual, but the Page knows he must hide when the King approaches. The Princess plays dumb when her father appears asking if she's seen a Page hanging around. Before she can lie to her father, the Page reveals himself and his true purpose for arriving in the kingdom. Vincent knew her audience. There had to be a way for love to win, so she created a most unlikely scenario: the Page is deliberately ineffective as a spy. Somehow, his honesty inspires the King to allow the Page to marry his daughter.

Obviously, the princess had to be played by herself. She had never gotten over her first performance as a princess and relished the idea of once again being given the exalted title. While not terribly original, the play was a huge hit with her classmates when it was staged by Gertrude Buck's "Techniques of Drama" class on May 12, 1917. The one-act verse play benefited from the poet's skill with meter and rhyme and her ability to revert to a childlike quality when the mood suited her.

The play's opening sentence, "I came here to read," was a bit of an inside joke among her peers. Everyone knew better than to interrupt Vincent while she was immersed in reading or writing. Falling upon Shakespearean devices of a prince being disguised as a peasant, it was clear that at least some of MacCracken's course was falling into her ears while the class read *Henry IV, Part Two*. Other elements, such as the mention of the quinces (a play on MacCracken's lecture on the role of Peter Quince in *A Midsummer Night's Dream*), and the couple having met earlier led MacCracken to also see elements of *As You Like It* and *Two Gentlemen of Verona* because all the male roles would have to be played by women. He could only laugh.

Again, Vincent was lauded, and her many scholastic sins forgiven. The triumph of *The Princess Marries the Page*, combined with her singing as Vigdis in *The Locked Chest*, translated into the enormous honor of being asked to write the Baccalaureate Hymn for her graduating class's week-long graduation festivities. She was doing well in her classes, receiving a stellar 3.8 average in the first semester of her senior year. Her latest romance was going well, and her poetry earned enough money to send some of it home to the great relief of her family. Despite all this, there was an ominous sense in the air that she chose to ignore amidst all the adulation.

* * *

Much to Vincent's delight, Norma's millinery skills brought her a lovely bonnet for Easter. Everyone adored it and suggested Norma might be the next great designer. The question was, what on earth was it made of? Vincent recognized the white cemetery wreath and the seaweed decoration but could not identify the rustic black felt. She was so taken with it that she promised to bring her "loved baby, blonde plum blossom" sister to New York and send her to the School of Design because Norma was, in the poet's estimation, the most talented of all the sisters.[477]

Even as she fantasized about sharing a flat with Norma, she was eager to share a recent Chinese import, a play called *Yellow Jacket*, with Kathleen, who was at the nearby Hartridge School. The poet had seen the play on an earlier trip into town. It was strange, absurd, beautiful, sad and altogether ravishing. Perhaps taking her younger sister to a performance would help mend the rift that seemed to be growing between them.

* * *

The ill wind had already caught up with her in April 1917, though it would take her a while to feel it. Vincent's increasingly haughty and imperious attitude reflected an illusory superiority that had overcome her tacit humility. Somehow, she thought she could get away with anything. Consequently, when the collegial twister fell upon her, she had no idea it was serious.

It all started innocently enough. She wanted to hear Caruso sing at the Metropolitan Opera in New York. Despite being told by the school's head warden that accepting Miss Dow's invitation to the April 18 performance was not a good idea, Vincent's sense of entitlement, bred by four years of getting away with murder, gave her leave to ignore the caution. It didn't help that she had lied about who invited her.[478]

Salomon de la Selva viewed Vincent as a woman with a deep inner sadness that he thought he alone could cure.[479] Although they had known each other even before their Thanksgiving weekend adventure, the pair had not been physical until that spring break in New York. The one-night stand was a disappointment for her, but he had become her slave. Hoping for a second chance, he invited her to the much-anticipated staging of Guiseppe Verdi's forty-six-year-old opera. Although she was scheduled to return to campus by

Wednesday, April 4, Vincent decided to remain in New York another fifteen days.

If Miss Dow had known about the poet's subterfuge, she would have seen to it that the poet returned to campus on time, but Vincent had reached a point where she was deaf to her patron's pleas. In fact, she didn't even tell her. She went from being her "Aunt Calline's" guest to being a guest of the Rice's, who were housing de la Selva. As far as Miss Dow knew, Vincent had left her apartment and caught the train north to Poughkeepsie. Consequently, when the warden called asking for the poet, the matron was as confused as the people at the college.

Vincent figured she'd deal with the repercussions of her tardiness in her usual way. MacCracken would scold her and then she would promise to do better. She was in for a surprise.

When the poet returned, she was met by Warden Palmer,[480] who directed her to report to President MacCracken immediately. Vincent did not know that a doctor was on call just outside his door lest the bad news she was about to hear was too much.[481]

"Well, you've done it now," he began as she walked into his office.

"Done what?" Vincent replied, smiling.

"The faculty has voted…"

The twenty-five-year-old poet couldn't believe her ears, so much so that she stopped hearing. Words like "campused" and "rest of term" broke through as MacCracken explained her punishment for not returning to campus when she'd been told to.

"After all I've done for the school?" she cried. Panic began to sink in.

"You're more than two weeks late coming back. Easter Break ended on April 4. It is now April 19." The exasperated president lit his pipe. "Listen, some of the faculty wanted me to kick you out entirely. You now have less than two months to stay out of trouble. Do you think you can do that? You will not leave campus until you have graduated. Understand?"

Vincent began to cry. MacCracken couldn't tell if she was acting or serious. He waited, watching for a telltale glance that said she was measuring his response. It came.

"Vincent, I told you when we first met that I would stick up for you, that I didn't want any dead Shelleys on my doorstep,"[482] he said firmly as he pulled a spare handkerchief from his desk drawer.[483] "I meant that. But I'm running a college. I also answer to your classmates, faculty and the governing board of this college."

She looked up, realizing the awkward position she had put him in. "I'm sorry."

"Now, you have a class with Dr. Washburn to attend and I expect you to do so. Is that clear?"

"As a bell," the contrite poet responded, wishing he knew how much she hated her psychology professor.

39. I Breathed My Soul Back into Me

1917

For several weeks Vincent was good to her word. She still snuck away to smoke in the cemetery, but she did not leave the outermost edges of the campus. The stares of her classmates and the snickers of her rivals saw to it that she felt well-chastised. Even her clothes seemed to take on a modesty they hadn't before. Some were cynical about her wardrobe choices, figuring that Vassar's top actress was merely posing to gain sympathy. Others thought she must have taken the admonition in a recent volume of the *Vassar Quarterly* to heart: "The lack of modesty in women's clothes emphasizes and appeals to the impulses and emotions in men that need no strengthening."[484]

No one knew how the poet scoffed at Anna Weinerson's piece on delinquency in the same volume, or how she truly felt about the punishment she had received. The fact was Vincent was angry. She had performed in all the best received plays, written two of them. She was president of the Spanish Club. She had published poems in their little magazine, thus limiting their appeal to paying magazines. She had won the senior song contest with "The Patient Periodical," a Gilbert and Sullivan style ode to Vassar: "We are an institution, for the further distribution, Among the aborigines, of spats and elocution."[485] She had written and was still rehearsing the 1917 Baccalaureate Hymn. She was three years older than everyone else. She wasn't a child! Damned Caruso!

Vincent would pace in her room when her three roommates were not there, mumbling with great fury at the injustice of it all. Yet in her heart she knew she had brought it on herself, so the person she was most angry with was the image in the mirror. She had spoiled a perfectly lovely final semester through her own hubris. Hadn't Miss Dow and Dr. MacCracken warned her about flaunting rules? Hadn't the warden told her not to stay in New York? Letters from Miss Dow expressing her disappointment and regret hurt more than being stuck on campus. Long talks with Drs. Haight and McCaleb did little to assuage her guilt.

On top of everything else, she was hard-up. The sixteen dollars she'd earned in December was long gone. Even adding a fourth person to a two-person room hadn't improved her condition much. Everybody wanted their loans repaid, even her own sisters, who probably needed cash more than she did.[486] She wished she knew who had sent her a huge, gorgeous bouquet from Saltford's.[487] That person might be able to loan her what she needed. The anonymous Valentine gift had cost at least $10, prompting Fran to exclaim, "I hate to think of the pair of boots you could buy with that." The poet thought the sender certainly ought to be thanked. But if it was someone like Elaine she might regret reaching out. Vincent knew her reputation had cost her dearly. Miss Dow hadn't been able to send her February allowance, let alone money for a cap and gown. The only saving grace was her final semester grades. If she could just hold on, she could make it out of Vassar with her "A.B."

But what about Kathleen? Dr. McCaleb assured her that if Kathleen passed her entrance examinations there would be a way to help her through Vassar as well. Yet Vincent knew Kathleen. Her sister would have even less patience with Vassar's many rules. It was true that Kathleen would put on a good show at first, but her sharp tongue was bound to get her in trouble sooner or later. Quietly, Vincent arranged for her youngest sister to start her freshman year at McGlynn's, just as she had done. She pleaded with MacCracken and others to be kind to Kathleen. Nonetheless, she realized her folly might haunt her sister. Only time would tell.

In the meantime, Vincent would bide her time. She did her utmost to appear chastened. She was doing so well after two weeks of confinement that she almost forgot her pledge to Dr. MacCracken.

* * *

Each year the senior class spent a weekend at Lake Mohonk, a scenic recreational area twenty miles from Poughkeepsie.[488] The tradition was seen as a kind of retreat, where graduates would bond, exchange contact information and offer referrals for possible jobs after graduation. Given that Vincent was already convinced she would have a position in a Greenwich Village theater company, she did not feel any desire to attend, and, with her roommate Charlotte Babcock, she decided it would be better for her to stay in and study.

After their other two roommates boarded an early morning bus, the resolute pair set about tending their remaining school duties.[489]

"Say, Charlie, what do you make of question four?"

"Just Washburn's didactic nonsense."

"Thanks. That's what I thought."

The two giggled and resumed working on their papers. Within minutes their self-discipline failed. Two older friends of Charlotte's appeared and, after a round of introductions, announced they had an automobile.

"A flivver!"

"Sweetest little Saxon Roadster you ever saw," the car's owner Gertrude Bruyn replied.

"Come on, Charlie," the other friend, Winnie Fuller, exclaimed. "Have breakfast with us."

"Would you like to come too?" Gertrude asked.

"I can't," Vincent replied through gritted teeth. Both interlopers were nearer her age, attractive and obviously had enough income to afford an automobile.

"Campused," Charlotte explained with a knowing nod.

"You poor dear," one of them said before Vincent watched the three of them slip out the door.

While they were away the poet fumed. She'd already been stuck in her personal "hellhole" for more than five weeks. In two and a half more she would graduate. It was more than frustrating. It was maddening. No one she knew at Vassar had an automobile—at least none of her classmates. The idea of getting outside on a gorgeous spring morning was delicious, but being by a lake and riding in a roadster with friends was positively ambrosial.

Ergo, when Charlie returned with an invitation to join them on the drive to Lake Mohonk Vincent jumped at the chance. She convinced herself that so long as she didn't spend the night no one would be the wiser.

The small two-seater was already crammed with three girls in it. A fourth required the women to design a sardine arrangement with two setting on top of the bench seat with their feet positioned between the driver and the passenger. After grabbing some sandwiches at the Hoot'n'Owl,[490] they began the journey through the verdant orchards and hills toward their destination.

The wind in her hair gave Vincent a chance to let out a whoop of freedom. Beside her, Charlie's cherubic face with high cheekbones and expressive eyes grinned so much that tears began to form in the corners of her eyes. Soon the poet was composing impromptu odes to the peach and cherry blossoms along the way.

After enjoying a picnic by the lake, all were so caught up in the fun that they decided they would spend the night at the home of Gertie Bruyn's family.

"I'll call Isobel and let her know where we are," Charlie said, knowing Vassar rules but forgetting entirely about Vincent's punishment.

"Yes, that will be good," the poet replied, certain that Isobel would cover for her.

Before long, the redhead was entertaining everybody with songs and piano music. Raucous laughter, smoking and drinks completed their revelry. After a scrumptious meal, Vincent and Charlie decided to see *Souls Triumphant* at the Fox theater nearby. It wasn't very good. They returned to the Bruyn's for a continuation of the evening's entertainment.

"Was the flicker any good?" Winnie asked as they walked in.

Both women began laughing. "Oh, my," Charlie cried, "You should have seen it."

"But was it good? Was it a comedy?"

"What was it about?" Gertie joined in. The poet and her roommate were practically falling over. Vincent tried to speak but was giggling so hard she couldn't start.

"No, no," Charlie laughed. "It was a drama, but it may as well have been a comedy."

"Let's...ha ha...let's show them," the poet suggested. "I'll be the husband. You be the Lillian Gish role and the old friend Hattie."

"What about the father? You've got to be the father."

The pair put their heads together and began their rendition of the film, starting with Vincent taking a glass from the table and wandering around like she was drunk.

Charlie stepped forward and batted her eyelashes. "Oh, Bob! Please stop drinking!"

"Why?"

"Because I love you."

"Why?" she said again, only this time like a three-year-old.

Their audience began to laugh.

"Because you're a drunk and I think it will be fun to fix you."

"Isn't that your father's job?" The laughter grew louder as the girls watched the redhead's drunk act. Vincent turned away from the audience and put a white handkerchief across her neck.

"My son, my son, my idiotic daughter loves you for some reason, but you simply must stop drinking."

"Oh, Daddy you may be the curate of St. Anthony's church but you're a drunk too, aren't you?"

"What makes you think so?" Vincent swerved across the parlor before returning to the role of Robert Powers.

By now the group was roaring with approval. When they'd finished the unlikely transformation of Bob to perfect dutiful husband, they could barely catch their breath. When Charlie started as Hattie, they could no longer contain themselves. During their performance, Charlie had given birth to numerous pillows and had joined Vincent in spinning around the room as Hattie, a dissipated harridan, before oscillating back to the long-suffering Lillian Vale.

By the time the group retired all had bellies sore from laughing and the antics of the roommates. Winnie, the daughter of a minister herself, had taken particular delight in their over-the-top performance.

The following morning, Winnie went to church and the remaining three friends piled back into the Saxon Roadster for a trip to the newly opened Ashokan reservoir on their way back to Vassar. After a brief opportunity to stretch their legs the trio made their way to West Shokan, where they stopped for a bite to eat at the stately Watson Hollow Inn, with its attractive gabled roof and abundant rose covered arbor. Relaxed, happy and playful, Vincent surreptitiously signed the guestbook.

40. Dark Disguise

1917

Vincent stood on the porch of the Flemish bond brick and sandstone president's house, waiting for the maid to answer the door. She had been summoned. Given that it was two days after her little adventure she thought nothing of it. Perhaps Dr. MacCracken wanted to discuss her examinations. Yet when she saw his face moments later, she knew something was very wrong.

He was sitting at the simple desk by the bay window in the office of his Tudor-style residence. "I suppose you know why you're here."

Vincent looked up at the dark wooden beams of the large room hoping to contain herself. She had been very good for nearly six weeks. She was gone for only thirty-six hours. She fixed her gaze upon the patient man and replied, "No."

"What were you doing last weekend?"

"Studying."

MacCracken peered at her face. He learned there were degrees of guilt that could register on a person's face. He could see that Vincent was guilty of something, but not what she was being accused of. "You were not at a hotel with a man?"

Vincent blanched and then laughed. "A man? Where did that idea come from?"

"Miss Palmer, the very same warden you ignored in April, saw your name beside a man's in the register of the Watson Hollow Inn. Do you deny you were there? Before you answer, Vincent, I'd like to caution you that receiving your diploma depends on your honesty."

The poet could hardly imagine what would precipitate so harsh a sentence, but she realized MacCracken was serious. "Charlie Babcock and I went to Lake

Mohonk and then spent the night with friends in New Paltz. The next day we stopped for lunch at the inn. That's all. Honest. Ask Charlotte."

"I have and she confirms your story. Nonetheless, I'm afraid the faculty has decided to strip you of your graduation privileges."

"You mean I won't get my degree!" she moaned, bursting into tears and flopping on the chair opposite him.

"Not so bad as that, but you will not be allowed to take part in the Baccalaureate Hymn and the other events, including the graduation processional."

"But I wrote the hymn," she sobbed over and over. How was she ever going to tell her family? What would Miss Dow say? She had finally managed to pay her costs to meet the college's requirement for graduation and none, *none,* of her patrons or family would be able to see her collect her diploma.

MacCracken stood up and pressed his hand on her shoulder. "I'm sorry it has come to this, but you promised to stay on campus. You did not. For four years you have ignored warnings, cut classes, flaunted regulations, and dismissed much of your classwork. If it weren't for your grades, you would have been dismissed long ago. You're a brilliant young woman, Vincent, but you lack discipline. Now you may stay here as long as you like to contain yourself, but I have a class to teach. Hannah will show you out when the time comes."

* * *

An hour later Vincent was sitting in Elizabeth Haight's office. Her eyes were red with distress, but she had stopped crying in favor of unleashing her fury.

"What do I care?" she demanded.

"From where I sit, I would say you care very much."

"I do, don't I?"

"Yes, you do." Dr. Haight's brief affair with Vincent had become a close friendship. Although never fully consummated, the closeness they shared was reflected in the poet choosing Dr. Haight as the first person she went to after getting the news.

"The faculty are to meet on Friday to discuss whether or not you will be granted your diploma," she said gently.

"But look at my grades! Look at all I've done for the college. How can they fail me?"

"It's one of those confounding things, I know, darling. If it wasn't for your ability to get exceptional results in your final examinations those grades would be a lot worse. Dr. Washburn has had it with your tardiness and lack of discipline."

"When a poem comes you must birth it. I can't help it if I heed my muse instead of spending hours being bored to tears by…"

Dr. Haight stopped her. "Vincent, if you wrote as many poems as you have missed classes over the past four years, you would have a volume larger than *War and Peace*!"

The poet laughed. It was true. She just hated lectures. While Cora's intent had been good, it had paved the road to the hell Vincent was now experiencing. All she could hear was her mother's endless directives. *"Now Vincent, you must practice every day."*

"Vincent, have you made sure to dot all your i's and cross all your t's?"

"Vincent, dear, you must write Miss Dow immediately." The poet had become a prisoner of her mother's expectations, and this had created a kind of love/hate relationship with both her mother and any sort of discipline. There were always deadlines and things she had to do. She'd had enough.

Dr. Haight was sympathetic. After all, she wrote poetry for *The Miscellany* herself when she was a student. The Latin scholar had edited the college's 1894 yearbook. She was active in school events, and although she was twenty years Vincent's senior, she had tried to keep up with changing trends. Nevertheless, she warned the poet that even if the vote went her way, Vincent would still likely get her diploma sent to her, "like a codfish."[491]

* * *

When the poet finally returned to her dorm room, all three of her roommates were anxious to know if the rumors floating around campus were true. All Vincent wanted to know is what Charlie Babcock had told "Prexy" MacCracken.

"Nothing except the truth. While the three of us had breakfast I got caught up in how much fun it would be to have you with us. I can't believe I'd be so careless. I shouldn't have asked you to go with us. I'm so terribly sorry."

Classmates cycled through their room for hours, all wanting the details. Was it a boy from West Point? Was it the husband of a professor? The stories were outrageous.[492] Vincent felt as if she'd been transported back to Camden. Eventually, she told them all to go hang except for the four willing to accept her side of the story.

One recommendation from a well-meaning friend suggested she study exceptionally hard for her final exams, which were to be held the following Thursday, May 31, 1917. This seemed to be a sensible opinion, so she made an extraordinary show of penitent study. Yet the faculty had grown cynical thanks to the acting abilities of the green-eyed poet.

It soon became apparent that Vincent's only hope rested with her classmates. The trouble was, not every woman supported the arrogant, rule-flaunting, small-town poet. There was plenty who had applied themselves and gone to class even when plagued by colds, menstrual cramps, exhaustion and homesickness. Her excuse of "birthing" a poem seemed frivolous by comparison.

Yet Isobel Simpson, Frances Garver, Katherine Tilt and many others thought it supremely unfair to deny the woman who had given so much to the school her moment in the sun at graduation. This was particularly true of Charlotte Babcock, who was guilty of almost the same offense—though minus ignoring being campused. All knew that Vincent was a bird who would die if her wings were clipped.

Marjorie MacCracken had gotten to know Vincent and admired her enormous talent. She shared her husband's fear of what would happen if the renowned poet were denied the opportunity to march with her peers to receive her diploma—let alone being denied a diploma altogether. She decided she would drop a bug or two in seniors' ears about starting a petition.

Meanwhile, Charlie told everyone that she was certain Vincent knew she shouldn't be away from campus overnight but probably thought, "Oh, I won't tell Charlie and spoil her fun."[493] This loyalty was offset by the firm stand of President MacCracken, who was feeling miserable about the position the poet had put him in.

Less than half her class signed the petition to allow her to graduate with the rest of the class. This number, 108 signatures, brought the beleaguered college president to a compromise he thought the trustees and faculty could live with.

On June 7 he took his motion to two faculty members: Ella McCaleb, Admissions Dean, and Margaret Washburn, psychology professor.[494] The two women represented the opposing sides of the of the debate regarding the poet's future. MacCracken showed them the petition and then asked their views.

"Vincent has always found college extremely difficult," Dean McCaleb noted.[495]

"And we've found her difficult," Dr. Washburn sniffed.

"Of course, there must be some repercussions for taking French leave," MacCracken acceded. "But what do we gain by suspending her indefinitely?"[496]

"We gain a lot less class disruption. I've been told by several students that it's about time we took this step."

"I agree. She might have known that it was a serious matter to just go off to New York instead of returning at the appointed time."

"It's more than that, Ella. She was campused. She's smart enough to know that meant she couldn't leave and yet she did, overnight and with a man."

President MacCracken explained that he believed she was innocent of the latter charge.

"For heaven's sake, Noble, she's certainly no virgin and I've seen how she manipulates people into doing her bidding. She probably has Charlotte backing up her cockamamie story."

"I think you're being too harsh, Margaret. Vincent has undoubted genius and ability and is absurdly childish in her attitudes toward the law, but let's hope that this vote to withhold the ceremonies—which has been bitter and trying for her, as well as her friends—may be a lesson of particular value."[497]

"Am I to believe you both think she shouldn't graduate?" MacCracken asked, hoping his face didn't reveal too much. Washburn nodded. McCaleb sighed her consent. This placed the president in a quandary. He had a compromise in mind that he now knew the faculty would not abide. By trustee vote he had the power to veto any faculty action, and in keeping with his personal management style he had resolved never to use it.[498] Yet here he was, faced with the feared Shelley on his doorstep. He had to go with his compromise decision regardless of faculty input.

"The fact remains any clever girl…" he began.

"Woman," Washburn corrected as Dr. Salmon had many times before.

"*Woman* could get by the wardens with ease."[499] We all agree Vincent is clever if unruly, do we not?"

The women nodded in unison.

MacCracken looked down at the petition. The signatures included the daughters of some of the college's strongest supporters. The idea of being confronted with weeping women made him miserable.[500] Professor Washburn was a noted scholar and a marvelous lecturer. Dean McCaleb was loved and respected by all the students and had taken a special interest in placing Vincent's sister Kathleen in the class of 1922.[501] Elizabeth Haight would likely encourage his compromise as punishment enough.[502] To this faculty weight the president added Cora's letter explaining that Vincent's expulsion, if final, would be "a blow from which she would never recover."[503]

Decision made, Dr. MacCracken politely excused the faculty and staff members before crafting a note to the rest of the staff. He began his June 8 letter by revealing that he had received a petition from 108 of Vincent's classmates and eighteen letters from individuals who believed the penalty was too severe, "first, in view of the leniency shown to Miss Millay before the spring recess: second, that false rumors regarding her reputation..."[504]

He paused and pulled two letters he had received from the poet on June 3 from under the pile of missives concerning her dilemma on his desk. As he read them, he found himself getting emotional. Here she was reminding him of their earlier meeting when he told her if she ever needed a friend he would be there. "If you don't want to see me, I should understand. But there is nobody else I want to go to. Mayn't I see you this evening—Sunday? If not, don't tell me it is because you are too busy; I shall know quite well why it is."[505]

MacCracken set the paper down. Was he being manipulated or was she truly contrite? He lifted the letter and kept reading, promising himself he would be watchful and balanced judge of her contrition. "I remember once that you chided me a bit for never telling people who are kind to me how kind to me I think they are, and it occurred to me that if I should die tomorrow, it would be rather shabby of me not to have blessed you. I shall remember till I am very old—if I live to be old—your great gentleness with me."[506]

Was she threatening suicide, praising him sincerely or manipulating him? He couldn't be sure. The educator could almost hear her in his head. "Oh, Prexy, I just had to cut in your class. I was in pain with a poem."[507] Yet an hour later she was performing splits and all sorts of fantastic capers under the Main

Gate. He thought she might be trying to kick out the light in the chandelier above the entrance. This triggered further visions of her jumping up in his English Drama class and almost shouting, "What fools these mortals be!" and "There is a tide in the affairs of men, which taken at the flood, leans on to fortune." Was she that high tide? He realized she was now at an ebb. He continued the letter he had begun composing.

"I have determined that Miss Millay has made a significant enough contribution to the college and, despite her low attendance, having received enough satisfactory remarks, that she will be allowed to graduate with her class on Tuesday, but not attend the Tree Ceremonies, the performance of "St. Vincent,"[508] the Baccalaureate Hymn she composed, or any of the other commencement events apart from receiving her diploma on June 12, 1917."

41. I Know the Path

1917

There were faculty members who understood the need for Dr. MacCracken's compromise solution, and there were others who did not. Vincent's art teachers, Tonks and Bye, were miffed when the poet took their mandatory class lightly, despite her work as a model the previous year.[509] They had already submitted their "C" grade when the president announced his King Solomon solution. If it wasn't too late, they would have given a failing grade to ensure that Vincent would not receive her degree.

Dr. Washburn was similarly aggrieved. In her own form of compromise, she lowered the "C" she had not yet posted for Vincent's social psychology class to a "D". In this way she felt she was honoring both the school and MacCracken's decision. Vincent was destined for something greater; Dr. Washburn could see that much. Whether it reflected on Vassar through infamy or talent she didn't know. It was MacCracken's cross now. She only hoped he had made the right decision.

* * *

As Vincent awaited word of her revered Prexy's decision, her worries were further compounded by her mother's melodramatic suggestion that she might not live to see Kathleen graduate.[510]

"Forgive me, dear, for turning the knife in the wound," Cora wrote, telling the poet that she was being robbed of the proudest day she had ever dreamed of seeing. It cut Vincent to the quick. She wept almost constantly, realizing she might have cost her mother's life. Norma had spoken of how sick Cora had been, how all the financial and emotional stress was slowly eating at their mother's health, how she had to wash Cora's face and hands, comb her hair and even help her up and down the stairs.[511] She wondered again how she could have been so selfish when her darling mother and sisters had sacrificed so much.

* * *

June 12, 1917, was a fine day.[512] The huge oak that served as a backdrop for the graduate procession gave a sun-dappled noon day light over the graduates as they marched toward the podium as their names were announced.

Vincent could hardly believe it. MacCracken had allowed her to graduate over the objections of most of the faculty and trustees. Classmates who agreed with them visibly snubbed her. Her allies gently patted her back and alternately held her hand. As the alphabet grew closer to "M," Vincent hoped Norma and their mother had honored her request to not tell Kathleen about her near expulsion until her younger sister took the Vassar entrance examination for the second time.[513]

Dean McCaleb hoped Kathleen would have a different attitude toward college. "If I did not believe this, I would not work to have her come here," the sixty-one-year-old dean admitted to the shaken poet.[514] The dean considered herself a liaison officer functioning between the college with its compacted interests and the outside world as represented by the alumnae.[515] As Dean of Admissions, it was her job to oversee all aspects of the social conduct and all things related to entrance examinations and graduation.[516]

Tears of relief began to spill quietly across Vincent's cheeks as she heard her name called. She did not want to give her detractors fuel for derision. The steps toward Dean McCaleb and President MacCracken were a blur. The murmurs of the audience slowly rose in volume. As she approached Ella McCaleb her hand froze at her side. Somehow, she wasn't sure if she should accept the sheepskin tube bound with a gray ribbon. Was this a dream? Would they take it away from her after all?

"Go ahead," McCaleb whispered as if reading the poet's thoughts.

Vincent lifted her hand and as the ticket to freedom touched her fingers a cheer rose up among those who supported her. Spontaneously, a few of her fellow graduates began to sing Vincent's Baccalaureate Hymn. Dean McCaleb guided her forward to where President MacCracken stood. His face conveyed a mixture of relief, pride and joy. "Congratulations, Vincent."

The poet took his hand and raised her eyes to look into his. MacCracken winked and used his free hand to sandwich hers. As the pleasure of his satisfied grip registered, Vincent finally recovered the words she found hardest to say.

"Thank you."

42. The World Stands Out on Either Side

1917

Vincent had made up her mind years before, but the decision had only become clearer in the intervening six years since nursing her father in Kingman.

She would not live as her mother had. She would not nurse other people's children. She would not take care of her own, that is, if she had any. She would not live hand-to-mouth, at the mercy of landlords and shopkeepers. She would not scrub until her hands bled or sew until her fingers ached.[517]

The courageous poet would work. She would work hard but dedicate her life to beauty. Other people could provide the everyday necessities. She would be the mistress of her own life.

Immediately upon graduation Vincent raced to Elizabeth Haight's apartment in New York. While there she made the rounds to see if she couldn't find work as an actress. She had to find work as soon as possible. She found new patrons in the husband wife couple of Edith Wynne Matthison and Charles Rann Kennedy, actor and playwright respectively, who foresaw a brilliant career on the stage.[518] They called fellow actors, theater managers and directors to suggest accepting an audition from the skilled poet and actress. She was given a home with them while studying with Edith and another famed actress, Laura Hope Crews. Whenever time allowed, she labored over a manuscript for Mitchell Kennerley.

Vincent wrote Norma admitting she could not come home until she had something in New York to come back to—if she came back to Camden at all. The poet added that she wanted her middle sister to tell Cora that the events of the past few weeks had nothing to do with money, and that everything had been sorted out.[519] Vincent's cherished Hunk could not believe it. She waited for her adored sister to arrive after all, but she soon learned that Vincent could no longer be contained by familial guilt.

Edna St. Vincent Millay, A.B., would never wear another hand me down, or hand down anything she had grown tired of to her sisters or mother. She would find employment as an actor, a playwright, a poet, a novelist, tutor, or even as a typist or stenographer,[520] if that's what it took to supply the necessities she would need in New York, things her mother and sisters had to slave for in Camden.

The poet had made a pact with herself. She would seek out the brightest minds in New York, the most stimulating and challenging puzzles in both her personal and professional life. She would not return to a small town rife with small minds. She would prove she was extraordinary.

Vincent had been blessed with a mother who nurtured her gifts. That was true. Norma had been a confidante and a friend as much as her sister in the family struggle. Perhaps Kathleen would make good at Vassar, at least better than she had, because "Wump" was more artful and disciplined than she had ever been. Vincent knew she had set a horrible example. She hoped her baby sister would avoid, whenever possible, making the mistakes she had made at Vassar. The more Kathleen followed her example, the more stupidly and unpleasantly people would talk.[521] But all of them, even her cherished father Henry, were an embarrassment at some level. While she loved them, she could not, would not sacrifice her plan for theirs.

She would rise above poverty, the shabby instability of grinding neglect that had wrinkled her skin and destroyed her beautiful hands as a teenager.[522] She would use her voice, her words, her cunning, her sex and her education to keep as far from Camden as she could.

Yes, the poet loved the beauty of those islands in the bay and the towering glory of Megunticook. She might even visit for a short time that summer, but New York would be her home. There *were* memories of better times in Maine. But she would not allow herself to end up six feet underground in the soggy earth worn down by endless labor at things which meant nothing to her.

Why did her family not understand that everything she had done to master the forces of wealth and art were done for their benefit, as much as hers? She knew it might seem cruel to them in the present, but they would thank her later. Why did they see her plan as selfish when her only intention was to save herself and them from a lifetime of insecurity? Perhaps all they could see were her new dresses.

Vincent's precious family couldn't see her plan had started with them. Cora had read James Whitcomb Riley, Robert Burns, the Brownings and Shakespeare to her when she was a toddler. Consequently, as far as Vincent was concerned, it was Cora's plan as much as hers; only her mother had forgotten that had been her purpose. Norma couldn't see how it was her purpose to make sure the poet read "Renascence" to Miss Dow and the others who lounged in the great dining room of the Whitehall Inn. The entire family had helped her with her plan. Even Kathleen had a role in its execution. She deflected the disappointments of Vincent's benefactors. Henry had helped her see there was a greater outside world. They all had a role to play in Vincent's story and, like a director, the poet had guided the production of her life's plan with skill and sacrifice.

Vincent acknowledged it may not seem like sacrifice to her family, especially when another income at home may have helped them avoid homelessness. All they saw was the way she managed to get away with every infraction while the family got away with nothing. Cora's hard work, the trudging from town to town seeking nursing and hair weaving clients, had never been enough and never would be. Vincent knew that. That is why she was now going to New York. It was a city that would embrace her, fete her and pay her handsomely—or so she believed.

While it would be years before the poet made enough income to allow her mother to retire and pay back relatives and friends for their assistance, Vincent would not be dissuaded. She was determined to be celebrated for who she was, not who others thought she should be. She would engage hearts and break them. She would employ her wiles and charm to finagle as much benefit as she needed to fulfill her plan.

Vincent Millay would be famous, and more importantly, she would be rich. That was the plan and so far, it had been moving gradually toward its fulfillment. The next logical step was conquering New York. She would move forward, not back. Her family would just have to understand.

Sonnet IX

I think I should have loved you presently,
And given in earnest words I flung in jest;
And lifted honest eyes for you to see,
And caught your hand against my cheek and breast;
And all my pretty follies flung aside
That won you to me, and beneath your gaze,
Naked of reticence and shorn of pride,
Spread like a chart my little wicked ways.
I, that had been to you, had you remained,
But one more waking from a recurrent dream,
Cherish no less the certain stakes I gained,
And walk your memory's halls, austere, supreme,
A ghost in marble of a girl you knew
Who would have loved you in a day or two.

End Notes

Chapter 1

[1] www.psychologytoday.com/us/blog/matter-personality/201601/neglectful-parents-and-eldest-siblings

"...In many of these families, childcare duties fall on the oldest of the siblings, who is pressed into service to take care of the younger ones. This situation is a setup for highly disturbed sibling relationships later on in their lives, after all of the siblings have grown into adulthood...

The older sibling, having no real power in the family and being ill-equipped to be a parent, becomes verbally or even physically abusive to the younger siblings. The younger siblings then come to resent the older one for two reasons: the abuse, and the fact that the older sibling is not the one they wanted taking care of them in the first place. ..."

www.thelancet.com/journals/lanpsy/article/PIIS2215-0366(19)30286-X/fulltext

"...Of psychosocial outcomes, the ten outcomes including the largest number of primary studies, ranging from seven to 45 primary studies, were included (e.g., adult sexual revictimization and substance misuse), whereas outcomes including fewer primary studies, ranging from two to six primary studies, were excluded (e.g., recent unprotected anal intercourse, online sexual offending compared with offline sexual offending, self-esteem, and hostility). There was some duplication of participants between anxiety and anxiety symptomatology, and depression and depressive symptomatology."

[2] millayhouserockland.org/about "Imagine Rockland, Maine in 1891, a rough and tumble coastal city, booming with rapidly expanding industries, including

lime, ship building, and fishing. Duplexes were springing up across the city to meet the demand for workforce housing. This is where our story about a young redhead begins. Edna St. Vincent Millay was born in a double-house at 198/200 Broadway, during a raging snowstorm, on February 22, 1892. The house was new and the first occupants of its north side were Henry Tolman Millay and his wife, Cora Buzzell Millay."

[3] Milford, Nancy. *Savage Beauty: The Life of Edna St. Vincent Millay* (New York: Random House, 2001) Page 15 "They both agreed their new place was entirely "D.E."—damned elegant!"

[4] Milford, Nancy. *Savage Beauty: The Life of Edna St. Vincent Millay* (New York: Random House, 2001) Page 15 "…In the parlor were Cora's piano…"

[5] https://www.flickr.com/photos/94058635@N04/16711022146/in/photostream/ Photo of Wellington. Singhi, photographer and the Millay's landlord.

[6] Milford, Nancy. *Savage Beauty: The Life of Edna St. Vincent Millay* (New York: Random House, 2001). P. 17 "But by then Cora had gone into labor. Restlessly pacing the floor, she complained of indigestion and asked Clem to call for Henry's aunt Lucy, who was a practiced midwife. Henry ran next door to tell their neighbors and raced through the snow to fetch the doctor."

[7] Millay, Edna St. Vincent. *Collected Poems* (New York: Harper Brothers, 1956) P. 575 "Sonnet xv"
"…Bizarrely with the jazzing music blended,
The broken shadow dances on the wall,…"

Chapter 2

[8] https://www.moongiant.com/phase/2/22/1892: www.astro.com

[9] Milford, Nancy. *Savage Beauty: The Life of Edna St. Vincent Millay* (New York: Random House, 2001). P. 18
"In the spring, when Vincent was just a few weeks old, the Millay's moved inland to Union, where Henry's parents still lived… His parents offered him a house in the center of town, close to the common. …"

[10] Milford, Nancy. *Savage Beauty: The Life of Edna St. Vincent Millay* (New York: Random House, 2001). P. 19-20 Note: Milford is quoting a remembrance written by Cora, which is why she put it in quotations. Given the

format of my book, I have taken the liberty of simply suggesting that was her opinion, minus the quotation marks.

"... William Millay was a converted Methodist and, Cora remembered, as hard-shelled as any Baptist that ever-braved water..."

[11] Milford, Nancy. *Savage Beauty: The Life of Edna St. Vincent Millay* (New York: Random House, 2001) Page 20 Note: Milford is quoting a remembrance written by Cora, which is why she put it in quotations. Given the format of my book, I have taken the liberty of simply suggesting that was her opinion, minus the quotation marks.

"...It wasn't much fun to go fishing with him because he wouldn't let her talk, but she remembered all her life the time he took her with him to his favorite fishing hole "and put me far enough away from him not to disturb his sport, and I caught the biggest trout of the morning." She said that in all fairness he was pleased, "though he did say, as he always did on the rare occasions when I won from him at cards, that it was beginner's luck." They were so different "that any crank on Eugenics would have said we were perfectly suited for the propagation of a family."

[12] Milford, Nancy. *Savage Beauty: The Life of Edna St. Vincent Millay* (New York: Random House, 2001) Page 25

"... for she knew the whole poem by heart, the beautiful 'Snowbound' of Whittier..."

[13] https://www.poetryfoundation.org/poems/45490/snow-bound-a-winter-idy

"And while, with care, our mother laid
The work aside, her steps she stayed
One moment, seeking to express
Her grateful sense of happiness
For food and shelter, warmth and health,
And love's contentment more than wealth."

[14] Note: Norma shared this wig with me when we first met in 1980

[15] Milford, Nancy. *Savage Beauty: The Life of Edna St. Vincent Millay* (New York: Random House, 2001). P. 20 NOTE: lines 3-4* of second stanza were added by Jenifer Kay Hood.

"Sometimes, when the day is dreary
    Filled with dismal wind and rain,
    Sometimes when the frame is weary,
    Filled with nervous ache and pain;
Then, across Earth's darkest shadows,
    Comes Life's dearest sweetest bliss
As with sweet red lips uplifted,
Baby whispers: "Onts a tiss."

Sometimes when no sun is shining,
    And my head is bowed with grief
    …
    [* When it seems the sun's aligning
    Never to bring me joyful relief]
Someone comes on weak feet toddling,
    Someone gives my sleeve a tug,
And with eyes and arms uplifted,
Baby whispers: "Onts a hug!'"

[16] Milford, Nancy. *Savage Beauty: The Life of Edna St. Vincent Millay* (New York: Random House, 2001) Page 21 "…Cora raced to lift Vincent from the pillows, under which lay Norma, her mouth stuffed with geranium leaves."

Chapter 3

[17] Epstein, Daniel Mark, ed. *Rapture and Melancholy: The Diaries of Edna St. Vincent Millay.* (Connecticut: Yale University Press, 2022). P. 57-58 Note: Although I am extrapolating from Millay's journals, I believe Auntie *Bine* was a real person.

"… And as I gazed, fascinated, the broad low house clung easily to the slope of the hill. It seemed to fit there, somehow, as if under the measured hammering of the years it had relaxed, unresistingly to become at last a part of the soil on which it stood.

Its whiteness, surrounded by the wonderful green of the grass, was fairly dazzling. ..."

[18] Epstein, Daniel Mark, ed. *Rapture and Melancholy: The Diaries of Edna St. Vincent Millay*. (Connecticut: Yale University Press, 2022). p. 57-58 Note: this description by Millay is one of the reasons why I believe Auntie *Bine* was a real person. Consequently, I left in some of Millay's own adjectives, e.g. "snowy washing spread on the short grass."

"...Where suddenly the old house opened its eyes and blinked sleepily at the setting sun and I caught my breath in an ecstasy of recognition. I know it now! The sunset on the window panes, the snowy washing spread on the short grass. ..."

Chapter 4

[19] Milford, Nancy. *Savage Beauty: The Life of Edna St. Vincent Millay* (New York: Random House, 2001) Page 21
"... Cora noted in her diary, 'Henry is not there when I am taken sick... The doctor is there long before Henry is. Mr. Gales comes to Union at about this time. ...'"

[20] Milford, Nancy. *Savage Beauty: The Life of Edna St. Vincent Millay* (New York: Random House, 2001) Page 22 Note: Milford is quoting a remembrance written by Cora. Given the format of my book, I have taken the liberty of simply suggesting that was her opinion, minus the quotation marks.
"Sat. *May* 22. ... Mr. Gales in just as we were eating dinner. Our dinner was real late. He was on his wheel and had a cap on, and looked real cute and boyish and happy."

[21] Milford, Nancy. *Savage Beauty: The Life of Edna St. Vincent Millay* (New York: Random House, 2001). P. 24-25 Note: Milford is quoting a remembrance written by Vincent. Given the format of my book, I have taken the liberty of editing Vincent's feelings down, minus the quotation marks.
"... and dropping directly before me a bottomless abyss in which every colour of ecstasy moved like a cloud, now drifting close, now inexorably drawn away,

and the winds from depths unthinkable pulling out my pinafore, and the tops of my doll-size slippers …"

[22] www.loc.gov/resource/gdcmassbookdig.unionpastpresent00unio/?sp=71 Note: This is based on stories I heard from Norma about there always being an instrument but rarely the same one.

"…The Smith Music Store is now occupied by the well-known firm of Cressey, Jones and Allen of Portland, with E. L. Staples, Esq., as manager…"

[23] Milford, Nancy. *Savage Beauty: The Life of Edna St. Vincent Millay* (New York: Random House, 2001) Page 25 Note: Milford is quoting a remembrance written by Vincent. Given the format of my book, I have taken the liberty of editing Vincent's feelings down, minus the quotation marks.

"We did not have the notes of it, it was something she knew by heart. I called her to help me with the chord, and she came in. She had been doing washing, and her hands, as she placed them upon the keys were very pink and steam rose from them. Her plain gold wedding-ring shone very clean and bright, and there were little bubbles on it which the soap suds had left, pink, and yellow, and pale green. …"

[24] Milford, Nancy. *Savage Beauty: The Life of Edna St. Vincent Millay* (New York: Random House, 2001) Page 22

"…Oh, he is such a brave man, and a good one. God bless him and his work. … He spoke this morning before his sermon of a certain something that attracts people toward each other and causes them to seek the society of each other; of scholar for scholar, artist for artist, etc. I think it is a true friendship. He called it elective affinity. I think there is such an attraction between us. He is my very dear friend."

[25] Milford, Nancy. *Savage Beauty: The Life of Edna St. Vincent Millay* (New York: Random House, 2001) Page 22-23

"… At last the church decided to call a meeting to decide whether his contract should be renewed. Cora was worried.

"However, a paper was drawn up by those who wanted him to stay, and Cora was asked to write it. … When Henry came home, he told her he thought the paper supporting Gales would work. …"

[26] Milford, Nancy. *Savage Beauty: The Life of Edna St. Vincent Millay* (New York: Random House, 2001) Page 26

"In the early spring of 1900, just before Vincent Millay turned eight, Cora sent Henry away."

[27] Milford, Nancy. *Savage Beauty: The Life of Edna St. Vincent Millay* (New York: Random House, 2001) Page 31 and https://www.realtor.com/realestateandhomes-detail/78-Lime-St_Newburyport_MA_01950_M46782-29110 Note: Both Milford and Epstein refer to Cora's Newburyport home as a bungalow, which is a small one-story building that sometimes has a second story with a sloped roof. This three-story, 3118 sf home, built in 1810, is far larger than a bungalow, and is more likely to be the home of the Todds and Buzzells. Cora may have used this as a stable address given how often she and the children were moving. Furthermore, given that Clem's description of these events indicated Cora arrived at the door with Rev. Gales and the uncles took him back to Cora's to pick up his luggage, it seems unlikely Cora lived in the same house. If so, they wouldn't have had to walk Rev. Gales anywhere.

"…In the fall of 1902 they moved again, to 78 Lime Street in Newburyport proper, closer to their great-aunt Susan Todd, and to Clem, who had been adopted by the Todds. It was on Lime Street that Mr. Gales came to call. …"

[28] Milford, Nancy. *Savage Beauty: The Life of Edna St. Vincent Millay* (New York: Random House, 2001) Page 31-32

"…The aunts were sitting in the living room at the Todd's when they heard Cora and Vincent's voices laughing at the door. 'but the third, evidently a male voice, was baffling. I opened the door just as Nell was reaching for the knob…. I recognized the man instantly.' Cora hesitated as she introduced him, and Clem leaped forward angrily."

[29] Milford, Nancy. *Savage Beauty: The Life of Edna St. Vincent Millay* (New York: Random House, 2001) Page 32

"I explained that he was the sanctimonious cheat who had violated all rules of decency by trading on Cora's love for music and her equal love for deep literary research. …"

… As Cora tried to speak, one of the Todds took Gales aside and told him he was not wanted in their home. They walked him back to Cora's house, retrieved his bags, and put him on the evening train."

[30] Note: Bromfield Street is in one of Newburyport's oldest neighborhoods and not far from Lime Street where Cora's relatives lived. As stated in End Note 27 above, it appears that Cora used the 78 Lime Street address for its stability, but I doubt they actually lived in the 3118-sf home. Biographers state Cora and her girls lived in a cute bungalow at this time. Bromfield Street's history is unknown but real estate records indicate the area was built-up at the end of the 1890s as a place where people of modest means lived and it is one of the few streets in Newburyport with bungalow style homes. I use Bromfield as a place marker for whatever their real address was.

[31] Milford, Nancy. *Savage Beauty: The Life of Edna St. Vincent Millay* (New York: Random House, 2001). P. 13, and 31-32

"Later Cora wrote that she cut her father completely out of her life. She remembered that her mother was madly in love and now she was free to become engaged to Gard Todd… "

And

"… For while these women were domestic enough to have six children, as Clementine had, or even three within four years, they were clearly neither submissive nor weak. Clementine Buzzell did not minister to household peace—no matter what *Godey's* magazine or *Ladies' Home Companion* advised; she was out in her buggy scouting for hairwork immediately after her divorce. When Vincent Millay heard the stories of her grandmother's lover—and her aunt's accusations about her mother's friend Mr. Gales—she knew the women and her family had been headstrong, that they had had the courage or the grit to achieve their independence at whatever cost to themselves and their children."

Chapter 5

[32] Milford, Nancy. *Savage Beauty: The Life of Edna St. Vincent Millay* (New York: Random House, 2001) Page 29-30

"That September, while Cora was still in Vinylhaven, Vincent wrote her a plaintive letter. She didn't feel well. Norma and Kathleen didn't either. Exasperated by her vagueness, Cora fired off this note: "You said you were almost sick, and that made me anxious about you. I cannot write much now as

I am very busy; but I want you to write me at once and tell me if you are well. … I am working awfully hard night and day, and cannot stand it if I have to fret about you."

[33] Milford, Nancy. *Savage Beauty: The Life of Edna St. Vincent Millay* (New York: Random House, 2001) Page 30

"… I cannot write much now as I am very busy; but I want you to write me at once and tell me if you are well. … I am working awfully hard night and day, and cannot stand it if I have to fret about you."

[34] Macdougall, Allan Ross, editor. *Letters of Edna St. Vincent Millay* (New York: Grosset and Dunlap, 1952). P. 3 Note: Imagined letter based on one cited.

"… I thought I would write to you and tell you how I am getting along all right in school but in my spelling-blank I had 10 and 10 and then 9 and I felt awful bad. …"

[35] Milford, Nancy. *Savage Beauty: The Life of Edna St. Vincent Millay* (New York: Random House, 2001) Page 29-30

"… That September, while Cora was still in Vinylhaven, Vincent wrote her a plaintive letter. She didn't feel well. Norma and Kathleen didn't either. Exasperated by her vagueness, Cora fired off this note: "You said you were almost sick, and that made me anxious about you. I cannot write much now as I am very busy; but I want you to write me at once and tell me if you are well. … I am working awfully hard night and day, and cannot stand it if I have to fret about you."

[36] Griffin, Nancy. Island Institute.org "How We Got Here: A History of Maine's Ferry Service" January 1, 2020

"We are the roads to the islands. We want to get everyone home," is how Mark Higgins, manager of the Maine State Ferry Service, based in Rockland, explains its role. Of course, ferries don't merely perform the vital function of getting everyone home. They also bring tourists, freight, in some cases the mail, and much more to the islands."

[37] Milford, Nancy. *Savage Beauty: The Life of Edna St. Vincent Millay* (New York: Random House, 2001) Page 30

"…She sat by their beds in a vigil that lasted day and night. She dozed sitting up beside them, stroking their burning faces with wet towels, rubbing down their feverish bodies with ice. She was completely alone with the children, for the neighbors were afraid of catching the disease. She watched helplessly as their fevers raged from September until the eighteenth of October, when each of the little girls was given up by the local doctor. It struck Kathleen, the youngest and most delicate, the hardest. All Cora could think of during the long vigil was the tiny starched dresses, 'freshly ironed, three sizes, hanging there, and all the little petticoats, three sizes, starched and sticking out. Typhoid!"

[38] Milford, Nancy. *Savage Beauty: The Life of Edna St. Vincent Millay* (New York: Random House, 2001) Page 30

"…Then the fever broke. Cora wrote, "They lived, and that was all." Exhausted, floundering, with winter coming on and without the stamina or the resources even to pack, Cora fled to Newburyport, Massachusetts."

[39] Epstein, Daniel. *What Lips My Lips Have Kissed: The Loves and Love Poems of Edna St. Vincent Millay*. (New York: Henry Holt and Company, 2001) P. 6
"First, during the winter of 1901 they stayed with Cora's brother Charles Buzzell and his wife, Jenny, on Ring Island while the girls went to school there."

[40] https://historyofmassachusetts.org/rings-island-salisbury-history/
"In 1835, the Amos B & John M. Coffin House, a Federal-style house, was built at 6 Second Street."

[41] Milford, Nancy. *Savage Beauty: The Life of Edna St. Vincent Millay* (New York: Random House, 2001) Page 31

"… To Vincent, however, the house and grounds seemed grander than anything they ever had 'and very romantic. The yard was infinite; in the back it ran right down to the marshes; but in front, it was infinite with something else. … the pheasant's eye narcissus, which I had never seen, and which I suddenly came upon in the grass there, was so much like a voice as a flower. Years later I learned it was called narcissus poeticus.'"

[42] Milford, Nancy. *Savage Beauty: The Life of Edna St. Vincent Millay* (New York: Random House, 2001) Page 31

"Norma remembered the home with a spacious attic full of her mother's books, 'and Mother allowed schoolchildren to walk in and up to the attic to read,' a real privilege because Mrs. Millay had a larger and finer collection than the local library. ..."

[43] Macdougall, Allan Ross, editor. *Letters of Edna St. Vincent Millay* (New York: Grosset and Dunlap, 1952). P. 5

"... Gentlemen: I wish to subscribe for Harper's Young People' and here enclose $2.00 for that purpose. I wish to begin with the next number and so have written as soon as I found your residence by reading one of your books. Respectfully yours, E. Vincent Millay."

[44] Milford, Nancy. *Savage Beauty: The Life of Edna St. Vincent Millay* (New York: Random House, 2001) Page 38

Note: This accounting comes from a story written by Millay as a child. It is also partially based upon a few hints Norma gave me. Many biographers have mentioned that Vincent individually may have suffered sexual abuse.

"... And once it took all three children, flinging themselves against the front door, to close it and bolt it, and just in time. ..."

[45] Milford, Nancy. *Savage Beauty: The Life of Edna St. Vincent Millay* (New York: Random House, 2001) Page 31 and

https://en.wikipedia.org/wiki/Seidlitz_powders

"... The little girls, young as they were, began to work folding and boxing Seidlitz Powders—a patent medicine for headache—to help their mother out. ..."

And

"The name 'Seidlitz powders' ultimately derives from the village of Sedlec in the Czech Republic. ...The municipality of Sedlec (somewhat confusingly) is also the source of Sedlitz bitter water... After ingestion, the powder combines with gastric juices to develop cathartic intestinal gases which can be somewhat helpful in evacuating the users' bowels."

Chapter 6

[46] Epstein, Daniel. *What Lips My Lips Have Kissed: The Loves and Love Poems of Edna St. Vincent Millay*. (New York: Henry Holt and Company, 2001) P. 6

"That winter was the coldest in memory, with temperatures plunging to forty degrees below, and Cora and her daughters returned to Newburyport in the throes of a coal shortage. Cora was too proud to take from the city supply of coal, although it was offered to them as it was to all the poor. Cora's youngest sister Clem bought them half a ton, and with coke from the gas house, and using shingles ripped from the ramshackle house next door, they were able to keep one fire going in their tiny kitchen. Cora would throw the shingles over the fence, and after school the girls would pick them up to put on the fire."

[47] Epstein, Daniel. *What Lips My Lips Have Kissed: The Loves and Love Poems of Edna St. Vincent Millay*. (New York: Henry Holt and Company, 2001) P. 7
"… 'For the little one to climb toward the blueberry pasture she needed help, and the queer limping hurried gait was sad to see. For the left leg would not do its part, not would the left hand, for it shook and trembled so that the only way she could keep it still, when she was eating, using the right, was to hold it between her knees.'

There at the farm Cora nursed Kathleen day and night, massaging her legs and arms several times a day with cocoa butter and giving the child infusions of skullcap 'to quiet the little shattered nerves.'"

[48] Milford, Nancy. *Savage Beauty: The Life of Edna St. Vincent Millay* (New York: Random House, 2001) Page 4 Note: It goes without saying that the eldest is in charge.
"… The house was close enough to their mother's aunt Clara Buzzell, a large, easygoing person who ran a boarding house for the mill hands, that she could keep an eye on the girls while their mother worked. …"

[49] Epstein, Daniel. *What Lips My Lips Have Kissed: The Loves and Love Poems of Edna St. Vincent Millay*. (New York: Henry Holt and Company, 2001) P. 8
"A man from Appleton who boarded at Aunt Clara's when he was staying in Camden owned a small rental house in the field downhill from Washington Street. … The dilapidated house in the field had been empty for some time. The man from Appleton said that Cora could have the little house for her and her children to live in. If they would just clean it and make certain repairs for which he would provide the materials—like painting and papering—he would give them a month's rent free."

[50] Millay, E.S.V. *Collected Poems*. (New York: Harper Brothers, 1956) P. 550
"Sometimes, oh, often, indeed"

"…You awake in wonder, you awake at half past four,
Wondering what wonder is in store.
You reach for your clothes in the dark and pull them on, you
    have no time
Even to wash your face, you have to climb Megunticook.

You run through the sleeping town; you do not arouse
Even a dog, you are so young and light on your feet.… "

[51] Milford, Nancy. *Savage Beauty: The Life of Edna St. Vincent Millay* (New York: Random House, 2001) Page 33

"Only Norma talked about her sudden rages. … She remembered, too, a conflict of wills between Vincent and their mother. Vincent was banished to the basement until she could apologize. She refused."

[52] Epstein, Daniel. *What Lips My Lips Have Kissed: The Loves and Love Poems of Edna St. Vincent Millay*. (New York: Henry Holt and Company, 2001) P. 9

"In autumn under the red maples and golden leaves of the oak trees the fields were colorful with staghorn sumac wild blue asters wild in pink orchids, fleabane, and goldenrod in the spring there would be violets and arbutus, dandelions and trilliums. In the summer, the sisters played hide and seek in the grasses that were never mown and swam in the river on days when the water was not tinted from the dyes that colored the cloths in the mill vats, fashioning water wings out of pillowcases blown up like bladders.

Cora recalled, 'Another joy in the tall grasses was when it was raining hard. Then there was nothing the girls so much liked as stripping and putting on thin print dresses and running out into the grass and leaping about in the rain, letting the summer showers soak them until it ran in little rivers from their hair and faces. Then they came in and stripped and I rubbed them down with a rough Turkish towel till they glowed and tingled amid their laughter.'"

[53] https://www.librarycamden.org/walsh-history-center/edna-st-vincent-millay-residences-and-map/ and Epstein, Daniel. *What Lips My Lips Have Kissed: The Loves and Love Poems of Edna St. Vincent Millay*. (New York: Henry Holt and Company, 2001) P. 9

Map and picture of 100 Washington Street

And

"But the house, neglected by the landlord, was brutally cold in the winter. When the rent was not paid up, Cora could not press too hard for repairs. 'The snow outside made as good a winter playground as the grasses in summer, but there is need of warm cover within reach to make playing in the snow drifts enjoyable this we had, but it did not cover the whole house.' ...

Their dwelling was no more than four small rooms. On the ground floor was the kitchen, which had the only indoor plumbing, a cold water sink that had to trickle constantly so the pipe would not freeze. ..."

[54] Epstein, Daniel. *What Lips My Lips Have Kissed: The Loves and Love Poems of Edna St. Vincent Millay.* (New York: Henry Holt and Company, 2001) P. 9-10

"Next to the kitchen was the dining room, which in good weather also served as the library and music room. There was a cooking stove in the kitchen, but in the coldest part of winter those lower rooms could not be heated. The main coal stove stood in the living room upstairs (where Cora and Kathleen slept), next to the bedroom of the older girls. Everything in the house had to be kept from freezing—milk, potatoes, onions, bread and butter—had to be taken upstairs to living room 'And this was a chore and did not add to the order of the room,' Cora remembered."

[55] Milford, Nancy. *Savage Beauty: The Life of Edna St. Vincent Millay* (New York: Random House, 2001) Page 37-38 Note: This is Millay's description.

...

"But they were afraid of nothing, which was important,—not of the river which flowed behind the house, coloured with the most beautiful and changing colours—dyes from the woollen-mills above—and in which they taught themselves to swim; nor afraid of that other river, which flowed past the front of the house, and which, especially on Saturday nights, was often very quarrelsome and noisy, the restless stream of mill workers, who never stayed long enough anywhere for one to know them even by sight. ... And once it took all three of the children, flinging themselves against the front door, to close it and bolt it and just in time. And after that, for what seemed like hours, there was a stumbling about outside and soft cursing. And after everything was quiet again the children lay awake for a long time, listening, and not making a sound, and thinking sometimes of the inconspicuous little path at the back of the house which they could follow in the blackest of nights, without making a sound, through the tall grass of the field to the banks of the river, and how there, if it should seem unsafe to cross the corduroy bridge a little further upstream, they could swim across as quietly as water-rats to the furthest banks, & ... hide themselves in less than a minute in any one of the ten places where nobody on earth—no, not even with a dog and a lantern!—and the mill hands never went about with dogs and lanterns—could possibly find them."

[56]   https://www.architectmagazine.com/practice/a-look-back-at-insulation-products-of-the-20th-century

"... In the 1900s, the design and construction of buildings with a thermal envelope began to improve human comfort, as well as to reduce energy costs, spurred the production of insulating materials. The use of cavity wall construction for housing across the country led to the development of materials from mineral sources that could be installed as loose fill, blankets, or sheathing panels the use of natural fibers extracted from wood and sugar cane produced a number of different insulating sheathing boards. Some of the earliest commercial insulation was made of mineral wool, a fibrous material spun from molten mineral or rock components such as slag. Mineral wool could be used to insulate piping and heating systems, as well as in general structures."

[57] https://en.wikipedia.org/wiki/St._Nicholas_%28magazine%29

"Saint Nicholas magazine was a popular monthly American children's magazine, founded by Scribner's in 1873 and named after the Christian St. The first editor was Mary Mapes Dodge, who continued her association with the magazine until her death in 1905. Dodge published work by the country's leading writers, including Louisa May Alcott, Francis Hodson Burnett, Mark Twain, Laura E Richards and Joel Chandler Harris. Many famous writers were first published in St. Nicholas League, a department that offered awards and cash prizes to the best work submitted by juvenile readers.

"Edna St Vincent Millay, F Scott Fitzgerald, E.B. White, and Stephen Vincent Benet were all St Nicholas League winners. In 1899, St Nicholas League began. It was one of the magazine's most important departments, and had the motto of "Live to learn and learn to live." Each month contests were held for the best poems, stories, essays, drawings, photographs, and puzzles submitted by the magazines young readers. Winners received gold badges, runners-up received silver badges, and "honor members", winners of both gold and silver badges, were sent cash prizes."

[58] Epstein, Daniel. *What Lips My Lips Have Kissed: The Loves and Love Poems of Edna St. Vincent Millay*. (New York: Henry Holt and Company, 2001) P. 15-16

"By 1906, she was filling notebooks with verses, and she began to send poems to the popular children's magazine *St. Nicholas*. This monthly offered not only publication to budding writers but medals and cash awards as well. In October of that year the magazine published her poem "Forest Trees," an eighteen-line ode that ends with the stanza:

> Around you all is change—where now is land
> Swift vessels plowed to foam the seething main
> Kingdoms have risen, and the fire fiend's hand
> Has crushed them to their mother earth again;
> And through it all ye stand and still will stand
> Till ages yet to come have owned your reign.

It was signed by 'Vincent Millay (Age 14).' This slice of mysticism shows the influence of 19th century romantic masters: Keats, Shelley, and Wordsworth. Five months later a much longer, more ambitious narrative poem, "The Land of Romance," not only appeared in the pages of St. Nicholas, but won the magazine's first prize, a gold badge."

[59] Epstein, Daniel Mark. *Rapture and Melancholy: The Diaries of Edna St. Vincent Millay.* (Connecticut: Yale University Press, 2022). P. 44

"*Monday, May 2nd* Weather Nasty

Nothin' doin'. I wish the weather didn't change its mind so often it's quite disconcerting. Mama is sick tonight. This rain is enough to make anyone sick. The Huckleberry Finners [girls Mark Twain reading club] meet Tuesday at Ethel's."

[60] https://glosbe.com/cy/en/genethod

"Genethod

Welsh-English dictionary

girls"

[61] Milford, Nancy. *Savage Beauty: The Life of Edna St. Vincent Millay* (New York: Random House, 2001) Page 34

"The Genethod was founded by her friend and Sunday school teacher Abbie Huston Evans. Abbie's father was Welsh, the pastor of the Congregational Church that the Millays attended. "Abbie," Martha Knight, Ethel's sister, remembers, "must quote must have been about 10 years or more older than Vincent. She was tall with chestnut hair and ... fragile she had an awful funny gait; she sort of sidled. I remember Ethel once saying this rhyme at one of our meetings of the Genethod: "Do little souls go upward /when little bodies die?" It was a silly little rhyme she'd made-up and we all laughed."

[62] https://camdenucc.org/about/history/

Original is image

[63] Milford, Nancy. *Savage Beauty: The Life of Edna St. Vincent Millay* (New York: Random House, 2001) Page 34 and Epstein, Daniel. *What Lips My Lips Have Kissed: The Loves and Love Poems of Edna St. Vincent Millay*. (New York: Henry Holt and Company, 2001) P. 14-15

"...She started the diary innocently enough at the suggestion of Ethel Knight. ...:

And

"... In the winter of 1905 through 1906, Mr. Wilbur, who had taught history, one afternoon found himself on the losing end of an argument with his most brilliant pupil. She would not be convinced and she would not be silenced. At last he shouted at her, "You have run this school long enough!" which may have come as a surprise to the other children, who fell to giggling and guffawing at his angry face, whereupon the school teacher threw a book at the red-haired girl.

It seems unlikely that Mr. Wilbur did not know Vincent's father, Henry Tolman Millay, was the superintendent of schools in nearby Union, where the family had lived before the divorce. Eventually Cora would appeal to Henry but not before marching to the square schoolhouse, with its old-fashioned peaked belfry and storming up the wooden steps into Mr. Wilbur's classroom. ... the principal of the Camden High School, a Mr. Mitchell, who agreed with Mr. Wilbur that Miss Millay was a good enough scholar to start right in with high school, thereby not wasting more of anyone's time in grade school on Elm Street."

[64] Milford, Nancy. *Savage Beauty: The Life of Edna St. Vincent Millay* (New York: Random House, 2001) Page 33

"Vincent began a diary she called *Rosemary*, …"

[65] Milford, Nancy. *Savage Beauty: The Life of Edna St. Vincent Millay* (New York: Random House, 2001) Page 34

…

"*June* 29 [1908]

I guess I'm going to explode. I know just how a volcano feels before an eruption. Mama is so cross she can't look straight; Norma's got the only decent rocking chair in the house (which happens to be mine); and Kathleen is so unnaturally good that you keep thinking she must be sick. I suppose this is an awful tirade to deliver but it is very hard to be 16 and the eldest of three."

[66] https://en.wikipedia.org/wiki/Jane_Cable and
https://www.gutenberg.org/files/12441/12441-h/12441-h.htm

"This is a story of American life the scene of which is laid in Chicago at the present time. Jane Cable, the heroine of the tale, is a beautiful and aristocratic girl, supposed to be the daughter of David Cable, a rich railroad magnate This, however, is not the truth, as in reality she was taken from a foundling hospital when an infant, by Mrs. Cable, who deceived her husband into believing it was her own child.

And

So on the morn there fell new tidings and other adventures. —Malory."

[67] Epstein, Daniel. *What Lips My Lips Have Kissed: The Loves and Love Poems of Edna St. Vincent Millay*. (New York: Henry Holt and Company, 2001) P. 17

"…She would write in her journal: "My soul is too big for the rest of me," which was poignantly evident from her poetry, her deep-throated voice, and the impression she made by her increasing appearances in local stage plays."

[68] Milford, Nancy. *Savage Beauty: The Life of Edna St. Vincent Millay* (New York: Random House, 2001) Page 38

"... and talk I must or my boiler will burst. ... It's Sunday and therefore it's Sunday School, and I don't want to go one bit. It looks like rain, and I hope it will rain cats and dogs and hammers and pitchforks and silver sugar spoons and hayricks and paper covered novels and picture frames and rag carpets and toothpicks and skating rinks and birds of Paradise and roof gardens and burdocks and French grammars, before Sunday school time. There!"

[69] https://www.jstor.org/stable/25089971

"Carl Little "The Life and Poetry of Abbie Huston Evans": An elderly, white haired woman came on the stage at the 92nd St. Y's Poetry Center in New York City on the evening of March 29, 1965. Somewhat tottering of gait, she leaned on the arm of poet Ned O'Gorman, who introduced her. This was Abbie Huston Evans, 84. In the pantheon of poets like Frost, Lowell and Eliot, she was not an icon though her devotees made up in passionate regard. ... A short lyric such as "Fringed Gentians" serves well as an introduction to Evans's rigorous eye and ear, each syllable cut at the extremist edge:

In run out ground in coveys
They startle; here and there
They put blue in italics
Where few stare.

On the bright edge of meadows
When orcheses have dried,
Where cranberries streak carmine."

[70] Milford, Nancy. *Savage Beauty: The Life of Edna St. Vincent Millay* (New York: Random House, 2001). P. 39

Note: There is no doubt Millay was a racist, though she supported the work of Paul Robeson, Langston Hughes and others later in life. She was a product of her time and imagining an Uncle Tom-like comforter would have seemed only natural to the unsophisticated, poverty-stricken New England teenager.

"...But that night, after her sisters had fallen asleep, she turned to her diary again and made a remarkable entry: she gave her diary a name. "

> I think I'll call her Ole Mammy Hush-Chile, she's so nice and cuddly and story-telly when you're all full of troubles and worries and little vexations. It's such a comfort to confide in her and let the cares roll off your mind. After this I'm going to talk right to her and not be content with a proxy.

For Mammy was there whenever she needed her, as her mother was not. ...

> I've written so many verses and keep on writing so many more that I became afraid that if I didn't write them into one big book I might forget some of them. ... I love my verses so that it would be like taking my heart out if I should wake up some morning and find that all I could remember of one of my most loved—was the name. O mammy, I mustn't let it happen, you mustn't let me, you dear old white-souled, black-faced cuddle-mammy. ..."

[71] Milford, Nancy. *Savage Beauty: The Life of Edna St. Vincent Millay* (New York: Random House, 2001) Page 39
"... And she was careful to admit no ambivalence; Not a touch of anger or resentment surfaced—she reassured herself that her real mother was a treasure.

> I make two cups of tea in the little blue China teapot, and we sit opposite each other and drink it nice and hot while we watch each other's faces in the fire-light of the crackling stove. It makes up for all the time she's gone. Mammy Hush-Chile; I forget all about the things that went wrong and she forgets about all the doctors and patients and the surgery and the sleepless nights."

[72] Milford, Nancy. *Savage Beauty: The Life of Edna St. Vincent Millay* (New York: Random House, 2001) Page 40-41
"During the two years that she kept the 'Poetical Works', she wrote out sixty-one poems in her clear slant hand in a brown copybook, with an alphabetical index at the back carefully noting the age at which she had written each poem. Forty of these poems were written before she turned sixteen; another ten would be added that year. She placed her gold-medal poem, 'The Land of Romance,' first."

[73] Epstein, Daniel. *What Lips My Lips Have Kissed: The Loves and Love Poems of Edna St. Vincent Millay.* (New York: Henry Holt and Company, 2001) P. 17

"… followed by 'Silver badge for poem 'Young Mother Hubbard' in August 1909."

[74] Epstein, Daniel. *What Lips My Lips Have Kissed: The Loves and Love Poems of Edna St. Vincent Millay.* (New York: Henry Holt and Company, 2001) P. 13

"… In the same space they had a Mason and Hamlin pump organ, which served Vincent for her first keyboard lessons, and as soon as they could afford it they would install a small upright piano. … The professors sight was failing and long after he had quit teaching her, after she had started taking lessons with Mrs. Leila Buckland French, she regularly visited the blind man and read aloud to him."

[75] Epstein, Daniel. *What Lips My Lips Have Kissed: The Loves and Love Poems of Edna St. Vincent Millay.* (New York: Henry Holt and Company, 2001) P. 13

"Cora's patient Mr. John Tufts, a composer and piano teacher retired from the New England Conservatory, heard Vincent play one of her own keyboard compositions in his living room in 1905, when she was 13. Impressed, he offered to give her piano lessons for free."

[76] Milford, Nancy. *Savage Beauty: The Life of Edna St. Vincent Millay* (New York: Random House, 2001) Page 42

"George Frohock, president of their class, son of the Baptist minister, and captain of Camden's first football team, was the leader of the boys devoted to mocking her. They laughed at her and mimicked her until the peak of malice was reached in at class elections. …"

[77] Milford, Nancy. *Savage Beauty: The Life of Edna St. Vincent Millay* (New York: Random House, 2001) Page 43

"Our class had a play this winter. He was my father. I put my arms around his neck and kissed him every night for weeks. Oh, I could strike my mouth! I can feel the touch of him now. I laid my head on his knee and clasped his hand. Oh, I loved him dearly in the play, but if I had known what I know now, my mouth would have burned him when it touched him. …"

[78] Milford, Nancy. *Savage Beauty: The Life of Edna St. Vincent Millay* (New York: Random House, 2001) Page 42-43

"When it was published, everybody loved it. They even told Vincent how much they admired it. Of course she didn't tell them she'd written the poem. When the time came for the writer of the class poem to be elected, the boys had an idea that Henry Hall was a poet and he—oh, he'll make a manly man someday, didn't have stiffening enough in his great fat sluggish stolidity to get on his feet and tell them that the only poem he had ever printed in his life had been half written, wholly made over, and published by me!"

[79] Milford, Nancy. *Savage Beauty: The Life of Edna St. Vincent Millay* (New York: Random House, 2001) Page 43

"Thwarted and angry, finding her rival repellent, she fell ill. No amount of oranges, sherry or milk could cure her."

[80] https://www.mainememory.net/record/72851

Original is a photograph

[81] Milford, Nancy. *Savage Beauty: The Life of Edna St. Vincent Millay* (New York: Random House, 2001) Page 42

"For she had suffered what she called … 'the first big disappointment of my life: I graduate in June—without the class poem…'"

[82] Epstein, Daniel Mark, ed. *Rapture and Melancholy: The Diaries of Edna St. Vincent Millay*. (Connecticut: Yale University Press, 2022). P. 24

"… One thing I like about you, Mammy, is that you never talk back. You are a big melting pot into which at night I pour my joys and sorrows, and which in the morning gives back to me a well-mixed pill to be chewed until I feel better. …"

Chapter 7

[83] Millay, E. S. V. *Collected Poems* (New York: Harper Brothers, 1956) P. 243 "Portrait"

"…

And bending it moments under the terrible weight of the perfect
 word,
Here in this room without fire, without comfort of any kind,

Reading aloud to me immortal page after page conceived and in a
    mortal mind...."

[84] Milford, Nancy. *Savage Beauty: The Life of Edna St. Vincent Millay* (New York: Random House, 2001) Page 58

"She was alone in the house when the telephone rang—a long-distance call from Kingman, Maine. The voice of the operator was scratchy and faint, but at last Vincent made out, 'Mr. Millay, your father, is very ill, and may not recover...'"

[85] Milford, Nancy. *Savage Beauty: The Life of Edna St. Vincent Millay* (New York: Random House, 2001) Page 48

"...Dear Papa, I am puzzled sore
To think why you don't send some more
Of that nice stuff you sent before.
...
But Papa, this is not a fluff
I've lived on sawdust long enough."

[86] Milford, Nancy. *Savage Beauty: The Life of Edna St. Vincent Millay* (New York: Random House, 2001) Page 57

"... I'm getting old and ugly. My hands are stiff and rough and stained and blistered. I can feel my face dragging down. I can feel the lines coming underneath my skin they don't show yet but I can feel a hundred of them underneath. ..."

[87] Milford, Nancy. *Savage Beauty: The Life of Edna St. Vincent Millay* (New York: Random House, 2001) Page 50

"... I am painstakingly trimming a rhubarb leaf hat with white-clover and butter cups, with which my lap is filled. Beside me are two long, slender white ones from which with primary elements of sharp teeth and nails I have been peeling the bark for ribbons. I taste again the sweetness of the smooth round stick in my mouth. I can see the moist, delicate green of the living bark. And into my nostrils I breathe the hot spicy fragrance until my very soul is steeped in it."

[88] Milford, Nancy. *Savage Beauty: The Life of Edna St. Vincent Millay* (New York: Random House, 2001) Page 50-51

"…Vincent made a schedule to reassure her mother that their topsy turvy household would be run efficiently and cheaply. "Do it now" was signed by each of the sisters, like a promissory note, but gleefully using their childhood nicknames—Sefe was Vincent, Hunk was Norma, and Wump was Kathleen. It ended with a notation that Kathleen was to bring in wood for the breakfast fires, Norma was to feed the cat, and 'Vincent kills flies'."

[89] Epstein, Daniel. *What Lips My Lips Have Kissed: The Loves and Love Poems of Edna St. Vincent Millay*. (New York: Henry Holt and Company, 2001) P. 53

"So Vincent threw some clothes and poems together into her Aunt Rose's borrowed suitcase."

[90] https://en.m.wikipedia.org/wiki/Bucksport_Branch

"…The Bucksport Branch is a railroad line in Maine that was operated by the Maine Central Railroad. It is now part of the Pan Am railway system. The Bucksport Branch junctions with the mainline at Bangor and continues south down the Penobscot River valley, passing through Brewer and terminating at Bucksport."

[91] https://images.app.goo.gl/PqcaeR7MKpMoU4Uj7

Original is an image

[92] https://en.wikipedia.org/wiki/Great_Fire_of_1911

"The Great Fire of 1911 took place in Bangor, Maine, United States, on April 30 and May 1, 1911. A small fire that started in a downtown shed went out of control and destroyed hundreds of commercial and residential buildings."

[93] https://images.app.goo.gl/q4ek5EmtW8CAHAu28 and

https://images.app.goo.gl/hqbAXKPguuenVxMS8

Originals are images

[94] Jackson, Timothy F. *Into the World's Great Heart: Selected Letters of Edna St. Vincent Millay* (New Haven, CT: Yale University Press, 2023). P. ix

"'No man could ever fill my life to the exclusion of other things,' she writes: 'I am one part brain, one part soul, and three parts flesh and blood.'"

[95] Epstein, Daniel. *What Lips My Lips Have Kissed: The Loves and Love Poems of Edna St. Vincent Millay*. (New York: Henry Holt and Company, 2001) P. 53

"… Vincent casually called it "the down underground poem."

[96] Milford, Nancy. *Savage Beauty: The Life of Edna St. Vincent Millay* (New York: Random House, 2001) Page 47 Note: Milford cites this as "Rosemary," but it is likely "Friends," the last poem she published with *St. Nicholas Magazine*.

"'Rosemary,' a poem she had written earlier that same year, was shot through with longing for childhood, a perfectly acceptable convention although at seventeen she was a little young to long.

> 'The things I loved I may go to see,
>   I may lie in them no more.
> But I stand at the door of the used-to-be
>   and dream my childhood o'er.'"

Chapter 8

[97] https://maineanencyclopedia.com/kingman/
"The settlements are along the Molunkas road. and at the village on the Mattawamkeag, near the center of town there are here a large sole leather tannery of F. Shaw & Brothers, a sawmill for long and short lumber, one for shingles, and a steam mill making short lumber. The increase in population has recently been considerable [185 in 1870 546 and 1880] and the town bids fair to become an important one."

[98] Epstein, Daniel. *What Lips My Lips Have Kissed: The Loves and Love Poems of Edna St. Vincent Millay*. (New York: Henry Holt and Company, 2001) P. 53 Note: Millay's journal records the name as Gannas Boyd, see Epstein, Daniel Mark, ed. *Rapture and Melancholy: The Diaries of Edna St. Vincent Millay*. (Connecticut: Yale University Press, 2022). p. 100

"Ella Somerville, the daughter of Henry Millay's doctor, met Vincent at the train station. Arrangements had been made for her to stay at Dr. Somerville's home. According to Vincent's diary, after a cup of coffee there, the doctor and Ella took Vincent to the place where her father was boarding, a pale blue house owned by Mr. and Mrs. Yannis Boyd. As Vincent walked through the doorway, she heard the sound of a man coughing upstairs. Only at that moment did she realize how long it had been since she'd seen her father—eleven years."

[99] Epstein, Daniel Mark, ed. *Rapture and Melancholy: The Diaries of Edna St. Vincent Millay*. (Connecticut: Yale University Press, 2022). P. 100-101

"… They kept telling me to brace up, and be calm, and things like that, which was really funny, as I was not in the least bit nervous and everybody else seemed very much upset."

[100] Epstein, Daniel Mark, ed. *Rapture and Melancholy: The Diaries of Edna St. Vincent Millay*. (Connecticut: Yale University Press, 2022). P. 100-101

Mar. 2nd [1912]

"It didn't seem to me that the man on the bed was my father, but I went over and stood beside him and said, 'Hello, Papa dear,' just as I had planned to say, only that my voice seemed higher than usual; …"

[101] Epstein, Daniel Mark, ed. *Rapture and Melancholy: The Diaries of Edna St. Vincent Millay*. (Connecticut: Yale University Press, 2022). P. 100-101

Mar. 2nd [1912]

"… and when he heard me, he opened his eyes—the bluest eyes I ever saw—and cried out, "Vincent, my little girl!"

[102] Epstein, Daniel. *What Lips My Lips Have Kissed: The Loves and Love Poems of Edna St. Vincent Millay*. (New York: Henry Holt and Company, 2001) P. 54

"That evening she wrote a card to her mother and sisters, telling them that she had 'found Papa very low.'"

[103] https://www.cardcow.com/images/set788/card00289_fr.jpg

Original in an image

[104] Epstein, Daniel Mark, ed. *Rapture and Melancholy: The Diaries of Edna St. Vincent Millay*. (Connecticut: Yale University Press, 2022). P. 101

Mar. 2nd [1912]

"The Somervilles are Newfoundland people. There are the doctor, whose name is Beverly and who is the spitting image of Andrew Carnegie, one of the jolliest and best men that ever were; his wife a short and stout woman who speaks with a decided accent and bakes all sorts of strange and delicious dishes, many of which (English puddings) were much too heavy for me, possessing a great deal of childlike credulity and almost no sense of humor tho she would laugh herself weak at Ella's and my fantastic celebrations; and Ella herself, who is twenty-four, a graduate of Kent's Hill, and very clever with the brush and palette. One painting a big copy of sad Landseer dog was simply fine."

[105] Milford, Nancy. *Savage Beauty: The Life of Edna St. Vincent Millay* (New York: Random House, 2001) Page 59

"But seeing his daughter had done him more good than any of them had counted on. On Friday, March 1st, the doctor hadn't expected him to live out the night. By Monday, March 4th, Vincent wrote home excitedly, 'Papa is better and they think he will get well.'"

[106] Milford, Nancy. *Savage Beauty: The Life of Edna St. Vincent Millay* (New York: Random House, 2001) Page 59

"… Dr. Somerville…took her driving every day…"

[107] Epstein, Daniel Mark, ed. *Rapture and Melancholy: The Diaries of Edna St. Vincent Millay.* (Connecticut: Yale University Press, 2022). P. 100-101

Mar. 2nd [1912]

"But he didn't die after all. In spite of everything, he got well. And my sojourn in Kingman turned out to be a visit to Ella Somerville whom I grew to like very much. I stayed there almost a month (I will stick dates in the margin), while Papa grew steadily better and Ella and I grew steadily better friends until by the time I came away, Papa was up and dressed and Ella was ready to cry to think of my leaving her."

[108] Epstein, Daniel. *What Lips My Lips Have Kissed: The Loves and Love Poems of Edna St. Vincent Millay.* (New York: Henry Holt and Company, 2001) P. 56

"During the entire second week of March, the Kickapoo-Laguna vaudeville medicine show played Kingman, and the girls went to it every day except for Tuesday, when they attended a lecture by the dean of education of the University of Maine. The Medicine Show's chief attraction was the Violin Man, described by Vincent 'from our near-front end seats … was a good-looking man of thirty or almost, tall, rather, and slim, rather, with peripatetic eyes, three gold teeth, black hair, and the handsomest feet and ankles I ever saw. We could not keep our eyes away from—his violin."

[109] Milford, Nancy. *Savage Beauty: The Life of Edna St. Vincent Millay* (New York: Random House, 2001) Page 60

"... The next letter came with an enclosed note from Norma that flashed with anger:

> Sister Millay,
> I am exceedingly ashamed of you for not letting us hear something from you. ... You have been up there almost three weeks and you haven't exerted yourself in writing letters to your family what is the matter, dear? Are you sick yourself? Just because you found your father must you forget all about your mother and us kids?"

[110] Milford, Nancy. *Savage Beauty: The Life of Edna St. Vincent Millay* (New York: Random House, 2001) Page 60

"Her mother continued to press her not only for news but for her return. Norma needed her help with French. 'I can only get along without you when I'm away; But home misses you awfully.' But Vincent was wasn't thinking of Norma's French or her home duties and she didn't respond to her mother's letters."

[111] Milford, Nancy. *Savage Beauty: The Life of Edna St. Vincent Millay* (New York: Random House, 2001) Page 59

"Dr. Somerville ... took her driving every day and sleighing miles upriver, where she saw deer hanging in a tree, killed by a bobcat. 'Papa says that now a bobcat is the only thing that can legally kill deer. He seemed rather skeptical."

[112] Epstein, Daniel. *What Lips My Lips Have Kissed: The Loves and Love Poems of Edna St. Vincent Millay*. (New York: Henry Holt and Company, 2001) P. 55

"'After that we slept together every night—at least we spent the nights together.' They talked, laughed, and giggled until the bed shook. They read poetry aloud including Vincent's new poem. Ella particularly enjoyed hearing Vincent read Robert Burns, because she rolled her tongue so easily and joyously around the words. She loved Vincent's tongue and her little fingers and it is not until the end of the month when Vincent had gone home and Ella, bereaved, starts writing her candid love letters that we realize just how Ella loved Vincent Millay."

[113] Epstein, Daniel Mark, ed. *Rapture and Melancholy: The Diaries of Edna St. Vincent Millay*. (Connecticut: Yale University Press, 2022). P. 100-104

Note: Millay's journal entry of March 2nd [1912] describes what drew Vincent and Ella Somerville together and the sort of games they played with each other.

As Vincent describes the previous night together, she lets it slip that they have been sleeping together every night. Between Vincent's apparent hold over Ella, and her husband's daily buggy rides with Vincent, it seems natural that Mrs. Somerville would catch on to what was happening and want Vincent gone. Please refer to the cited reference for more details.

[114] Epstein, Daniel Mark, ed. *Rapture and Melancholy: The Diaries of Edna St. Vincent Millay*. (Connecticut: Yale University Press, 2022). P. 102-104

Mar. 2nd [1912]

"… There was a funny little clock in my room that had to be wound whenever you thought of it. It was a customary, in passing, to give it a turn or two by way of perfunctory greeting. But at night the task would always fall to me, as would also the raising of the window that always let in a shivery gust—and, if we weren't to read in bed, the 'dousing o' the glim.' For Ella was always ahead of me in turning in: she didn't do so many things to herself before the mirror. But one night, when we had talked ourselves tired were almost asleep, Ella struck her elbows into my back and asked me if I'd wound the clock.

"No," said I. "I ain't. And I ain't a-go'n' ter."

"Oh, dear," said Ellen [sic]. "That clock has got to be wound."

"That's true," said I.

There was a heavy silence. I knew she was thinking how she hated to get up I was thinking how glad I was I didn't need to.

After a minute or two the bed creaked, and a minute after that I heard Ella plowing around over the by the bureau. It was pitch-dark but she didn't want to strike a light because the shades were up and she didn't want to put down the shades because then she would only have to put them up again. If Ella hadn't been so disinclined to exert herself more than necessary, I should never have mentioned the clock at all. (In other words, this is a story that would never have been written.)

"Where's the stand?" asked Ella in a startled voice after a futile five minutes of scratching and pawing about the other end of the room.

"Where's the stand?" I repeated.

"Where's the wall? You want to find that first. You're drunk, Ella."

Now the truth of the matter is this: the stand where on the clock was wont to rest, habitually stood halfway between the bureau and the little wood stove.

In fact, if it had never been moved from that position while I was there—except once; and that 'once' was the night before.

We had been intending to write a letter after we went to bed: that is, we were to compose it together, but I, who slept on the front side, was to do the writing. So we wheeled the stand over to the bed—and the little funny clock came too! Ella had forgotten all about its having been changed, but I—I could have reached up one hand and wound it without turning in bed. But I was sick of winding it. It was Ella's turn."

[115] Milford, Nancy. *Savage Beauty: The Life of Edna St. Vincent Millay* (New York: Random House, 2001) Page 60

"In that inevitable tug between parents, especially those who have divorced, one parent wears the mantle of the victor and the other becomes the vanquished. Henry was clearly the vanquished. But there is a peculiar susceptibility children have to the fallen, to the not victorious, particularly if it is the father and they are girls. Henry had been irresponsible. He hadn't supported them, and Vincent knew it. But now, for the first time since she'd been very young, she was in his world, and she was thriving."

[116] Epstein, Daniel Mark, ed. *Rapture and Melancholy: The Diaries of Edna St. Vincent Millay*. (Connecticut: Yale University Press, 2022). P. 107

"*Sunday, 22 Sept. 1912*

I have been trying to think why it is that I feel so physically lonely and I have about decided that it is the coldness of the room ah, but I love the warmth! It is such a friendly thing. …"

[117] http://bangorinfo.com/Focus/focus_1911_fire.html

"…Within only a few years, downtown Bangor rose once again. Bangor Public Library opened the doors of its new home on Harlow St. in December 1913, only a few months after the new Bangor high school opened next door. Although the library had lost irreplaceable documents on the city's history, its collection grew to more than 80,000 by the end of the decade. The Universalist Church rebuilt over the ashes of the old structure. The federal government built a new and larger post office, but at the junction of Harlow and center streets instead of at its former home on the Kenduskeag Stream. The city turned that land and the land on which Norumbega Hall had stood into a parkway and firebreak…"

Chapter 9

[118] Milford, Nancy. *Savage Beauty: The Life of Edna St. Vincent Millay* (New York: Random House, 2001) Page 62
"Vincent raced back to Camden. She helped Norma with her French, and she helped her mother move into their new home at 82 Washington Street, across from the high school. …"

[119] Epstein, Daniel Mark, ed. *Rapture and Melancholy: The Diaries of Edna St. Vincent Millay*. (Connecticut: Yale University Press, 2022). P. 104
"*April* 1st
Began moving into 82 Washington [in Camden]. Dear place. Moved in the 8th."

Chapter 10

[120] https://camdenarea.pastperfectonline.com/Archive/D738D3A6-9522-43F5-91A9-701225673340#gallery
Original is an image

[121] Epstein, Daniel. *What Lips My Lips Have Kissed: The Loves and Love Poems of Edna St. Vincent Millay*. (New York: Henry Holt and Company, 2001) P. 61
"That June, Vincent was joyfully preparing for Norma's graduation—sewing, baking, and rehearsing some duets they would perform at the commencement in the Opera House. Several of her friends, including Ethel Knight, were getting married and there were wedding showers and weddings to attend and gifts to be made for the brides.

…

… It was generally believed that the apotheosis of [Edna] St. Vincent Millay that year and the next was a thing that happened to the girl from Camden, a series of peculiar coincidences of which she was less an active participant than a passive spectator. This is far from true. From the day she received her first letter from *The Lyric Year*, the ambitious poet worked the situation for all it was worth, and it turned out to be worth a fortune."

[122] Milford, Nancy. *Savage Beauty: The Life of Edna St. Vincent Millay* (New York: Random House, 2001) Page 64

"Vincent had gone into a nearby meadow to pick blueberries for supper, and when she had a pailful she came home to find her mother waiting anxiously on the doorstep with a letter in her hand. It was addressed to E. Vincent Millay, Esq., and it was from the editor of *The Lyric Year*. On July 17, 1912, he accepted "Renascence" as one of the best one hundred poems in the contest."

[123] Milford, Nancy. *Savage Beauty: The Life of Edna St. Vincent Millay* (New York: Random House, 2001) Page 64

"… She waited less than a week to answer, addressing her letter to Mitchell Kennerley, the New York publisher under whose aegis the prize had been announced: 'It may astonish you to learn that I am no 'Esquire' at all, nor even a plain 'Mister.' In fact, that I am just an aspiring 'Miss' of twenty.'"

[124] Milford, Nancy. *Savage Beauty: The Life of Edna St. Vincent Millay* (New York: Random House, 2001) Page 64

"If I were a noted author, you would perhaps be interested to know that I have red hair, and five feet-four inches in height, and weigh just one hundred pounds; that I can climb fences in snowshoes, am a good walker, and make excellent rarebits. And if I were a noted author I should not hesitate to tell you that I play the piano—Grieg with more expression than is aesthetic, Bach was more enjoyment than is consistent, and rag-time with more frequency than is desired."

[125] Milford, Nancy. *Savage Beauty: The Life of Edna St. Vincent Millay* (New York: Random House, 2001) Page 65

"He said he hadn't been alone in finding her poem very fine, original, strong, impressive. But he'd had certain reservations about it. He'd come upon other poems by 'Mr.' E Vincent Millay, and they had been so unequal to "Renascence" that he'd suspected some sort of forgery was being palmed off on *The Lyric Year*. He hadn't liked the other poems, so he'd taken "Renascence" to a friend of his, 'author, critic and attorney, to see if he could detect a clue. The next day, I came across a strong short piece: "then why the appetite—why the fruit".'

The strong, short piece he was referring to was her mother, Cora Millay's, not Vincent's, but he didn't know that—and no one was about to tell him."

[126] Millay, Edna St. Vincent. *Collected Poems* (New York: Harper Brothers, 1956) P. 13 "Renascence".

"...
The world stands out on either side
No wider than the heart is wide;
..."

[127] Milford, Nancy. *Savage Beauty: The Life of Edna St. Vincent Millay* (New York: Random House, 2001) Page 67

"As High Street rises away from the center of Camden, there was, and still is, a large white-frame summer hotel called the Whitehall Inn. It sprawls across a broad lawn rimmed with fir trees and wild roses, its long porches sleepily watching the bay. It was there in the summer of 1912 that Norma Millay took a job as a waitress.

Since she'd never worked as a waitress before, I asked her why she had taken the job.

'Mother said I could go. And, well. I guess as always, it would be nice to make a little money. And, too, it was just as a sort of a lark. ... The guests got interested in me. What beautiful hands I had, when I served from a tray, or the way I spoke. Anyway, as soon as they asked me about myself and my family, I said I had a sister who was a poet. I said she had a poem in *The Lyric Year*.'"

[128] Milford, Nancy. *Savage Beauty: The Life of Edna St. Vincent Millay* (New York: Random House, 2001) Page 68

"Vincent wore a tiny black velvet mask with rosettes of red crepe paper at the sides where the tie was fastened. Her costume had a short, full skirt made of yards of white cheesecloth fitted smartly at her waist, with the low-cut sleeveless bodice with black pompoms down the front. She won the prize for best costume, and Norma got the prize for best dancer."

[129] Milford, Nancy. *Savage Beauty: The Life of Edna St. Vincent Millay* (New York: Random House, 2001) Page 68

"... Vincent gave me a dirty look, the looked that meant—you've been tattling! What are you up to? ..."

[130] Milford, Nancy. *Savage Beauty: The Life of Edna St. Vincent Millay* (New York: Random House, 2001) Page 69

"Well, yes. Now things were happening very fast. The next day they had her up to lunch and I waited on her. Then they began taking us out sailing. That sort of thing. And mother, who was nursing one of the guests upstairs at the hotel, came down and did the silver for me, so I could leave to sail. You see, we were different. We were different from all the others."

[131] https://prabook.com/web/day_allen.willcy/1082924

"Willey, Day Allen was born on August 6 1860 in Rochester, NY, United States. Died December 14, 1917. Began as reporter, and became city editor, *Rochester Democrat* and *Chronicle*. Removed to Baltimore, 1890. Editor *Baltimore World*, and assistant editor *Manufacturer's Record*."

[132] https://www.findagrave.com/memorial/16320515/frederick-august-geier

"… In 1887, Frederick Geier returned to Cincinnati to settle his father's estate. One of the tasks he had to do was collect a debt from the owners of the Cincinnati Screw & Tap Co. Intrigued by what he heard about the new milling machine they were going to make Geier bought into the tiny company for $7000. When Frederick died he was company president and successfully guided the company to be America's largest machine tool manufacturer, Cincinnati Milling Machine. The "Mill", as it was known, changed its name in 1970 to Cincinnati Milacron."

[133] Epstein, Daniel Mark, ed. *Rapture and Melancholy: The Diaries of Edna St. Vincent Millay*. (Connecticut: Yale University Press, 2022). p. 111

"*October 24, 1912*

Letter from Miss Geier.

I wish I had written things down as they happened: they were—and are—so wonderful! The bare facts, of course, call up to my mind all the wonder of it, but I'm just too tired to write it down. … I have all the letters and all the cards and all the souvenirs, and I shall never forget a bit of it, --so what's the sense of scratching it all down?"

Chapter 11

[134] Milford, Nancy. *Savage Beauty: The Life of Edna St. Vincent Millay* (New York: Random House, 2001) Page 69-70

"On September 3, Vincent's editor sent her two snapshots, but he was still teasing her, for on the reverse of one he wrote:

(to Miss Edna Vincent Millay
from The Editor of
The Lyric Year.
with her—(his?)—best compliments.

A tall, narrow man with thick straight black hair sharp dark eyes, and a crooked grin was standing with his wife: in the other photo he holds their baby daughter. By the middle of the month, he said that if he were a sport, 'I should wager odds on 'Renascence' for first honors'; and he returned a carbon copy of 'Renascence' with his comments in red pencil. …

… On the twenty-first, she received proofs of her poem. It was not until September 25 that he revealed he was Ferdinand Earle and assured her she would be pleased with the results of the contest. 'Several have prophesized that you have the best chance for the first prize.' Which, unbeknownst to her, was exactly what he'd suggested to torrents three weeks before."

[135]. Milford, Nancy. *Savage Beauty: The Life of Edna St. Vincent Millay* (New York: Random House, 2001) Ibid. Page 69

"A tall, narrow man with thick straight black hair sharp dark eyes, and a crooked grin was standing with his wife: in the other photo he holds their baby daughter."

[136] Milford, Nancy. *Savage Beauty: The Life of Edna St. Vincent Millay* (New York: Random House, 2001) Page 70.

"Their letters flew back and forth, and every other day, Earl seemed to have some fresh delight to offer her. … But what he truly admitted was that 'if I could believe that I have encouraged and helped you with my big clumsy venture. And when your name is pronounced only with a whisper of awe, it will be my secret pride to believe that I had the privilege of discovering your worth, before anyone else.'"

[137] Milford, Nancy. *Savage Beauty: The Life of Edna St. Vincent Millay* (New York: Random House, 2001) Page 70

"... As for his venture, he must never call it clumsy, 'Say, rather, your big, splendid venture. O, but it's great to be a man! You made this year so ...miraculous to me!'

Savoring her spunk, he wrote to her as his 'Dear Tom Boy', admitting that 'the big, central thrill of the whole affair was digging you out of oblivion.' His single note of caution fell in his letter of September 29:

> 'I have no right to promise you a prize, as that depends mostly upon Mr. Wheeler; aren't you bursting to learn the November decision? I am.'"

[138] Milford, Nancy. *Savage Beauty: The Life of Edna St. Vincent Millay* (New York: Random House, 2001) Page 71-72

"Millay had told him a great deal about herself, but she had said remarkably little about "Renascence" itself. Only this once. And even here she said more about his effect on her: "If it will make you the least bit happier to know just what your friendship has meant to me, then please understand this: the sky had to cave in on me, of course, before I could write "Renascence", and I dug my man up because it wasn't pleasant to leave him there, not because I had come up too. It was you who, in your enthusiastic 'discovering,' accidentally exhumed me. Now we won't talk about that anymore."

[139] Milford, Nancy. *Savage Beauty: The Life of Edna St. Vincent Millay* (New York: Random House, 2001) Page 72

"Two days later, he sent her proofs of several of the other contesting poems. But again he cautioned her, 'You must promise me, dear, dear, Tom Boy, never, never to write to a strange man as you have written me.' He didn't say what she'd written that had disturbed his wife, and he admitted later in the same letter that he wasn't really a stranger to her, that he was, even, attracted to her. He was writing to her, he said, for the sake of his own part in her future development and to protect her from herself."

[140] Milford, Nancy. *Savage Beauty: The Life of Edna St. Vincent Millay* (New York: Random House, 2001) Page 72

"...

> (If you could know how—almost annihilatingly I want to hear you play that violin! Or how I could come straight back home again and be *tamed*

for the rest of my life, if just for one evening I might listen to Wagner's music with a man who knew how to love it! Savage passion! There could be no savage passion in you that would not find itself again in me! I am not big enough to love things the way I do.)

If that didn't jar Mrs. Earle's sense of propriety, it's hard to imagine what would. Poor Earle. He had no idea what he was up against in trying to restrain Edna St. Vincent Millay. 'But there,' she sweetly assured him,

'I had not meant to say so much. It was shockingly bad form to be so unreserved. Dear me! What will you do with me now, Mr. Ferdinand Earle? Scold me, or shake me, or pat me on the head? (don't dare! O, I have to giggle!)'"

[141] Milford, Nancy. *Savage Beauty: The Life of Edna St. Vincent Millay* (New York: Random House, 2001) Page 73

"What he wanted, he told her on October 14, was to 'flame back into silence, leaving a trail of fire across your dreams. I would leave you a mingled peace and unrest.'"

[142] Epstein, Daniel. *What Lips My Lips Have Kissed: The Loves and Love Poems of Edna St. Vincent Millay.* (New York: Henry Holt and Company, 2001) P. 63

"Her love letters were so full of wit, badinage, and sexual wordplay that he did not know exactly how to take them ... 'I beg of you to write me immediately ... a frank, serious intelligible letter. Remember in spite of all you may suspect, I am just a baby boy in the woods. You must take me by the hand and lead me to the light. There is something bewitching about you ... You see, I need a letter, crystal clear!' This is an ultimatum. He is calling her bluff in this letter that is breathless with schemes about his sneaking into Camden or her coming to New York, this letter in which he coyly and parenthetically remarks, 'Think of it while I am writing you: I know the decision of one of the two other judges.'

In her letter of October 28, 1912, furious, she lambasted him as 'the Patch-Work Letter Man', asking him to return her last love letter, of which she was proudest, granting him permission to read the others aloud to his wife, and offering to send all his letters back to him (she didn't). She wanted a flesh and blood lover, not a nervous moralist."

[143] Milford, Nancy. *Savage Beauty: The Life of Edna St. Vincent Millay* (New York: Random House, 2001) Page 73-74

"... Her anger and dependence are everywhere in this letter, and by its close, the child voice is the dominant one:

> 'Then what if you wrote an indiscreet letter (partly because you ...didn't know whether you dared or not, and partly because you wanted to see just what your editor would say, and partly...Oh *lots*, because you were the only twenty) and your editor wrote back an indiscreet letter that made you want to baby him—tho you really couldn't help it—and at the very end of it said, 'Will you hate me if you don't get any prize'; then, why then you wouldn't hate him, of *course* but wouldn't you want to cry on him? Please, that isn't wicked, is it? It's just that men are so much more comfortable to cry on—and you're the only man-friend I have. I haven't in all the world one friend who is stronger than I. I need someone to make me do things, and keep me doing things, and keep me from doing things.
>
> I guess I shall never see you in all this world. O, dear, I feel so it an' small an' all shrunked up. I guess you couldn't see me if you were here. I'm honest 'fraid you'd have to use a big nifying glass! I...please, sir, I'm sorry for my badness, and will you write me a letter purpose to cry on?'"

[144] Milford, Nancy. *Savage Beauty: The Life of Edna St. Vincent Millay* (New York: Random House, 2001) Page 74

"What she couldn't have known was that Earle had written to Kennerley on the 15th, just after he'd written to her, placing 'Renascence' second. But even then he had equivocated, 'Renascence' could easily deserve first honors."

[145] Milford, Nancy. *Savage Beauty: The Life of Edna St. Vincent Millay* (New York: Random House, 2001) Page 74

"Then he wrote her a peculiar letter, cut and pasted together, telling her that most 'friendships, relations, acquaintance-ships are bloodless, frigid, and stark, with no becoming drapery in the form of mystery and romantic atmosphere, with no bared elbows and throats.' He did wish he could tell her 'about the prizes'—the question, however, is still an open one (shut at the outside ends!)

She didn't write him for three weeks. Or, more precisely, she drafted three letters and sent none. She kept them, and she waited. Her drafts tell us how she felt as she waited:

> 'I am asking you to return to me a letter which I, a short time ago, wrote to a friend of mine, and which you, a complete stranger, seem to have received by mistake. The letter can mean nothing to you, as you are incapable of understanding it: but to me, who wrote it in all sincerity and candor, it means much—and it annoys me to think of it being in your possession.'

She gave him permission to read all her letters to his wife."

[146] Epstein, Daniel. *What Lips My Lips Have Kissed: The Loves and Love Poems of Edna St. Vincent Millay.* (New York: Henry Holt and Company, 2001) P. 63

"She wrote him the crystal-clear love letter that he demanded. It scared the daylights out of him. He left the billets-doux from the shameless Camden girl poet lying somewhere where his wife could find them, and she read him the riot act then during the last week in October he wrote a craven note in which he apologized for any part that he might have played in encouraging her amorous wanton schemes."

[147] Milford, Nancy. *Savage Beauty: The Life of Edna St. Vincent Millay* (New York: Random House, 2001) Page 75

"Indignantly, relentlessly, she pressed on:

> 'I am wild, if you like; But I stayed in my burrow a long, long time—nibbling your straws and snapping at your fingers, but always just a little out of reach. Until at last I got to trust you so much that one day I ventured out for a minute... And you threw rocks at me. And I will never come out again.'"

[148] Milford, Nancy. *Savage Beauty: The Life of Edna St. Vincent Millay* (New York: Random House, 2001) Page 76

"This, then, is what I have been waiting for, from day-to-day… In such a way as I had not known I could experience. This is the answer; this is the end. I wonder why I am not crying. My mother is crying. Did you ever hear your mother cry as if her heart would break? It is a strange and terrible sound, I think I shall never forget it."

[149] https://en.wikipedia.org/wiki/Jessie_Belle_Rittenhouse
"… From 1914 to 1924, she conducted lecture tours. In 1914, Rittenhouse helped found the Poetry Society of America, of which she was secretary for 10 years."

[150] Milford, Nancy. *Savage Beauty: The Life of Edna St. Vincent Millay* (New York: Random House, 2001) Page 76
"He told her that there was something better than a prize: Jesse Rittenhouse, a force in American poetry, who was an officer of the Poetry Society of America and 'perhaps our most distinguished critic', had written Earle to tell him that Millay's 'Renascence' was '…the best thing in the book… in fact, one of the freshest and most original things in modern poetry.'"

Chapter 12

[151] Daniels, Elizabeth A. *Bridges to the World: Henry Noble MacCracken and Vassar College*. (Clinton Corners, New York. College Avenue Press, 1994.) P. 159
"Edna St. Vincent Millay, 23 years old when she arrived at Vassar, had grown up as an eccentric genius in Camden, Maine. But because she challenged the authority of one too many teachers in her local high school, she was barred from attending classes and had to complete her secondary education by herself. Besides that, she lacked the training to construe Latin prose and to present certain other traditional credentials required for Vassar admission in 1913. To prepare herself for Vassar, she attended Barnard College in New York City from February to June 1913 as a non-matriculated student and was conditionally admitted to Vassar over the summer of 1913 into the class of 1917."

[152] Milford, Nancy. *Savage Beauty: The Life of Edna St. Vincent Millay* (New York: Random House, 2001) Page 77-78.

"Miss Dow hedged. She was uncertain if there was a vacancy for the year, and while she assured Vincent of her own impartiality, she said there were some very good reasons why Smith might not be as 'helpful to you as Vassar.' But she gave only one: 'the country life.' Her best news she saved for last: 'I have about $400.00 promised for your first year, and feel no doubt about getting the rest.'"

[153] Earle, Ferdinand. *The Lyric Year: One Hundred Poems.* New York: Mitchell Kennerley, 1913). P. 235.

"…As unto lighter strains a boy might turn, from where great altars burn, and Music's grave archangels tread the night, So I, in seasons past…"

[154] Earle, Ferdinand. *The Lyric Year: One Hundred Poems.* New York: Mitchell Kennerley, 1913). P. v.

"The terms of the competition called for a first prize of five hundred dollars and two second prizes of two hundred and fifty each, and they have accordingly been awarded as follows:

First Prize Mr. Orrick Johns

Second Prizes Mr. Thomas Augustine Daly, Mr. George Sterling

November 1st, 1912"

[155] Epstein, Daniel. *What Lips My Lips Have Kissed: The Loves and Love Poems of Edna St. Vincent Millay.* (New York: Henry Holt and Company, 2001) P. 67.

"… The winner himself, Orrick Johns, embarrassed, wrote, "I realized it was an unmerited award. The outstanding poem in that book was renaissance by Edna St. Vincent Millay, immediately acknowledged by every authoritative critic as such."

[156] Thesing, William, ed. *Critical Essays on Edna Dt. Vincent Millay.* (New York: G. K. Hall, 1993.) P. 29-32 Note: Quote's Untermeyer's essay, "Why A Poet Should Never Be Educated".

"In the following review, originally published in the *Dial* magazine on 14 February, 1918, Untermeyer praises the collection "Renascence and Other Poems" as an extraordinary work in which the reader finds 'a direct and often dramatic power'."

[157] Milford, Nancy. *Savage Beauty: The Life of Edna St. Vincent Millay* (New York: Random House, 2001) Page 76.

"Two weeks later, in the Holiday Book number of *The New York Times*, Jessie Rittenhouse—while praising Earls and Kennerley's effort and commitment to modern American poetry—singled out and saved for the conclusion of her full-page review Millay's 'Renascence':

> '*The Lyric Year* has, however, a poem so distinct … that it seems to me the freshest, most distinctive note in the book. This is "Renascence" by Edna Vincent Millay. Miss Millay's defects are the healthy defects of youth, time will take care of them; but that so young a poet should have so personal a vision of humanity, nature and God, such a sense of spiritual elation, of mystical rebirth, and present it to us with the freshness of first view—is certainly worthy of recognition and one could wish that the judges had seconded Mr. Earle in his choice of this poem for one of the awards.'"

[158] Epstein, Daniel Mark, ed. *Rapture and Melancholy: The Diaries of Edna St. Vincent Millay.* (Connecticut: Yale University Press, 2022). P. 115.
"*December* 12

…

Evening
Letter from the Poetry Society of America, asking for some unpublished (save the mark!) poems, to be read aloud at the next meeting. I sent some stuff—of which more anon!"

[159] YWCAnyc.org/history

[160] Milford, Nancy. *Savage Beauty: The Life of Edna St. Vincent Millay* (New York: Random House, 2001) Page 78.

"On December 18, 1912, the president of Smith College offered her a full scholarship for the following year. When Miss Dow learned of Smith's offer, she wrote immediately, 'I have on hand enough money for the first year at college and it seems to remain for you to decide whether you will go to Smith or Vassar.' …

Two days later, Miss Dow made her condition clear: 'Since there since three of the largest gifts for your education came from people who expected you to enter Vassar, I shall have to write them and find out if the gift would still hold if you went elsewhere.'"

[161] Milford, Nancy. *Savage Beauty: The Life of Edna St. Vincent Millay* (New York: Random House, 2001) Page 78
"…Vincent wrote to her mother in Rockland:

> 'Isn't this fierce? She puts in her little word about the country life at Vassar, but leaves the matter entirely in my hands. … Mother I knew it would come to this!… my head is a howling wilderness. And every once in a while I have to shriek with laughter over the dead funny side of it!'"

[162] Jackson, Timothy F. *Into the World's Great Heart: Selected Letters of Edna St. Vincent Millay* (New Haven, CT: Yale University Press, 2023). P. 27 Note: This is from a letter dated October 1912 to Millay's friend Gladys Niles.
"… What an egoist I am! I have spread my incoherent self over more than two sheets of note-paper. And I know you are interested in what I am doing and am trying to do and am going to do! And it's really all I can think of or talk of now… The things that have happened to me. It's like a fairy tale! And truly I have been very, very busy—typewriting, and writing out music (the most exasperating task) and—ahem—keeping my numerous appointments with the upper crusters. Someday I will astonish you by answering the letter promptly, and by filling it with experiences aspirations, and anticipations other than those of your friend, Vincent Millay"

[163] Epstein, Daniel Mark, ed. *Rapture and Melancholy: The Diaries of Edna St. Vincent Millay.* (Connecticut: Yale University Press, 2022). P. 116.
"*December 25*
Had a fountain pen, three boxes of Crane's Linen Lawn different kinds, a paper-knife, books and things, oh a lovely Christmas. Mr. Ficke's breaking the bonds came the day before I think.
December 26
I think Mr. Ficke sent me a copy of William Blake, of who he has been astonished to learn that I had never heard. Mr. Ficke is a dear!"

[164] Epstein, Daniel Mark, ed. *Rapture and Melancholy: The Diaries of Edna St. Vincent Millay.* (Connecticut: Yale University Press, 2022). P. 117
"*Dec. 29*

Spread. During the festivities my yellow chiffon, gradually but inexorably, fell from me, in ribbons. Poor Cinderella! How she must have felt when the clock struck 12! My yellow chiffon is now but a souvenir."

[165] Epstein, Daniel Mark, ed. *Rapture and Melancholy: The Diaries of Edna St. Vincent Millay.* (Connecticut: Yale University Press, 2022). P. 117-118 Note: Millay made three journal entries on December 31, 1912.

"*December 31, 1912*

… The last mail of the year! Wasn't it lovely?…

December 31, 1912

(Mother just brought up the mail, the evening mail, the last mail of the year and something indescribably unspeakable came in it, but I can't tell about it now because I've got to wait until I catch up to it and there is a lot between, and, anyway, I'm going to the movies with Norma and [her boyfriend] Kenneth, so I can't write any longer now. I'll sit up and watch the New Year in, and finish this record. There's a lot to tell. I hope I shan't have to lap over. But I shall probably get all caught up before tomorrow night, when I shall have to write the first New Year's entry. I think I'll make a resolution to write in my diary every day. No, I guess I won't.)"

Chapter 13

[166] Epstein, Daniel Mark, ed. *Rapture and Melancholy: The Diaries of Edna St. Vincent Millay.* (Connecticut: Yale University Press, 2022). P. 123
"*Jan. 6 [1913]*

Someone (I think it may be Mr. Kennerley) sent me a copy of the January *Forum*. When I first caught sight of it, I thought that it might be a sample copy, and then wondered if there could be anything about my poem in it. So I looked down the index—and there was a review of *The Lyric Year* by one Charles Vale. So I hunted up the page (Mit hands vot zhook) and happened to strike the end of the article first so that I caught a fleeting glimpse of a whole page of my poem. After which, very calmly (!), I proceeded to hunt up my beginning and find out what was said about me. Almost all of "Renascence" was quoted and the comments were quite satisfactory. I wonder if any of the other January magazines will have mention of the book. I must look them up."

[167] Epstein, Daniel. *What Lips My Lips Have Kissed: The Loves and Love Poems of Edna St. Vincent Millay.* (New York: Henry Holt and Company, 2001) P. 67

"In her hillside bedroom overlooking Camden harbor, the young woman had prayed to a mysterious spirit, a dream lover, to come and rescue her from the loneliness and bitter life of futile toil. In that same room where she made love ritually to a ghost, she also summoned Erato, the muse of love poetry. She had cast a spell over her room, her notebooks, pencil and paper, the air around her, and the streets of her hometown. Now through her poetry she was casting a spell over the whole world.

On January 10, 1913, in the dark early hours of the morning, Vincent gazed at her guttering candle. She braided her long red hair into one pigtail. She pulled the tarnish ring from her finger, placed it in a little box and holding the candle at an angle spilled a drop of molten wax into the box with the ring."

[168] Epstein, Daniel Mark, ed. *Rapture and Melancholy: The Diaries of Edna St. Vincent Millay.* (Connecticut: Yale University Press, 2022). P. 125

"*Friday night, Jan 10, 1913*

My little ring is all tarnished now, my candle is almost gone, and I never come to you as I used to on the third of the month—but I love you. Some people think I'm going to be a great poet, and I'm going to be sent to college so that I may have a chance to be great—but I don't know—I'm afraid—afraid I'm too…too little, I guess, to be very much, after all. I'm not joking a bit. I don't want to disappoint people and perhaps tomorrow I won't feel like this, but it seems to me that all I am really good for is to love you…and that doesn't do any good. Perhaps I could be a great poet or nearer to it if I had you and you wanted me to."

[169] Milford, Nancy. *Savage Beauty: The Life of Edna St. Vincent Millay* (New York: Random House, 2001) Page 81

"… Perhaps I could be a great poet or nearer to it—if I had you, and you wanted me to. I have some big thoughts.

Darling, Darling, Darling, I could kiss you now, and *now* I could kiss you, and *now*, and *now!* … Dear, I think if I once you I could write and write and write! If I once could just hear you over the phone wire—and know it was you. –I could work and work and write and write!"

[170] Epstein, Daniel Mark, ed. *Rapture and Melancholy: The Diaries of Edna St. Vincent Millay.* (Connecticut: Yale University Press, 2022). P. 126
"*Friday night, Jan 10, 1913*
Now I'm going to take my ring and a drop from the candle and seal them up together in a little white box, and never open it perhaps, perhaps not open it till I get my real ring.

I did it. And I pricked my ring finger and dropped in a drop of red, red blood. (I shall always have to do things like that. It is my *self* that does it.)"

[171] Epstein, Daniel Mark, ed. *Rapture and Melancholy: The Diaries of Edna St. Vincent Millay.* (Connecticut: Yale University Press, 2022). P. 125
"*Friday night, Jan 10, 1913*
Darling, Darling, Darling, I could kiss you now, and *now* I could kiss you, and *now*, and *now!*"

[172] https://politicalstrangenames.blogspot.com/2016/10/zelma-merwyn-Dwinal_1884
"The son of Fred and Luetta Briggs Dwinal, Zelma Merwyn Dwinal was born on March 12, 1884, in Mechanic Falls, Maine. He would attend local schools and later studied at Bates College, graduating in the class of 1906. Following his leaving college Dwinal settled into an educational career that saw him serve as principal in several Maine school districts, including those in Richmond (1906-09), Livermore Falls (1909-11), and Camden (1912-17). He married in December 1907 to Harriette Newall (birth-date unknown), with whom he had three children, Charles, Barbara, and Lucille.

Zelma Dwinal was called to a very different area of public service during the early 1910s, being selected by then U.S. Senator from Maine William P. Frye to be a member of the U.S. Senate police force. Dwinal's appointment was successful and he served at the Capitol from 1910-1912, during which time he also studied at Georgetown University. Dwinal continued to serve at the Capitol until the year following Senator Frye's death, afterward returning to Camden, Maine."

[173] Epstein, Daniel Mark, ed. *Rapture and Melancholy: The Diaries of Edna St. Vincent Millay.* (Connecticut: Yale University Press, 2022). P. 127
"*January 12*
Got my Smith application filled out.

Sunday January 12

Saw Mr. Dwinal and got Smith application filled out wrote Miss Bannon, Miss Dow, Mr. Ficke and my Editor. Mother was up this afternoon. It seemed so good to see her she's going to try to come up every Sunday. Kenneth is up. There was no rehearsal on account of a howling blizzard which has been pleased to visit us today."

[174] Milford, Nancy. *Savage Beauty: The Life of Edna St. Vincent Millay* (New York: Random House, 2001) Page 69

"You see, we were different. We were different from all the others."

[175] Epstein, Daniel Mark, ed. *Rapture and Melancholy: The Diaries of Edna St. Vincent Millay.* (Connecticut: Yale University Press, 2022). P. 127

"*Tuesday, January 14*

Nothing happened today. No mail, no anything. Doc and Madolin were up a few minutes this afternoon hunting for sun enough to take a picture in. Went to the moving pictures with Norma and Kenneth. Mother sent up by Kenneth some little scruffy straw slippers for all of us girls and Madolin. I must go try mine on."

[176] Epstein, Daniel. *What Lips My Lips Have Kissed: The Loves and Love Poems of Edna St. Vincent Millay.* (New York: Henry Holt and Company, 2001) P. 19-21 and

https://archive.org/details/Dr.JekyllAndMr.Hyde1912_201312

"…Millay describes the experience of being called away as a professional actress:

> 'Not that the paint stick, and the rouge-paw, and the eyebrow pencil and all the varied apparatus that bring about the theatre's nightly illusion were up to that time unknown to me.'"

And

"*Doctor Jekyll and Mr. Hyde* (1912) is a short horror drama, based on the story of Robert Louis Stevenson. It is included in our program to illustrate the work and contributions of Florence La Badie, a star of Silent Hall of Fame."

Copyright Disclaimer Under Section 107 of the Copyright Act 1976:

"Allowance is made for 'fair use' for purposes such as criticism, comment, news reporting, teaching, scholarship, and research. Fair use is a use permitted by copyright statute that might otherwise be infringing."

[177] Epstein, Daniel. *What Lips My Lips Have Kissed: The Loves and Love Poems of Edna St. Vincent Millay.* (New York: Henry Holt and Company, 2001) P. 21.

"… She had many close girlfriends, including Abbie Evans, the preacher's daughter, with whom she taught Sunday school for years, and Corinne Sawyer, Ethel Knight, and Stella Derry, all members of both the Sunday school class at the Congregational Church and at a reading group they called the "Huckleberry Finners." Jesse Hosmer, one of the reading group, told a journalist that Vincent was "the life of the party wherever she went.' The girls took nature walks on Mount Battie and around the harbor' in good weather they swam and went rowing and sailing in Penobscot Bay, and took picnic lunches to the nearby islands. Stella Derry remembered: 'My mother used to ask me why I liked washing dishes and making potato stew at the Millay's when I hated doing those things at home. It was because Vincent made everything wonderful fun. She was always making up songs and games, and on walks she would make birds and plants and wildflowers as fascinating as people. She could be a spitfire if she thought something wasn't fair. No one ever heard a word of gossip from Vincent, or a swear word.' (All her life she was known as an inviolable confidante.)"

[178] Epstein, Daniel Mark, ed. *Rapture and Melancholy: The Diaries of Edna St. Vincent Millay.* (Connecticut: Yale University Press, 2022). P. 128-129.

"*Thursday, January 16*
Heard from R. Seymour again this morning, and 'signed the page.' He says that the January *Poetry* has a very unusual review of my poem. That wasn't the word he *used*. Went to the pictures with Mart. Norma & Kenneth went to the dance."

[179] Epstein, Daniel Mark, ed. *Rapture and Melancholy: The Diaries of Edna St. Vincent Millay.* (Connecticut: Yale University Press, 2022). P. 129.

"*Friday, January 24 [1913]*
… Kenneth was up and we all played poker. We have rigged the study up sporty and rechristened it 'The Poker Joint.' Norma tacked a great big and

awfully cute Velvet Tobacco ad up on the wall. Mary Emery called with a friend Mrs. Getchell of Waterville."

[180] Milford, Nancy. *Savage Beauty: The Life of Edna St. Vincent Millay* (New York: Random House, 2001) Page 79.

"Vincent told her mother she was picking Vassar because it would be great to know girls from Persia, Syria, Japan, India, and 'one from Berlin Germany'; besides, she wrote her mother, 'There isn't one 'furriner' in Smith.' But the real reason was 'Lots of Maine girls go to Smith; very few go to Vassar. I'd rather go to Vassar.'"

[181] Epstein, Daniel Mark, ed. *Rapture and Melancholy: The Diaries of Edna St. Vincent Millay.* (Connecticut: Yale University Press, 2022). P. 130

"*Saturday, February 1*

Am spending the night with Aunt Rose and Uncle Bert. Went to Rockland this afternoon & brought home my suit, my hat, a brown leather traveling bag and a pair of tan rubbers. An express package from Miss Dow came this came tonight it doesn't seem possible the things are really for me. Letters from Miss Dow and Ella."

[182] Milford, Nancy. *Savage Beauty: The Life of Edna St. Vincent Millay* (New York: Random House, 2001) Page 78-79

"In the end, when Vincent had chosen Vassar, the grace and generosity with which Miss Bannon took her news was a signal of the attachment she had developed for her young poet. It was ardent:

> 'I do not want them to conventionalized your spirit…one can learn anywhere…but I want you to learn to think and dream for yourself. Do not think everything that is told you is necessarily true…because what you want is freedom to think and freedom to range among dreams.'"

[183] Milford, Nancy. *Savage Beauty: The Life of Edna St. Vincent Millay* (New York: Random House, 2001) Page 79.

"This was from a woman she'd never met, who knew her only through her poems and their correspondence. 'I shall always be interested in you…if anything happens that you cannot go to Vassar write me at once and I shall be your friend again…and again.'"

[184] Macdougall, Allan Ross, editor. *Letters of Edna St. Vincent Millay* (New York: Grosset and Dunlap, 1952). P. 33.

Note: What follows is based on a letter Millay wrote her family on February 6, 1913. Parts of the next few pages are almost verbatim as she described the overnight journey aboard the State of Maine Rail Line of the Boston and Maine Railroad. (see https://en.wikipedia.org/wiki/Boston_and_Maine_Railroad):

"… I rested beautifully in my birth last night. (I tipped the porter too, this morning, a dime.) The train was an hour and a half late. In the night we stopped somewhere and I reached out and raised the shade a little so as to peak [sic] and leaned on my elbow and looked and saw a big sign all lighted up on a big dark factory—'Brockton Die Company', I think it was. We stopped there a long while. George met me at Portland and carried my bag and got my sleeper berth (lower 10 in *A*) and came down with me afterwards. Just think, I traveled Pullman all the way. It didn't seem very long, I was so lovely and comfortable. This morning … they made me go to bed when I got here and after a while a maid came in with my breakfast on a tray and raised the shade and told me what time it was and went out and I had more fun. I'll bet when the chamber boy put away my kimono & slippers and cap she thought they were cute. I found the kimono on a hanger in the closet and the slippers under it and the cap over the corner of the mirror. Send my comb along, will you? –I forgot it and have had to borrow one."

And from Wikipedia re Boston and Maine Railroad:
> "A new alignment to Portland opened in 1873, splitting the old route at South Berwick, Maine. B&M flourished with the growth of New England's mill towns in the late 19th and early 20th centuries, but still faced financial struggles it came under the control of J.P. Morgan and his New York, New Haven and Hartford Railroad around 1910, but antitrust forces wrested control back."

[185] www.american-rails.com/81-82.html and www.visitportland.com/blog/2020/03/12/maine-maritime-and-transportation-history/.

"The State of Maine Express was another of the many joint ventures carried out by the Boston and Maine and New Haven serving the populated coastal areas of northern New England. It operated on a year-round schedule running an abbreviated routing in comparison to some of the regions more well-known trains. The overnight run, inaugurated in the early 20th century, interchanged in central Massachusetts and also had a daytime running mate (which operated only during the warmer months)."

And

"58 passenger service through Union Station emphasized connections to Boston until the New York, New Haven and Hartford Railroad introduced convenient long distance train travel in 1913 with State of Maine overnight sleeping car service to Grand Central Terminal in New York City."

[186] https://www.bmrrhs.org

"The invention of the steam railroad in the 19th century gradually expanded human mobility and commerce. By 'annihilating distance', the railroad forever changed the American landscape and patterns of business and domestic life originating in the idea of constructing a continuous inland route between Boston and Portland, the Boston and Maine railroad gradually gained control of other lines until the B&M system linked hundreds of cities, towns, and villages in Massachusetts, Maine, New Hampshire, Vermont, and New York."

[187] Macdougall, Allan Ross, editor. *Letters of Edna St. Vincent Millay* (New York: Grosset and Dunlap, 1952). P. 33 and https://www.american-rails.com/81-82.html.

"… Rested beautifully in my birth last night. (I tipped the porter too, this morning, a dime.) The train was an hour and a half late. In the night we stopped somewhere and I reached out and raised the shade a little so as to peak [sic] and leaned on my elbow and looked and saw a big sign all lighted up on a big dark factory—Brockton Die Company, I think it was. We stopped there a long while. George met me at Portland and carried my bag and got my sleeper berth (lower 10 in A) and came down with me afterward. Just think, I traveled Pullman all the way. It didn't seem very long, I was so lovely and comfortable."

And

"If one lived in the northeast New England during the early 20th century virtually any town of notable size could be reached by rail. The on board accommodations were equally impressive with comfy reclining seat coaches, full dining services, relaxing lounge cars, and Pullman sleepers. The State of Maine Express was one such train, operated by the B&M and New Haven connecting New York City (Grand Central Terminal) with Portland, Maine at a distance of 343 miles."

[188] Milford, Nancy. *Savage Beauty: The Life of Edna St. Vincent Millay* (New York: Random House, 2001). P. 87.

Note: Grand Central had opened just three days before Vincent's trip. For a fascinating look at its press reception, go to
https://www.pbs.org/wgbh/americanexperience/features/grandcentral-opening/.

"She arrived in pigtails at 7:00 in the morning of February 5, 1913, having forgotten her hair combs in the rush to leave Camden."

Chapter 14

[189] https://en.wikipedia.org/wiki/Grand_Central_Terminal and
https://www.thedailybeast.com/grand-central-terminal-100-years-100-facts.

"Grand Central Terminal was designed and built with two main levels for passengers: an upper for inner city trains and a lower for commuter trains. This configuration, devised by New York central vice president William J Wilgus, separated intercity and commuter rail passengers, smoothing the flow of people in and through the station. The original plan for Grand Central's interior was designed by Reed and Stern, with some work by Whitney Warren of Warren and Whitmore. The main concourse is located on the upper platform of Grand Central, in the geographical center of the station building the 35,000 square foot concourse leads directly to most of the terminals upper-level tracks, although some are accessed from passageways near the concourse."

And

"Grand Central terminal opened its doors at midnight on February 2, 1913.

Perhaps the terminal's best known feature, the celestial ceiling of the main concourse depicts the Zodiac. The view is of the Mediterranean winter sky. The stars #2500."

[190] Milford, Nancy. *Savage Beauty: The Life of Edna St. Vincent Millay* (New York: Random House, 2001) Page 87.

"She looked, in fact, about 12. Mary Alice Finney, an aide to Miss Dow who had come to meet her, never forgot Millay standing in the middle of Grand Central Terminal awestruck, like a little girl, and wearing a broad-brimmed hat not at all in the fashion of the day, totally unaware of that fact. Finney whisked her off to Huyler's for an ice cream soda before taking her to the national training school for the YMCA on Lexington Ave. and 52nd street where she was promptly put to bed and told to rest."

[191] Milford, Nancy. *Savage Beauty: The Life of Edna St. Vincent Millay* (New York: Random House, 2001) Page 88.

"Miss Dow had not been idle. There was more than $1200 deposited in Millay's account at Barnard, and she had persuaded Dr. Talcott Williams, the director of the new School of Journalism at Columbia University, to write to the registrar at Barnard presenting Vincent Millay as a non-matriculating student in his school, so that her entrance exams had been waived. '…You see,' Vincent wrote home later, 'thanks to the pull I had, I am a very, very irregular *Special*.' The week before her arrival, Williams had written to the Dean of Barnard, Virginia Gildersleeve, 'Let us by all means have Miss Millay here and handle her gently.'"

[192] Milford, Nancy. *Savage Beauty: The Life of Edna St. Vincent Millay* (New York: Random House, 2001) Page 88.

"Caroline B. Dow was stout, proper, and generous; unmarried and childless and now in her late forties, she respected order and believed in restraint and self-discipline. She cherished the arts and was deft at organizing people on behalf of the things she believed in, whether the YWCA, the Poetry Society of America, the McDowell Club, or Vincent Malay. Having no use for disorder, extravagance, or wastefulness, she was a natural administrator.

From the beginning, Miss Dow suspected a certain instability or wildness in her young charge, which she felt was due to her environment as much as to her immaturity. It was, she said, 'in a certain sense… and asset, but it must be offset by very careful plans as to her personal surroundings.' In other words, Vincent Millay was to be cautiously nourished. Miss Dow felt that to have just missed *The Lyric Year*'s prize was good medicine for her character: 'She will be distinctly more on her mettle to reconstruct and polish her work. Successes are not always the best tonic for young authors or artists.'

Within a week of Millay's arrival, Miss Dow had was writing to the registrar at Barnard with a certain proprietariness:

'I appreciate keenly the kindliness you which you have shown my little protege she needs guidance, and I am glad to have my responsibilities shared.'"

[193] Macdougall, Allan Ross, editor. *Letters of Edna St. Vincent Millay* (New York: Grosset and Dunlap, 1952). P. 33.
Note: According to a letter the poet sent her family on February 6, 1913, Millay's actual guide was a Miss Doerin, but for the sake of simplicity, I'm using the name of the person Nancy Milford designated as her guide from the train station.

"This is the first chance I've had to write, and I can't write very much now, because I'm tired and I have to get up early in the morning to go to school. Yes, so quick! Miss Doran took me over to Columbia this afternoon to see a professor and he sent me to the registrar at Barnard (with a note) and she sent me to the bursar with a slip, and we went to see the Dean and she was at a committee meeting, so will have to see her tomorrow, and I'm all registered, and I have a class ('English 24,' they call it) at 10 in the morning. I am in room No. 840, on the eighth floor of the National Training School—the loveliest place and one of the biggest I ever saw almost, that is—I've seen some pretty big ones already …

From my window in the daytime I can see *everything*—just buildings, tho, it is buildings everywhere, seven and eight stories to million and billion stories, washing drying on the roofs and on the lines strung between houses, way up in the air;—they flap and *flap!* Children on roller skates playing tag on the sidewalks, smokestacks *and* smokestacks and windows and windows, and signs way up high on the tops of factories and cars and taxicabs,—and noise, yes, in New York you can *see* the noise."

[194] https://operations.cufo.columbia.edu/content/pulitzer-hall
"Address: 2950 Broadway, New York, NY 10027
Architect: McKim, Mead & White
Year Built: 1913
Major Occupants: School of Journalism"
[195] https://en.wikipedia.org/wiki/Talcott_Williams
Original is an image
[196] Milford, Nancy. *Savage Beauty: The Life of Edna St. Vincent Millay* (New York: Random House, 2001) Page 88.
"… The week before her arrival, Williams had written to the Dean of Barnard, Virginia Gildersleeve, 'Let us all by all means have Miss Millay here and handle her gently.' Earlier he had written to Miss Gildersleeve that not only had Miss Dow already raised $400.00 toward Millay's education, but my experience has been that Miss Dow uniformly completes what she undertakes.' There was no doubt at all that she had undertaken Vincent Millay."
[197] Milford, Nancy. *Savage Beauty: The Life of Edna St. Vincent Millay* (New York: Random House, 2001) Page 89.
"The only person Edna St. Vincent Millay was dependent on was Caroline Dow, and with Miss Dow she intended to be careful. 'Miss Dow,' Vincent wrote to her mother, 'is going to start right in getting me everything I need.' She would provide for her charge, and she would orchestrate her introduction.

> Well, now I've come to yesterday we bought everything at Lord and Taylor's, and this is what we bought. … A pair of black satin pumps with eleven story heels (New York slippers, you see) and big rhinestone buckles; rubbers to fit (it was sort of wet and I would have had to cross the pavement to the cab, and back later), white kid gloves, sixteen button length way up ones, and a scarf, a beautiful soft big white silk one with pale yellow roses on it—didn't I drape it tho!—as it wasn't an *awful* dress affair, we decided that Non's yellow would do if I wore the scarf all the time to cover where it's too big in the back."

Chapter 15

[198] Jackson, Timothy F. *Into the World's Great Heart: Selected Letters of Edna St. Vincent Millay* (New Haven, CT: Yale University Press, 2023). P. 47. Note: This is from a letter dated March 20, 1913, to Norma Millay.
"… So we'll say that I got with my birthday money:
> …
> International Art Ex. $0.25 & car fare $0.10."

[199] Milford, Nancy. *Savage Beauty: The Life of Edna St. Vincent Millay* (New York: Random House, 2001) Page 91-92.
"The day after Millay's arrival in the city, she had written to Louis Untermeyer, who had reviewed "Renascence" as a triumph. 'Here I am! … If you sent me a note some morning, would I get it in the afternoon?' By return mail she had heard not only from both Mr. and Mrs. Untermeyer but also from the poet Sara Teasdale, whom they had alerted of her arrival.
…
Sara Teasdale invited her for tea, asking that Vincent meet her at the Martha Washington, a hotel for women, where she stayed when visiting from her home in St. Louis. 'And in order that I may know you and all the crowd of women in this unlovely place, sit as near as possible to the desk. As for me, I wear glasses and have red brown hair.'"

[200] Milford, Nancy. *Savage Beauty: The Life of Edna St. Vincent Millay* (New York: Random House, 2001) Page 88.
"…You see, Vincent wrote home later, thanks to the pulls I had, I am a very, very irregular S*pecial*. …"

[201] Millay, Edna St. Vincent. *Collected Poems* (New York: Harper Brothers, 1956) P. 66 "Journey":
> "Ah, could I lay me down in this long grass
> And close my eyes, and let the quiet wind
> Blow over me—I am so tired, so tired
> Of passing pleasant places! All my life,
> Following Care along the dusty road,
> Have I looked back at loveliness and sighed;
> …"

[202] https://allpoetry.com/Helen-Of-Troy

"There is no rest. The gods are not so kind
To her made half-immortal like themselves.
It is to you I owe the cruel gift,
Leda, my mother, and the swan, my sire,
to you the beauty and to you the bale;
For never a woman born of man and maid
Had wrought such havoc on the earth as I,
Or troubled heaven with a sea of flame
That climbed to touch the silent whirling stars
And blotted out their brightness ere the dawn.
Have I not made the world weep enough?
Give death to me. Yet life is more than death;
How could I leave the sound of singing winds,
The strong sweet scent that breathes from off the sea,
Or shut my eyes forever to the spring?"

[203] Millay, Edna St. Vincent. *Collected Poems* (New York: Harper Brothers, 1956) P. 3 "Renascence".

"All I could see from where I stood
Was three long mountains and a wood;
I turned and looked the other way,
And saw three islands in a bay.
…"

[204]. Epstein, Daniel Mark, ed. *Rapture and Melancholy: The Diaries of Edna St. Vincent Millay.* (Connecticut: Yale University Press, 2022). P. 134.
"*Feb. 17*

Letters from Mr. Ficke and Ferdinand Earle, who is going to Europe, or rather, to start for Europe or rather, to sail for Europe on the 27th. Shall perhaps see him before he goes at the meeting of the Poetry Society, which is, I think, the 25th.

Monday, February 17

Went up to Barnard and had luncheon there. Letters from Norma, Mr. Ficke, Mr. Earle, and a review from Mr. Untermeyer. Hateful, *hateful,* cold. Hate everybody."

[205] Epstein, Daniel Mark, ed. *Rapture and Melancholy: The Diaries of Edna St. Vincent Millay.* (Connecticut: Yale University Press, 2022). P. 135.

"*Tuesday, February 18*

Cold a little better. Hate most everybody; like a few people. Abed all day. Went to college today. Had a terrible spell of nerves and cut class to go for a walk—up Riverside Dr. My first peek; glad I was alone."

[206] Epstein, Daniel Mark, ed. *Rapture and Melancholy: The Diaries of Edna St. Vincent Millay.* (Connecticut: Yale University Press, 2022). P. 135.

"*February 20*

Tonight saw and heard my first grand opera, 'Madame Butterfly,' at the Metropolitan Opera House. Geraldine Ferrar sang Butterfly and other big ones did the other big parts. Wish I could hear it again tonight (am getting this mixed this being really the 21st, you know); wish I could hear it again tomorrow night and the next night."

[207] https://en.wikipedia.org/wiki/Geraldine_Farrar.

"Alice Geraldine Farrar (*February* 28, 1882-March 11, 1967) was an American lyric soprano who could also sing dramatic roles. She was noted for her beauty, acting ability, and 'the intimate timber of her voice.' In the 1910s, she also found success as an actress in silent films. She had a large following among young women, who were nicknamed Gerry-flappers."

[208] Epstein, Daniel Mark, ed. *Rapture and Melancholy: The Diaries of Edna St. Vincent Millay.* (Connecticut: Yale University Press, 2022). P. 135.

"*Feb. 20 [1913]*

…Truly. I really ought to hear it three times right off. It is the most wonderful thing period but there! Ma'am. I did not wait. The lady who accompanied me and whom Miss Dow warned that I *might* weep, did weep! Well, well! I never cry at the theatre. It seems to me I feel things far too deeply, too deep down in my heart, too splash."

[209] Epstein, Daniel Mark, ed. *Rapture and Melancholy: The Diaries of Edna St. Vincent Millay.* (Connecticut: Yale University Press, 2022). P. 136-137.

"*Saturday, February 22nd, 1913*

Twenty-one today. And my first birthday away from home. Last night and this morning had twelve letters and -six cards. And some of my presents came, too, and some of them are in the office now, I know, and will have to wait until Monday. Still it will be a lovely Monday. Tonight at dinner one of the girls as George Washington (stunning!) and I as Martha (!) went in together and I had a big surprise birthday cake, and afterward we danced the minuet. Loveliest time! I wonder what will come Monday."

[210] Macdougall, Allan Ross, editor. *Letters of Edna St. Vincent Millay* (New York: Grosset and Dunlap, 1952). P. 34.

Note: This is from a letter dated February 9, 1913, to Arthur Davison Ficke.

"… I have learned to glare with a wild hunted expression all about me at a corner, to elbow fiercely on occasion those fellow creatures whom I love as myself, and to run and grab—literally grab a streetcar! I have been here since Wednesday and I am become a hardened citizen of a heartless metropolis."

[211] Jackson, Timothy F. *Into the World's Great Heart: Selected Letters of Edna St. Vincent Millay* (New Haven, CT: Yale University Press, 2023). P. 47.

Note: This is from a letter dated March 20, 1913, to Norma Millay.

"I'm very much afraid that if I told Miss Dow about it she would say that I ought to be willing to do what I could to help. And of course I am. So we'll say that I got it with my birthday money:

Money order to P.S. of A $1.03"

[212] Macdougall, Allan Ross, editor. *Letters of Edna St. Vincent Millay* (New York: Grosset and Dunlap, 1952). P. 34.

"… How do I like New York? O, inexpressibly! Yes, the Public Library is! No, the subway *isn't*! O, the St. Patrick cathedral! Quite too sweet, I assure you! And the view—charming, charming! So many roofs and things, you know; warships, and chimneys, and brewery signs—so inspiring! Yes, to the Madison Avenue Presbyterian! Doctor Coffin is *wonderful*. O, my dear, tremendous!"

[213] Macdougall, Allan Ross, editor. *Letters of Edna St. Vincent Millay* (New York: Grosset and Dunlap, 1952). P. 34.

Note: This is from a letter dated March 6, 1913, to Arthur Davison Ficke.

"…

I am not being Bohemian. I'm not so Bohemian by half as I was when I came. You see, here one has to be one thing or the other, whereas at home one could be a little of both. And whereas heretofore I have amused myself in idle moments by the diffusing of indiscreet letters which I would now give half my kingdom to recall, I am at present (unless indeed that confession may has made this letter also indiscreet) prudent to the point of Jane Austen. ..."

[214] Milford, Nancy. *Savage Beauty: The Life of Edna St. Vincent Millay* (New York: Random House, 2001) Page 95.

"Mr. Earle I saw and talked with only once and then only for a few minutes, at the February meeting of the P.S. of A. He sailed for Europe a day or two later. For reasons which I'm sure you can understand I preferred to meet him for the first time at the Society meeting. I preferred saying, 'I am very glad to meet you, Mr. Earle' to saying, 'O, *we* know one another!' That is why I let him keep writing to Camden instead of giving him my address here. ..."

[215] Epstein, Daniel. *What Lips My Lips Have Kissed: The Loves and Love Poems of Edna St. Vincent Millay.* (New York: Henry Holt and Company, 2001) P. 74.

"The day after she attended her first opera, *Die Walküre*, at the Met, she cut classes at Barnard so she could attend the luncheon at the Poetry Society of America where she met Witter Bynner and other well-known poets, such as Alfred Noyes and Edwin Markham. She must have been intrigued by young Bynner, his high, intelligent forehead, his heavy-lidded eyes, and his sensitive good looks. But it wasn't until the society's party in her honor at secretary Jesse Rittenhouse's, on Sunday the ninth, that Witter Bynner engaged her in conversation.

'Do you mind if I smoke?' he asked.

'Not in the least,' she replied."

[216] Macdougall, Allan Ross, editor. *Letters of Edna St. Vincent Millay* (New York: Grosset and Dunlap, 1952). P. 36.
Note: This is from a letter dated March 13, 1913, to the Millay family.

"... but Sunday night I was very much taken up with Witter Bynner, with whom I had a long chat; and Mr. Walker, early in the evening, was lassoed and tripped and thrown by a sweet young thing from boarding-school who came with Miss Thomas—and who is so exactly like Josephine Hobbs in every way you can think of that it's absolutely startling. So that Mr. Walker & I have not yet 'gone on', as it were.

Yes, I have seen and talked with Witter Bynner. He has said to me, 'Do you mind if I smoke?' and I have said to him, 'Not in the least.' He has proffered me his cigarette case and I have said, 'No, thank you.' He raised his eyebrows and said, 'O, you don't smoke?' And I have replied, 'Not here, certainly.'

He: Then you have no prejudice against it?

I: None whatever

He: I'm glad of that. My sister used to think it dreadful, but now she smokes more than I do."

[217] Epstein, Daniel Mark, ed. *Rapture and Melancholy: The Diaries of Edna St. Vincent Millay.* (Connecticut: Yale University Press, 2022). P. 139.

"*Sunday, March 9*

Party at Miss Rittenhouse's. *Lovely* time. Mr. & Mrs. Edwin Markham, Mr. & Mrs. Louis Ladoux, Dr. & Mrs. Ralph Wheeler, Sara Teasdale, Anna H. Branch, Edith M. Thomas, Gertrude Hall, three or four others, Witter Bynner, and Dugal Walker. Yes, I met him. I don't think he loves me *yet*. But then! Witter Bynner is delightful. Talked with him a long time. He read my poem 'Renascence' aloud, beautifully. Mrs. Trowbridge went with me."

[218] Milford, Nancy. *Savage Beauty: The Life of Edna St. Vincent Millay* (New York: Random House, 2001) Page 79.

"Are you at liberty to name the author? The little item about her in the back of the book is a marvel of humor. No sweet young thing of twenty ever ended a poem precisely where this one ends: it takes a brawny male of forty-five to do that. Don't, however, fear that Bynner and I are going about bud-mouthed with dark suspicions; if it's a real secret, we respect the writer of such a poem far too much to want to plague 'her.'"

[219] Macdougall, Allan Ross, editor. *Letters of Edna St. Vincent Millay* (New York: Grosset and Dunlap, 1952). P. 35-36.

Note: This is from a letter of March 13, 1913, to the Millay family.

"Saturday—Went to International Art Exhibition. Impressionistic school, you know, and perfectly unintelligible things done by people they call the

"Cubists" because they work in cube shaped effects. Everything they do looks like piles of shingles. I'll get some postals of the pictures, I think—especially the one called "Nude descending the stairs", and if you can find the figure, outline it in ink and send it back to me."

[220] Epstein, Daniel Mark, ed. *Rapture and Melancholy: The Diaries of Edna St. Vincent Millay.* (Connecticut: Yale University Press, 2022). P. 140.

Friday, March 14

"…Miss R. says that Witter Bynner said some very nice things about me. I didn't ask what they were, tho I'm dying to know."

[221] https://en.wikipedia.org/wiki/Sara_Teasdale

"… From 1911 to 1914 Teasdale was courted by several men, including the poet Vachel Lindsay, who was truly in love with her but did not feel that he could provide enough money or stability to keep her satisfied. She chose to marry Ernst Filsinger, a long-time admirer of her poetry, on December 19, 1914."

[222] Epstein, Daniel Mark, ed. *Rapture and Melancholy: The Diaries of Edna St. Vincent Millay.* (Connecticut: Yale University Press, 2022). P. 139-141.

"*Monday, March 10*

… Letter from a crazy kid in Texas.

…

Saturday, March 15

Mr. Monroe called tonight. Just as much of a kid as I knew he would be, but a nice kid I think, and a smart kid I know conductor fell over my umbrella today and broke it in two, I said it doesn't matter I don't think I'll need it this morning how did I happen to say that?"

[223] Macdougall, Allan Ross, editor. *Letters of Edna St. Vincent Millay* (New York: Grosset and Dunlap, 1952). P. 35.

Note: This is from a letter of March 6, 1913, to Arthur Davison Ficke.

"I'm quite settled down. I run in my rut now like a well-directed wheel. Sometimes, it is true, I feel that I am exceeding the speed limit. But I seldom skid, and when I do there is very little splash."

[224] Epstein, Daniel Mark, ed. *Rapture and Melancholy: The Diaries of Edna St. Vincent Millay.* (Connecticut: Yale University Press, 2022). P. 145.

Friday, April 4 Cut French.

"8 P.M. I'm crying because I was studying my Horace like a good girl, it got later & later and I didn't know it because I didn't have any clock, and the bell didn't ring and nobody called me and so I didn't get any dinner. You can talk about all you want about virtue being its own reward, but it's darn unsatisfying when you're hungry."

Chapter 16

[225] Bruccoli, Matthew J. *The Fortunes of Mitchell Kennerley, Bookman.* (Orlando, Florida: Harcourt Brace Jovanovich Publishers, 1986) P. 25.
Note: It is intriguing that Kennerley hung himself on Millay's 58th birthday, February 22, 1950, and that she died seven months later, October 18, 1950. Information about the quaint town of Mamaroneck can be found here: https://en.wikipedia.org/wiki/Mamaroneck_(village)%2C_New_York and here: https://townofmamaroneckny.org/.
"… Helen's inheritance was no doubt responsible for a change in the Kennerley's style of living. In 1903 they rented a summer home in Mamaroneck, which Helen bought in November—paying $16,000 for the house and 27 acres. The staff of the large house included a coachman, gardener, nursemaid, cook, Helen's personal maid, and other servants. Mamaroneck—about twenty miles from the city in Westchester County—became their main residence. Kennerley enjoyed the life of a country gentleman and kept horses. There were weekend visitors from the literary world."

And

https://en.wikipedia.org/wiki/Mamaroneck_(village)%2C_New_York
"Along with the other shore communities of Westchester, the Mamaroneck was at one time the location of summer residences for wealthy families from New York City."
[226] Epstein, Daniel. *What Lips My Lips Have Kissed: The Loves and Love Poems of Edna St. Vincent Millay.* (New York: Henry Holt and Company, 2001) P. 77-78.

"... In any case they were destined to meet soon, as both belonged to that society of avant-garde artists and writers centered around Mr. and Mrs. Kennerley's mansion in Mamaroneck, New York. Kennerley is a story in himself. He was one of the bold publishers—along with Alfred Knopf, Horace Liveright, and B. W. Huebsch—who were balancing lists of great French and Russian authors in translation and homegrown radical talents like Theodore Dreiser and Walter Lippman with money makers like romantic novelists and writers on spiritualism. Kennerley was the chief rogue among these booksellers, a fast-talking hustler who liked to traffic in highbrow fiction, poetry, and sex; In Edna St. Vincent Millay he had the hunter's instinct that he had found all three rolled into one. It was Kennerley who brought D. H. Lawrence's scandalous *Sons and Lovers* to this country in 1913, and Kennerley who went toe to toe with Anthony Comstock's Society for the Suspension of Vice over a tawdry novel about a fallen woman, *Hagar Revelly*. Kennerley won the first major decision against censorship laws not long after he met Millay, who was to become one of his principal moneymakers."

[227] Bruccoli, Matthew J. *The Fortunes of Mitchell Kennerley, Bookman.* (Orlando, Florida: Harcourt Brace Jovanovich Publishers, 1986) P. 26, 60.

p. 26

"... Kennerley's cousin Arthur Hooley performed most of the editorial functions, from reading manuscripts to working with the authors. A shy man with a speech impediment, Hooley published his own work as Charles Vale. Before coming to America, he had collaborated with Bennett on two plays. He was closely associated with Kennerley's ventures for more than twenty years; But in the early years of their connection he had reservations about his flamboyant cousin, writing to William Wood Kennerley: 'I find myself interested in his pose, but indifferent to his personality, and quite unimpressed by his ability.'"

p. 60

"... Writing in *The Forum* is Charles Vale, Hooley hailed the volume as a literary event and printed a long excerpt from "Renascence". He concluded in a burst of metaphors: 'There have been some suspicions that the soul of

America was becoming flat, but the sky will not cave in while there are such poets to uphold it, with the stars shining, as *The Lyric Year* reveals.'"

[228] Epstein, Daniel Mark, ed. *Rapture and Melancholy: The Diaries of Edna St. Vincent Millay.* (Connecticut: Yale University Press, 2022). P. 142 and https://daytoninmanhattan.blogspot.com/2012/04/lost-1907-madison-square-presbyterian.html.

Note: Although Millay's journal says Dr, Parker was the speaker at the Madison Square church, the actual pastor's name was Parkhurst. It is this sort of simple mistake that may account for some of the other possible discrepancies I have found in Millay's accounts.

"Sunday, March 23rd

Easter

Beautiful day in every way. Went to three churches. first to Trinity Chapel, which is almost Catholic. The service there was dreadfully oppressive & Miss Barnwell and I got out as soon as possible and went over to Dr. Parker's [sic] church, Madison Square. ...."

And

"But the impressive brownstone Gothic Revival Madison Square Presbyterian Church sat on the site. The churches congregation was composed not only of wealthy and influential New Yorkers, but it was headed by the highly regarded and powerful Rev. Dr. Charles H. Parkhurst. Their church was, in fact, most commonly called 'Dr. Parkhurst's church.'"

[229] Epstein, Daniel Mark, ed. *Rapture and Melancholy: The Diaries of Edna St. Vincent Millay.* (Connecticut: Yale University Press, 2022). P. 142.

"Sunday, March 23

Easter

... This evening to Calvary Church, Organ Recital, beautiful and wonderful choral & all kinds of singing by men & boys. They sang the *Hallelujah Chorus*. I honestly believe, as truly as I believe in fairies, that *angels always join in that*. They always sing the *'Hallelujahs.'* I'm sure of it!"

[230] Epstein, Daniel Mark, ed. *Rapture and Melancholy: The Diaries of Edna St. Vincent Millay.* (Connecticut: Yale University Press, 2022). P. 141-142.

"Monday, March 24

Am tired to death. Went with Mrs. Trowbridge to look at dresses. Everything that is pretty is too expensive. I am *cursed*, and I know it, with a love for beautiful things. I can't *bear* anything that looks cheap or feels cheap or is over-trimmed or coarse. I hate myself all the time because I'm all the time wearing things I don't like. It's wicked & it's ungrateful, but I can't help it. I wish I had one *graceful* dress."

[231] Epstein, Daniel Mark, ed. *Rapture and Melancholy: The Diaries of Edna St. Vincent Millay.* (Connecticut: Yale University Press, 2022). P. 142.

"*Tuesday, March 25*

I've got it. O, my heart! The *sweetest* thing. Makes you think of summer & iced tea on the lawn & men & girls & once in a while a breeze. I am—I am *languorous* in it. I have to be. It's that kind of dress. ..."

[232] Epstein, Daniel Mark, ed. *Rapture and Melancholy: The Diaries of Edna St. Vincent Millay.* (Connecticut: Yale University Press, 2022). P. 143.

"*Thursday, March 27*

Moved from room 860 to room 863, just around the corner. I love my room & my wonderful down-town view. But room 863 has one peculiarity which sets it apart from every other room in the building, one advantage which more than offsets every deficiency, and I am looking forward to a joyful sojourn here. For in this my new room the hot water comes out of the cold water faucet. Such a feeling of comradeship as it give[s] me! Here I am at home. The room is surely mine,--made for me."

[233] Macdougall, Allan Ross, editor. *Letters of Edna St. Vincent Millay* (New York: Grosset and Dunlap, 1952). P. 38. Note: This is from a letter dated April 11, 1913, to Cora Millay.

"It seems as if this has broken my hoodoo of 'all praise and no profit.' The two poems were the one beginning 'O, World, I cannot hold thee close enough' and the one called 'Journey.' Louis Untermeyer and Sara Teasdale are crazy about them both. William Rose Benét of the *Century* told me that there were some things in them he should hate to have the *Century* lose, but that there are several obscurities in them that I'll have to clear up a bit, and as some of the obscurities happen to be the best things in them, I sent them off just as they were to the *Forum*, so the *Century* has lost them for good."

[234] Milford, Nancy. *Savage Beauty: The Life of Edna St. Vincent Millay* (New York: Random House, 2001) Page 98.

> "Promise me, please, that with some of this you'll do something to make something easier for yourself. Shoes, dear, or have your glasses fixed if they're not just right. Please, please, do something like that. And I'd like it so much if each one of you would get some little tiny silly thing that she could always keep. But that's just a whim; the other isn't."

[235] Epstein, Daniel Mark, ed. *Rapture and Melancholy: The Diaries of Edna St. Vincent Millay.* (Connecticut: Yale University Press, 2022). P. 146.

"Monday, April 14 [1913]
Party here tonight. Had the first really *hectic* time I've had since I've been here. Have fallen in love again,—thank goodness! I won't feel so lost, like now-- with the red-headed boy who sat next to me at dinner. He's not really red-headed, not nearly as much as I am, and I'm not so very myself. A kid, graduated from Yale last year, and a—a *darned sweet kid*. And it's fun to talk just plain nonsense to him because he is sure to understand & answer back. He has a *real* sense of humor, and he loves music. I—I think I honestly hope I'll never see him again, because I'd be awfully likely to spoil him. I wish I were a really *nic*e girl!"

[236] Macdougall, Allan Ross, editor. *Letters of Edna St. Vincent Millay* (New York: Grosset and Dunlap, 1952). P. 38. Note: This is from a letter dated April 11, 1913, to Arthur Davison Ficke.

> "Right here, and apropos of 'The Birds and Flowers of Hiroshige,' which I love best of all, and with which I am drunk at this moment, right here let me say that you are the only person I know whose poems about flowers and birds and skies and things, filled as they are with your own so evident Earth-Ecstasy, quite satisfy my Earth-Ecstatic soul. The colors in that poem fairly make me stagger. …"

[237] Jackson, Timothy F. *Into the World's Great Heart: Selected Letters of Edna St. Vincent Millay* (New Haven, CT: Yale University Press, 2023). P. 32. Note: This is from a letter dated December 15, 1912, to Arthur Davison Ficke.

"… You need not wish to be a painter, my friend; you are one. And truly a poet. I am very glad you wrote me. And very, very glad to have 'The Earth-

Passion.' The earth passion! I have always had that. Perhaps that is why I love the book so well. I thank you for it and for the scribble on the fly-leaf."

[238] Bruccoli, Matthew J. *The Fortunes of Mitchell Kennerley, Bookman.* (Orlando, Florida: Harcourt Brace Jovanovich Publishers, 1986) P. 60.

"… *The Lyric Year* was freighted with flowery diction along with the free verse. Kennerley announced in August 1912 that annual volumes of *The Lyric Year* would follow, but none appeared."

[239] Epstein, Daniel Mark, ed. *Rapture and Melancholy: The Diaries of Edna St. Vincent Millay.* (Connecticut: Yale University Press, 2022). P. 148.

"*Wednesday, April 23rd*
Lovely letters from Mother, Aunt Clem, Norma and Mr. Ficke. And arbutus from the *Maine Woods!*"

[240] Millay, Edna St. Vincent. *Collected Poems* (New York: Harper Brothers, 1956) P. 323 "English Sparrows (Washington Square)".

"…
Breathing with quiet pleasure the cool air cleansed by the night,
    lacking all will
To let such happiness go, nor thinking the least thing ill
In me for such indulgence, pleased with the day and with myself.
    How sweet
The noisy chirping of the urchin sparrows from crevice and shelf
Under my window, and from down there in the street,
Announcing the advance of the roaring competitive day with city
    birdsong.

…"

[241] Jackson, Timothy F. *Into the World's Great Heart: Selected Letters of Edna St. Vincent Millay* (New Haven, CT: Yale University Press, 2023). P. 45. Note: This is from a letter dated March 20, 1913, to Norma Millay.

"Have just got your letter. I wish I hadn't said a word about coming home. I didn't know you'd think I really could. I wouldn't ask to for anything. It isn't as if the Vanderbilts were sending me to college, you know. There's quite a lot of money, but it's not unlimited. My opera *cloke* isn't new. It was somebody's else I don't know whose and was fixed over for me. But it is lovely, just the same. ..."

[242] Epstein, Daniel Mark, ed. *Rapture and Melancholy: The Diaries of Edna St. Vincent Millay.* (Connecticut: Yale University Press, 2022). P. 149.

" *Friday, April 25* (S.)
Went down all alone this morning to look for opera cloaks for Norma. Went to Wanamaker's in the subway & then came out on the street & asked a policeman where was Broadway & then found my way up to Lord and Taylor's, getting nervous but not stumped at 14th St., when Union Square butted in. I knew that Broadway runs up town from East to West so I picked up the scent again all right. Did some more work for Miss Adams. 2 hours."

[243] Epstein, Daniel Mark, ed. *Rapture and Melancholy: The Diaries of Edna St. Vincent Millay.* (Connecticut: Yale University Press, 2022). P. 149.

"*Saturday, April 26*
Went to Staten Island with some of the girls here. Saw the Goddess of Liberty. Saw Sailor's Snug Harbor. Walked around in the grass & got homesick."

[244] Bruccoli, Matthew J. *The Fortunes of Mitchell Kennerley, Bookman.* (Orlando, Florida: Harcourt Brace Jovanovich Publishers, 1986) P. 196.

"… Kennerley characterized Hooley as 'undeniably a genius' in his statement to the press. 'Few men had the sympathetic insight and pure taste for what is abiding and distinguished in literature.'"

[245] Epstein, Daniel Mark, ed. *Rapture and Melancholy: The Diaries of Edna St. Vincent Millay.* (Connecticut: Yale University Press, 2022). P. 151.

"*Friday, May 9* Cut French.
Today (I wish I had red ink to write in) I saw Sarah Bernhardt in *Camille*. It was only the last act (she is in vaudeville here) but the last act is the best, and it is the most wonderful thing I ever saw, heard, or imagined. Ever since I can remember I have cut out pictures of her, and longed terribly, and hopelessly, to see her. And now, I cannot express my happiness or gratitude to the people who, with quite another end in view, have made this thing possible. *I have seen Bernhardt. Seen & heard her.*"

[246] Epstein, Daniel Mark, ed. *Rapture and Melancholy: The Diaries of Edna St. Vincent Millay.* (Connecticut: Yale University Press, 2022). P. 153.

"*Monday, May 19*

Stayed all night. Mrs. K. brought me in the machine this morning and called for me this afternoon to take me out again. Wonderful ride both ways. Saw the other man again. Came home this morning just in time to go with the girls on a picnic to Coney Island. Road on the flying horses. Nobody would ride with me. They just stood around to chaperone and I did it all alone. All all alone, because there wasn't a single soul but me on any horse. For five cents I had the music & the tide & two men & all the horses."

[247] Epstein, Daniel Mark, ed. *Rapture and Melancholy: The Diaries of Edna St. Vincent Millay.* (Connecticut: Yale University Press, 2022). P. 153.

"*Friday, May 23rd*
Dinner with Alene Stern. Got lost in Central Park on my way there, pouring rain, no umbrella, getting dark,—it was wonderful."

[248] Epstein, Daniel. *What Lips My Lips Have Kissed: The Loves and Love Poems of Edna St. Vincent Millay.* (New York: Henry Holt and Company, 2001) P. 79.

"And on Monday, back in the city, packing to leave school for home, she wrote: 'It must be I'm getting terribly calloused in soul. I don't seem to be regretting very much.' Against her better judgment she went back to Mamaroneck, at Helen Kennerley's insistence, to a liaison that lady must have encouraged, but which had already scandalized Miss Dow, who somehow had gotten wind of it.

'Miss Dow called up. She's heard some new cussedness about me and is about heartbroken. Damn them I wish they'd keep their mouths shut.'"

[249] Epstein, Daniel Mark, ed. *Rapture and Melancholy: The Diaries of Edna St. Vincent Millay.* (Connecticut: Yale University Press, 2022). P. 154.

"*Sunday, May 25* (B & M)
It must be about one o'clock. I have not yet begun to regret this day & night, but I shall be sick about it in the morning. I have been intemperate in three ways, I have failed to keep, or rather fulfill an obligation, and I have deliberately broken my word of honor.

The cocks are crowing. It's later than I thought. I must get to sleep before I get to thinking."

[250] https://en.wikipedia.org/wiki/Battle_Creek_Sanitarium

"… The Battle Creek Sanitarium was a world-renowned health resort in Battle Creek, Michigan, United States. It started in 1866 on health principles advocated by the Seventh day Adventist Church and from 1876 to 1943 was managed by Dr. John Harvey Kellogg. The 'San,' as it was called, flourished under Dr. Kellogg's direction and became one of the premier wellness destinations in the United States."

[251] Epstein, Daniel Mark, ed. *Rapture and Melancholy: The Diaries of Edna St. Vincent Millay.* (Connecticut: Yale University Press, 2022). P. 154-155.

"Friday, May 30

… Borrowed a black silk bathing suit which made me glad I'm red-headed. …"

[252] https://www.city-journal.org/article/love-and-glory-in-east-aurory

"… The next morning, newspaper obits brimmed with the deceased's achievements—and aphorisms: 'Many a man's reputation would not know his character if they met on the street to avoid criticism, do nothing, say nothing, be nothing.'"

[253] Bruccoli, Matthew J. *The Fortunes of Mitchell Kennerley, Bookman.* (Orlando, Florida: Harcourt Brace Jovanovich Publishers, 1986) P. 25.

Note: Helen Kennerley was not cut off completely. Her father's will left his money in lifetime trust, with a clause that only her children or siblings could inherit any residuals.

"There was no way Kennerley would ever get his hands on the principal. Still his wife would draw from an income from 22% of a multi-million-dollar estate. Helen's inheritance was no doubt responsible for a change in the Kennerley's style of living.

[254] Epstein, Daniel Mark, ed. *Rapture and Melancholy: The Diaries of Edna St. Vincent Millay.* (Connecticut: Yale University Press, 2022). P. 155

"Sunday, June 1

… Miss Dow called up. She's heard some new cursedness about me is about heartbroken. Damn 'em. I wish they'd keep their mouths shut."

[255] Epstein, Daniel Mark, ed. *Rapture and Melancholy: The Diaries of Edna St. Vincent Millay.* (Connecticut: Yale University Press, 2022). P. 155.

"Monday, June 2

Didn't rest much last night. Came down to breakfast looking like a ghost. Felt like dying and couldn't do anything."

[256] Millay, E. S. V. (pseudonym Boyd, Nancy). *Distressing Dialogues*. (New York: Harper & Brothers, 1924). P. 22.

"… On the twentieth of September Goddard came to me and announced, having first exacted from me a promise of adamantine silence, that he was leaving for New York on the midnight train."

Chapter 18

[257] Epstein, Daniel Mark, ed. *Rapture and Melancholy: The Diaries of Edna St. Vincent Millay*. (Connecticut: Yale University Press, 2022). P. 156.

"*Saturday, June 7*

As Torchy says, 'Nothing doin'…' Torchy is one of the four, a little red-headed Jew, with beautiful brown eyes and an instant feeling of liking and fellowship for me."

[258] Epstein, Daniel Mark, ed. *Rapture and Melancholy: The Diaries of Edna St. Vincent Millay*. (Connecticut: Yale University Press, 2022). P. 157

"*Sunday, June 15*

Henry waited till this morning and I *did* go out home with him. To Collinsville. Rather unconventional even for me, I suppose."

[259] Epstein, Daniel Mark, ed. *Rapture and Melancholy: The Diaries of Edna St. Vincent Millay*. (Connecticut: Yale University Press, 2022). P. 157

"*Sunday, June 15*

… We went canoeing for about four hours. It was simply perfect. Henry is a nice boy, and I was a nice girl."

[260] Epstein, Daniel Mark, ed. *Rapture and Melancholy: The Diaries of Edna St. Vincent Millay*. (Connecticut: Yale University Press, 2022). P. 157.

"*Wednesday, June 18*

Back in New York. Lovely long talk with Miss Dow. Everything's going to be all right. …"

[261] Epstein, Daniel Mark, ed. *Rapture and Melancholy: The Diaries of Edna St. Vincent Millay*. (Connecticut: Yale University Press, 2022). P. 158.

"*Saturday, June 21*

At Aunt Clem's in Newburyport. Got across Boston all alone—the first time I ever was there, since I can remember. I'm getting to be so self-reliant and resourceful!"

[262] Milford, Nancy. *Savage Beauty: The Life of Edna St. Vincent Millay* (New York: Random House, 2001) Page 16

"While Henry was gone, Cora and Clem would visit Marcia and ramble with her along the country roads and through the fields, harvesting herbs and wildflowers. They learned when to pick pennyroyal, tansy, chamomile, yarrow, and bone set, and how to dry or soak and steep the great leaves of the mullein plant and the hairy stems of alkanet for their curative properties. They made ointments, decoctions, oils, and syrups carefully and kept them even more carefully."

[263] Epstein, Daniel Mark, ed. *Rapture and Melancholy: The Diaries of Edna St. Vincent Millay.* (Connecticut: Yale University Press, 2022). P. 158

"*Sunday, June 22*

Went 100 miles in The Magic Carpet, Aunt Clem's automobile. Went to Gloucester and all around,—to Beverly Farms. Had a lovely time, but I've got to get home. *I wan' my Mama!*

[264] Milford, Nancy. *Savage Beauty: The Life of Edna St. Vincent Millay* (New York: Random House, 2001) Page 27

> "Separation was Nell's goal, and she told Henry to go and not return; this was a one-sided affair… I was rebellious about this, and Nell never was allowed to lose sight of the fact that my loyalty to Henry was first, last, and always and that we, of her family, were firm in our opinion that she had… thrown away a life-time royalty of happiness and deprived her little girls of their birthright of happiness, good cheer, and wealth of unselfish interest from him to them."

[265] Epstein, Daniel Mark, ed. *Rapture and Melancholy: The Diaries of Edna St. Vincent Millay.* (Connecticut: Yale University Press, 2022). P. 158

"*Tuesday, June 24*

Corinne was up to supper. Bless her. Have a hateful cold. They say everybody does when they first get home. Mart was up in the evening.

Wednesday, June 25

Sick with my cold. Kenneth up. Mother went on a case for Dr. Wasgatt in Rockland.

Thursday, June 26
Went to 'Thursday Night Dance' with Hunkus [Norma]. She and I did the tango and were afraid of getting put out of the hall, but weren't. I love those disreputable dances."

[266] Epstein, Daniel Mark, ed. *Rapture and Melancholy: The Diaries of Edna St. Vincent Millay.* (Connecticut: Yale University Press, 2022). P. 159
"*Saturday, June 28*
Sunday School Picnic. Norm and I went, just to see Abbie, Ethel and the old crowd. My cold kept getting worse and worse and I wept and sniffled all the way home."

Chapter 19

[267] Epstein, Daniel Mark, ed. *Rapture and Melancholy: The Diaries of Edna St. Vincent Millay.* (Connecticut: Yale University Press, 2022). P. 159
"*Friday, July 4*
'The Glorious 4th.'
Kenneth up to dinner. We four went paddling in the afternoon."
[268] Epstein, Daniel Mark, ed. *Rapture and Melancholy: The Diaries of Edna St. Vincent Millay.* (Connecticut: Yale University Press, 2022). P. 160
"*Saturday, July 5*
Aunt Sue down from Portland, motored down, unexpectedly. Cleaned up the house from garret to cellar as soon as Mother called up to let us know she was on her way. Great to see her."
[269] Millay, E.S.V. *Collected Poems.* (New York: Harper & Row, 1956) P. 142
'Portrait by a Neighbor'.
"Before she has her floor swept
    Or her dishes done
Any day you'll find her
    A-sunning in the sun!
…"

[270] Milford, Nancy. *Savage Beauty: The Life of Edna St. Vincent Millay* (New York: Random House, 2001) Page 105.

"Dearest old neglected Muvver and Wump,

Bincent he's going to be good again once more like he used to be. ... But I've been having such a good time that I've just been selfish. Besides I've been in love.... His name is Arthur Hooley and he's the *Forum*'s 'power behind.' So help me I was in love with him, for a week, and I've written some lovely poems which the *Forum* will never see. It's all off and all over, since I left him wringing his hands in the station yesterday, but it was all the more acute for not being chronic (forgive it). ..."

Chapter 20

[271] Epstein, Daniel Mark, ed. *Rapture and Melancholy: The Diaries of Edna St. Vincent Millay.* (Connecticut: Yale University Press, 2022). P. 160.
"Thursday, July 8
Did a lot of tiresome little duties I've been putting off and putting off for ages. ..."
[272] Epstein, Daniel Mark, ed. *Rapture and Melancholy: The Diaries of Edna St. Vincent Millay.* (Connecticut: Yale University Press, 2022). P. 161.
"*Sunday, July 20*
Had the grandest time. Went sailing, Norma, Kenneth, Mother, Kathleen, Fritz & I. There were showers and we got soaked. Went ashore at Oakland Park, to get something to eat.

Perfectly lovely time."
[273] Epstein, Daniel Mark, ed. *Rapture and Melancholy: The Diaries of Edna St. Vincent Millay.* (Connecticut: Yale University Press, 2022). P. 159
"*Tuesday, July 1*
Mr. Boehler called. It's nice to have him here this summer and he makes another man."
Thursday, July 3
"Went to the dance with Mr. Boehler. I wish he could dance."
[274] Epstein, Daniel Mark, ed. *Rapture and Melancholy: The Diaries of Edna St. Vincent Millay.* (Connecticut: Yale University Press, 2022). P. 162 and

Milford, Nancy. *Savage Beauty: The Life of Edna St. Vincent Millay* (New York: Random House, 2001) Page 105.
"*Sunday, July 27*
Fritz and Kenneth up. … Fritz has a gray suit that exactly matches his eyes."

And
"…She and Kathleen spent an entire day on the Perry's yawl, *The Comfort*, bound for Great Spruce Head Island. There were thirty-one in their party, …"
[275] Milford, Nancy. *Savage Beauty: The Life of Edna St. Vincent Millay* (New York: Random House, 2001) Page 106
"When Miss McCaleb wrote to Vincent in mid-July, she said she had a larger problem in her entrance work than most of the other girls. …"
[276] Milford, Nancy. *Savage Beauty: The Life of Edna St. Vincent Millay* (New York: Random House, 2001) Page 106
"… If you are really so desperate and ill-prepared as your letter suggests, then perhaps you have no right to try for Vassar this year—the disappointment of those who are interested in you would be nothing compared with the possibility of your attempting too much. …"
[277] Milford, Nancy. *Savage Beauty: The Life of Edna St. Vincent Millay* (New York: Random House, 2001) Page 106
"… She had to work up Latin prose composition, mathematics, the equivalent of a third language, and some ancient history. She couldn't possibly do it all in one summer. She suggested that Vincent focus on American history and mathematics or Latin. Vincent must have written back to her in desperation or panic, for a month later Miss McCaleb replied."
[278] Epstein, Daniel Mark, ed. *Rapture and Melancholy: The Diaries of Edna St. Vincent Millay.* (Connecticut: Yale University Press, 2022). P. 163
Note: The Comique was one of two local movie theatres in Camden.
"*Wednesday, July 30*
… Norma, Hazel and I went swimming over at the island.
Thursday, July 31
Norma & I went to the Comique [?]. Kenneth came up when he was told not to, so we left him to sleep in the hammock.
Friday, August 1

Saw Mildred Perry & Marion Prescott. They want us to go swimming with them from their bath-house.
Sunday, August 3
…

    Norma & I and the boys went paddling.
Monday, August 4
Norma & I went swimming all alone. …
Tuesday, August 5
We three girls went in swimming with a whole crowd. Swam out to the float. Pretty good swim. I guess we can really swim.
    Went sailing with the Perrys."

[279] Macdougall, Allan Ross, editor. *Letters of Edna St. Vincent Millay* (New York: Grosset and Dunlap, 1952). P. 99 Note: This is a self-portrait Millay shared with her friends John Peale Bishop and Edmund Wilson some years later. "E. St. V. M."

"…
A long throat,
Which will someday
Be strangled."

[280] Epstein, Daniel Mark, ed. *Rapture and Melancholy: The Diaries of Edna St. Vincent Millay.* (Connecticut: Yale University Press, 2022). P. 164

"*Thursday, August 14*
Algebra
Saturday, August 16
Algebra."

[281] Macdougall, Allan Ross, editor. *Letters of Edna St. Vincent Millay* (New York: Grosset and Dunlap, 1952). P. 47-48. Note: This is found in the editor's note.

"From the summer of 1913 on, with the entrance to Vassar in view, Miss Millay applied herself to her studies. She was being tutored in Latin by correspondence with the professor of Latin at Vassar, Elizabeth E. Haight, and at the same time cramming up on other subjects in order to prepare for the entrance examinations."

[282] Jackson, Timothy F. *Into the World's Great Heart: Selected Letters of Edna St. Vincent Millay* (New Haven, CT: Yale University Press, 2023). P. 57 Note: From letter dated July 12, 1913, to Arthur Ficke.

"…
I have a fearful amount of study ahead for this summer. I must pass examinations in mathematics and American history, and I always just—just *skun*, as you might say, through algebra, and all I know about American history is one verse of the Star Spangled Banner. …"

[283] Paine, Thomas. *The Thomas Paine Reader* (excerpt). New York: Penguin Classics, 1987) P. 79

"Of more worth is one honest man to society and in the sight of God, then all the crowned ruffians that ever lived."

[284] Epstein, Daniel Mark, ed. *Rapture and Melancholy: The Diaries of Edna St. Vincent Millay.* (Connecticut: Yale University Press, 2022). P. 164

"*Saturday, August 9*

Studied all day. Norma brought up Stewart Cottman and a Mr. Neil. Men are an awful bother. They interfere with my studies. It's got to stop."

[285] Epstein, Daniel Mark, ed. *Rapture and Melancholy: The Diaries of Edna St. Vincent Millay.* (Connecticut: Yale University Press, 2022). P. 164

"*Sunday, August 10*

Fritz and Kenneth were up. Fritz and I went driving. Told Fritz he can't come up anymore. He's dreadfully cut up about it. I wonder if I've done anything terrible. I didn't mean to. I think it will kill me to know I had hurt anyone like that."

[286] Epstein, Daniel Mark, ed. *Rapture and Melancholy: The Diaries of Edna St. Vincent Millay.* (Connecticut: Yale University Press, 2022). P. 165

"*August 24*

We four & Wump paddled over to Sherman Point in the evening. Made coffee & had a late supper on the rocks. Put out for home at about eleven in a pretty stiff wind, Fritz & I paddling. Couldn't get her more around into the wind to save our lives and had to turn back and haul her up for the night in a little cove & walk home. About three miles.

Mother was crazy. Never no more."

[287] Ibid.

[288] Epstein, Daniel Mark, ed. *Rapture and Melancholy: The Diaries of Edna St. Vincent Millay.* (Connecticut: Yale University Press, 2022). P. 166
"*Tuesday, August 26*
… Gwendolyn saw her fist today for the first time and hit herself in the eye with it. Then she looked at me as if I'd done it, and howled. I'm sore yet from laughing.

[Note by Norma Millay: Gwendolyn is Ellen Young's baby. They were staying with us....]"

[289] Epstein, Daniel Mark, ed. *Rapture and Melancholy: The Diaries of Edna St. Vincent Millay.* (Connecticut: Yale University Press, 2022). P. 167
"*Tuesday, August 26*
Wrote a few letters. It's colder than anything you can think of. I have a new sweater that I love, sort of green & orange mix, and I wore it all day. ..."

Chapter 21

[290] Milford, Nancy. *Savage Beauty: The Life of Edna St. Vincent Millay* (New York: Random House, 2001) Page 107

"Her history exam now lies in the vaults of Vassar's Rare Books Library, where C. Mildred Thompson gave it a 1-, with the following comments: 'No understanding of history, grand epithets.' Millay had begun by writing, 'I was prepared in American history at my home in Camden, Maine, in the hammock, on the roof, and behind the stove.'"

[291] Milford, Nancy. *Savage Beauty: The Life of Edna St. Vincent Millay* (New York: Random House, 2001) Page 106

"… You see it is not because of any hatred of you that this summer work is demanded but because every Vassar girl has to take certain subjects in her first year, and there is no justice or pleasure in admitting a girl if she is not ready to go on with the required work....."

[292] Milford, Nancy. *Savage Beauty: The Life of Edna St. Vincent Millay* (New York: Random House, 2001) Page 107

"… She wrote home immediately afterward:

"It's all right. I belong here and I'm going to stay. I'm sending Kathleen the geometry examination. Perhaps she can pass it. I couldn't. But Miss McCaleb says it doesn't matter. I'm admitted anyway, if I flunk 'em all. … So you can send my snowshoes.

At last she met Miss McCaleb. After the exams, all the girls were to tell her how they thought they'd done.

I waited in line till my turn came and then I went in, and she looked at me a minute and then sort of smiled and said, 'Well, my dear, what did you do? And I answered, very solemnly, 'Miss McCaleb, I did my darndest.'"

[293] Millay, E.S.V. *Collected Poems*. (New York: Harper & Row, 1956) P. 550
"Sometimes, oh, often, indeed."
…
The path up the mountain is stony and in places steep,
And here it is really dark—wonderful, wonderful,
Wonderful—the smell of bark
And rotten leaves and dew! And nobody awake
In all the world but you!—
Who lie on a high cliff until your elbows ache,
To see the sun come up over Penobscot Bay."

[294] Milford, Nancy. *Savage Beauty: The Life of Edna St. Vincent Millay* (New York: Random House, 2001) Page 108
"Among the first girls Vincent met was Agnes Rogers, 'my sophomore … the most wonderful Sophomore there is, they say,' she wrote home. In August, Agnes had written to welcome a number of freshmen to Vassar in the fall, wondering 'what sort of girl each one is from her name'; but in Vincent's case, not wondering at all."

[295] Epstein, Daniel Mark, ed. *Rapture and Melancholy: The Diaries of Edna St. Vincent Millay*. (Connecticut: Yale University Press, 2022). P. 169
"*Sunday, September 21*
A wild time in room. About fifteen of us, planning a spread for Friday. Adele & Dorothea Campbell, Kim Tyler from *Bal'more,* Annie Hope Smith from

Tennessee, Bianca Scheuer, Harry [Harriet] Wiefenbach, Olive Burke, (my roommate) and I can't remember the rest.
   ..."

[296] Milford, Nancy. *Savage Beauty: The Life of Edna St. Vincent Millay* (New York: Random House, 2001) Page 109

"…While she was rich in talent, nerve, and ambition, they were rich in everything else.…"

[297] Milford, Nancy. *Savage Beauty: The Life of Edna St. Vincent Millay* (New York: Random House, 2001) Page 108-109

"… Her German teacher, Florence Jenney, never forgot the first moment she saw her that fall: 'Running footsteps overtook mine on the path between Rockefeller Hall and the Quadrangle, and a slight figure paused beside me. I had noticed especially that pale, eager face and gold reddish hair in a large section of Beginning German, and remembered that she signed her papers 'Vincent Millay.' 'I just wanted to say something to you,' a rich, vibrant voice began. 'I am going to love German. I know my work has not been very good yet, but it is going to be. By Christmas I shall be the best in the class.'

'She was, easily. And by Thanksgiving, not Christmas.'"

[298] Ibid.

Chapter 22

[299] https://alookthrutime.com/womens-fashion-in-1912/ *and*
https://glamourdaze.com/history-of-womens-fashion/1900-to-1919
"… Just two years earlier Fortuny patented a special process of pleating and dying that he called delphons."

And

"By 1912, the silhouette had achieved a more natural line. Women wore long line corsets as foundations for day dresses which were tight-fitting and flattering."

[300] Milford, Nancy. *Savage Beauty: The Life of Edna St. Vincent Millay* (New York: Random House, 2001) Page 111

"Flirtation was a practiced art, and Millay was adept at handling the girls. Her room was at the head of the stairs, and as she was dressing,

'I heard a masculine giggle & looking down saw *Jack* ... watching me. The *best* looking boy.

'You horrid thing,' said I. 'I shall close my door at once.'

'No, you don't,' said he. 'I'm coming in.'

'You can't,' I screamed, 'it's not proper! –All right then, come in, and see if I'm all hooked up.'

'Jack', who was Margaret, stood there gazing at Millay—who wrote home that without either her petticoat or her corset, 'Honestly, you don't know how cute & slim I look.'"

[301] Milford, Nancy. *Savage Beauty: The Life of Edna St. Vincent Millay* (New York: Random House, 2001) Page 111

"The girls dressed like men tucked their hair in their collars and posed with chocolate cigarettes stuck jauntily in their mouths. Millay refused the chocolate, afraid she'd give herself away."

[302] Epstein, Daniel Mark, ed. *Rapture and Melancholy: The Diaries of Edna St. Vincent Millay.* (Connecticut: Yale University Press, 2022). P. 170

"*Wednesday, September 24*

My roommate upset her ink bottle tonight all over everything, after which she had a crying fit and 'wanted her mother.' Poor kid! I have done just the right things and just said the right things, (somehow I must have been inspired) and got her quiet again."

[303] Ibid.

[304] Epstein, Daniel Mark, ed. *Rapture and Melancholy: The Diaries of Edna St. Vincent Millay.* (Connecticut: Yale University Press, 2022). P. 174

"*Friday, December 5*

...

People, my friends and hers, are very much interested in a seemingly new friendship which has sprung up between Catherine Filene & me. Handsome great big child!"

[305] Lisicky, Michael J. *Filene's: Boston's Great Specialty Store.* (Charleston, South Carolina: Arcadia Publishing. 2012). P. 11

"When William Filine opened his first Boston store in 1851, he probably had no idea what would come to of his business. By the turn of the century, William Filene's sons' company earned the title' world's largest specialty store'. Contrary to most people's perceptions, Filene's was not a department store. It carried merchandise for women and children exclusively, although it expanded later to include menswear. Two of William's sons, Edward and Lincoln, were responsible for much of Filene's success. Not only did they have a flair for merchandising and advertising, they were pioneers in employee relations and community service.

By the time Filene's landmark store opened on Boston's Washington Street in 1912, the company employed 2500 people and had annual sales of 4.5 million. On opening day, 235,000 customers visited the store."

[306] Epstein, Daniel Mark, ed. *Rapture and Melancholy: The Diaries of Edna St. Vincent Millay.* (Connecticut: Yale University Press, 2022). P. 170

"*Thursday, September 25*

Olive has been called up on campus. She is broken-hearted. I am not. I wanted a lonesome room in the first place."

[307] Macdougall, Allan Ross, editor. *Letters of Edna St. Vincent Millay* (New York: Grosset and Dunlap, 1952). P. 48 footnote, *and* from early 1914 letter to Arthur Davison Ficke, also on P.48.

"'…Vincent fulfilled all these conditions and then built her course around her own interest. English studies were its foundation, and they included a wide range and great teachers: old English and Chaucer with Christabel Fisk, 19th century poetry and later Victorian poetry, and invite advanced writing course with Katherine Taylor, English drama with Henry Noble McCracken, the techniques of drama with Gertrude Buck… then she enriched her knowledge of literature by many courses in foreign languages: both Greek and Latin, French, German, Italian, and Spanish. Besides the course in general European history, she elected Lucy Maynard Salmon's course in 'Periodic Literature: Its use as historical material' and she had a semester in Modern Art… one in social psychology… one in music.'"

And from 1914 letter
"...
I hate this pink-and-gray college. If there had been a college in *Alice in Wonderland* it would be this college. Every morning when I awake I swear, I say, 'Damn this pink-and-gray college!'"

[308]. Millay, E.S.V. *Collected Poems*. (New York: Harper & Row, 1956) P. 340 "Rendezvous".

"...
That is to say, in rooms less bright with roses, rooms more
    casual, less aware
Of History in the wings about to enter with benevolent air
On ponderous tiptoe, at the cue 'Proceed.'"

[309] Milford, Nancy. *Savage Beauty: The Life of Edna St. Vincent Millay* (New York: Random House, 2001) Page 111

"When Millay sent the snapshots home, she concentrated on Catherine Filene: she was bossy, she was domineering, she was 'too executive'; 'Catherine can't do a thing with me … because I don't let her see that I resent her manner of Authority, I just plain do as I like and don't notice her. She'd give a lot, I think, to have me chase her around. I don't go near her.' …"

[310] En.m.wikipedia.org/wiki/1913_in_music *Note: Listings of popular recordings in 1913.*

"Popular recordings

- *The Spaniard That Blighted My Life* by Al Jolson
- *Till the Sands of the Desert Grow Cold* by Alan Turner
- *When the Midnight Choo-Choo Leaves for Alabam'* by Collins & Harlan"

[311] Epstein, Daniel Mark, ed. *Rapture and Melancholy: The Diaries of Edna St. Vincent Millay*. (Connecticut: Yale University Press, 2022). P. 172
"*Tuesday, October 21*
Was physically examined. Am five feet one, and weight one hundred and one.
…
Friday, October 31

Halloween Ball here at McGlynn's. Some of the girls met the dearest boys. They all sent flowers and we really dressed. I had a perfectly lovely time. I wouldn't have believed it possible."

[312] Note: This is a bit of literary license. Because Millay had many people with similar names in her life (Kathleen Millay, Catherine Filene, Katherine Tilt, etc.), I chose to give Catherine Filene the nickname Fil. Given that Millay knew a "Jack" (Margaret) and "Charlie" (Charlotte Babcock Sills), it seemed natural that Filene would give herself a masculine moniker just between them. I trust it will also help the reader identify the characters.

[313] Epstein, Daniel Mark, ed. *Rapture and Melancholy: The Diaries of Edna St. Vincent Millay.* (Connecticut: Yale University Press, 2022). P. 173

"*Friday, November 7, 1913*
Dead to the world.

Came home from German—cut it and went to bed. Too tired to go to the first Hall Play.

Geometry test. Didn't pretend to do it. Instead spent the time writing a letter to Miss Cummings. Hope she's pleased with it. Perhaps I'll be expelled.

Saturday, November 8
Washed this morning. Studied History in the library all afternoon. Miss Conrow, my French instructor, told somebody that I am a very brilliant girl who probably won't stay the year out. She doesn't know that there's nothing else for me to do."

[314] Milford, Nancy. *Savage Beauty: The Life of Edna St. Vincent Millay* (New York: Random House, 2001) Page 111-112

"… One night I came along in my blanket bathrobe with some books in my arms and started down the hall.

'Oho,' said Catherine Filene. "Where are you going?' 'Where do you s'pose?' said I. And tramped up stairs. You see, it bothers her. Sometimes she comes up when I'm up there—knows I'm up there—and says, 'O, I *beg* your pardon! Perhaps I interrupt. *You two turtledoves!*' And there you are. She's a handsome thing, very boyish, deep rough laugh, but the sweetest, most charming smile when she wants to be decent for a while. Really a fascinating type. Isn't she *wonderful* in that picture? Couldn't you die in her arms? –Fancy two dances with her in that rig and a third one *begged* and almost sworn about right after we'd finished the second! She actually made love to me, the devil, in her uninterested, insolent way."

[315] Milford, Nancy. *Savage Beauty: The Life of Edna St. Vincent Millay* (New York: Random House, 2001) Page 112

"… 'People, my friends & hers, are very much interested in a seemingly new friendship which has sprung up between Catherine Filene & me. Handsome great big child! … People are very disturbed.'

The following day, her entry was even clearer: 'Went down town with Katherine Tilt. … Told her about Catherine Filene purposely to make her jealous, because she's been telling me how much she likes somebody else. It worked beautifully.'

The next day was Sunday, a 'Horrible day' she wrote in her diary. And why? She and Katherine Tilt gave a tea, and Agnes Rogers, her 'sophomore,' among others, came to it. Afterward, 'I just came home & howled over a little thing Katherine did. However, Catherine Filene came in & consoled me beautifully.'"

[316] Milford, Nancy. *Savage Beauty: The Life of Edna St. Vincent Millay* (New York: Random House, 2001) Page 112

"… She's a handsome thing, very boyish, deep rough laugh, but the sweetest, most charming smile when she wants to be decent for a while."

[317] Epstein, Daniel Mark, ed. *Rapture and Melancholy: The Diaries of Edna St. Vincent Millay.* (Connecticut: Yale University Press, 2022). P. 174

"*Monday, December 8*
Katherine felt nervous about what she did last night. She will feel nervouser before it's over. And it will be good for her."

Chapter 23

[318] Epstein, Daniel Mark, ed. *Rapture and Melancholy: The Diaries of Edna St. Vincent Millay.* (Connecticut: Yale University Press, 2022). P. 175

"*Saturday, December 13*
Did 12 in my math note book. Had a nice call on Miss Coggeshall. Was invited to & attended a very exclusive dance in Catherine Filene's room. She & Adele & Harry & I, and the Victor. And some eats. Heaps of fun. Love to dance. And

Catherine makes a wonderful man. She was *swell*-looking & swell-*feeling* last night."

[319]. Epstein, Daniel Mark, ed. *Rapture and Melancholy: The Diaries of Edna St. Vincent Millay.* (Connecticut: Yale University Press, 2022). P. 175
"Friday, December 12
… Wore my tan satin with the train and not much of anything else & felt just like dancing. …"

[320] babel.hathitrust.org/cgi/pt?id=mdp.39015066660336&seq=15&q1=calendar P.5, #15 Note: Original is an image of Vassar's College Calendar indicating that December 19, 1912, was beginning of Christmas break.

Chapter 24

[321] http://nywbry.com/history/
"…Under New Haven control, the New York, Westchester and Boston railroad went through many changes from its original plan. Because the original NYW&B had already spent a considerable amount of real estate and construction, they chose to use its franchise, though somewhat modified. With recent successes in electrifying its mainline, it was decided that the NYW&B would also be all electric. Two additional tracks for Westchester were built along the Harlem River Branch from West Farms to the New Haven's existing Harlem River passenger terminal.

The next two years saw the most magnificent railroad property ever constructed suddenly appear on the landscape of Westchester County. Banking that the city would continue to grow northward, and that large populations would be moving to the suburbs, the NYW&B stood ready to serve them. It can be argued that the facilities were the most attractive built new for any railroad of the time.

The NYW&B opened for service in May 29, 1912. Even though construction crews rushed to finish the work not all the facilities were completed in time for opening day. The large E 180th St. station was not ready in time, so trains left from a temporary arrangement at Adams St. until the grand depot opened. The White Plains terminal was not ready either, so trains terminated at Mamaroneck Avenue until July."

[322] Milford, Nancy. *Savage Beauty: The Life of Edna St. Vincent Millay* (New York: Random House, 2001) Page 113
"Christmas break provided her with another chance to sharpen her wiles: Witter Bynner and Arthur Hooley would both be spending part of the holidays with the Kennerley's in Mamaroneck. This time, meeting Bynner's train, she arranged herself against the door of the Kennerley's car—'sort of leaning out & when I caught sight of *Him* I leaned out taller & just looked at him & when he caught sight of me he—he—he just *gusp* & lunged right at me &—oh, it was wonderful—he didn't take his eyes off me a minute,—I apologized for my 'décolleté'; by which she meant she hadn't worn a petticoat."

[323] Milford, Nancy. *Savage Beauty: The Life of Edna St. Vincent Millay* (New York: Random House, 2001) Page 113
"… Oh, girls, I have wanted Witter Bynner to really—*put down his paper & look at me* --& now he has."

[324] https://www.bynnerfoundation.org/witterbynner/index.htm
"… His long career began during his undergraduate days at Harvard, where he was graduated summa cum laude in 1902."

[325] Millay, E.S.V. *Collected Poems*. (New York: Harper & Row, 1956) P. 34 "Sorrow."

"Sorrow like a ceaseless rain
    Beats upon my heart.
People twist and scream in pain, —
Dawn will find them still again;
This has neither wax nor wane,
    Neither stop nor start.

People dress and go to town:
    I sit in my chair.
All my thoughts are slow and brown:
Standing up or sitting down
Little matters, or what gown
    Or what shoes I wear."

[326] Epstein, Daniel. *What Lips My Lips Have Kissed: The Loves and Love Poems of Edna St. Vincent Millay.* (New York: Henry Holt and Company, 2001) P. 87

"She arranged to spend a day or two again with Hooley at the cottage in Mamaroneck after Christmas 1913. She would always go to him under the cover of a weekend visit to the Kennerleys, who countenanced the affair. It may indeed have given Mitchell a bargaining edge in purchasing the poet's first book.

Arthur made a crackling fire in the hearth. He admired her long green dress and made a fuss over her 'princess slippers'."

[327] Jackson, Timothy F. *Into the World's Great Heart: Selected Letters of Edna St. Vincent Millay* (New Haven, CT: Yale University Press, 2023). P. 73

"[September 6, 1915]

…

Arthur, I have the most beautiful blue cape with a hood on it,—bright light blue. You would love it. It was bought in London,—at Liberty's—& given to me. —Do you remember my princess slippers?

…"

[328] Epstein, Daniel. *What Lips My Lips Have Kissed: The Loves and Love Poems of Edna St. Vincent Millay.* (New York: Henry Holt and Company, 2001) P. 87

"Arthur made a crackling fire in the hearth. He admired her long green dress and made a fuss over her 'princess slippers.' He was sad, always sad. The Englishman longed for his native land, and spoke nostalgically of the hills and heaths and castles, quoting for her the new verses of Rupert Brooke: 'If I should die, think only this of me: / That there's a corner of a frozen field / That is forever England.'"

[329] Jackson, Timothy F. *Into the World's Great Heart: Selected Letters of Edna St. Vincent Millay* (New Haven, CT: Yale University Press, 2023). P. 85

Note: From a letter dated January 1, 1916, to Arthur Hooley.

"… This year, for a course in philosophy, I read the Descartes *Second Meditation* in the original Latin—from pure vanity, Arthur, and a passion, which is strong in me, for intellectual adventure."

[330] Epstein, Daniel. *What Lips My Lips Have Kissed: The Loves and Love Poems of Edna St. Vincent Millay.* (New York: Henry Holt and Company, 2001) P. 87-88

"'In you there are so many beautiful possibilities—I would be loathe to leave you with any memory that you might ever wish to obliterate,' he said in his doleful, lisping voice."

[331] E Millay, E.S.V. *Collected Poems.* (New York: Harper & Row, 1956) P. 14 "Interim".

"…

… Here 'twas if a weed-choked gate

Had opened at my touch, and I had stepped

into some long-forgot, enchanted, strange,

Sweet garden of thousand years ago

And suddenly thought, 'I have been here before!'"

[332] Millay, E.S.V. *Collected Poems.* (New York: Harper & Row, 1956) P. 17 "Interim".

"…

That day—that day you picked the first sweet-pea,—

And brought it in to show me! I recall

With terrible distinctness how the smell

Of your cool gardens drifted in with you.

I know, you held it up for me to see

And flushed because I looked not at the flower,

But at your face; and when behind my look

You saw such unmistakable intent

You laughed and brushed your flower against my lips.

…"

[333] Millay, E.S.V. *Collected Poems.* (New York: Harper & Row, 1956). P. 18 "Interim".

"…

That first sweet-pea! I wonder where it is.

…"

[334] Epstein, Daniel. *What Lips My Lips Have Kissed: The Loves and Love Poems of Edna St. Vincent Millay.* (New York: Henry Holt and Company, 2001) P. 88.

"The first night she visited the brown-shingled cottage with the big fireplace, she took a seat across from the glowing hearth and he said to her: 'Don't sit there Edna—I might want you there always.' He recited some verses of his own, and then she read aloud to him Swinburne's 'Triumph of Time.'"

[335] Milford, Nancy. *Savage Beauty: The Life of Edna St. Vincent Millay* (New York: Random House, 2001) Page 113 and Epstein, Daniel. *What Lips My Lips Have Kissed: The Loves and Love Poems of Edna St. Vincent Millay.* (New York: Henry Holt and Company, 2001) P. 88.

"... On her last night, Arthur Hooley, who had stayed up after everyone else had gone to bed, delighted her with a compliment. I'm not in love with him, exactly, she wrote home. I love him, he's such an old dear, and half the time such an old bear."

And

"... She recalled one night in the lamplit library of her publisher's mansion, when Arthur drew her aside and bid her smell his linen handkerchief, *'saturated*, it must have been, with eau de cologne.' And he wickedly told her, who was giddy with love for him: 'One can get on without women, if he has perfumes… and vermouth,' a remark that she fondly recalled as unpleasant but characteristic, thrillingly decadent."

[336] Epstein, Daniel. *What Lips My Lips Have Kissed: The Loves and Love Poems of Edna St. Vincent Millay.* (New York: Henry Holt and Company, 2001) P. 88.

"... He recited some verses of his own, and then she read aloud to him Swinburne's 'Triumph of Time.'"

[337] Millay, E.S.V. *Collected Poems.* (New York: Harper & Row, 1956) P. 575 "Sonnet xv".

"…
Yours is a face of which I can forget
The colour and the features, every one,
The words not ever, and the smiles not yet;

But in your day this moment is the sun
Upon a hill, after the sun has set."

Chapter 25

[338] Epstein, Daniel Mark, ed. *Rapture and Melancholy: The Diaries of Edna St. Vincent Millay.* (Connecticut: Yale University Press, 2022). P. 176.
"*Wednesday, December 24*
Went to the Knights of Pythias dance with Norma and Wumps—and drew the turkey! Didn't even know there was a turkey till they handed around the little slips. But, oh, what fun to bring it home to mother! Christmas dinner! And we hadn't really known what we were going to have."

[339] Epstein, Daniel Mark, ed. *Rapture and Melancholy: The Diaries of Edna St. Vincent Millay.* (Connecticut: Yale University Press, 2022). P. 175-176.
"*Friday, December 19*
'Lower 3, please,' the conductor just said and I handed out my tickets through the slit in the green curtain. —I am on my way home. Had 'seven hours in New York' this afternoon & spent them at the Training School. —I am going to write a story about a girl in a sleeper who pins her skirt to the curtain & pins a man's back right in with it. His coat, I mean. —Well, when I wake up, I can say, 'Today I'll see them.'"

[340] Epstein, Daniel Mark, ed. *Rapture and Melancholy: The Diaries of Edna St. Vincent Millay.* (Connecticut: Yale University Press, 2022). P. 176.
"*Saturday, December 20*
… For the bridge was down at Wiscasset & we all had to pile into automobiles & be toted across the other bridge to So. Newcastle (I guess) where another train was waiting for us. …"

[341] Epstein, Daniel Mark, ed. *Rapture and Melancholy: The Diaries of Edna St. Vincent Millay.* (Connecticut: Yale University Press, 2022). P. 176
"*Tuesday, December 23*
Went up to Uncle Bert's and stayed all night with them. I wonder why people love me so."

[342] Ibid.

[343] Macdougall, Allan Ross, editor. *Letters of Edna St. Vincent Millay* (New York: Grosset and Dunlap, 1952). P. 38
"April 12, 1913
Dear Spiritual Advisor,—
…"

[344] Millay, E.S.V. *Collected Poems*. (New York: Harper & Row, 1956) P. 35 "Tavern".

> "I'll keep a little tavern
>> Below the high hill's crest,
> Wherein all grey-eyed people
>> May sit them down to rest.
>
>> …"

[345] https://knightsofpythias.com and http://pythias.org
"…Our fraternal order follows three distinguishing principles, *Friendship, Charity, and Benevolence*."

[346] Epstein, Daniel Mark, ed. *Rapture and Melancholy: The Diaries of Edna St. Vincent Millay.* (Connecticut: Yale University Press, 2022). P. 176
"*Wednesday, December 24*
Went to the Knights of Pythias dance with Norma & Wumps,—and drew the turkey! Didn't even know there was a turkey till they handed around the little slips. But, oh, what fun to bring it home to Mother! —Christmas dinner! & we hadn't really known what we were going to have."

[347] *The Ellsworth American* newspaper. Vol. LIX No. 52, December 24, 1913 Note: From photostat of old paper. Weather report in second column mid-page below 'Local Affairs':
"… Weather in Ellsworth for week ending at Midnight Tuesday, December 23, 1913 … Wednesday…12 m 36 …"

[348] Epstein, Daniel Mark, ed. *Rapture and Melancholy: The Diaries of Edna St. Vincent Millay.* (Connecticut: Yale University Press, 2022). P. 177
"*Friday, December 26*
Had a little party for the old crowd but it stormed terribly & and only Mart & Jesse who lived near came.

Fritz sent me a book that we had talked about last summer & I hadn't read. Good old Fritz. So he doesn't forget.
_____ "

Chapter 26

[349] Macdougall, Allan Ross, editor. *Letters of Edna St. Vincent Millay* (New York: Grosset and Dunlap, 1952). P. 48 Note: From early 1914 letter to Arthur Ficke:
"…

I hate this pink-and-gray college. If there had been a college in *Alice in Wonderland* it would be this college. Every morning when I awake I swear, I say, 'Damn this pink-and-gray college!'"

[350] Millay, E.S.V. *Collected Poems*. (New York: Harper & Row, 1956) P. 286 "Childhood Is the Kingdom Where Nobody Dies".
"…

Nobody that matters, that is. Distant relatives of course

Die, whom one is never seen or has seen for an hour,

And they gave one candy in a pink-and-green stripéd bag, or a
    jack-knife,

And went away, and cannot really be said to have lived at all.
…"

[351] Note: Arthur Hooley stopped editing Kennerley's The Forum in 1915, but Millay was writing him in late December that same year, when he would have turned forty-one. Millay also wrote to him as late as 1917 and in a letter dated April 1928, she wrote Kennerley expressing her shock that Arthur was dead. Consequently, I am guessing that he is over dramatizing whatever was ailing him. He may have been sickly given his heavy smoking and drinking, but I doubt he was dying in late 1913.

[352] https://prabook.com/web/arthur.hooley/1084167

"… Hooley, Arthur was born on December 29, 1874 in Newcastle-under-Lyme, England. Son of Samuel J and Ellen Barlow (Wood) Hooley. Educated Newcastle high school and University of London. Unmarried. Came to America, 1908. Editor the forum, July, 1910 to October, 1915."

[353] Jackson, Timothy F. *Into the World's Great Heart: Selected Letters of Edna St. Vincent Millay* (New Haven, CT: Yale University Press, 2023). P. 84 Note: From December 27, 1915, letter to Arthur Hooley.
"…

Arthur, do you know who said; 'I sometimes think that all great passion is like a kiss in mid-battle, —a difficult peace between oil and water, between candles and dark night'? Do you not think it very beautiful?—'A *difficult peace'!"*

[354] Epstein, Daniel. *What Lips My Lips Have Kissed: The Loves and Love Poems of Edna St. Vincent Millay.* (New York: Henry Holt and Company, 2001) P. 89

"He scolded her for this, and for childishly surprising him at work at his desk, and for the way sometimes she would cross her fingers about her knees, pulling one knee toward her. 'Don't do that, Edna, it makes your hands look ugly.'"

[355] Millay, E.S.V. *Collected Poems.* (New York: Harper & Row, 1956) P. 243 "Portrait".

"…

Here in this room without fire, without comfort of any kind,
Reading aloud to me immortal page after page conceived in a
   mortal mind.
…"

[356] Scott, Sir Walter. *Ivanhoe. (*eBook: www.gutenberg.org, June 2, 2021.) Chapter 33

"'…And there is mine in return,' said the Knight, 'and I hold it honored by being clasped with yours. For he that does good, having the unlimited power to do evil, deserves praise not only for the good which he performs, but for the evil which he forbears. Fare thee well, gallant Outlaw!' Thus parted the fair fellowship: and He of the Fetterlock, mounting upon his strong war-horse, rode off through the forest.
…"

[357] Jackson, Timothy F. *Into the World's Great Heart: Selected Letters of Edna St. Vincent Millay* (New Haven, CT: Yale University Press, 2023). P. 91 Note: From letter of February 28, 1916, to Arthur Hooley.

"This is a strange place. I had known, but I had not realized, until I came here, how greatly one girl's beauty & presence can disturb another's peace of mind, —more still, sometimes, her beauty and absence. There are Anactorias here for any Sappho,—and I am glad, whenever I think of it. That I have never felt moved to say harsh & foolish things about an ancient Greek philosopher or a modern English poet, whom the world has condemned & punished. It might better have been said, not 'let him who is without sin among you' but 'let him among you who has sinned all sins, cast the first stone.' —But perhaps a poet does not need to sin at all, except in the heart, in order to know that it is no question of stone-throwing at all. And it often happens that I am very, very sorry for everybody.

Since this is an observation, & not a confession, it is not irrelevant. For up here, while some of us are thinking of the rest of us, the rest of us are thinking of you, & men like you,—I mean to say, unlike you."

[358] Milford, Nancy. *Savage Beauty: The Life of Edna St. Vincent Millay* (New York: Random House, 2001) Page 126

"I want to write to you. I have nothing to say,—except a thousand things which I may or may not have said when this letter is done. But I am sick of never speaking to you any more. Once I knew you, and loved to be with you, and I would love to be with you tonight. I shall live quite comfortably to the end of my life—after tonight—without you, without ever seeing you again; I shall marry one of the three men that I love, and have a wonderful time; but tonight I would rather write to you. ...

Arthur, don't say to me, 'Child, child,' I am not a child in love with you, to be patted and sent away, or to be scolded and shaken. I am an almost reasonable human being, who has not spoken to anyone for a long time. ..."

[359] Epstein, Daniel. *What Lips My Lips Have Kissed: The Loves and Love Poems of Edna St. Vincent Millay.* (New York: Henry Holt and Company, 2001) P. 89

"Most of all he scolded his 'child' for loving him, even as he drew her to him. He was ill, he was getting old, he was dying of some mysterious illness neither he nor any physician could understand and that neither drug nor time nor love could cure. She must leave him, she must not telephone or write; they must be content with a love spiritual, above the flesh, eternal and divine. But then he sent her love poems, and after months of tormented correspondence on both sides he would wearily consent at last to another tryst at his apartment on Lexington Ave. in New York. There in the darkness he would let her have her way with him, and he might use her in the way he would use a wicked little schoolboy who would not do as he had been told."

[360] Jackson, Timothy F. *Into the World's Great Heart: Selected Letters of Edna St. Vincent Millay* (New Haven, CT: Yale University Press, 2023). P. 88 Note: From February 3, 1916, letter to Arthur Hooley.

"…

I have nothing to say to you, —though I fancy that if I were with you that might be different. —It is only that I do not wish you to wonder why I do not write—which perhaps you had not noticed at all.

…

'The fire is out and spent the warmth thereof.' It is true. —The fire is out by which you stood & said aloud those lovely verses—and your voice shook at the end. —The fire is out by which we sat while I read to you—the *Triumph of Time* or *Anactoria*. —The fire is out which burned that first night in your little house, when you said to me, 'Don't sit there, Edna. I might want you there always.' —and again, 'It's great fun living alone, sometimes.' —You did not really love me then. —But I think you do now. —Now that the fire is out."

Chapter 27

[361] Macdougall, Allan Ross, editor. *Letters of Edna St. Vincent Millay* (New York: Grosset and Dunlap, 1952). P. 33 Note: From a letter to Arthur Ficke dated February 9, 1913.

"…

Yesterday I got a note from Sara Teasdale, inviting me to take tea with her. Whaddayouknowaboutthat! …"

[362] https://www.vassar.edu/specialcollections/exhibit-highlights/2016-2020/millay-austerlitz/checklist.html

"Case 1: Acting

26 October 1914: Princess Daisy of Pretentia in the 1914 Sophomore Party

- Program
- Party Invitation from the Class of 1917 to the class of 1918
- Photograph of Millay and fellow actors by Edmond Wolven"

[363] Milford, Nancy. *Savage Beauty: The Life of Edna St. Vincent Millay* (New York: Random House, 2001) Page 113
"The *Miscellany* is offering four prizes of fifteen dollars each for the best poem, best story, best essay, & best play,' Vincent wrote home on her return to Vassar in January. ..."

[364] Milford, Nancy. *Savage Beauty: The Life of Edna St. Vincent Millay* (New York: Random House, 2001) Page 114
"A month and a half later, on February 23, she wrote her mother again about 'Interim.' This time she'd made-up her mind: 'It would make a bigger hit in a college full of women than anywhere else in the world and might do a lot for me, help me get a scholarship for next year, you know.'"

[365] Epstein, Daniel. *What Lips My Lips Have Kissed: The Loves and Love Poems of Edna St. Vincent Millay.* (New York: Henry Holt and Company, 2001) P. 47
"... 'Interim' is a curious and enigmatic poem, an elegy for a departed girl. When Millay submitted the piece to a writing class at Vassar in 1914, it so stymied the professor that he suggested she add the Browning-esque stage direction 'A Man Speaks'. She graciously agreed, to please him, but later she deleted the stage direction when the poem was published in her first book.
...
Like 'Lycidas,' 'Adonais,' and other classic elegies Millay admired, 'Interim' mingles memories of the lost beloved with meditations upon death, mortality, and the dynamics of faith."

[366] Millay, E.S.V. *Collected Poems.* (New York: Harper & Row, 1956) P. 8 "Renascence".
"...
Into the earth I sank till I
Full six feet under ground did lie,

And sank no more,—there is no weight
Can follow here, however great.
…"

[367] Epstein, Daniel. *What Lips My Lips Have Kissed: The Loves and Love Poems of Edna St. Vincent Millay.* (New York: Henry Holt and Company, 2001) P. 47-48
"We know the book, the table, and the room very well. This is a picture of Vincent's own bedroom and secret diary, an 8 ½-by-6 ½-inch, brown bound notebook, and the description of writer and handwriting ('You were so small and wrote so brave a hand!') and other details indicate that the subject of 'Interim' is the poet herself. …"

[368] Epstein, Daniel. *What Lips My Lips Have Kissed: The Loves and Love Poems of Edna St. Vincent Millay.* (New York: Henry Holt and Company, 2001) P. 46
"… For instance, her first substantial long poem, 'Interim,' a mysterious elegy of more than two hundred lines, was written in late September of 1911, in the same notebook that contains an extraordinary 'Essay on Faith.' This thousand-word essay is a precise philosophical statement of Millay's belief system, as it emerged out of her recent crisis of faith.

> 'Things are real only as we believe them. Just as surely as each is the center of his universe, just so surely is his universe bounded by the circumference of his life. His believings are the radii he sends out to the edge of things and on the edge of things does each find its corresponding belief. …"

[369] Millay, E.S.V. *Collected Poems.* (New York: Harper & Row, 1956) P. 13 "Renascence".
"…
The world stands out on either side
No wider than the heart is wide;
…"

[370]. Milford, Nancy. *Savage Beauty: The Life of Edna St. Vincent Millay* (New York: Random House, 2001) Page 114
"Don't worry about your bad, bad run-away child. … All that keeps me from writing long, long letters about Vassar is that I'm getting so crazy

about Vassar & so wrapped up in Vassar doings, that I don't have so much time as I used to have when I just liked it well enough. ... But oh, I love my college, *my* college, *my college!* Last night by the light of the moon we ran into a band of Seniors & a few others whom we knew out in the athletic circles on the bleachers, strumming the mandolin & singing, & we got boosted up along o' the rest and sang, too, —and the moon shined bright as day & the warm wind blowed, and oh, didn't we love our college! —I thought—Lord love you—'If Mother could only see me now!'"

[371] Epstein, Daniel Mark, ed. *Rapture and Melancholy: The Diaries of Edna St. Vincent Millay.* (Connecticut: Yale University Press, 2022). P. 177
"*January 19, 1914 Memoranda*
Tonight Katherine and I came together with a crash that smashed us all up, and when we picked up the pieces we put them together as they should be and now everything is quite wonderful. God, if you are looking, bless her, please[.]"
[372] Macdougall, Allan Ross, editor. *Letters of Edna St. Vincent Millay* (New York: Grosset and Dunlap, 1952). P. 50 Note: From letter dated February 24, 1914, To Cora Millay.
"...We hate to go to chapel, and cut whenever we can, and we *do* miss something, though I couldn't for the life of me say what, that we ought to have. We've got so sort of sceptic [sic] and scoffy here that if anybody has a real thought she's ashamed of it & keeps it to herself & we don't get to know each other's best. ..."
[373] Macdougall, Allan Ross, editor. *Letters of Edna St. Vincent Millay* (New York: Grosset and Dunlap, 1952). P. 49 Note: From letter dated February 24, 1914, To Cora Millay.
"Dear Mother,
    Will you lend me, and send to me, your Bible? ..."
[374] Milford, Nancy. *Savage Beauty: The Life of Edna St. Vincent Millay* (New York: Random House, 2001) Page 115
"...
'O girls, I have saved the best for last! It is what I needed more than anything else in the world, perhaps—an afternoon dress. Sweller than anything you ever saw, simply regal in every scrap of material, unquestionably this seasons. ...*O, girls*!

...'"

³⁷⁵ https://vintagedancer.com/1900s/1910s-capsule-wardrobe-what-clothing-cost/

"... Clothing was replaced only as needed, not because the fashion trends changed."

³⁷⁶ Macdougall, Allan Ross, editor. *Letters of Edna St. Vincent Millay* (New York: Grosset and Dunlap, 1952). P. 50-51 From letter dated 1914 to the Millay family.

"... Next week is mid-years and if I perish I perish. I shall flunk everything but French and that only because no one in the French department would have the nerve to flunk me,—after promoting me & putting [me] into the French Club ...

O, about flunking my exams,— I shall flunk History and probably Geometry, and I may pass German and possibly Old English. That's the way I stand at the present. ..."

³⁷⁷ Note: Suffragist Inez Millholland (1886-1916) was married to Eugen Jan Boissevain at the time. He would marry Millay in 1923.

³⁷⁸ Daniels, Elizabeth A. *Bridges to the World: Henry Noble MacCracken and Vassar College* (Clinton Corners, NY: College Avenue Press. 1994) p. 16-18.

"... The ringleader of the faculty revolt, which had already been well underway when McCracken arrived at Vassar, was the maverick Lucy Maynard Salmon, a distinguished historian and one of the leading spokespersons of the faculty. Completely unbeknownst to McCracken, who had not met her prior to his arrival at Vassar, her sentiments about reorganizing college governance had been placed before the national reading public in September 1913 when *The Popular Science Monthly* had published an article entitled 'The Next College President.'

Although it was attributed to a 'Near Professor' and published anonymously, the article was definitely written by Vassar's Lucy Salmon, who was no 'Near Professor', but a most unconventional Full' one, who had been at Vassar since 1887. ... Continuing her analysis of various categories, she found that the force of tradition is strong and tradition makes the student, at least in theory passive and receptive rather than active and creative. ... The article, in short, constituted an indictment of the archaic, authoritarian system that prevailed in colleges and universities just before World War I and colorfully expressed a belief that a more organic system could take its place, under forward-looking presidents of the future."

[379] www.Poetryfoundation.org/poets/harriet-monroe

"... Monroe's commitment to this approach ensured the magazine's [*Poetry*] success: 'The Open Door will be the policy of this magazine—may the great poet we are looking for never find it shut, or half-shut, against his ample genius! To this end the editors ... desire to print the best English verse ... being written today, regardless of where, by whom, or under what theory of art it is written.'"

[380] Milford, Nancy. *Savage Beauty: The Life of Edna St. Vincent Millay* (New York: Random House, 2001) Page 116

"It was only this once that Cora indicated how beyond mere indebtedness to Miss Dow she felt herself to be. 'I shall be on my knees crawling around after Miss Dow, yet.'"

[381] Jackson, Timothy F. *Into the World's Great Heart: Selected Letters of Edna St. Vincent Millay* (New Haven, CT: Yale University Press, 2023). P. 60

"April 27, 1914

Dear Kathleen,

Can you ever forgive me for not writing you a letter on your birthday? —I have been expiring with tooth-ache, hon', & you know what that means. I have had to stay away from classes for two days, in spite of my good resolution not to cut this spring."

[382] Milford, Nancy. *Savage Beauty: The Life of Edna St. Vincent Millay* (New York: Random House, 2001) Page 116

"But the news in the last letter of Vincent's freshman year was the best. On May 21, 1914, she was notified that 'Interim' had won the Miscellany Prize Contest for best poem. She sent the prize money right home.

> 'Please, please don't feel bad that I've let it go for so little. I shall do more, much better, or it won't matter. And it will mean a great deal to me here, both with the faculty and the girls. Please don't mind, dear.'"

[383] Millay, E.S.V. *Collected Poems.* (New York: Harper & Row, 1956) P. 562 "Sonnet ii".

"Time does not bring relief; you all have lied
Who told me time would ease me of my pain!
I miss him in the weeping of the rain;
I want him at the shrinking of the tide;
The old snows melt from every mountain-side,
And last year's leaves are smoke in every lane;
But last year's bitter loving must remain
Heaped on my heart, and my old thoughts abide.
There are a hundred places where I fear
To go, --so with his memory they brim.
And entering with relief some quiet place
Where never fell his foot or shone his face
I say, 'There is no memory of him here!'
And so stand stricken, so remembering him."

[384] Macdougall, Allan Ross, editor. *Letters of Edna St. Vincent Millay* (New York: Grosset and Dunlap, 1952). P. 51-52

"[May 7, 1914]

Dear Mother,

I love you. In a few minutes I'm going to be home. We've drawn lots for next year's rooms, and I have a perfectly wonderful single in North, a corner room with two windows & lots of room for everything. North was the most popular hall."

[385] Milford, Nancy. *Savage Beauty: The Life of Edna St. Vincent Millay* (New York: Random House, 2001) Page 107-108

"Her history exam now lies in the vaults of Vassar's rare books library. Where C. Mildred Thompson gave it a 1-, with the following comments: 'No understanding of History, grand epithets.' Millay had begun by writing, 'I was prepared in American History at my home in Camden, Maine, in the hammock, on the roof, and behind the stove.' That was not guaranteed to win a serious young instructor of history to her side. Her examination paper was six pages long, marked by cheek and ignorance. At its close she added this note:

'At precisely that point the pleasant lady in an Alice-blue coat, who I wish might be my instructor in History, requests us all to bring our papers to a close. As I know a great deal about American History which I haven't had a chance to say, I am sorry, but obedient.'

There is every reason to doubt her. Thirty-eight years later, C. Mildred Thompson, who had saved the examination and was then dean of Vassar College, explained why she reckoned it as a Failure. The answers were 'at large.' ... and did not bear any particular relation to the questions asked.' That attitude, with its saucy insolence, was a signal of the success and failure that would mark Vincent Millay's entire career—with both faculty and students—at Vassar."

[386] Milford, Nancy. *Savage Beauty: The Life of Edna St. Vincent Millay* (New York: Random House, 2001). P. 107

"She had won Miss McCaleb to her just as surely as she had Miss Dow. But when classes began on September 22, Vincent learned that although she passed geometry, 'I flunked—just flunked' both algebra and history. She'd been certain she had passed history, 'but Miss Thompson was funny & didn't like the way I did it. She told me so. We stood on the campus an hour day before yesterday, swapping insults. We are born enemies.'"

Chapter 28

[387] Macdougall, Allan Ross, editor. *Letters of Edna St. Vincent Millay* (New York: Grosset and Dunlap, 1952). P. 52 and 55-56 Note: From May 7, 1914, letter to Cora Millay.
"...But I tell you I'm all ready to be home.—What a wonderful summer we'll have, 'spite of Latin Prose, & all the rest! ... "

And
November the seventeenth, 1915
My Dear Dr. McCracken,

I have written to my mother, telling her what you said to me yesterday about the possibility of Kathleen's coming here. Kathleen herself is not at home now, and unless Mother is able to get together the information you want, I may not be able to get it to you until sometime after Thanksgiving.

...
    If the entrance requirements are made as sympathetic to my sister as they were made to myself—then there will be no doubt about her preparation to enter next fall. I had my arms full of conditions when they let me in,—but they are all gone now—except that I flunked gym last spring! —If they will only be as nice to her—after she is once *in* here there will be no question about her suitability—as her high school record will show you."

[388] Macdougall, Allan Ross, editor. *Letters of Edna St. Vincent Millay* (New York: Grosset and Dunlap, 1952). P. 52 Note: From May 7, 1914, letter to Cora Millay.

"...
I shall have the cutest room. I am going to get me a little alcohol tea-kettle so I can have tea, and bring back my lovely tea-set for show, & use my cute one. I'm going to subscribe for a couple of good magazines & a newspaper, so the room will look alive, so to speak. And I'm going to try most always to have a flower. I'll have to buy a little furniture—we get it here second hand from the seniors. Desk and extra cot, etc."

[389] Milford, Nancy. *Savage Beauty: The Life of Edna St. Vincent Millay* (New York: Random House, 2001) Page 117

    "But her modesty had its limits. 'Besides having beautiful hair, an extraordinary good forehead in spite of the freckles, an impudent, aggressive, & critical nose, and a mysterious mouth,' she wrote, 'I have, artistically, & even technically, an unusually beautiful throat.'"

[390] Milford, Nancy. *Savage Beauty: The Life of Edna St. Vincent Millay* (New York: Random House, 2001) Page 97

"... Then, too, Norma was 'Sick of staying in Camden Burg *all* the time meself. Bah. (graceful gesture here.) ... Do you ever feel like you wanted to see Muvver, Wump & Hunkus? Don't believe you have half time enough to get lonesome do you? Gorry I do & don't care one dam who knows it.'"

[391] Epstein, Daniel. *What Lips My Lips Have Kissed: The Loves and Love Poems of Edna St. Vincent Millay.* (New York: Henry Holt and Company, 2001) P. 89

"On September 8, 1914, Vassar sophomore Edna St. Vincent Millay sat down to breakfast in the dining room of the new Plaza Hotel on Fifth Avenue with her friend the dapper publisher. Mitchell Kennerley had grown up in England and she admired his accent. When they finished their cantaloupe and sweet rolls, their toast and marmalade, they sipped coffee and Mr. Kennerley offered the poet a cigarette from a silver case. She declined, concerned there might be someone in the room, 'who knows I do not smoke.' But as soon as they returned to the publisher's office downtown she gratefully accepted her first cigarette of what had already been a long day."

[392] Ibid.

[393] Ibid.

[394] Epstein, Daniel. *What Lips My Lips Have Kissed: The Loves and Love Poems of Edna St. Vincent Millay.* (New York: Henry Holt and Company, 2001) P. 89

"… Then back at his office he made such a fuss over her she had to laugh: he found a jar of Page & Shaw orange candies and stuck it in her bag. He pulled a big novel off the shelf he wanted her to read, along with a box of imported chocolates; and as the gifts piled up he rang for his stenographer to ship all of them to Vassar. He wanted her to know what else he could do for her."

[395] Millay, E.S.V. *Collected Poems.* (New York: Harper & Row, 1956) P. 83-87 "The Poet and His Book".

"Me, by no means dead
 In that hour, but surely
When this book, unread,
 Rots to earth obscurely,
And no more to any breast,
 Close against the clamoring swelling
 Of the thing there is no telling,
Are these pages pressed!

…

Boys and girls that lie
 Whispering in the hedges,
Do not let me die,
 Mix me with your pledges;
Boys and girls that slowly walk
 Into the woods, and weep, and quarrel,

>   Staring past the pink wild laurel,
> Mix me with your talk,
>
> Do not let me die!
> …"

Chapter 29

[396] Milford, Nancy. *Savage Beauty: The Life of Edna St. Vincent Millay* (New York: Random House, 2001) Page 118.
"Being on campus was more expensive than McGlynn's. Vincent's twenty-dollar-a-month allowance from Miss Dow went like water, but it made 'such a difference in knowing people, and North is *full* of the best people in our class… and some awfully nice Juniors.'"

[397] Milford, Nancy. *Savage Beauty: The Life of Edna St. Vincent Millay* (New York: Random House, 2001) Page 118
"… One of those Juniors was Elaine Ralli. From her first mention of Elaine, her diary entries are full of ambiguity. But the crucial note will be her use of the masculine pronoun—Elaine has become a boy.

> 'Elaine is jealous when Bad Vincent loves anybody but hisself. He is almost even jealous when Bad Vincent loves *him*, because that is his nature.'

She doesn't explain who the jealous Elaine is until her next letter home, on November 4, 1914.

> 'She's Elaine Ralli, a Junior, another hockey hero, cheer-leader, rides horseback a lot, very boyish, & makes a lot of noise, not tall, but all muscle.'"

[398] Milford, Nancy. *Savage Beauty: The Life of Edna St. Vincent Millay* (New York: Random House, 2001) Page 122
"On her birthday, Elaine had sent her a great armful of roses, 'big tan-pink roses mixed with pussy willows.'"

[399] Milford, Nancy. *Savage Beauty: The Life of Edna St. Vincent Millay* (New York: Random House, 2001). P. xv Note: Milford recounts Norma explaining how hard it was to burn Millay's ivory dildo. However, there is also this unconfirmed tale! canecdotes.blogspot.com/2008/04/whatever-happened-to-edna-st-vincent.html

"… There was an ivory dildo which Norma admitted was difficult to burn, but she had managed."

And

"The Holy Grail, if you will, of literary relics, is an ivory dildo once owned by Edna St. Vincent Millay. The dildo's existence first entered the popular imagination in 2001 with the publication of Nancy Milford's Savage Beauty, a Millay biography. In Milford's preface we get an excerpt from a letter written to her by Edna's sister Norma, in which the latter admits to having burned the famous pole—though it wasn't easy. 'I tossed it in the fire, but it wouldn't catch. It just kept getting blacker and blacker. You know how long it takes to burn one of those things? A lot longer than it takes to cool one down, I'll tell you that much.'

Most people figured that was the end of it; the dildo was buried in a Maine dump, cracked, and finished. But that's just not the case. That dildo's been Canadian-owned for more than fifty years. And if it could speak…Gwen Davies'd [sic] sue it for copyright infringement.

Edna's ivory dildo is kind of a legend in the Canadian literary community."

[400] Millay, E.S.V. *Collected Poems*. (New York: Harper & Row, 1956) P. 292 "Aubade".

"Cool and beautiful as the blossom of the wild carrot
With its crimson central eye,
Round and beautiful as the globe of the onion blossom
Were her pale breasts whereon I laid me down to die.
…"

[401] Millay, E.S.V. *Collected Poems*. (New York: Harper & Row, 1956) Note: Here I have combined the poems "Sappho Crosses the Dark River into Hades" (P. 294) and "Tristan II" (P. 478), so they fold into the narrative in a way that illustrates the extent of Vincent's relationship with Elaine.

From the poem "Sappho Cross the Dark River Into Hades"

"…

That supple back, the strong brown arm,

That curving mouth, the sunburned curls;

…"

And from "Tristan II"

"I still can see

How you hastily and abstractedly flung down

To the floor,

Having raked it, arm after arm,

Over your head,

Your lustrous gown;

And how, before

Its silken susurration had subsided,

We were as close together as it is possible for two people to be.

…"

[402] Milford, Nancy. *Savage Beauty: The Life of Edna St. Vincent Millay* (New York: Random House, 2001) Page 118

"She's just naturally taken me, for better or for worse, and Lord knows why. And the way she treats me is killing. I'll be talking, in the middle of a crowd of people, and if Elaine wants me for anything, the first thing I know she has come and got me, just plain lugged me off to another part of the field. Everybody recognizes the situation, and accepts it unquestioningly, and there's no fuss about it. They just go on talking. And I say, 'Hello, Elaine.'"

[403] Milford, Nancy. *Savage Beauty: The Life of Edna St. Vincent Millay* (New York: Random House, 2001). P. 121 and Macdougall, Allan Ross, editor. *Letters of Edna St. Vincent Millay* (New York: Grosset and Dunlap, 1952). P. 50 Note: From a 1914 letter to the Millay family.

"Finally, Vincent wrote to her 'Dear darling adored Family' on March 8, 1915. Her news was entirely about her performance as Marchbanks in Shaw's *Candida.*"

And

"... no one in the French department would have the nerve to flunk me,--after promoting me & putting into the French club & having me write poems for them and a' that.—Last week they asked me to write a little farewell song to Miss Conrow who is to be gone next semester, & I did, to the tune of 'Au Claire de la Lune'—it's *Little Friend Pierrot* in the school year song-book— & they sang it & everybody was crazy about it, they told me (I was tired and didn't go) and Agnes Rogers told me that M. Bracq said, 'C'est exquis!'"

[404] https://libraryguides.missouri.edu/pricesandwages/1910-1919 Note: See images

[405] Milford, Nancy. *Savage Beauty: The Life of Edna St. Vincent Millay* (New York: Random House, 2001) Page 123-124

"'Elaine is going to ask her mother if she can come to Camden in the summer and *board with us!* She knows all about us. Her people don't, but she does. And I told her like as not she wouldn't get anything to eat. But she says she can live on grape-nuts and salad. She would hire a sail-boat and have a real time. Of course, it's a crazy idea and probably her mother wouldn't let her anyway.'"

[406] Milford, Nancy. *Savage Beauty: The Life of Edna St. Vincent Millay* (New York: Random House, 2001) Page 123

"... 'I'd go anywhere I got the chance. Mother is over her nursing I guess— We will owe three months' rent the first of April and they have been making a deuce of a fuss over it.'"

[407] Milford, Nancy. *Savage Beauty: The Life of Edna St. Vincent Millay* (New York: Random House, 2001) Page 121

"When there was still no word from Vincent, she wrote again just before Vincent's twenty-third birthday, 'Why have we not heard from you? Kathleen can have the Coe fellowship, if I could manage the rest of it. We are trying to see some way out, but you must let them know very soon.'"

[408] Jackson, Timothy F. *Into the World's Great Heart: Selected Letters of Edna St. Vincent Millay* (New Haven, CT: Yale University Press, 2023). P. 93 Note: From letter dated [Spring 1916] to the Millay family.

"I have three poems in the May *Forum* for which Mr. Kennerley has not paid me. I think he has not forgotten it.—At this time of year in college one needs money."

[409] Jackson, Timothy F. *Into the World's Great Heart: Selected Letters of Edna St. Vincent Millay* (New Haven, CT: Yale University Press, 2023). P. 93 Note: From letter dated [Spring 1916] to the Millay family.

"… I have been posing for the art class, and earning a little money that way. It is pleasant, but very hard work."

[410] Jackson, Timothy F. *Into the World's Great Heart: Selected Letters of Edna St. Vincent Millay* (New Haven, CT: Yale University Press, 2023). P. 72 Note: From a letter dated July 1, 1915 to Vassar Dean Ella McCaleb.

"The college treasurer has sent me last semester's bill which he says must be paid before the fifteenth of next month. Of course, as my allowance is not continued during the summer, I have no money with which to pay it. Can it not be carried over until my autumn allowances begin to come? Otherwise I must forfeit my right to my room, it seems. I would have written to the treasurer, but I was afraid he would not understand as well as you would do.

This is the first summer for four years when I have not had to study. And I am resting. It seems so good.

It will be all right about the bill, won't it?"

[411] Milford, Nancy. *Savage Beauty: The Life of Edna St. Vincent Millay* (New York: Random House, 2001) Page 122

"When we *did* get a letter from you, Mother made the remark 'All she said about me was to ask how I was—no other special message—and the letter wasn't even to me.' Please address your letters to her once in a while. You might as well know what she says—Wump and I get it all the time. … Mother said it seems as if you have gone right out of her life … and if Kathleen goes next fall she will probably be the death of me. … You will remember when you went back you were going to send Mother some of the money she lent you. I believe she gave you all she had but you have never even *mentioned* it. How easily you forget."

[412] Milford, Nancy. *Savage Beauty: The Life of Edna St. Vincent Millay* (New York: Random House, 2001) Page 124 and https://vcencyclopedia.vassar.edu/interviews-and-reflections/maccracken-millay/

"But she did. 'The two of them seemed to have made all the arrangements without consulting the mother's about it,' Daisy Rowley wrote to Cora."

And

"You see she was two persons: she was very slatternly most of the time; she looked as if she ought to be thrown in the ash can and on the other hand, she was neat and exquisite and fantastic in her makeup."

[413] Milford, Nancy. *Savage Beauty: The Life of Edna St. Vincent Millay* (New York: Random House, 2001) Page 11

"If Cora looked more like her father than her mother—her hair was a deep brown like his, and her eyes were gray—she was very like her mother in temperament. She was impulsive and possessed what one of her sisters, in an unpublished memoir, would one day call 'a driving force that carried all before it.'"

Chapter 30

[414] Milford, Nancy. *Savage Beauty: The Life of Edna St. Vincent Millay* (New York: Random House, 2001) Page 124

"Girls, I want you to be all beautiful when we get home. Not too gorgeous, you know. Just shirtwaist & skirt, —simple, you know, and your hair all *simple*, Non, not frizzed & false. You see at college, no one ever *hears* of false hair. And don't be *too* powdery. Please excuse me. Wump, you see to it that Non is not too artificial, and Non, you see to it that Wump is not too much in earnest about anything. And both see that Mother is particularly beautiful. Fix her hair lovely, Non, & have everything she wears just as *dainty* as possible, because I want Elaine to fall in love with her, & first impressions mean so much."

[415] Ibid.

[416] Milford, Nancy. *Savage Beauty: The Life of Edna St. Vincent Millay* (New York: Random House, 2001) Page 124 Note: In truth, Vincent warned them about using Djer-Kiss before she came home. I created this scene as a means of illustrating the poet's growing snobbishness toward her sisters and the embarrassment she felt.

"She even fretted about the smell of the house: 'Burn something so it will smell all *homey*, coffee or a cigarette, you know. And if you have *anything* Djer-Kiss about the house or anything that even remotely suggests it, drown it! This is no joke. It makes me sick to vomiting.'"

[417] Jackson, Timothy F. *Into the World's Great Heart: Selected Letters of Edna St. Vincent Millay* (New Haven, CT: Yale University Press, 2023). P. 66-67 Note: From a letter dated December 2, 1914 to her sister Kathleen written by Elaine Ralli. It is fascinating to note this level of familiarity, particularly when later in life Millay's husband performed the same function.

"[In Elaine's hand] Vincent should have written long ago, but as she never yet has done what she should she probably won't begin now. However, 'take it from me' (Excuse the colloquial) she's 'all to the good' (Excuse again). I really can talk straight, and if she wasn't pursuing Greek with such a vengeance she might (?) be writing herself—
Au revoir—
    I'll leave the rest to her
        E.P.R."

[418] Milford, Nancy. *Savage Beauty: The Life of Edna St. Vincent Millay* (New York: Random House, 2001) Page 125 Note: I created this scene based on this photograph. The nature of the couple's relationship would have been obvious and engendered a good deal of gossip in a small town.

"In a snapshot taken that summer, Elaine is sitting at the helm of her little knockabout sloop, *Watch Your Step*, hunched and absorbed, her left hand steady on the tiller. They're sailing directly into the sun. Norma looks away from the camera, while Vincent gazes directly into it, smiling wanly. Elaine's gaze is absorbed and level; her right arm is draped nonchalantly over Vincent's shoulder, her hand just grazing her breast. Vincent tilts her head slightly, leaning into the crook of Elaine's arm."

[419] https://www.sushi-rider.com/friends-of-dorothy/lesbian-terminology-timeline.html

"… Lesbian Term: **Boston Marriage**: Merriam Webster definition of *Boston marriage* = a long-term loving relationship between two women. First known use of *Boston marriage* = 1893, in the meaning defined above (but no citation given).

Although Henry James never used the term *Boston marriage* within his book it is most likely the term *Boston marriage* is derived from his popular novel *The Bostonians* (1886), which centers around a long-term relationship between two unmarried women living together in Boston."

[420] https://www.sushi-rider.com/friends-of-dorothy/lesbian-terminology-timeline.html

"… Queer Term: **Invert**: *Sexual inversion* was a term used by late 19th and early 20th century sexologists, to express the inborn reversal of gender traits i.e., taking on the gender role of the opposite sex."

[421] Milford, Nancy. *Savage Beauty: The Life of Edna St. Vincent Millay* (New York: Random House, 2001) Page 125-126

"…Certainly she was never unaware that he edited one of the finest literary publications in America, but while she played him just as much as he played her, that summer her equilibrium was disturbed, and she let him know. Not *why;* that she cloaked."

Chapter 31

[422] Milford, Nancy. *Savage Beauty: The Life of Edna St. Vincent Millay* (New York: Random House, 2001) Page 127

"Of course, you are the mistress of yr. own productions and as always I do not want to… make unreasonable demands, but tho' I am not a literary woman there are some ways in which I might be of help thro' various friendly avenues. It seems important to me that the next year or two you should guide yr. self & yr. products pretty carefully if the future brings what I believe it should. More of my friends have seen you now and their influence is to be had—if—your trend is in the right direction."

[423] Milford, Nancy. *Savage Beauty: The Life of Edna St. Vincent Millay* (New York: Random House, 2001) Page 127.

"She then suggested that Millay was unaware 'of your dangers both from physical & temperamental conditions.' She did not mean by this that she should guard herself against illness: 'Absorbing attentions from individual students are a hindrance in spite of the pleasant things they bring. Those very things are not the best for yr nature.'"

[424] Milford, Nancy. *Savage Beauty: The Life of Edna St. Vincent Millay* (New York: Random House, 2001) Page 128

"Because of yr. gifts, Vincent, life will present some complicated problems for you—I believe you will have both courage & strength & yet I see such pitfalls. ... I want you always clean, sweet & pure & ready to return your talent to the world enriched by an idealism which means ennobling the lives of others. ..."

[425] Milford, Nancy. *Savage Beauty: The Life of Edna St. Vincent Millay* (New York: Random House, 2001) Page 128

"While she did not define those great fundamentals, it was clear that neither "The Suicide" nor Elaine Ralli was among them. 'This may sound like a sermon,' she continued, 'but is it but it is not so intended; It only means love and interest in a great gift and its setting.'"

[426] MacCracken, Henry Noble. *The Hickory Limb*. (New York: Charles Scribner's Sons. 1950). P. 95 and Milford, Nancy. *Savage Beauty: The Life of Edna St. Vincent Millay* (New York: Random House, 2001) Page 128

"... Other enterprises were later successfully started by students. The Hoot'n Owl, a snack bar, started in Main as a candy kitchen, became a successful after-show tavern, competing with off campus in spite of temperance rules."

And

"One day I was going over to pageant rehearsal & as I came out of Main I met Fran Garver going in. 'Come on back,' she said, '& get some fudge I've made some in the candy-kitchen, & I give it to the people I love.'"

[427] Ibid.

Chapter 32

[428] Epstein, Daniel. *What Lips My Lips Have Kissed: The Loves and Love Poems of Edna St. Vincent Millay.* (New York: Henry Holt and Company, 2001) P. 97

"It is hardly an exaggeration to describe Vincent as the queen of a cult of personality at Vassar. There are romantic photographs in the college archives of her sophomore-year triumph in *The Pageant of Athena*. She stands with a golden crown and necklace, her dress designed after one of Maxwell Parrish's faerie queens, with a long, coarse white cotton skirt gathered into an elaborate girdle belted low on her hips. Two starry-eyed handmaidens in dark tunics and tights hold the corners of her ten-foot-long train. The pageant came as near to a literal coronation of their idol as the sophomore class could devise."

[429] Ibid.

[430] Milford, Nancy. *Savage Beauty: The Life of Edna St. Vincent Millay* (New York: Random House, 2001). P. 24 Note: The *Romeo and Juliet* passage is found in Act 5, Scene 3.

"… What she called "My first encounter with Poetry' was a curiously physical experience: 'I know that it knocked the wind clear out of me, and left me giddy and almost actively sick … when, on opening at random my mother's gargantuan copy of Shakespeare, I read the passage from Romeo and Juliet about the 'dateless bargain' and Death keeping Juliet as beautiful as she was in life, to be his 'paramour.'"

Chapter 33

[431] Milford, Nancy. *Savage Beauty: The Life of Edna St. Vincent Millay* (New York: Random House, 2001) Page 129

"I think no feeling, ever, has come so strongly over me as the all-gone-choking sensation I have when I'm in your room,—when you're gone. The only time I ever felt anything like that was when my mother, whose breath I had been watching for half an hour, smiled at me happily & closed her eyes. I knew she was dead. … Vincent dear, it was because you had the same beautiful expression in your eyes as my dying mother did, that I couldn't bear to have you look at me the night you were so tired. I didn't write to you Thurs night because I knew I'd make love to you. …"

[432] Epstein, Daniel. *What Lips My Lips Have Kissed: The Loves and Love Poems of Edna St. Vincent Millay.* (New York: Henry Holt and Company, 2001) P. 97

"… The letters and diaries reveal unequivocally that she was engaged in both serial and simultaneous sexual relationships with Katherine Tilt, Catherine Filene, Isobel Simpson, and Elaine Ralli. There may have been others who left no paper trail, but certainly those four would have sufficed to keep Vincent entertained when she was not hard at work."

[433] Millay, E.S.V. *Collected Poems*. (New York: Harper & Row, 1956) P. 66 "Journey".

> "Ah, could I lay me down in this long grass
> And close my eyes, and let the quiet wind
> Blow over me—I am so tired, so tired
> Of passing pleasant places! All my life,
> Following Care along the dusty road,
> Have I looked back at loveliness and sighed;
> Yet at my hand an unrelenting hand
> Tugged ever, and I passed. All my life long
> Over my shoulder have I looked at peace;
> And now I fain would lie in this long grass
> And close my eyes.
>
>   Yet onward!
>   Catbirds call
> Through the long afternoon, and creeks at dusk
> Are guttural. Whip-poor-wills wake and cry,
> Drawing the twilight close about their throats.
> Only my heart makes answer. ...
> ..."

[434] Milford, Nancy. *Savage Beauty: The Life of Edna St. Vincent Millay* (New York: Random House, 2001) Page 129.

> "... If you don't marry when we're out of V.C. I shall earn a million and you shall write & we'll divide the money & when it pleases you you'll visit me and do exactly as you wish—"

[435] Milford, Nancy. *Savage Beauty: The Life of Edna St. Vincent Millay* (New York: Random House, 2001) Page 121

"Finally, Vincent wrote to her 'Dear darling adored Family' on March 8, 1915. Her news was entirely about her performance as Marchbanks in Shaw's *Candida:*

A great many people said I made them cry. And certainly in other places I made them laugh.—It's a queer part, you know, of a boy of eighteen, a poet, terribly sensitive to situations and atmosphere, in love with the wife of an English clergyman. ... I had a dark blue Norfolk coat and dark blue trousers that fitted me perfectly and a tan soft shirt and black tie tied in an artist bow—long ends, you know—and those old brown rubber-soled shoes I had last summer & black stockings. Everything fitted me perfectly and I felt *perfectly* at home in the clothes. People told me I reminded them of their brothers the way I walked around and slung my legs over the arms of chairs, etc. ..."

[436] Milford, Nancy. *Savage Beauty: The Life of Edna St. Vincent Millay* (New York: Random House, 2001). P. 129-130. Note: It's worth mentioning that after graduating from Vassar in June 1916, Dr. Elaine Ralli became an authority on diseases of the metabolism and nutrition, as well as an associate professor of medicine at University and Bellevue Hospital, New York. They remained in touch after Vincent's graduation and became lifelong friends. See https://archives.med.nyu.edu/node/3042.

"Elaine was struggling with her own feelings about Millay. In an undated and unsigned, but initialed, letter she began:

'You will excuse the paper I know—You see I must find some common way to begin altho' why I cannot say for certainly you are the most uncommon of people. ... How I want to come back to you—yes I know I have just left—but the longing in me never leaves and this is a night that seems for you and me. ... If I'm not careful I will be covering this paper with words that make a poor endeavor to tell you I love you—the reason I repeat so often those words is because I can really find nothing to express the hunger, the yearning and oh! the love for you—and you are so small! ... You have not spoken to me for so long about your poems and I dare not ask—will you not say something—surely some day you will find time to say something to me. Have you heard the rain? It is cold to-night and I'm too restless for the rain—only for the touch of you—will I ever not want that.'

She told her, again and again, in a tone that became increasingly desperate, not only how much she loved her but that Vincent must never doubt her, that she was the only person in the world for her. And that she was Vincent's child.

A friend who knew Ralli much later in her life said that after a while Elaine 'knew Vincent had dropped her. She had, then or shortly thereafter, but while at Vassar... a serious crack up."

[437] Millay, E.S.V. *Collected Poems*. (New York: Harper & Row, 1956) P. 602 "Sonnet xlii".

"What lips my lips have kissed, and where, and why,
I have forgotten, what arms have lain
Under my head till morning; but the rain
Is full of ghosts to night, that tap and sigh
Upon the glass and listen for reply,
And in my heart there stirs a quiet pain
For unremembered lads that not again
Will turn to me at midnight with a cry.
Thus in the winter stands the lonely tree,
Nor knows what birds have vanished one by one,
Yet knows its boughs more silent than before:
I cannot say what loves have come and gone,
I only know that summer sang in me
A little while, that in me sings no more."

Chapter 34

[438] Epstein, Daniel. *What Lips My Lips Have Kissed: The Loves and Love Poems of Edna St. Vincent Millay*. (New York: Henry Holt and Company, 2001) P. 103

"But her English lover's stone heart was unmoved. By the end of the month she had chosen another tack, challenging *his* sexuality, his notion of her as a woman, and his idea of himself as a man. He suggested to his 'child' that if only if she were a man she could understand his sadness, his ennui, and his torment."

[439] Epstein, Daniel. *What Lips My Lips Have Kissed: The Loves and Love Poems of Edna St. Vincent Millay.* (New York: Henry Holt and Company, 2001) P. 105

"Arthur responded quickly and kindly, eager, it would appear, to play the role of her sexual confessor in a matter he thoroughly understood. 'Edna, Edna, even if you *had* cared for a girl, and even if you had given yourself (so far as you could) I do not think I should care, greatly. No, I should not.'"

[440] Millay, E.S.V. *Collected Poems.* (New York: Harper & Row, 1956) P. 148 "The Philosopher".

"And what are you that, wanting you,
    I should be kept awake
As many nights as there are days
    With weeping for your sake?

And what are you that, missing you,
    As many days as crawl
I should be listening to the wind
    And looking at the wall?

I know a man that's a braver man
    And twenty men as kind,
And what are you, that you should be
    The one man on my mind?

Yet women's ways are witless ways,
    As any sage will tell, —
And what am I, that I should love
    So wisely and so well?"

[441] Milford, Nancy. *Savage Beauty: The Life of Edna St. Vincent Millay* (New York: Random House, 2001) Page 131

"…
But more than that I do not wish to be. … You said once that there are so many beautiful possibilities in me that you would be loath to leave with me any memory that I could wish to obliterate. God knows, I wish no such

memory of you.—But no memory that any man could leave me could really touch me. –I am sure of this. And why am I so sure, is because none has. …—Although I have been faithful to you—in my fashion. (Not that you have desired my faithfulness; or that faithfulness is in any way a virtue.—It is oftener a stupidity, I think.) But nothing has ever hurt me. Nothing can. In that respect, surely, I shall always remain a child.'

Then she told him an anecdote with a point: a friend of the Kennerleys had once watched her and another woman together and come to the conclusion that if the other woman should marry she would stop writing, 'but that under the same circumstances I would not. As far as I am concerned, that is true. No man could ever fill my life to the exclusion of other things.' She was, for someone as young as she was –twenty-three to Hooley's forty—entirely clear about her yearnings. She was as accurate as it was rare to acknowledge."

[442] Milford, Nancy. *Savage Beauty: The Life of Edna St. Vincent Millay* (New York: Random House, 2001) Page 131-132

"It was as close to a confession as Edna Millay would ever make in writing. Arthur wrote back immediately:

'Edna,
Even if you had cared for a girl, & even if you had given yourself (so far as you could), I do not think I should care, greatly. No, I should not. … '

That note drew blood—or he would have written something more that was not saved—for on March 10 she wrote him a savage little note:

Indeed, —I will be very careful from this day,—for of course you must not really love me. That would spoil it all,—& we have had such a beautiful game. —It is 'no fair,' as we say, to love me.

As for myself, —God forbid that I should give my heart to a dyspeptic Englishman!"

[443] Jackson, Timothy F. *Into the World's Great Heart: Selected Letters of Edna St. Vincent Millay* (New Haven, CT: Yale University Press, 2023). P. 90-91 Note: From a letter dated February 28, 1916, to Arthur Hooley.

"It really isn't necessary that I should be a man, Arthur, in order to know what the word *girl* sometimes means to you. —What do you suppose the word *man* sometimes means to me? —In a place like this? —It is silly, I think, to say that a man & woman cannot understand each other. —They can understand each other quite as well as they can understand themselves."

[444] Jackson, Timothy F. *Into the World's Great Heart: Selected Letters of Edna St. Vincent Millay* (New Haven, CT: Yale University Press, 2023). P. 99. Note: From a letter dated October 2, 1916, to Arthur Hooley.

"…

Arthur, do not let me go from you—hold me—I swear to you that no one else can bring me back to myself—whatever myself may be—a child that you loved, I think. If only you could *look at me* for a minute!"

[445] Jackson, Timothy F. *Into the World's Great Heart: Selected Letters of Edna St. Vincent Millay* (New Haven, CT: Yale University Press, 2023). P. 88 *Note:* From letter dated February 3, 1916, to Arthur Hooley. It is interesting to observe the couple were caught up in a common emotional trap. He hadn't loved her when she most loved him, but now that the fire was out for her, it was sparking in him. The trouble is, he was probably incapable of fully reciprocating because he was either gay or a pedophile who lost interest as Millay's bloom faded.

"… —The fire is out which burned the first night in your little house, when you said to me, 'Don't sit there, Edna. —I might want you there always.' … You did not really love me then.—But I think you do now.—Now that the fire is out."

[446] Milford, Nancy. *Savage Beauty: The Life of Edna St. Vincent Millay* (New York: Random House, 2001) Page 133

"…

Last night we gave the play of which I once spoke to you, *Deirdre of the Sorrows*. It was very real to me, as always. In the last act I stood beside the grave of the man I loved, who had been killed in battle, and with his knife killed myself.—I did it with all my heart,—and when they picked me up from the floor after the fall of the curtain, I found that I had actually driven the knife right through my little leather jacket."

[447] Epstein, Daniel. *What Lips My Lips Have Kissed: The Loves and Love Poems of Edna St. Vincent Millay.* (New York: Henry Holt and Company, 2001) P. 104-105

"Reporters got wind that something special was on the boards in Poughkeepsie the night of March 13, 1916—this girl wonder who wrote 'Renascence' and those other poems that had been appearing in *The Forum* was chewing up the scenery as Deirdre in Synge's tragedy. They showed up in force, not only the daily critics from the nearby *Eagle* and the *Enterprise*, but also the drama reviewer from the *New York Tribune*.

'Deirdre small and bewitching... lovely in her little Irish costume, clinched the attention of the audience and the whole play with the increasing intensity of her acting, building to a successful crisis.'

(*The Eagle*, March 12, 1916)"

[448] Epstein, Daniel. *What Lips My Lips Have Kissed: The Loves and Love Poems of Edna St. Vincent Millay.* (New York: Henry Holt and Company, 2001) P. 105

"She needed him, and the exact nature of her need is expressed in many of the letters. She wanted him to look at her, to listen and speak to her as an equal, as no one else could. 'Nobody speaks to me. People fall in love with me, and annoy me and distress me and flatter me and excite me and—and all that sort of thing. But no one speaks to me. I sometimes think that no one can. Can you?' She had created such a dense and mobile mask, layer by layer, that almost no one could penetrate it. But now she had told him everything. She was quick to add that it was not a confession but an observation, not at all irrelevant but in no way shameful."

Chapter 35

[449] Milford, Nancy. *Savage Beauty: The Life of Edna St. Vincent Millay* (New York: Random House, 2001) Page 133-134

"Vincent wrote home immediately after *Deirdre* but said very little about it because she just received the news that they would have to leave their Washington Street house. 'Never mind,' she wrote Norma.

> 'dear old loved. ... Of course I could just weep all day at the thought of leaving the house,—but I'm not going to let myself. ... I can't ever let myself *think* of that hedge of morning-glories, & the morning air coming in the bath-room window. —But we can't help it, dear. So never mind. It doesn't really matter at all,—if you just think of it that way.—Dear Sister, I love you very much.'"

[450] Milford, Nancy. *Savage Beauty: The Life of Edna St. Vincent Millay* (New York: Random House, 2001) Page 130

"'Millay was a seductress. Oh, I should think so! You have only to look at those poems. I see nothing wrong with that in her. She drew people to her. She liked to draw people to her. ... Elaine felt there was a ruthlessness about Vincent. That her work came first. ... She always thought Vincent had an eye on herself, her future. ... She felt it was her first love, and perhaps her only one: her poetry.'"

[451] Epstein, Daniel. *What Lips My Lips Have Kissed: The Loves and Love Poems of Edna St. Vincent Millay.* (New York: Henry Holt and Company, 2001). P. 101-102

"... Unlike the athletic Ralli, Simpson shared Millay's passion for books. The letters abound in allusions to Kipling's *Jungle Books* in particular, as they addressed one another as 'Best Beloved.' She called Isobel the 'Little Sphinx' when she did not call the younger girl her 'child' or her 'daughter.' Isobel in turn called her sexual mentor her 'Little Mother,' and more often 'Dearest Little Slimey Serpent,' reminiscent of the letters of Vincent's inamorata Ella Somerville."

[452] https://vcencyclopedia.vassar.edu/faculty/prominent-faculty/woodbridge-riley/

"... In 1908, Riley joined the Vassar philosophy department. There, he impressed students with his insights and with his satirical bite. He shared with his students his analytical and critical capacities, instilling in them his deep dislike of fraudulent or sloppy thinking. As his natural abilities led him toward philosophical history and criticism, he was excellent at outlining philosophic movements and demonstrating how they developed over the course of the centuries."

[453] https://www.nyshistoricnewspapers.org/lccn/sn91066542/1916-03-07/ed-1/seq-8/ Note: This comes from the local news section. Mr. Reardon was the local undertaker.

"… C. B. Reardon has a new Studebaker hearse for his business. We have not heard any [sic] our people say that they cared to ride in it."

[454] Millay, E.S.V. *Collected Poems*. (New York: Harper & Row, 1956) P. 400 "Song of the Nations".

"Out of
Night and alarm,
Out of
Darkness and dread,
Out of old hate,
Grudge and distrust,
Sin and remorse,
Passion and blindness;
Shall come
Dawn and the birds,
…"

[455] https://archive.org/details/americanphilosop00rile/page/126/mode/2up

"… Outwardly, Edwards was an advocate of cold ratiocination, of the strict metaphysical way of reasoning; inwardly, a philosopher of the feelings, a fervent exponent of the dialectic of the heart; traditionally he has been known as the preacher of the cold austerities of Puritanism; in reality he was an advocate of the interior or hidden life which results in an intimate union between the individual and the absolute. … Between Edwards the philosopher and Edwards the theologian there may be granted a certain intellectual duality."

Chapter 36

[456] Milford, Nancy. *Savage Beauty: The Life of Edna St. Vincent Millay* (New York: Random House, 2001) Page 134

"'Vassar was not a college for rich girls, then or now,' one of Millay's classmates told me many years later. It was for the intellectual girl with a social conscience. 'You see we all wore middies, which were a sort of leveling uniform. Although it is true that one knew, if one were at all observant, that certain middies were from Wanamaker's. Or they might be from Filene's.'"

[457] Milford, Nancy. *Savage Beauty: The Life of Edna St. Vincent Millay* (New York: Random House, 2001) Page 134

"… The astonishing thing is that she invited Elaine Ralli's brother to be her date. Victor Ralli was no one's idea of a prince—he was shy, hardworking, short, and swarthy—and he agreed immediately. …"

[458] Jackson, Timothy F. *Into the World's Great Heart: Selected Letters of Edna St. Vincent Millay* (New Haven, CT: Yale University Press, 2023). P. 62 Note: This is from a letter of Fall 1914 to the Millay family.

"… Went home with Elaine mid-year weekend. Had the best time yet. Friday night was Vassar Alumnae Play. Victor had the leading part, I told you, I think, and Elaine and I were ushers, the *only* undergraduate ushers. You will find our names on the program I'm sending you under separate cover. Victor is perfectly great in the play and when the play comes to Po-kips and all the girls go crazy about him and see me trotting around campus with him—Elaine and Dave are going to give him a party—I think I shall die gloating. …"

[459] Macdougall, Allan Ross, editor. *Letters of Edna St. Vincent Millay* (New York: Grosset and Dunlap, 1952). P. 49 Note: This is from a 1914 letter to Arthur Davison Ficke.

"They trust us with everything but men, —and they let us see it, so that it's worse than not trusting us at all. We can go into the candy-kitchen and take what we like and pay or not, and nobody is there to know. But a man is forbidden as if he were an apple."

[460] Milford, Nancy. *Savage Beauty: The Life of Edna St. Vincent Millay* (New York: Random House, 2001) Page 134

"... He told her he had to read her letter of invitation several times to make sure she meant him. He apologized in every note to her for being inarticulate. He said to be her 'suitor' he'd be happy to bunk with a janitor. ..."

[461] Jackson, Timothy F. *Into the World's Great Heart: Selected Letters of Edna St. Vincent Millay* (New Haven, CT: Yale University Press, 2023). P. 89 Note: This is from a letter dated February 3, 1916 to Arthur Hooley.

"I am having up a very nice man, with whom you would not get on at all, —and I shall wear a dress of pale yellow chiffon, with butterflies on the shoulders, and fur around the bottom —(which is about eight inches from the floor!)—*and gold slippers—pure gold, truly*, Arthur, I think they must be,— they *shine* so!."

[462] Epstein, Daniel. *What Lips My Lips Have Kissed: The Loves and Love Poems of Edna St. Vincent Millay.* (New York: Henry Holt and Company, 2001). P. 103

"She goes on at length to defend the license of Greek philosophers and English poets from Plato to Oscar Wilde, and all those lovers the narrow-minded world has condemned for their homosexual acts and affections. ..."

[463] Jackson, Timothy F. *Into the World's Great Heart: Selected Letters of Edna St. Vincent Millay* (New Haven, CT: Yale University Press, 2023). P. 91 Note: This is from a letter of 'February the Twenty-eighth 1916 to Arthur Hooley.

"... It might better have been said, not 'let him who is without sin among you' but 'let him among you who has sinned all sins, cast the first stone. ...'"

[464] Milford, Nancy. *Savage Beauty: The Life of Edna St. Vincent Millay* (New York: Random House, 2001) Page 135-136

"That May of 1916 she won the Intercollegiate prize for 'The Suicide,' the writing of which had become a piece of drudgery, she wrote home... And Mitchell Kennerley published three of her poems in *The Forum*. ...

Yet the sonnet 'Bluebeard,' a grim parable about female obedience, was far more revealing. Millay wrote in the first person, in the voice of the murderous king, but there are no murders here. ..."

[465] Millay, E.S.V. *Collected Poems.* (New York: Harper & Row, 1956) P. 566 "Sonnet vi *Bluebeard*".

"This door you might not open, and you did;

So enter now, and see for what slight thing
You are betrayed. ... Here is no treasure hid,
No cauldron, no clear crystal mirroring
The sought-for Truth, no heads of women slain
For greed like yours, no writhings of distress;
But only what you see. ... look yet again:
An empty room, cobwebbed and comfortless.
Yet this alone out of my life I kept
Unto myself, lest any know me quite;
And you did so profane me when you crept
Unto the threshold of this room tonight
That I must never more behold your face.
This now is yours. I seek another place."

Chapter 37

[466] Milford, Nancy. *Savage Beauty: The Life of Edna St. Vincent Millay* (New York: Random House, 2001) Page 136
"That summer, short of money as always, Cora was barely home. She was canvassing for hair work on the islands off the coast of Maine. ..."

[467] Milford, Nancy. *Savage Beauty: The Life of Edna St. Vincent Millay* (New York: Random House, 2001) Page 136-137
"... Her letter was fierce:

> 'And it doesn't make any difference whether you wash their heads or their floors, they have nothing on us, unless we give it to them. As long as we consider ourselves their superior & they can't get the idea out of our heads...they have nothing on us, & can't get anything, you see. The girl is a nonentity at Vassar,—*I am not.*
> ..."

Chapter 38

[468]https://archive.org/details/lockedchestsweep00maserich/mode/2up?ref=ol &view=theater P. 22

"The Locked Chest

Scene: A room. A chest used as a bench. A table, etc. Vigdis embroidering a cloth.

 Vigdis

 [singing]"

[469] Epstein, Daniel. *What Lips My Lips Have Kissed: The Loves and Love Poems of Edna St. Vincent Millay.* (New York: Henry Holt and Company, 2001). P. 118

"... Millay's fame as an actress had spread far beyond the halls of Vassar. Her performance as Vigdis in the premiere of John Maysfield's *The Locked Chest* (December 9, 1916) brought praise from the laureate himself, who wrote from England to tell Miss Millay that his theatre friends in New York had informed him she had been superb in his play. And he wanted to see her poetry. ..."

[470] Jackson, Timothy F. *Into the World's Great Heart: Selected Letters of Edna St. Vincent Millay* (New Haven, CT: Yale University Press, 2023). P. 115 Note: This is from a letter dated October 18, 1917 to Kathleen Millay.

"...

 You are making a mistake, dear, which I wish you would not make,— playing too much with the few people you already know there, & not getting sufficiently acquainted with new people. It is a serious mistake & one that you will regret all the next three years. —You should avoid whenever it is possible making the mistakes I made, & make mistakes of your own; the more you follow after me the more stupidly & unpleasantly people will talk. I *know*.

 ..."

[471] Macdougall, Allan Ross, editor. *Letters of Edna St. Vincent Millay* (New York: Grosset and Dunlap, 1952). P. 57-58 Note: This is from a letter dated November 26, 1916, to Norma Millay.

"...

Did I tell you that Salomón is teaching the Spanish language at *Williams College*? And that Prof. and Mrs. Rice, great friends of Salomón, have invited me up for the week-end of the 1st of December? I hope I can go.—Miss Palmer, the head warden, says it is very hard to get off for that week-end—because on account of Thanksgiving holiday—one day!—they have switched Thursday classes to Friday & Friday classes to Saturday! —I could oath! …"

[472] Epstein, Daniel. *What Lips My Lips Have Kissed: The Loves and Love Poems of Edna St. Vincent Millay.* (New York: Henry Holt and Company, 2001). P. 115

"Salomón faithfully gave her his best, and would have given her anything she asked of him. He showered her with gifts, some of them extravagant. 'I have received, from England, a little flask of Attar of Roses. …' This perfume, then the most costly in the world, was the Christmas present with which he hoped to lure her to Williamstown. Not that she was indifferent to his company and his fascinating conversation. But physically he was not her type, so between them there arose an uncomfortable pressure of his sublimated desire."

[473] Jackson, Timothy F. *Into the World's Great Heart: Selected Letters of Edna St. Vincent Millay* (New Haven, CT: Yale University Press, 2023). P. 93 *Note: This is from a letter dated Spring 1916 to the Millay family.*

"… —At this time of year in college one needs money. I have been posing for the art class, and earning a little money that way. …"

[474] Macdougall, Allan Ross, editor. *Letters of Edna St. Vincent Millay* (New York: Grosset and Dunlap, 1952). P. 59 Note: This is from a letter dated [December 5, 1916] to Norma Millay.

"…

Never mind, sixteen dollars aren't many dollars—but oh, I can use them all right! —This room of ours has cost awfully—I have to write many more poems before I am straight—& be very sparing from now on—else I shall find myself in wrong.

…"

[475] Daniels, Elizabeth A. *Bridges to the World: Henry Noble MacCracken and Vassar College* (Clinton Corners, NY: College Avenue Press. 1994) p. 159-160.

"... But because she challenged the authority of one too many teachers in her local high school, she was barred from attending classes and had to complete her secondary education by herself. ...

... As a substitute for a more conventional final exam taken by the other students in his class, MacCracken encouraged her to compose a play that would reflect her comprehension of the course."

[476] Milford, Nancy. *Savage Beauty: The Life of Edna St. Vincent Millay* (New York: Random House, 2001). P. 137

"She had a fine time senior year. She took two courses in Spanish (and became president of the Spanish Club), took English drama with President Henry Noble MacCracken and the technique of the drama with Gertrude Buck. Her play *The Princess Marries the Page* was written for that class and performed on May 12, 1917; she was the princess. She even took one term of Italian, having taken every other language course Vassar offered. And, in what was a great honor at Vassar, she was asked to write the Baccalaureate Hymn for her class of 1917, which was to be sung at commencement. She did not, however, hear it sung."

[477] Macdougall, Allan Ross, editor. *Letters of Edna St. Vincent Millay* (New York: Grosset and Dunlap, 1952). P. 61 Note: This is from a letter dated March 24, 1917, to the Millay family.

"Norma, my hat is just the cutest thing, —everybody *adores* it. They really do—they mention it themselves, —and, baby, old blonde plum-blossom, if I get a good job here sometime in the near future you're coming out here & get a job & study at the School of Design, because it's wicked for you not to. You're the most talented one of us all, & you've got to have your chance, too. ..."

[478] Epstein, Daniel. *What Lips My Lips Have Kissed: The Loves and Love Poems of Edna St. Vincent Millay.* (New York: Henry Holt and Company, 2001). P. 111

> "All the way through college Vincent had found it extremely difficult to live according to college regulations, and she had been forgiven possibly too often. I kept hoping she would grow into a sense of responsibility for daily engagements, and into a more cordial support of college laws, and possibly we were too easy with her. ... When the Warden's department

placed her under penalties for calmly staying in New York to go to the Opera instead of returning at the appointed time at the end of spring recess, she ought to have known that it was a serious matter, but when the impulse came to go off on a lark, she yielded as any little child might have done, hoping that she would not be found out."

[479] Epstein, Daniel. *What Lips My Lips Have Kissed: The Loves and Love Poems of Edna St. Vincent Millay.* (New York: Henry Holt and Company, 2001). P. 114 Note: It wasn't just men who felt a need to 'rescue' Vincent. Nearly all of her intimates felt they could cure Vincent's inner wounds.

"… Most of her lovers apprehend a sadness in her beyond anything she will admit to. Evidently she projected a tragic sense in her lovemaking, which I believe was compounded by her own deep conviction that love, so precious, cannot last, and her lovers' contrary desire to capture the woman and keep her forever. Edna appeared sad to Salomón, as she would to dozens of other men, because she made *him* sad—she was a promise of paradise too good to be true, the consummate femme fatale."

[480] Milford, Nancy. *Savage Beauty: The Life of Edna St. Vincent Millay* (New York: Random House, 2001). P. 137-138

"… One of the college wardens lunched at the same hotel and saw Vincent's name in the register, directly below that of a man. She thought the worse and reported her. …

Henry Noble MacCracken had become president of Vassar in 1915. He later recorded that Millay cut classes regularly, and while some faculty members excused her, others did not. He called her in to reprimand her but was none too persuasive."

[481] MacCracken, Henry Noble. *The Hickory Limb.* (New York: Charles Scribner's Sons. 1950). P. 81

"Women's tears were new to me, as weapons of defense. Vassar tears flowed like a river. I sat silent and miserable while student or teacher wept on. The little handkerchief was soon a drench, and my own big one called into play. I began to keep an extra one in my desks right hand drawer, in the wax candle box where Prexy Taylor had kept a revolver. I soon stocked up. They became regular equipment for my interviews with students. Knowing nothing of women, I had read that it was good for them to 'cry it out.' So when it started,

I would just pull out the drawer, get a good big handkerchief, and silently handed to the sufferer."

[482] Milford, Nancy. *Savage Beauty: The Life of Edna St. Vincent Millay* (New York: Random House, 2001) Page 138

"'... I ... told her, 'I want you to know that you couldn't break any rule that would make me vote for your expulsion. I don't want to have any dead Shelleys on my doorstep and I don't care what you do.' She went to the window and looked out and she said, 'Well on those terms I think I can continue to live in this hellhole.' ... What do you do with a girl like that?'"

[483] MacCracken, Henry Noble. *The Hickory Limb*. (New York: Charles Scribner's Sons. 1950). P. 81

"Women's tears were new to me, as weapons of defense. Vassar tears flowed like a river. I sat silent and miserable while student or teacher wept on. The little handkerchief was soon a drench, and my own big one called into play. I began to keep an extra one in my desks right hand drawer, in the wax candle box where Prexy Taylor had kept a revolver. I soon stocked up. They became regular equipment for my interviews with students. Knowing nothing of women, I had read that it was good for them to 'cry it out.' So when it started, I would just pull out the drawer, get a good big handkerchief, and silently handed to the sufferer."

Chapter 39

[484] *Vassar Quarterly*, Volume II, Number 2, 1 February 1917. P. 85
"... On the other hand, the lack of modesty in women's clothes emphasizes and appeals to impulses and emotions in men that need no strengthening."
[485]

https://ia903205.us.archive.org/34/items/vassarion00vass./vassarion00vass.pdf Note: This is a link to the Vassar College 1917 Yearbook. See P. 63

"As a Stimulus to musical composition, two prizes are offered each year. On Founder's Day at Song Contest the banner is awarded to the class which sings best a song composed by one of its members. The cup is given for the best contribution offered during the year by an under graduate, and may in form be; a song, dance music or orchestral composition. Last Founder's Day, May 9th,

1916, the banner was awarded by the judges to the class of 1917 for its singing of "The Patient Periodical" by Vincent Millay, and the cup was given to Miriam Marsh (1916), for the music written for Class Day dances.

I

The patient periodical.
So zealous and methodical.
Concerned with post-impressionistic
    Matters and pre-diplodical.
Has turned its perspicacity
And tangle foot tenacity
Toward Vassar, and is writing us up,
    Regardless of veracity.

    We see in the "Times"
    That pickled limes
    Are Vassar's delight.
    And at the fall of the night
    To see the Seniors weeding the
        begonias in the circle
    Is a beautiful sight.
    It is a beautiful sight;
    Oh, the daisy-chain marshal wears
        a rose and gray dress
    That costs a million dollars, not a
        red cent less,
    ("The Post" inserts this item as
        they gallop to press.)

II.

Now if there is a particle
Of truth in any article

About our movements, social, academic,
    or Delsartical,
We are an institution
For the further distribution
Among the aborigines, of spats and
    Elocution.

    We see in the "Sun"
    Our greatest fun
    Is taking our beer
    Beneath the evergreens near:
    "The Herald" has a column
    On the savage rites and solemn
    Of sororities here.
    Of our sororities here;
    Every girl in the choir takes an
        afternoon nap
    In a long-sleeved nightie and a
        boudoir cap;
    Oh, in this information, girls, there
        isn't a gap
        Words and Music by Edna St. Vincent Millay."

[486] Jackson, Timothy F. *Into the World's Great Heart: Selected Letters of Edna St. Vincent Millay* (New Haven, CT: Yale University Press, 2023). P. 102-103 Note: This is from a letter dated February 17, 1917, to the Millay family.
"… but if my bills aren't paid before commencement I can't graduate, so I'm trying hard to get a little money. … I owe $10 to Hilda Strouse for the money to send to Clem, which I sent directly on my return here. I owe a tremendous amount for laundry,—which no lady can very well help. My photo-graphs were something over $14.00, but I had to have them, or be the only girl in the Senior class without her picture in the Vassarion. And everybody who had pictures taken had enough to give to her friends besides, you know. And I have had to buy food because I couldn't be the one in the alley-way not to, and so I have run a big bill at Carey's for chocolate and condensed milk and crackers

and innumerable cans of condensed heat, while my room-mates with ready cash have kept the fruit-basket filled with grape-fruit and tangerines, etc. It's been sort of terrible,—I've had to borrow money for everything: stamps, type-writing paper, everything. I just haven't had a penny in months, except that dollar which you sent me, and which I almost wept to see. You see, Wump, I owe $2.75 still for the stockings I sent you, and I've had to have stockings myself, one does. And I owe $8 for my boots, which also I had to have, because one can't wear white rubber-soled sports shoes all winter. I am very sorry, dear. If I had the money at all I would send it to you, although it would be a very foolish thing to do, because no matter how much you may want the dress, and no matter how much of a bargain it may be, you cannot really be said to *need* it, as I need, for instance, to get my bills paid before commencement. ..."

[487] Jackson, Timothy F. *Into the World's Great Heart: Selected Letters of Edna St. Vincent Millay* (New Haven, CT: Yale University Press, 2023). P. 103-104 *Note: This is from a letter dated February 17, 1917, to the Millay family.*

"But first I want to tell you about the Valentine I got, the most beautiful box of flowers I have ever seen, I think: I don't know who sent them, there was no sign of a card, but they came from Saltford's, so it looks as if it were some girl here. I am crazy to know, of course, because she certainly ought to be thanked. It is an enormous corsage of English violets and orchids, it completely covers the front of me,--it is beautifully made up with some lovely green leaves, and there are baby orchids attached to the long ribbon streamers. ... When Fran, my room-mate first looked at it she said, 'Well, I hate to think of the pair of boots you could buy with that.' ..."

[488] https://vcencyclopedia.vassar.edu/vassar-off-campus/lake-mohonk/

"... Vassar's relationship with Mohonk dated from 1872 when Frederick Thompson, a banker and Vassar trustee, invited students and faculty to the hotel.... He wanted to give the students the opportunity to leave campus and the Smiley resort must have seemed ideal for a weekend excursion from Vassar... Due to the number of students, Mr. Thompson invited the juniors and seniors one weekend in mid-May, and the freshmen and sophomores the following weekend."

[489] *Vassar Quarterly*. December 1960 Babcock-Sills Letter P. 25-26 Note: this description of the events of the next two days comes from Charlotte Babcock

Sill's letter to the editor of the Vassar Quarterly, forty-three years after the 1917 events.

"Most of the letters in this department are concerned with timely questions or problems. This letter is written in an attempt to clarify an incident that took place more than 43 years ago and yet seems to be of current interest.

'I was a classmate and senior year roommate of Edna St. Vincent Millay. In the spring of 1917 our class was preparing to go on the traditional annual trip to Lake Mohonk. Vincent and I decided not to go, but to stay on campus and work on some topics and papers. Our roommates were up early and left with the class after breakfast in buses for Mohonk. Soon after their departure two old friends appeared in what was then an exciting vehicle. A car! I think it was a Saxon roadster. The car belonged to Gertrude Bruyn, a Mt. Holyoke graduate who was at that time a social worker. The other friend was Winifred fuller, now Winifred Byrd, of the class of 1915 at Vassar. Both lived in Kingston, N.Y at that time.

'I had breakfast off campus with these three friends and they persuaded me to take a drive with them. It was such a beautiful May Day—why work? We asked Vincent to go with us, we picked up some sandwiches, and soon we were off across the river in the direction of the hills around Lake Mohonk. We drove around the countryside, Vincent composing verses about the cherry trees and peach trees then in radiant bloom, and I wrote my fiancé late that night, 'we talked and sang and just yelled for joy as we skipped along uphill and down dale in the blessed little Saxon.'

With Gertrude, we called on some of her problem children and then decided to accept the Bruyn's invitation to spend the night with them. I telephoned one of our roommates at college to tell her where we were. We had a good supper and Vincent and I were hilarious. We went to a movie and then returned to the house to sit by the fire, Vincent played piano and sang charmingly, and there was good talk. I have had recent letters from Gertrude and Winifred and they both write that they have always considered that evening a cherished memory.

The next day was Sunday; Winnie, a ministers daughter went to church, and Gertrude drove Vincent and me around the Ashokan Reservoir, then new and interesting, and we stopped at an attractive inn which Winnie tells me is still there—the Watson Hollow Inn I don't remember whether or not we all signed our names in the guest book, but Edna St Vincent Millay did, and, it is said, after a man's! At any rate a day or two after we returned to college that Sunday evening a Vassar warden stopped for lunch at the inn, saw Vincent's name, and the storm soon broke; For Vincent had been campused for cutting classes or some similar infringements of rules, and as a penalty for being away from college on this expedition the faculty voted to spend her from college indefinitely and it was just before commencement!

Miss Elizabeth Haight has written of this event, calling it a 'tale of an A. B. Degree nearly lost,' and her story will appear in her memoirs which she is now completing. Miss Haight's story is not quite correct: Vincent did not go driving with a college friend and her mother, nor did the car break down. Dr. McCracken has also written about the episode in his book, *The Hickory Limb*; He tells of his part and that of the faculty in voting to let Vincent return for Commencement but not for the other festivities. So Vincent received her diploma but she did not stand with her class to sing the Baccalaureate hymn for which she had composed words and music. She was heartbroken about it.

I do not remember whether or not I knew that Vincent should not have been away from college overnight. I'm sure Vincent remembered it but probably thought, 'Oh, I won't tell Charlie and spoil her fun.' Many stories about our expedition have persisted through the years. And just recently a friend sent me a clipping from a Chicago newspaper with a new tale. It seems that a woman at a Vassar club meeting in October said that she heard that Vincent had crossed the Hudson to meet a cadet beau at West Point. That was a new version to me—and one that Vincent would have thoroughly enjoyed!

Charlotte Babcock Sills '17'"

[490] MacCracken, Henry Noble. *The Hickory Limb*. (New York: Charles Scribner's Sons. 1950). P. 95

"… Other enterprises were later successfully started by students. The Hoot'n'Owl, a snack bar. started in Main as a candy kitchen, became a successful after-show tavern, competing with off campus in spite of temperance rules."

Chapter 40

[491] Macdougall, Allan Ross, editor. *Letters of Edna St. Vincent Millay* (New York: Grosset and Dunlap, 1952). P. 63 Note: This comes from a letter dated June 6, 1917, to the Millay family.

"What I mean is this,—I can't stay here at all for Commencement. I can't graduate with the class,—my diploma will be shipped to me, as I told Miss Haight, 'like a codfish',—& it all seems pretty shabby, of course, after all that I have done for the college, that it should turn me out at the end with scarcely enough time to pack and, as you might say, sort of 'without a character.' ..."

[492] *Vassar Quarterly*. December 1960 Babcock-Sills Letter P. 26 Note: this description of the events is based on the memories of Charlotte Babcock Sills sent in a letter to the editor of the Vassar Quarterly, forty-three years after the 1917 events.

"I do not remember whether or not I knew that Vincent should not have been away from college overnight. I'm sure Vincent remembered it but probably thought, 'Oh, I won't tell Charlie and spoil her fun.' Many stories about our expedition have persisted through the years. And just recently a friend sent me a clipping from a Chicago newspaper with a new tale. It seems that a woman at a Vassar club meeting in October said that she heard that Vincent had crossed the Hudson to meet a cadet beau at West Point. That was a new version to me—and one that Vincent would have thoroughly enjoyed!"

[493] Ibid.

[494] Milford, Nancy. *Savage Beauty: The Life of Edna St. Vincent Millay* (New York: Random House, 2001) Page 139 Note: MacCracken's own account says it was June 8, 1917.

"On June 7 [sic], MacCracken sent a letter out to the faculty telling them that 108 members of the class of 1917 (somewhat less than half the class) had sent him a petition asking that 'Vincent Millay be permitted to remain for Commencement, inasmuch as she has contributed largely to our Commencement activities and we feel that the penalty inflicted is too great.' It was accompanied by letters from eighteen individuals urging that the penalty imposed was too severe, particularly 'in view of the leniency shown to Miss Millay before the spring recess; second, that false rumors regarding her reputation' would be stopped by allowing her to take her degree with her class."

[495] Epstein, Daniel. *What Lips My Lips Have Kissed: The Loves and Love Poems of Edna St. Vincent Millay.* (New York: Henry Holt and Company, 2001). P. 111

> "'All the way through college Vincent has found it extremely difficult to live according to college regulations, and she has been forgiven possibly too often. ...'"

[496] MacCracken, Henry Noble. *The Hickory Limb.* (New York: Charles Scribner's Sons. 1950). P. 96

"French leave almost cost Edna St. Vincent Millay her diploma. After the faculty had asked for her indefinite suspension for unauthorized absence, I was in a quandary. By trustee vote I had the power to veto in faculty action, but had resolved never to use it. In this one instance I did so, but only after a stupid delay, which kept Vincent from her own Class Day and Baccalaureate. ..."

[497] Epstein, Daniel. *What Lips My Lips Have Kissed: The Loves and Love Poems of Edna St. Vincent Millay.* (New York: Henry Holt and Company, 2001). P. 111 and Milford, Nancy. *Savage Beauty: The Life of Edna St. Vincent Millay* (New York: Random House, 2001) Page 140-141.

> "'... I kept hoping she would grow into a sense of responsibility for daily engagements, and into a more cordial support of college laws, and possibly we were too easy with her. ...'"

And

"... The entire experience had been both 'bitter and trying for her friends as well as for herself,' and McCaleb hoped that Kathleen would take a different attitude from that of Vincent. ..."

[498] Ibid.

[499] MacCracken, Henry Noble. *The Hickory Limb.* (New York: Charles Scribner's Sons. 1950). P. 45-46.

"I began to refuse to carry out penalties left to my discretion to execute. I urged teachers to let up—I transferred to student government, with faculty approval, all responsibility for honesty in written work. In all this Professor Lucy Salmon was my unfailing support. 'Call them "women", not "girls",' she urged, 'and you will see that they will act like women....'"

[500] MacCracken, Henry Noble. *The Hickory Limb*. (New York: Charles Scribner's Sons. 1950). P. 81

...I sat silent and miserable while student or teacher wept on.

[501] MacCracken, Henry Noble. *The Hickory Limb*. (New York: Charles Scribner's Sons. 1950). P. 73 and Milford, Nancy. *Savage Beauty: The Life of Edna St. Vincent Millay* (New York: Random House, 2001) Page 141

"...It meant much to me that Professor Washburn, probably our most famous scholar and certainly our best lecturer, could at last have her own building when the Vassar Brothers Laboratory was vacated by the Physics Department. ..."

And

... and McCaleb hoped that Kathleen would take a different attitude from that of Vincent. 'If I did not believe this I could not work to have her come here.' A full scholarship for her first year was promised, but beyond that nothing was assured."

[502] Milford, Nancy. *Savage Beauty: The Life of Edna St. Vincent Millay* (New York: Random House, 2001) Page 141

"After commencement, Vincent fled to Miss Haight's apartment in New York, from which she wrote to Norma: ..."

[503]. Milford, Nancy. *Savage Beauty: The Life of Edna St. Vincent Millay* (New York: Random House, 2001) Page 139.

"...

But now, this awful thing seems more than I can bear. It does not seem that it can possibly be true that my girl will not be with her class-mates on Thursday. You cannot realize what it means to us. Such a possibility never occurred to us, and it is a terrible shock. If it must be, if your decision is final, it is a blow from which I shall never recover."

[504] Milford, Nancy. *Savage Beauty: The Life of Edna St. Vincent Millay* (New York: Random House, 2001) Page 139 (Note: MacCracken's own account says it was June 8, 1917.) and

https://vcencyclopedia.vassar.edu/interviews-and-reflections/maccracken-millay/

"On June 7 [sic], MacCracken sent a letter out to the faculty telling them that 108 members of the class of 1917 (somewhat less than half the class) had sent him a petition asking that 'Vincent Millay be permitted to remain for Commencement, inasmuch as she has contributed largely to our Commencement activities and we feel that the penalty inflicted is too great.' It was accompanied by letters from eighteen individuals urging that the penalty imposed was too severe, particularly 'in view of the leniency shown to Miss Millay before the spring recess; second, that false rumors regarding her reputation' would be stopped by allowing her to take her degree with her class."

And an account by MacCracken published in The Vassarion.
"… The President of the Class got a petition signed by practically every girl in the class. I then had it manifolded and sent it out and sent out to the Faculty. I did not insult them by insisting on a special meeting over Vincent. I knew that would make them so mad they would vote something worse. When you just get a letter which says something to this effect: I have received the enclosed petition and the undersigned request an immediate answer; after all they're all certified to graduate and I think their opinions should receive your consideration. Under the circumstances I recommend that the petition be granted but please express your own thoughts about the matter on the enclosed blank. A large majority of the faculty signed and I immediately cancelled the suspension. …"

[505] Jackson, Timothy F. *Into the World's Great Heart: Selected Letters of Edna St. Vincent Millay* (New Haven, CT: Yale University Press, 2023). P. 108 Note: This is from a letter dated Spring Semester 1917 to Vassar President Dr. MacCracken.

"You told me once that if I ever needed a friend to let you know.—I need one now. And I want to see you. May I?—If you don't want to see me, I shall understand. But there is nobody else I want to go to.

Mayn't I see you this evening.—Sunday?—If not, don't tell me that it is because you are too busy; I shall know quite well why it is.

But you must know that I wish very much to see you.
..."

[506] Milford, Nancy. *Savage Beauty: The Life of Edna St. Vincent Millay* (New York: Random House, 2001) Page 140

"'... I remember that you chided me a bit for never telling people who were kind to me how kind to me I think they are and it occurred to me that if I should die tomorrow it would be rather shabby of me not to have blessed you just.'"

[507] Daniels, Elizabeth A. *Bridges to the World: Henry Noble MacCracken and Vassar College* (Clinton Corners, NY: College Avenue Press. 1994. P. 160.

"Drama 220 was a lecture course. ... However, this did not deter Vincent from getting up and spouting Shakespeare when the occasion moved her to it. Physicians considered women frail in those days and sick excuses could be sent to class for almost any reason. Miss Millay used this convenient means to cut her eight o'clock drama class one morning. Dr. MacCracken saw her performing splits and all sorts of fantastic capers about an hour afterward under the Main gate. He remarked teasingly when he saw her later in the day on her 'quick recovery from illness.' She replied, 'It just so happened that at the time of your class I was in pain with a poem.'"

[508] MacCracken, Henry Noble. *The Hickory Limb*. (New York: Charles Scribner's Sons. 1950). P. 96.

"... After the faculty had asked for her indefinite suspension for unauthorized absence, I was in a quandary. By trustee vote I had the power to veto in faculty action, but had resolved never to use it. In this one instance I did so, but only after a stupid delay, which kept Vincent from her own Class Day and Baccalaureate. For the latter she had composed both words and music of a hymn which she called 'St. Vincent.' Her diploma, however, was duly presented to her at Commencement in defiance of faculty opinion. ...."

Chapter 41

[509] https://vcencyclopedia.vassar.edu/interviews-and-reflections/maccracken-millay/

"The president of the Class got a petition signed by practically every girl in the class. I then had it manifolded and sent it out and sent out to the Faculty. I did not insult them by insisting on a special meeting over Vincent. I knew that would make them so mad they would vote something worse. When you just get a letter which says something to this effect: I have received the enclosed petition and the undersigned request an immediate answer; after all they're all certified to graduate and I think their opinions should receive your consideration. Under the circumstances I recommend that the petition be granted but please express your own thoughts about the matter on the enclosed blank. A large majority of the faculty signed and I immediately cancelled the suspension."

[510] Milford, Nancy. *Savage Beauty: The Life of Edna St. Vincent Millay* (New York: Random House, 2001) P. 140

> "What are they thinking, dear? Is it absolutely final? ... Is there nothing that can move them so that I may not be robbed of that proudest day I have ever dreamed of seeing? I may not live to see Kathleen graduate. Tell them so, those people. Forgive me dear for turning the knife in the wound. ..."

[511] Milford, Nancy. *Savage Beauty: The Life of Edna St. Vincent Millay* (New York: Random House, 2001). P. 122

"Norma would have none of it. She wrote sharply to Vincent on March 16, 'Dear Vincent, please pay a little attention to this in spite of all your *busyness*. Mother is sick. ... I have to wash her face & hands & comb her hair & help her up the stairs to the bath-room and every little thing like that.'"

[512] https://www.extremeweatherwatch.com/cities/new-york/year-1917.

Day	High (°F)	Low (°F)	Precip. (inches)	Snow (inches)
June 12	77	62	0.00	0.0

[513] Macdougall, Allan Ross, editor. *Letters of Edna St. Vincent Millay* (New York: Grosset and Dunlap, 1952). P. 63 Note: This is from a letter dated June 6, 1917, to the Millay family.

"... I don't want Wump to know until after she is through there, if we can help it.—This will make no difference about her. If she passes her exams she has next year here for sure. ..."

[514] Milford, Nancy. *Savage Beauty: The Life of Edna St. Vincent Millay* (New York: Random House, 2001) P. 141

"... and McCaleb hoped that Kathleen would take a different attitude from that of Vincent. 'If I did not believe this I could not work to have her come here.' ..."

[515] MacCracken, Henry Noble. *The Hickory Limb*. (New York: Charles Scribner's Sons. 1950). P. 42, 44 and

https://vcencyclopedia.vassar.edu/distinguished-alumni/ella-mccaleb/

"... She kept her motherly hand on all the branches of her own work, however, it was not easy to develop the bureaus of admission, of student employment, and of registry of marks, as they should be. Faculty action as well as my influence had to work by indirection before much was done.

For Miss McCaleb a good college meant a college of what she called 'nice girls.' She was right, I thought, in her emphasis on personality, but wrong in her choice of attributes. ...

...Under Miss McCaleb's management the admission was by school certificate only, the dean closing the list of applications whenever the list contained twice the number for which Vassar had room. ..."

And

"... Speaking at the time of her death in 1933, President MacCracken recalled, 'she considered herself a liaison officer functioning between the college with its compacted interests and the outside world as it is represented by it alumnae.'"

[516] Vcencyclopedia.vassar.edu/distinguished-alumni/ella-mccaleb/

"Deans at small colleges, Stewart noted, presided over 'the supervision of conduct and studies, attendance at chapel, and the control of all matters pertaining to graduation and discipline.'"

Chapter 42

[517] Milford, Nancy. *Savage Beauty: The Life of Edna St. Vincent Millay* (New York: Random House, 2001) Page 57.

"...

> I'm getting old and ugly. My hands are stiff and rough and stained and blistered. I can feel my face dragging down. I can feel the lines coming underneath my skin. They don't show yet but I can feel a hundred of them underneath. I love beauty more than anything else in the world and I can't take time to be pretty. ... Crawl into my bed at night too tired to brush my hair—my beautiful hair—all autumn colored like Megunticook."

[518] Epstein, Daniel. *What Lips My Lips Have Kissed: The Loves and Love Poems of Edna St. Vincent Millay.* (New York: Henry Holt and Company, 2001). P. 118 Note: The actor's last name was spelled 'Matthison' and was married to the playwright Charles Rann Kennedy.

"... Edith Mattison *(sic)* embraced and kissed the proud girl, and prophesied for her a brilliant career on the stage. She offered to do anything in her power—as teacher, as sponsor, as patron—to get Vincent started on the road to fame in the theatre world. Soon after her graduation, the Kennedys began calling upon powerful friends, theater managers in New York and in regional theaters, to audition the budding actress as soon as possible."

[519] Milford, Nancy. *Savage Beauty: The Life of Edna St. Vincent Millay* (New York: Random House, 2001) Page 141

"After commencement, Vincent fled to Miss Haight's apartment in New York, from which she wrote to Norma:

> 'Tell mother it is all right,—the class made such a fuss that they let me come back, & I graduated in my cap & gown along with the rest. Tell her it had nothing to do with money;—all my bills have been settled for some time. —Commencement went off beautifully & I had a wonderful time. Tell her this at once if you can.
>
> ...
>
> You see I have to start right in working as soon as I can get a job, —& I may not be able to come home at all. We mustn't be foolish about these

things. ... But I *can't* come home unless I have something sure here to come back to, —you understand.
..."

[520] Jackson, Timothy F. *Into the World's Great Heart: Selected Letters of Edna St. Vincent Millay* (New Haven, CT: Yale University Press, 2023). P. 111-112, 114, 116 Note: This citing consists of two letters and two notes by Timothy Jackson. It begins with a letter from July 26, 1917, to Dr. Elizabeth Haight, Millay's Latin professor, followed by a note by Timothy Jackson citing an advertisement Millay placed in the *Camden Herald* offering typing services.
"... The check is still intact, but the money I earn tutoring and typewriting, a not inconsiderable amount, is speedily requisitioned here at home—girls need so many gol-darn things; so I'm not getting ahead very fast, and am too busy to be getting much dress-making done. ..."

And note by Jackson:
... Millay advertised her typing services in the *Camden Herald* in 1917. 'Edna St. Vincent Millay / Typewriting / 12 Limerock St. / Camden / Telephone 328-6' (this example from July 6, 1917, 7).
This citing is followed by a letter dated August 27, 1917, to Henry Seidel Canby, on P. 114.
"... I have no other verses on hand just now in which I think you would be very interested, and I am in a great hurry to have you publish When The Year Grows Old, so that there will be no trouble about its being published in the collection of my poems which Mr. Mitchell Kennerley is to publish later this fall. ..."

The citing concludes with a note by Jackson on P. 116 citing Miriam Gurko's account of the staging of Millay's plays, "The Princess Marries the Page" and "Two Slatterns and a King" at the Bennett School in October 1917. Ms. Gurko is the author of the biography, "Restless Spirit: The Life of Edna St. Vincent Millay." (published by Thomas Y. Crowell, 1967, p. 75).
"Millay was at the Bennett school in October 1917. Miriam Gurko notes that she spent a week there helping with the production of her plays, *The Princess*

Marries the Page, and *Two Slatterns and a King*, and giving a reading of her poetry one night. She received another fifty dollars for her week's work. ..."
[521] Jackson, Timothy F. *Into the World's Great Heart: Selected Letters of Edna St. Vincent Millay* (New Haven, CT: Yale University Press, 2023). P. 115 Note: This is from a letter dated October 18, 1917, to Kathleen Millay.

"...

Next week I shall be at the *Bennett School* in Millbrook, very near you, coaching the students—alumnae—in the production of my two plays—*The Princess* and *The Slatterns* & also to give a reading of my poems. I shall doubtless get over to see you. —

You are making a mistake, dear, which I wish you would not make,— playing too much with the few people you already know there, & not getting sufficiently acquainted with new people. It is a serious mistake & one that you will regret all the next three years. —You should avoid whenever it is possible making the mistakes I made, & make mistakes of your own; the more you follow after me the more stupidly & unpleasantly people will talk. —I *know*."
[522] Milford, Nancy. *Savage Beauty: The Life of Edna St. Vincent Millay* (New York: Random House, 2001) Page 57.

I'm getting old and ugly. My hands are stiff and rough and stained and blistered. I can feel my face dragging down. I can feel the lines coming underneath my skin. They don't show yet but I can feel a hundred of them underneath. I love beauty more than anything else in the world and I can't take time to be pretty. ... Crawl into my bed at night too tired to brush my hair—my beautiful hair—all autumn colored like Megunticook."